T0369479

BADON

Stephen Lonsdale

iUniverse, Inc.
New York Bloomington

BADON

iUniverse books may be ordered through booksellers or by contacting:

iUniverse
1663 Liberty Drive
Bloomington, IN 47403
www.iuniverse.com
1-800-Authors (1-800-288-4677)

Because of the dynamic nature of the Internet, any Web addresses or links contained in this book may have changed since publication and may no longer be valid. The views expressed in this work are solely those of the author and do not necessarily reflect the views of the publisher, and the publisher hereby disclaims any responsibility for them.

ISBN: 978-1-4502-7057-1 (sc)
ISBN: 978-1-4502-7058-8 (ebk)

Library of Congress Control Number: 2010916410

Printed in the United States of America

iUniverse rev. date: 11/17/2010

Dedicated to my wife, Debra.

PREFACE

There are many theories about whether there was a historical King Arthur. There are so many views on the subject one scholar opined that anything could be said about the subject because we just don't know. I have cherry-picked what historical facts and theories I liked best and have woven them together to present a unique version of the age-old story.

Badon is the story of a Celtic tribal chieftain who leads an army of rival Celtic tribes into an impossible battle of overwhelming odds against the invading Saxons, Frisians, Jutes, and Angles in the sixth century. He hails from what is now North Wales and gains the support and authority from the High King of Southern Briton, the Roman-Briton, Ambrosius Aurelianus, who was then 74 years old. This Northern Celtic tribesman was never a king and his name was not "Arthur."

The resulting clash of cultures, religions, politics and lore, provide for a powerful story of love, loyalty, honour, betrayal and violence that climaxes with the battle of Mount Badon.

Mons Badonicus in Latin; Mynydd Baddon in Cymraeg, the Welsh language, is the mysterious mountain or hilltop that was a pivotal battleground between Britons and Saxons. Mysterious, because its location has never been proven.

Cymraeg (what the Celts speak):

CH- *as in the Scottish word "loch" or the composer's name "Bach"*

DD- *a"th" sound as in "thin"*

F - *sounds like "v"*

FF- *is "ef"*

G - *is hard like in "go" never soft like in "giraffe"*

NG- *is as in "song"*

LL- *is similar to shaping your tongue to say "L" but blowing air instead*

PH- *is "f"*

R - *is rolled on the tongue*

RH- *is like saying "R" but blowing air*

W-*is like "oo" as in "cool"*

An example: *Myrddin*; Mer-th-in

Old English (what the Saxons speak):

SC- *is "sh"*

C - *is usually hard like "k"*

G -*usually pronounced "y"*

H - *is never silent but like throat clearing as in "Bach"*

AE- *as in "band" or "fan"*

I - *as in "feet"*

An example; *Ceolwulf*; kay-ol-wolf

Latin (what the Romans and Romano-Britons speak):

Latin is pronounced pretty much as it is spelled. Some differences though are, V as in W, i as in y and g as in "gap"

Chapter 1

Lying in the dirt of the forest floor, cold and cramped, his enemies in front of him, Owain tried to remain focused. He and his men had travelled many miles through the dense forest. The cold was biting into him and he was taunted and tormented by the thought of a warm meal. It was one moon after *Samhain*, the end of Harvest, the beginning of the Dark Months, and in another month it would be Winter Solstice, what the Christians called the Christ Mass. Owain lay motionless, trying to assess the danger.

Owain first thought the trail he and his men had been following was made by a group of warriors. It was a certainty that only a band of well-armed men would have a chance at attacking his village. But now the signs told Owain that he and his men were on the trail of a single man. Owain rubbed his eyes. The cold crept deeper into his bones. It had begun to snow. The trees of the Great Forest creaked, their bare limbs rattling like a corpse's bones. Owain chanced a quick look at his men hidden about. The tension was palpable.

His captain, Dyfyr, made his way to him and leaned close to his ear.

"Footprints," he whispered quietly. It took the two men a long time to move soundlessly through the dead underbrush to the spot where two more of their warriors lay hidden. The men looked at the site and were puzzled. Clearly, the trail of the man they were tracking led back to their own overnight camp deeper in the Great Forest. Dyfyr motioned to the men lying unseen on the forest floor. They were going to move out quickly.

After hours of running through the forest without making a sound, the handful of men slowed as they approached their own camp. Everyone moved into position. Dyfyr looked to Owain for the order to charge down. A yell split the deep silence of the forest. Archers were instantly ready, their powerful yew longbows notched with deadly arrows, drawstrings pulled taut, were quivering with tension. They waited for Owain's order to shoot.

Dyfyr saw one his men, Guto, down at the camp. Owain signalled the archers to stand down while he and Dyfyr took two men and sprinted down to the scene. Guto was surprised to see them. One of the young village warriors lay dead at his feet. Just beyond was a prone figure, presumably the man Owain had been tracking. One of Owain's men raised his lance to thrust its blade into the stranger and so ensure his death.

"Hold!" ordered Owain in a booming voice. Dyfyr looked up at Owain with surprise. It was unusual that Owain had not already ordered the stranger killed. After all, the stranger had invaded their lands and killed one of their own men, as the scene before them testified. The look in Owain's eyes told Dyfyr the situation had just become more complicated. Stifling an inward groan, Dyfyr slapped the warrior closest to him on the back of the head.

"No one does anything until Owain commands it!"

"Is he dead?" Owain nodded his head toward where the stranger lay, asking of the warrior closest to the stranger. The man roughly kicked at the stranger with his deerskin boot. A look of surprise raced across the man's face, he bent down to the stranger. Straightening, he looked up to Owain.

"He lives," was all he said. Owain looked to his captain and Dyfyr immediately ordered warriors to bind the man to prevent any escape. It seemed they were to have a prisoner.

"What are you doing?" asked Dyfyr. "The men are not going to be happy keeping this bastard alive while one of their own lays dead. And don't forget, he was in the forest. You know that makes him all the more a dead man in their eyes!"

Dyfyr was trying hard to contain his anger and frustration. In the years he had known the young Owain, he had come to realise that this man, while he had many good traits, could be wildly unpredictable. But flouting tribal customs as serious as this was beyond being quirky and unpredictable; it was dangerous.

"I want him alive," said Owain quietly. He looked at his trusted captain and saw the worry etched in his face.

"There is a lesson here, something we can learn from this stranger. Surely, you want to know if there are anymore like him in our lands? Don't you think it strange that he would show up in the midst of the forest by himself with no other warriors with him as though he knew the secrets?" Owain stared at Dyfyr waiting for the implications of what he was saying to dawn on the old soldier.

"But the men, they will want blood. Already they are grumbling that the Old Laws are being broken..."

"You deal with the men, just see to it that nothing happens to the prisoner. Tell them we will have a Gathering upon our arrival home and I will ask that Rhiannon speak on the matter to those assembled."

Dyfyr stood looking at Owain trying to gauge the leader's mind. Turning away abruptly, he ordered the prisoner slung over one of the ponies they had kept hidden near their encampment. Guto walked alongside the pony carrying the body of their man. Low voices could be heard murmuring their disapproval of the prisoner. Dyfyr gathered his own pony and rode to the front. He told the men of Owain's decision to call a Gathering and allow Rhiannon to speak to the issue of the prisoner. This assuaged the feelings of the men. It was written in their tribal laws that only a Druid, which is what the villagers called the priests of the Ancient Religion, could advise a leader in circumstances such as these. And Rhiannon, in their opinion, filled that role aptly. She was revered as a healer, a warrior, and one who was possessed with the Sight. Some thought her to be a Druid priestess, though Rhiannon never spoke of it one way or another.

Snow began to fall heavily now and the way home was cold and long. The men trudged on silently; the mood was solemn. The cold light of the day's dying sun began to fade as the signs of their village appeared. An outrider from the village rode forth and greeted them.

Caerwyn warriors who returned from patrolling the Great Forest were always heartily welcomed back home. Fires were lit and food was prepared as the men entered the village. Their ponies were led away by the village boys to be fed and brushed. Orders were issued to ensure the prisoner was looked after, an unused storage shed was quickly turned into a makeshift gaol, and guards were posted.

Fresh warriors, ready and alert for new dangers, now protected the village. The wooden palisade was manned and the round huts with their thatched roofs were safe within. Watch fires were burning at different points providing illumination and warmth. Shadows of men and women danced across the white-wattle walls of the village huts. There was a hut near the centre of the village and it served as a *dafarn*, a meeting place serving ale, cider, and mead in exchange for war booty and bartered items. Men were regaling each other with tales of bravery and prowess with their mighty yew long bows. In the distance, the sound of a crying child could be heard mixed with the barking of a hunting hound. Throughout the village this night, tired men would take their pleasures in their own ways as best they could. The snow had stopped.

The village of Caerwyn was nestled in a meadow that bordered on the deep and mysterious Great Forest. The forest provided good protection to the village because no man could navigate the depths of those mysterious woods without knowledge of its secrets. Many had tried and in so trying, they had died. The village was near the shores of Llyn Tegid that provided the people of Caerwyn with pike, roach, perch, and eels. And there was always the chance of catching a whitefish that roamed the deep, clear, waters of the lake. The ample meadows grew grains for beer, bread, gruel and grazing for the animals. The hills were but a day's walk away and the hunting there was good. Caerwyn was a thriving village of circular huts made with mud brick and wattle walls, conical shaped thatched roofs and earthen floors. The inside of the huts were comfortable and simple with wooden tables, a chair perhaps and a pallet piled with animal skins that served as a bed. The inner walls were whitewashed. Some villagers covered their walls with designs of stylistic animals and intricate patterns of swirls and interlacing designs.

In the centre of the hut was a fire pit and the smoke from the cooking fire drifted up through the hole in the thatch. The village huts were warm, dry, and very cosy. Of course, some of the wealthier villagers made their huts from stone and were more sophisticated than the common huts. There was a great two story stone hut, the largest in the village, belonging to Owain and his wife, the Lady Gwenhwyfar.

Like Caerwyn itself, Gwenhwyfar had captured Owain's heart from his first sight of her. She was quite simply, beautiful. Her hair was the colour of dark honey and it fell unfettered about her smooth white shoulders. The Lady Gwenhwyfar was nearly as tall as Owain, but she moved with a sultry grace made even more intoxicating because she was unconscious of her movement. Her figure was womanly and curvy with soft milk white, breasts that amply filled her long flowing dresses. The Lady was no will-o'-the-wisp; there was a strength in her that was as evident as her sexuality. Gwenhwyfar eyes were blue and captivating. Intelligence and merriment shone through them and Owain often wondered if his thoughts were read, then dismissed as a small boy's fantasy.

Gwenhwyfar's family was revered amongst the people of Caerwyn. Bard's sang songs about her ancestors and how they had founded Caerwyn so long ago. And if one listened carefully to the bard's words, it was the mother goddess Dôn herself who had bequeathed the village and its lands to Gwenhwyfar's ancestors. The villagers called the stars of Cassiopeia that shone in the night sky over Caerwyn, Llys Dôn. *Aranrhod*, a daughter of Dôn was the goddess of inspiration and re-birth, her stars were found in the northern sky and called *Caer Aranrhod*. The villagers saw the son of Dôn as the Milky Way that they called *Caer Gwydion*. But the most renowned of the mother goddess Dôn's children was her son *Llud* and to the Britons he was a Zeus. The family of Gwenhwyfar, being thought as favoured by Dôn, gave the villagers a sense of privilege and ownership that was reflected in their stewardship of the land and the pride with which they carried themselves.

Owain dismounted from his horse and surrendered the animal to a sleepy youngster charged with the animal's care. The young Owain had married Gwenhwyfar on the Summer Solstice, fifteen years ago. Owain's father Yrthyr Pendragon, chieftain of Gwynedd, had arranged his marriage to the Lady Gwenhwyfar of the Segontiaci tribe. The Romans had left the Misty Islands of the Britons eighty years ago and since that time the tribes of the North had been fighting each other. Yrthyr wanted his son Owain to rule the village of Caerwyn and the surrounding area. This he thought would bring peace to the tribes of the Deceangi, Demetae and the Silures. With his son guarding his flank and placating the rival tribes, Yrthyr would be free to rule Gwynedd from his hill-fort in Berth. The strategy had worked well these past years. It had not always been so.

The famed Roman IX Legion had quieted the wild and barbarous Picts and Scotti. The rebellious tribesmen had remained north of the Wall, named after the Emperor Hadrian who had relied on the large stonewalls to keep the frontier secure. In the year 410, Rome ordered her legions to return and protect the imperial city from the onslaught of the Visigoths. The Picts and Scotti seized the opportunity and breached the Wall; they laid waste to the surrounding countryside.

Gwrtheyrn, an immoral man rumoured to have impregnated his own daughter, became leader of the Council in the year after the last legion had returned to Rome. While the *civitas,* Roman settlements, in the southern lands near the coast remained relatively safe, their Roman ways intact and commerce thriving, the Northlands were left to fend for themselves. Gwrtheyrn's solution to the problem was to invite the Germanic tribes of the Frisians, the Jutes, the Angles and the Saxons to act as mercenaries, what the Romans called *foderati*. It was an unpopular tactic and one that would ultimately lead to his ruination.

Gwrtheyrn had been slow to pay what he had promised the *Sacsonaidd,* as the Britons called the Germanic tribesmen. He allowed them property and land which had placated many of their number for a time, but they wanted more. Soon Gwrtheyrn was facing armies of Picts, Scotti alongside discontented Sacsonaidd. More deals were struck and more land given away. The attacks of the Picts and Scotti stopped. The conflicts between the Britons and the Sacsonaidd however, became increasingly frequent. The two sides fought pitched battles with each other that went unabated for years. The misery of the common Briton caught between these forces was heavy. Gwrtheyrn's strategy was to contain the Sacsonaidd in the *Cantii* lands of the south and to land in the midlands. But the Sacsonaidd were not happy. An uprising began and more bloody battles were fought.

The Romano-Briton aristocrat and general, Ambrosius Aurelianus, arrived from Amorica, across the channel and on the coast of Gaul. He was furious that an unscrupulous degenerate such as Gwrtheyrn was chopping up his beloved Britannia, as the Romans called the islands. Not being able to stand what he considered to be blasphemy any longer, Ambrosius attacked the forces of Gwrtheyrn and war between the two broke out. Ambrosius and Gwrtheyrn fought each other viciously for years. Finally, Ambrosius caught Gwrtheyrn in his fortress at Ganarew and burnt it to the ground with the tyrant trapped inside. Battles still raged on between the Britons who were being pushed westward and the Sacsonaidd who held ground deeded to them by Gwrtheyrn in the south. The Sacsonaidd continued claiming Briton's traditional tribal lands renaming them Wesseaxe, Susseaxe and Esseaxe.

A great battle, though some said it was a gross slaughter of men on both sides, was fought between the Britons and the Sacsonaidd at a place called Wippedsflete. The carnage was so gruesome causing such heavy losses to both armies that no one side could clearly be called victorious. The Sacsonaidd retreated to live in the Cantii lands on the south eastern shore between the Tamesis and the Afon rivers and on the Isle of Thanet. For a time, there was peace between them and the Britons.

In the last few years, however, the wild northern tribesmen had again begun raiding and ravaging the towns and villages. The tribes were at each other's throats since Yrthyr had died.

While Owain was the heir, he did not have the support of the other tribal leaders. Even amongst Owain's own kin, there was dissent. They argued and bickered amongst themselves, the Picts and Scotti's made their raids even more daring. Sacsonaidd from the Cantii lands were pressing further west and though Caerwyn was so far unaffected; it could only be a matter of time. Owain and the warriors of Caerwyn remained on constant vigil.

Owain's main concern had been to comply with his father's wishes and placate the rival tribes. This had always been a complex and delicate task because many of the tribes had converted to the new religion of Christianity while others remained passionate followers of the Old Ways. His marriage to Gwenhwyfar had been meant as a means to assuage the tribes, at least those in the immediate area. Now after more than a decade of relative peace, Owain felt that the clouds of war were once again gathering.

"I think Owain has made a mistake in keeping this barbarian," said the shorter of the two men guarding the prisoner.

"That may be little Derfel, but master Owain is our leader, we have found no more of the invading bastards and we are out of harm's way. So, we are at leisure to do, as we will. No harm indulging in a little curiosity. And, little Derfel, that," the taller of the two men jabbed his thumb backwards over his shoulder indicating the prisoner, "cannot be executed without the say so of a Druid. That is the Ancient Law. Of course, our holy monks, if there were any around, would not wish him killed unless he refused to convert to their god. So he stays alive until Owain decides otherwise."

"Dyfrig, how can you be so bloody stupid," cried Derfel, slightly insulted about being called little.

"He had a battle axe and look at his clothes and his long hair and beard; he must be one of those bastards they say killed all of those monks over in the East! Surely any of the monks that are around will want him dead!" The man made a quick gesturing of his hand across his body in a strange pattern.

"That may be, but since the Law has been called into question, we've no right to kill him yet! That is as Owain, our leader and chief wishes it, so let that be an end to the matter!" Dyfrig nodded his head to indicate the discussion was ended. He shifted the long bow to a more comfortable position on his back. The two companions set about their duties, tending the fires and keeping watch on their charge. Derfel looked angrily at his slightly taller friend.

"You know Dyfrig, I hate those bastard dogs from the South," he spat his contempt for the prisoner, "and you know why as well!"

Guto pulled off his tunic and unwrapped his leggings. His wife was putting some barley bread and leek soup on the table. Her dark brown hair was thick and swirled about her shoulders as she moved. Not a small woman, she amply filled her plain woollen dress. She bent over the table to pour more cider for her husband, her breasts swinging freely, threatened to spill from her dress. As she turned her swaying hips away, Guto grabbed her roughly around the waist from behind. She tried to struggle free, complaining that there was more work to be done. Guto's rough grasp was far too strong. He spun her around and backhanded her across the face, his big meaty hand calloused from war, ripped her skin. As she fell whimpering to the dirt floor, her husband kicked her in the ribs. Dragging her to her feet Guto hit her repeatedly before throwing her back to the floor. Grabbing her hair from behind, he forced himself into her, giving no thought to her cries or her tears or her blood.

Across the village in another warrior's hut, children were sleeping in the wooden bed under an old wolf's skin. A fire was burning brightly in the hearth as Rhys watched his wife busying herself with cutting a piece of salted meat for him. Her thick tawny hair was pulled back from her face and tied with a brightly coloured strip of cloth. She wiped her hands on her apron and passed the plate of salted meat, hard bread, and pungent cheese to her husband.

"You should let me wash that cut," she said, a look of concern flickering over her face.

"Aah, *cariad*, it's not that bad is it?" Her husband asked using a term of endearment that never failed to bring a smile to his lovely wife's lips. He looked at the gash on his biceps with mock horror.

"Rhys, stop," his wife's concern for him written on her face, "if you don't let me wash it clean and bind it with a poultice, it will become putrid. Now come here and be still!"

"Right, cariad, you are always right," conceded her husband, as he offered his arm to her ministrations. She took some water that had been boiling on the fire, and with a clean cloth, she washed the wound. She then bound it tightly with a poultice of musky smelling herbs. Rhys gazed appreciatively at his pretty wife; reaching out his good arm, he gently took her by the hand and pulled her close, breathing in her scent. She giggled and bent her head down to kiss him more fully and openly on his mouth, her hair cascading around both of them as she freed it from the cloth. Fumbling their way out of their clothing, the happy couple managed to find their way to their pelt covered wooden bed. Laughter and giggling sang out in loud abandon and soon gave way to cries of passion and pleasure.

"Husband, welcome," Gwenhwyfar said although it was more a purr as that from a playful kitten. She had a fire burning in the fireplace to warm them and it's dancing yellow light made patterns with the shadows. There were sweet smelling woods burning and their pleasing scent filled the room. The Lady Gwenhwyfar herself was freshly washed with warm scented water and she was wearing a simple white woollen nightdress that did nothing to conceal her feminine shape. She approached her husband and assured him their children were well and safe in their own room. Her man had taken off his warm woollen cloak, leather belt, gauntlets, knife, and sword. Gwenhwyfar glided sensuously to him and began taking off his leather tunic, wool shirt, breeches, and leggings.

"You look tired, husband. Come wash your self in this warm water and wrap up in this wolf's fur." Her hands helped wash her husband's body caressing him with the warm, scented water. As she began to dry him off with a thick warm cloth, she playfully bit his ear lobe.

"Ow! What is this? I brave untold dangers in the Great Forest only to be eaten alive by my own wife?" cried Owain in mock indignation.

"Can you think of a better way to meet your end my Lord?" she breathed into his ear. Owain laughed.

"No cariad, no in truth I cannot." Owain ran his fingers through his wife's thick honey coloured tresses, pulling her closer to him. They melted into each other embracing as one before they kissed, their tongues swirling and searching. Falling onto the large wooden bed heaped with furs, they made love to each other alternating between sweet tenderness and unbridled passion.

"So, my husband," Gwenhwyfar said as she untangled herself from her husband's arms, leaving the warmth of their bed to put another log on the fire.

"What is this I hear about a captured barbarian and why don't you think he should be killed for invading the forest and killing one of your men? Surely, he is one of those from the tribes in the south and you know they killed the holy monks in the east. Has this anything to do with your feeling that troubles are about to beset us and soon?"

It always amazed and astonished Owain how his beautiful wife knew so much that was going on in his world. He had heard the rumours that she too had the gift of Sight and that because of her lineage; hers may even be greater than that of Rhiannon. The two women were very close friends. But when he asked her directly about such things she managed to answer without adding anything to his knowledge. Owain did not believe the tales of magic, mystery, and intrigue surrounding his wife and her ancestors. He suspected she had her own informants who provided her with gossip, news, and rumours. But this night he was startled and unnerved by her insights.

"Cariad," he said entreatingly to her, "come back to bed, it's cold."

"Then it's true you feel it, that we are about to enter into Dark Days".

Owain frowned and decided he may as well talk; his wife seemed to know his thoughts anyway.

"Something is not right that is to be sure. We have a man dead. I did not see it happen; the deed was done by the time we got to him. What troubles me about the scene was that he was stabbed from behind. I would have expected the barbarian to use his axe, but again the scene is troubling since the barbarian was found unconscious near by and his axe was clean and sheathed behind his back. His knife was also sheathed behind his back and it too was clean. I don't completely understand but I think something ominous is going on." Owain was now sitting on the side of the bed wrapped in a wolf's fur.

"I think, husband, that changes are coming to Caerwyn. I feel that the tribal chiefs will soon be at each other's throats vying for the scraps like great hounds at the hunter's table. They will be blind to the storm that is already beginning." Gwenhwyfar poked the fire one last time before returning to her husband.

"You are right, cariad, as always." Owain looked quizzically at his beautiful wife, her insight again startling him.

"The tribes are gathering and they are looking to our lands as easy pickings. It is as it has always been. We war and quibble amongst ourselves whilst others lay in wait to attack when our forces are divided and we are at our weakest. If only the tribes would put aside petty differences and come together for the good of all! The Romans showed us that if nothing else!" Gwenhwyfar smiled as she listened to her husband. She never doubted his passion but it amused her hearing him sound so pompous.

"Husband who was it that found the dead warrior, who was standing closest to him when you arrived?"

"I'm not sure; it was Guto, I think. Yes, Guto found him and immediately yelled for help, we all of us heard him. We scoured the forest and we made our way to the camp were we found the dead warrior, Guto and the barbarian."

Gwenhwyfar frowned and turned from her husband. She watched the fire dance over the logs, hissing and crackling, filling the room with warmth.

Owain's arms encircled her and she felt his warm hardness press against her. It had taken only seconds for her to fall in love with her husband. Fifteen summers ago, when she first saw him standing with his father Yrthyr Pendragon, she knew he was special. Her father, Bevan, had beamed with pride at the arrangement he had made with Yrthyr. Gwenhwyfar knew she was the key to a political strategy. An alliance between the tribes, under the auspices of Yrthyr Pendragon, would strengthen her tribe's position; maybe even bring peace to the land. What thrilled her more was the strength of character that shone in Owain's handsome face.

There was one villager though, who seethed with anger at the proposed match. Gronw was well known in Caerwyn as a cunning individual. He had gathered prestige, possessions, and a little power through shrewd deals and manoeuvres. It wasn't completely clear what his objections were regarding the marriage between Owain and Gwenhwyfar but he had been loudly protesting to any who would listen. Whether from misplaced pride or ignorance, some villagers had taken up Gronw's cause. The day came when Owain and Gronw came face to face. Gronw had said something about the pride of the men from Caerwyn inferring Gwenhwyfar was too good for Owain. Neither Bevan nor Yrthyr had been present, a fact not unnoticed, by Gronw and his men. Owain stood looking at Gronw; a few villagers who were present began shouting at Gronw. They were unhappy about any disparaging remarks that even remotely insulted Gwenhwyfar. Gronw hotly defended Gwenhwyfar making it clear that his displeasure was with Owain and not the beloved Lady herself. His men began pushing and shoving the villagers as a crowd gathered. It took a moment for Owain to understand what was going on. Gronw's men were manipulating the gathering crowd so that he would be cut off from any who were friendly to him. From the corner of his eye Owain saw two of Gronw's men heading for him. Owain began walking to his right, putting a family of villagers between him and Gronw's men; he managed to delay their flanking manoeuvre.

"What exactly is your grievance?" Owain asked of Gronw in a loud voice. He kept moving and changing directions slowing the advance of Gronw's men.

"My grievance? My grievance is that you are not of our village! You do not know our ways nor do you know anything of our Great Forest!" There was a murmur of approval from those supporting Gronw. They continued to push and shove and bully the other villagers.

"Well and good then!" cried Owain, "I stand ready to defend my right to be here as one of you!" He had effectively evaded Gronw's men and was now nearly face-to-face with Gronw himself.

"You impudent bastard!" Gronw was red in the face and shaking with rage.

"This is my land as much it is yours! Though this is not my own village, we all share the vast bounty of this great land. We should learn to live together for the greater good of all! We should not kill each other over petty squabbling! We are *Cymry* and as compatriots we should live together in peace and harmony!" Now there was a murmuring of approval amongst the villagers for the words of Owain. The crowd had grown as word of what was going on had spread through the village like wild fire.

Gronw looked confused. He glanced about for his men. They were effectively cut off from their leader by the crush of bodies anxious to see what they hoped would become the ancient ritual of single combat.

Owain felt the subtle change in the crowd and saw that Gronw's men were unable to help their leader. He stepped forward and with arms spread wide, a disarming smile on his face, played to the crowd. This of course infuriated Gronw. He lunged at Owain. A glint of reflected sunlight caught Owain's attention just as the hidden knife in Gronw's hand sliced through his tunic cutting him. Gronw slashed at him, but Owain deftly evaded. Again, Gronw sliced the air in front of Owain's face, but Owain managed to move back just out of the blade's path.

"Hmmm, smart that one is," said an old warrior to his young son as he intently watched the battle unfold.

"What do you mean, Da? He looks afraid to me. He keeps stepping away from Gronw."

"And wisely too, my little man. You always move away from a man with a small weapon. You only move in when the weapon is big like a spear, lance or a battle axe."

"Why is...." The young boy's question was drowned out by the noise of the other onlookers as they reacted to Gronw's move. He had feigned a thrust at Owain's right side only to pull back sharply and slash in a back handed movement across Owain's upper left chest, cutting him deeply. Owain stumbled and went down on one knee, his hand clutching at the cut in his chest. It was deep enough to flow red with blood that was seen by all, especially Gronw. He wasted no time and lunged quickly. His arm high, hoping to come in over Owain's bowed head and stab him through his exposed back and into his heart. But Owain anticipated the move and shot up, his left arm deflecting Gronw's knife arm as his right hand grabbed the front of Gronw's tunic and his head slammed into Gronw's face.

Gronw was stunned and he staggered back, blood pouring from his smashed nose, blinding him. But Owain held him firmly by the tunic. With his left hand, Owain pulled down hard capturing Gronw's knife as he pulled the man off balance and spun him around. Now Gronw, still stunned, was on his knees, his back to Owain whose right arm was now pulling the tunic tightly across Gronw's windpipe cutting off his air. In Owain's left hand was Gronw's knife, tightly held against its former owner's throat. The knife drew a thin red line of blood across Gronw's exposed throat. A hush fell on all who watched.

Gwenhwyfar stirred in her husband's arms as she broke her reverie of those horrible events from years ago. She had arrived too late to stop the fight between her husband and Gronw and the crowd slowed her. But she had stood in horror and witnessed the end of the combat.

"What is it cariad?" Owain asked, concern creeping into his voice. "Why do you have that troubled look on your sweet face?"

"I was remembering when we first met." Gwenhwyfar turned from her husband moving her back to him so that his strong arms encircled her.

"And that brings you sadness?" mocked Owain playfully. Gwenhwyfar snuggled closer her to her lover, her husband and her chosen. She pulled the wolf's skin around them both and again nuzzled her husband.

"Having found you has been the greatest treasure of my life, the greatest gift the Goddess ever bestowed to me. No, husband I am not sad at having found you but only of the circumstances of that day."

"Well, as I recall," said Owain continuing in his playful tone, "you didn't find me nor was I a gift from the Goddess. My father arranged our getting together with your father. But I appreciate your fondness of me! I am now more puzzled, however, that you are so sad, what with all of these pleasant memories." Gwenhwyfar elbowed her husband sharply in his stomach.

"That's for your insolence," she said and then delivered another hard elbow, "and that is for insulting the Goddess. An arrangement between our fathers, please! Who do you think put such a notion in their heads if it was not the Goddess herself?" Laughing, Owain covered his stomach with one hand while with the other he tried to stop another elbow being delivered.

"I was thinking," continued Gwenhwyfar, "of the fight you had with Gronw."

"Surely you never doubted my survival or were you afraid I would lose and thwart the Goddess's plan?" Owain knew his humour had crossed the line when he felt his wife's body stiffen.

"Never say such things even in jest," she said, her face looking drawn and serious. Owain said nothing but simply hugged her tightly and kissed her neck.

"Cariad, come I am only trying to lighten your mood. Tell me what troubles you." He finally said, after a moment. His own face now showed concern.

"Has my decision to bring the prisoner in alive displeased you? I know the men are angry, but surely you can see the wisdom."

"Owain, you should have killed him."

Owain looked at his wife. He was unused to her being so maudlin. It was from his fear for her well being that caused him to speak sharply.

"I will not kill him, Gwenhwyfar! I will not!" Owain used her full name and she knew instinctively he had become angered with her.

"There is something I can learn from this man," her husband was saying as he jumped from their bed and began stalking the room.

"What it is I cannot be sure but there is a lesson for me here. I know there is something foreboding about the death of our man and the appearance of this stranger. Killing him will not help me or make me wiser. Keeping him alive for the time being is no threat to you or to Caerwyn. Do you think me such a fool that I would willingly bring danger to our midst? Do you think I have dung between my ears, that I would allow any danger to threaten us? I have worked hard to see to it that we not only have a safe life here, but that the surrounding lands are also safe. My father demanded that of me! I love you very much and I know the strain you bear, the responsibility you have to your ancestors to keep this place alive and free. I would do nothing to threaten that.

You know I have spent these last years doing my best in service to you and Caerwyn. You have always trusted my judgement and I have always trusted your knowledge no matter how you come by it! Why should you go against me now? Have you information about this man I do not?"

Owain's voice had risen to a shout in his frustration. He was exasperated. He could not fathom the reason for his wife to wish him to kill the prisoner. And then suddenly Owain realised what it was.

"Cariad the man who was killed was he a cousin of yours? I had no idea! But cariad the scene is a complex one and to be honest I cannot say with surety that this prisoner killed your cousin. Had I the evidence it would be a dead barbarian out there in the shed! Believe me we searched the area of the Great Forest where we found this barbarian and there was no sign of intrusion by any force of men. He was alone which is highly suspicious. And that is what I would learn from this man, why is he here?"

Gwenhwyfar looked quizzically at her husband. She gently shook her head, her thick honey-gold hair swaying with her movement.

"No, husband," she said solemnly, "I do not doubt you. How could I? It was your honour, your soul that I fell in love with when we first met. Of course, I know how hard you have worked and I fear nothing when I have you by my side. I dare say most of the villagers feel the same as I in that regard. No, husband, I do not wish your prisoner dead and that poor man who was killed was not my cousin. In truth I do not wish your prisoner to be killed at all and think you are wise to keep him alive and learn from him what you might."

"What then are you saying, cariad?" Owain was stupefied.

"You should have killed him, husband. Gronw. You should not have let him live when you had him at your mercy those years ago." Gwenhwyfar had never trusted Gronw and a deep resentment of him burned in her. Owain never understood her feeling and was left wondering what she really meant. Gwenhwyfar placed her hand on her husband's chest, her fingers tracing the jagged line of the scar that wended its way across his torso. An old scar it was now, its white and raised mark tracked across his flesh. She looked up into her husband's eyes and then turned to kiss him more deeply. They held each other tightly, no words passing between them. They loved, their passion soared taking them to a place that was safe and warm and sweet. It was a holy place full of light, music, and pleasing scents. A place they wished they could live forever.

Chapter 2

Rhiannon was well respected by the tribesmen of Caerwyn. They believed her to possess the Sight, a power to see the hidden truths in men and discern the future. The ancient Druids had possessed these gifts in the time before the Romans. The villagers of Caerwyn had not seen a Druid for many decades. The Romans had hunted the priests of the Old Religion, killing them wherever they were found; such was their fear of the priest's power over the people.

On the sacred isle, *Ynys Mon*, where the Druid centre of learning had been, Roman soldiers butchered the entire caste of ancient priests, leaving nothing but charred bodies and burnt out buildings as warning to all who followed the Old Ways. That was well over a hundred years ago and since then, no one in Caerwyn had actually seen a priest of the Old Ways. It was always rumoured the Druids, still watched over the devout. But that they did so from afar waiting for the time to come again and announce themselves so saving the faithful from their misery.

Rhiannon never spoke of such things. She helped those whom she could in her own way. Her healing powers were strong and her knowledge of healing herbs was vast. The respect of the villagers was well earned. When her husband had been killed during an attack by a rival tribe many years ago, Rhiannon had picked up his sword, jumped on his horse and rode out, bare breasted, to avenge her husband's death. She had killed the enemy in her husband's name and in so doing, had garnered the villager's respect, attaining stature that rivalled the Lady Gwenhwyfar. Rhiannon often disappeared from Caerwyn for weeks at a time and it was supposed she was communing with other Druid's, perhaps receiving their powers as one of their order.

By order of Owain, the dafarn was to be used to house the gathering of his advisors and soldiers. Normally, a council meeting would be held in the two-storied stone structure he shared with Gwenhwyfar but Owain wished this council to be more informal. He wanted the members to be comfortable and thereby be more malleable. Gwenhwyfar sat beside her husband and his advisors. The room was filled with armed warriors draped in their traditional woollen cloaks woven in the yellow and black squared pattern favoured by the tribe. Their mood was sullen and angry. Rush torches burned and smoked in their wall sconces. A hearth-fire cast a warm yellow glow into the room. The prisoner had been brought in and he was lying unconscious on the floor in a heap of rags.

One of the guards kicked the pile, but he got no response. Owain signalled to Dyfyr who gave orders to two guards to remove the rags and bare the prisoner concealed within. The prisoner was a well-muscled man of indeterminate years, though clearly he was not a youth. Many battle scars criss-crossed the warrior's chest, back and arms. A knife wound, a sword cut and there, a mended bone. Water was thrown on the prisoner and a camp girl was told to clean him as best could be.

"Well," quipped one of the tribesmen, "it seems he isn't quite as invincible as *Morrigna*, the warrior goddess and killer of our enemies." There was a smattering of laughter from the men until they caught the look on Owain's face. Their laughter quickly subsided. A groan signalled the prisoner was coming to his senses. Silence fell on the men.

The prisoner drew a long breath and glared from behind his grey mane. He slowly looked around. Getting to his knees was difficult and blood ran freely from an open gash in his side, but he managed to stagger to his feet.

He was a large framed man with thick shoulders and his muscles rippled under his skin. Sinews showed like ropes of iron running down his arms. Although he was clearly a captive and must know his future was bleak at best, he showed no sign that he acknowledged such facts. There was a haunted look in his eyes. It was not fear Owain saw in the big man's face but a look showing no concern whatsoever for the circumstances of the moment. He was locked in his own private hell from which there was no escape.

Rhiannon, tall and beautiful, strode gracefully into the midst of the gathering. Her black hair was long and flowed in an unfettered mane behind her as she walked. Rhiannon's movements accentuated her muscular body leaving no doubt of the strength at her command. Her white marble skin, gleamed and her blue eyes sparkled in the firelight. The men could not avert their eyes and she knew they drank in her every move. The silence was broken when Rhiannon threw some small animal bones onto a hide she had laid down for the purpose of divination. This was something the men had not seen in ages; awe and wonderment perhaps an undercurrent of apprehension swept through the fire-lit dafarn. Gwenhwyfar stifled an enigmatic smile as she took in the scene.

Rhiannon bent close over the jumbled bones and seemed to sniff at them. Mumbling words, only she could understand, Rhiannon began to sway back and forth, a cry rising from her throat.

"A once proud and mighty warrior, a leader of men, not the best in his land but respected nevertheless," she managed to mumble almost incoherently. A skin of watery ale was offered her and thirstily she drank of it. Wiping her lips, she smiled slyly at the prisoner and began to sing.

"Sights seen, tasks preformed,
victories won and
lost friends mourned.
Battles fought, honour sought,
brave and true
in deed and thought.
Warm hearth, but cold bed,
meat and wine though
love alas not here it's dead.
New found bed, soft'n sweet,
time stands still
when two lovers meet.
Lovers love and together play,
know not they
of the price yet to pay.
Quarrels wound, remove the spice,
now not lovers

too high's the price.
Love now gone, or has it yet?
No matter now,
for too steep's the debt.
Warrior not, man now mad
and this because
love once sweet now is bad.
Sword broken beyond repair
man ashamed
soon will drown in his despair."

She stopped suddenly and laughing hysterically, Rhiannon pointed at the prisoner. All of the tribesmen were laughing now; even Owain was beginning to smile. A low rumble faint at first, not heard over the laughter, began to rise. The prisoner threw his head back and howled like a wounded bull. The laughter stopped, men grabbed their weapons, and two of Owain's guards threw themselves in front of him as protection from whatever unseen demon had entered the dafarn.

The wild-eyed gaze of the prisoner caused fear and panic in the tribesmen. Now they thought him truly mad. In fear, a guard raised his spear and struck a mighty blow with its haft to the prisoner's head sending him sprawling face down into the dirt. Owain acted swiftly to prevent his men from beating the prisoner to death. He ordered the prisoner bound, clothed and his wound's tended. Owain's guards bristled at the tribesmen's grumbling but the guards' half-drawn swords ensured the villager's obedience.

"What do you make of that?" one of Owain's advisors asked him.

"If he is mad surely he should be put to death. That is our law and in any case of what use is he?" Dyfyr fidgeted uncomfortably trying to keep his opinion to himself. Other advisors where milling around Owain. They were acutely aware of Gwenhwyfar and Rhiannon and kept their comments civil and respectful in tone.

"He is not completely mad and I think there is a lesson for me here." Owain cast a knowing look first to his wife and then to Rhiannon.

"I think his deepest wounds are in his soul and that he has lost his honour but not on the battlefield. I am curious as to how a man like him can regain such a loss. That indeed might be the lesson! But of course I would want to know where he came from, what he was doing alone in our forest, and how many more of them there may be. And if it's the law you are concerned with, I will say this; our Druids decreed an execution or a sacrifice could not be undertaken without one them being present. I would say that the Ancient Law you so casually mention can be satisfied more properly by holding this man alive. Especially so, since we have had this examination of our prisoner, in the presence of the Lady Gwenhwyfar and the Lady Rhiannon." Rhiannon nodded her head and smiled ambiguously, her twinkling blue eyes revealing nothing of her thoughts.

"My husband is right," the Lady Gwenhwyfar, stood and in a clear voice declared.

"The Lady Rhiannon has used her powers and has been satisfied that the Ancient Law has not been violated. On behalf of my venerated Ancestors, I decree that the prisoner will be bound over alive in the charge of Owain."

Unnerved the advisor took a sloppy drink of ale and left the dafarn. Dyfyr and the others saw to it the dafarn was cleared and the prisoner placed under lock and key once again.

Outside the snow fell silently.

Lydia had just finished her chores in the kitchen when she was called to the hut of one of the villagers. One of Owain's warriors was injured and her skills as a healer were needed. The man of the hut had struck his head hard while riding through the forest on patrol earlier in the day. He had fallen off his mount but had been able to regain his senses enough to continue his duties. Now that he was home, he discovered his vision was blurred and his head ached terribly. Still reluctant to seek help, the warrior had tried eating the food his wife had prepared for him on his return. When the wife saw that her husband could not keep his food down, she had sent for help. Rhiannon though was busy at the Gathering and so Lydia had been called upon.

Lydia quieted the man's wife, who was out of her wits with fear for her man.

In truth, she feared for herself as much as for her husband; life would be the harder for her without him. The water was boiled and Lydia made an herbal drink to calm the woman. She examined the man and then used the rest of the hot water to concoct a drink made with willow bark, to treat the pain in the man's head. She instructed the wife to keep her husband laying down where he could remain quiet and calm. Lydia gave the woman the rest of the willow bark concoction with instructions to make a brew for her husband every four hours. And while he remained prone and quiet, under no circumstances was she allowed to let him fall asleep. Not until morning when many hours had passed, could she allow her man to sleep. Lydia was quite firm on that point.

When she left the hut, Lydia heard the woman talking quietly to her man and praying to the Great Mother Goddess Dôn, for her husband's recovery. Lydia frowned. The Ancient Ways, ever on the surface of daily rural life, had remained close to many of the villager's hearts, despite the teachings of the new Christian religion. This made some of the more pious Christian villagers uneasy and they usually called on Lydia, herself a devout Christian, to administer to their sick. But in times such as this when Rhiannon was unavailable, followers of the Old Ways also sought Lydia.

Lydia was an attractive woman, voluptuous, with thick, long black hair and olive complexion. Her eyes were coal black, accented by her high cheekbones and slightly slanted like the eyes of a doe. She came and went in the village as she pleased, a benefit derived from her close relationship with the Lady Gwenhwyfar. It was the Lady herself who had saved Lydia from death when the poor girl had been found left for dead by the edge of the Great Forest. It was rumoured in the village that Lydia was from the South and had been captured by the barbarians who were fighting and occupying the crumbling Romano-Briton civitas of the southern lands. She had suffered in their hands but had escaped. The journey had been cruel and hard for the poor girl but she never spoke of these hardships to anyone.

Lady Gwenhwyfar had been on the edge of the Great Forest with her guards and entourage when Lydia was found all those years ago. Seeing the pathetic state of the girl, Gwenhwyfar immediately acted to save Lydia, tending her wounds giving her food and water and wrapping the girl in her own wolf skins. Gwenhwyfar believed since that day that she and Lydia were spiritually connected despite the fact Lydia was a Christian. Since that time Lydia had been allowed a small hut of her, own. There she grew herbs and prepared remedies to ease the pain and suffering of her adopted neighbours. At times, she helped in the kitchens. She was especially helpful when the village warriors were returning from patrol late at night, tired, cold and hungry. Owain always made sure that those of his men who did not have a woman to look after them were fed something hot upon their return from duty. And there were always wounds needing tender care.

The prisoner lay in a heap in the centre of the hut used to hold him. Two guards lounged in the doorway, a rush torch cast a flickering amber light on the scene inside.

His head ached terribly from the blow he had received earlier. His body shivered with cold and blood still ran from the gash in his side, but he barely noticed any of these things. His soul was being eaten by the shame and guilt of his captivity. He got up to his knees. The guards stirred uneasily at his movements.

"Law, he's moving!"

"I can see that, can't I? He's a big bugger too!"

"What should we do?" asked the smaller of the guards as he notched an arrow in his great long bow.

"Math! Un-notch that bow! You'll go straight through the bloody hut with that arrow!"

"I've never missed anything I have notched my arrow against in all my life as you well know!" spat an offended Math. Llew had stood up himself and moved off to the side carrying with him a large club.

"Our orders were not to let him escape but we are not to kill him either! So un-notch that arrow pick up your club and move to the other side. If he gets out, we'll come at him from two directions and beat the bastard to his knees. Now do as I say!"

The prisoner looked at both men. They were shorter than he was but they would still have been considered huge by Roman standards. The tribesmen were powerfully built and battle-tested. They both had dark brown hair worn to the shoulders, rough beards and blazing blue eyes. He thought they were clever to have put down the huge bow and move away, each taking a different direction. That would make it near impossible for him to attack without getting struck down by one them. He saw their woollen cloaks with the curious black and yellow squared pattern and marvelled at the artistry of their cloak pins. The colourful patterning of the men's clothing amused him. He saw that their leggings were bound at the ankle to allow for warmth and comfort as well as freedom in battle. Their weapons though, he noted carefully, the warrior within him ever alert, were well cared for; the knives, the swords and spears were clean and sharp. The warrior also paid heed to the clubs and especially to those huge long bows.

"Now there is an interesting weapon," he thought to himself. He had seen bows before, the Jutes used them and even some warriors in his own tribe had become proficient with them. But he had not seen such big ones; these weapons were the height of the warriors wielding them.

The prisoner got up from his knees. The rags on his body fell away leaving only a brief cloth around his waist.

"*Ic grete ge! Ceolwulf is min nama!* " He stated his name loudly so that his gods would hear him and know who was facing death this day.

"I greet thee, Ceolwulf is my name!" he yelled again, shaking his fists at the two guards, "come on, come in here and fight me, Ceolwulf, a man who spits on you *waelas,* you barbarians! Come, I bid thee, fight, and I will hand you your heads!" The warrior had both fists clenched and was beckoning the two guards.

"Llew, what the hell is he barking at?" asked Math, concern in his voice.

"How the bloody hell should I know what he's saying? What has got him so worked up?" Llew was also anxious.

"Hey you! Big bugger...sit down and be quiet or we'll beat you to a bloody pulp, you dog!" Llew punctuated his rough remarks with a shake of the club he carried.

The prisoner stood tall and with outstretched hands and head held high, began his prayer of death.

"O, Mighty *Woden*, All Father, *Hael to Woden*! I ask you welcome me to your Great Hall! I ask you allow me my place among my people at your bountiful table, that together we may live forever and tell tales of our courage in your Great Hall!"

"Llew, he's going to charge the cage!"

"He wouldn't dare, Math, he's not that stupid!"

The prisoner's body slammed into the wooden cage with a mighty crash, shaking the entire hut. Math jumped back and again notched his great bow. Llew immediately swung his club at the prisoner's head, missed but caught the man's hand.

"Don't loose your arrow, Math or we'll be dead! Grab that club and help me beat him back!" yelled Llew to his smaller companion.

"You said he wouldn't charge, Llew! That's what you said! I think we should just kill him now and get it over with!"

"Math, our orders! If we kill him we'll forfeit with our lives, now help me beat him back!"

The prisoner's body crashed into the cage again. Blood now flowed freely from the raw wound in his side. Again, Llew swung his club and this time he struck a terrific blow to the side of the prisoner's head. The blow sent the prisoner sprawling in the dirt. He tried to regain his footing but Math thrust the haft of a lance through the cage from the other side striking the prisoner in the stomach, driving all air from his lungs.

As Lydia passed the hut now being used to cage Owain's prisoner, she heard Llew yelling at Math, two men she knew to be friends of long standing. Curious, she stopped by the hut and peered into the opening. What she saw appalled her!

"Llew! Math! What in the name of all that is Holy is going on here?"

"Ahh, Lydia...you shouldn't be here! This is not your business..."

"Don't you tell me my business Llew! I asked you a question and I want an answer!"

"It's not what you think...."whined Math, "we are just doing as we were told."

"And who told you to torture a man as though you were agents of the Devil himself?" demanded an enraged Lydia.

"We are not torturing him! And you have no right to say something like that to us! If you must know, master Owain himself told us to guard this creature, so you can just climb down off your high horse, my lady!" spat an equally perturbed Llew.

"Master Owain told you to beat this man to a bloody pulp?" asked Lydia, sarcasm dripping from her words.

"We didn't beat him, we only prevented him from escaping. Our orders are not to kill him, but to keep him from getting away. That's right isn't it, Llew?"

"Right as rain! Math and I are only doing as we were told Lydia, that's all. This bugger nearly brought the whole hut down on our heads. We had to do something!"

"Well, " Lydia said again, sarcasm evident her tone, "if keeping this man alive is part of your duty then you may yet have failed master Owain!"

The two men were anxious and upset despite their show of bravado in front of Lydia. Neither man would be willing to admit it, but they were grateful that Lydia had appeared when she did for they were worried they had killed their charge. Lydia bent down and began washing the prisoner using the water from the guard's drinking skin and the clean cloth she carried. She was not concerned with his bruises and cuts. They would not be difficult to heal. Even the gash in the prisoner's side could be stitched and with a poultice, she could guard against the wound worsening. The bruises would heal in time and the bone beneath the skin seemed unbroken. It was the lump on the side of the prisoner's head, which concerned Lydia. He was still unconscious and his eyes rolled in his head when she tried to look at them.

"I am going to get some help. I will need another pair of hands and some things from my hut. Don't hit him again, Llew or you will kill him. I am sure master Owain would not be impressed if that should happen!"

"Don't give me orders, Lydia! I know my duty! You just go and get what you need and get back here quickly!" Llew's pride had been stung by Lydia's words.

"You'll keep a civil tongue in your head, Llew or I'll go straight to Owain and tell him you've beaten his prisoner to death!"

"Llew," whispered Math, "be polite to her. If she goes to master Owain with this, it'll look bad for us both!"

"Well, I know my duty! No one tells me my duty! Now, Lydia you just go and carry on...get what you need and come right back. We'll not hurt the creature. If he tries to escape again we'll shoot him through, right Math?"

"Right, Llew! We'll shoot him through! I've not missed anything I've ever notched an arrow against as well you know!"

Lydia left quickly. She knew the two men were badly shaken and that they would not do anything else to the prisoner as long as he stayed still. She was sure the poor wretch would not move and prayed she was not to late to help him.

Much to the surprise of Llew, Lydia returned with Rhiannon. Lydia was not often seen in the company of Rhiannon as many villagers thought Lydia considered Rhiannon to be a sorcerer of some kind. Everyone in Caerwyn knew Lydia was devoted to the new religion and that she thought the Ancient Ways were pagan and unfitting. It was odd to see the two women side by side on the same mission.

"It will not bode well for you two should this prisoner die." Rhiannon's piercing blue eyes transfixed Llew and frightened poor Math nearly to death. The two men were dumbfounded and could say nothing in their defence.

"Still I detect some life in him yet, perhaps...." Rhiannon looked around the hut, spying the dying fire and the cauldron above it, she ordered the two men to stoke the fire.

"What are you doing?" she asked of Lydia.

"Why, I am praying for the health of this man of course. He seems to be important to master Owain and he looks such a wretch," replied Lydia.

"I fear you may overtax your god. It is beyond me how you think only one god can be responsible for all that goes on in this world. There are many problems and we need many gods to help us deal with them all. Even the gods will not help if first we do not try to help ourselves. Now go and fetch some clean water. Take the little one with you and bring some more firewood as well," said Rhiannon as she indicated that Math should assist with the job.

Turning her attention to Llew she ordered him to open the cage so that she could better examine Owain's prisoner. Llew was about to protest that without Math and proper precautions he would not willingly open the cage. How could he disobey Rhiannon? He opened the cage door and stood aside, his hands now firmly on the shaft of his spear.

Rhiannon stripped the prisoner and examined every inch of his body. She seemed dismayed by his unresponsiveness. Llew was now getting more anxious about the condition of his charge after seeing the grey pallor of his skin, the deep wound in his side and the blue-black bruises on his head, face and back.

Lydia entered the hut, Math in tow, carrying the firewood and water. She instructed Math to start another fire in an iron brazier on the opposite side of the hut, while she poured the water into the cauldron over the fire. Soon the hut was bathed in the warmth and light of the two fires.

Passing Llew, who gave her a weak smile, she entered the cage and helped bathe the prisoner. Rhiannon placed a poultice of elfwort over the wound in the prisoner's side explaining that it would further clean the wound and help prevent fever. She applied wood betony to soothe any headache and joint pain, even helping the prisoner to drink some of the potion so his blood would be purified. Vervain was applied to ward off any fits or seizures, calm the prisoner and further reduce any headache.

Rhiannon winked at Lydia and said, "I have used this herb many times for love enchantment." She pulled back the wolf's skin that they had used to cover the prisoner and gazed at his exposed manhood. "I wonder if it will have such an effect on our man here?" She grinned mischievously and replaced the wolf pelt. Lydia blushed deeply, Math and Llew pretended not to hear.

"Well, Lydia, I have seen many men in such a state of slumber as this. Sometimes they wake and sometimes they die. It will be up to the Mother Goddess Dôn, may she protect and watch over this one!"

The two women cleaned the area, bundled up their patient against the cold night air, and left the cage. Before they left the hut Lydia turned to Llew.

"Now you listen to me, Llew. We have done as much as we can for this man. There will be no more beating, sticking or stabbing from you or Owain will be told of your incompetence!"

"You've no place telling me off, Lydia! I was only doing what I was told. Master Owain did not want that barbarian to escape! Math and I were only doing what we were told!" Math was nodding his head in agreement with his friend.

"Well," said Rhiannon, "you two had best keep that hut warm and take better care of your charge. Pray to the Goddess Dôn that she may look after this man in his slumber lest he escapes into the afterlife! Perhaps *Arawn*, God of the Underworld, will steal him away to his home in *Anwn* where he may join the Hunt!" Laughing fitfully, Rhiannon walked through the doorway into the snowy night. Lydia followed her after first pausing to say a prayer to her One True God.

Chapter 3

The morning was bright and the air coldly embracing. Owain hoped it would be a short winter. That was a good thing to contemplate he thought. It would be good to get all of Caerwyn thinking of the upcoming planting and the work involved in their farming and metalworking. But the Solstice was still a week or so away which meant winter had not yet peaked.

He decided to go to the lake, Llyn Tegid, and check on his son Cynglas. Owain had his captain Dyfyr take Cynglas to the lake. That area needed to be patrolled and Dyfyr said he would take some men and make sure no rival tribes had braved the frigid waters. Cynglas had begged to tag along.

Owain was proud of his son. The boy was thirteen summers old and a young warrior in training. He had hopes that his son would learn reading, writing, and thinking. It was Owain's opinion that a warrior needed more than a sword; he needed his wits about him if his name was to be remembered.

Owain's daughter Gwyneth had been the first-born. She was nearly fifteen years old now. Owain smiled at the thought of his tousle-haired daughter. He always called her "Princess" and took great delight in seeing her helping in the village. Today, Gwyneth was working in the kitchens with the other women, learning to cook and prepare winter foods.

Sadness passed over Owain. He wished he could spend more time with his children; time spent playing with them and teaching them. His duty to Caerwyn and to the memory of his father, Yrthyr, meant that he was often away from his children. Owain wished secretly for a more ordinary life. He wanted to farm and hunt and raise his children. Would it be so bad thought Owain to simply protect and provide for his family, enjoy the fruits of his honest labour and celebrate a life together with his wife? Could not someone else worry about the status of Caerwyn, the alliances with the other tribes and his father's lands? Owain sighed. He knew he was his father's son and that nothing could change that.

Cynglas and Dyfyr were waving and shouting to him. He ran to meet them. Cynglas was very excited; he was jumping about with what looked like a fish on the end of his spear. Dyfyr was beaming and slapping Cynglas on the back in congratulations, obviously proud of the boy.

"Da, Da," cried Cynglas, "look what I caught, look!"

"And just how did you manage to catch such a large fish in winter time? Did you resort to some sort of magic?"

"No father, I did not! I was just brave, strong and quick, and I listened to the advice of Dyfyr who knows everything!"

"Really," said Owain, "and Dyfyr, just what advice did you give young Master Cynglas?"

Dyfyr swallowed hard and began fidgeting about and looking as though he was caught in some form of trap.

"It was really quite safe, master Owain." That was the giveaway. Dyfyr always called Owain, "master Owain," when he felt he had crossed the boundary of his authority in some manner. In the heat of the many battles in which the two men had fought, Dyfyr was much less cordial. Indeed, he was at times very obscene and insulting.

"Out with it Dyfyr, what have you and my son been playing at?"

"We were not playing at anything Da. We caught dinner for tonight, surely that is a noble thing to have done?"

"Er...surely the boy is right Master Owain?" stammered Dyfyr.

"Surely indeed my friend. Humour me and explain just how this noble feat was accomplished."

"Da, it was very simple. Dyfyr and I went to the lakeshore. There was no sign of any boats or anything suggesting intrusion or signs of strangers."

Owain threw a scowl at his friend. The idea was to take Cynglas to the lakeshore only after it was determined to be safe. In no way were they to go looking for any signs of trouble. That was why there were patrols. Dyfyr blanched under the fierce look on Owain's face.

"Then," continued his son, "when we knew there would be no problems, Dyfyr showed me where some fish might be hiding in the water near the rocks. So, we went over, I climbed out to the end of the rocks, and sure enough, I saw some fish! I used my spear and got the second largest one with my first try!"

"And tell me my son, how is it you came to be wet?" Owain had just now realised that his son's leggings and tunic were soaking wet.

"Oh, Da," said the exasperated young warrior-in-training, "I slipped on the rocks. But not to fear, Dyfyr had tight hold of me most of the time!"

"Did he indeed?" Owain was becoming less and less amused as he heard the details of his son's exploits.

"Well, perhaps my friend, Dyfyr and I should have a talk while you young Cynglas run up to the hall and get out of those wet clothes and stand before a fire with a wolf's skin wrapped around you. You will be no good to us if you come down sick!"

"Father, I am not a child. I do not need...."

"Son, this is not a request to a child but rather the rites of the wily fisherman who has provided for his family." Owain looked to Dyfyr for help.

"Er, quite right young master Cynglas. Your father is quite right. The heat of the fire symbolises the warmth of renewed life having feasted on a courageous battle with the Sacred Lake. And the wolf skin is ...is... er...."

"Symbolic," chimed in Owain, "of the gratitude to all living things on earth, that they sacrifice themselves so that we may flourish..."

"Quite right master Owain, quite right...."

"So, young Cynglas, my young warrior, get a move on now before you pass this honour by and displease the gods." Cynglas looked at Dyfyr, who nodded solemnly. The boy then searched his father's face for some assurance and was pleased to see his father beaming proudly down at him. Off he went with a young man's purposeful walk, a warrior, and hunter in the making.

Owain looked at his friend. Dyfyr knew it was serious for there was no emotion showing on Owain's face. He had seen Owain look this way before, but it was usually in battle at a time when men were killed in the blink of an eye.

"Never," said Owain very quietly, "never put my child in danger."

Dyfyr knew better than to voice an opinion or give argument and reason to explain his actions, not when Owain acted like this. He would never dare speak his mind and tell his leader that Owain was mollycoddling the young lad and that if he wanted a warrior he needed to give the lad a warrior's responsibilities. No if he valued his life, Dyfyr would never be so dangerously presumptuous. He lowered his eyes.

"I understand."

"Good! Now come with me up to the hall and break your fast with Gwenhwyfar and me!" Owain clapped his friend on the back. Dyfyr breathed more easily, knowing the danger had passed and that all was forgiven...as long as he never again put Cynglas in a situation in which Owain might consider dangerous. Such a strange man this Owain, thought Dyfyr.

After breakfast, Owain occupied the rest of his day with checking and reorganising the patrols. He even took a ride out into the forest to see for him self that all was safe. Later he checked with the cooks and asked them their opinion on the winter supplies. Though Owain wished for a short winter, he wanted to know just what the food and provision levels were for one could never completely rely on nature to co-operate. He was nevertheless pleased with the answers. No one in Caerwyn would go hungry this winter. His mind turned next to military matters. Was Caerwyn safe from rival tribes? Were there more men like his prisoner out in the depths of the Great Forest laying in wait? Owain had been informed that Lydia and Rhiannon had tended to his prisoner. He decided to summon Lydia to his and Gwenhwyfar's house and speak with her.

Gwenhwyfar and Owain were sitting in chairs by a warm fire when Lydia arrived.

"Well, master Owain, I am not sure," said Lydia in response to Owain's questions about the prisoner's health.

"He has been very badly beaten, he has a gash in his side, but it is his head that is worrisome. I must tell you Rhiannon is concerned for him. She has seen men who have been struck on the head in battle and she thinks that with careful and proper care he may survive. There is no guarantee of it." Lydia had been received into the hall, provided food and drink although she would not accept anything stronger than watered barley beer. She was seated near the fire facing Owain and the Lady Gwenhwyfar.

"And what do you think, Lydia?" asked Gwenhwyfar.

"I have seen wounded men many times in my life and with many different wounds. Cuts can be stitched and as long as they are kept clean and free of pus, the wounds mend. Broken bones can be straightened and bruises all heal in time. But with head wounds it is not so easy to tell. I think that when the wound is not obviously fatal then the man's life is in the hands of God. Oh! I am so sorry, my Lady!" A look of concern flashed across Lydia's face as she realised what she had said to the woman most people in Caerwyn though of as being of divine lineage.

"Not at all dear Lydia. What you say is true. We may look upon things differently but the sentiment is a good and noble one. I am sure the Goddess Dôn will watch over him too! Please continue." Gwenhwyfar smiled graciously and put Lydia at ease with her disarming charm. The bond between them remained intact despite their religious differences.

"Yes," said Owain, "tell us what you have noticed about this stranger."

"Well I am sure I cannot add much to what Rhiannon has already told you..." Lydia was still shaken by her accidental slip of the tongue.

"Be that as it may Lydia, but I would be interested in your thoughts. You possess a unique perspective among us." Owain said with a smile.

Lydia blushed, lowered her eyes and continued.

"Yes, master Owain, I am unique here in Caerwyn. From what I remember from my youth in the South, this prisoner is most probably one of those from across the sea, from the continent. It has been an age since I heard such coarse language and I was not able to understand much of what he said. He said very little to be sure. But I will listen hard and try my best to understand his tongue."

Owain jumped to his feet.

"An excellent idea my dear Lydia! Rhiannon will look after his wounds and you will talk with him and report to me all that you may learn!" Owain was very pleased.

"But husband, Rhiannon has gone."

"That's right master Owain. The sorcerer...er...Rhiannon has gone off and has not been seen in the village this day." Lydia took a drink of the watery ale thankful she had recovered from another verbal slip.

Owain tried to cover his surprise and frustration.

"No matter! Lydia you will be in charge of the prisoner and nurse him back to health. I will assign good and strong men to assist in guarding the prisoner. You will report only to me what ever you may learn from this man. Is that understood, dear Lydia?"

"Yes, master Owain." Lydia did not look at all happy.

The Lady Gwenhwyfar looked softly at her and with compassion.

"Dear Lydia. Such a hard lot you have had in your life. If there is anything, I may do to ease your burden I bid you come to me so that I may help. In the meantime, if my husband has finished his business with you..." She looked at Owain commanding him with her eyes. Owain appeared not to have noticed but he smiled and nodded his head.

"Then perhaps you would accompany me to my room where we may talk of feminine things."

Lydia lowered her eyes to Owain, who stood, walked over to her, and kissed her on both cheeks as a brother would. Lydia blushed and was lead away by Gwenhwyfar.

Math and Llew had finished a long shift guarding the warrior. They had done as was asked of them. Two braziers were burning one on each side of the cage. Skins had been thrown into the cage for additional warmth and Llew had placed a pot of broth to simmer over a fire. Their work completed and relieved of duty by fresh guards, the two friends decided to go to the dafarn for food and drink. They sat quietly along a wall and were soon engaged in serious conversation. Math was extolling the virtues of cider whilst Llew was giving freely of his opinions on the superiority of ale as the drink of choice. Only once did Geraint the dafarn owner need to come over to the men. Their quiet conversation had escalated into a near brawl when Math had thrown Llew's ale onto the dirt floor. Not taking kindly to what he considered sacrilege, Llew had grabbed his friend by his tunic, threatening to punch him in the face. Fortunately, the appearance of Geraint had served to calm the situation. Cooler heads had prevailed and the two men were again friends, each enjoying their favourite drink. Nevertheless, both were careful not to bring up the subject of which drink, cider or ale was the more superior. The common ground shared by both men was they agreed mead was horse piss.

The other men in the dafarn had stopped their discussion when Math and Llew had entered. After closely observing Llew and Math's drunken dispute over their drinks, the group of three men continued their whisperings ever conscious of the two men whom they considered Owain's lackeys. One of the men in the group saw Math vomit on Llew's foot. The three of them laughed at the sight and made a few choice and off-colour remarks. They continued with their conversation without paying Math or Llew further mind.

"So, Gronw is coming back to Caerwyn then?" one of them asked their leader.

"I am sure of it," said March, "our Gronw has heard about this prisoner of Owain's and he does not like it one bit!"

"Well, what does this mean, what will happen?" asked the third man of their party, a small scruffy looking individual wrapped tightly in a greasy, worn, grey woollen cloak.

March shrugged his shoulders and opening his rough hands.

"I really don't know my friends. I am sure he will want the prisoner killed; you know how he is! He will probably invoke the Old Religion and draw on the sentiments of the Lady Gwenhwyfar."

"That's right," laughed the scruffy one, "he will probably want a Council of Druids to pronounce sentence on the prisoner! Perhaps even resurrect the ancient rite of *Galan Mai* and have the bastard draw the burnt bread!"

The rite of Galan Mai was the old celebration held at summer's eve, the first day of May. It was held to welcome back *Bel* the Sun God. Throughout the south of the island, the rite was called, *Beltane*. The celebration was marked with singing, dancing and feasting. Large bonfires were built in homage to Bel. It was deemed good luck to jump through the fires and get singed by them. In some villages, herds of cows were channelled through two fires where the beast's sides were mildly singed by the heat, all in the name of good fortune. The festivities ended with the bannock bread passed amongst the gathering. The individual who took the burnt piece of bread was the one who was to be sacrificed to the Sun God and so succour good will for the coming harvest. That at least was the popular story passed down amongst the villagers. No one in Caerwyn had ever seen such a thing with their own eyes, it was simply something sung about in songs and told as stories around the campfires.

All three men laughed at the prospect of the Galan Mai being invoked and the prisoner being sacrificed.

"Yes, that would serve the bugger well!" Their laughter was raucous now.

"Maybe Owain could help by volunteering himself as the sacrifice!" March glanced furtively over at Llew and Math as his friends roared with laughter. He smiled as he saw Math vomit again as Llew stumbled to help his friend through the dafarn's door.

Owain and Gwenhwyfar had spent a wonderful night together with their children. It was a rare night indeed that allowed Owain the luxury of spending time with his family. They had shared a meal together at the big table and then moved to chairs around the fireplace. The children warmed themselves by the fire and pulled furs over themselves for added warmth as they told their parents what they had learned that day. Owain listened to Cynglas describe his plans for the future security of Caerwyn. Both parents had been amused and proud by the young boy's bravado and sincerity. He was growing up fast and soon would undergo proper instruction in the art of war. Tradition demanded that Cynglas become a war leader like his father.

However, Owain wanted only that his son would become a good man among men, strong, wise, courageous and temperate. And of course, he wished his son all happiness. Cynglas had finished telling his parents how he would chase any invader into the Great Forest where village warriors could pick them off and so save Caerwyn from attack. The boy sat back down in his chair and pulled the wolf skin around him. Owain's daughter was eager to have her turn to speak.

Gwyneth was, in her father's eyes, the fairest, most virtuous and by far the most charming young lady in the land. Owain's love for his daughter had been apparent from her birth. The great chieftain Owain had been smitten by the fragile beauty of his small baby girl and ever since she had her father, the great and mighty war leader securely wrapped around her finger. Owain smiled and squeezed his wife's hand as he had listened adoringly to his daughter discuss the day's lessons in her thoughtful manner.

"So you see Da, that when applied correctly and in the right amount, the boiled down bark of the willow tree can ease pain in the body and especially pain in the head." Gwyneth sat down with the confident self-assurance of youth.

Gwenhwyfar was proud of her daughter. Rhiannon told her that Gwyneth was doing well in her studies. Lydia too had told her how helpful Gwyneth was becoming. Gwenhwyfar knew though that the time was fast approaching when her daughter would be sought after for marriage. Gwyneth was already filling out her feminine shape and her mother noticed the young men of Caerwyn were aware of that fact. Gwenhwyfar knew instinctively that Gwyneth would soon be seen as a prize to be had by the heads of the clans. She had so much left to teach her daughter. The responsibilities of her ancient lineage demanded more than the challenges of an ordinary wife of Caerwyn.

The fire was warm and the heavy supper was making Owain's family sleepy. The parents took the rare opportunity of seeing their offspring to their beds. Cynglas had protested that he was a young warrior and did not require being escorted to his bed. His father agreed and after allowing the young boy to accompany him on one last check of the village, kissed his young son on the forehead and wished him good night. When the boy was safely in his bed, Owain crept back. The father stood over his sleeping son filled with pride and love, grateful for the moment. Owain watched his son breathing, the boys' eyes moving with his dreams. It was a brief moment of a father's desire to protect his son from the world. Owain knew in his heart that his little boy was indeed becoming a man. His time was nigh.

Throughout the next day, Owain had worn a smile every time he remembered the precious moments of the evening before. He had risen just before first light so that he could go about his duty checking and re-checking supplies, reorganising the patrols and ensuring the safety of the village for another day. Before mid-day, he stopped in to see his prisoner and speak with Llew and Math. The two men had risen early and had been guarding the prisoner since first light. And that on top of the night they had spent at the dafarn.

Owain was surprised to see the prisoner sleeping so late in the day. He was told by Lydia that the prisoner's wounds were serious and though she would not normally allow a man with such a wound to the head sleep so long, there was little she could do for him. He slipped in and out of consciousness and had spent a bad night. Lydia herself was looking tired and worn and that worried Owain. He replaced Math and Llew with Dyfrig and Derfel, leaving Lydia in charge of the prisoner's well being.

Outside the hut, away from the eyes and ears of the rest of the village, Owain managed to speak with the two tired guards. Llew told Owain what they had overheard in the dafarn the night before.

"And you are sure they did not suspect you were eavesdropping? You clearly heard them say Gronw was coming back to Caerwyn?" Owain's questioning was intense.

"Well, sir" began Llew, "they were very cautious at first, but we fooled them into dropping their guard. And yes that is what we heard them to say, they expected Gronw to return to Caerwyn." Carefully Llew described the subterfuge he and Math had acted out in order to get the information Owain had requested.

"Oh yes, sir," added Math gleefully, "I had them right fooled didn't I, Llew? Yes sir! I vomited on our Llew here to make it look real. Twice sir! Twice I did! You see, master Owain, I can vomit at will! Would you like me to show you...owww!"

Llew had elbowed Math sharply in the ribs to get him to shut up.

"Er, no, thank you Math. That won't be necessary. I know your talents and that is why I chose you and Llew here for this very important job. Well you are both doing too!" said Owain slapping Math on his back. He turned and left.

Math beamed with pride from ear to ear.

"Why the bloody hell did you tell our Master Owain that you puked on me? Are you completely daft?" demanded Llew. "You silly bugger!"

"Well, our Master Owain is a very wise man, Llew and he chose me because I have talent. So you just mind yourself my little man, when you speak to me like that!" Math shook his great bow at his friend. Llew just looked up to heaven, shook his head and opened his arms as though begging the indulgence of the Goddess herself.

Chapter 4

Inside the hut the prisoner stirred. Dyfrig and Derfel looked over at him while Lydia went to the pot and came back with a small bowl of broth.

Ceolwulf opened his eyes. Still seeing double, he had to wait a minute for his vision to clear. He rubbed his eyes and then shook his head and that motion caused him to vomit. The buzzing in his head became louder. He could see the two dishevelled men guarding him were well armed and walking towards his cage. They were trying to say something, but Ceolwulf could not hear them. He clenched and unclenched his fists. Placing his hands on the floor, he tried to gain his footing, stumbled, and tried again. The room spun and suddenly he was gazing at the roof of the wooden cage. Something warm passed his lips and ran soothingly down his throat. He felt a cool damp cloth, wipe across his face a few times and then a warmth as a hide was drawn up over him.

"Is he dead, Lydia?" asked a concerned Dyfrig.

"Did you do something to him wench, something you shouldn't have?" menaced Derfel who received a sharp look from Dyfrig.

"No, he is not dead and of course I didn't do anything to hurt him, you ignorant little man!" Lydia shot back at Derfel. She glared at him, angered that he would question her integrity and her loyalty to Owain. He resented being called a "little man" by someone who was not from Caerwyn.

Derfel had never liked Lydia. It was known that Lydia was from the south and had been captured by the *Sacsonaidd*. To Derfel, that made her untrustworthy.

Many years ago, raiders from the south had killed Derfel's entire family. Derfel, his wife and children along with cousins and other kin had decided to migrate south of Caerwyn. They had crossed the mountains and rivers and were awed by the beauty of the land. In their travels they had even had seen a gathering of Druid's praying in a sacred oak grove. Or at least that's what Derfel said every time he got drunk. No one had ever wrested any more detail from him drunk or not. The small group of family and kin eventually made it into the tribal lands of the Dobunni.

One day Derfel's family was out foraging for food while he stayed and talked with some of the tribesmen. As he talked the day grew long until nightfall was very near. Derfel was mad with worry for his family's safety. Finally he was able to convince a few of the tribesmen to accompany him in searching the meadow where his family had last been. There in the flattened grasses were the signs of a fight. Derfel found his wife first. It was a sight he had wished to never see. His beloved wife had been beaten and raped unmercifully. Her knife was still clenched in her hand and the amount of blood present suggested she had fought valiantly. A few paces away confirmed this as the body of one of her attackers was lying face down. One of the Dobunni turned him over and it was clear he had been repeatedly stabbed. Derfel did not recognise the tribe this scum had belonged to. The Dobunni told him that this was a *Sacsonaidd*. The tribesman noted sardonically that his grandfather had been present thirty years ago when the great leader Gwerthyrn had persuaded the Council to invite these tribes of Sacsonaidd from the continent to act as mercenaries against the Picts and Irish invaders.

"Who will protect us from these Sacsonaidd dogs, now? Mark my words, these vermin will be at war with us all soon, very soon!" The Dobunni spat harshly into the grass. He then went about searching the dead Sacsonaidd for valuables. Derfel had to enlist help to bury his family members. Broken hearted and alone Derfel made the long and arduous journey back to the only home he knew, Caerwyn.

It was a sign some said, a miracle said others, that he had survived the return journey alone and distraught. Now every time Derfel laid eyes on the prisoner he remembered his loss anew. He was in control of himself enough to know he could not give in to his fury and butcher the Sacsonaidd bastard he was forced to guard. Instead, he allowed his anger to wash over poor Lydia, ironically the only other person in Caerwyn who, under other circumstances, could empathise with him.

"Now you listen to me, I am in charge of this man's welfare. Master Owain and Lady Gwenhwyfar specifically asked me to do this task. And I am to report and answer to no one but master Owain himself! If anything befalls this prisoner master Owain will not be amused and you both will forfeit your lives, that I promise you!" Lydia was a force to be reckoned with when she was angry. Not only did she have her own righteous Christian duty to assist the sick, but also in this case she had the direct instructions from both the military leader of the village and the head of the divine pagan ancestral line that had founded it.

"Why Owain would want this maggot alive, I don't know!" began Derfel as he menaced the prisoner with his spear.

"That is no concern of yours! I have been given instructions by master Owain to keep this man alive..."

"Sure he's not just for you to rut with? After all it's cold out and you're all alone!" quipped Derfel.

"...and that is what I will do! What? What did you say to me?" Lydia would have struck Derfel had not Dyfrig stepped in and directed her to the cauldron. Over his shoulder he yelled at Derfel to go and get more firewood.

"Sorry about Derfel miss! He can be a bit of a bast...er, I mean a bit awkward at times."

"If anything happens to that prisoner," said Lydia through clenched teeth, "you're both for it! Do you understand?"

"Yes, miss I do. And have no fear. Although Derfel hates those pig fu...er I mean those men from the south, he is loyal to master Owain. And Miss, I know that he would lay his life down for the Lady Gwenhwyfar. He thinks she is favoured by the Goddess Dôn herself!"

"Well, I will take you at your word and hold you responsible for the prisoner's safety. Make sure your friend honours his loyalty to Owain and the Lady Gwenhwyfar!" Lydia suppressed an urge to make the sign of the cross.

"Now get some more heat in here. I will set myself in that corner over there. You two sort yourselves out as you wish. Just you mind what I said!" Lydia was livid and shaking with rage, but she had to do as Owain ordered. Stoically, she busied herself with prodding the fire and seeing to the broth in the cauldron anything that would take her mind from what Derfel had said to her.

The prisoner had regained his senses enough to hear the conversation, but the words were garbled to him. He lay quietly in his cage trying to make sense of what was going on. Cold fingers of fear crawled up his spine. What if his injuries had somehow made him unable to understand? He quickly put that thought aside.

"These strange people are no doubt speaking in their own tongue," he thought to himself, "and that is why I am unable to make sense of what they say."

He had to keep his wits, if he wanted to survive this hell. The question was did he want to survive at all? Would not death be better than whatever these bastards had in mind for him? What about his honour? With a rush and a shudder, images of snow, cold and white, flooded his mind. He realised that his own blind ambition had caused him to be here in this cage. He had bargained like a merchant for the chance to increase his stature and power. There could be no honour in that.

No, torture could not match the pain of the shame he was already feeling. He vomited, coughed and then though he was delirious, he tried to stand. The once mighty warrior managed to get to his knees and with his arms outstretched he beseeched his gods for a quick and honourable death.

"*Eala! Hael Woden*, All Father, pray take me to your Great Hall this day! Allow me a warrior's death or at least a huntsman's fate! I have served you well, O Father! Allow me to take part in the Great Hunt and be amongst my own brave people in your Great Hall!"

Ceolwulf stopped mouthing his words and hung his head. He felt he had not lived well enough to be worthy of asking his god, Woden, for mercy. Ceolwulf knew his vices were more numerous than his virtues. The thought that his capture might very well be punishment for losing his honour suddenly occurred to him. What could be worse than to be consigned to this lifeless, dull existence? No, it was beneath him to beg Woden for anything! After all, Woden, the God of War, the Wild One, the Inspired One, prized self-reliance above all else!

Ceolwulf decided he would not kill himself. He instead would endure the unendurable and prove himself worthy as a follower of Woden. He would only seek a death befitting of his stature as a thane and a leader of men thereby regaining his lost honour.

"What the hell is he saying? What is he doing? Should I stick him, Dyfrig?" Derfel was ready to spear the prisoner, but held his weapon in dutiful abeyance.

"No, Derfel...."

"No! No! Do nothing!" Lydia yelled as she got up quickly and ran to the cage. "Just wait, he is too sick to do anything, just wait!"

As though by command the prisoner's eyes rolled in his head and he collapsed on his face more vomit running from his mouth. Lydia managed to persuade Dyfrig to help her roll the prisoner onto his side, while she wiped the vomit from him.

"Dyfrig this is dangerous!" Derfel said nervously.

"Never mind Derfel it will be all right!" said Dyfrig. "Put down your spear. Instead, you just notch your bow and stand back. You can cover me from there. If it is a ruse and this bastard tries to escape, loose your arrow. Mind you hit him or that arrow will go right through the wall!"

Derfel quickly put his spear down, grabbed his bow, notched and arrow, and backed away to a good firing position. Dyfrig turned back to help Lydia. She appeared more shaken than he expected. He thought that since she looked after the sick in the village, that she would not be so rattled by the sight of puke or a man passing out. Dyfrig wondered if she had understood some of what the prisoner had said and the thought made him nervous.

"It's alright," Lydia said, "he is sleeping fitfully again. He is still too weak to be of any real harm and in truth he may not ever recover; it is in the hands of God." She and Dyfrig exited the cage and Derfel lowered his great bow.

"You understood him didn't you?" Dyfrig challenged her with his question. Upon hearing this, Derfel was about to scream at Lydia, his pent up loathing barely controlled. Dyfrig's hand on his shoulder prevented him.

"You did understand him?" Dyfrig asked again, pinning Lydia with his angry brown eyes.

"No," Lydia said without blinking, "that is, I didn't understand anything but a word or maybe two."

"Can you understand his language," said Derfel tightly, "I am asking you a direct question, can you understand him?"

"I don't! I heard only a word and maybe two that sounded familiar, that's all!"

"What...."

"Where is he from, then?"

"....words, Lydia?"

Lydia threw her hands up in despair. The two men's barrage of questions, the prisoner, the tension between her and Derfel, it was all too much for her.

"I cannot discuss this anymore. Master Owain has given me specific instructions not to talk about anything that goes on here until he first hears of it for himself." She finished cleaning the prisoner and left him sleeping soundly on his side. Curtly Lydia ordered the two men to put more wood on the fires and take up their positions for the night. She crawled under the furs that piled on the wooden pallet she used as a bed. Lydia decided she needed to rest a while and think of what she thought the prisoner had said. She was badly upset, confused, and needed to think through what had happened.

There was a commotion outside. There was someone making a noise as though they were deliberately trying to get the attention of those inside the hut. Derfel notched his bow while Dyfrig grabbed his spear and made ready to battle anything coming through the door. He glanced quickly over his shoulder to make sure Derfel was in position and that Lydia and the prisoner were out of harm's way.

"Who's there?" he yelled, standing to one side of the entrance.

There was some more noise and perhaps, he thought someone was sobbing. Dyfrig pulled open the door a crack and tried to peer out into the darkness.

"Please help! Is Lydia in there? We need her!"

Dyfrig recognised Katryn the wife of Rhys. She was tightly clenching a yellow and black cloak about her against the biting cold of the night.

"What is it you want of her Katryn?"

"Dyfrig is that you? We need Lydia to come look at Guto's wife. She is badly hurt. He beat her again and this time it is truly bad!" Katryn was in tears as she pleaded with Dyfrig. Behind him, Lydia made a move to go but Dyfrig motioned her to stay put.

"Katryn, I'll send her out, but first get your husband to fetch his bow and spear and come to me. We've a job to do here and I will not abandon my duty to Owain!" Katryn replied that she had already sent her son to fetch his father from the dafarn.

Lydia was now gathering her herbs and healing powders, readying herself to go out into the cold night. Secretly she welcomed the chance to get away from the men and she knew the prisoner would be no trouble. Katryn had hurried across the village to get back to tending to Guto's poor wife. Derfel was alert and ready; bow in hand, arrow notched and eyes blazing fiercely. Dyfrig was holding his spear and peering into the darkness. He knew Katryn's husband, Rhys. They had stood watches together in the Great Forest and Dyfrig knew him to be a good man whom he could count on well enough. Derfel had gone on a few patrols with Rhys and although they did not agree on many things, Derfel also knew he could trust Rhys's judgement and count on his courage.

Dyfrig would not let Lydia leave until Rhys arrived, but they did not have long to wait. Rhys and his son were quick to get to the hut. Lydia hurried away as fast as she could to Guto's hut, Rhys's son leading the way and carrying her medicines. Rhys and Derfel simply looked at each other and nodded. Dyfrig was glad to see Rhys and asked him what was going on in the village.

"Well, I don't know! We had just come in from a two-day patrol in the forest and of course, we went to the dafarn. Well, I stopped at home first, you know to check on everyone and to say hello to my dear wife," here Rhys smiled and looked back at the door in the direction of his hut.

"Then I made my way to the dafarn for some ale and good cheer. I'd only been there a short time when my son burst in to tell me of Guto's wife being in a bad way and that his mother, my good wife," Rhys smiled again, "was all upset and crying about the woman's condition. He told me to come directly here with my bow. Well, I didn't have my bow with me, just my knife. I hurried here in any case, as duty would require, and here I am!"

Dyfrig slapped Rhys on the shoulder and thanked him. Rhys was a tall lithely built man, battle-tested, and used to a warrior's life. He was dressed in a dyed red leather tunic that fitted over a faded blue woollen shirt, grey woollen breeches and worn deer skin leather boots. A worn leather belt cinched his waist, its ends looped over and through. Rhys had no cloak; it must have been the one Katryn had been wearing. He thought to himself that it was a good thing that Rhys did not have his bow with him, for Rhys was not feeling the cold. Dyfrig could smell the ale on his friend and noticed him swaying ever so slightly. Still, Dyfrig knew Rhys would be able to handle himself if necessary and that his knife and one of the spare spears would be armament enough if it came to that.

"So this is what all the fuss is about eh? I was on patrol when that bastard was brought in and so I didn't get a look at him. Why, I wonder, doesn't Owain just kill the bugger and be done with it?" asked Rhys, brushing snow from his long brown hair.

"Well, your question is a good one. I suppose Owain has his reasons for keeping him. Maybe he wants a pet!" Quipped Derfel and the men laughed.

"Oh, I don't know," said Dyfrig, "I think master Owain thinks a bit more deeply than that. He has something in mind no doubt. Still, no harm done really. We've plenty of food to last the rest of this winter and this one's not eating much anyway." They all nodded and Rhys was curious and decided to walk around the cage and get a good look at the prisoner.

"Well he certainly looks like a barbarian. Has he said anything as yet?" asked Rhys.

"Lydia says she may understand a word...."

"And she should know!" growled Derfel his anger returning.

"Now, now, good Derfel. Lydia has been a good addition to our village. She fills in when Rhiannon is not about and why look at the situation tonight. Without Lydia, who knows what might have happened to Guto's poor wife!" Rhys always played the role of peacemaker, forever trying to get squabbling villagers to agree with each other for the common good. Some saw this as a weakness, but those who had fought side by side with the good natured Rhys knew he was far from weak. Rhys was a formidable warrior with a slight ruthless streak in him when the blood was up. Derfel knew this as well as anyone and if truth were told, he did have a grudging respect for the man.

"I pity the woman, I really do. Why that bastard Guto has to mistreat her so is beyond me. Still he's a good man in battle and a good provider as well. I suppose it is his business after all."

"Very true and well said good Derfel. I too wonder why he is so miserable to his woman. Now you take my situation, now I love my cariad and I wouldn't dream of harming her! The reason I am on this good earth is to love my cariad and provide for her and my darling children. I give thanks everyday that I am able to do so!" Rhys was filled with pride and happiness. And despite the ale he had earlier imbibed, his sincerity was real.

It was a long time before Lydia finally arrived back at the hut. She went straight to the cauldron and washed her face and hands. The men turned from guarding the prisoner and gaped at her flustered condition.

"Well? What have you to tell us?" demanded Derfel.

"Softly, good Derfel, softly." Rhys said soothingly. "Surely you can tell that good Lydia here is distraught and the news cannot be at all good."

Lydia glanced at Rhys and smiled weakly, unspoken thanks for his sensitivity.

"Dear Rhys is correct. It is bad. Though I must say the poor woman will survive...this time! I have done what I can for her, she is bandaged, a poultice placed on her bruises and balm on her cuts. I gave her a soothing herb to help her sleep tonight. How a man can beat a defenceless woman so, leaves me cold inside! And you lot, standing around knowing this goes on, and doing nothing about it! You are just as much to blame as Guto!" Tears began flowing down Lydia's cheeks. The stress of the last few days was taking a toll. Having to deal with the prisoner, his guards and now this, it was all beginning to drain her spirit.

"But you cannot blame us for what a man does in his own hut!" Dyfrig spluttered.

"It's just that type of talk that gets a woman hit in the first place!" Derfel added.

Rhys winced visibly at that remark and put his hand on Derfel's shoulder.

"Lads, lads, let us tread softly here. Good Lydia is tired from her duties and it has been a trying night for all. Let us give her privacy and allow her to rest and take some nourishment." As he said this, Rhys handed Lydia a bowl of broth from the cauldron. The others backed away and took up their guard positions.

He looked again at the prisoner lying on his side in the cage.

"Now lads, you have a job to do here watching over this man for our master Owain. So you look to your duty to him and mind what good Lydia says. She has been charged with the responsibility of keeping this warrior alive for our Master Owain and his good Lady Gwenhwyfar." With that he looked directly at Derfel knowing his reverence for the Lady Gwenhwyfar. The men muttered their agreement and settled in for the rest of the night. Rhys tended to Lydia with kindness. Her wolf skins were arranged comfortably and she had more hot broth and a generous hunk of hard bread in her hand. The fires in the braziers were burning brightly casting shadows on the walls. The atmosphere was heavy but warm and protection enough against the cold night air. Rhys satisfied that all that could be done for the occupant's comfort had been done left the hut. There was a cold look of determination on his face.

The dafarn was full for the late hour and Geraint beamed, thinking of his profits while he and his wife Angharad served ale and cider to their customers. Between serving and pouring, he tallied the accounts and recorded who owed what. There was labour promised in the forthcoming springtime, a fox fur, some smoked fish and salted meat. One or two scrawny rabbits that did not please him much, but there were two cloak fasteners, the kind the Romans would have called *fibulae* in the old days that made him very happy. Customers who paid with bobbles like that were favoured and doted on by Geraint and his wife. Gold and metal were payment in substance, something Geraint could hold in his hands. It was quite awkward at times reminding patrons they owed a week's labour and sometimes the foodstuffs such as smoked fish, especially the smoked fish, seemed a little less than delectable. Gold and metal, now that was commerce and overall he was quite pleased with his profits.

A young boy stoked the hearth-fire and tried vainly to keep the smoke from filling the room. There was much banter and horseplay amongst the men. A few serious conversations were taking place in the corners, especially amongst men associated with Gronw.

Guto burst through the door and stood glaring in the middle of the smoke-filled room. Angharad giving Guto a look that could have killed; passed him and quickly closed the thick wooden door against the cold night air. Guto sullenly walked over to a rough-hewn wood table where three men sat. He unceremoniously plopped himself down on the plank bench at the end and called for a jug of ale. Geraint came over with a mug of strong ale but before he laid it on the table, and knowing the character of Guto, he asked for payment first.

Guto leaped to his feet shaking with rage. It appeared he would attack Geraint on the spot. Silence fell on the room and some men moved for their knives. Guto reached in his cloak but instead of brandishing his knife, he held up a heavy silver ring between his thumb and dirty forefinger.

Geraint was delighted, his fear vanishing at the sight of the exquisite and obviously valuable ring. He promptly slapped down the mug along with a full jug of ale, telling Guto he could have all he wanted here tonight and the next four. Guto grabbed Geraint's wrist menacingly and pulled him closer. Geraint, sensing the seriousness of the current negotiations added breathlessly that of course, Guto had paid enough to drink what he wanted for a fortnight and of course, a meal would be cooked especially for him as well! He then frantically signalled for his wife to bring over some hot broth and hard bread for this, his newly favoured customer. Things calmed down once Guto sat and slurped a mug of ale washing down a huge bite of bread dripping with broth gravy, though he was hard pressed to find any meat in the broth.

Math and Llew had been patrolling the village. After stopping in to see Derfel and Dyfrig, they had checked the perimeter one more time before being relieved of duty by fresh guards. The two friends decided to go over to the dafarn for ale, cider and some food before heading to their respective huts. A few men were leaving on wobbly legs, making room for the friends to sit together at a table. They had settled up with

Geraint the other night and could now order on account. Geraint came over with a jug of ale and one of cider as well as salted pork, bread and cheese. It was on their third cup each, that they noticed they were across the table from Guto. Both Math and Llew had shared warrior's duties with Guto and they knew him to be a rough and miserable bastard. Still, he was a good man with a weapon and courageous enough; what he did in his own hut was his business. They nodded gruffly to him in acknowledgement.

"What the bloody hell, are you two whelps staring at?" Guto yelled drunkenly. Math looked hurt by the remark, Llew's face however reddened with anger over the insult.

"Hello, Guto, how are you?" asked Math trying to placate the situation, having noticed his friend's changed demeanour.

"Bugger off you little goblin! And you little man, you keep staring at me like that and I'll give you a beating you won't soon forget!"

"Aaah well said good Guto! Well, said!" cried Rhys who had kicked open the dafarn's door swirling his retrieved cloak with dramatic flourish. He sauntered over to the aid of his two friends. Angharad swore and moved to slam the heavy wood door closed again. Rhys smiled belying the seething anger and contempt he bore the wife-beating Guto.

"Pray tell, would that be the same sentiment you expressed to your good wife, before you nearly beat her to death? I wonder if a man, who beats a woman so badly, is not angry about something else? Perhaps he made promises to his woman, his manhood could not live up to?" Rhys had been standing arrogantly with hands on his hips, feet wide apart and what is more important, just outside the reach of Guto.

Guto roared and upturning the table, grabbed Math by the wrist and punched him viciously in the face, sending the smaller man sprawling into the dirt floor. Llew lunged at Guto, smashing a jug into the side of his head. Guto simply shook his head, suffering no ill affect from the blow. Rhys grabbed the big man with both hands bringing Guto to his feet and kneed him mercilessly in the groin. Guto instinctively grabbed onto Rhys for balance and the two men fought in the middle of the room. Rhys managed to hit Guto with his elbow splitting Guto's lip. Another elbow missed, but Guto lost his balance anyway and fell to the dirt floor. Rhys came in with a hard right-handed blow that Guto barely managed to block. From his knees, he thrust his right hand between Rhys's legs grabbing his belt at the back. His left forearm smashed against Rhys's throat as he pulled hard with his right hand toppling Rhys backwards smashing the back of the man's head hard into the dirt floor.

Guto went for his knife, but Llew saw the glint of the blade and kicked hard into Guto's breadbasket. This time Guto dropped, gasping for air and Llew grabbed two handfuls of hair and pulled down as he brought his knee up forcefully, smashing Guto's nose. Guto was now on his feet but bent over, both hands holding his broken nose. Llew went to strike him with wide right-handed punch, but Guto brought both his hands up sharply, blocking the punch. Guto grabbed both sides of Llew's head and pulled forward delivering a devastating head butt to the bridge of Llew's nose. Blood splayed everywhere. Tables were overturned, men jumped to their feet shouting and bellowing with rage, encouraging the combatants in a chaotic frenzy.

Llew was nearly unconscious, but still on his feet. He knew if he fell now Guto would kick him to death. He wobbled and moaned trying desperately to see through the blood and the pain. Guto suddenly cried out in pain and dropped to the floor. Rhys had regained his senses and from his back had kicked out against Guto's knee toppling the big man. Quickly, Rhys was on him holding him tightly around the neck and punching repeatedly into Guto's ribs. The two men fought hard both filled with rage. Guto was struggling to free Rhys's hand from his neck. There was a flash, as the firelight glinted off Guto's drawn knife. He had reached into his leggings and pulled out a secreted blade. Cries of protest filled the air as the men in the dafarn realised what was about to happen. Guto managed to slice into Rhys's arm causing him to scream out in pain and surprise. Llew jumped in trying to control Guto's knife hand so he wouldn't be able to finish Rhys off. He managed to grab hold with his left hand while he punched hard with his right hand. Guto blocked the punch and elbowed Llew in the teeth. As Llew slumped, Guto grabbed him from the front and spun him around. Now Guto had hold of Llew's hair from behind and was prepared to cut his throat with the knife he held in his right hand.

Unexpectedly, Guto dropped, screaming to the ground but still clutching on to Llew. An arrow protruded from Guto's right arm, the knife clutched in his right fist. Silence. Then all eyes turned to the doorway. Standing there was an enraged Math holding his great yew bow notched with another deadly arrow.

"Now you miserable, wife-beating bastard! You just let my friend Llew go or by the Blood of Christ, I will loose this arrow through your miserable throat!"

The men stood stock still and stared at Math, who was white with rage, making the red blood pouring down from his broken nose stand out all the more. His great yew bow was bent, the bowstring quivered with tension ready to deliver death.

"I told you to release our Llew! I will loose this arrow and God knows I have never missed anything I have notched an arrow against!"

Guto stood up, blood dripping from his own crooked nose, his right arm dripping blood from the arrow sticking out from it, a look of belligerence on his craggy face. Llew had finally dropped to his knees, but was slowly gaining his senses. Rhys, on the other side of the smashed table, was also coming round, slowly getting up from the floor holding his arm tightly trying to stop the flow of blood.

Guto, who no longer had hold of Llew, suddenly kicked Rhys savagely in the chest driving the air from his lungs. He spun the helpless Rhys around and held the knife against Rhys's exposed throat. The knife began it's cut, a thin red line just beginning as Guto looked defiantly at Math.

"To hel..."

The rest of what Guto was going to say ended in a gurgle as Math's arrow sprouted suddenly from Guto's throat. Guto fell backwards onto the floor; the knife, with which he had intended to cut the throat of Rhys, fell to the floor. It took several minutes for him to die as he writhed in agony and drowned in his own blood.

Chapter 5

One hand holding his nose, Llew shakily moved toward Math and gently put his hand on his friend's arm, lowering the huge bow. Rhys was still gasping for breath, blood drenching his tunic from the cut on his arm and the smaller one on his throat. A few of the other men in the dafarn helped him to his feet. Geraint was nearly hysterical. He ran from one to another of the men.

"There will be a reckoning for this mark my words! There will be questions and master Owain will not like this one bit, I can tell you!" He screamed; Angharad was doing all she could to quiet her husband. The men in the dafarn helped Rhys to move, but he refused to be taken to Lydia, saying she needed her rest this night. Instead, he insisted on being helped home to his wife. Math put his great bow in its place, tethered on his back. He put his arm under Llew's shoulder to help his friend to Lydia so she could mend him. Llew did not want Lydia to see him this way, something that confused Math. Llew, like his friend Rhys, insisted on being taken to his own hut.

Gronw's men, who until now had done nothing to bring attention to themselves, hovered over Guto's body talking excitedly amongst themselves. Without Gronw's leadership they did not know what to do until one man stood up. Clydog, the biggest man amongst them, took charge and ordered the others to take Guto's body to Owain.

"There will be a reckoning for this act and on that you can count!" He spat the words at no one in particular, but Geraint seemed to take the remark personally and became agitated again. The big man continued shouting.

"A life for a life, that's what the law says! And you will pay for this!" Clydog motioned the men to take up Guto's body.

"We'll see what Owain has to say about this, then we'll come for you!" He and his men half carried, half dragged the body out of the dafarn and began to make their way to Owain and the Lady Gwenhwyfar's hut.

Owain's personal guards would not allow Clydog and his men in to see their master. Extra guards, men loyal to Owain and in his service, had been roused from their slumber and ordered to assist their comrades. Their mood was decidedly foul at having their rest disturbed by a mere dafarn fight. Clydog and his men were out numbered and out manoeuvred. Insolently, he dumped Guto's body at the feet of the leader of the guards and with his men in tow, stomped off into the night.

Elidir, the Captain of the guards, suppressed his anger and the urge to throw his spear through the back of the insolent bastard. His men were angry too and spoiling for a fight. Elidir reminded them their duty was to safeguard Owain and the Lady Gwenhwyfar, not fight with other warriors, drunk from spending too much time at the dafarn and too little time in their own beds. He told them it was important that Owain get some much needed rest this evening. More to the point it was the wishes of the Lady that this be so. That calmed them.

He ordered Guto's body to be put into a cart in the courtyard and posted a guard.

Meanwhile he sent a patrol out into the village to make sure there was no more fighting. He made sure to send guards to the dafarn; the place was to be closed until further notice. Elidir was certain from the look on the faces of the teulu there would be full compliance from the villagers; there was no more deadly a creature, than a warrior whose precious sleep had been disturbed.

Gwenhwyfar looked down at her sleeping husband. Owain had been gone from first light and had only just got back from his duties. His wife did not think her husband had fully rested from the extended patrol he had been on when he captured the prisoner. Since bringing the prisoner to Caerwyn, Owain had been even more restless; something was on his mind something more than what he had shared with her the night he had returned. Owain had not heard about Guto and his poor wife or the fracas at the dafarn. This evening, upon his return from patrolling the village, her exhausted husband had fallen asleep right away, well perhaps not right away. She still glowed from their lovemaking.

Gwenhwyfar was grateful to the Goddess for giving her Owain as a husband. While he could certainly be moody and insufferable at times, he was a man after all and could not help his nature, but he was a man of noble principle. Owain had a strong sense of right and wrong and tried always to do what was right for the benefit of her, the children, and Caerwyn. And he didn't beat her. Not that she would stand for that abuse! The Lady Gwenhwyfar apart from being beloved by both pagan and Christian alike, was the matriarch whose ancient ancestors had ties with the Goddess and had founded the village of Caerwyn. She was also an expert with a knife and would not hesitate to use her skill in defence of her children, Caerwyn or herself.

"Sleep my love, sleep," she thought as she stroked her husband's hair, "for you will need all your wits about you come daylight." It was Gwenhwyfar who had ordered Elidir ap Alun Dyfed the captain of the night guard, that under no circumstance save for direct attack was Owain to be disturbed this night.

The sun was warm on his back; he took of his tunic and deliciously soaked in the gentle warmth of this spring day. The meadow was a yellow sea, gently rolling to the rhythm of the wind. He could smell the fragrance of the growing grain and the wildflowers that sprouted in random abundance through out the meadow. A short distance away was Caerwyn and just beyond stood the first great trees of the forest, silent sentinels guarding the village as they had done for centuries. The tree line's dark green and shadow offered promise of cool respite from the warm sun. Birds sang and butterflies danced all about. Figures appeared moving from Caerwyn towards the meadow. He could see Gwenhwyfar, Cynglas and Gwyneth. They were waving to him.

Owain quickened his pace as he ran lightly towards them. He was looking forward to a leisurely day spent with his wife and children. The children ran to him and he gathered up his daughter in his strong warrior's arms as she reached him. Putting her down he tousled his son's hair that quickly escalated into a rough and tumble, wrestling match between father and son. The mock combat ended with Cynglas on his back, Owain straddling him tickling unmercifully. Howls of laughter filled the air and frightened the birds. Gwenhwyfar pulled out a bundle of cloth she had been carrying. She spread the cloth on the ground revealing what was held within, breads, cheeses, a salted fish and a small flask of ale. The family gathered around and picked at the food. Owain drank the ale as Gwenhwyfar produced another flask of watered cider that she and the children drank.

The family talked together, not of important issues, just of things they had done or would do, feelings about the days gone by and of days yet to come. Owain lay on his back with Gwenhwyfar beside him gazing at the clouds. The white clouds played with each other against the vast blueness of the sky. A hunter seeking his prey, a rabbit running, a hound lying down, a man with a long beard, all of these shapes and scenes could be found within the shape-shifting clouds. Owain thought he could see a table full of bounty with men sitting down to a feast. Just as he began to make sense of the sky-picture, it changed. Now he saw the frightening visage of an enraged bull! This gave him a start! He was about to turn and comment to his wife when the blue sky turned dark. A bright light ripped the sky apart. Cynglas and Gwyneth came running from their play to the safety of their parents. Gwenhwyfar stared in wonder; Owain was himself transfixed as he saw a four-horned goat with blazing yellow eyes peering down at them. Fire erupted from its mouth and his children screamed. Gwenhwyfar was frantically reciting a prayer to the Goddess. The ground around them shook from being struck by a bolt of lightning. All four family members were now clinging to each other for safety. Owain chanced to look skyward and was horrified to see that Caerwyn had been struck by a fire bolt and was engulfed in flames. Where could they run for shelter? Where could they turn to save themselves from this fury raining down? He glimpsed a huge fireball coming straight at them...

It was at that precise moment Owain woke from his troubled sleep. He was bathed in sweat and shaking violently. He tried to hide that fact from Gwenhwyfar, who was sitting up in their bed, a look of worry and concern on her face. She stroked his hair again.

"Dyfyr ap Alun Dyfed is here, cariad. He needs to speak to you about last night."

"I had a very bad dream my love," he blurted out. "Very bad indeed. I don't know what it means or if it means anything at all."

A coquettish look passed over Gwenhwyfar's face, briefly hiding her concern for her husband's state of mind.

"Well, cariad, after you speak to Dyfyr perhaps you will tell me your dream that I may explain it for you?"

"Yes," Owain was trying to cover his embarrassment for mentioning his dream. Warriors should not allow themselves such weaknesses.

"Yes, I suppose I might tell you later. It could prove useful to make sense of the foul thing, though I doubt it was anything but gas! Now, what is this? What happened in the night that Dyfyr should wish to see me so early?"

Though still concerned for her husband, Gwenhwyfar suppressed a smile at his weak attempt to dismiss the dream that had so disturbed him.

"Early," she pretended to scold him, "early, you say? It is many hours past first light, my sleepy head! The day is nearly done and you lay here like some decadent potentate!" Gwenhwyfar was now grinning at the shocked look on his face. "Still I suppose you would not have slept so long if you had not required the rest. I suppose if I had not ordered your guards to ensure you were not disturbed then perhaps you may have risen before midday. Now get up, Dyfyr is waiting!"

Owain managed a smile through the haze caused by the dream and the realisation his wife had bested him...again.

"Well, you best not let the old bugger stand on ceremony out in the cold on my account! You know how insufferable he can be, invite him in for breakfast, woman, and be quick about it!" It was of course said in jest and it was received within the same context.

Nevertheless, there was a slight icy glint in Gwenhwyfar's eyes as she turned from her husband. Owain noticed but pretended not to, it didn't help his position that she had already done as he requested without him requesting it. Gwenhwyfar went to sit with Dyfyr and share the bread, ale and hard cheese she had readied for him. Owain got himself ready for the day ahead.

"You missed a bloody wild time last evening, I can tell you!" Dyfyr shouted as he saw Owain approaching the warmth of the fire.

"Bloody wild time indeed! You know Guto's been killed?" Dyfyr loosed the question between bites of bread and cheese and great gulps of ale.

"No, I did not know!" Owain shot a cold glance at his wife, "tell me how that came about?"

"Aaah, well, they were at the dafarn and you know what a bastard that Guto can be at times! Well he starts in on Rhys...."

"Rhys? But he is a peace maker not a trouble maker what did he do to incite a fight?"

"That's right Owain! Rhys the Peacemaker to be sure! But Guto, that wife-beating bastard, was in no mood for pleasantries! He had already started on Math and Llew when Rhys showed up to help his mates. Dyfyr went on describing the fight at the dafarn. He stopped when he came to the part about Clydog bringing Guto's body to the hall and demanding to see Owain.

"Guto beat his wife again?" he looked at his Gwenhwyfar inquiringly and was troubled to see that icy look still in her eyes.

"Oh aye, he did indeed! And according to Lydia, it was a right brutal pasting as well! Not to worry, Owain, your prisoner is safe. Derfel and Dyfrig stayed throughout the night so all is well on that score. But this Guto business, well the bastard won't be beating anyone anymore thanks to Math and his bow. *Myn Duw*! My God! That lad can shoot! Oh, sorry My Lady!" Dyfyr apologised to the Lady Gwenhwyfar, the divine inspiration of Caerwyn, for using one of the New Religion's expressions.

Gwenhwyfar was mildly surprised to hear the expression from their friend. She had not realised Dyfyr had at his age become interested in the new religion. She nodded to him graciously and waved for him to continue his report.

"So what do you want done now then, Owain? I suppose Math will need to be talked to and the dafarn owner, Geraint, was making a stink over the damages to his place. And of course, there is the curious claim by Clydog that Guto was unjustly killed. What the connection is between those two buggers, I am sure I don't know! Very strange indeed!"

"And let us not forget about Enid!" said Gwenhwyfar forcefully as she reminded the men of Guto's poor battered wife.

"Of course. We will take care of Guto's wife Enid directly, cariad, never fear." Owain stroked his wife's hand reassuringly.

"Who is with her now Dyfyr?" he asked.

"Last I heard Lydia was there with your daughter, Gwyneth."

"Really and at what time did she go there pray tell?" Owain seemed to be getting angry and Gwenhwyfar looked a bit surprised by his reaction.

"Just before first light I think. She must have risen before you and hearing of the tragedy late last night, hurried to Lydia to see what she could do. No harm in that surely?"

Owain was not placated.

"I do not relish the idea of my young daughter running around in the wee hours of the morning unescorted! Especially with fighting and bloodshed going on!"

"She was not unescorted, Owain. Elidir walked her over to Lydia and stayed to make sure all was right with her and with your precious prisoner."

Owain's voice had gone quiet in that menacing way of his, an indication of the violence he was struggling to keep in check.

"I am not impressed by the fact that my own young daughter walked out in the dangers of the night with a man!"

But Dyfyr also had his anger building. Elidir was his son and Owain was talking as though he were a common scoundrel! Dyfyr pushed back from the table, about to stand, his face red with rage. Gwenhwyfar spoke out.

"Owain, cariad, are you not forgetting that Elidir is one of the captains of your most trusted guards? He discharged his duties last night most competently. By not allowing Clydog to provoke a scene last night he avoided a difficult and politically charged situation. Elidir ensured Caerwyn was secure and that there was no more fighting or disturbances; what is more important he ensured the safety of our daughter and me. This fine young man, son of your most trusted warrior and dear companion, who sits here in front of you this morning, did all of this without waking you, allowing you a much needed night of rest!"

Owain and Dyfyr were now standing, their bodies coiled ready to fight and to kill. Finally, Owain breathed out a long sigh.

"I am an idiot! Please forgive me, my dear friend! I had a very bad dream as I awoke a few moments ago and I fear I am still under its mysterious spell. Certainly there is no one besides you yourself, in all of our beloved land, I would prefer to have watching over me and mine, than your own honourable son, Elidir, the captain of my night guard. Please accept my hand on the matter." Owain leaned forward and proffered his hand to his trusted friend.

Dyfyr stood still for two more heartbeats while the thoughts of what just happened and what could have happened turned over in his mind. Then he slowly leaned forward, took Owain's hand in both of his, and clasped tightly. Owain pulled his friend close and hugged him hard.

"You are a strange breed of man, master Owain!" The two men howled with laughter, drained their ale, and poured more filling their tankards. The near disastrous situation was all but forgotten. Gwenhwyfar remained placid but her face only hid her troubled mind from the two men hugging and guffawing in front of her. Sometimes she thought to herself the minds of men are more mysterious than all else in the cosmos.

"Now what of this dream, Owain?" asked Dyfyr.

Their laughter subsided as Owain once again swallowing his embarrassment recounted his dream for his wife and his friend. When he was finished with his tale, their boisterous mood had vanished giving way to a more sombre frame of mind. Owain and Dyfyr were now looking to the Lady Gwenhwyfar for insight into the matter of Owain's dream.

"Well, I think, my love, that your dream can be interpreted to mean that you wish for goodness, abundance, joy and a happy future. The world is not always so easily bound simply by the wishes of men. Familiar things can sometimes hide dangers. One minute they are good and joyous and then in the blink of an eye, due to the whims of nature or the nature of men, wickedness befalls you. Now I cannot tell you if this is what you are simply thinking or if they are leftover thoughts enhanced by what you already know or suspect. I cannot say if this dream is a portent of things yet to happen. That will be for you to determine."

Owain had to wait for a few minutes before it was quiet enough for his words to be hear.

"Well, that certainly gives me something to think about!" He said it with a bravado he did not feel. "Now perhaps, dear friend, you can round up our three hooligans, Rhys, Llew and of course our archer Math. Tell them I wish to see them after their midday meal this day. Clydog and two of his men may apply here for judgement on any grievance they may harbour. Oh, and keep the dafarn closed until further notice. I'll see Geraint today as well. We will need to meet with the Council to discuss this barbarian and our dead warrior. There has been too much death in this village in too short a time and I want answers! Tell me my good friend," Owain put his arm on Dyfyr's shoulder, "do you think something is amiss in all of this or am I just suffering from an unexplained dream?"

Before the old warrior could answer, Owain smiled.

"Perhaps after a proper rest and nourishment, your Elidir may accept a captaincy on the day watch? Why don't you and your son join us for a feast after all of this business has settled? Cariad, do you think you and our young Gwyneth will be ready by sundown?" Gwenhwyfar beamed nearly as much as Dyfyr.

"Fine, it's settled then. Call the Council we must talk, but first I am going to see my prisoner, my daughter and poor Enid. Cariad?"

Gwenhwyfar nodded, agreeing to accompany her husband and lend assistance and comfort where she might. Dyfyr rose and bowed to his hosts and lieges, turned on his heel and went to go about his duties.

Gwenhwyfar and Owain had toured the village on horseback because Gwenhwyfar thought it important to offer encouragement to the people of Caerwyn after they learned of Enid's beating and the circumstances of her husband's death in the dafarn. With the barbarian in their midst, many villagers were frightened. Some thought the killing in the dafarn the night before was caused by the presence of Owain's captive. Owain reflected on how his wife was right to advise they check on the people in person. As they rode by Owain could feel tensions ease. He knew the villagers were comforted seeing his wife, the Lady Gwenhwyfar.

The Council meeting began just before sundown. The meeting was important and as such Gwenhwyfar was present along with Owain's trusted advisors and captains, Anwas Adeinoig, Cadyreith ap Saidi, Cadwy ap Geraint, a cousin of the dafarn owner and not as the name suggested his son, Caradog Freichfras named for the famous chieftain leader Caradog who had fought the Romans, Bedwyr, the brothers Nudd, and Owain's foster brother, Cai ap Ceinfarfog. These men were all battle hardened, intelligent and had proved their valour often.

Anwas Adeinoig was strong, tall with a black beard to match his black mane of hair. He had travelled across the land to rescue a sister of one of the villagers who had been given in marriage to another tribe. The man she wedded mistreated her terribly and she was used as a slave in contempt of the honour of Caerwyn. Anwas had killed the man and a number of his tribe before returning to Caerwyn with the young bride safe and in good health.

Cadyreith ap Saidi had travelled the breadth of the land to track down the ancient cauldron that had a special, some say magical, significance to Gwenhwyfar's late mother. He was wiry, auburn haired and sported a small beard, a look that belied his strength and tenacity. Cadyreith had survived much hardship on his search for the stolen cauldron. Finding it amongst a small village in the West, he and his men negotiated for its safe return.

Cadwy ap Geraint was the youngest. He was of average height, very agile and very quick on his feet. During one of the worst storms in village memory, fire swept through Caerwyn destroying all in its path. In the midst of the charred and blackened aftermath, lay an old Bard close to death. The Bard had lost his beloved harp, an instrument he had used to brighten the spirits and inspire the people of Caerwyn for a generation. He was broken hearted and his sadness overwhelmed the village. The loss of the harp and the despondency of the old Bard deeply affected the village. Young Cadwy, merely a boy at the time, braved the hot embers of the burnt out village, searched, and searched through the charred ruins. He burnt his feet, he burnt his young hands, and yet he kept looking. Cadwy found the old Bard's harp safely tucked inside a scorched leather bag. Seeing the old man reunited with his prized instrument lifted the spirit of the people and gave them the strength to rebuild. The credit for the transformation was due to the tenacity of young Cadwy.

The two Nudd brothers were different. They were tall and well-muscled men and fearsome fighters. They were inseparable, which was just as well for Edern was hot-tempered, and a troublemaker at times. He was valuable as an invincible warrior and as a shrewd strategist, but at times, he went too far especially, if he felt his honour had been besmirched. His brother Gwyn, an awesome warrior in his own right, was also a gifted peacemaker and negotiator. Whenever the two brothers agreed action was to be taken against an enemy, a bloodbath was sure to ensue!

In the days before the Romans, a Druid would have been present to advise the chiefs of the tribe at such an important Council. Even during Roman occupation and after the Druids were all killed or exiled, the Romans held little influence at such gatherings in villages as ancient and as remote as Caerwyn. The Ancient Ways was that strong in the hearts of the people. These days the Council would be as Owain dictated. Often the Lady Gwenhwyfar or Rhiannon would be present representing at least the sentiment of the Druid. Sometimes, as concession to the changing times, a Christian priest might be present.

In the warm days of summer, the Council convened outdoors, at the back of the two storied stone Hall that was Owain and Gwenhwyfar's home. Tables and chairs arranged for the Council set out for the members of the Council and the villagers would gather round and sit on the grass. Councils always met just before sundown so as not to interfere with the daily running of the village.

This was winter and the Council met in the Hall itself, which was little more than a converted horse barn, though it was made from stone, and decorated befitting the solemnity of the occasion. At one end, a large hearth-fire provided warmth and along the walls, sconces holding burning rush torches cloaked the scene in a warm yellow light. Three wood plank tables were erected, one in front of the hearth, and one on each side. The air was warm and the straw that was strewn over the hard-packed dirt floor smelled sweet. The preliminary investigation began while guards made ready to receive the villagers who would be let in for the hearing of the grievances. Guards were posted outside to prevent any disturbances and control the number of villagers who could safely be let in. This night the Hall would be crowded and the guards would surely be kept busy.

The Council was underway and testimony was being given.

"All I know is that we were on patrol in the Great Forest," Anwas was saying. "We were on the look out in case any of the men from *Iwerddon*, had slipped in from the South..." The island of Iwerddon lay off the west coast and its inhabitants often raided the shores of Cymru.

"Wouldn't those bastards come from the west and in from the sea, I mean why were you so deep in the southern part of the Forest?" Edern had been riding along the shoreline and wanted to know in his usual rough manner why manpower was being wasted.

"We, that is master Owain and I had heard rumours that the men from Iwerddon had landed to the south and might decide to sneak up on the landward side of us, not knowing of course the way through our Great Forest. In any case, it turns out they had met one of the other tribes and were stopped where they landed." Dyfyr's clarifying interjection calmed Edern who nodded slowly taking in the information. Anwas continued.

"We were spread out a bit thin, but we all knew to meet at the shelter we had built in a small clearing, you know the one. In any case, it turns out Dyfyr and Owain had been tracking a trail through the forest with a patrol of men. The trail led them back to the clearing where we joined forces. We saw Guto standing over a body and we ran down to investigate. Guto came up to me and said that Dafydd had been killed and that he, Guto, had killed the assailant. Well, of course we gathered a scouting party and went looking. Sure enough, we found Dafydd's body and the barbarian. It was obvious from the start that the barbarian was not from Iwerddon and when we went to turn him over to have a better look at the bugger...damn if he wasn't alive!"

A murmur swept through the council and Edern grumbled out loud that the barbarian should have been killed on the spot.

"You forget yourself Edern!" Owain was visibly angered and his voice went low and quiet. Dyfyr and Cai fidgeted in their seats and exchanged looks.

"It was by my order the barbarian should remain alive. I want information that a dead man cannot give me." Turning to Anwas, Owain asked, "the barbarian was in the condition you found him when you brought him to me?"

"Well no, we stripped him of weapons and..."

"You made sure he was not a threat?" Owain had turned back and was looking at Edern but his questions were directed to Anwas.

"Yes, we er...made sure he was no threat."

"His weapons, they were an axe, a sword and what else?" Owain continued staring at Edern as he curtly fired his questions at Anwas.

"Yes," replied Anwas uncomfortable with the tension in the air, "he had a battle axe, a sword and a long knife tucked behind his back. I found no shield or helmet."

"The weapons were intact and not bloodied?"

"That's right, they were still in his belt, the big axe tied with leather across his back, why?"

Owain turned his attention now to Anwas.

"His wounds, of what nature were they?"

"Well, it's hard to say...er.. He had what looked like a stab wound in his side and he was battered about the head and face. You saw that when you had him examined by Rhiannon and that camp girl." Anwas was confused by the tone of the questioning but he knew he had answered Owain and Edern honestly.

"It seems to be a bit of a puzzle," stated Cai simply. "Guto claims Dafydd was killed by this barbarian, who he, in turn killed. Yet, the barbarian is alive and Guto sadly is no longer with us. Dafydd is dead and the barbarian's weapons are clean. I find it curious that of the three men, the only weapon to have been bloodied, belonged to the now dead Guto. Now, I hear Clydog, who is Gronw's man, wants to make a claim on behalf of Guto. Gronw himself seems to have a hand in this. His name keeps popping up." Cai looked around at the others on the Council. His gaze stopped on Owain.

"There is something very much wrong here," Owain spoke as he rose, "and we need to get to the bottom of this. For now let us agree that the barbarian should remain alive unless he proves to be a threat. And let us deal with last night's incident but with an eye to anything that may seem peculiar. We cannot increase the patrols for that would leave us unprotected in the village. Do we agree?" Owain looked at each member on the Council.

"You are saying that there is treachery among us! You suspect Guto or Gronw and the barbarian is the key." Gwyn looked hard at Owain and then searched his foster brother's face to gauge his response. Edern was lost in his own thoughts and did not catch his brother's quizzical look.

"I think we may learn more with the barbarian alive," said Cai, "and we should be on our toes during this hearing of grievances."

Gwenhwyfar had remained quite while she listened to the men speak. Now she stood and spoke to the Council.

"Indeed we shall all listen hard to what shall be said during this grievance hearing. My husband is quite right to keep the barbarian alive until we can discover what if anything is the meaning of the recent events. Let us then hear the grievances." The warriors stood and bowed their heads respectfully to Gwenhwyfar.

It was unusual for there to be so many villagers gathered at night, but these past few days had not been of the usual variety. The entire village had heard of the killing at the dafarn. Many sympathised with Math, as he was much liked amongst the people. Some villagers were even glad that Guto was dead. He had a reputation, well earned of being a rough brute of a man. The womenfolk were especially horrified at how he had beaten his poor wife. There were those men who had fought and hunted with Guto and looked to his courage and skill as virtues. They were not concerned with what a man did within the confines of his own hut. And they were less impressed that an arrow had killed Guto, in what they had perceived to be a fistfight. The villagers crowded around the Hall of Gwenhwyfar's home to hear the Council.

Math, Llew and Rhys were standing apart from Geraint the dafarn owner, their wounds still raw and red. Enid stood alone. To the side Clydog and March mumbled to themselves.

"Now then," said Owain, "we have a serious matter before us and we have heard all regarding this matter. The dafarn will remain closed for one more day. When it opens no weapons will be allowed inside. You," Owain pointed to the owner, "will see to it!"

"But sire..." Geraint whimpered.

"Quiet! The captain of the guard will assign a man to check in twice during patrol. You may report to him any breaches of the peace. As to compensation, with what did Guto pay you?"

Geraint blanched at the question. What if Owain knew of the ring Guto had given him? Now he had to decide to lie or tell the truth. Looking around and noticing the grim looks of the Council, especially the look on the face of Edern, he decided that telling the truth was best.

"It was with this silver ring that Guto paid me," he said holding up the ring.

Owain ordered the ring to be passed around for inspection. It was noted that the ring was exquisite in its detail and heavy in weight...and far too rich for the boorish Guto who had never been known to have anything of value.

"What do you make of this ring?" asked Owain.

"Well," began Cai, "it is not from around here, the design is different, foreign to our artworks. It is good workmanship, but I think if is from the hands of another tribe, perhaps the Essylwg. I wonder how our Guto got possession of it?"

Owain gave the ring back to Geraint. He allowed the dafarn owner to keep the ring in compensation for damages. Geraint shuffled off to the side happy he was able to come out of the melee with a profit. He was concerned about the weapon ban but reasoned with himself that with Owain's promise of a patrol, it might just work out.

"You three," Owain said pointing at Rhys, Math and Llew. Owain waved them to the centre as the villagers craned their necks in anticipation of the next judgement.

"A life has been taken. That death prevented a killing and a warning had been issued." Owain looked hard at the three men. Math looked straight at Owain and nodded his head.

"Then the killing does not deserve another death in payment." A murmur of agreement swept through the crowd. But there were a few, Gronw's men all, who disagreed. Clydog tried to intervene.

"But master Owain, it was three to one and Guto was shot through with an arrow, he had no..." Owain put up his hand to silence the man.

"It was a fist fight, until your man pulled a knife. By doing so, he showed his intention to kill. He would not stop even when Math fired a warning shot. Instead, he carried on, intent on taking a life. He cut one of my men, tried to cut a second man and then had the audacity to try to cut the throat of the first of my men he had attacked. This was prevented and the peace preserved, when he was shot through. Now I want to know why this concerns you?" The tension in the air was so thick as to be stifling.

"The man was a friend. We all knew Guto well! He served the village and was a good warrior. He deserved better!" growled Clydog.

Owain was becoming angry; his voice had gone low.

"Your friend assaulted one of my men and tried to kill two of my trusted guards. So it seems I have a stake in this fracas. If your grievance weighs so heavily upon you, perhaps you would wish to call on me personally for payment?"

The crowd went silent.

Owain had thrown the gauntlet, he had challenged Clydog to fight to the death or abandon his claim! Owain's teulu and his captains were taken by surprise and were visibly shaken. They bristled ominously, their hands moving to their weapons. Seeing this, and realising he had pressed the issue more than he intended, Clydog decided to try to get out with his dignity intact.

"I was thinking of the value of Guto's service was to you. If you are content that all is even, I have no complaint but one." Clydog's tone was unusually smooth.

"What complaint is that?" Owain's men were prepared for a fight. Edern had to be physically restrained now by his brother in order to preserve the peace of the proceedings.

"That Guto's wife should now find herself without a man to look after her needs. This demands compensation." The crowd now stirred daring to breathe again. Owain looked concerned, as did Gwenhwyfar. Clydog continued.

"I would gladly take her to my household, so that she may not want for food or comfort."

A voice was heard shouting out. It was Math.

"Master Owain, it was my arrow that killed Guto and my responsibility. I acknowledge Guto was a sound man on patrol, in battle and on the hunt. He had no right to use a knife. He had no right to fight with any of us. And he had no right to beat his wife. I will take responsibility for her and I will see she is provided for...if she will agree ... and with your permission."

Llew could do nothing but stare at is friend with his mouth open. Rhys positively beamed and slapped Math on the back. Math looked meekly at Enid.

"You have our permission and our thanks for your gallantry," said Gwenhwyfar, who then looked at Enid. "And you poor Enid what is it you wish?"

Enid looked up from her hooded black cloak and surveyed the gathered crowd. She stood and moved a few paces forward. Standing there quietly, proudly, and with great dignity, Enid commanded without words that all eyes turn to her. She took her hood down and all present saw the torn and bloodied lip, the blackened eye, the cut cheek, and the bruised and swollen flesh that a day before had been a beautiful face. She gracefully walked toward Clydog stopping mere inches from him. Villagers jostled for position, Owain's guards fidgeted with their weapons. All expected something ominous to occur. Enid stood looking into the eyes of a man she knew to be made of the same character as her late husband. Clydog returned her gaze, boldly defiant at first. As Enid unfalteringly peered into his very soul, Clydog became unnerved. He looked around trying to garner support, still Enid held her gaze. He raised his arms in mock futility, playing to the crowd, but Enid's unwavering dignity made him appear foolish and weak. She finally spat at his feet and abruptly turned her back. Enid walked proudly to her place and turned now, facing toward Math. Almost imperceptibly, she nodded her head in agreement to what Math had proposed and then she pulled her hood back up, hiding her battered face yet cocooned in grace and dignity.

"Then it shall be so!" decreed Gwenhwyfar. With that the Council was over and the matters decided upon.

Owain took Cai aside, "We will need to keep an eye on Clydog. He knows something. Also, since we don't know what is going on under our own noses we best be prepared for anything. We need to thwart any surprise action, so let Clydog know he is being watched. Tell Edern to look after it personally."

"You think that wise?" Cai asked surprised at Owain's request. "You know what a hot-headed bastard Edern is."

"Yes, but I also know how cunning he can be when intrigue abounds. It is an unusual mix of characteristics, is it not?" Owain was now smiling at Cai who simply gazed at him shaking his head.

"You are a very strange man, Owain."

Math did not know what to say or do. After he had escorted Enid to her hut, he left her there to be tended to by Lydia, Katryn and some of the other women. Rhys had accompanied him and Llew to their hut.

"It was indeed a gallant and noble gesture you made agreeing to look after Enid." Rhys slapped Math on the back again, beaming from ear to ear.

"I don't know if I've done the right thing at all," said Math mournfully. "What if it's thought that I killed our Guto just so as I could have his wife? What then?"

"Now you listen to me," Llew was quite angry, "you bloody well saved my life and certainly our Rhys here owes his life to you! There are those that saw this thing take place and they will remember what they saw clearly. So you just put such a thought out of your head. In any case if anyone objected they would have made a case against you in front of Owain and Lady Gwenhwyfar."

"That's right, good Math, that's right!" beamed Rhys.

"Oh, what am I to do now?" Math was distraught at the predicament in which a few moments of bravado had placed him.

Chapter 6

Ceolwulf opened his eyes. It was dark and smoky. Through his cage, he could see the woman crouched at the steaming cauldron hung over the hearth fire. Taking a surreptitious look around the dimly lit hut, he could see he was still guarded by two warriors, one on each side of the cage. They were well armed and alert. Both men wore the black and yellow checked cloaks he had seen before and they carried spears, knives, and long bows. Ceolwulf closed his eyes again and sighed. The sound brought one of the guards to his feet. Ceolwulf could hear the man speaking, the language sounded like he was trying to clear his throat of some phlegm and yet there was an almost pleasant singsong quality to its cadence. He lay back down quietly without any further sighs.

The pain in his head had lessened somewhat though he still felt groggy. His side ached and burned but he was not concerned about that as much, he had been cut before. His headache bothered him. Not the pain of it, but the inability to orient, the queasiness and weakness that prevented him from being strong. This he had never experienced before. He drifted out of consciousness.

Ceolwulf dreamed he was lost in a great forest. His men had refused to enter with him and he had derided them for their cowardice. The forest was dense and the snow that fell silently blanketed the forest floor. He thought the sight of it was beautiful. There were shadowy figures hiding just out of sight and moving amongst the trees. Danger was near, of that he was sure. He decided to make his way toward them and confront the shadowy creatures head on like a man, a warrior searching for valour. But there were no shadowy creatures, only a man, one lone man and he stood with his hand open, an exquisite heavy silver ring lay in his open palm. And then everything went black.

Ceolwulf regained consciousness, looked around the hut. Nothing had changed; the guards eyed him suspiciously until he closed his eyes again. This time he dreamt of home and the curious events that brought him to these misty islands.

The slatted wooden huts with their thatched roofs were clustered haphazardly behind a tall wood planked palisade. Wood smoke wafted, adding to the smell of pig dung and balancing the aroma of fresh cut hay, baked bread, and fresh hewn wood. The Great Hall stood in the centre of the scores of simple huts. It was a commanding structure, the largest within the wooden walls. The Hall provided a focal point in the lives of the people. The shire, as the people called their assembly of huts, was for the moment quiet.

This was the young Ceolwulf's home. He and his clan believed their little shire provided them protection against marauding bands and tribal rivals. The tribal fighting was endless. There was always one king, willing to lead his tribe into battle against another. The peasants were the ones who always paid the price. Their work in the fields left them vulnerable to the butchery of invaders. When all the grain was burned and the cattle stolen, it was the men and women and the children toiling in the fields who starved. Today, wood smoke swirled about as the peasants tended their chores, feeding livestock mending farming implements and working the small fields. Tradesmen worked at their trade, shaping leather, cloth and metal and wood into useful items. Children scampered back and forth while harried mothers chased after them. Great hounds wandered the compound scavenging for food in the refuse.

Ceolwulf was young and not yet aware that his father's political machinations with the nobleman of the shire had been successful. There was an agreement that Ceolwulf's older brother Eanwulfing may be selected for the Hearth Troop, selected warriors who acted as personal guard to the nobleman. This was good news for it would bring prestige to the family.

Ceolwulf's father Eanwulf held the rank of a *thane*, a warrior of standing with the clan's nobility. As a thane, Eanwulf was expected to provide five armed warriors for the common war host. When a thane served his master well, he was rewarded with a ring or some token of esteem. Continued loyalty and good service by the thane to the nobleman was rewarded with small parcels of land.

Eanwulfing was but three summers older than his brother and already he was a proven warrior. The boy was tall and well muscled with an arrogance easily seen in his walk. The young man's hair was long, straight, and blonde like his mother's. His light beard was worn close cut to hide its' youthful sparseness. Eanwulfing was a feared fighter with a mean and cruel temper. Eanwulf hoped that by providing his noblemen with a fine warrior like his son, Eanwulfing, he might add to the family's holdings. Eanwulf hoped providing his son, as a member of the Hearth Troop would be a very good political move. Eanwulf was a very political man.

Ceolwulf's family had done very well for themselves in the shire. They owned a small parcel of land that grew enough vegetables for them to eat with some left over to sell. A shrewd business deal had garnered a small herd of pigs that they also raised on the land. The sale of pork and vegetables supplemented the earnings from Eanwulf's masterful work with leather had done much in keeping hunger from their door. It also provided strong weapons to the family's warriors. Freya, the wife of Eanwulf and Ceolwulf's mother, had come to her husband with a good dowry that had also provided comfort for the family.

Ceolwulf was a summer shy of manhood. He was a youth who had not yet proven himself a warrior. With envy, he looked upon his older brother as a hero. The other four warriors of his father's retinue were Ceolwulf's cousins. All of them were adept at killing and had proven their worth and their skill many times over. The men were well fed and clothed in plain wool shirts under leather jerkins, cinched with wide leather belts, woollen breeches, leggings, and leather foot coverings. Thick grey woollen cloaks with plain metal clasps hung around their shoulders. Eanwulf's expertise with leather meant that his men possessed gear that was strong, functional and handsomely befitting their standing in the shire. Another of Eanwulf's deals, this time with the shire's metalworker, provided his men with swords, spears, axes and fine *saexes*, fighting knives, that were of good quality, nothing fancy just sharp, strong and deadly.

A curious thing happened when Ceolwulf was nearly of age. He had a quarrel with an older, bigger lad. The source of the disagreement was not remembered, but egos were hurt and had to be assuaged with fighting. Horst, the older youth was getting the better of young Ceolwulf, who had already been bruised and bloodied, his left eye blackened. The two lads had dropped to the ground and were fiercely fighting each other for control. Horst won and got on top of Ceolwulf, raining punches down on the younger lad's head.

Somehow, Ceolwulf managed to get a leg free and with all his might and his newfound leverage, he rolled free. Scrambling to his feet, he was able to connect a kick to Horst's groin doubling the boy over in pain. They circled each other warily, Horst still in pain from the groin kick. Without warning, Horst flew at Ceolwulf, his head striking at the smaller boy's stomach driving all air from his lungs. They crashed to the ground, again.

Suddenly, the sound of drawn steel was heard and Horst's saexe appeared in his hand. He slashed at Ceolwulf who squirmed away narrowly evading the attempted cut from his rival. Again, Horst slashed and again Ceolwulf's agility saved him. Horst's momentum however caused him to stumble off-balance and he sprawled headlong into the dirt. Ceolwulf wasted no time, jumping on his fallen enemy and with both his hands seized Horst's knife hand. He used his knee to deliver devastating strikes to Horst's groin. Only two of the five knee strikes found their target but it was enough. Horst lost his grip and Ceolwulf recovered the saexe. Pulling Horst's hair back with his left hand, Ceolwulf's right hand gripped the fighting knife and poised to cut the boy's throat. The cheering from the other boys who had been watching and goading the two combatants went silent. Ceolwulf hesitated a fraction of a second and then made his cut. A red mark appeared on the exposed white throat of Horst. There was no blood. Ceolwulf had only marked the boy. Laughter filled the air.

The beating Ceolwulf received from his brother and his father was vicious. While nothing had been broken, the bruises and cuts had taken five days to heal and he had lost two teeth. They had been furious about his fight with Horst. The lesson Ceolwulf had to learn was that in a fight there is no quarter given. Once your enemy is at your mercy, you kill him! Ceolwulf should have cut Horst's throat, for according to his father and warrior brother, he had created a life long enemy. If he had killed Horst outright there would have been nothing said. Oh, perhaps a *wergild*, a small fine for the taking of a youth's life to be paid as compensation to the boy's father. Better that than the taking of Horst's honour, a crime much worse than a killing.

"You stupid dog! When you fight, you fight to kill! Do you hear me?" his father had raged as his fists crashed in to Ceolwulf's prone body. A final brutal kick to his ribs and his father stomped off in search of a drink. Ceolwulf was left unconscious and bleeding, a battered heap on the dirt floor of their hut. Ceolwulf's mother had remained silent, minding her business and not interfering with the men. Now she tried to tend her son, wiping away the blood. Eanwufing, for his part held a begrudging respect for his little brother though his blows were delivered just as viciously as his father's. Ceolwulf had after all disarmed and defeated a bigger and stronger enemy. Still Eanwulfing knew his father was right. Such things as this, leaving alive an enemy but taking his honour, only lead to a blood feud and more fighting. Ceolwulf left his father's house that day.

In need of food and shelter, Ceolwulf asked the blacksmith of the shire for work. Whether from pity for the battered young boy or respect for the lad's determination, the man agreed. Ceolwulf would work for him. Sigurd, the smith, gave Ceolwulf the job of cutting wood, hauling water and cleaning the tools. He told the young lad that if he proved his worth he would learn to use hammer and tong. Ceolwulf slept in a lean-to near the furnace. It was warm and dry and he could help Sigurd's huge hound guard the tools and metals at night. He got used to the smells of the burned coal and coke and he even became oblivious to the hound's fleas.

Sigurd's wife saw to it that he was fed once a day. She laughed seeing the young lad scratch furiously at a fleabite and told him to boil water and bathe himself. The days passed quickly and the hard work made Ceolwulf stronger. He had learned much from old Sigurd. Scyld, the younger son of Sigurd, was trying to fill in for his older brother who had been killed in battle a summer ago. Sigurd had been thankful for Ceolwulf's help these past months for it gave Scyld time to grow into the role for which he was destined. Sigurd was impressed how fast Ceolwulf had learned the trade and what was more important, how he had taught his son Scyld. Ceolwulf had taught the young Scyld how to work the bellows and how technique could compensate for the youngster's lack of strength when cutting wood. The younger Scyld looked upon Ceolwulf as the brother he had lost. Ceolwulf and Sigurd knew their situation would soon change. It had been many months, almost a year really since Ceolwulf's arrival. Soon Ceolwulf would need to return to his father and obey his bidding. Eanwulf was after all a thane.

It was time. A battle was brewing. Battles were a common thing. Angli, from the peninsula jutting into the bay of Kiel, fought Jutes and Saxons north of them. Sometimes they fought the Frisians from the seacoast below the Elbe, but one thing was certain a battle was always brewing. It would be Ceolwulf's time to become a proven warrior

He went to his father's hut and waited outside in the rain. Eanwulfing, after quite some time, came out and walked around him. Ceolwulf remained motionless, drenched to the bone in cold rain and kneeling in the mud. His brother sized him up, noticing how Ceolwulf had filled out. The hard work at Sigurd's village forge responsible for Ceolwulf building muscles and sinew. Eanwulfing suddenly wheeled around and punched his younger brother in the midsection. Ceolwulf grunted, and then gasped for air but remained kneeling in the mud. Eanwulfing punched Ceolwulf in the face, bruising his jaw, but Ceolwulf remained stoic and unmoving. Eanwulfing laughed and then punched his brother again in the face, harder than before. Ceolwulf shook his head to clear the cobwebs, but remained kneeling, his hair matted with mud, rain, and now blood. His brother spun and aimed a tremendous kick at Ceolwulf's stomach. Ceolwulf blocked the blow with both forearms, trapped his brother's leg, and wrenched it, bringing the older man down hard, face first into the cold mud. Ceolwulf was instantly on top of his big brother's back and pulled his muddied hair back. His face was close to this brother's ear.

"This is not a fight and I am unarmed. You are not obliged to kill me nor I to kill you!"

Eanwulfing looked enraged. His countenance suggested that killing Ceolwulf, his brother, was exactly the course of action he wished to take!

It was another heartbeat before Eanwulfing scrambled to his feet and looking at Ceolwulf slapped him heartily on the back.

"He'll do Father!" he cried, "He'll do just fine!" He seized his brother in a bear hug as though they were long comrades-in-arms already victorious in battle.

Eanwulf had appeared at the hut's door. Ceolwulf knelt on one knee in obeisance. Looking down at his young son and then into the shining eyes of his eldest, Eanwulf grunted. One of Ceolwulf's cousins came round the side of the hut, his arms full of leather harness, gauntlets, shield and sword. Another cousin appeared carrying a great double bladed battle-axe. The weapons and equipment were unceremoniously dumped in the mud at Ceolwulf's feet.

"Use these well and remember, to be counted by Woden for his Wild Hunt, you must achieve honour in battle! Do not shame me!" Eanwulf turned on his heel and stomped back into the hut.

Strangely, Ceolwulf was more afraid before the battle than when engaged in it. The thought of battle and death was worse in his mind than the reality he now faced. Lined up in the muck and mire with a cold rain beating down, the enemy stood arrayed in a line a few yards away. They were at the edge of a forest lined up facing Ceolwulf's kinsmen from across a brief meadow. The weather was foul, cold and wet. The battle gear was heavy and uncomfortable to Ceolwulf, the novice warrior. The enemy was a rival clan trying desperately to improve their holdings. The fighting men were yelling taunts and insults, their jibes mixing with the sound of the rain and the fidgeting of the warrior's equipment. One of the men began banging his spear against his shield. The sound increased as other warriors followed suit. Soon all the warriors including Ceolwulf were madly banging their spears and swords against shields. The din was raucous and deafening. A warrior broke rank and made a mock charge against the enemy. He ran forward, full out, his long braided hair flowing behind him whilst his thick, strong arms hefted his great axe. Immediately, a spear ripped through the front of his body, its leaf shaped blade grotesquely sprouting out his back. The dying man crumpled into the mud with a gurgling sound.

Another warrior charged. At midfield, the enemy met the man. Swords held high they ran screaming at each other. The clash of the bodies was mighty. Repeatedly they traded blows, the ring of steel on steel and the clanging of sword to shield was heard over the battleground. A wild swing of a sword, an arc of death and a spray of blood rose in a cloud where once a haughty head had ruled. Warriors on both sides roared. Two more enemy warriors broke ranks and came roaring at Ceolwulf's cousins. A spear took one in the leg, he screamed in pain. Writhing in agony, he was cut nearly in half by a mighty swing of double bladed battle-axe wielded by a kin of Ceolwulf. The battle was on! Men were running and screaming at each other crashing together in a chaotic crush of bodies. The meadow's grass and earth churned with rain and blood.

Ceolwulf caught the battle fever and ran bellowing at the enemy. He came up fast face to face with an older man, though he looked more a demon. His long brown hair was matted with blood and mud, his face streaked with red and contorted in rage. A spear thrust narrowly missed Ceolwulf's stomach as he spun. Swinging his new battle-axe in a mighty arc, he felt the sudden shock through the haft of his dreadful weapon as it chopped through bone. The enemy screamed in pain as his spear-arm fell from his body and landed in the mud at his feet. Ceolwulf raised his axe and brought the dreadful thing down onto his enemy's head, splitting the man. Without stopping, without thinking, Ceolwulf ran to the next enemy. His mighty axe swung in a terrible arc and a head plopped in the mud. Ceolwulf ran.

A spear haft caught him in the stomach and all breath was driven from his lungs. Losing is grip, his axe slipped into the mud as he collapsed forward gasping for air. Ceolwulf was on his back trying desperately to get air into his lungs. Instantly, a warrior was on him. The foot on Ceolwulf's throat pinned him, as the sword was quickly raised for a stabbing deathblow. Ceolwulf rolled and squirmed to his side, the sword pierced the reddened earth where once his head had been. Clutching at a knife he had secreted in his leggings, Ceolwulf slashed upwards. The warrior screamed in pain and surprise as Ceolwulf's blade ripped into his inner thigh. Stumbling to his knees, sucking for air, Ceolwulf rooted in the reddened mud for his axe. His wet gloved hand clasped onto the shaft of his battle-axe and he fought to get to his feet. He swung his axe and felt the sudden thump as its hideous blade bit deep into his enemy's back. Standing with feet apart, battle-axe readied for more killing, Ceolwulf tried to see through the blood and rain. He was still gasping for a lungful of air. A horn blew a discordant chord. Another blast. The air was now filled with the cacophony of blaring war horns and screaming men. Combatants pulled apart, lines of warriors disengaged. Banners flew, battered by the wind and rain. Ceolwulf stood bewildered. Bloodied men were pulling themselves from the filth and muck to make their way back to their thanes. The battle was over.

Ceolwulf and his kin gathered in the Great Hall of their king. The funeral pyres had been lit, songs for the dead had been sung. The bodies of the fallen were stripped of their gear and burned with honours due their station in life. War booty was given to the king. Celebration for the victory of Ceolwulf's clan was in full swing. The smoke-filled hall was heavy with the smell of battle-weary men caked in sweat, blood and filth. Torches burned, a great fire roared in the hearth and men sat lined on benches at the long tables. Hounds slunk between the rows of tables scavenging for dropped food. Huge haunches of venison, pork, and beef were paraded by serving girls. Mead and ale flowed and bone-tired warriors drank their fill. The chaos and roar of the Great Hall rivalled its smell.

Roasted meat, baked bread, ale, and mead mixed with the foul odour of warrior's sweat, shit, piss and blood. Nevertheless, a sort of order remained. Warriors sat at the mead benches according to their rank and station. Eanwulf's rank as a favoured thane allowed Ceolwulf, his brother and cousins to sit only a few rows removed from their nobleman's table. Mixed among them according to rank were other thanes and their retainers. Ceolwulf ate, drank and pounded the table with the others. He noticed that many of the men around him bore freshly sewn wounds, black and purple bruises, bloodied faces and bandages, few men remained unscathed.

Eanwulfing, his own face sporting a gash, his nose broken, was standing proudly expounding his victory over five of the enemy, sending them all to an ignoble end. The men pounded the wooden plank tables in uproarious approval. The serving girls laboured to keep the great haunches of roasted meats and loaves of bread circulating amongst the warriors. Their progress impeded by constant gropes from the men.

Eanwulf stood and pounded the table with the pommel of his saexe. His kinsmen quieted to hear the words of their thane. Above the tumultuous din of the hall, Eanwulf spoke loudly of the battle and the great victory won for their king. More pounding, war whoops and roaring ensued. Eanwulf raised his arms in acknowledgement to the cheers of his people, his face red and hot streaked with blood and mud, a slashed leather tunic revealing the savage cut wending its way down his chest. Standing on the mead bench, Eanwulf grabbed Ceolwulf by the back of his tunic and dragged him up to his feet.

"Today," bellowed Eanwulf, "my youngest son, Ceolwulf, becomes a proven warrior recognized by his clan!" The roaring was deafening, the tables threatened to splinter under the pounding. Other warriors strained to hear what the new commotion was about. Word passed from one to another that a youth had this day proven his mettle in battle and with three kills no less! The hall erupted in singing, yelling and banging. Ceolwulf jumped onto the table, his cloak furling behind him as he stalked up and down, arms thrown wide receiving the loud acknowledgement of his kinsmen. He strutted with full-blown pride, welcomed into the company of men in front of his own father and their nobleman!

That was his first battle many summers ago. Time had passed and the fullness of that time, Ceolwulf, youngest son of Eanwulf had himself become a thane. Eanwulfing had become the family patriarch when their father died the winter past. The old man had been at the Great Hall sitting on a mead bench, drinking horn firmly grasped in his hand, loudly stating his opinion to other proud warriors from past wars. In the midst of his boast, Eanwulf crumpled and fell to the dirt floor still clutching his drinking horn, not a drop of mead spilled from it.

Eanwulf's legacy was that his political ambitions had been realised. Eanwulfing had become a member of the Hearth Troop and the family was in good standing within the shire. The elder son had the ear of the clan's nobleman and had been well rewarded for his battle skill and his sound advice. However, the clan's fortune in their homeland was waning. The tribe's population had increased and many battles were constantly being fought over land and possessions.

A generation ago, a call had gone out for Saxons, Angli and even Jutes and some Frisians to leave their lands and travel to the Misty Islands of the Britons off the West coast. A self-proclaimed head of the Council of Britons had need of fighting men to quell disturbances along his northern borders. Warrior leaders were told of fertile lands that would be given to those who fought valiantly against the wild tribesmen of the Briton's Northlands. The call was heeded and many warriors indeed sailed west. Rumours came back that the fighting was easy. The strange blue-painted, north men were fierce, but no match for Angli-Saxon and Jutes.

Years passed by, more warriors from the peninsula and the coast travelled to the Misty Isles. More rumours circulated at home. The fighting may not be as hard, they said, as receiving their due payment for providing a mercenary force, as was requested. Frustrations festered. Soon their countrymen were seizing Briton lands as their own.

Ceolwulf had kinsmen who had answered the call to arms in the employ of the Briton Council leader. Twenty-odd years ago, an uncle and some of his cousins along with others from surrounding villages had sold their service to the Britons. They had not been heard from since. It was thought they had done well for themselves. Ceolwulf's father had decided against moving his family to the Misty Islands. He had reasoned that he would raise strong sons who would do their fighting for their king and their homeland! Eanwulf had looked forward to basking in the accomplishments of his life and the honour earned from his many battles. If Woden smiled on him then he would die in a battle beside his sons and feast at the Great Hall in the Valhalla. All would sing songs of his valour and drink to his tales of bravery and courage. Eanwulf vowed to never leave his shire! It was his home, his family's home and he would not abandon it!

Another call for arms had been issued! The Angli, Saxons and the Jutes had won lands in the south of the island. More men were needed to secure the holdings and to add to them. The lands were fertile and rich. A man, it was said, need only plant the crop, spit and duck as fields of golden grains sprung up from the fertile ground. The temptation was great and many men of Ceolwulf's village had succumbed to the allure of the adventure and the promise of rich land.

Eanwulfing now had a wife and two young sons of his own. Ceolwulf was yet unmarried. He was respected in the shire and spent much time talking with the craftsmen and the older warriors. What he learned from these men concerned him. He began to realise the family land, indeed the shire itself, was not so stable as his late father had thought.

Times had changed and Ceolwulf wondered if his brother realised just how much things had changed.

The clan's nobleman was old. He still had the ear of the king but the men of the shire thought his influence had long since waned. To increase the shire's worth, and his own standing with the king, the clan nobleman decided to invade a neighbouring village to the North. It was a large village and rich. Many said the metalworkers of that village produced the finest rings, goblets, and armbands in all the shires thereabouts. Their fields and cattle were the best. But to invade and conquer this rich village, their nobleman would need to make an alliance with two other villages to the East and West. The new allies were to be enticed with war booty. Success meant that Ceolwulf's shire would be in the position to increase their largesse with booty and increase their influence and standing by providing their king with rich lands.

Of course the king would be pleased, and would no doubt justly compensate the nobleman for his boldness, for it would be his shire and not the king, who would shoulder the risk.

Negotiations had already begun. A war council was convened and strategies were being discussed. An undertaking this size with so much at stake required a proper battle plan. Eanwulfing was not pleased he had been chosen to negotiate with the other villages.

"This is something Father was good at, but I am a warrior, a member of the Hearth Troop! I have not the temperament for this!" Eanwulfing complained.

"Brother, don't you see, that is why you have been chosen. Many have heard of our father. His reputation is sung about in other villages and shires. It is his memory you need draw on, for the fact that you are his son stands you in good stead. The others know you can influence the nobleman. That means what you say reaches the King's ear. With you negotiating they can count on wise council that carries with it some weight. More importantly your presence offers another layer of buffering for the King thus providing him further protection should this plan fail."

Eanwulfing's face darkened.

"I am a scapegoat, then!" He paced around the wooden table and slammed his drinking horn down in anger.

"I am nothing more than a herald, a messenger boy!"

"You are," soothed Ceolwulf," a necessary political tool, safeguarding the honour of our King and the memory of our father."

They were words that rang hollow for Ceolwulf. He spoke them only to quiet his older brother's temper. Eanwulfing would need his wits about him to survive the political quagmire in which he was now trapped. Unlike his father, Ceolwulf had no political ambitions, and unlike his brother, he could usually sense when the political ambitions of others were shaping his world. He could sense the dangers and determine how to act accordingly. The effect such machinations had on his sense of honour disgusted Ceolwulf. He was still young.

Lately, Ceolwulf found his thoughts did not come easily to him. He felt distracted. There was a reason for this; her name was Yetta. To the young Ceolwulf, serious thinker and fearsome warrior, she was poetry personified. Her long brown hair and soft, sensuous body had cast a spell on Ceolwulf. All he could think of were Yetta's sea green eyes, the swell of her breasts and the sway of her hips, as she moved about the shire.

It was difficult for him to approach the fair maiden. He had responsibilities as a proven warrior, a thane, a protector of the shire and a commitment to the black smith. Scyld had replaced his ailing father and he often asked help from his mentor that kept young Ceolwulf busy. He found he rarely saw the pretty Yetta long enough to strike up a conversation. Not that he could do so in any case. To date, whenever he had occasion to bump into the young girl, Ceolwulf found himself unable to speak. He spluttered and stuttered like a drunken fool or remained stupidly silent like some dumbstruck peasant. To make matters worse, Yetta's father kept his daughter at his disposal. The old man watched his daughter like a hawk. Especially, it seemed, when Ceolwulf was around.

There was an added problem. Yetta had a brother. Horst.

Often Ceolwulf thought that his brother and father had been right those many years ago. Perhaps he had made a lifelong enemy. Certainly, nothing had transpired between the two young men since that fateful day of their fight, but friends, they were not.

The following weeks were busy ones filled with preparations for war. Ceolwulf managed to see Yetta only twice during that time. She had stopped by the smith's to pick up a copper basin Scyld had made at her father's request. Ceolwulf happened to be there and had handed Yetta the basin. In so doing their fingers touched. They lingered. Yetta smiled at him and Ceolwulf thought his heart would explode. Scyld blundered in on them before Ceolwulf could make any intelligent sounds.

Their last meeting occurred in the mead hall. Ceolwulf, his brother, and their kinsmen were rowdily drinking and telling battle tales fortifying themselves against the horror of the war waiting for them. Warriors from the other villages, allies in the upcoming battle, entered, nodded their acknowledgements. The day was dying but it had been glorious. A warming sun, clear blue skies, and crisp air laden with pine scent and wood smoke had provided good cheer for the men. Moving deeper into the mead hall they had commandeered benches and piled shields and spears and battle gear nearby. The hearth fires burned fiercely throwing a yellowed light through the smoky haze. Warriors continued shouting for mead and meat. Laughter and singing filled the hall. The men were comfortable.

Yetta was among the serving girls plying the warriors with mead, ale, and haunches of meat and loaves of coarse dark bread. Eanwulfing caught Ceolwulf's furtive glances in Yetta's direction and dug his brother playfully in the ribs. Ceolwulf pushed back at his brother careful not to do so too roughly. He did not wish his brother to feel challenged in front of his men. On the pretence he needed to urinate, Ceolwulf left their company. Once away from the raucous singing of his fellows, he searched the kitchens for the lovely Yetta. She was cutting meat when he came up to her.

"I have wanted to speak with you for some time," he stammered awkwardly.

Yetta stopped what she was doing and moved away from the table and her chores. She now stood with her back against the wall of the kitchen out of the line of sight of the other girls and partially covered by shadow.

"And tell me Brave Warrior," she said coyly, "what has kept you from speaking?" Her green eyes sparkled with humour.

"Well my precious one, I am not used to speaking with Fair Maidens. My manners are rough and coarse and I did not wish to be seen as a lout." Ceolwulf managed a sheepish smile.

"Do you think you have succeeded?" She smiled up at him and poor Ceolwulf thought certain his heart would pound straight through his mail shirt.

"I have done my best," was all that he could say. "It is you who must judge my success or failure. My experience and my judgement only pertain to battles and war I am sorry to say." He blushed. Yetta saw this and felt drawn to the young man in front of her. The Proud Warrior, the Feared Fighter, even she knew the name of his dreaded axe, "Mansplitter." And yet, there was something in his eyes, something other than bloodlust and conquest.

Ceolwulf looked at her with almost uncomfortable intensity and yet there was something else, something other than simple lust. Could it be vulnerability? Unconsciously, he stroked her long unfettered brown tresses. Still without thinking, he brushed his lips against her cheek, she pressed into him. The moment became their universe and nothing else existed.

A loud noise! Another loud noise and it was closer this time. Now they could hear voices and laughter and the sounds were getting closer. Men looking for mead entered the kitchens. Startled, the two would-be lovers separated awkwardly.

It was two men, two fighting men from the alliance and they were drunk. Negotiations were dragging on and the men brought by chieftains as their retinue were restless. The mead hall could not hold their interest for long and these two had come looking for amusement in the kitchens.

"Hans look! Now there is a fine looking wench! Be thou hale young girl!" The bigger of the two men had not noticed Ceolwulf who had leaned back into the shadow. The men came closer, the smell of the mead wafted about them.

"You're a beautiful girl aren't you? Would you like to share a drink with me and my friend here?" The warrior had come closer. He was suddenly startled to see Ceolwulf in shadow.

"*Ela*! What are you doing here, skulking in the shadow like a thief in the night?" the man blustered angrily. His friend, the other warrior stopped short and now stood his ground some feet away, anger mixed with surprise.

"You may have forgotten, but this is my shire and my mead hall." Ceolwulf answered curtly, moving fully into the firelight and bristling with hostility.

"And you have forgotten, boy, that we are here because this shire is too weak to fight its own battles! While our nobleman decides if we will save your miserable hides, we will amuse ourselves! Now out of my way, boy!" The warrior reached out and grabbed Yetta by the waist. He roughly pulled her to his side, his right hand yanked her hair back exposing her throat and forcing her to look up into his leering face. He kissed her full on the mouth.

Ceolwulf forgot all about negotiations, alliances, and politics. In his rage, Ceolwulf grabbed a handful of hair with his left hand and pulled the man forward unbalancing him. Yetta squirmed free from his grip. Ceolwulf had already plunged his saexe into the exposed back of the warrior, spinning the dying warrior so that his back was now to him. Still clutching hair with his left, Ceolwulf's right hand drew the deadly saexe across the throat. Blood splayed a grotesque pattern on the wooden wall.

Yetta did not scream. She was on her knees where she had fallen, when Ceolwulf tore the man away from her. Ceolwulf was standing over her guarding her from the nearly headless body of her defiler.

He had forgotten about the man's companion. The muted clanging of metal caught his attention as he straightened to see the sword wielding warrior mere yards away. The man's arms had gone limp, his sword had fallen from his grasp and there was a surprised look in the man's eyes. A gurgling sound came from his lips as blood appeared and dripped down the corners of his lips. The man fell in a heap on the dirt floor.

Ceolwulf now looked into the ice blue eyes of Horst. Blood still dripped from the saexe Horst had plunged into the back of the warrior. The two men stood staring at each other over the corpses of their would-be allies.

"You saved my sister," said Horst simply. He wiped the blood from his saexe and slipped it into the sheath behind his back.

"That doesn't change anything between us. However, I cannot find it in myself to kill you this instant. If you survive the battle and if I too am alive at battle's end, then you must leave this shire. If you do not, then my kin will kill yours until you and yours are no more."

"You credit yourself too much," Ceolwulf growled. "I am not in the habit of running from a challenge, perhaps you have heard?" With this Ceolwulf arrogantly kicked the body of the man he had killed. The head nearly rolled free from the body.

"I know your reputation! Listen to me! Surely, you must see the reality of this situation we are in? This alliance will never hold," here Horst pushed his foot against his kill, rolling the corpse onto its side. Our nobleman is old and feeble and this...this war, it is nothing but the desperate act of a dying man trying to hold onto a power he never really possessed! The king knows this! Nothing good will come from this battle!" Horst spat into the dirt for emphasis.

"That is a coward's talk! I will fight for my honour! Men will sing my name in praise!" Ceolwulf was angry. He edged forward menacingly.

"No! You will stay and die in a pointless battle. There will be no glory in your death and no praise heaped upon you for no one will remember your name. You will have died for the bargaining of dried up old men who care for nothing save their own comforts." Horst smiled.

"Or you may indeed survive the battle. Then you will have to fight me to the death! If you are successful in that, you will live only to see the decay of your beloved shire. And thane no more, you will die a lowly peasant in miserable servitude to a fool!"

Ceolwulf was thoroughly confused. He knew well what Horst said about the battle was true; it was his own feeling as well, despite what he told his brother. What was Horst after? It was clear his rival had something up his sleeve.

Horst saw all of this play out on Ceolwulf's face. He again smiled. The boy may be astute, but he had no guile in him.

"I want you to take Yetta and a few chosen of your men to the Isles of the Britons. You would have a chance there of a better life and my sister would at least be safe. I intend to die here, the last of my line. It is my duty to my dead father." Horst was staring hard at Ceolwulf. There was intensity in his gaze that disquieted.

Ceolwulf would have none of it!

"What of my honour? I am a thane! My duty also lies here in my shire! I will not shirk my duty!"

"There is honour in making bad alliances to fight useless battles for weak political gain? We are not talking about a just cause, an honourable and glorious death, a place at the mead table of the Great Hall of our Ancestors!" Horst paused to let Ceolwulf weigh what he said. He continued in a more conciliatory tone.

"I am telling you I would consider my honour satisfied if you take my sister to another land away from this miserable dung heap. I say to you with honour, your name will be remembered by me and mine, as a hero, a brave leader of men who left the confines of a dying shire to blaze a trail of his own choosing. You will be sung of as a man who was not afraid of the unknown, but who valiantly took his new bride to a foreign land so that he may write his own destiny! It's that or die ignobly here in this dung heap." With that, Horst gestured over his shoulder. Two of his kinsmen stood with spears poised.

Ceolwulf took no notice of the spearmen. He looked into the eyes of Yetta. The firelight bathed her in a warm yellow glow. He noticed the shadows flicker over the smooth skin of her face. Ceolwulf saw too that her face was tear streaked and her eyes glistened with tears and an unspoken wish for a brighter future.

"I will answer you after the battle," he said tersely to Horst.

The battle was brutal and bloody. Ceolwulf survived with only a gash across his back. The objective had been lost, their nobleman had been killed, and the alliance was broken. Ceolwulf's shire was now in the possession of a rival nobleman, a former ally, now and a sworn enemy. The king, of course, remained in power and above reproach. His rule was not impinged by the battle or the treachery. For Ceolwulf and his kinsmen there would be no victory celebration, no drinking, or feasting in honour of the fallen and the victorious. They could only pick their broken, chopped bodies out of the stinking filth of the battleground and painfully make their way home.

Their shire was no longer their home.

Stumbling round once familiar huts, Ceolwulf found Horst and two of his kinsmen. Horst was sitting on rock. He was pale and caked in mud and blood. His kinsmen were needed to steady Horst as he sat; otherwise, he appeared whole and unscathed by battle.

"It seems we are homeless," Horst stated simply, waving with an open hand toward the devastated shire. Huts still burned orange, roiling thick black smoke toward the grey leaden sky. Dead cattle lay where they fell.

"We have lost," Horst grimaced in apparent pain for a brief moment and then quickly regained his composure.

Ceolwulf looked upon the grim scene and knew Horst was right. The shire had been attacked while its war host fought the battle. They had been betrayed.

"I am a member of the Hearth Troop but I have no one to protect. You Ceolwulf, are a thane with neither men to lead nor land to hold." It was said without malice but the truth of what Horst said sat heavy on Ceolwulf's heart.

"I say there is nothing here for you to do," Horst was saying, "but to leave at once for the Isles of the Britons. You have a few bits of armour, one or two weapons. You can go to the islands with my sister at your side, some food, and some arms and write your own destiny. What say you to that?"

"What of my brother Eanwulfing," Ceolwulf cast round like a drowning man looking for something to clutch on to. "He will want to raise an army and seek revenge! His honour and the honour of the shire demand it!"

"Your brother, Ceolwulf, is lying on his shield. He is dying and will join your father in Woden's Great Hall this night." Horst grimaced again and slumped slightly. His kinsmen helped keep him righted.

"What of you?" asked Ceolwulf. It was not meant to sound unkind.

"I am not long for this world, Ceolwulf. All the members of my family are dead. Yetta and a few cousins are all who remain alive. My men will...." Horst grimaced and he spat frothing red spittle to the ground.

"My men will wait for the inevitable and then go their separate ways. You...you must save my sister." The two men stared at each other. Horst removed his glove and slowly stretched out his hand toward Ceolwulf. They grasped arms in brotherly bondage. Ceolwulf saw the blood leaking through Horst's woollen shirt. It was a great deal of blood. Horst's grip weakened, his arm slipped from Ceolwulf's hand.

Chapter 7

Briton was not what Ceolwulf had expected. While he hadn't really believed the fabulous stories he had heard, he had expected the land to look, well, more foreign. The long low ship Ceolwulf and Yetta had set sail in had made landfall in the south of the Misty Isles. They were among their own, other Saxons who were making the treacherous trip across the rough narrow seas to Saxon-held lands just north of the great River Tamesis. The crossing was a rough one. Ceolwulf was surprised that Yetta was so uncomfortable during the trip. She had vomited a lot and her skin was clammy and pale with a tinge of green. He had talked with others, mainly peasants, but no one really knew what to expect from the mysterious island. He decided to keep his status to himself partly for strategic reasons, no need for everyone to know his business until he himself had a plan and knew the lay of the land. Ceolwulf harboured another secret. He was ashamed he had not stayed in the shire to fight for his place among his ancestors. The decision to leave his homeland haunted him despite the wisdom of it.

He and Yetta along with a few others rested at a small hamlet, gathering their strength for what they were told would be an arduous inland trek. They were to follow the great meandering river westward. This path, according to the self-appointed leader, a big rough-hewn man with long locks of red hair tinged with silver, would lead them to a frontier where they could start fresh.

His name was Günter and he described to Ceolwulf the sight of a large city made of stone. Indeed, after a few days of rough travel overland keeping the great river in sight, the motley group of travellers skirted the city. Ceolwulf noted the crumbling walls and could see in the distance, the great stone buildings, roads of stone, stonewalls, and swirling black smoke all the signs of many, many inhabitants. Günter called the city, *Londinium,* and said it had always been a great city, a gathering of people even in ancient times. The smell, Ceolwulf noted, was foul, pigswill and dung, offal and human waste. He was glad to be moving on keeping to small tracks through meadows, forests, and the bordering marshes.

During their trek, they chanced to stop many times at small enclaves though they were more hamlets and could not be called shires. Ceolwulf talked to the men he found there and to his surprise many understood his words. The language was the same save for an accent. When talking to some of the younger lads who had been born in this land, Ceolwulf found their accents difficult to follow.

It was clear that his Briton-born countrymen lived on a frontier in a land that had been claimed by their peoples not far north from the riverbank, but much west of their original landing. Looking around Ceolwulf saw the chance of good game, clear water and land suitable for farming. In speaking with the men folk, he realised his talents and skills as a leather worker combined with what he knew of metal work, thanks to his apprenticeship with Sigurd, would allow him a living. He spoke to Yetta who had not recovered fully from the sea journey. It was Ceolwulf's mind that he settle here, a place as good as any, where a man could start anew. As it happened, Yetta was in no mood for more travelling.

The two young people from the continent were made husband and wife in a hand-fasting ceremony attended by their newfound neighbours. There was merriment and drinking of mead and some of the local wheaten ale. One of the old women in their company, unsteady on her feet from the mead, took Ceolwulf's arm. Laughing up at him, she toasted the young man and his new bride for their good fortune. When Ceolwulf laughingly asked the wise old woman what exactly she meant, she told him his new wife was with child. Ceolwulf was surprised, but delighted.

Life in the village was for the most part tranquil allowing Ceolwulf to focus on providing for his wife and soon to be born son. The skills he had learned from his father and what he had learned at Sigurd's household stood Ceolwulf in good stead with the villagers. He was able to make and repair harnesses, belts, and war equipment. He was becoming adept at producing small metal items such as clasps, fasteners, and saexe. The villagers paid with food, drink, and bartered for other items that Yetta needed for their modest wood-slat house.

Ceolwulf's house while not ornate or luxurious was nevertheless clean, warm and dry. A simple wood table with wood benches served as the focal point in the one room dwelling. The hearth in the middle of the house was serviceable and provided for cooking and warmth. Smoke meandered upward filtering out through the hole in the thatched roof. The hut was built facing the sun to capture its warming rays. The standard wooden plank palisade surrounded the small village provided at least some protection for the thirteen modest wood huts contained within. The Great Hall also was modest and could hardly be compared to Great Hall of Ceolwulf's homeland. This was where the leader of the village and his retinue lived.

There was the occasional call to arms. The men of the village were required to put up a small force of arms that would go on patrol. The men were told they were to look for robbers or any invaders from the West or North. They were particularly on the look out for hostile *waelas,* an insulting Saxon word for foreigners that the villagers used to describe the Britons. Ceolwulf heard the old men of the village recount tales of battles between Saxon and Britons. They told him of the battle at *Crecganford* when their own leader, Hengest, had fought to a glorious victory over the Britons. The "Wild Stallion" as he was called, went on to become King Hengest of Kent, lands to the south of where the ship Ceolwulf sailed in had landed. They spoke in hushed tones of the battle of Wippedesflot. The Britons claimed victory in that battle, but the carnage was so great on both sides, the armies refrained from fighting anew. That was over two decades ago and since then the Saxon war chief, Aelle, had landed in the south of the island, driving the Britons into the *Weald,* the Saxon word for woodlands. The chieftain Aelle and his men had been expanding the Saxon holdings into lands they called Sussseax. The ambitious war chief pushed further driving the Britons ever westward. The waelas fled as game flee a forest fire. After the bloody battle of Mercredesburne, a fleeting friendship had been entered into between Briton and Saxon. So far this begrudging truce had held.

Ceolwulf did not trade on the fact that he had been a thane in his homeland. He preferred to start a new life here in this new land and earn whatever respect was his due. In truth, Ceolwulf was broodingly ashamed that, though he was a thane, he had chosen to leave his home. This thought caused him anguish and the weight of his decision never left him completely. Somehow, though, Ceolwulf's former status had become a whispered rumour in the village. A few men respected him for earning the honour back home, others were jealous. There were one or two men who had caught a strange look in his eye and had decided to give Ceolwulf a wide berth.

Otherwise, life in the small village was very pleasant. Ceolwulf and Yetta already had a small garden and Ceolwulf had made a few shrewd bargains trading his metalworking skills for things they needed. His son was born on a beautiful summer's day. It was a day that was Ceolwulf's happiest memory. Yetta had survived the childbirth and was in fine health, tended to by the midwives and young maidens of the village. Ceolwulf was beaming from ear to ear with pride. The men were slopping mead into their drinking horns and singing the songs of valour and glory of their homeland.

"What are you going to name the lad?" asked Manfred, slapping Ceolwulf on the back good-naturedly.

"I...er...I hadn't really given it much thought..." stammered Ceolwulf, a stupid grin on his face. The rest of the men roared with laughter and began singing louder and louder, banging on the tables and spilling mead and ale everywhere.

"Well, you had best think of it and fast for he is here now and bellowing for his food!" a very drunk Günter said before he slipped and fell over onto his arse.

"Yes, well...er ... I think I will name him Aethelwulf."

"Well, that's a very powerful name," another slap on the back and Manfred gulped down a horn of beer between guffaws of laughter. Ceolwulf went into the hut to see Yetta and hold his newly named son.

In the months that followed, Ceolwulf became quite busy. The bargains he had made within the village provided food and shelter as well as some moderate comforts. He and his family were very comfortable. And yet, Ceolwulf was uneasy. He had begun to feel a burning desire that he should somehow leave a legacy of some sort for his son to follow. He wished to leave Aethelwulf, his beloved son, something of value, not money or land per se, but something honourable. Ceolwulf was unable to explain what that thing might be for he did not know himself. All he knew was that there was an anxious feeling in the depths of his being that would not allow him any peace. Ceolwulf still brooded over leaving the shire of his homeland.

Ceolwulf had taken over leading the patrols and training recruits. The need for more patrols was increasing and there was a general feeling of unease in the air. All the men felt it. They sensed that something dreadful was about to happen. More of their countrymen had made the treacherous journey across the narrow sea seeking to better their lives in the new land. It was not just their countrymen either, but those of the Angli, the Frisians and the Jutes. Stories circulated that the Angli had already been given lands in the North as reward for fighting the Picts and the Scotti tribesmen.

In the borderlands between the Angli-Saxon immigrants and the Britons, villages could be found that held mixed marriages and progeny that shared Briton and Saxon blood. The two cultures mingled.

However, in remote villages, skirmishes had broken out between Angli-Saxons and Britons. The long held truce was wearing thin.

"So," Manfred was saying between great draughts from his drinking horn, "things are quiet now. Hear me when I say, with these waelas, you never know! They allow us to occupy lands along the shore. We can expand a bit to the West, East and South, not too far, mind! Yet, every now and then, they attack us!" Manfred's manner grew rough as he continued railing against the Britons.

"When our Aelle landed on the southern shores, he pushed the bastard waelas west into the Weald! Woden's Wisdom! They are the ones who asked, no begged, our people to come and fight their battles with the wild ones north of the Wall!" Manfred was drunk now and he was living in his memories of his lost wife. She had died in a raid on their village in the Southwest. Günter had told Ceolwulf the story. He said Manfred's wife had died a horrible death at the hands of the enraged Britons. It was rumoured that her head had been missing from her body. From time to time when Manfred was in his cups and the subject of the Britons arose, he relived his tragedy.

Ceolwulf allowed Manfred to go on about the waelas. He patted his friend on his back and left with the other warriors to patrol the area. Glancing back, Ceolwulf saw Manfred waving his arms wildly as he continued his tirade against the Britons.

Aethelwulf was growing strong and doing very well. Ceolwulf could not be more proud of his son. The worry was the boy's mother. Yetta had become sullen. She withdrew her affections, no longer did she make love to her husband, and always she refused his lustful advances and instead busied herself solely with looking after her son. When Ceolwulf was home from patrol and village business, he took Aethelwulf around the village showing his little boy off to his men. Yetta, instead of using the respite to attend to her man, turned to working in the kitchens helping the younger women. Ceolwulf tried to be compassionate and understanding, he knew he was away much of the time. He was trying to build something of long standing, something he could be proud and that would cause his people to remember his family name. He wanted to build something that would shower his wife and son with honour and respect. It had been a very long time since he had felt any affection or gratitude from his wife and a very long time since he had enjoyed her. Many men would have simply taken what they wanted without consideration. Ceolwulf was not like that; he did not condone rapine by his men when they happened upon unguarded Briton women. He certainly would not force his own wife.

In his resentment, he recalled the days when Yetta's passion had swept him away. Certainly, she had been passionate when she wanted a child. Ceolwulf made up his mind to speak to her when he returned from patrol.

Travelling through the forest was a dangerous task for him and the patrol he was leading. Waelas were known to attack from the cover of the deep woods. The trees were large and dense but Ceolwulf had seen thicker woods in his homeland. Nevertheless, he was wary and his warrior's senses were on full alert. Ceolwulf felt the familiar tension he experienced ever since his first battle so long ago.

His horse snorted. Ceolwulf and his small band of warriors were mounted troops. He had personally picked experienced men for his patrol and argued more land could be covered by horseback. His people customarily marched to battle and fought on foot and not on horseback.

Only professional soldiers were provided with mounts, hence Ceolwulf's insistence his men be experienced warriors. Back in his homeland, Ceolwulf had learned horsemanship from his brother, though he had only a few occasions to practice. Now Ceolwulf led his men from the back of a chestnut mare.

The mare snorted again, then pawed the ground nervously with her hoof. Ceolwulf held his hand up to stop his men's movement. He listened. A whooshing noise preceded the scream from one of his men. Quickly turning, Ceolwulf saw the warrior behind him fall from his mount, an arrow protruding from between his shoulder blades.

"Ambush! Look to cover!" the cry went up. Arrows rained down all around. Another of Ceolwulf's men fell gurgling to the hard ground, an arrow imbedded in his throat. A horse screamed and was felled by a dozen of the deadly quills. A blinding pain in his left shoulder caused Ceolwulf to spin in agony. He dropped to the ground just as three more arrows hit the tree behind him with a resounding thunk.

Silence. No more whizzing of arrows, only the groans of the wounded could he hear now.

"Let us go and get those waelas bastards," cried one of his men, "let us kill them all and send them to the Otherworld!" The angry warrior spit into the dirt to underscore his rage.

"No!" yelled Ceolwulf wincing as he moved to get back into his saddle.

"No, that is just what they want us to do! They want us to follow them deeper into the forest. Then they will have us at their mercy. No! We must get back to the village and warn them. Later we can come out in force and track them down."

"You are a coward!" He was a young warrior full of pride and his own importance. He had been successful on a few other patrols but Ceolwulf noticed an impulsive tendency in the boy. Riding up to the young warrior Ceolwulf spoke gently.

"It's all right, Ethelbert, we too are enraged. We must control our emotions and not fall for their ruse."

"You are a coward! You are afraid to go deeper into the woods after those waelas!"

The boy was red in the face and shaking with rage. More importantly, Ceolwulf noticed the effect he was having on the others. Some of them were impressed by the young lad's show of bravado and they were beginning to pay attention to him.

"No," said Ceolwulf patiently, "I am not afraid, I am wise. I have been in many battles and I have...."

"Did you run from those battles as well?"

"...seen this sort of thing before. What..?"

"You heard me! I asked did you run from those battles too!" The sneer on the boy's face was what angered Ceolwulf. He could forgive ignorance born of inexperience, but his own pride would not allow him to forget he was once a thane. With his good right hand, Ceolwulf grabbed the youth by the hair and with strength that surprised the onlookers, yanked the younger man from his horse. Blood flowed freely from the arrow wound in his left shoulder. Ignoring the pain and the blood, Ceolwulf viciously kicked the young warrior in the back. Yelping with the force of the blow, the boy rolled up on his feet and charged at Ceolwulf.

Ceolwulf spun to his right and his good arm wrapped tightly around the boy's neck, while his right hip struck the boy hard in the stomach. Continuing the motion, Ceolwulf threw the boy over his right side. The wind expelled from the lad's lungs as Ceolwulf's body crashed down onto him. Using his right elbow, Ceolwulf smashed it in to the young warrior's face, breaking his nose and stunning him. Ceolwulf struggled to his feet, the left side of his tunic now soaked with blood.

The sound of a sword being drawn was heard by all present. The youngster stood, blood streaming from his smashed nose, his sword held over his right shoulder. He was moving toward Ceolwulf. The young warrior, sensing Ceolwulf's injury was taking a toll on him, swung his sword. The overhead arc of shimmering steel threatened to cut Ceolwulf in twain. There was a sickening sound, a thud followed by a splay of blood.

Ceolwulf had reached behind his back and loosed his battleaxe. Spinning away from the deadly arc of the young man's sword, Ceolwulf used his momentum, his one good hand gripping the haft of Mansplitter and swung. The razor sharp blade of his battleaxe buried its self in the top of the youth's head.

Ceolwulf's put his foot in the centre of the body's chest and pulled hard freeing his lethal axe. The body fell backward into the dirt.

"Mount up!" Ceolwulf looked hard into the eyes of the remaining warriors. Only when they were back in saddle did he secure Mansplitter behind his back. One warrior had picked up the body and slung it across his own horse. The mounted warriors rode silently back to the village.

Things were decidedly different after that incident. Nothing was said to Ceolwulf when he and the remaining men returned to the village. The men were sullen and kept to themselves. Ceolwulf regrouped with fresh warriors and horses, forming a new mounted patrol. He tracked down the small band of waelas responsible for the ambush and true to his word; he and his men killed every one of them. The men now knew Ceolwulf had been right and a begrudging respect for him developed amongst the warriors. Ceolwulf, once a thane in the old country, was now in a position of power and authority again.

Yetta continued to be withdrawn. She was well liked by the other women in the village and was always there to help them with their chores or communal projects. She kept Ceolwulf's hut clean and warm and him well fed. Their son was well looked after and healthy. Ceolwulf had nothing to complain about. Yet, he was not happy. Yetta was distant and unresponsive to any advances he made toward her. They had not made love for many months, not a kind word did she offer him, nor a comforting embrace or even a show of support. Yetta's attitude toward her husband had become one of bemused tolerance bordering on contempt. This attitude was beginning to grate on Ceolwulf.

Ceolwulf would not have admitted to his unhappiness, he was a warrior and he thought of himself as such. Warriors did not have petty thoughts. He had seen his men take their pleasure with women who were unwilling. Ceolwulf had never done so, he never thought why, it was simply not his way. Instead, he spent increasingly of his time at the mead hall drinking. Often he became surly and arrogant, peasants and serfs gave him a wide berth, and only his warriors could talk to him. Patrols under his leadership were taking more risks. Ceolwulf was becoming a dangerous man.

Word came from a visiting band of warriors fresh from the chieftain Aelle in the Southeast. Manfred and Ceolwulf met with the war-leader who claimed he was a representative of Aelle. He told Manfred that Aelle wanted more land and the establishment of a real kingdom. Nothing substantial was agreed on but the underlying sentiment was clear. Aelle expected loyal Saxons to press their advantage and expand their lands and holdings.

Manfred had been carefully watching Ceolwulf these last few months. He had become jealous of him as he felt his own influence with the villagers wane. He began to think that getting Ceolwulf out of the way for a while would allow him to convincingly re-secure his place as village leader. If, Manfred, unaided by this thorny thane Ceolwulf, expanded his lands perhaps Aelle would take notice.

A patrol was needed, Ceolwulf was told, and it would be dangerous. Manfred had selected the warrior band all rough battle-tested and seasoned men and he placed Ceolwulf in charge of them.

Manfred had selected an ambitious patrol for Ceolwulf. He was to cross the great meandering River Tamesis and head Southwest to scout the ancient lands of the Dumnonii. The danger lay in the fact the Romano-Briton, Ambrosius Aurelianus, had taken over much of the region. Ambrosius was as a king to the Romano-Britons, even now in his old age. He had, many years ago, fought gruelling battles with Gwrtheyrn the very same leader of the Council who had "invited" Angli-Saxon-Jutes and Frisians to fight as mercenaries for him. Ambrosius had besieged Gwrtheyrn in his caern at Ganarew and then burnt the fort down upon him. Since that time, Briton tribesmen had harried the Saxon clans, even to the point of raiding their lands given them by Gwrtheyrn. Ceolwulf was not to engage either tribesmen or any of Ambrosius's warriors, his mission was to gather information and report to Manfred within a fortnight.

Rumour had it that many Britons had fled to the West coast of the continent, a place they called Amorica. King Erbin of the Dumnonii had seen his kingdom fracture, the Roman cities were decaying and in ruins, his people near starvation. The king had abdicated his throne in favour of his son Gerren Llygesoc. Manfred sought an assessment of this situation that he secretly thought would be a valuable bargaining tool with Aelle.

Ceolwulf's band of Saxons came across a village not far from what was once a medium sized Roman *civatas*. Looking at the stonewalls, the stone buildings and paved paths, now crumbling from neglect, Ceolwulf could only imagine the life the inhabitants once must have led. Certainly they were better protected inside stonewalls than a rickety wooden palisade. Of course, with a Roman governor installed in the region, no tribe dared breach the peace and attack for to do so would be to bring a Roman legion down upon them. Such criminals died very badly at the hand of Roman justice. He turned his thoughts back to the task to which he was charged. This patrol, he thought, was a waste of time, a wild goose chase. The only people he had seen were poor starving serfs and former slaves eking out an existence in the shadows of past glory. They were no threat and there certainly was nothing valuable to be taken, not even their holdings.

They were walking their horses along an old Roman path, some crumbled walls spilled haphazardly in their way. Poorly constructed wooden hovels were scattered randomly amongst the ruins. Ceolwulf caught glimpses of gaunt frightened inhabitants here and there. A half-starved hound with its ribs showing through its mangy hair, scuttled about in search of some meagre thing to eat. Smoke wafted about the barren earth and wended its way amongst the scattered shelters. One of his Saxons, Beorn, a large boned burly warrior had discovered a priest rummaging about apparently tending to a patch of earth. A few undersized vegetables were gathered in his filthy, stained brown robe. Beorn walked arrogantly up to the holy man and unceremoniously grabbed the front of his dirty robe. He began interrogating the priest demanding to know if there were any warriors about, if there were any supplies worth stealing. Of course, the priest could not understand the Saxon tongue, he answered in Briton. This added to the chaotic scene, especially as Beorn could not understand Briton. Frustrated, Beorn threw the priest to the ground and began kicking him viciously in the ribs.

"Hold," barked Ceolwulf, "why do you torment a priest?"

"Of what concern is it of yours?" snapped the surly warrior.

"I lead this band and I do not condone the torture of priests or holy men!"

"Then you are an idiot!" replied Beorn contemptuously. "These *wogs* entreat the others to fight against us, they need to be cowed to show we mean business!" The term "wog" derived from the word "waelas" and was an even greater insult. The priest lay moaning in the dirt and mud, blood dripping from his battered face.

"He is a holy man of their religion. He guides them in their prayers. He is no threat to us!"

"Only Woden makes idols," swore Beorn, using an Old Saxon saying. With that he brought his great axe down, burying it into the unfortunate priest's chest. The holy man died wide-eyed in surprise and agony.

Ceolwulf instantly realized why Manfred had sent him on this sortie to Dumnonii. It was a trap. His leadership and authority were being challenged and his very life was now in jeopardy. Ceolwulf was not meant to survive the journey. He looked at the huge warrior standing astride the butchered holy man, his great axe still dripping the priest's blood.

"Perhaps I should help you lead these men. Maybe the job is too taxing for you!" The surly Beorn sneered. The other warriors could hear what was happening and came to see if Ceolwulf would meet the challenge.

Beorn was now circling Ceolwulf and turning his bloodied axe over in his hand as he smiled.

"Come, great thane or have you lost heart since I am no youngster whose head you can so easily split!" The others laughed at the taunt. Ceolwulf felt his face redden and his blood begin to boil.

The big man kept moving round Ceolwulf; the others closed in to better witness the combat. Suddenly Beorn swung his mighty axe, the sharp blade slicing horizontally through the air. Ceolwulf spun clear of the deadly arc, but he was a shade too slow. Beorn's axe grazed Ceolwulf's tunic slicing through the wool fabric. Ceolwulf swung his own axe in an underhand motion the blade ripping upwards toward Beorn, narrowly missing his groin. The men were yelling and shouting with each strike. Beorn swung his axe in an overhead strike, trying to bring the weapon down on Ceolwulf's head. Quickly Ceolwulf sidestepped to avoid the strike, turning and swinging his axe horizontally at Beorn's midsection. Missing, he had just enough time to bring the shaft of his axe up to block another downward strike from Beorn. The strength of the big man's strike splintered the shaft of Ceolwulf's axe, Mansplitter.

Beorn sensed the kill and swung again, but the now unarmed Ceolwulf spun away. Relentless now, Beorn swung his battleaxe repeatedly. It was all Ceolwulf could do to avoid death as Beorn's sharp blade cut deadly arcs in the air ever closer to Ceolwulf's skin.

The two men were drenched in sweat. The air was heavy with tension and the anticipation of death. Ceolwulf was older and without his axe. Beorn in contrast was younger, well muscled and swung his killing axe with ease. Beorn missed again, sunlight flashed on Ceolwulf's saexe. He had reached behind and pulled the traditional fighting knife from its scabbard. The blade sliced through Beorn's arm spurting blood and causing the big man to bellow in surprised pain. Beorn quickly brought the shaft of his axe up slamming its wooden butt into Ceolwulf's jaw. Stunned, Ceolwulf fell to one knee. His arm dripping blood, Beorn rushed in with a mighty overhead strike. As though he were about to chop wood, Beorn aimed his dreadful axe swing at Ceolwulf's exposed neck. Ceolwulf timed his movement perfectly. Darting onto his left side, Ceolwulf avoided the swing of Beorn's axe. The big man was off balanced as his axe blade bit deeply into the dirt. Still on his left side Ceolwulf used his left foot to trap Beorn's right ankle. He kicked out hard with his right foot striking Beorn on the right knee. With his ankle trapped by Ceolwulf's foot, his knee took the full force of the strike and dislocated. Beorn screamed.

Scrambling to his feet, Ceolwulf took hold of the shrieking Beorn's hair and pulled his head back. The saexe buried itself into the chest of Beorn. Ceolwulf pulled his saexe from Beorn's chest, but still held onto the hair of the once mighty warrior. He looked up at the surrounding men.

Defiantly, Ceolwulf drew the sharp blade across the throat of Beorn. The wound was grievously deep, blood splayed out and Beorn gurgled hideously before he died. Standing upright bathed in sweat and drenched in Beorn's blood, his bloodied saexe gripped in his right hand, Ceolwulf looked into the eyes of every man present. None could hold his gaze. Nothing was said. Two men picked up Beorn's body and tied it to his horse. The rest of the men gathered their gear and sat on their mounts silently waiting for Ceolwulf's orders. The grim band of Saxon warriors turned their backs on the Dumnonii lands and rode for home.

Ceolwulf's reputation grew and his influence increased. Manfred decided to leave the village taking supporters and some seasoned warriors with him. He had his mind set on settling lands south and west of the

Tamesis close to the Dumnonii lands that Ceolwulf had scouted that fateful day. Ceolwulf was again a Thane in charge of a band of warriors, villagers, men, women, and children.

Things with Yetta did not get any better. She was even more distant and cold towards him. The mead hall was Ceolwulf's home on many nights. The drinking was not what he was after. Berit was a buxom maid at the hall who had caught his fancy. She was a curvy woman with waist length blond hair cascading down her simple blue woollen dress. Her white skin enhanced her yellow hair and made her lips the more red and inviting. She worked hard in the kitchens and the mead hall serving drinks and food to the warriors and men. Her tongue was sharp and her temperament fiery as any man who tried to dally with her soon learned. Berit, though, was quite enamoured with Ceolwulf's exploits and often spoke of him as though he were already a hero at Woden's table in Valhalla. The stories circulated and Ceolwulf's stature grew. He liked being appreciated and acknowledged. Ceolwulf found it more intoxicating than the mead Berit served in the hall.

It was late one evening Ceolwulf was sitting on a bench near a wall. He was situated so that he had full view of who entered and left the hall. The wooden wall protected his back but he was not so far in the corner that he could be trapped. His drinking horn, it was his father's and the only memento he had brought from the homeland, was nearly empty. The mead hall itself was nearly empty. Many of the men had already gone to their huts. Berit came over to him with a jug of mead. She leaned in to refill his horn and as she did so her breasts swayed and bulged from her dress. Ceolwulf was mesmerised. Berit pulled her long locks from her face with her left arm the movement causing her breasts to sway even more seductively. She spilled some mead on Ceolwulf while trying to balance the heavy jar of mead. Berit put down the jug and took a rag of cloth from the belt at her waist.

"I am sorry master Thane," she said as she gently washed the mead from his arm.

"I am usually more careful," she smiled invitingly at Ceolwulf. Her hand moved to his face and gingerly wiped his cheek and close-cropped beard. She stood back up slowly and Ceolwulf drank in her scent, the curve of her hips and the bountiful swell of her milk white breasts. As Berit turned to go back to her duties she threw her hair back over her shoulders, glanced back at Ceolwulf and disappeared behind the leather curtain.

Ceolwulf looked around the mead hall. There were only three other men present and they were drunk. He watched as they gathered their gear to leave. Ceolwulf adjusted his leather tunic, his belt, and sword. Standing quietly, he moved toward the leather curtain of the kitchens. The smell of the herbs, roasted meat and baked breads mingled with the heat of the cooking fires. The feeling was one of warm homecoming and it cheered the heart. The kitchens were lit by torchlight and of course cooking fires and all cast a warm yellow light throughout. Ceolwulf moved toward Berit who he saw scrubbing tin plates in a wooden washtub. Her hair flowed down her back in a mass of delightful curls and her hips swayed invitingly with the motion of her work. Ceolwulf's heart pounded in his ears, his breath was coming short, as his desire took hold of him. He walked up behind Berit and pulled her into him kissing the side of her neck as his hands cupped her ample breasts. She pressed her body into his, her hand over his while the other groped for his manhood. The two older women in the kitchen went about their business discretely and out of the way of the lovers. Berit guided Ceolwulf to the back of the kitchen were there was more privacy in the shadows. There was also a cot. Soon their tentative and furtive explorations gave way to the rhythmic pounding and moaning of lust and groans of pleasure.

From that day on, Ceolwulf could be found at the mead hall when not on patrol or tending to village business. Yetta did not complain, in fact she seemed relieved that she no longer had to contend with her husband's amorous advances. Berit continued to help in the kitchens and from then on, she seemed always to be in or near the mead hall. Ceolwulf was content with the arrangement and for a time, his foul temper seemed much muted.

Heretoga was one of the few men Ceolwulf trusted. Heretoga had something he wished to tell his thane, something important. He made his way to the mead hall in search of his leader. The day was cold. The villagers could feel it in their bones, winter was coming, and summer had died. The hall was warmed by hearth-fires and mead was warming the drinkers. Men who had come in from the fields were eating food and enjoying the warmth of the hall, the mead and the company of friends.

Songs of the old country were sung loudly and with pride. Serving girls carrying boards of roast boar, venison and great loaves of dark bread, wended their way through the press of customers.

Heretoga found a mead bench where he sat and kept to himself, as Ceolwulf was not yet in the hall. After two tankards of mead, Heretoga's body relaxed with the inner warmth. He reached for a loaf of the dark bread and another tankard of mead just as he spied Ceolwulf. The Thane had entered through the kitchen; Berit hanging on his arm a glow surrounded them both as they laughed at some private joke. Berit untangled herself from her lover and went to help the servers. Ceolwulf made his way to Heretoga nodding at warriors here and there in acknowledgement. The two men, Thane and warrior, greeted each other with a hearty slap on the shoulders and shared a warrior's toast. Heretoga drained his third tankard whilst Ceolwulf drank from his huge drinking horn.

Wiping his mouth with the back of his hand, Heretoga leaned forward so that only Ceolwulf could hear him. He told Ceolwulf of his foray into the Northwest very near the end of the mighty River Tamesis and close to the Mearc.

The Mearc was the boundary, the frontier forming between Angli-Saxon held lands, the lands they had designs on and the Briton lands. The Britons had been pushed to the West with the expansion of Angli-Saxon ambitions. The lands of the Mearc were mountainous, dotted with moors and wooded river valleys. While in these wild frontier lands, Heretoga had been approached by a waelas. Though not a chief or tribal leader, this man, this Briton, claimed to have great influence within one of the tribes. He claimed to want to open negotiations with a Saxon king. He thought, so he told Heretoga, he could offer a deal to the Saxons that would be of benefit. The Briton wanted Saxon backing for his tribal faction in return for security in the region and a large parcel of land, a fair proposition. It was though, a dangerous notion, given the mistrust and hatred between Saxon and Briton especially in the Mearc. This waelas promised if the Saxon king could come over the Mearc, across the mountains and moors to the Great Forest, he would be met and guaranteed safe passage. Surely, said the waelas, it was worth talking about.

Heretoga told Ceolwulf all of this and offered the opinion that the entire scheme could very well be a ruse. Ceolwulf sat with his drinking horn half empty, his eyes closed as he contemplated what he had heard. Heretoga, interpreting this as hesitation, placed an exquisitely crafted silver ring into Ceolwulf's hand.

"The waelas said this was given in good faith. He said it was a sign that his words were true and could be trusted, that the bargain was to the benefit of all." Heretoga leaned back and drank from his tankard, stretched his back and kept his eyes on Ceolwulf.

Ceolwulf laughed and slammed his drinking horn down.

"He said all that did he? Well may be I will think hard on the proposal." He turned the ring over in his hand admiring its craftsmanship, weight, and obvious worth.

"Perhaps I might offer an other opinion?"

Ceolwulf stopped laughing, dropped the ring into his pouch and looked sharply at Heretoga. It was unlike the man to be so formal and Ceolwulf wondered what was coming next.

"I have spoken to some who have heard of this region. It might well be profitable to us if we were able to acquire it. I think force of arms would outright fail, whereas guile may just win the day."

Ceolwulf drained the mead from his drinking horn and signalled to a girl he wanted a refill. She smiled, blushed and ran over with a large jug and a wooden board piled with venison. Taking a great bite of roasted venison, Ceolwulf washed it down with a mighty draught of mead. He looked at Heretoga over the rim of his drinking horn.

"It is not like you to wax so poetic nor to be so mysterious."

Heretoga smiled and then broke into laughter.

"Forgive me I couldn't resist. It does sound mysterious. There is truth in what I say. That is a very nice ring and I understand there is much more of the same to be had. Perhaps it would be worth a few trusted men having an informal look into the area. They could report back what they find and we could make a better decision."

"What you really think is that we should keep this little offer to ourselves. Perhaps just you and I and one or two of your men might have an extended hunting trip to the Northwest, to see the lay of the land?"

"That is what I was thinking," smiled Heretoga.

"Did your friend give any information about this trade?"

"He did mention a meeting could be arranged. He also said it would be dangerous and insisted only a very small band should make the trip."

Ceolwulf frowned. His eyes blazed as his mind turned over the possibilities and implications of this new offer. Rich new lands and a profitable alliance with a Briton tribe would certainly put him in good stead with Aelle. And there was the possibility of plunder.

"And what of this meeting?" asked Ceolwulf.

"Well, I have been told how I can get you to the forest. It will be a long trip and it will not be an easy one. With a very few men you are to follow specific instructions and when you get to the edge of this great forest you are to walk one in for half a day and wait. There, a man will approach you from their tribe. He will open his hand. You are to place the ring in his hand and that way he will know a Saxon king has arrived to make an alliance."

"But I am not a Saxon king," Ceolwulf said sardonically.

"Oh, but you will be if you can bring about an alliance with a tribe wishing to help us take new lands. Besides, despite what they say, they do not really expect a real king to place himself in such a dangerous position. They have their own ambitions and we have ours which they do not need to know."

Heretoga drank from his tankard. He kept his eyes on Ceolwulf, but could not determine what his Thane was thinking.

Chapter 8

Ceolwulf woke from his dream, bathed in sweat and feeling weak and sick to his stomach. He tried to get his bearings and determine just what was happening. Time seemed to have stood still, how long had he been here in this wooden cage? He stirred and tried lifting his head, a wave of nausea swept over him. Bile rose in his throat, Ceolwulf feared he would empty his stomach again but the feeling passed. Through blurry eyes, he saw the woman had brought him a bowl of broth. Two guards flanked her. The warriors at her side were menacingly holding spears in front of them. They were ready to pierce him should he do anything other than meekly accept the offering. With careful and deliberate movements, Ceolwulf reached for the bowl. The broth was good. Ceolwulf looked at the woman and noticed she was studying him. It seemed she was waiting for him to say something.

"*Eala*! This smells very good," he said obligingly.

Lydia was startled, but quickly regained her composure lest the guards, one of whom was Derfel, became aggressive. She did not understand the words clearly; it had been ages since she had heard the language of the invaders. In truth, Lydia had tried hard to block those memories from her mind. In any case, the prisoner's accent was not quite, what she remembered. It suddenly occurred to her that he might not be from the South at all. Perhaps he had recently arrived in the South from the continent. "I wonder if this is important," she thought to herself.

"You are welcome to the broth," she said to the prisoner, "master Owain has told me to keep you well."

Ceolwulf could not understand any of what the woman said, but surmised that she was talking about the food, telling him he was welcome to it.

Ceolwulf thanked her. Lydia was again startled as she recognised the word. Quickly she hid her surprise and returned to the cauldron. Ceolwulf noticed her look of surprise and wondered if he had been understood. With nothing to loose and nothing better to do with his time, Ceolwulf began to talk to Lydia.

"My head hurts," he said slowly, "I have never felt like this before and I have been in many battles and have survived many great wounds." He looked at her intently and saw she was listening and watching him.

"My head hurts and I feel like I have had much too much mead," he smiled at her and saw immediately that her face relaxed.

"Will I die? Will your man kill me? Am I to be tortured to death for the amusement of your warriors?" Ceolwulf's face was serious, but his blue eyes were sparkling as though he were amused.

Lydia looked concerned and then confused. She touched her own head with her hand.

"You have had a terrible blow to the head. It may have cracked your skull. You may die, but I think not. If God wills it, you will recover, but of course, it will take some time. You will be weak for a time and you will vomit and have a great pain in your head. The herbs should help with the vomiting and ease your ache. *Understandan*?"

It was Ceolwulf, who startled this time. Hearing a word in his own language, he snapped his head around to look at Lydia. The sudden movement caused another wave of nausea to sweep over him.

"The woman can understand my tongue," he thought to himself as he passed out.

The voices of the man and the woman arguing broke through Ceolwulf's grogginess. He had no idea how long he had been unconscious. Instead of moving, Ceolwulf lay still with one eye open, listening to the harsh singsong language. The woman who was always present was yelling at one of his guards. The other guard Ceolwulf assumed was watching him from across the hut, he remained motionless. With his one open eye he saw that the woman was crying, tears streaked down her high cheekbones.

"I don't know how you can minister to that piece of dung the way you do, not after what they did to you!" growled Derfel.

"Do you think it is easy for me? Do you? What do you know of me? Have you ever before asked about me? Have you ever before cared anything at all about my burdens? Then don't you dare bring them up now, you twisted little man! I am doing what master Owain commanded. He and his good wife asked that I look after this prisoner," she sobbed again her shoulders shaking uncontrollably.

"I don't remember much of what happened to me because I choose not to," she cried again. "This man is not the one responsible for my misery. That I know. I owe it to my Lady Gwenhwyfar to assist in whatever way I can. What is more important I owe it to God to be forgiving and charitable..."

"Awww!" Derfel spat into the dirt floor. "I have no use for that rubbish!" he growled and moved away. Derfel was intolerant of the new religion, but the mention of the Lady Gwenhwyfar had made him uncomfortable as he realised Lydia was doing the Lady's bidding. This was something he could not argue against.

Dyfrig moved from his position and roughly shoved the haft of his spear into Derfel, gruffly motioning him to take up his post. Dyfrig walked over to Lydia and put an arm around her to comfort the sobbing woman.

"No," she said through tears and violently pushed away from him. Dyfrig looked hard at Derfel, disapproval, and anger on his face.

Lydia stood up, wiping away her tears she moved to the cage to check on the prisoner. She was surprised to see him staring at her. Smoothing her luxurious hair back from her tear-wet face she smiled tentatively at him.

"Good day. How are you?" she asked in Cymraeg adding, "How long have you been awake?"

Ceolwulf stared at her not understanding what it was she was saying to him. He shrugged his shoulders and sat up happy to find he wasn't as nauseous as he was before.

Lydia noticed the slight improvement and commented.

"You seem to be better. The herbs are working by the good grace of God." Lydia knew he probably did not understand her words but she chattered on anyway. It helped her rid her mind of the pain her conversation with Derfel had caused.

Lydia heard the guttural speech of the prisoner and was again shocked that she had understood the word "lady" in what Ceolwulf had asked. But she wasn't sure of anything else, just the one word.

Ceolwulf saw the change on her face and so asked again only slowly this time.

"My lady, who are you?"

"What did you say to me about a lady?"

Ceolwulf closed his eyes; the strain in trying to understand another language in his condition was giving him a headache. Knowing that only a word or two of his was being understood at best was frustrating to him. He opened his eyes and looked up at Lydia surprised to see new tears flowing down her cheeks. Ceolwulf opened his hands palm up in a gesture of offering help. He wanted to show sympathy to the one person he believed was trying to help him. Lydia caught sight of the gesture and recognising it for what it was intended she began to cry anew. She was tired, bone tired. The strain of dealing with these men, the tension in Caerwyn and her own demons were draining her strength and her spirit. The isolation she felt from most of the villagers denied her any comfort. Her shoulders shook with her sobs and for a brief moment, she gave into her misery.

In truth, no one in all of Caerwyn could possibly understand Lydia's grief. The task with which Owain had charged her was stealing her serenity if not her sanity. The proximity to the prisoner, she was forced to endure caused such bad memories to flood back into her mind. The pain was almost unbearable for poor Lydia.

She had been a child living with her family in the ruins of the Romano-Briton civitas of Camulodunum far to the South. Her family farmed crops and grew what vegetables they could to stave off starvation. Her father and other citizens scrounged the stone buildings of the civitas trying desperately to rebuild their lives. Daily life was hard and the family's time was preoccupied with getting enough food to eat. They bartered with other families for goods and scraps eking out an existence in the shadow of former glory. Many families had run off into the forests to fend for themselves the way their ancestors had done many hundreds of years ago. Other families were devastated by the loss of children and old people to disease and starvation that swept the region.

Lydia's family maintained faith in the new Roman God and they increasingly centred their lives on one of the few priests that were left in the tattered community. Her father was killed along with her brother, fighting against roving bands of thugs and killers. Lydia and her mother sought protection and comfort from the only source left to them, a kindly old priest of the One True God. Lydia did not know his real name and only ever addressed him as "Father." He was a large robust man with long white hair and a bushy grey beard. The Father good-naturedly scolded his flock of poor, desperate followers.

"So, do you think you are Christian if you keep the poor downtrodden? Do you think you may be Christian if your riches are made on the backs of others? Perhaps you think yourselves Christians if you make your gold from the blood, sweat and tears of those less fortunate. No, my friends, no, a real Christian cannot stand idly by while a poor man is oppressed. A Christian is one whose hut is available to all and whose bountiful table is shared with those less fortunate." Then with a wink of his eye and mischievous nod of his head, he would move amongst his flock sharing what bread or vegetables he had with them.

The good Father had many converts and just as the Church had taken hold in that part of the country. The Church deliberately used many of the same days of celebration as the Pagans. This practice made conversion more palatable, much easier and therefore more successful. Both old and new religions agreed on the idea of right and wrong and the existence of an afterlife. The writings of the Celtic Bishop Pelagius that had so enraged the Roman Bishops, was the Celtic idea that men and women could gain salvation and heavenly reward based on their own efforts and good and charitable deeds and not through preordination. Pelagius was subsequently murdered and excommunicated years ago and his teachings declared as heresy by Rome. Even the ancient Celtic idea of the sacred number three represented and represented in Celtic artwork for centuries had now become the Christian concept of the Holy Trinity. It had been written about many years ago by a Celtic Gaul named Hilary of Poirier who became a Roman Bishop. Of course, the Celtic cross, known as a wheel cross, a symbol predating the new religion of Rome by thousands of years, became synonymous with the cross of Christ the Saviour. These images and teachings were already familiar to the Britons who found it an easy thing to convert to the Roman religion. The Church had grown in influence until the Romans departed. After that, hordes of Britons returned to the religious beliefs of their past or to some amalgam between ancient and new.

The day the strangers from across the rough straits arrived in their long ships was the saddest day Lydia had known. The huge leather clad strangers surged through the crumbling civitas easily taking it under their control. They burned the wooden structures and killed any of the men who stood in their way. The good Father calmed his frightened flock assuring them God would protect them. After all, there was nothing of value in the civitas. Certainly nothing, that would entice violence from these strange men. The Father, fearless and humble, arranged to speak with the leader of the invaders. He offered what food and drink his flock could spare and explained their poverty to the men from the long ships as best he could. Holding his carved wooden cross, which hung on his neck before him, the good Father entreated the strangers to leave the people unharmed.

The leader just laughed, cursed, and yelled a Saxon curse. The big man with the long yellow hair took a large knife from a scabbard behind his back and with a chain-mailed fist placed on the Father's shoulders, rammed the big knife into the stomach of the priest. The gathering of invaders stood around laughing as the poor priest writhed in agony in the dirt. One of the men, a big brute with braided red hair and thick bush of a beard, held the priest down with his boot, loosened his leather breeches, pulled out his penis and pissed on the tortured Father. The flock of the faithful broke and ran in all directions trying to escape the bloody massacre they knew was coming.

That was the last time Lydia saw any of her family. A searing pain in her head knocked her to the ground. Before she could regain her senses, a foul smelling monster of a man was on top of her crushing the life from her. The stink of him invaded her nostrils and she was nearly sick. A sudden searing pain and she knew she was being raped. The filthy man finished his business and with a leering grin kissed her face, his spittle leaving a trail like a slug on a rock. Lydia tried valiantly to move but another warrior kicked her hard driving the breath from her lungs. She felt the same pain again as this man also raped her and then her defiler struck her in the face.

Another fetid invader violated her but this time she was numb and for a moment passed out mercifully. A sharp slap to her face brought her back into her hell. A large brute of a man with thick braided red hair straddled her, his leather breeches already pulled down. He stood laughing above her mocking her pain, her fear and her misery and readied himself for his turn with her. A chain-mailed fist struck the side of her defiler's head and he crashed to the ground. Lydia had no idea what was happening. She could vaguely make out yelling and shouting and saw shadows and movement but that was all she could comprehend in her beaten and dazed condition. She was already in shock.

The man with the mailed fist roughly picked her up out of the dirt and filth and bundled her in a warm wolf skin cloak. Half dragged, half carried, she was thrown haphazardly onto the wooden floor of his long ship. Lydia passed mercifully into unconsciousness.

Lydia spent months of hellish captivity cleaning, cooking, and fending off advances from drunken men. She was fortunate in that no man tried to force himself on her again. The man with the mailed fist made sure of that. The woman in charge of the Great Hall did not harm Lydia, apart from the occasional beating. As weeks rolled into months, Lydia began to get sick. Every morning she vomited and during the day, she was lethargic and found it difficult to keep up with her duties. At first, the woman in charge beat her more frequently for not working hard enough. One day the woman grabbed Lydia's face with both hands. She spoke quietly in the language Lydia did not understand. After that, two more women came and put their hands on Lydia examining her and finally leading her to a bedchamber. They chattered incessantly to each other. Lydia felt hot, the room was stuffy and fetid and the constant dirge of the woman's voices disoriented her. She fainted.

It was many hours later that Lydia regained consciousness. She was in her sleeping quarters. There were extra blankets that were not there before and something else. She had a small jug of fresh water and an extra piece of bread nearby. Startled by these unusual comforts, Lydia realised it was morning. She normally began her work before the sun came up and yet the sun was already on the horizon and the woman in charge had not roused her. Lydia rose just as the woman appeared.

There was more talk in the foreign language and with many hand gestures the woman made Lydia understand that she was pregnant. From that moment, Lydia was assigned lighter duties and the woman did not beat her.

Once she began to show her condition, Lydia was kept almost isolated. She never saw any of the warriors or any sign of the man with the mailed fist. The woman in charge and two of her helpers were Lydia's only companions. She became even more withdrawn.

Her pains began and she was taken to a warm room where the women helped her giving her herbs to reduce the pain. She was tied down to the bed her legs apart. The birth was very hard and the pain terrible, more than Lydia thought she could endure. She survived; her baby son did not.

Lydia had always been quiet and withdrawn amongst her captors but now after the stillbirth of her son, she withdrew even further into herself. The women watched her go about her duties showing no emotion, no response, or reaction to anything. The woman in charge did not beat or berate her not even if she failed in her work. The others gave her a wide berth. The women expected Lydia to soon die.

One night Lydia took some bread and salted meat. She wrapped the food in a cloth and placed the bundle inside a worn woollen cloak that was left unattended. With another stolen cloak wrapped tightly around her and clutching her bundle of food, Lydia walked out of the Great Hall and into the cold night. No one noticed. She walked and walked. Headed north after weeks of weary travel she had ended up inside the Great Forest of Caerwyn. She was lost.

Lydia looked at the prisoner in the cage; tears flowed freely down her cheeks. The memories of her past brought crashing back into her mind because of this man and the cruel words of Dyfrig threatened to undo her resolve and her duty to the Lady Gwenhwyfar.

The door to the hut flung open and in stumbled Llew. His face was still swollen and sore and he was decidedly not feeling his best. The days of healing had helped and now he wished to see Lydia. He moved over to her and saw she was crying, tears streaming down her face. Gently, very gently Llew placed his hand on her shoulder, she did not pull away. Llew wrapped his arms around the poor woman's shoulders and held her close. He had always harboured feelings for Lydia but never had he the courage to admit to them not even to his friend Math. He had hidden his true emotions under a guise of roughness and disinterest. Math's startling actions the day of the Council changed all of that. Now seeing Lydia tired and crying, Llew broke through his awkwardness and released his pent up feelings for her. Looking down at Lydia, her face buried in his shoulder, he felt a sudden surge of rage shudder through his body for he guessed the cause of Lydia's heartbreak.

Llew looked over at Derfel who had occupied himself with tending the fire in the brazier. Dyfrig caught Llew's eye and tried to make a gesture suggesting nothing could be done about his colleague's temperament. Llew was having none of it though. He guided Lydia to the pallet of skins she had used as a bed and covered her with a warm pelt. Walking past Dyfrig without acknowledgement, Llew continued to where Derfel fidgeted with the fire. He did not touch Derfel but simply leaned forward and spoke to him in a low tone.

"If you cause this good woman to cry again I will gut you like a fish." The two men locked eyes for a moment and then Derfel lowered his gaze and stood watching the fire leap in the brazier.

Llew walked back to Lydia this time nodding to Dyfrig as he passed. In a louder voice that all could hear he told them of a visitor to Caerwyn.

"There is a priest with a party of travellers close to the village about a half days ride perhaps less." Lydia quickly looked up at Llew searching his face to determine the truth to his words.

"I just heard of the news myself, the patrol came into the dafarn whilst I was there," his face grew hot as he gazed lovingly down at Lydia.

"I heard them say Owain had been informed and that we are going to have a bit of a feast." He looked down at the now radiant face of Lydia.

"I thought you might wish to know." The look in Lydia's eyes warmed his heart and right away Llew knew how important a visit this would be to her. Dyfrig was rubbing his hands and commenting on the chances of getting some decent food. Derfel made a noise and was about to say something. Llew turned sharply to look at him. Derfel stopped whatever it was he was going to say. Holding Llew's glare, he spat rudely into the dirt before turning to tend the fire.

Chapter 9

The mood was festive as the villagers crowded into the Hall. Rush torches burned in their iron sconces on the wattle walls adding their flickering yellow light to the warming glow of the large hearth fire at the end of the Hall. The Hall had been swept clean, benches and tables arranged and scented herbs were hung all in preparation for the gathering. Sweet smells of fresh roasting venison, baked breads, and stewing leeks mixed with the tapestry of smells that filled the air. It was a pleasant evening, the snows had stopped a day or two ago and the air was no longer so bitterly cold. Math and Enid sat close together flanked by Rhys, Katryn and their children. Llew was not with Math or the group, but hovering around Lydia who was close to the guest of honour, the priest. Owain and his Lady had instructed her to take time off from her duties with the prisoner and attend the Gathering. Both Owain and Gwenhwyfar were concerned for Lydia and they thought a visit with this priest might be the tonic Lydia needed. She sat with Llew, a cup of leek soup in hand and looking forward to a piece of venison. It was the best she had felt in days. Her smile beamed and that sight alone warmed the heart of Llew.

The priest had arrived hours ago and was escorted into Caerwyn by Owain's warriors. He had with him two younger men and a woman as part of his travelling entourage. They had not shown up empty handed for across the back of one of their mangy ponies was a large deer. This gift was well accepted and one of Owain's men immediately took the animal to the village cook. The priest was a man of average height, shorter than Owain, wiry with a ring of unkempt grey hair that wreathed his head, the top of which had been shaved. His shaved pate was now sporting grey stubble, as was his otherwise clean-shaven face. He wore a plain woollen shirt and brown woollen and hooded robe which he wrapped tightly around him and was well worn, patched, stained but serviceable and a visible reminder of his status as a Roman priest. On his feet were thick leather sandals. The cross of wood, the simple symbol of the Christians, hung from a piece of leather around the priest's neck. He was energetic and animated, possessing a boyish charm that served to amuse and disarm those whom he met. The gift of fresh venison also helped ingratiate him with Owain's warriors. Owain's men discretely checked for signs of a ruse but were satisfied that the man was who he said he was. Once vetted by the teulu, the priest had been introduced to the Lady Gwenhwyfar.

"Welcome, welcome, how are you all?" sang Gwenhwyfar welcoming the guest and asking how he fared. Gwenhwyfar asked for the priest's name. The priest thanked Gwenhwyfar and told her his name was Bedwini, then there were hugs, kisses and sharing of beer. Everyone was in good humour. A small crowd of villagers had gathered eager to hear news from the rest of the region. The Christians of the village were of course hoping for a blessing and perhaps the chance to make their confessions to the Father. They had not been able to catch his attention or make their way to him.

Owain, Gwenhwyfar and the priest were sitting in chairs arranged to take advantage of the hearth fire's warmth. A harpist played some light songs but the strains of his music were lost in the general murmur of the gathering. Owain's son Cynglas helped redirect the attentions of two great hounds that were getting more than a little frisky. The smell of the cooking meat was making them anxious. Gwyneth sat close to her mother assisting at times to bring ale to her father and the priest. Council members dropped by, Dyfyr and his son Elidir were present and seated close by Owain and the Lady Gwenhwyfar. Cai had stopped in to pay his respects before leaving Caerwyn to lead his men on patrol. He and his men were sent packing with a haunch of venison, bread and small covered pot of leek soup and flasks of ale.

The priest was laughing raucously and talking non-stop to Lady Gwenhwyfar. Owain thought it amusing that the Christian Man of God should be so engaged with the Lady Gwenhwyfar whom the villagers thought to be directly related to the Goddess Dôn. He had not known what to expect, but had supposed that the priest would have been cold and reserved in the presence of a Pagan. Seeing him now with Gwenhwyfar laughing merrily, the two of them with their heads together enjoying some bawdy joke was shockingly amusing to Owain.

A signal from the cooks indicated that the rest of the venison was ready to be cut and handed out. Behind the cooks lined up by the kitchen opening was an army of serving girls with boards of breads, cheese and bowls of broth, and leek soup. It was not only the great hounds that were salivating, everyone in the hall was anticipating some small bit of venison or at least gravy to accompany the dark bread, leek soup and some cheese.

Gwenhwyfar stood and all in the Hall went silent in respect. In her clear sing song voice, Gwenhwyfar gave thanks to the Goddess Dôn for the venison, the health of those gathered and the fact they could enjoy a hearty meal in companionship. She reminded the gathering of the triune nature of the Goddess, the power of life, death, and rebirth. The Lady spoke of the energy of the three worlds, the Otherworld of the Ancestors, the Earth itself, where all men lived, and of the Heavens, where the Gods lived.

"Realise," she said, "that you are all part of the land and of nature. You are all as one, not separate, but connected to each other as a part of the whole."

A few villagers squirmed uncomfortably hearing her words. The Christian villagers respected the Lady Gwenhwyfar and their own cultural heritage, but they had been converted a long time ago to the Christian view and had been taught not to pay heed to ancient Pagan ways.

The Lady Gwenhwyfar had opened her arms to the Universe, now she gracefully held them at her side and invited her guest the priest to say a few words before they enjoyed his gift of venison.

The priest stood up and with calm clear blue eyes he surveyed the Great Hall taking in the crowd gathered in the warmth and revelling in the enticing smells of bread, mead, ale and meat. The upturned faces of the long haired and bearded men, the unfettered tresses of the women and the innocence of the children running amok playing and frustrating their parents, created a scene of harmonious village life that touched him. The dazzling colours of the four cornered woollen cloaks, the colourful breeches, shirts and tunics, the bits of coloured cloth the village women wore in their hair or around their necks delighted his senses. The villagers of Caerwyn were well fed, well clothed, content, and happy. This the priest could clearly see for himself. He bowed his head for a moment and the Hall reminded quiet.

In a rich baritone voice he intoned his own prayer of thanks that he spoke in the Church's Latin language. He ended his prayer with "*in nomine patris et filii et spiritus sanctii amen.*" The Christian villagers made the sign of the Cross in front of their bodies as though they understood the priest's words. They did not. They only recognised the familiar sounds of the prayer's end. The priest, ever joyful, raised his leather tankard of ale and the people cheered and began talking again.

With a wink of his eye, the priest spoke in Latin to Owain, Gwenhwyfar and those nearest to him.

"Oh, was I speaking Latin again? Sometimes it just slips out!" Gwenhwyfar did not understand Latin, nor did many of the others, but Owain, who had been schooled in the Roman tongue, laughed aloud. Together, he and the priest slammed their tankards together and laughing, drank down their beer in great gulps.

Lydia had understood some of what the priest said and she smiled. It was good to see the villagers laughing and singing she thought to her self. The capture of the prisoner had cast a pall over Caerwyn. The fight in the dafarn that resulted in Guto's death had added to that sense of dread, Lydia could feel it in her bones. The effect could be seen in Owain's face. He looked older these days, she thought, as she tried to imagine the thoughts of the leader of Caerwyn. She shook herself and rubbed her arms promising herself not to think about such things this evening. Tonight was a happy occasion and Lydia would not entertain thoughts that were not about music and happiness. Already a villager was up on a table singing an amusing song of two lovers. The harpist was laughing and having difficulty keeping up to the timing of the singer's cadence. Lydia looked over at Owain, Gwenhwyfar and the priest Bedwini. All three were laughing uproariously.

Most of Caerwyn had turned out for the Gathering and so there was not much food for each person. The venison was cut into thin strips and passed amongst the revellers with bowls of broth made from the roast drippings. Some women had brought bread and kettles of soup, which were added to from the stores kept in the Hall. The wily efforts of Rhys and his cousins resulted in a deal struck with Geraint the dafarn owner. The men would not speak of the details of the deal but the look on poor Geraint's face as he brought in a keg of ale and one of cider suggested he had not made the profit he thought was his due.

Nevertheless, he was hoisted on the shoulders of a few appreciative villagers and hailed as a hero. Slowly a smile came to his face as he beamed with pride at the accolades heaped upon him. A song was even started honouring his generosity. While not a sumptuous feast by Roman standards, no one went hungry or thirsty and everyone shared in the bounty.

One of the men brought a flute fashioned from a ram's horn and he began playing a tune on it. The harpist and two whistle players along with three men with thin drums made from goat skin that had been stretched over a round wooden frame that they struck with a small piece of wood the size of a spoon, joined in. The villagers clapped in time and the lively tune lilted along building in crescendo. Ale and cider flowed like water.

The priest Bedwini got up on a table and with a leather tankard of hearty ale in hand he began to sing a soulful lament. His song was the story of two lovers, a boy and girl from different tribes who had against their families wishes fallen in love. They saw each other only once a year at the annual gathering of the tribes. One year they decided to run away together. They managed to get to the Great Forest and then without hesitation they boldly entered the dark woods. Days then weeks then months and finally years went by without a trace of the two young lovers. Then one day a maiden who was travelling with her family and an escort of warriors, came across the bodies of the two lovers beside a stream deep in the Great Forest. Their bodies, now mere skeletons, were huddled together in one last forlorn embrace. From then on, all maidens with problems of the heart came to pray at the same stream. They brought flowers and votive tokens in the hopes of obtaining advice from the spirit of the dead lovers. Tragically, so the song told, those poor maidens who could not see any hope in their love affairs threw themselves into the fast waters of the stream and drowned. There was not a dry eye in the Great Hall and a melancholy silence had descended upon the people. Looking around at the sad villagers the priest took a great gulp of beer.

Father Bedwini wiped his eyes and with a wink, sarcastically asked for a towel. Hearing the priest ask for a towel and realising he was kidding them, the villagers began laughing, the melancholy lifted and the musicians launched into another jaunty tune. Soon there was dancing, stomping of feet and clapping of hands.

Elidir leaned down, said something to Gwyneth, and then pulled her to her feet. The two young people began dancing and were soon jostling for room in the crowded Hall. Owain was scowling as he watched his sweet young daughter dance with her young man. Gwenhwyfar saw her husband's expression and pulled him to his feet despite his vigorous protestations. The villagers cleared a circle and clapped in time with the music as they laughed and watched. Owain whirled and dipped with Gwenhwyfar as they danced and danced with carefree abandon. Finally, their exertions caught up with them and they stopped at their seats for a much needed drink of ale. The two of them watched as their daughter continued dancing with Elidir.

"They do make a fine looking couple," said Gwenhwyfar to her husband.

"Yes, they do but I think Gwyneth is much too young for this sort of thing." He began to rise as though he was about to put a stop to his daughter's dancing but Gwenhwyfar pulled him backwards. She pulled so hard that they both fell back over the chairs and landed unceremoniously on the straw strewn dirt floor.

Dyfyr and the priest ran over along with two of Owain's teulu. They arrived only to find Owain and Gwenhwyfar laughing raucously, hugging, and kissing each other on the ground.

"Hmmm", said the priest Bedwini, "Perhaps it is time to end the festivities." He bent down and pulled the two of them to their feet and with a wink and a nod told his slightly drunk hosts to get along to their bed. Owain was still laughing as he and Gwenhwyfar, arm in arm assisted by two of the teulu, walked around the gathering calling out good night. Couples linked arms and strode off in small groups.

Some of the men had to be carried home for they had too much cider and ale to drink. The musicians were carrying their instruments and talking to each other about their music as they walked slowly out of the Great Hall.

Elidir looked down at Gwyneth. He was anxious, uncertain how to act and confused about what he should do, but certain that he would lay down his life for the beauty standing before him. Gwyneth looked adoringly into the blazing blue eyes of the handsome young warrior, her face flushed and her heart fluttered but she did not move. The awkward moment that threatened to stretch to an eternity was brought suddenly to an end by the appearance of Dyfyr.

"There you are boy! Well, come on let's get the lovely lady home safe, there's work to be done before we retire!" The father looked at his son and though nothing was said, all was understood. Dyfyr was happy that the two of them should be so fond of each other but this was a tricky situation. Dyfyr knew it was a dangerous situation, if not handled in the proper way. The three of them walked out of the Hall and around to the entrance of Owain and Gwenhwyfar's home. Elidir was embarrassed and Gwyneth was simply demure as Dyfyr kissed Gwyneth on the cheek and handed her to her mother standing just inside the door. Owain was tending the hearth fire stoking it to a fine warm blaze. He had a piece of dark bread in his hand and was still laughing about the incident with his wife.

"Ah, Dyfyr," he stopped as he noticed Elidir by his friend's side and suddenly realised what was going on, "and Elidir! Come in, come in and have a last drink with me by the fire!" He turned quickly away and indicated the flask of beer by the hearth. Owain calmed himself remembering his good and wise wife thought it appropriate that their daughter should be courting. Owain decided that Gwenhwyfar was right about the young couple. And he would be right in selecting the son of his cherished friend as suitable suitor for his daughter's hand.

That's the way he saw things now and his mind was set. Turning back to his guests he had in his hands two tankards of ale and he thrust them into their hands before they could object. The three men stood there, ale in hand, facing each other while behind them a warm fire burned brightly in the hearth.

Dyfyr and Elidir were speechless as father and son sensed their leader and their host had come to some important decision about something, which they were not yet privy. Owain rescued them from the awkward moment.

"To all things right and proper, eh?" He slammed his tankard into the two of theirs, but his eyes bore into Elidir's. There was no mistaking the unspoken message. Elidir did not waiver, he stared straight back into the eyes of his commander.

"To all things right and proper!" He downed his ale in a gulp. Dyfyr and Owain drank down their ale emptying their tankards and remained looking at each other.

A pact had been made. An agreement amongst men and warriors had been reached and the deal was sealed. Owain put down his tankard and stuck his hand out to Elidir. Stunned Elidir cast a quick glance to his father, but Dyfyr just stood smiling. Elidir took Owain's hand in both of his and said again with a slight bow of his head, "To all things right and proper!"

Rhys, Katryn, their children, Math and Enid left together. The children scampered ahead in the dark giggling and laughing happy to be up so late. Rhys had his arms around his wife and was singing her a bawdy love song but he was off key, much to the amusement of the others. Math and Enid walked close to each other.

They had been together ever since Math had stood up in front of everyone and declared he would take care of her. He was still self-conscious about how the two of them came together, but if the truth were known, he was in love with Enid. She was nearly as tall as Math and robust in a voluptuously feminine way. Math adored her long coal black hair and the exciting sway of her hips as she walked. Above all else it was Enid's self evident dignity expressed in her calm manner and quiet ways that Math loved so well. He hadn't noticed before, certainly, he was not in the habit of leering at other men's wives, but he thought Enid to be quite beautiful.

In any case he would not leave her side for a moment. Enid, though she never spoke much, seemed to enjoy the attention of gentle Math. His gentle nature so endeared him to her heart. She had not known that about him at the Gathering when she chose to go with him. After all he had shot an arrow into the throat of her husband. The alternative, to be the kept woman of the leering Clydog, was not an option and so she had gambled that Math was genuine and honourable. Enid had lived for years with a man who other men feared. Guto had acquired a fierce reputation in Caerwyn and though many thought him a great warrior, Enid knew him only as a brute. It was taking time for her to become used to the gentle ways of Math. There were men in the village that considered Math a simpleton, the cur that followed Llew around. Enid had heard these things and she used to think of Math as bemused and perhaps a bit slow. Since the incident at the dafarn men spoke differently of Math. Now tales were being spun of how deadly accurate Math was with his great yew long bow. Men were saying a terrible rage lay deep in the soul of Math. Some were careful not to look him in the eye for fear of angering him. No one wanted to fall victim to his deadly long bow for it was said he could shoot a man through at five hundred paces even if the man was in his hut and lying in his own bed!

Enid was beginning to understand the truth. Math enjoyed the simpler things in life and he appeared slow only because he savoured life in an unhurried fashion. It was not rage, which lurked in the heart of Math, but a deep-seated sense of honour. Enid was finding she loved him for it.

"Well, cariad what do you think of my sweet song?" Rhys was not staggering but it was obvious that he had enjoyed one or two more ale than he could manage.

"That was not so sweet a song, you were off key!" laughed Math. Katryn and Enid nodded their agreement and giggled.

"That's your opinion, but I don't recall you lending voice to any ballads this evening!" retorted Rhys.

"True, but then I don't fancy myself a singer!"

"Nonsense! What self-respecting Cymry does not fancy himself a singer?" With his hands on his hips, swaying ever so slightly, Rhys was the picture of mock indignation.

All of them were laughing now and the children came running back to see what the commotion was all about. Katryn grabbed her youngsters, hugged them and in the process fell down in a heap with them. Enid helped her up and hugged the children as she sorted them from the tumbled pile. Rhys grabbed hold of Math's arm.

"You two make a handsome couple. I wish you both all the best. My good wife and I will be for home just now but I wanted to tell you I hope your lonely nights and Enid's painful days are all behind the two of you." It appeared Rhys was going to burst into tears.

"Rhys, thank you but you are drunk. Now take Katryn home before you both catch your death of cold!"

Rhys nodded, smiled, and squeezed Math's arm. He then went over to Katryn and put is arm around her and began to sing again to the groans of his children. They walked off towards their hut in a faltering, giggling gaggle.

Math and Enid laughed and laughed all the way to Enid's hut. Unconsciously Math put his arm around her as they walked. Enid moved close to him allowing him to wrap his arm more tightly, around her warming her against more than just the night air. Math had in the past dallied with his share of womenfolk from the village.

There were one or two women he had found in other villages, during the many years he had been in service to Owain. Generally, he had lived a solitary soldier's life, taking his pleasure when he could, sharing a hut with Llew his friend, both of them eating with the other single men when coming home from patrol. Sometimes the two of them would go eating and drinking at the dafarn amongst other warriors. This was the first time Math had felt something other than lust for a woman. He was unsure now of his role or how he should act. Math had moved into Enid's hut, it had seemed the prudent thing to do. He was uncomfortable, as he knew well that this was once Guto's hut and he felt sure, the other villagers would look upon him as an interloper. Everyone knew of course the oath he had sworn to protect and provide for Enid but he was still worried about gossip. He hesitated slightly at the entrance to the hut; Enid gently took his arm and guided him through the doorway.

The inside of the hut had been swept and cleaned meticulously. Enid walked to the fire and poked the embers until they glowed before putting on a new log and coaxing it to burn brightly filling the hut with a warm glow. Without saying a word, she walked over to Math and wrapped her arms around him. Her warm cloak fell to the ground in a bundle and she pulled Math closer to her body. Enid had never before felt so safe with a man. She had never before experienced the feelings welling up inside her now as she held on to this man she barely knew. Math reached down and brushed her hair from her forehead with his lips. He breathed in the intoxicating scent of this woman he now held tightly in his arms. Their lips hungrily searched for each other, once met, they kissed deeply. As passion overcame their anxiety and transformed their shyness, the newness of their being together gave way to intimacy. Hastily they threw their clothing on the floor and fell into the warm bed, giggling like naughty children and pulling the wolf pelts over themselves. Math wondered at how natural it felt to have Enid in his arms. He kissed her again and gently sucked on her breasts. Enid gasped with pleasure and pulled her lover down onto her. A tear glistened on Enid's cheek but for the first time in her life, it was not a tear of misery but one of absolute joy.

Llew was walking close to Lydia, listening as she was speaking Latin to the priest, Father Bedwini. The priests companions two men and a woman were all about the same age neither youths nor quite adults. They laughed and joined in the conversation. Lydia was asking the Father questions about himself. She asked the priest where he was from; using the rudimentary Latin, she had learned in her childhood.

The priest was amused at Lydia's enthusiasm though he understood it all too well. The Church had been established throughout the island for nearly two centuries. Yet, many Britons still clung to the old ways especially here in the West. Father Bedwini understood Lydia and those Christians like her were starved for the Word of God. Since the Roman Legions had left, many Britons had returned to the Pagan ways of their ancestors. The gods of Briton were not the only deities worshipped. The priest had come across those who still worshipped the sacred rites of Mithra, the mystery cult of the Legionnaires that had rivalled Christianity until the Emperor Constantine had declared himself a Christian. From that time on, Christianity had become the official religion of the Roman Empire. The decree had not wholly succeeded. Father Bedwini hoped to change that here on the island.

"I am from Deva just east of here. I must say I have travelled more than I care to remember." The priest said with a smile. He told Lydia of some of his travels and how tired he and his entourage were and how happy it made them to be so kindly welcomed here at Caerwyn.

"My duty to God is this poor attempt to bring the Word of God and the Teachings of His Church to the villages. I am impressed that you speak Latin my dear."

Lydia blushed, "I speak a little Latin. It is only what I remember from my childhood in Camulodunum, from a Father I knew there."

Llew was getting impatient. He did not understand Latin and felt totally left out of the conversation, a stranger in his own village. The Father sensed his frustration and anger and asked in Cymraeg.

"Where is the chapel? I thought I would perform mass tomorrow morning." The Father saw immediately how the poor child lit up at the mention of a mass.

"Oh, Father that would be wonderful!" Lydia was close to tears and Llew moved closer to her putting his arms around her shoulders.

"Father, we do not have a chapel. Not a proper one. We just go from hut to hut or sometimes we meet outside and make a little prayer. What shall we do?" Llew squeezed her shoulders in reassurance as poor Lydia began crying.

"There, there my child, we will make do! Please do not worry yourself so. I will have a word with your master Owain tomorrow about this neglectful situation." Llew was now holding Lydia up with both his arms wrapped tightly around her as she sobbed. The Father stepped forward, placed both his hands on either side of Lydia's face, and kissed her softly on the forehead.

"Good night!" he said as he threw his arm around the woman in his entourage. The two of them walked off towards the hut where they had been billeted leaving the two male companions to fend for themselves.

Llew gently lifted Lydia up so she could walk and helped her to the hut. Inside he saw that the prisoner was asleep and the two guards were well armed and alert. He walked Lydia to her bed and laid her down covering her with a warm bear pelt. In a surprising show of affection, Llew bent over and gently kissed Lydia on her cheek. She smiled slightly and squeezed his hand. Lydia was thankful for his kind support and warmed by his attention and affections to her.

Realising he was being watched Llew stood up and walked over to the guards. He generously offered to take up their posts allowing them to go outside one at a time take in the night air and stretch their tired muscles. It was a much-needed break for the guards and each man thanked him profusely. Llew was not tired and he stayed the night in the hut talking with the men. He kept a loving eye on the sleeping Lydia. Llew was glad that the poor woman could finally sleep.

It seemed to Owain that the morning light came too early this day. The sun was up and warmed the air so that there was hardly much snow left on the ground. The bed was warm but Gwenhwyfar was not there, instead he could hear her humming over by the fire.

"It is a lovely day," said Owain as he opened his eyes again.

Gwenhwyfar looked over at her husband, "Good morning, my love. Yes, it is a lovely day and soon to be over! If you do not hurry; you will miss it!"

Owain gave a pained look. Gwenhwyfar walked over and put a small cup of ale and some bread in his hand before kissing him on the head.

"Thank you."

"Thank you" for what, cariad?"

"Why for last night my love, though it pains me to think such a wonderful time meant more to me than to you as you seem to have forgotten already."

Owain jumped up and grabbed his wife around the waist pulling her down on top of him.

"After all our time together, cariad, there is no need to thank me for loving you well, for it is indeed my pleasure." They laughed again together and untangled themselves so Owain could ready himself for whatever the day might bring. Owain valiantly ignored the nagging headache that throbbed behind his eyes refusing to believe it had anything to do with the last night's festivities. He of course did not mention his discomfort to his wife.

It wasn't long before the days' business revealed itself to Owain. Gwyn ap Nudd had come with news for Owain's ears alone. He had been shown in and given beer and bread, but he was eager to speak to his leader. Owain entered the room and greeted him, together they walked out into the sun.

"My brother has some news that may be of value." Gwyn said simply waiting to see how Owain would react.

"What might that be pray tell?" asked Owain in an even tone.

Not being able to gauge his leader's mood or how he might accept his news, Gwyn continued.

"It seems Clydog was very interested in the ring Guto had in his possession...."

"Ring? What ring is this? The one he paid to the dafarn owner?" asked Owain impatiently.

"Yes, it is the ring with which Guto generously gave to the dafarn owner in exchange for food and drink. Apparently, it comes from the tribe of the Essylwg. Yet, it has the markings of the tribe of the Dobunni from the South. These barbarians like your prisoner, place much value on the giving of exquisite rings. Now how Guto came in possession of such a thing is anybody's guess. That bastard never had anything of value in his miserable life. I would wager it came from your prisoner."

"Is that so? Why do you think that?"

"Well, just a thought, Guto may have simply plundered it although why he didn't just kill the prisoner outright and raise the alarm...."

"What do you mean?"

"Guto did not call out when he found the prisoner. Dafydd was there as well and yet no alarm was sounded. One of them was not surprised to find your barbarian walking around in the Great Forest. I think it was Guto."

"So tell me," said Owain more than interested now, "how much of this do you know for certain and what does it mean?"

Gwyn swallowed hard and looking a bit uncomfortable, he tried as calmly as he could to explain to Owain what his brother found out.

"It seems that Edern had a bit of a conversation with Clydog the other night."

"I gave orders for him to keep watch over Clydog that is all! Now what is going on?"

"He did keep watch on him but you know how he gets when he thinks danger is at hand, he becomes...impulsive." Gwyn smiled sheepishly. The look on Owain's face indicated he was not amused and Gwyn thought it best to get to the point.

"He decided to talk to Clydog and on the pretence of going on a patrol through the village he offered him some cider. So they stopped by at the dafarn and got a skin of cider from the owner before the lads took him and a few barrels off to the gathering. It was a quiet night because of the gathering so Edern and Clydog were able to drink quite a bit. At least Clydog drank a lot anyway."

"The point, Gwyn the point?" Owain was growing irritable. Whether it was trying to follow Gwyn's meandering story or his headache he did not know...or care. Owain wanted to know what Gwyn thought was so important. His voice was low and husky and he desperately wanted a drink of cool water.

"The ring, according to Clydog, belonged to Gronw."

"You said that Guto had it and that he got it from the prisoner." Owain was getting more frustrated trying to follow what it was Gwyn was saying.

Gwyn simply nodded his head.

The importance of Gwyn's information dawned on him.

"That means that the prisoner got it from Gronw!"

Owain had jumped to his feet and was walking fast and in the direction of the hut where the prisoner was being kept. He had forgotten his headache.

Chapter 10

"Good morning!" The voice was unmistakably that of Father Bedwini. What irked Owain even more than what would now be an unwanted interruption in his day was the gaiety and the energy contained in the good Father's voice. Owain remembered he had matched the priest ale for ale the night before. Now the bright sunshine on this clear cold morning hurt his eyes and did nothing to ease his headache. He stopped his brisk walk across the cold earth of the village and turned toward the priest.

"Good morning, Father," called out Owain as brightly as he could pretend.

"You seem to be in a hurry this morn, master Owain." Father Bedwini nodded to Gwyn who returned the gesture respectfully. Though reluctant to engage in idle banter with the priest, Owain was polite. He hoped he could keep the conversation short so that he could get on with village business.

"Yes, I am sorry, but there are some things which require my attention just now...."

"Oh, could it have anything to do with the *Sacsonaidd* you have under guard?" deadpanned the good Father.

Owain froze instantly in his tracks. The look on his leader's face made Gwyn very nervous and he was glad his brother was not here to catch sight of Owain's reaction to the priest. For if Edern had been present and decided that the priest had affected his leader so, then poor Father Bedwini would surely be struck dead where he stood. Already

Gwyn had his hand on his own knife and had moved to the blind side of the Father. Owain kept his piercing eyes trained on the priest.

"Now don't get yourself upset, I mean no harm. I am here to offer my services."

If the good Father was afraid he certainly did not show it, he just beamed his beatific smile at Owain.

"No disrespect Father Bedwini, but the village's business is my concern and I shall deal with the situation in my own way guided as I am by my good wife, the Lady Gwenhwyfar."

"Yes, yes, I know all about Gwenhwyfar's family history. Such a touching story, such love for family, it really is inspirational. But did you really think you could keep such a secret as that of a captured Sacsonaid'd, from the likes of me? Come now, I offer my services and some news to boot, I dare say!" He laughed and his voice boomed with bonhomie. A good back slap was all that was missing to complete the hearty scene. But Father Bedwini was no fool and he did not move to touch Owain even in jest and good will, not with his man Gwyn so close.

Owain was angry that the priest was sticking his nose into the business of Caerwyn. He had no time to deal with this priest. He was focused on the security of the village, priest or no, Owain would trust no man with the lives of those he had sworn to protect.

"The prisoner, the Sacsonaidd, what is he to you, priest? He is not of your faith!" Owain's tone had turned curt and his voice was menacingly low.

"Oh, of that I am sure dear master Owain! Of that, I am indeed very sure! No! I do not offer the sacraments to this stranger. No, but I do offer my services to you as translator. I speak your prisoner's language, I speak *sacsoneg*!"

"And the news, Father Bedwini, what news may that be pray tell?" Owain tried to keep the surprise from his face as his mind raced with the new information about this priest.

"We'll speak of that later dear master Owain, but first let us hear what your pet has to say for himself, eh?"

Owain was trapped. He had no choice but to allow the priest to speak with his prisoner. While this would be a boon to Owain, it also meant that whatever the prisoner said, whatever secrets he may hold and whatever the implications to Caerwyn as result of any conversation, the priest would also know. The priest was not from Caerwyn. Owain wished to keep such information as might be forthcoming to himself so that he could ponder and mull over any strategies. He did not like to act rashly. If this priest could speak directly to the prisoner and understand him the information would be valuable. Poor Lydia was trying her best but she could not understand the prisoner completely and she had thus far not been able to give Owain any worthwhile information. The strain of her task was taking its toll on her health. Owain had noticed how run down Lydia was looking. Gwenhwyfar had noticed too and had asked her husband to do what he could to lighten poor Lydia's burden.

"Gwyn, fetch your brother. We shall meet in the hut and hear what this prisoner has to say." Owain had made up his mind. Gwyn paused for half a heart beat; his eyes bore into the priest. Then he turned abruptly and left to find Edern.

"Now Father, what else is on your mind?" asked Owain congenially as the two men walked through the bustling village towards the hut.

"The chapel." The priest said it simply as though the mere mention of a chapel would make its' meaning self-evident to Owain.

"Yes, well we don't have one. It has never been a problem as we all go about our own business here in Caerwyn. Pagan and Christian alike get along well with each other, neither group trying to out do the other and all enjoying a simple celebration of observed days of devotion regardless of beliefs. It has helped matters that you Christians choose the same days to celebrate as Pagans." Owain thought his was a good answer, it was true what he said and he could not help wonder what the priest's intentions were in mentioning Caerwyn's lack of a chapel. He did notice the priest scowl when he mentioned the common days of observance.

Father Bedwini, ever an astute negotiator for his cause, felt the stubbornness in Owain and decided now was not the time to press the issue. It was much better he thought to simply and delicately mention that there was an issue and leave things at that...for the time being.

Owain and the priest entered the hut where the prisoner was being held. The priest saw that Llew was lying beside Lydia with his arm around her as she slept. Owain instantly took note that the two guards were alert, armed and in position. Llew had spent the night and had frequently spelled the guards allowing them the luxury of walking about, stretching their stiff muscles, and taking the occasional quick nap. The hut was warm; the fires had been kept lit against the cold. Porridge was simmering in a blackened pot over one of the hearth fires filling the meagre hut with its inviting smell.

Father Bedwini broke the spell as he loudly cleared his throat. The sound woke Lydia and startled Llew who leaped to his feet, knife in hand. The quickness in which it appeared and the obvious readiness of Llew to cut the throat of any man to come close enough impressed Owain. The priest was frightened by the sudden and violent display. He jumped back and Owain was certain he heard a squeal of shock from the Father. The two guards of course had seen Owain and the priest approaching and had been at the ready. Owain noticed they smirked at the priest's reaction to Llew's knife.

"Good morning" said the priest after a minute, composing himself as best he could, and hoping no one had heard his cry of surprise.

"How are you?"

"Fine, thank you very much Father," replied Lydia. Owain thought she looked decidedly embarrassed and he wondered if anything was going on between her and the man Llew. He made a mental note to ask Gwenhwyfar what she knew of the situation.

Father Bedwini had recovered his composure fully and did not seem to be phased by Lydia's embarrassment or the circumstances of it. He seemed to have a light in his eye that had not been there before.

Lydia hurriedly got up, casting a quick look of reproach at Llew. He had a sheepish look on his face and was now sheathing his blade. Quickly Lydia began with her duties, stoking the fire, stirring the porridge, and offering some to Owain and the good Father. She then went to the makeshift cage and checked as best she could on Ceolwulf. He seemed asleep and impervious to the goings on around him.

Ceolwulf had been awake for hours but had found it useful to feign sleep. He could not understand the language but understood full well, that someone important had just arrived. He studied the tall, lean, hard man with the close-cropped beard and long brown hair, a warrior he thought immediately. He took note of the leather tunic, woollen shirt, leather gloves and boots, warm woollen breeches cinched tight with leather belts one of which held a sheathed long sword and a smaller fighting knife. Here was a dangerous man.

Ceolwulf turned his attention to the smaller man, the one with the ring of unkempt grey hair and stubble of a grey speckled beard. He could see the brown robe tied with a rope at the middle and the worn leather sandals. He was not as clean as the other man and he smelled, but unlike the tall warrior, this man seemed quite jovial. Which one of the men was more important? Ceolwulf was not sure. The others in the hut were all watching the small man, especially the woman. The guards were standing alert and on edge but they too were watching the robed figure with the peculiar hair. Ceolwulf's head cleared and his thinking sharpened. Of course! The smaller man was a priest, a Holy Man! How much power if any did he wield over the warrior?

He knew the woman was staring at him looking for some sign of improvement in his health. She caught his eye and as she did so he winked at her and smiled. The woman was startled and then quickly tried to cover her reaction. Llew noticed the change in her mood and was quickly at her side staring malevolently at Ceolwulf. Owain took note of that. So too did the priest.

Owain was anxious about what the priest could learn from the prisoner. He wanted to find out everything the good Father knew. The idea that this priest could talk directly to his prisoner burned in Owain's thoughts. He was impatient to start the questioning. The priest was looking around the hut intently as though he were assessing it. Owain did the same and noted the hut was in good repair, warm and dry, he assumed Lydia had seen to that. The makeshift cage of stout wood was in the centre of the hut and it too was warm, dry, and clean. The prisoner, Owain noted finally allowing his keen eyes to settle on his captive, looked cleaned, dry, bandaged, and wrapped in a warm wolf pelt. Of course, his long grey hair was tangled and lay limp down his back, his bushy grey beard was in need of brushing, but there was no dried blood or dirt present. The bruises on his body were purple, black, and blue, but he seemed whole. The prisoner was sitting up; his intelligent eyes were taking in the scene around him and missing nothing. A fleeting thought burst through Owain's mind that this man was not that different from himself. He certainly seemed engaged in the very same activity at present, the sizing up of the enemy.

Owain's impatience and frustration grew. He wanted to begin questioning the prisoner immediately. If he refused to answer, well Gwyn was on his way with his brother. Owain would have his answers of that he was quite confident. He did not wish to be cruel and it was not his nature to be brutal but the safety of Caerwyn was at stake. It was his duty to learn what he could to protect his wife, his children, and the village. Owain was getting anxious and where was Gwyn and Edern?

Just then the priest spoke.

"Now master Owain forgive me if I speak out of place, but perhaps I might suggest we move to more comfortable surroundings?"

Owain was dumbfounded. The gall of the little man! Looking around Owain saw that the others were staring agape at the presumptuous priest, even Lydia looked upon him, her   mouth open in shock and surprise.

"Now you just listen to me," began Owain, his voice ominously low, "you will start with questioning this man. I want to know from where he hails, what others are with him and what his intentions and plans were..."

Owain was interrupted by the arrival of Gwyn, his brother Edern and Cai, along with Dyfyr. Owain turned to acknowledge them and motioned them to enter and be still. Turning back to the priest he continued in the same stern tone. Edern, sensing Owain was angry with the priest, began to move in the priest's direction, his knife already held free in his gloved hand. Owain raised his own hand; Edern obediently hesitated, his eyes never leaving the priest. That was just the time Gwyn needed to clamp down on his brother's arm and hold him fast, whispering something into his ear as he did so. Cai had his hand on his sword ready to defend Owain's flank.

The priest had now turned ghostly white and had begun to shake. Lydia was shocked that the priest should be so threatened. Llew ever by her side kept his right hand on the handle of his fighting knife. The two guards had their spears gripped in their calloused hands ready to spring into action. Ceolwulf smiled. He was amused at the scene unfolding before him. Swords, knives, and spears bristled in the men's hands as tension taunted them to act.

"If you please, master Owain, I am only trying to help! I mean no harm!" To the priest's credit, though he was obviously frightened, his voice remained even. He slowly raised his arms not in a gesture of submission but to calm the fears of the jittery warriors. Owain took a breath and exchanged looks with his foster brother Cai. Motioning the men to stand down, he turned and spoke quietly to the priest.

"Father Bedwini, I am tired...what is it you have in mind and what is your interest in all of this? Tell me now or my man here," Owain pointed with his thumb to Edern, "will have words with you."

Father Bedwini looked around the hut. Seeing clearly the situation he realised it would be better if he simply and truthfully told Owain what was on his mind. The priest sat down next to the fire. Lydia scuttled over with a warm bowl of porridge, her concern showing for the poor priest. She was mortified that Owain could speak to a priest in such a rough and threatening manner. Lydia, too, was frightened by the display of violence from Owain's warriors. Her head was spinning trying to understand the actions of these men.

"All right...! Fair enough! You want information from this man, am I correct?" Owain simply stared straight at the priest.

"Well then," continued the priest, "the best way to get information is to make the man comfortable, ply him with food and drink and simply engage him in conversation." The priest looked back at Owain as a craftsman would look at a slow-witted apprentice. "You would be surprised how men open up when they think there is no threat. A little beer to loosen the tongue and some meat to induce a satisfied contentment, before you know it you have the man's life story."

"And your interest in this matter?" Owain still held the priest with his piercing blue eyes.

"My interest," said the priest in a serious tone not heard from him before, "is that these Sacsonaidd killed my Abbot and friends. They raided the village, they raped the women, and they plundered what they could. After they burned the huts to the ground, they routed out the brethren, my brethren, and killed as many as they could in the most gruesome of ways. They did not spare my Abbot nor did they leave the monastery standing. I would wish to know the reason why."

"Why is the reason so important? Surely the barbarians kill for the simple pleasure of it?" Owain's voice had taken a softer tone on hearing the priest's story.

"If I knew the reason," said the priest solemnly, his voice quiet and thick with emotion, "I would better be able to pray for their souls and then my Abbot and my friends will not have died in vain."

Ceolwulf's head hurt trying to understand the jabbering that was going on around him. He felt something of importance was being discussed and that somehow he was not in immediate danger. In any case, he could do little. He looked over at the woman and was surprised to see she was ashen in colour. Whatever the men were saying that had caused them to bristle so with their weapons had clearly upset her. Catching her eye, Ceolwulf again winked boldly at her and was amused anew at her shocked reaction. She began busying about the hut stoking the fire and preparing more food. More men entered the hut and Ceolwulf thought they would need to move to larger quarters if this kept up. Two armed men quickly left the hut as though they were on some mission. One of them returned, two large pitchers of beer in his hands. He watched as the woman produced two leather tankards and poured a generous amount of frothy ale into each.

"*Eala*! So this is their torture! To drink their fill of ale while I go without and in plain sight!" Ceolwulf laughed aloud. His laughter was cut short when Lydia thrust one of the tankards through the makeshift bars. Cautiously he accepted the gift and drank the ale down in a mighty gulp.

Two guards were standing with spears at the ready, swords sheathed and it was apparent to Ceolwulf he was to be moved. One of the guards opened the door for him and motioned that he should come out of the cage. Ceolwulf took a breath and decided he would face whatever his destiny had in store for him with the dignity due his position as thane. After all the skein of his life had been woven long before his birth and his fear would not change the outcome.

The group of armed warriors wended its way amongst the other huts of Caerwyn. Their leather-booted feet marched over the frozen ground. The sun seemed bright to Ceolwulf and he enjoyed its warmth on his face. It had been a lifetime since he had breathed anything but the fetid air of captivity. He savoured the smell of wood smoke that hung in the cold brisk air. The warrior in him made note of the villagers going about their business, stopping to stare at him and the accompanying warriors as they passed by. The group stopped short outside a hut that was decidedly bigger than the one he had previously been confined. Ceolwulf did not know it was the home of Owain and Gwenhwyfar and where the Gathering had taken place the night before.

Entering the hall Ceolwulf noticed there was no cage, only a large hearth fire warming the area. There were a few trestle tables and wooden chairs scattered around and some warm inviting skins piled on a floor strewn with sweet smelling herbs. One of his guards motioned that he should choose a seat. Ceolwulf walked to a pile of wolf skins on top of which lay a straw filled cushion. He flopped down leisurely allowing his legs to sprawl out comfortably in front of him. He was surprised that his arrogance was rewarded with a tray of food and a tankard of ale. Looking around he saw that the men and the woman with them were eating and drinking. Ceolwulf noticed too that there were guards stationed some distance away armed with those huge long bows, spears and swords. He counted four armed men discretely placed in the shadows of the great room.

"Friend I say to you King Owain greets you in friendship." said the priest to Ceolwulf in heavily accented language of the prisoner.

Ceolwulf's surprise was comically seen in his face as he nearly spit a mouthful of ale on himself.

"Who are you?" the good Father asked noting with pleasure the shock on Ceolwulf's face and the ale in his unkempt beard.

"Ceolwulf is my name." It was all Ceolwulf could manage to say, so surprised he was to hear his own tongue being spoken.

"Peace favour your sword, Ceolwulf," said the priest politely. He picked up some bread and cheese and offered it to Ceolwulf along with more ale.

Ceolwulf thanked the priest. He was impressed with the manners of this little man and he began to feel more at ease. He thought to himself that if they wished to give him food and ale and treat him like a man, a thane, then he would reciprocate and converse with them politely.

"I greet you! I ask who are you?" Ceolwulf thought he might as well know the name of the man he was talking with, perhaps he could learn something useful himself."

"Bedwini is my name. I am a priest of the One True Religion and...."

"Woden makes idols!" spat Ceolwulf using a common phrase. "Woden is the Chieftain of Speech, the Mainstay of Wisdom and the Comfort to Wise Ones! He is every noble warrior's hope and happiness! Do not speak to me of your puny god, priest, you do not own the truth!"

The priest's face turned red with rage and anger. He shook and bristled with violence as he shouted at Ceolwulf.

"*Nihil curo de ista tua stulta superstitione*! I am not interested in your foolish religious cult! You are to answer the questions I put to you or..."

"Enough!" Yelled Owain, "You will confine your questions to the subjects I wish to know about! I do not want to hear religious doctrine nor do I want you to conduct a sermon, do you understand me?"

The priest was shaking with anger, his face red and blotched with his rage. These emotions quickly gave way to anxiety as the priest took note of the two archers, bows drawn, arrows notched and aimed directly at his heart. Father Bedwini collected himself, smoothed his dirty brown robe, walked to a table and poured a tankard of ale from one of the pitchers. The eyes of the archers and the point of their arrows followed his every move. The priest took a moment to gulp some ale and noticed the smug look on Ceolwulf's face. Owain was angry himself and was having second thoughts about allowing the priest to continue with the interview. Cai had tight hold of Edern's arm. Gwyn came up and whispered into his brother's ear yet again. Edern quieted himself obediently but his eyes blazed at the priest and his hand was on the hilt of his battle sword.

"Owain this is good! The prisoner will be more confident now and we can play both of them, the priest and your prisoner against each other," whispered Gwyn to Owain, keeping his voice low and his hand in front of his mouth so the priest would not hear. He had told his brother the same.

Owain did not acknowledge Gwyn but motioned to the priest to continue. He also indicated to Lydia that she should replenish everyone's tankards with ale; everyone except the archers and the Nudd brothers.

"Father Bedwini, remember your mission. Now continue and don't worry about your outburst. It should not matter since you were speaking to him in Latin in any case." Owain smiled at the priest and the tension in the room lessened as a result. Lydia had tears in her eyes as she served the men. She was appalled that Owain would treat the good Father in such a disrespectful way.

"Woe is me!" said the priest, trying to do his best to regain control of the conversation.

"Yes, woe is me! I dare say I am excitable when it comes to religious matters, I do apologise."

"So? What you speak of is true, you are excitable about religious matters but then are not all men so afflicted?" Ceolwulf was feeling generous enough to smooth over the priest's ruffled feathers. Now he knew that the priest had no real power. The tall lean one with the long brown hair and small beard was the one in charge. Interesting, he thought to himself.

"I don't know. Let us not dwell on such matters! How is it you happen in our lands?" The priest was glad that the big man held no grudge against him. He decided to be more forthright and come to the point.

"Alas, yes! Let's do talk of other things. How is it I am here, you ask? I am lost. I left my village far to the South to see the country for myself. Beware of the Waelas, my kin told me, but I would not listen." Ceolwulf was playing for time while trying to make up his mind if there was any danger in telling this priest and his master the truth.

"No! I don't think what you say is entirely the truth." The priest thought it possible that Ceolwulf had become lost in the Great Forest. There could be some truth to that. However, he was quite sure there was an underlying reason for his presence, something other than idle curiosity about new lands.

"No! What you speak of is true. At least what you are thinking is true. I did get lost in the forest, but my coming here was no accident. I was invited. I am here to negotiate an alliance or at least to determine if an alliance is possible between your local tribe and us."

"Yes, an invitation you say? Who, pray tell, invited you?" Father Bedwini was excited now as he thought he was getting to the information that was of keen interest to Owain.

"Alas! I do not know!" Ceolwulf was carefully playing a cat and mouse game with this priest. He wanted to maintain the interest in his story but at the same time he did not wish to divulge more than he had to. He needed time to figure a strategy. He did not think the priest would accept his last statement but in truth, Ceolwulf did not know who had invited him. He had been instructed to find his way to the edge of the Great Forest where a man would meet him. He was to show the ring to this man, who would then lead him through the forest to the meeting with the one who had the influence to broker the alliance. Ceolwulf's blind ambition drove him to such an absurd and dangerous meeting. If he could broker an alliance with a northern tribe, he could bring pressure to bear on the surrounding tribes. Such an alliance even if it held only for a short time would allow his compatriots to advance into new lands. The king would be very appreciative of that surely. How much of this he could reveal to these men Ceolwulf was not sure. He thought there was a chance to continue with negotiating an alliance. On the other hand, there was the danger that they may think him to be the vanguard of an invasion force and simply put him to death.

The priest did not look convinced.

"Friend! I ask you...would you have us believe you came all this way risking certain death on a perilous journey and yet you don't know who it is you were to meet?" Father Bedwini looked pained at having to accept the weak story being offered to him by the prisoner. The look on his face conveyed disappointment and bemusement to Ceolwulf.

"Yes...I do not know who was to meet me. An alliance would be important," Ceolwulf looked over at Owain as he spoke to the priest trying to gauge any reaction to his words. "Important and beneficial to both our peoples. In any case, I took up the adventure, for glory is the reward of a true warrior!"

Here he paused and again set his gaze steadily on Owain.

"The trip was hard and fraught with danger of course. I had agreed to make my way with but a few men to the edge of a huge forest. There I was to venture in alone as far as my courage would allow. I was told I would meet a man. He was to open his hand and I was to place into it a ring of which I was the bearer. The ring had been given to me by one of my men who had in turn been given it by a *waelas*. It was a symbol of recognition. This man was to be my guide and he was to take me to meet with a man who wielded some influence with the tribe. I saw such a man and gave him the ring but that was as far as I got. I was hit on the head from behind and do not remember anything afterwards."

Ceolwulf had told the truth such as he knew it to be. Now he looked around the room to assess the effect of his tale. There was nothing more for him to do but observe. He shrugged his shoulders, gulped down his beer, and turned his eyes back to Owain.

The priest held up his hand to signal the end of the conversation. He called to Lydia so that she might re-fill Ceolwulf's tankard with ale. Father Bedwini then spoke to Owain and translated for him what Ceolwulf had said. Owain nodded his assent as Cai spoke putting pieces of the puzzle together.

"That's it! Gronw travelled south traded for the ring and then contacted these Sacsonaidd. His intent was to make an allegiance with them, which would strengthen his bid to take Caerwyn! Guto was the man who would lead this prisoner to Gronw. That's how he got the ring. Dafydd must have come across them accidentally and was killed by Guto who then tried to cover up by killing the prisoner. Thinking himself successful in that, he kept the ring as payment to himself. Clydog knew this or at least suspected as much and tried to retrieve the ring after Guto had been killed, not knowing that Guto had stupidly paid his bill at the dafarn using the ring. So now, we know that Gronw is trying to take over Caerwyn by force using another tribe and an alliance of Sacsonaidd mercenaries. Clydog and Guto were part of the conspiracy and those other bastards with them can be counted as part of the treachery as well!" Cai stopped, took a huge draught of ale and thoughtfully wiped his mouth on his sleeve.

Owain looked sharply at Edern. The message was clear and Edern and two of his men left the hall in search of Clydog. Dyfyr seized the chance to speak his mind to Owain.

"We have no choice now but to kill this prisoner! Not only that, Owain, but also we must do something with Clydog and the others or we will be seen as weak. The thing of it is we need to know who else is involved. Certainly, Gronw could not wrest control of Caerwyn without help. Which one of the other tribes is plotting with him against us? We need to know now!"

Owain looked around his hall and motioned to Lydia to bring him more ale. He took a deep breath, his demeanour, belying the tension and stress he felt.

"I want you to think," he said looking at every man in the hall. "I want you to calm yourselves and think for a moment. Soon Edern will bring Clydog here to us and we must decide what to do not just with him, but as Dyfyr has said we need to deal also with this man." Owain pointed to Ceolwulf. "Remember we searched the Great Forest and we found no signs that there were any other Sacsonaidd present. There were no signs of any intruders at all, Cymry or Sacsonaidd. There are no forces present to support Gronw and his plans and we know he cannot harass us on his own. I suggest we have thwarted a plan in the making. We may yet be ahead of the game. I do not think there is any imminent danger to us...yet."

"But what do we do with Clydog and this prisoner?" Dyfyr was clearly agitated.

"Dear friend," said Owain quietly to his man, "we will do as we must do and what we do will be what is right and proper. Please inform my wife I wish to see her on an urgent matter." Owain needed more time to think. Owain and the Council would need Gwenhwyfar, no matter what decision was to be made, and sending Dyfyr for her would give his friend something to do. Owain knew Dyfyr as a man of action and presently there would be something of a wait before any action could be decided upon. Owain gulped ale and peered over his tankard to see that Ceolwulf was watching him intently.

Chapter 11

The Lady Gwenhwyfar arrived at the Council gathering resplendent in a blue woollen dress and wolf fur cape draped around her shoulders for warmth. The blue of the dress and the grey-silver of the wolf fur set off her blazing blue eyes. His beautiful wife looked outwardly calm but Owain detected a slight seriousness in her. Indeed this was a serious situation and one Owain was impatient to understand. He needed to understand so that he could take the proper action that his duty as leader required of him. Dyfyr and two other guards accompanied his wife, Gwenhwyfar. Lydia rushed to her and gave the Lady some ale and bread while the warriors ensured she was comfortably seated next to Owain.

"So you see cariad, we are in a ticklish spot," Owain whispered to into his wife's ear after explaining what had been translated by the priest.

Gwenhwyfar nodded and looking again at Lydia, she smiled. She noticed when she entered the hut that Llew was being very attentive to Lydia and that the woman seemed to grow in confidence under his ministrations. Poor Lydia she thought to herself, happiness was long overdue in her life. The Lady turned her thoughts back to the crisis at hand, a slight frown appeared on her face. No one noticed but her husband.

Edern entered and walked to the centre of the hall. Standing there one hand on his sword, he motioned to his men and their charge standing just outside of the hall.

"Come! Come! You swine! You traitor!" he harshly called out. Two of his men pushed and dragged a badly beaten Clydog into the hall unceremoniously throwing him at the feet of Edern.

Gwenhwyfar, ever compassionate, motioned for Lydia to tend to the wounds of the injured Clydog. Edern arrogantly moved as though to stop Lydia who had anticipated the Lady's concern and was already moving toward the new prisoner, cloth and healing herbs in hand. Edern caught the eye of Llew and saw he was glaring at him, his hand on his fighting knife. The look of outrage in Llew's eyes caused Edern to look up whence he noticed the mood of all in the hall had changed to shock. He noticed too, that the archers had nocked their bows and their arrow points were aimed at his heart. Turning his head to the Lady Gwenhwyfar, Edern saw in her eyes a look of hurt and disappointment. Owain's countenance had changed to a hard steely glare, his hand was on the hilt of his sword and he was about to stand but for the gentle touch of his wife upon his sword arm.

Edern immediately dropped to one knee and bowed his head. His face was pale for he now realized what he had done. He had never intended to insult the Lady Gwenhwyfar nor go against the wish of his liege lord Owain. By moving to block another carrying out the wishes of the Lady, Edern had done just that.

"Excuse me, please, I am sorry..." the now chastened warrior said. The tension in the hall lessened considerably with Edern's show of humility. To Ceolwulf, it was unfathomable and he could not see any clue to what was going on in the priest's face. Something important was happening and he was at a loss to understand except that in some way he knew it concerned him.

"Yes, of course..." said the Lady Gwenhwyfar as she motioned Lydia to continue. Owain's eyes never left Edern. Nor did Llew's.

Edern stepped away from Clydog allowing the responsibility for his prisoner to lie with the two guards. He walked over to his brother, head slightly bowed. There he stood for a moment and then slowly he brought his head erect, pride returning to him once again. His hands however he kept well clear of his knife and sword. Owain noticed and was content.

Owain knew Edern to be a loyal and trustworthy man. It was just that the man's passion, while useful, was at times too explosive. Owain thought of him as a hunting hawk being trained to the glove. The same delicate patience was needed dealing with the warrior in Edern. Too much freedom and the hunter gave up control; too much restraint and the predator instinct would be stifled. Turning his attention now to Clydog, Owain noted that the wounds he had looked much worse than what they really were and Lydia was doing a good job of cleaning them. Clydog stood in the centre of the hall all eyes upon him.

"Now then," began Owain, "we have reason to believe you are conspiring with Gronw to usurp power here in Caerwyn. What do you say to the charge?"

"Go to hell," Clydog retorted defiantly, "I've done nothing wrong! It's true I am not as fond of you, Owain as you would like but that does not make me a traitor! You have no proof of this charge and I demand to be let go, now!" The sweat on Clydog's brow betrayed his words and it did not go unnoticed.

"Do you know this man?" Owain pointed to Ceolwulf who upon seeing he was being talked about, stood up straight. This caused the archers to again pull their strings taut, arrows nocked and pointing at the Sacsonaidd. Ceolwulf smirked at the sound of the bows. The priest whispered to him in sacsoneg to sit back down. Ceolwulf sprawled out as before, the smirk firmly planted on his face.

"Of course, I do not know him! He is a Sacsonaidd! How would I know him?" Clydog's voice was loud and steady yet still he sweat.

"Indeed, you are right. Then how did you know he was Sacsonaidd?"

"Well...I mean...everyone knows that...the priest...he told everyone... In any case it is common knowledge who and what he is!" Clydog was getting dry of throat and Gwenhwyfar signalled to Lydia to give the man some ale. Lydia went about her duty but under the watchful eye of Llew.

"What of the ring you sought?" Owain's voice was low and even, an ominous sign that his patience was wearing thin. It did seem plausible that Clydog's explanation could indeed be the truth but Owain did not believe the man.

"Ring? What ring?" Clydog opened his arms in a gesture of innocence.

"Come now Clydog, the ring you wanted to obtain from Guto's body. That is why you made your case against his killing is it not? You told Edern the ring belonged to Gronw, is that the ring you wished to have in your possession?"

"I have no idea what you are talking..." Clydog's lie was cut short as he saw what Owain held in his thumb and forefinger. It was the ring. Edern had brought it from the dafarn owner Geraint before going to retrieve Clydog. Owain had received it from one of Edern's men.

"I could have you killed immediately for treason, Clydog." Owain stated this in a matter-of-fact tone as he looked evenly at the battered man before him.

"But you cannot! You have no proof! This ring means nothing, nothing at all! You cannot under the law have me killed on such trivialities!' Clydog was white and sweating profusely now his voice raspy and desperate.

"Is that true, Cai? Can I cannot have this traitor killed?" Owain had turned to ask his foster brother, beginning the ruse.

"Strictly speaking, master Owain, no, you cannot. There is not enough evidence against him to support the charge." Cai never allowed his gaze to waiver from the eyes of Clydog.

"Father Bedwini, in the eyes of the Church should I kill this man for treason?" Owain asked the priest keeping mockery from entering his voice.

"No, master Owain," said the priest in Cymraeg and then switching to Latin he said, "*legum servi sumus ut liberi esse possimus*; we are slaves to the law in order that we may be able to be free."

Lydia made the sign of the Cross instinctively upon hearing the words from the Father. Llew put his hand on her shoulder to calm her and lend support.

"Cariad, my Lady Gwenhwyfar, you have heard the charge and the thoughts of us who present the charge, now what would the Old Ways have us do?" Out of the corner of his eye, Owain saw the priest blanch at the question he put to his wife.

Gwenhwyfar stood up, her head was held high and proud and she regally walked amongst the gathered warriors. She spoke softly but with absolute authority and confidence. Even the Christians amongst the men were awed by her presence for she commanded respect in her every move, her every nuance. It was her gift.

"In Old Times before the Romans came when the Great Standing Stones glistened blue in the shining sun, our chieftains would gather under the moonlight to hear counsel from each leader. No decision could be made without the consent of the druid. No king could decree an order without first obtaining approval of the druid. They were the arbiters of the Ancient Law. They were the Wise Ones and they knew the philosophy, the history, and the law of our people by heart. It would be for them to decide guilt or innocence. The Romans killed our Druids. We have not seen one in a generation. The Ancient Laws still stand and they serve the people in times of need. My family have long been tied to this ground this earth. The village of Caerwyn has been given to my Ancestors some say by the Goddess Dôn herself. Yet, I am not a Druid. Rhiannon would be good counsel. She and I share some of the gifts of the Druids, the Healing, the Sight, she has ridden in battle and is a slayer of our enemies. Alas, she is not present. As my ancestry requires of me, I would counsel that this dilemma be decided by the Goddess Dôn. This is what the Ancient Law would state." Gwenhwyfar walked back to her seat her movement almost haughty.

Owain watched his Lady as she made her way to her seat beside him. The hall remained silent. Gwenhwyfar's words were working their way into the men's hearts. Her husband was thinking about what his wife had said and what her words meant. Gwenhwyfar's suggestion that the Goddess Dôn should be the final arbiter presented a way out of the situation in which Owain found himself.

The implication was that a deal to usurp the power of Caerwyn existed between the Sacsonaidd prisoner and the man Clydog. While the Sacsonaidd was being vague, Clydog was thought to be outright lying. The evidence was not strong. The Ancient Laws that the Lady Gwenhwyfar talked about were predicated on the idea that truth would always be stronger than lies. Therefore, under Ancient Law and since no Druid was present to decide the matter, it was written that the two men be compelled to fight to the death. The truth would win. The survivor would be allowed to live free of the charges against him.

"So it shall be done! Prepare them both!" Owain said in an even solemn voice.

The archers on the second floor were alert and their bows ready arrows at hand. A few more warriors had slipped into the hall to take up positions in the shadowy corners. The decision of this contest of truth may be up to the Goddess but Owain was taking no chances. The wooden tables and chairs, the cushions and skins had all been cleared from the centre of the hall. Ceolwulf was standing now; he knew his time had come.

"At last," he thought, "an opportunity for glory in Valhalla!" He smiled contentedly. Clydog stood shaking, unable to believe what had just taken place. He had counted on being released; he knew Owain did not have enough evidence against him. He looked over at the priest. Father Bedwini was speaking Latin so no one around him understood what he said. It was clear he was very agitated. The others in the hall, Owain, Gwenhwyfar, Lydia, Llew, Cai and the members of Owain's advisors sat on chairs creating a large ring around the two men. Gwenhwyfar and Owain had four guards standing directly behind them spears in hand. Owain took his Lady by the hand and stood. He raised his hand and began to speak.

"You have been accused of treason by trying to usurp power here in Caerwyn. You are believed to be in a conspiracy with Gronw who will be dealt with soon. And you", he pointed at Ceolwulf, "we believe you to be involved somehow with this man. We believe you to be a vanguard of an alliance made to assist this man and Gronw in the taking of our village. The proof is not strong enough to have you put to death. The Ancient Law is what will guide us in troubled times. It is the Ancient Law that decrees when judgement cannot be made, the Truth can be found in combat. It is an Ancient tradition and it will be upheld. You will engage each other in single combat to the death! The survivor will be set free. That is all! Give them each a knife!"

Father Bedwini could hold his silence no longer. This spectacle of death, this Pagan ritual was more than his Christian sensibilities could bear.

"Master Owain, Lady, please I beg you do not allow this thing! It is an affront to decency. It is not a Christian thing to pit two men against each other in a death match! Please I beg of you reconsider..."

Owain was confused by the priest's supplications on behalf of the Sacsonaidd. He would have thought the priest would be glad that the prisoner faced death. The story the priest had told of the butchery against his brethren and the village at the hands of Sacsonaidds surely cried out for vengeance. Owain told the priest so.

"Which is greater, master Owain, the power of hate or the power of love?"

"You are telling me," said Owain incredulously, "that you love this man whose people you say butchered your friends?"

The priest smiled at Owain through his tears. "I am saying that I choose to act from love rather than from hatred. As an act of love, I pray for the souls of those who killed my brothers. If they come to see the Light and repent their sins, they will be welcomed into the Kingdom of Heaven. Their souls, dear master Owain, would then be saved for all eternity. That is the mission of our order and in accomplishing this small feat my brothers will not have died in vain and I will have lived to see their work fulfilled!"

Lydia between sobs was also beseeching Owain and Gwenhwyfar. She had nursed the prisoner back to health. She now felt responsible for him and would feel guilty if he were to be slaughtered.

"Please, Lady this is not the Christian thing to do," the poor girl sobbed.

Gwenhwyfar held up her hands. Silence descended upon the hall as she stood.

"You are correct dear Lydia, it is not a Christian thing we do. However, I am not a Christian. Nor is my husband. These are the Old Ways. They have worked for us long before your new religion touched our shores. There is no other way out of this situation save that we kill both men with our own hand. I think it more prudent more compassionate to call upon the Mother Goddess Dôn for assistance. We do not wish for unnecessary bloodshed and in that, we are all in agreement Father Bedwini. Whosoever survives this ordeal will have been chosen by Her as the Truthful One."

Gwenhwyfar stroked Lydia's hair and with her eyes signalled Llew to take hold of her and calm her. Turning to Father Bedwini the Lady nodded slightly as a token of respect. Llew guided Lydia back and cradled her head as she sobbed uncontrollably. The priest stood his ground. He took a halting step forward toward the prisoners. He wanted to shield the men from the sentence levied against them. He stood tall, his face toward Heaven, his voice clear and strong reciting Latin prayers. Owain signalled and one of his warriors used his spear to herd the priest back to the edge of the circle. The archer's bows were pulled taut and nocked with their deadly arrows. The priest heard the sound and saw the archers on the second floor. There was nothing more he could do. The priest slumped his head, dejected. Owain was not done with him even yet.

"Tell the barbarian that we have decided the only way to determine the truth about this situation is for him to engage in mortal combat with Clydog. If he survives, we will free him. These are our ways and our Laws. Tell him!" Owain's voice was calm and low but held a finality that compelled the priest to do as he was bid. The priest's words had unsettled Owain.

Despite the Ancient Law, he did not believe in his heart this contest was the best solution. It was, however, the only one presented that he could accept. Owain could not question his decisions now. It had been his decision to keep the Sacsonaidd alive and having done so he now knew of the plot. He had learned of Gronw's scheme, Clydog's complicity to seek a Sacsonaidd alliance. There was more to be learned. One of the tribes was involved that was to be sure. Gronw could not have acted alone he would have needed a tribe to make the offer of a Sacsonaidd alliance more attractive. Owain's suspicions had now been confirmed. He could act now to protect the village. Owain had allowed himself one wistful thought. If only the tribes would come together in alliance under one leader, to form one nation for the good of all. It was his wish. It was his dream.

Ceolwulf listened to the priest. He took the news that he was to fight to the death calmly. He was glad that he would have the chance to survive but more than that, he was thankful he could now die like a warrior. In that, he had already won. The priest looked at him without comprehension. Of course, the priest could not know that for a warrior it was not important whether he lived but rather how well he died. The priest did mention one thing that surprised Ceolwulf. The Holy Man questioned Ceolwulf about a massacre of a village and of a community of Holy Men like himself. This bothered Ceolwulf.

As a warrior, he was accustomed to death. He was certainly no friend to followers of the weak and arrogant religion of this priest. For

Ceolwulf there was no honour, no glory in burning innocents. Warriors should fight warriors. That was the way to glory, the way to Valhalla and a place at Woden's table. If there was to be a burning it should be to stop the waging of war and not for sport. Ceolwulf knew of no such activities. No one under his command had done such a thing. He had himself avenged the senseless killing of a priest by a warrior. Ceolwulf told the priest this and saw the priest was surprised.

He allowed no more time for such thoughts. Instead, he began to think of the fight and standing up he began to stretch his body. Taking stock of his condition, he realised he was still weak and his wounds would hamper his ability.

Clydog had stood up upon seeing Ceolwulf moving about. Clydog had not counted on things turning out as they had and Gronw had not mentioned this possibility. These thoughts preyed upon his mind. Still he thought he would be able to kill the barbarian. If he could not, well it was better to die in battle than to be slaughtered like a sheep. Clydog picked up the fighting knife that had been thrown in his direction. He held it in his hand appreciating the balance and weight of the weapon. He twirled it and made some slashes in the air. It was a fine weapon.

The two men were bare-chested each armed with a fighting knife. They were directed in to the centre of the hall by Owain's guards. Outside the sun had died leaving only the hall fires to light the hall. The flickering yellow firelight cast an eerie hue as shadows danced on the walls. There were no catcalls and no jeering that would normally have accompanied a common fight. The room was silent and solemn in reverence for the ancient ritual, which was about to unfold. The two men circled each other.

Clydog feigned to his right and then smartly moved to his left, his knife slicing the air in front of him making a swishing sound. Ceolwulf barely moved only slightly leaning his body away from the errant slash. Again, Clydog attacked. This time he lunged at Ceolwulf and missed. Ceolwulf deftly managed to stay out of Clydog's range. He moved his knife so that the spine of the blade was held firmly against his inner right wrist; the hilt toward is attacker. The knife was invisible to Clydog, who again slashed at Ceolwulf. Suddenly, he changed directions and back slashed. He missed again. The men circled.

Clydog lunged, his knife in front of him, its target Ceolwulf's chest. Ceolwulf parried with his left hand and at the same time swung downwards with his right hand. The blade he held against the underside of his wrist sliced through the inside biceps of Clydog's right arm. Instead of following through in an arc, Ceolwulf reversed the direction of his knife and stabbed twice just under the right arm of Clydog. The cut itself was probably fatal, slashing as it did through a main artery. The twin stabs were definitely mortal wounds for they had punctured through the unprotected flesh of the underarm allowing the blade to penetrate deeply into Clydog's body. Ceolwulf still did not hesitate, but grabbed Clydog's hair, pulled him backwards and plunged the knife into the top of Clydog's chest.

It was over.

Ceolwulf was all smiles. He was well, unharmed and gulping down the rest of the ale left in his tankard. He wiped his lips with the back of his hand. Impervious to the sombre silence of the hall, the dragging away of Clydog's bloody body going unnoticed by him, Ceolwulf stood up and began to speak.

"My honourable friends, my dear friends, Alas, the snake came crawling and struck at none. But Woden took nine glory twigs and struck the adder so that it flew into nine parts." Ceolwulf saw the look of surprise on the faces of his captor's and noted even the priest had not understood the meaning of his words. The big Sacsonaidd shook his head sending his grey locks swirling as he laughed uproariously before sitting himself back down.

Owain gave orders to two of his guards that Ceolwulf was to be taken into the Forest and set free. The route to be taken was to be a little used path, one most villagers would have forgotten existed. Owain was bound by the Ancient Law and his own oath to allow the prisoner his freedom. The Law however did not dictate the manner in which the freedom should occur. The prisoner had won his freedom nobly to be sure. Freedom was his. Owain was simply returning the Sacsonaidd to the Forest a free man. If the Sacsonaidd could find his way out of the Great Forest then he would live to enjoy that freedom which he had so bravely earned. The Ancient Law was satisfied. Owain had kept his oath. Caerwyn would no doubt soon be even safer.

Some jugs of ale were passed around and food was brought to the hall by serving girls. Gwenhwyfar was comforting Lydia whilst Llew hovered between seeing to Lydia and helping the men return the hall to normal. Several village women were trying hard to clean the blood from the floor. There was so much blood. It made a trail from where Clydog was felled to the door where his body had been dragged. More women came with water and cloth. The gruesome scene played out in the flickering firelight of the hearth fire.

The priest sat silently in the corner. He had blessed the carved carcass that had been Clydog. The priest was moved to tears by the violence that had played out in front of him. The Holy Man wept at not being able to put a stop to carnage. He rocked back and forth.

"Lord have mercy, Christ have mercy." He said to himself. A serving girl noticed him and took pity offering him a tankard of ale. The priest took the tankard that was pressed into his hands. He did not look up. Finally, he gulped down the ale.

Cai took Owain aside and told him it was too dark, too dangerous to take the prisoner to the Forest. They would have to wait until morning. Owain was not happy but saw the wisdom in his foster brother's words. He beckoned the priest be brought to him. He instructed the priest to inform the Sacsonaidd that he would have to spend one more night under guard for his own safety. The priest looked at Owain with accusation in his eyes.

"Fear not Father Bedwini, the Ancient Law will stand and my oath to this man will be upheld. In the morning, he will be escorted to the Great Forest and freed. Until then he may eat and drink his fill and all comfort shall be afforded him."

"But he shall surely die in the forest," the priest said pleadingly.

"He is to be freed, put back where we found him with a full belly and in good health! What more can be demanded of us?" Owain's voice was low and it rumbled malevolently through the hall. The priest could only move to Ceolwulf and translate what was to happen to him.

Upon hearing the news Ceolwulf stood up again and spoke in a strong voice, the strange guttural language cascading over his hosts.

"I give you thanks my Lord, my Lady...your hospitality and generosity with your drink is most appreciated!" Ceolwulf laughed but not as boisterously as before, he was more wary now. He knew it wise not to travel in unknown forests in darkness and he was glad of the decision. Ceolwulf realised the choice was more to protect this leader's men than any consideration for him. He also knew that releasing him to the forest even in daylight meant his chances of survival were slim. It would take all his wits to figure a way through the dense forest and he was sure the guards would not make that task the easier. Still he wished to be free from this place.

Owain turned to his men. He gave instructions that Dyfyr and Llew were to prepare to leave at first light. It would be their task to take Ceolwulf deep into the Great Forest and "free" him. The journey would be six days long, three in and three back to Caerwyn. Guards were assigned to escort Ceolwulf to another hut. He was now more a guest than a prisoner. He would not be caged, but he would still be guarded. Owain saw no sense in making the Sacsonaidd spend the night in a cage. The priest may be right. The man might feel free to talk some more if he were comfortable. Food and ale was sent to the hut ahead of Ceolwulf's arrival.

Owain instructed that the priest and Lydia should remain with the Sacsonaidd overnight. If he did say anything, Owain wished to hear of it. They were encouraged to engage the Sacsonaidd in conversation. The rest of the men were ordered away. Everyone could do with a good rest. It had been a trying day for the small village. Cai gathered a few men to have a last look around the village. Edern went with Cai while his brother Gwyn and the rest of the warriors went off to their families. The unmarried men went to the dafarn. Llew was reluctant to leave Lydia's side. Father Bedwini told him that Lydia would be safe but that was little comfort to Llew, as he did not entirely trust the priest. He was not sure why this was so, it was just a feeling that nagged at him. Llew had no choice but to obey Owain's orders and so he left to prepare the journey with Dyfyr.

Ceolwulf settled into the new hut, hearth fire burning brightly, table full of food and ale. He felt optimistic for the first time in weeks. He took another gulp of ale and wiped his mouth with his arm ignoring the ale that trickled down his beard. The room that was the hut was warm, dry and pleasant smelling. A pallet piled with skins served as a bed and Ceolwulf lounged on it in comfort. The priest and the woman sat in chairs made more comfortable with straw filled cushions and thick woollen blankets. The woman was stoking the fire. The priest looked miserable.

"Friend, I say to you...that you do not look well. Is there something wrong?" Ceolwulf said as he lay back comfortably on the skins.

"No, there is nothing wrong." Father Bedwini murmured. Ceolwulf caught the priest's eye and saw a flicker of hatred pass fleetingly in the priest's gaze.

"Friend, forgive me but you look at me with hatred and yet I cannot think of what I have done to cause such offence. Is it the difference in our beliefs or the blood spilled this night? For that I cannot apologise as clearly it was a case of kill or be killed. I am a warrior, a thane after all!"

"No, please forgive me I am a man of God," said the priest softly, "and it is my duty to strive for peace and for love to be present in my bosom always. What you say is true...you are a warrior, mighty and brave. I have witnessed that for myself. While I cannot condone the killing and I grieve for the loss of life, I know it was justified according to the Ancient Laws of this island. I wish it were not so. I wish God's laws and no others commanded all men. Perhaps someday, men will see the error of their ways. I do not care for your beliefs, but I would know more about you that I might better pray for your eternal soul everlasting as it is my duty to God to do so."

Father Bedwini again told Ceolwulf the sad tale of the massacre of his Abbott's fate, his friends, and their village. He told Ceolwulf what he knew of Lydia's light and watched to see what sort of reaction Ceolwulf might have to these woeful tales. It was difficult to gauge the warrior's feelings and the priest supposed that the man's heart was stone.

Taking another gulp of ale, Ceolwulf stood up, wiped his mouth again and spoke in a strangely soft voice.

"I ask you, in times of conflict, in the heat of battle, when warriors are filled with bloodlust, is it so unusual that tragic things should happen? Whatever the reason for conflict for war, warriors such as me must face death and mutilation, as is our duty. Rarely though is the fight of our choosing. Kings and nobles make the wars and men such as me do as our duty and loyalty dictate. Fear, pride, anger, and lust for glory in battle make fighting men dangerous and unpredictable. Some men even become cruel and barbarous. Perhaps this is a good thing, lest men devote all their time and energy to wreaking war and destruction. I do not know. Death in battle is better than death in servitude. How else can a warrior take his place at Woden's table in Valhalla?"

Ceolwulf noticed the priest's look of disgust.

"I cannot say anything about your comrade's sad plight or that of this woman's. I can only tell you truthfully it was not at my hand nor the hand of any who I commanded that such tragedy befell you and yours." Ceolwulf looked hard at the priest and then turned his gaze to Lydia. She had not understood much of what he had said but instinctively knew she was being talked about. In the context of conversation between these two men, she could guess what was being said about her. Lydia blushed.

"Even in your darkest hour, my lady...was it not a warrior...who came to your rescue and saved you?" Ceolwulf moved closer to Lydia, bending forward he kissed her lightly on the forehead. "My lady...remember my people came here many years ago at the behest of your own king. He hired us to fight your battles and to keep your lands safe. When he refused payment, we had to act and do what we had to do to obtain what was rightfully owed to us. I would not have harm come to you, never would I wish harm on such a beautiful woman. I owe you a debt of gratitude for my recovery and my safety. I thank you my lady." He kissed her again this time on the cheek.

Father Bedwini gulped down some ale. He was parched after translating all Ceolwulf had said. The Father thought Ceolwulf to be more complicated than he had first credited. Certainly, he seemed interested enough in Lydia. Of course, that was only natural, since it was she, who had spent the most time with the warrior, nursing the big man back to health. There was something in the way the warrior spoke his words to the woman that made the Holy Father believe there was something more, something of a romantic nature in his words. Strange that he could not determine what the warrior was feeling when he was told of the tragedies his people had caused in the land. The big man had not flinched or shown any sign of compassion or empathy upon hearing those sad tales. Yet, here was a hint of feeling being demonstrated freely toward the woman Lydia. He is a complicated man, thought the priest.

Chapter 12

The morning came all too soon. Dyfyr and Llew were in the hall gulping ale and eating bread and gravy left over from the night before. The fires had burned out and a girl was scurrying about trying desperately to rekindle the main hearth fire. It was morning but only barely so. The thin sliver of daylight was only just beginning to glow a dull red, it would be hours yet before the sun warmed the cold winter air. Dyfyr and Llew checked their equipment between taking bites from their loaves of bread.

Two men of Caerwyn stood patiently by the doorway. They had already broken their fast and were waiting for their orders. They were wearing their bright coloured yellow and black chequered woollen cloaks for warmth. Over their shoulders were slung long yew bows for protection, along with their knives, swords, and quivers of arrows. Their breath fogged in the cold. They had brought Ceolwulf to the hall, fed and clothed him and were ready to get the day started. The priest and Lydia entered the hall. They had being praying together outside with the priest's small entourage. Llew walked over to Lydia and kissed her lightly on the cheek. Ceolwulf watched keenly and the priest made note of Ceolwulf's interest. A young boy came into the hall to tell the men that the horses were packed. The time had come for the group to start on their journey into the Great Forest. As warriors grabbed their gear, Ceolwulf could not help feeling naked at being unarmed. The priest told the big man in his native tongue that Dyfyr would return his axe when they freed him three days hence.

The Father was nervous, he had been ordered to accompany the men so that there would be no misunderstandings due to language on their adventure. Llew walked over to Lydia standing by the hearth fire that had finally caught flame and promised to throw heat into the room. He put his hands on her shoulders and kissed her gently, on the cheek again. Lydia smiled. Ceolwulf looked up, noted the kiss, and then frowned noticing the fire was now lit and the men had to leave its promised warmth. The priest made the sign of the Cross in the air as he turned to follow the men, the prisoner, Dyfyr and Llew out the door.

After the warriors had left and the chores in the hall were completed, Lydia decided to go back to her hut. Nothing needed doing right away and she still felt weary from her ordeal. It was only just after daybreak and a short nap would be just the thing she needed.

Lydia's dreams took her back to the time she was captured by the Sacsonaidd. They were troubling dreams full of terror and pain. Looking after Ceolwulf had brought back a flood of memories and conflicting feelings. At first, she thought of only the welfare of the captured man. She could not stand idly by and let another person be wantonly mistreated. It was contrary to her religious beliefs and an affront to her common decency. Yet, when Owain asked her to talk to the prisoner and learn what she could from him, she had felt a loathing at being so close to the Sacsonaidd. Lydia had tried over the years to completely forget her time in captivity. Troubling dreams from time to time plagued her and she was never able to cast off the melancholy that clung about her like a shroud.

She had difficulty understanding the Sacsonaidd despite all the time spent nursing him to health. Now that he was gone, Lydia remained conflicted in her feelings. One thought in particular kept running around in her mind. Ceolwulf had said that it was a warrior, who had saved her from her attacker, had kept her safe for those many months of captivity and drudgery in his Great Hall. In truth, that man, that warrior, had saved her and the treatment she had received at his hall was no different than that of the other Sacsonaidd women living there. Lydia had never thought of that before. The kisses Ceolwulf had given her were still fresh in her memory. Lydia felt a strange tingling, an odd stirring in her. She had hated the killing last night, the brutality and the swiftness in which death was dealt. Part of her could not help admiring the skill and courage of the big man. She wondered if she would ever see Ceolwulf again. The tingling continued.

Meanwhile life in Caerwyn was returning to normal after the excitement of the last few days. Each day was warmer than the last. This day was already warmer than the day when the men had left for the Great Forest. That had only been two days ago. Surely, this meant the time for planting could not be many weeks away. Tools were repaired and sharpened and roofs were being thatched. Owain had instructed men to go hunting for a deer; if the priest and his lot could find a deer, then the men of Caerwyn could as well. Math and Enid were seen throughout the village and it seemed they were never apart from each other. It was heart warming to see Enid happy. She had blossomed with the attention and kindness shown her by Math. All of Caerwyn took great delight in the couple's happiness and contrary to Math's fears, not one word was said against him.

To many in the village, Math was reckoned as a hero for saving his friends from a deadly and vicious traitor and bringing Enid to the happiness she deserved. The two of them were the talk of the village.

Owain had stopped by the dafarn for a quick drink and to check on the owner Geraint. Owain saw that the men had stacked their weapons neatly by the door of the dafarn as he had ordered. There had been some complaining by the men about the new rule, for they did not like having to give up their swords and knives. Edern ordered one of his men to take charge of the dafarn's peace. Once it became known that Edern's man regularly patrolled the dafarn, complaints and arguments over the new rule ceased. No one wished to challenge Edern in the discharge of his duty to his liege.

Owain was surprised to learn that Rhys was going to be a father... again. Rhys was talking rapidly and to any, who would listen, telling them all how happy he was about the new arrival to be. He certainly beamed from ear to ear, but whether that was from happiness at the prospect of again being a father, or from the drinks he had been given in celebration of the news, Owain was not sure. The men were glad to see Owain amongst them. Things had been very tense the last few days and it comforted the men to see Owain as one of them, drinking and celebrating with Rhys.

Owain continued his rounds, stopping to talk to the villagers as they went about their work. Edern and Cai supervised their warriors mending their equipment, sharpening their blades, and practicing their martial skills. Horses were being groomed, exercised and fed. Owain talked with his captains and accepted a mug of ale or two from them as they discussed possible strategies and plans. Owain enjoyed the walk around the village; his spirits were lifted. He could sense that the mood in the village had been raised. The sun had warmed the day and the afternoon was fast waning. Owain returned to his hall.

"Well, husband, I see you have made the rounds," said the Lady Gwenhwyfar. "And from the smell of you I can guess where you have spent most of the afternoon!"

"Nonsense, my love, I have only drank that which was given me in celebration." Owain beamed sure he was that his wife had not yet heard the news of Rhys's impending fatherhood.

"Celebration? Oh, you must have heard that Katryn is going to have another baby! If I am any judge of these things I would say it is to be a boy!"

Owain nearly fell over as he leaned against a wooden fence post. It was not from drink that he lost his balance, Owain rarely allowed himself to get that intoxicated and never would he do so walking alone in the middle of the day. No, it was the shock that his wife seemed to know everything before he did and try as he might he had yet to give her news of something she had not already heard.

"Come cariad," she said laughingly, "allow me to help you home, you poor man. Did you know that the children are out and the servants are all busy in the village?"

"No, I did not know that, but then is there anything I could know that you would not already have knowledge of? I think not!" Owain managed to note the twinkle in his wife's eye as he linked arms with her.

It was late the next morning, when Owain finally got out of bed. Gwenhwyfar had been up for hours, seeing to things and making sure her children were busy with their chores. She noted to herself how much like a young woman her daughter was becoming and thought again of her husband's agreement with Dyfyr's son Elidir. They made a handsome couple, daydreamed the Lady. The Goddess Dôn was wise to inspire the couple to love. Gwenhwyfar was thinking of how happy she was and what a splendid wedding day feast she could make for her daughter. As the happy thoughts skipped through Gwenhwyfar's mind, she dropped a flask she had been cleaning. The flask slipped from her hands. Gwenhwyfar saw it as it happened, almost as though the flask were defying gravity and slowly floating to the stone flagged floor. Owain appeared at the door and called her name. The flask hit the stone floor at that precise moment and shattered into thousands of pieces. Gwenhwyfar stood stock-still, white with fear and shaking uncontrollably.

"Cariad, what..."

"War....war...."

"Cariad what are you saying?"

"War, husband, it will be war." Her eyes were glazed over and the look of her frightened Owain through to the bone. He shook her trying to break whatever power had taken possession of his beautiful wife. As Owain stood shaking his wife, a voice cried out from downstairs. It was Cai.

"What is the matter?" Owain barked angrily as he turned from his wife to confront his foster brother.

"There's been an ambush. Our men who were escorting the Sacsonaidd have been attacked! Two men were killed and one of them was Llew. The wounded are on the way back and should be here in Caerwyn before nightfall." Cai looked worried.

"What of him, the Sacsonaidd? Is he dead or did he have a hand in this?" Fear and anger gripped at Owain. It was his decision to allow the ritual that had ultimately released the Sacsonaidd. Had he been wrong? Was he, Owain, responsible for the deaths of his men?

"I don't know. We won't know anything until the patrol returns with the survivors. Owain, I think we had best prepare for an attack."

Owain looked at his wife who had regained her composure. He was struck with awe. How was it that she could have known such a thing as this would happen? There must be some natural explanation, his mind told him. Yet, Gwenhwyfar now stood with such a calm and serene look about her as though she knew all along the outcome of the future.

By late afternoon, word had spread through the village of what had happened. Defences were being built while barriers, were strengthened and all available men were armed and ready. The men and women of Caerwyn worked tirelessly throughout the early evening. Watch fires burned brightly on the perimeter surrounding the village casting a yellow hue over everything. Shadows danced and writhed on the wattle and daub walls of the village huts. Food was kept warm so tired men and boys could be given nourishment. Fear hung in the air like a mist settling over the people of Caerwyn. Owain was everywhere seeing to defences, ensuring the fires were lit, the men armed, water stored in case of fire. As the sun slowly sunk in the sky, a shout rang out from one of the sentries. There was movement in the forest edge. Men rushed to their posts, it had to be the patrol returning, no one else could come through the forest everyone knew that. Fear thickened and settled on the villagers.

A signal! Small and weak but someone was waving a piece of cloth. Just at the tree line, two warriors could be seen. The small patrol had found the survivors. Men from the village ran out to help. The wounded were brought directly to Owain and Gwenhwyfar's two-storied dwelling. The hall had already been prepared to accept the injured. The hearth fires were blazing, pallets were arranged as beds, blankets, pelts and cushions ready to give warmth and comfort. Water was boiling, healing herbs arrayed near by and broth simmered in great pots hung over the fire. The whole hall was warm and well lit. Lydia was there, supervising other women including Gwyneth all ready to heal the broken bodies of brave men.

Owain gasped when he saw his friend the dour Dyfyr. The poor old warrior's chest had been slashed open to the bone. The tight drawn look on his face was evidence his friend was in great pain.

"Will he survive?" Owain whispered to Lydia as she instructed the women to remove the man's clothing and fetch the boiling water, bandages and clean cloths. She pushed Owain unceremoniously out of the way without answering. She busied herself with cleaning the terrible wound in the old warrior's chest. His tunic and breeches were soaked. Dyfyr was nearly drained of his blood and the poor man's colour was white as the snow. No one had told her yet of Llew's fate.

Owain left her to her work realising any intrusion on his part might delay the care being given his most trusted friend. He went to the other casualty and gazed down on the figure of the Father Bedwini.

The Father's leg had been rent open by a sword. He was in severe pain, screaming, and cursing, which meant he was very much alive. The priest screamed first in Cymraeg, then in Latin and sometimes even in Sacsoneg.

"Cachu....cachu...uffern dân......meum crus nocet!......scitan.... scitan......!"

The barrage of language was heady indeed and had the circumstances been otherwise, it would have been quite humorous to hear the priest use such a mix of expletives. A village woman was tending to his gaping wound, cleaning it with hot water and clean rags. There was much blood. Another woman worked feverishly with needle and thread trying to close the torn flesh. Lydia had overseen the boiling of thread and needles and made sure only clean cloths were being used. She could not remember where she had learned this. Owain ordered some ale and he was soon holding the priest's head helping him gulp down the offered drink.

He looked over at the men who had brought the wounded in and demanded information. He was told there was no sign of Ceolwulf. Owain wondered if this attack had been the work of other barbarian Sacsonaidd trying to rescue Ceolwulf. The irony struck him that the reason for his men being in the forest was to free the barbarian. Owain had to tell the priest to speak Cymraeg for he had slipped into sacsoneg again.

"Where is the Sacsonaidd? Was this the work of his men? Are there more of the bastards hiding in the forest?" Owain peppered the poor Father with questions one after the other not allowing the priest to answer one before he asked another. Gwenhwyfar came over to her husband and put her hand gently on his shoulder. Owain looked up and realised what he had been doing. He took a big breath and held another cup of ale for the priest.

"No... Owain! It was not the Sacsonaidd or any of his men! It was another tribe! It was Cymry! Of that I am sure.... he saved my life... aaahhhh.... yes.... the man whose people I hold responsible for the massacre of my Abbot.... owwww.... yes, him, he saved my life..." The poor priest passed out from the pain.

Owain hurried back to the bedside of his friend Dyfyr. The women looked frightened. Owain looked down at his friend. It was not good. He could see his friend was at his end. Gwenhwyfar was by her husband's side, she could see the pain and anguish that washed over him. She could also plainly see that poor Dyfyr was not long for this world. He was cut to the bone, his insides visible, and his lungs unable to fill with air. The once proud and dangerous warrior lay gasping for air like a landed fish. Finally, mercifully, the gasping stopped.

"Call me when the priest wakes up," Owain said curtly to the guard in charge. Turning to Gwyn who had just careened into the hall he barked, "Get me your brother and the rest of the men and meet me here quickly!"

"But Owain...."

"NOW! Do it, now!" No one had ever before heard Owain speak in such a manner or with such rage. The Christians in the hall crossed themselves while the rest just stared open mouthed.

The Dark Times had descended upon them.

Owain went to where young Elidir had been standing post. He was cold, tired, and afraid but he had marshalled his men and the area was secure. Owain watched as his friend's son talked to his men encouraging them, keeping them focused. He was a man and a good warrior. Elidir looked up and noticed Owain staring at him. The leader made his way to the young warrior and hugged him hard. Holding him then at arm's length Owain looked deep into Elidir's eyes and told the young man of his father's death. Elidir bore up well under the news though he was clearly shaken. Owain told what he believed to be his future son-in-law that he was now responsible for Owain's family and that he Owain was counting on him to discharge his duties well. Elidir nodded solemnly.

"Your father was like an older brother to me. I shall miss him greatly. I am very happy that his son will soon be part of my own family and I have every confidence in you."

Elidir nodded again looking up into Owain's face.

"All things right, and proper." He thrust his hand into Owain's and though tears now streamed down his young face, he remained strong and confident, every bit the hardened warrior he would need to be very soon.

The war leader of Caerwyn made his way back to his hall. He waited for Edern. The Lady Gwenhwyfar looked for her husband. He had gone to their hut and she found him upstairs sitting on a stool with his head in his hands. She tried to comfort him. Standing over her husband, she grasped his head in her hands and held it tightly to her bosom.

"He was a dear friend, cariad, a very dear friend. I should never have sent him. I should have kept him here at my side in Caerwyn. The man was getting on in years and he had done more than his share of duty."

"Yes, husband, he was getting on in years as you say, and he knew it. Take some comfort from knowing he would have wanted to die as a soldier, a warrior, in your service, tall and proud. He would not wish to have spent his last days as an old man of no use to anyone simply giving advice to those who did the deeds he no longer could."

"How will I honour him?"

"The best way that you can my husband, the best way you can."

Gwenhwyfar had already sent a servant to prepare Owain's battle gear and provisions. She could hear the arrival of Cai, Gwyn, Edern and the rest of her husband's trusted warriors. Gwenhwyfar moved away and came back with a flask of ale and some food for her man. Her movements seemed subdued as though she carried some great weight.

Gwenhwyfar had seen that Lydia learned of Llew's death. She had hugged and consoled her, but Lydia was strong and through her tears, she pushed gently away from Gwenhwyfar and turned to continue her duties ministering to the injured. Gwenhwyfar went next to tell poor Math about his dear friend Llew. The man was dumbstruck by the horrible news. Tears streamed soundlessly down his cheeks as he listened to Gwenhwyfar recount what Tad Bedwini had told her and Owain of Llew's last moments.

Llew had fought valiantly. He had killed many of the attackers helping the Sacsonaidd and saving Father Bedwini's life. Dyfyr had already killed two men when a sword cut wielded by a younger warrior felled him. A spear had found its mark and Llew bled heavily from the wound it made in his chest. The Sacsonaidd fought with him side by side and when Llew gave out, the Sacsonaidd killed the last attacker. His axe stroke cleaved a head from the body saving the priest from a lethal sword thrust. Then it was over.

The attackers disappeared. Ceolwulf did what he could for Llew, but it was too late he had died. Turning his attention to the Father, he managed to wrap the priest's leg. Dyfyr was also wrapped in cloth and what little Ceolwulf was able to do no doubt prolonged the old man's life at least until he could die in his own village amongst his beloved people. Then the strange barbarian, the Sacsonaidd from the Southeast, disappeared into the falling snow.

It was heart wrenching to see Math so distraught. Yet, it warmed Gwenhwyfar's heart to see Enid so attentive and lovingly supportive of her man. Truly the two of them belonged together and Gwenhwyfar knew they would need each other's strength to survive what life would now bring to them. Gwenhwyfar discretely left their hut as Math began to breakdown, held firmly in Enid's strong embrace. He clutched her like a drowning man.

Enid remained silent but her grip on Math remained tight. Gradually she let go of him and busied herself with preparing Math his favourite drink of cider and she placed some food on a plate for him. Poor Math was so bereaved he could neither eat nor drink, he just sat there in his chair staring. Enid stood quietly behind him. Eventually she wrapped both her arms around him and again pulled his head to her bosom. Bending forward she gently kissed Math's cheek and caressed his head. Math tried to say something but nothing escaped his lips other than a dry cracked sound. Enid shushed him and held him closer until finally she heard the sobs. They held each other like that for a minute or two.

The warning cry was heard.

It was the signal that Caerwyn was under attack. Math straightened upon hearing the alarm. He kissed Enid and hugged her again. She took notice of the change in his eyes. The sadness was gone replaced with a cold deadly look that frightened her.

"Cariad," she said using the word for love for the first time, "promise me you will be careful." Math's eyes softened for a moment hearing the term of endearment coming from her lips. He kissed her again and then picked up his great bow and went out into the chaos.

"Elidir will be responsible for the safety and well-being of my family." Owain was addressing the men who had gathered to hear his plans and learn their part. They were sitting as their ancestors had done, on hides set on the floor in a circle, a fire in the middle. Their war gear was piled behind them watched over by a retinue of men loyal to each of them.

"He will choose his men. Anwas Adeiniog will be in charge of Caerwyn assisted by Cadyreith ap Saidi and Cadwy ap Geraint. The rest will come with me. Cai will be my second in command and I will be accompanied by the brothers Edern and Gwyn ap Nudd." The men nodded their heads in agreement. None of what Owain had said thus far had surprised them but they were anxious to know more about the actual plan.

"So Owain, do we know which tribe attacked and when do we hunt them down...."

"No, we must prepare Caerwyn for the attack. Obviously, that is what they will do now. They think they have cut off our retreat by hiding in the Great Forest...."

"...that would be something of an accomplishment...."

"They must have had help from someone who knows the woods...."

Owain raised his voice over his men.

"Listen..."he said, "From what I have learned from Tad Bedwini, they were attacked by men related to the Essylwg. The Sacsonaidd had nothing to do with the attack. He saved the priest's life and fought gallantly with Dyfyr and Llew. It saddens me to know we have lost our dear friend Dyfyr as well as a good man like Llew. I will mount an all out attack at first light. We will move in force against these bastards and finding them we will kill them all!"

Owain quietly revealed his plan. The tumult of voices caused by the passionate dissent of his men was almost painful to the ears. Not a single man amongst them agreed to the plan as Owain had outlined it and they were angrily letting him know that they were opposed to his idea. The smile on Owain's face grew wider until he could no longer contain himself but burst into laughter. It was a cold sounding laugh!

Everywhere villagers prepared for an attack. Working hard, the village's men, women and children, doused their thatched roofs with water, soaked fence posts and palisades. Strongmen sank sharpened wooden staves into the half-frozen earth to hinder and impale their enemy. Spears, swords, and shields along with sharpened scythes and anything else that could be used as weapons were piled ready to use. Archers were strategically placed throughout the village. The women had plenty of bandages and Lydia was supervising the preparation of healing herbs. Young Gwyneth worked side by side with the women. Gwenhwyfar had again visited the grievously injured Father Bedwini.

She had helped where she could and then moved about the village stopping to assist and working side by side with her daughter and Lydia. She was a welcome and calming sight to both Pagan and Christian villagers alike. People were afraid but there was no panic to be seen.

Owain and his family gathered around the hearth fire of their hut. Ale and food were readied for them and they ate a hasty supper. Owain hugged his children and ignored the embarrassed discomfort that such a show of affection caused his young son. He saw a tear in his daughter's eye and at the sight of it; he thought his heart might break. Owain tried to speak but could not so he feigned clearing his throat. Gwenhwyfar saw her husband struggling with his emotions and she hugged him tighter still.

"I have a plan," he said finally his voice shaking with constrained emotion. "I think it is a good plan and that it will save the day. It requires that I be absent from you much longer than any of us would expect. It is my duty and as a man I must do what it is my duty to do."

"Cynglas," he continued as best he could, "I am counting on you to safeguard your mother and your sister." He looked hard at his young son his worry nearly breaking through at thrusting so great a responsibility onto him at such a young age. The danger that threatened his family was nearly more than Owain could bear. He swallowed hard.

"I want you to listen well to Elidir. He is soon to be part of this family, I think." Owain looked at his beautiful daughter who was now weeping silently in her mother's arms.

"He is a good man, as good a man as his brave father and that statement I do not make lightly, so you mind his word." Little Cynglas nodded firmly. The lad was becoming a warrior and now he had to learn to take orders from his leader.

"I won't let you down father." The little warrior said in a clear voice, his chin ever so slightly quivering. Owain quickly hugged them all to mask his own tears and then with a kiss on the cheek to each, he was gone.

It was just before dawn that the first blazing arrow struck the fence. It was followed by a barrage of flaming arrows that lit up the still darkened sky casting shadows of frantic men and women hurrying to put out the flames. The din rose, as the warrior's cries grew closer. Children began wailing, the fierce hounds of Caerwyn barked angrily and the village's men folk began banging on their shields with their swords and spears. It was a sound reminiscent of ages past, long before the invasion of the Romans, when warring tribal chiefs fought each other for power and land.

The enemy watched the men of Caerwyn ride behind Owain their leader and disappear into the Great Forest. Then they attacked! The still faint light added to their advantage. The Essylwg warriors knew that Owain's bravery and pride would compel him to retaliate for the death of his men. It was what they had counted on as they watched him charge into the Great Forest after the archers. They knew that his plan would be to use the depths of the Forest against them. Which is why their main force had remained hidden. The Essylwg hoped Owain's pride would be his downfall.

The leader of the Essylwg turned to the thin man at his right.

"Your knowledge of the Great Forest and the nature of the man Owain has proven valuable, Gronw. Even without the Sacsonaidd and his tribe we will have victory this day!"

"Yes, the secrets of the Great Forest that I have shared with you will give your men the advantage," Gronw sat in his saddle astride his war pony, a peculiarly decorative spear in his hand.

"I too, am sure we will have victory. You just remember that while this may gain you the kingship it is I who will rule Caerwyn!"

"And you remember," spat the Essylwg leader, "that you will owe allegiance to me or I will not only take this village, but your life as well!"

The barrage of flaming arrows abated. The attacking force moved toward Caerwyn. The Essylwg tribesmen rode war ponies, running along each side of the ponies were fleet-footed warriors keeping a quick pace by holding onto the foot straps of the rider. In their free hand, they held a spear. The first wave had just reached the defences of the village and they were met with a hard fight. As the running Essylwg warriors faltered a second wave of their tribesmen rushed forward.

Inside the village of Caerwyn, men were running back and forth slashing with swords, stabbing with spears, and using scythes and farm implements to cut down the ranks of the invaders. Women and old men were trying valiantly to put out the fires started by the barrages of flaming arrows.

Hounds were let loose and they sprang at the invading warriors ripping and slashing with their powerful jaws. The ancient hunting hounds of Briton had long been revered even in Roman times. The hounds of Caerwyn were their blood descendants. Two of the huge beasts cornered an Essylwg warrior who had breeched the wooden palisade. One of the hellhounds ripped into his thigh. As the screaming warrior raised his sword to kill the beast, another leapt at his throat. The two hounds tore the Essylwg to bloody pieces.

Math was perched on a roof near the fence line, his now famous bow bent, its bowstring pulled taut and an arrow nocked and aimed. With him, he had three spears and an old Roman short sword. His bowstring sang as he fired one after another of his deadly arrows. Every one of Math's shots found its mark. A villager had given Math two full quivers of arrows and Math had another two by his feet. The villagers all knew that Math had never missed what he notched his arrow against in all of his life.

Elidir ordered his two best men to guard Gwenhwyfar and Gwyneth. They were housed not in their own hut but one close to the outskirts of the village. Elidir selected the hut because it would be the least suspected place to find the Lady and her daughter. It also provided a quick escape should the defences of Caerwyn fail and the village become overrun. After seeing them safely hidden, Elidir took to the roof of another hut in the same manner as Math and with as many arrows. Elidir was also a keen shot with the long bow but his real talent lay in his swordsmanship. A long well balanced and deadly blade was strapped on his back. From the thatched roof, Elidir could see that the defences of Caerwyn were holding. Anwas had done a brilliant job organising the men. It was then he saw the second wave of Essylwg attackers.

Cynglas was not with his mother. Instead, he ran to help the old men keep the fires at bay by fetching heavy buckets of water. He was armed and prepared to fight and an old Roman short sword swung from his belt. Grimy from the soot of the fires and weighted down with buckets of water the little warrior strained to keep up with the men.

Rhys had taken his family to the dafarn. The drinking establishment was in the centre of Caerwyn and was relatively safe. Wounded warriors would be brought there as well as to the hall of Owain. Katryn and her children were ready to help tend the injured. Rhys had no time to mourn his friend Llew since Katryn had told him the grim news. Rhys had stood there with his mouth agape as all his humour left him. The sight of that alone was enough to bring Katryn to tears. Rhys silently and methodically armed himself and joined the fray along with Derfel and Dyfrig just as the invaders breeched the fence. Rhys was slashing and hacking with his long sword. An Essylwg warrior clambered through the wooden fencing and swung his sword at Rhys. He missed. Rhys's sword slashed through the man's right clavicle and bit straight through his chest.

In the flickering firelight, Rhys' face devoid of any human emotion resembled a demon. He spun, expertly avoiding another slashing Essylwg blade. His own sword rang as he parried yet another strike before he counter-spun and drove his sword point through the heart of the invader. Stuck, his blade buried in the chest of the man he had just killed, Rhys brought his foot up and kicked the dead body from his sword. Rhys's face now registered rage. Blind rage. He slashed, thrust, and hacked as the dead piled up at his feet.

A third wave of attacking Essylwg warriors were preparing to shore up the assault the second wave had begun. A gap had opened in Caerwyn's defences under the relentless attack of the invaders. The Essylwg leader turned to Gronw and laughed. His forces rushed to press their advantage over the weakened villagers. He was certain of victory now!

Chapter 13

The Essylwg warriors were attacking in force at the weakened defences of the village. Bloodlust was up as battle sounds rang in their ears and blood frenzy coursed through their veins. It would only be a matter of time before the village was theirs! It sounded like thunder at first. Low and rumbling, the sound rose from the cold earth instead of the dark sky. It was not thunder. The Essylwg tribesmen did not heed the "thunder." The dim light of the grey dawn tried in vain to cut through the black smoke of the burning village. The attackers at the back of the Essylwg ranks heard the rumble. Some turned to the sky, others turned to peer through the battle haze. Movement. That was all the faint dawn light would reveal. More rumbling was felt as well as heard, closer this time and louder. A shout rang out. It was not a battle cry; it was fear. The sound of chaotic movement was unmistakable now. The attackers faltered. Confusion swept through the Essylwg warriors. The Caerwyn defenders used the hesitation to their advantage and bolstered their ranks. Panic gripped the attacking Essylwg and the rear ranks broke and ran. It was too late.

A line of riders broke through the smoke and haze of the dimly lit morning. The scene was surreal as cold mist, smoke from burning thatched roofs, and wood fences swirled about frightened men. Horses broke through the battle haze at the gallop snorting early morning mist through their nostrils. The huge beasts resembled Otherworld demons as they bore down on the attackers. The "thunder" was deafening, nearly drowning out the screams of those men who were trampled down under the onslaught of horseflesh and iron.

The third wave of Essylwg warriors faltered. They were in complete disarray and trampled their own men trying to escape the hooves of the charging Caerwyn cavalry. As they ran for their lives a second line of cavalry thundered at the Essylwg invaders from their right flank. They were trapped. They were being trampled by the beasts and hacked to pieces by Owain's warriors.

Escaping Essylwg warriors ran haphazardly back the way they came and towards the open ground of the meadow. They ran unknowingly towards the line of Owain's archers. Terrifying sounds of screaming men, the throaty twang of the mighty yew bows, the thundering hooves of horses and the ring of steel on steel, made a dizzying cacophony of sound. The archers let loose several carefully aimed volleys of deadly arrows calculated to do the most carnage and create the most confusion. Then the men re-slung their long bows across their backs and drew swords and spears as they methodically moved forward.

"Hold the line!" was the order as the line of Owain's warriors slashed and stabbed at the terrified Essylwg tribesmen, pushing them back toward the crushing hooves of the Caerwyn cavalry.

The cavalry began to pull back, for they were now in danger of trampling their own men. The fighting was brutal and gruesome, blood mixed and churned with the earth creating a grotesque mud. Owain swung his sword cutting open an Essylwg warrior intent on impaling him with his spear. The sudden evasive move toppled Owain from his mount and he landed with a thud in the bloody mud. He wheeled and dodged a sword thrust coming from his right. Spinning and hacking, Owain was filled with a rage that lent strength to his sword arm and cold determination to his will. Essylwg warriors fell dead at his feet as the leader of Caerwyn fought for the survival of his family.

A shadowy figure came out of the battle haze, straight at Owain's back. Owain was dodging a spear thrust from the front and slashing at a sword-wielding warrior from his left. Both men died from the blade of Owain's long sword just as the haft of a spear caught him in the middle of his back. He had caught the movement of the spear wielding Essylwg warrior and had managed to twist away from the deadly spearhead. The blow from the spear haft drove the air from his lungs and dropped Owain to his knees gasping for air. Through the great din of battle Owain recognised the voice.

"Now, master Owain, you will die as you should have done all those years ago." It was the voice of Gronw.

A searing pain bit deeply into Owain's shoulder as he tried to roll away from the voice. The spear was viciously pulled out of his body and Owain heard himself scream. Owain was on his back gasping for air and reeling from the pain of the spear thrust. He looked into the blazing eyes of his enemy.

"Gronw..." gasped Owain, "Gronw.... why...why betray your own..."

"You are not "*my own*," Owain!" His eyes burned with hatred and spittle flew from his lips as he spoke.

"You were never of our village and yet you stole from me what was rightfully to have been mine! You took from me what was mine and then you made me a laughing stock! You humiliated me! You sanctimonious, arrogant bastard!"

"What are you talking about," gasped Owain desperately trying to keep away from Gronw's spear tip, "what was it I stole from you?"

"GWENHWYFAR!" Gronw screamed. "You stole Gwenhwyfar from me! She should have been mine, not yours! You had no right to her, you don't even belong among us!" Saliva was frothing from Gronw's lips as he screamed aloud for the first time what had so long been his heart's desire.

"Now, she will be mine this day!" Gronw raised his arms clutching his curiously decorated spear. The magical writings and symbols written along the spear's shaft glinted in the new day's light. The deadly weapon was thrust toward its target.

Owain kicked out hard. His foot smashed into Gronw's knee buckling it and causing him to fall. As quick as his pain would allow, Owain scrambled to his knees. He pulled a knife from his belt and slashed wildly in front of him. Gronw was struggling to get to his feet; his leg was damaged but not broken. Gronw clutched his decorated spear. He thrust the weapon at Owain, to keep him at bay and give himself time to stand. Owain, despite his pain was on his feet, crouched low with his knife barely visible in his hand. Dodging the thrust made by Gronw, Owain leaped forward. Gronw, expecting Owain to keep retreating, was taken by surprise. Owain's knife entered Gronw's right side between his ribs, causing him to gasp and fall to his knees. The strangely decorated spear fell harmlessly to the mud.

Owain quickly withdrew his knife and slashed the blade upwards cutting the inside of Gronw's right biceps, severing the artery. Owain continued his fluid motion and plunged the knife into Gronw's back. Now, grabbing Gronw around the neck from behind, Owain began to cut his enemy's throat.

A strong arm firmly grabbed Owain's knife hand. Struggle though he might Owain's waning strength could not free his hand from the grasp. Through the bloodlust pounding in his ears, Owain heard his name being called. Faintly at first, growing as the blood fever subsided. Looking up, Owain saw Cai a look of concern and disgust on his face.

"Enough! Owain, enough, the man is dead! We have won!"

The early morning sun was straining to burn through the smoke of battle that lay thick over the village of Caerwyn. Owain stared without seeing. His men were re-forming and Edern was already gathering a band of warriors to chase down the few Essylwg who had escaped. The rest slowly gathered around Owain, their leader.

Bloodied, mud splattered and wounded, Owain stood and forced his mind to make sense of the scene. All around him were dead men. His warriors were starting to yell and cheer in victory. The pain in Owain's shoulder had not hit him yet. He was still in shock. One of his men saw that there were many dead Essylwg at Owain's feet. There must have been a dozen corpses piled where the leader of Caerwyn was standing. Another of his men quipped that Owain had fought like an enraged bear. It was a boastful comment. Warriors often speak bravely after battle. The mood of the battered and tired fighting men was fast turning into a celebration of their victory. The numbing fatigue of battle, the strain of the all night preparation, the cold, the hunger and the pain of the wounded slowly gave way to shouts of victory. They gathered round their war leader. Another of the men commented on the many dead Essylwg at Owain's feet. Someone else said Owain fought like a bear. The comment was repeated. It rippled amongst the men that their leader fought with bear-like ferocity. A lone warrior, eager to be heard by his compatriots, began yelling about Owain's prowess as a fighter. A few of the Pagan warriors began banging their spears on their shields and chanting. They chanted a word in the old Briton tongue.

"Art gwr, Art gwr!" It meant "Man of the Bear." In Cymraeg, the word was *"Arthgwr"* and sounded like "Arth-gur." It was an old title and a common one, used by military men to describe the valour and ferocity of a deadly fighting man. The Caerwyn warriors began chanting and banging their shields, the joy of winning a hard earned and bloody battle swept over them. They picked up their wounded leader and headed to his hall. The chant was deafening.

"Arthgwr! Arthgwr! Arthgwr!"

Gwenhwyfar's concern for her husband did not show on her beautiful face. She knew Owain would survive the wound in his shoulder. Lydia was already cleaning out the muck and filth from the hole the spear tip had made in Owain's right shoulder. The spear tip had not hit any major arteries and it had shattered no bones nor cut any ligaments or tendons. Owain had been lucky. Lydia finished the thorough cleaning and dressed the wound under the supervision of Gwenhwyfar. She did not show her concern for her husband, but she felt it nevertheless.

Cai had told Gwenhwyfar of the strange decorative spear that Gronw had used as a weapon. Gwenhwyfar had instinctively known it was designed as a magical tool with one purpose, to kill her husband. Gronw had wished to guarantee Owain's death because the object of his hatred of Owain was his obsession with her!

To be the object of lust for such a vile creature as Gronw sickened Gwenhwyfar. She had known Gronw all his life. She knew his family, they were crafty and kept to themselves, but they were not evil. She wondered what had poisoned Gronw's mind so that he would betray his own village. The Lady Gwenhwyfar shuddered under her thick wool tunic.

It had been hours since the end of the battle for Caerwyn. Owain had no fever and the wound was cleaned and dressed. There were no complications. Gronw must have made a mistake in copying the design in the strange writing on the shaft. In any case, Gwenhwyfar was certain Gronw had failed and that her husband would live. She thanked the Goddess Dôn for her divine intervention. Gwenhwyfar did this silently, keeping the prayer to herself, deciding not to tell her husband the meaning of Gronw's decorative spear.

Owain and Gwenhwyfar's hut was full to the brim with revellers. The whole village was celebrating and there was a momentary lull in the work of rebuilding. All the fires had been put out. The dafarn had survived. There were only two huts in the village that had been destroyed. Other than that, a few places in the wooden palisade and some minor storage huts had been damaged in the attack. One elder had died in the raid and there were several people injured, but no other villagers had been killed. Prayers were said to the Christian God and to the Mother Goddess; the people of Caerwyn were grateful.

The dafarn was full. Gwenhwyfar and Owain's two-storied hut and hall were full and still people crowded in. Food, ale, and cider were passed from one to the other as villagers bolstered their spirits in an impromptu celebration. Songs of victory and tales of heroism were being raucously sung by drunken warriors. The sun was close to setting now as the day passed into night. And what a day it had been!

Chants of "Arthgwr! Arthgwr! Arthgwr!" started up and did not abate until Owain managed to stand and was seen by the villagers. Then the din rose even louder. Spears and swords were banged on shields, ram horn flutes were sounded, and a great cheer rose giving way again to the chant.

An old man standing on a table, began speaking of the battle and the prowess of Owain. He regaled the crowd as those around him quieted down to listen to the storyteller. With his long white hair swirling around him, the old man spoke with passion of the bear-like ferocity of his leader. Stamping a spear shaft on the wooden table, alive with passion, the elder continued his story of the "nine hundred" enemy dead that lay at Owain's feet. It was in this, the embellishing style, of the Old Ways that the old grandfather recited his tale of battle. His voice was loud and melodic, his passion contagious, as he banged the spear haft in time to his cadence. His white beard bristled and blue tattoos were visible on his still muscular arms. He had captivated the hall with his telling. He paused for dramatic effect and to take a much needed gulp from his tankard. Ale dripped from his beard as he became a teacher and educated his people of the importance of the name, "Arthgwr."

"Yes, "Arthgwr," it means "Bear Man" and describes a fierce warrior! What's more," he said between generous gulps of ale, "if you young ones knew your own heritage, you would understand that in Old Times, many of the tribes worshipped as Bear cults." The Christian villagers, though fascinated by the story and the telling of Owain's brave tales, crossed themselves when they heard talk of animal gods and goddesses.

"Yes, there was.... hmmmm.... *Dea Artio*, the "Bear Goddess," and.... er.... *Artgenos,* whose name meant "Son of the Bear." Even in the new tongue "Arthgwr" means Bear Man! Yes, my friends, these gods and goddesses were worshipped deep in our Great Forest! These names of gods were always given to warriors and heroes whose prowess on the field of battle was terrible to behold! Fierce as a rampaging bear!"

There was a general murmur of approval for Owain and the chant, "Arthgwr! Arthgwr! Arthgwr!", broke out again. Laughter erupted as the storyteller, taking a huge gulp of ale, lost his balance and came crashing down to the earthen floor of the hut.

From the makeshift bed in the corner of the hut not far from where the storyteller had fallen, the voice of Tad Bedwini was heard. He had been made comfortable and the ale had deadened his pain and inspired his thoughts. He had been moved by the storyteller and swept away by the history lesson the older man had given.

"Yes, my children," the injured priest began speaking in Cymraeg right from the start for a change, "and the name, *"Arcturus,"* can be seen as the Greek derivative, meaning "Keeper of the Bears." It can also be used to describe the Great Bear, *Ursa Major,* and the Star of the North. Such a name as Arthgwr, indeed, tells of a great fierce warrior-hero hailing from the North and perhaps even from the Great Forest of yours!"

The crowd grew restless as the Good Father added his learned words to the old man's recounting of history. He grew exhausted and searched for his cup of ale drinking thirstily not noticing that his educated speech was beyond the ken of his listeners. Suddenly, he remembered his position in the Church and realised that blasphemous talk of gods and goddesses taking the shape of bears, abounded.

"Glory in Highest to God!" Father Bedwini shouted in Latin. In his state of injury, exhaustion and inebriation propped himself up as best he could. He continued muttering to himself in Latin.

"I am not interested in your silly religious cult! *Confiteor deo omnipotent beate Mariae simper*...I confess to God Almighty to Blessed Mary forever!" He yelled defiantly.

The poor priest fell back on to his pillow, exhausted. The tending women wiped his brow with cool cloths and helped him drink some broth and cool water. Father Bedwini's piety was wasted, lost in the noise of the celebration. Warriors whooped and shields were banged with spears and swords and the chanting started. Owain stood again and with his beautiful wife at his side, he raised his good arm to the cheers of the villagers.

"Arthgwr! Arthgwr! Arthgwr!", rose the chant.

The people began to return to their huts. Neighbour helped neighbour in this time of need and no one was without shelter or food. Guards were posted and sentry fires were re-lit casting a flickering yellow light over the village. It was comforting firelight this time. The night was cold but not as cold as past nights, a cause for hope to the people. Morning would come soon and the job of repairing and fortifying Caerwyn would start in earnest. Now was a time for celebration and celebrate they did, these happy villagers of Caerwyn.

The rising sun burnt off the morning mist and chores had been underway for hours. Caerwyn was bustling with activity. A sense of relief and hope and gratitude cloaked the village. Many Christian villagers had already worshipped, the injured priest managed to give a blessing. Lydia took comfort from having attended the mass and staying to minister to the Father. Roofs were being re-thatched, fences mended and the grounds cleaned up. What needed to be done was being done. Cai had ensured Caerwyn was secure, a patrol of warriors had just returned and reported to him that all was well. Edern was still out tracking the retreating Essylwg and there was no news of his progress or even when he would return. There really was not much for Owain to do for the moment. He ate and drank and had his bandages changed. Of course the villagers still flattered him and this caused him discomfort. Gwenhwyfar saw to it that her husband was kept relaxed and humoured. It was important that he regain the strength of his sword arm.

Orders from Gwenhwyfar to Cai ensured her husband was not disturbed. However, she encouraged Owain to walk about and be seen. She used the pretence that Cai wished to show her husband Caerwyn's defences. Gwenhwyfar was acutely aware just how much the villagers had need of a hero figure for the moment. She knew that the attack was not the war she had predicted to her husband. While she did not yet mention it to him, Gwenhwyfar feared much worse was yet to come.

The people of Caerwyn went about their work joyfully because of the victory Owain had won. The singing and merrymaking soothed everyone's jangled nerves. Shouts of "Arthgwr!" rang out as Owain walked by aided by Cai. A young boy ran up to Owain and handed him a tankard of ale. Cai smiled as Owain drank the offered beer. Though injured and in pain Owain maintained an aura of calm confidence about him as he walked with his foster brother. Cai chuckled, when on more than one occasion, Owain answered to the name "Arthgwr." It seemed natural and Cai understood the villager's need for a larger than life hero. He assumed the role of supporter to his now famous foster brother. That too, seemed natural and Cai did not mind.

As the days since the attack passed, Anwas carried out many of the village duties. Elidir assisted him. The young man had grown since the news of his father's death. He had hardened and it showed in his gaunt face and in the way he carried himself. Young Elidir was always a capable warrior, a captain of Owain's guard, but now he was more. Elidir carried out Anwas's orders with confidence and authority. His ideas and thoughts were listened to by Anwas and conveyed to Owain. The young man was excessively serious and did not suffer fools. The one soft spot in his heart was Gwyneth. His face lit up whenever she was around and it was obvious to all that the young couple was very much in love. Owain smiled when he saw them together. It warmed his heart that his precious daughter had found a good man in young Elidir. He knew his friend Dyfyr, the boy's father, would also smile.

More than a week had passed since the attack before Edern returned with his men. Only a few were injured and none seriously. Cause indeed for another impromptu celebration. During the drinking and singing Edern was amused by the chants of "Arthgwr!" He quickly saw how the new name was a point of pride with the men. It was their rallying cry. Edern reported to "Arthgwr", as Owain was now called, that he and his men had attacked and killed a few retreating Essylwg invaders the first few days. Then he thought it more prudent to hide silently and track the attackers to see if they regrouped with a larger force. He and his men tracked the remaining invaders to a village several days' travel from Caerwyn. It was more a settlement than a village and contained a motley band of men, women and children who appeared loosely related to the ancient tribe of the Essylwg. They were not organised and appeared to be in disarray without a proper leader. Edern left a few men to keep an eye on the group while he and the rest of his men returned to Caerwyn for instruction and provisions. He again smiled as a warrior approached and addressed Owain as "Arthgwr."

Edern followed his leader into the yard behind the hall of the two-storied stone hut. Gwenhwyfar and Lydia who were already present and sitting with two serving girls acknowledged him. Cai soon joined them and nodded in acknowledgement. "Arthgwr" stripped off his tunic and began a series of exercises. Edern could not help notice the angry wound, red and swollen from the stitching. It was a serious injury. Arthgwr picked up a sword and began swinging it in circles slowly at first, then in controlled combat with the other warrior. Lydia and the Lady Gwenhwyfar put their heads together and discussed the injury of their leader. Both marvelled at his recuperative powers and though they at first hesitated to approve the activity so soon after being badly wounded, they were forced to admit the exercise did Arthgwr good.

"That was a very wise thing for you to have done, Edern," said Arthgwr. He smiled to himself as he thought of the time he had told Dyfyr what he had thought of Edern's ability to strategise. He dearly missed his old friend and it was a burden he bore with sadness.

It had not gone unnoticed that "Arthgwr" seemed more distant, more sombre since the attacks. Putting aside his sad thoughts, Arthgwr looked to Edern and told him to prepare his men. Turning to Cai, he ordered a meeting of all the captains and advisors to be convened by tomorrow's night fall.

"We should think clearly about what our duty might be for us and for our village in the days to come. We will need to make a proper plan for I believe there is much more in store for us then what we may have thought." He glanced over at Gwenhwyfar. She masked the sudden surprise she felt at hearing her husband speak out loud the fears she dreaded in her own mind.

Cai looked up quizzically, he had never heard his foster brother speak in such enigmatic terms. He wondered if more than just Owain's name had changed with the battle. Catching sight of Cai's surprised look, Arthgwr smiled.

"Come my brother, you surely don't think Gronw's warped ambitions were the driving force behind the attack? No, there is more going on here. Gronw was a small player in a much larger game."

"Certainly," replied Cai trying to mask his feelings. "I think I should tell you that it would be a good thing if you took the men to this village in force. They are without a leader now and we do not want a rabble of armed men at our doorstep. If they regroup or join with others we will be attacked again. We need to drive home the point! We are not to be trifled with and any who dare shall be put to the sword! If we show weakness now after this attack we will forever be the prey of others!" Edern nodded his agreement.

Arthgwr paused and looked hard at his foster brother. Cai fidgeted under the unnerving gaze convinced more than a change of name had taken place.

"Gather the men, we will talk of this!" Arthgwr said curtly. He then turned his back and threw himself into his martial exercise renewing his wife's concern for his health.

Lydia had been kept busy ministering to the wounded especially to Father Bedwini. Since Llew had been killed, Lydia had seemed less animated, she moved lethargically through the village as though all reason for living had been drained from her soul. It worried Gwenhwyfar and she had mentioned her concerns about Lydia to her husband in the hopes that together they could determine what they could do to help. Arthgwr said he would speak to Father Bedwini about the matter. He felt that as a Christian priest, the good Father would have a better insight into the matter.

The priest had been healing well. His leg wound closed nicely around the stitching and he did not become feverish or sick. The priest rested most days, though he did give morning mass and some evening benedictions to those villagers who asked.

As he became stronger, Father Bedwini tried to help out in more substantial ways. The members of his entourage had been taken in and worked in the kitchens, fixing roofs, fences and helping with livestock. The priest was now feeling up to the task. He maintained his sleeping area in Gwenhwyfar's hall and availed himself of the food and drink, especially the drink.

Arthgwr came upon the priest as he sat sharpening farm tools. He was working with others and doing a good job of earning his keep. The villagers appreciated his efforts though some of the more pious Christians thought it beneath the priest's station to work as a common labourer. Arthgwr approached and unceremoniously plopped himself down beside the busy Father. Casually hailing the priest, Arthgwr did not wait, but launched into his concern about poor Lydia. Arthgwr paused and asked the priest for his thoughts. The priest did not look up from his work. He did not even acknowledge Arthgwr's presence.

"Getting used to the new name are you?" he said curtly, without looking up.

Arthgwr contained his annoyance at the priest's arrogant attitude and tried to answer.

"Well...er.... I suppose I am...yes. Gwenhwyfar seems to have no trouble with it but I think by children snicker at me when they address me. Gwenhwyfar says it inspires the villagers and I should learn to accept it. I suppose there is some merit to that."

The priest glanced up and then immediately continued his work.

"Indeed, indeed. You wear your new name as the title of "Arthgwr" the "Bear Man From the North" while your wife Gwenhwyfar is revered as something close to a deity! Such silly superstitious nonsense! Are you letting all of this...this...flattery go to your head?"

Anger flashed through Arthgwr. He wanted to strike the insolent priest for his insults. The man Edern had assigned to watch over Arthgwr, moved toward the priest with just that thought in mind. Arthgwr raised his hand to stop him.

Struggling to remain calm, he looked at the priest and answered.

"No, I don't think so!" His voice was low and firm. Edern's man again moved forward but was signalled to stop by a look from Arthgwr.

"Well, I suppose that is a good thing!" said the priest stopping what he had been doing and finally turning his whole attention to Arthgwr.

"Listen, priest, if you have something to say to me, say it plainly! Say what it is you mean and be clear! I do not like these games of yours!" Arthgwr's face was red with anger, his voice low and menacing.

"Just who do you think is playing games here?" The priest was angry too and it could be heard in his voice. Arthgwr had to put a hand in the chest of Edern's man to keep him from running the priest through with his long sword.

"All I am saying," said the priest in a more chagrined tone, taking note of the hostility in Edern's man, "is that pride can be the downfall of any man. It would be a pity to see a good man like your self fall prey to such a thing. That is all."

"Father Bedwini," Arthgwr addressed the priest formally, "do you think me such a fool that a mere name would swell my head and cause me to forget my duty? Is it not a sign of humility that I have sought you out this day to ask your opinion on a matter dear to the hearts of my wife and I?"

The priest stared at the man in front of him. He looked into the blue eyes set in the rugged face and noticed the beginnings of a smile appear at the corner of the man's mouth.

"Words," he spat, "just words! If you really want to live up to the adulation that seems to be pouring down upon you then you need to act!"

"Act? What do you mean, act?" Arthgwr lost the beginning smile and his anger came rushing back.

"That quiet anger of yours could be your undoing," the priest realised he had pushed as far as he could; it was time to come to the point.

"I could suggest an act that would demonstrate to all your sincerity, your humility, qualities that would earn the love of your people."

"What are you talking about?"

"A chapel." There the priest had said it, he had revealed his intentions.

"A chapel? That would not win me the hearts of those people who do not follow your Christian god. Why should I build a chapel?"

"Many reasons, for a start, it would bring the village together, Pagan and Christian alike and it would certainly lift the spirit of poor Lydia."

Arthgwr looked at the priest and marvelled at his shrewdness and his courage. It was true that a chapel would lift the spirit of the religious villagers and especially Lydia. But not all the villagers were Christians.

"What you say has some merit Father Bedwini," declared Arthgwr in a measured tone, "but how do you suppose that building a chapel will bring Pagans and Christians together? Certainly only the Christians would benefit from such a thing. Those who follow the Ancient Ways do not need such a thing as a chapel."

"Because, my dear Arthgwr," the priest used the new name with only a hint of sarcasm, "you would build the chapel to honour your friend Dyfyr who was beloved by all. Yes, loved by all and yet he was a Christian." Father Bedwini watched Arthgwr as the weight of what he had just said settled on him. For a brief moment the priest thought he could see tears welling in the warrior's eyes.

Arthgwr remained motionless for a heartbeat and then he curtly nodded his head to signify he would think about what the priest had told him. He turned on his heel and briskly walked away. Father Bedwini watched the leader of Caerwyn guarded by his warrior, walk back to his home. He could just see Arthgwr rip off his tunic and begin his martial exercises. There was no doubt he was a dangerous man, a fierce warrior. He was a strange man too, thought the priest.

Chapter 14

The council met the next night in the hall of Gwenhwyfar's ancient family home. Arthgwr's advisors were all present. The anxious tension that filled the great room was palatable. Flickering torchlight bathed the gathered warriors with yellowish light while roaring hearth fires warmed the stone hall. The fighting men arranged themselves in a traditional circle, just as their ancestors had done many hundreds of years earlier. Sitting on heaps of animal hides, their battle gear piled behind them, discussing the issue at hand, the discovery of the village by Edern. It was argued that a small well-armed war party should be sent against the Essylwg settlement to destroy it, in retaliation for the attack on Caerwyn. The discussion was heated and passionate. Cai and Edern did not want Arthgwr to lead the war party lest he reopen his wound. Other captains said their leader, as war chief, was duty-bound to lead his warriors in an attack.

Arthgwr listened carefully to the discussion and advice of his men. He listened for hours and carefully pondered all they had to say. Now it was time for a decision. Arthgwr stood up to speak.

"I have heard what all of you have said and I thank you for your thoughts and advice. My decision is this; I will lead a party of men. We will ensure enough of a force is left to protect Caerwyn. We do not ride to destroy these people but to implore them to join with us for the good of all. I will not allow any lawless acts of vengeance. I want that plainly understood! If you ride with me, you will abide by my rules. No one is to be killed without good reason. Womenfolk are to be protected always; there will be no raping or mistreatment of women.

189

"In our past women, have led men into battle and won glory for their tribe. That demands respect and dignity. There will be no burning of any crops or settlements. We may be compelled to slay the tyrant but we will not wreak havoc on those forced to do his bidding! Above all we will act according to all things right and proper!"

The reed torches flickered and hissed in their sconces, the hearth fire roared at the end of the hall, two hunting dogs fought briefly over a scrap of meat and for a moment they were the only sounds heard in the hall. Then the men erupted, shouting disagreement, yelling approval, it was chaos. Arthgwr sat back down and allowed tempers to run their course. It was another two hours before a general agreement was reached. The men were quiet now.

On his feet again, Arthgwr addressed his men.

"Before we take our leave, all of us will swear by whatever god or gods he holds dear that he will obey these rules I have laid down to you. When we ride, we ride as one! One heart! One will! One law!"

The men jumped to their feet yelling agreement, banging their swords and shields, the din was deafening! Slowly they quieted down again seating themselves on their animal skins. Cai remained standing. All eyes followed him as he solemnly walked to his foster brother and knelt at his feet, his hand on his sword hilt. In a clear voice, Cai pledged his allegiance to Arthgwr and the Law he had just laid down before his men. They had never been very close. "Arthgwr," even when he was known as Owain, had been aloof, almost dismissive of Cai. He did not mean to be so; it was simply that he was pre-occupied with responsibility. Arthgwr did trust his foster brother and harboured genuine affection and respect for him. Cai now knelt, head bowed at his foster brother's feet, his hand on his sword hilt. Arthgwr clapped his hand on his foster brother's shoulder and pulled him to his feet. The two men embraced to the cheers of the company.

Elidir rose next. The young captain walked confidently up to Arthgwr. When the hall was again quiet, the youth spoke.

"My father trusted you. He rarely understood you but he trusted you. I grew up respecting you because of my father's trust in you. I am in love with your daughter and will do all in my power to keep her safe. I hereby pledge my sword to you, Arthgwr, Leader of Caerwyn! I will uphold your Law!" He stood and saluted Arthgwr with his sword then returned to the circle.

Arthgwr was humbled by the actions of his dead friend's son and the loyalty of his foster brother. He bowed his head and remained still and silent. He lifted his head and he saw that the warriors in the hall were kneeling, their hands on the hilts of their swords in obeisance.

"We will leave at first light," ordered Arthgwr.

The banging and yelling started up again. The hall was filled with the singing of men of action, warriors all, who were glad to be of service to their war leader. They gulped down the last of their ale, happy to be part of something bigger than themselves. They had each sworn allegiance to Arthgwr and they took their oaths seriously. Now they were ready to put their oath of honour to the test.

Arthgwr and his warrior band left Caerwyn in the cold dawn's meagre light. The leader of Caerwyn travelled with Cai, Edern, and his brother Gwyn and their men. Caerwyn he safely left in the hands of Anwas and Elidir and their men. The band of warriors travelled fast, stopping only to rest and water their horses. They slept from necessity, a stolen hour maybe two in the depth of the night. Thankfully, the weather held. It was four days of hard riding before they came to the place Edern described as being the site of the village. While it was true that Arthgwr did not wish to lay waste to the settlement in revenge for the attack on Caerwyn, he was obliged to drive home the point that the men of Caerwyn would brook no threat to their homes. It was important that these marauders understand that Arthgwr and his men could crush their enemies if they so wished. The plan was to ride in hard from two directions and take advantage of the ensuing chaos. No motley band of would-be raiders could stand against a full cavalry charge, much less two!

At midmorning, Arthgwr and his men rode through the settlement at full gallop. The thundering hooves and din of crashing war-horses, shields and spears and swords shocked the inhabitants into submission. There was little resistance and only one casualty. A young man had foolishly drawn his sword in defiance. He threatened Edern instead of dropping his weapon as ordered. Edern decapitated the young warrior without hesitation or even a backward glance at his handiwork. Arthgwr's archers dismounted and formed a loose perimeter, their great yew long bows at the ready. The others rode their horses through the settlement and corralled the inhabitants. The huddled wretches looked up in fear at the war leader. Cai ordered two of his men to question the men folk of the settlement and determine who, if anyone, was leader and assess the settlement's strength. All useful information was then reported to Arthgwr.

As it turned out, the peasants were not in as bad a shape as they looked. They had food reserves that would, with care, last them until spring. Their farming tools were in good repair and water was in good supply. The land they occupied was fertile and with some skill, it would yield a crop. There were a few cows, pigs and poultry, several hunting hounds, two oxen, but no horses. With some hard work and good management, this settlement would thrive. The leader of these people, loosely held together by tribal ties to the Essylwg, was a chief named Manw. He had wanted to attack Caerwyn to extend his influence and impress the chief of the region, a hard man called Dunirix. Manw thought success might earn him the rank of War Leader and with that, the chance of increasing his power, perhaps gaining control over other villages. He would become rich and powerful. By supporting Dunirix at the next Gathering, Manw would be favoured and his reward, great.

The shrewd leader had persuaded his people to support his ideas by telling them of Gronw, an important man in the very village he wished to attack. Manw told the village elders, Gronw had made an alliance with the Sacsonaidd who he said wished a peaceful expansion of their lands into the North. The key to victory over Caerwyn was Gronw and his knowledge of the Great Forest. With Sacsonaidd allies and the secrets of the Great Forest, Manw was assured of victory! That meant riches and wealth to all the villagers.

Many villagers thought there were too many ways for the scheme to fail and the risk, which ultimately would be born by their families, would be greater than the benefit Manw sought. Now that Manw had been killed leading the attack on Caerwyn, their worst fears were realised. They were leaderless and many of their best warriors had been killed in battle. All of their horses had been taken for the military enterprise, none had returned. They huddled and cowered before the Arthgwr, the leader of Caerwyn. Their fate was sealed!

Arthgwr stood up on a wagon so that all could see him. Wood smoke wafted through the settlement, while hounds nosed through madden heaps, searching for scraps of food. The sun was high and warmed the air. It should have been an ordinary day. The crowd cowed before him. Children cried, women sobbed and men looked down at the ground in shame. Arthgwr looked at the misery before him. His shoulder pained him, reminding him how close his own village had come to ruin.

"I will not put you to the sword nor will I burn your village!" Arthgwr paused and looked at the now hopeful faces of the villagers. Small children clung to their mothers, whimpering. Young sons stood fearfully alone, their fathers killed in the battle for Caerwyn. Old men tried valiantly to stand proudly, despite bent backs, their gnarled hands gripping wooden staffs. Smoke from the cooking fires curled upward and the faint aroma of boiled pork was carried on the wind.

"You may live in peace if you will agree to live under my guidance!" He paused again to gauge the effect of his words.

"It is my plan that we forge an alliance. Not just between our two villages but with others in the region. Commerce and a common law will allow security and prosperity for all! To accomplish this some of you," Arthgwr looked at the very few able bodied men and boys, "will be required to accompany me and my men as we visit each village and ensure the alliance. There may be some fighting. If we hold to a vision of peace and prosperity for our children, I am confidant an alliance will hold. It has always been my belief that Cymry should not fight one against the other but that we should unite as good compatriots for the benefit of us all!"

The gathered villagers fidgeted uneasily. Most were simple folk and they did not grasp the meaning of Arthgwr's words. The quick-witted amongst them instantly realised they were not going to die and began praising their saviour, Arthgwr. Children happy to see their mothers relief, scrambled to play and run amok. Young boys confused by the sudden change of fate stood mutely, fear haunting their eyes. The village elders grappled with the idea Arthgwr presented, that the opportunity to improve their future was through commerce not conflict. Many were sceptical. Arguments ensued and voices grew loud as the old men argued the merits of the words that had been spoken. Arthgwr's men became nervous at the commotion. The horses snorted and stomped their hooves, churning the ground into mud. Cai calmed his men, seeing to it swords were sheathed and spears lowered. Arthgwr remained motionless and did not speak further.

It was imperceptible at first, drowned out by the arguments of the old guard. It grew louder as the realisation of their salvation dawned on the villagers.

"Arthgwr! Arthgwr! Arthgwr!" The chant soon became deafening.

In this, his second victory, the leader of Caerwyn truly became Arthgwr, the Bear Man, the Fierce War Leader from the North.

Cai and his men made a reconnaissance of the area and talked to the men folk about distances and routes to other villages. It was now dusk, the general excitement of the day was over and the villagers were settling down. Arthgwr had taken for himself a large hut near the centre of the village. Edern and a few hand picked warriors moved in to provide security for their leader. Two of the men were with him; close enough to render aid, but just far enough away to give Arthgwr the illusion of privacy.

He sat down heavily on a stump of wood. The leader of Caerwyn looked up into the night sky at an unobstructed view of the stars. Looking up to the heavens Arthgwr wondered what his wife was doing. He imagined her to be looking at the same stars. He thought of his children and how grown up they had seemed, especially Gwyneth. The implications of what he had said to the villagers and to his own men was beginning to settle on his mind. By saying the things he had said this day Arthgwr had inadvertently committed himself and his warriors to a monumental task. Whatever else lay down the road he had just chosen, it was sure that Arthgwr would not see his family for a long time. How long he would need to stay on this quest, he did not know.

In the gathering darkness, alone but for his guards, Arthgwr was suddenly unsure of his commitment. Insecurity was a weakness that a strong leader could ill afford. Arthgwr wished he could speak to his wife Gwenhwyfar or even his old friend Dyfyr. It was not that he was incapable of making decisions, but rather that he had committed to a course of action without thinking it through properly. This was beyond his experience and the cause of his self-doubt. What would Gwenhwyfar say of all this? He could not rid himself of the feeling that he would not see his beautiful wife again for a long time. Arthgwr grew miserable at the thought.

After many moments of soul searching, Arthgwr began to feel that what he had done had been necessary. It was as though all his life had been in preparation for what he was about to undertake. The feeling was not altogether unwelcome. It was familiar. Shaking off the lonely feeling of sadness, Arthgwr walked over to one of the watch fires. His warriors stood on seeing their leader approach and they offered the tired looking Arthgwr food and ale, which he accepted. Looking around at his warriors and the villagers scurrying about with food and drink, stoking the fires and keeping the night warm and bright, Arthgwr felt something had changed. He thought his men were more sombre and formal with him. The villagers, he noted, could barely look him in the eye. It made Arthgwr uncomfortable to think of it, but he was beginning to feel these people were holding him in awe.

The next few weeks were difficult. Arthgwr's army had travelled around the region visiting the various outlying tribes and villages parlaying with the chiefs and chieftains. The notion that an alliance of tribes was in the best interest of all concerned was a hard idea to sell. Arthgwr's reputation preceded him and for the most part the chiefs did not have the courage or the resources to resist Arthgwr's position. There were however one or two incidents where individuals were unwilling to listen to Arthgwr's reason.

In one village, in a large round building once a stable, a meeting with the chief and his advisors was convened. A warrior called Gluneau stood up and began to question Arthgwr's reputation. The warrior's tone was arrogant. His questions turned increasingly to insults and personal attacks on the character of Arthgwr. Edern was incensed. He had to be restrained by his brother and two others, lest blood was spilled and Arthgwr's position reduced to force instead of reason. Gluneau continued his tirade on Arthgwr.

For his part, the leader of Caerwyn remained calm and courteous, and yet unbending in his resolve. His main point, hammered home repeatedly, was that Cymry should not fight each other, but strive for unity. Gluneau's verbal assault continued unabated and Arthgwr's blood began to boil. Gwyn spoke into Arthgwr's ear.

"This is a trick; they all want to see what you are made of and this Gluneau is the bait! You must do something or they will think you a coward."

Gluneau had continued speaking, but changed tactics.

"What can be said of the woman of such a man?" His voice dripped contempt. "Surely that is a sad ignoble creature, to have whelped and yet never to have known a real man? Perhaps I should offer a more personal union before there is more talk of uniting tribes?"

Arthgwr stood up abruptly. His men went deathly quiet, even Edern stood still; the shock of the insult was so great. Arthgwr walked to the centre of the circle and stood glaring at Gluneau. The host chief was agitated and excitable; he knew things had gone too far. The men were now all jabbering excitedly amongst themselves. Gluneau strode into the circle.

The flickering torchlight cast shadows and distortions onto the white washed, stonewall. At the centre of the circle of men, two champions stood facing each other with murderous intent in their hearts. This was single combat; an ancient ritual and nothing could stop the drama or the two champions now bound by destiny.

Neither man wore armour. They were both armed with knife and sword, but neither had picked up a shield. They circled each other slowly. Gluneau had a sarcastic smirk on his face. Arthgwr's expression was unfathomable. Those who knew him well however, could see Arthgwr masked a burning rage at hearing his wife, the good Lady Gwenhwyfar insulted. Arthgwr's men were outraged by the insult, but their own rage was impotent for it fell to Gwenhwyfar's husband to defend her honour.

Gluneau held the naked blade of his sword above his head as he circled Arthgwr. Suddenly, he brought the blade down diagonally cutting Arthgwr's tunic. Arthgwr deftly escaping serious injury, circled to his left, his own sword held midlevel in his right hand. Gluneau attacked with a side cut left to right, continuing the momentum so that he brought the blade downward barely missing Arthgwr's shoulder. Without pause, Gluneau brought his sword in a diagonal upward strike; he was now moving quickly forward, his sword cutting through the air in overlapping circles of death.

Arthgwr managed to move backward keeping himself just out of range of the deadly iron ring of death. As Gluneau cut sideways again, Arthgwr timed an underhanded cut of his own that sliced through the sleeve of Gluneau's tunic cutting into his arm and spurting blood.

A loud cheer went up from Arthgwr's men.

Gluneau quickly moved backwards disengaging his attack to assess the situation. Arthgwr kept his momentum and pressed his advantage. He lunged forward with a powerful thrust then suddenly spun to his left bringing his sword down hard in an overhead cut. The manoeuvre gained him precious reach, but Gluneau managed to parry the blow with his own sword. Without breaking his momentum Gluneau swung hard, his sword strike missed Arthgwr, who hammered his assailant with the pommel of his sword. Fortunately, Gluneau had still been moving and the blow, although hard, glanced off his head without serious injury. The blow nevertheless stunned him and Arthgwr quickly moved in to attack, spinning in the opposite direction and thrusting his sword at Gluneau's side. Gluneau managed to parry the blow. The two men disengaged and circled each other.

Gluneau darted forward with a powerful downward strike. Arthgwr sidestepped and cut sideways, this time cutting his attacker across the right side of his torso. Without hesitation, Arthgwr continued in a smooth motion and cut down, his blade slicing down the right side of Gluneau's back. Gluneau bellowed in pain and blindly swung his own blade sideways to his rear trying to cut Arthgwr's throat. Arthgwr parried the blow and cut down, his blade biting deep into Gluneau's right leg. He kicked Gluneau viciously knocking him down to the ground. Reversing his grip and clenching his sword with both hands, sword tip pointing down, Arthgwr stabbed downward plunging his blade into Gluneau's back. It was a deathblow.

Gwyn, his brother Edern, and their men quickly drew their swords and confronted the chief and his warriors. There was to be no more fighting. The chief and his tribesmen agreed to the terms of the alliance. Arthgwr and his men were again victorious.

Chapter 15

Weeks had passed since Arthgwr's fight with Gluneau. Many villages had been visited by the "Bear of the North" and his army, most had entered into an alliance readily, awed by the stories of Arthgwr's victories.

Indeed, Arthgwr's army was composed of many different tribal chieftains and their supporters all of whom had pledged allegiance to him. They knew that their fiefdom's enjoyed the protection of Arthgwr's army. Many of the minor chiefs and chieftains embraced Arthgwr's vision of unity for the Cymry. They had even begun talk that Arthgwr should claim the position of High King of Briton.

These sentiments had begun to worry at Arthgwr. He spent increasingly more time alone contemplating the future and evaluating his choices. Cai and some of the men who were close to Arthgwr started to worry about their leader's health. It was noticed that he was not eating much, that he was drawn about the face and looked tired, rarely smiling, never laughing. No one dared brave the leader's wrath by expressing such concerns to him directly. Arthgwr may have looked drawn and tired, but he was not weak or frail. He seemed to be made of the same steel as his long sword, hard, unbending, sharp, and able to cut to the bone.

The lazy days of summer were promised on every warm breeze that caressed the earth. Spring planting was completed and the peasants enjoyed a short respite from their backbreaking toil. The crops would ripen in the warmth and wet of the summer and then harvest time would be upon the land. For now, men and women rejoiced in the warming, sunshine and children danced and chased the butterflies that darted in and out between the crop rows. Warriors had brought with them their families and now hundreds of men, women, and children travelled with Arthgwr. Wherever they set camp, the site became its own village. Arthgwr had the army make camp in the mountains above the meadowlands where the children and butterflies played. Up high, the air was chill and bracing. Warriors tended to their duties and perimeters were set up to safeguard the people. Horses were rigorously brushed and rubbed down and fed sweet hay. Boiled pork, leeks, cheese, and dark bread were fed to the men. The purple cloak of night gathered and spread over the land. Firelight flickered in the darkness like flecks of golden thread amidst the dark of blue-dyed wool. Arthgwr could not sleep. He looked at the many campfires and thought of the hundreds of people who now looked to him for their safety and wellbeing. The thought weighed heavily on him.

It was close to dawn and a thick wet mist hung about the camp. Arthgwr had slept only an hour or two and had remained awake most of the night. He shivered in the damp, pulling his thick cloak tightly around him. It was no use. He rose and stretched, trying to shake off the cold morning. A sliver of red broached the horizon and Arthgwr hoped it would be a warm day. He walked around the encampment deep in thought, nodding hello to other early risers. Sunlight spread gently and gradually warmed the air. Sounds of mothers preparing to break fast with their husbands and children collided with the chopping of wood and bustle of men starting their day's work. Arthgwr had meandered over to see to his horse. He absently stroked the beast's nose and offered some strands of hay to the animal's inquisitive snout. Both the horse and Arthgwr startled at the sound of a sudden shout. Arthgwr immediately began running toward a group of peasants, a fighting knife already clenched in his hand.

"What is the matter?" He yelled as he approached the small gathering. Edern and some men had already cleared a path and were standing in front of someone not yet identifiable. Arthgwr was battle-ready and prepared for anything. Anything, that is, but what he now saw in front of him.

It was Rhiannon.

She stood there in plain sight, arms open to show she did not carry any weapons. Like a vision from ancient times, Rhiannon was resplendent in a long woollen dress dyed blue, a gold cord tied around her waist, a black hooded cloak clasped with an exquisite silver fastener shaped as a boar. She stood with her unfettered raven black hair, flowing in the gentle morning breeze. Her arms adorned with silver and gold bracelets, still outstretched as though she were a goddess welcoming her children.

The men did not know how to act. The Christians in the crowd saw a Pagan woman vane and provocative; their mood quickly turned ugly. This prickled the sensibilities of the Pagan soldiers, Edern among them. Arthgwr acted quickly. In plain view of all, he approached Rhiannon, bowed respectfully, and then embraced her heartily. The gathering quieted considerably at seeing Arthgwr show such high regard to the woman. Because their leader's warriors also treated this stranger with much respect, was further cause for wonder and did much to ease tensions. The intensity that shone in the fighting men's eyes as they prepared to lead the woman to Arthgwr's tent was enough to clear a path and put a stop to further grumbling. No frightening looking warriors could stop womenfolk from talking amongst themselves. Those who did not know Rhiannon supposed she was Arthgwr's wife. This was proved they said by the passion contained in the embrace they had witnessed. Their belief was seemingly confirmed, as Arthgwr walked Rhiannon arm in arm straight to his tent. That meant, so went the gossip, that Rhiannon was herself a queen.

Food was prepared for Arthgwr's guest and his men crowded into his tent to catch a glimpse of Rhiannon and perhaps hear some news of home. A gathering of warriors and families spilled out from the large tent of their leader. Rhiannon took the attention paid to her in stride. Regally, she walked among the people touching each man she met on the shoulder and whispering some intimate detail of life as it went on in their home, Caerwyn.

Rhiannon appeared different to Arthgwr since he had last seen her. There was an underlying power in her elegance and grace he had not noticed until now. When he looked into her ice blue eyes, he felt a faint urge to do her bidding. Nevertheless, it was grand to see her and Arthgwr was overjoyed to hear news from home.

Gwenhwyfar, Gwyneth, and Cynglas were in good health and doing well. He was glad to hear Elidir was performing his duties admirably and that the young man had easily grown into the role thrust on him, by the sudden death of his father.

"So you have recently been to Caerwyn, then?" Arthgwr asked as he and Rhiannon shared a moment out of earshot from the men.

"If you do not trust me to correctly report the news to you *"Arthgwr,"* just say so and I will stop immediately." Arthgwr thought he detected a hint of amusement when she used his new name. He had the distinct feeling he was being mocked.

"It seems you have adjusted well to your new name. I must say the entire region has heard of the Great Warrior, Arthgwr, the Bear Man from the North."

Surprised by her words and the underlying tone, Arthgwr fumbled over his response. He was sure she mocked him but could not understand why. They had enjoyed a good relationship in the past and there was no question that he had always shown her all proper respect. Arthgwr was becoming angry.

Rhiannon continued talking as if nothing had happened. She told Arthgwr more about his wife; she knew that was what he wanted to hear about more than anything else. Moving out of the tent, Rhiannon spoke to a few men, regaling them with a humorous story of Geraint, the dafarn owner. It seemed his wife had caught him dallying with a hired serving girl.

"Yes, that is right," she said noticing the incredulous stares of the men, "business was so good that old man Geraint hired a serving girl. His appetite, however, has left him in trouble with his wife!" The story caused the men to laugh for they knew Angharad and her temper! Poor old Geraint had certainly bitten off more than he could chew!

"Not that we don't appreciate news from home, but is there any other reason why you should find yourself alone out here in the wilderness?" Arthgwr's voice was gentle, but it belied a certain seriousness lurking just below the surface. Edern ap Nudd sensed it immediately and he looked up sharply at his brother. Gwyn ap Nudd sensed the same tone and was watching Arthgwr closely.

Rhiannon gave no outward sign that she was offended by Arthgwr's inference. She stood and allowed a servant to refill her cup with ale. She looked about her at the gathered men, warriors all, and then sipped her ale. Leaning down she whispered into Arthgwr's ear.

"There is someone who wants to meet with you."

Arthgwr was surprised. He was about to ask the identity of this mystery person, but Rhiannon had already moved off to mingle with the men. She was fully engaged in lively conversation and the men were laughing and pounding their sides. The fighting men of Caerwyn, Christian and Pagan alike, were genuinely happy to see Rhiannon. They remembered her as a warrior who had fought along side them, killing their enemy in revenge for the death of her husband. Many of the men regarded her as a priestess with mysterious connections to the Wise Ones. Her beauty and vivacious charisma captivated their imaginations and she held them in her power. Regaling them with stories of their home, she told tales rich in detail and vividly personal to each man she spoke to in turn. Arthgwr knew Rhiannon had been travelling for weeks and he wondered how she could possibly know all that was going on in Caerwyn. He was especially curious how she knew the details described to each man.

Of course, the men themselves were not concerned with such things; they were simply glad for happy news and entertained by Rhiannon's story telling. Begrudgingly, Arthgwr had to admit that the men were more relaxed and happy than he had seen them in weeks. It was probably good for their morale that Rhiannon had come along and Arthgwr put the matter from his mind.

The day wore on and Arthgwr's men were again consumed with the mundane tasks of tending the horses, making repairs to tents, armour, and weapons. Rhiannon kept busy talking with the warriors, visiting with the womenfolk and even speaking with some of the Christian peasants. She had healed a few of the men of their aches and pains, in return the people provided her with a tent for her own use. It was bare of fancy furnishings and more like a soldier's hut. It was warm and dry and contained a cauldron and a small table where she could cook and prepare her healing herbs. Rhiannon napped at mid-afternoon and was not seen again until nightfall. Arthgwr was becoming increasingly curious about this mysterious person who so wanted an audience with him. He had sent patrols out from camp in different directions with orders to report anything suspicious. The perimeter guard was fortified.

There had been nothing to report. No one had been seen, friend or foe. Everything was quiet and calm in the camp. Fires were lit to stave off the night chill that hung about the highland.

The plan had been that the main force of the army would travel through a known pass near the mountain's peak and on into the next village on the other side. It would be three to four days hard ride. Once the new village was secured the rest of Arthgwr's army and it's entourage would follow. Arthgwr was sure that Rhiannon's sudden appearance would now interrupt those plans. He had gathered his trusted warriors for a conference with Rhiannon that evening. Arthgwr wanted Rhiannon to speak plainly. He wanted to know what her intentions were and to have her reveal them in the presence of his advisors.

The company gathered in Arthgwr's large leather tent. Braziers burned the chill from the air and bread, cheese and ale circulated amongst the gathered men in an attempt to quell their appetite and warm their bones. Rhiannon sat on a pile of skins next to Arthgwr. She wore her black hooded cape over a plain grey woollen dress cinched at the waist with a thick leather belt of the type a warrior might wear. Wrapped over her shoulders was a wolf skin. Her black hair fell loose down her back. No man escaped her beauty; it radiated from her like light from the sun.

"Well, then Rhiannon, you have supped with us and entertained us grandly with your news and stories from our home. I dare say you have been a welcome sight and we all, every man of us, have been warmed by your presence. Now, you told me that there is someone who wishes an audience with me and I wonder if you are now going to change our present plans?"

Rhiannon gracefully rose from her seat fully aware all eyes were on her. Like some wild cat, she stretched and arched her back. Her ice blue eyes searched out each man of the council. She saw they were all good men, true to their word, honourable and confident. Without speaking or moving Rhiannon looked long into every man's eyes. The pride she felt for these brave warriors burned through her eyes and into the fighting men's souls. Each man felt as though he had spoken privately and directly to the beautiful woman-warrior-priestess and had received her praise.

"Yes, Arthgwr. I would ask you to delay your plans and accompany me further into these mountains, but in a southerly direction. Someone wishes to meet with you. He possesses important knowledge and information that may change your life. You may bring two men with you on the journey, but you must take this meeting alone. I will take my leave now and you may inform me of your decision in the morning." Then she left.

It took a moment for the spell to break and the men to begin speaking. They had been held enthralled by Rhiannon and now her sudden absence allowed them to argue the merits of her words amongst themselves. It was chaos. There were those who did not want Arthgwr to delay any further but to continue with the plan already agreed upon. Others believed Arthgwr should delay since nothing of great value would be lost in so doing and there may be greater value in gaining insight, perhaps even knowledge they at present did not possess. There were warriors who, despite their great admiration for Rhiannon, did not like the idea of blindly accepting a meeting on terms too vague to make an intelligent decision. It was a complex situation and discussions waged well into the night.

In the end, it came down to trust. Arthgwr made the argument that Rhiannon had proven herself as one of the children of Caerwyn. She had been born there and had fought for her village alongside her husband who had died protecting their home. She had over the years comforted and healed the villagers of Caerwyn. Many said she was in league with the Wise Ones, some villagers even believed her to be a Druid herself. This argument held no sway for the Christians for they did not hold with Pagan ways. They were convinced of Rhiannon's character only by Arthgwr's arguments and were persuaded by him to accept her as a brave and wise woman of Caerwyn and not as a sorceress. They threw their support and approval in with the Pagans. The decision was made. Arthgwr would delay the plan and embark on this mysterious quest at Rhiannon's request. The army and the camp would stay put until Arthgwr returned. Arthgwr decided against taking any member of his council with him. Instead, he chose two young servants to accompany him.

The council reluctantly agreed all. Edern, however, was furious at not being chosen to accompany his leader. He wanted to provide protection for the leader of Caerwyn. It was all Gwyn and Cai could do to convince Edern that the decision was Arthgwr's to make; that in this, Arthgwr had the last say.

By midmorning of the next day, four figures were cutting through the mountain mist moving in a southerly direction. The sun slowly burned through the morning shroud, warming the air as the day grew long. The travelling was not too hard for the four.

Rhiannon looked at Arthgwr.

"Why have you not asked me who it is that wishes to speak with you?"

"For one thing I didn't think you would answer a direct question and for another I assumed this person is some envoy of the High King."

Rhiannon's deep and raucous laughter filled the thin mountain air.

"Well, Arthgwr, I suppose I do have a reputation for not answering questions. It is very astute of you to think that I want you to meet an envoy of the king. You are not too far wrong, though he is not an envoy, but rather an unofficial advisor." Rhiannon turned her head to better look at the progress of the two servants. Turning back to face Arthgwr she smiled.

"Rhiannon, why all this secrecy? We have known each other many years and I thought we shared a mutual respect for each other and that if we were not outright friends we were friendly."

Rhiannon pulled her horse up to a stop and looked straight at Arthgwr.

"I have respect for you Arthgwr and I always have considered you a friend. If I seem a bit distant or aloof, it is because I have many burdens to carry. Secrecy is but one of them, but I assure you all will be revealed to your satisfaction. You know, we are not too different you and I. We both are different from those around us and we both act as though we are above their petty concerns. You have Gwenhwyfar and the children, but I find my station in life lonesome. I miss my husband and since his death I have never felt the same towards another man."

Arthgwr was astonished. He had never heard Rhiannon speak about personal matters and he was slightly embarrassed by her candid confessions. Arthgwr realised his earlier anger toward this remarkable woman was unwarranted. He suddenly felt guilty. Pulling his horse up to hers, he leaned over and holding her head in his strong hand, he kissed her forehead.

The awkward moment was soon over and they resumed their journey in silence.

It was late afternoon on the third day when Rhiannon told Arthgwr that they were near their destination. The spot was well chosen. The height of the mountains was not so great as to be impassable and yet they provided the feel of a fortress. Below, where their small party stood, was a small mountain meadow, and Arthgwr could see scrub brush, lichen, and heather. Some rugged sheep were foraging for food. A thin trail of wood smoke curled its way upward; the revealed source was a small stone hut with a pasture containing a few goats and a pony. Rhiannon indicated that was where they were going and she abruptly nudged her horse forward pushing past Arthgwr. The winding mountain trail took some time as well as some skill to negotiate. The path was a steep descent fraught with rocks, loose brush, and scrub. As Arthgwr saw the hut from a closer viewpoint he realised it was much bigger than he had first thought. From what he could tell, the hut had several rooms and it looked surprisingly inviting and hospitable. Arthgwr's tired bones caused him to imagine what a great luxury it would be not to have to spend another night in the open. He turned to assess the progress of the two servants and judged they too would be thankful for shelter.

The smell of cooking food, some sort of meat, greeted their party as they rode up on their tired steeds. Arthgwr dismounted and signalled the others to do the same. The two servants quickly grabbed the reins of the horses and walked them to the small pasture at the back of the hut. Rhiannon and Arthgwr approached the door. Rhiannon knocked briskly and not gently on the wood door. Looking back at Arthgwr, she winked and put her shoulder to the door bursting the door open. Laughing, Arthgwr and the two servants followed her into the hut. It was warm and inviting inside, the smell of whatever was cooking set their stomachs rumbling in anticipation. Rhiannon motioned that they should find themselves a seat, while she rummaged around to discover the source of the enticing smell was indeed a meaty broth. She immediately began spooning the delicious smelling soup into wooden bowls she had found and they all tucked into the best hot food they had eaten in days.

Arthgwr was startled when Rhiannon suddenly jumped up and ran to the door. It opened just as she reached out with her hand to open it. In strode a fit looking man with iron, grey hair worn long down to his broad shoulders. His cheeks were covered with a short white beard, which contrasted with his weather worn face. He wore a simple homespun woollen cloak of deep brown over a nondescript grey woollen tunic. A wide black leather belt cinched the tunic under which he wore faded brown leather trousers with leggings and worn leather boots. He carried with him a walking staff and a bag full of what looked like herbs. He was certainly not a young man, but neither was he old. His age was very difficult to guess. Dropping the staff and the bag, the man and Rhiannon hugged and giggled speaking to each other in a language unknown to Arthgwr.

As though he just noticed Arthgwr in the room, the older man winked at him and spoke words that were not understood by Arthgwr. The puzzled look on Arthgwr's face must have registered with the old man and he attempted to change to a language Arthgwr could understand, working his way through several dialects.

"*Yntertanment..........failte.........failt royd.........*" the older man was trying, but he could not find words Arthgwr could readily decipher. The merriment in the old man was slowly turning to frustration. "…. *Altachada beatha...degermer mat...*" the older man continued, despite his rising frustration at not being understood,".... *croeso.*"

"Thank you for your welcome," cried Arthgwr, happy that finally he could understand the man in whose home he stood.

A big smile spread over the face of the man as he shook Arthgwr's outstretched hand welcoming him.

" I am Cymry and thank you for welcoming me to your home," said Arthgwr

"Aaaah," said the old man, "good health to all Cymry. Pardon the long way 'round, but I don't often have guests and I sometimes forget which language I am speaking!"

The man giggled, his blue eyes twinkled, and he looked over at Rhiannon who had not stopped laughing since he had arrived. It was contagious and Arthgwr soon found himself laughing with them.

Between giggles, he told the old man not to worry, that he knew someone else who had the very same problem.

Hearing this, the man laughed even harder and slapped Arthgwr on the back. Arthgwr was shocked at the power of the older man's hand as the breath was all but knocked from his lungs. The man made his way over to a shelf and ferreted until he found what it was he was looking for. With a flourish, he produced some leather tankards and a flask of mead.

"And how is Father Bedwini these days?"

The laughter froze on Arthgwr's face.

He began sputtering trying desperately to form the question that begged to be asked. Rhiannon and the old man simply laughed and laughed. They paid no heed to Arthgwr's distress and shock. Arthgwr cautiously drank down the golden honey liquor. He had never liked mead before, but now found he enjoyed the taste, the smoothness and the slight burning sensation as the honey liquor warmed his insides.

"Aaaah, that's better!" said the old man after guzzling a full tankard of mead before offering the jug around to Rhiannon, Arthgwr, and the two servants. He had motioned for the two of them to be as comfortable as they could, the room boasted a chair, and a bed and many hides piled on the floor. The stone hut had more than a few rooms and was much larger than it appeared from the outside. Rhiannon had stoked the fire and the room was pleasantly warm. Rhiannon was puttering about looking for ingredients to add to the broth they had been sipping. She threw some dried herbs and salted rabbit meat into the pot and for good measure added a generous amount of the mead. The old man did not seem to mind and he produced another full pitcher of the stuff along with some hard bread.

Arthgwr was still stunned from the question the old man had asked about Father Bedwini. How had the old man known about the priest? More disconcerting to Arthgwr was that when he looked up at the old man from time to time he sometimes did not look so old at all. He watched as the man moved about helping Rhiannon and marvelled that sometimes he looked even older than he first appeared.

When the light hit him just at the right angle, the man looked as old as a leathered corpse. Then just as suddenly, when Arthgwr looked fully at him with both his eyes focused wide, the man appeared as an older man who had kept much of the vim and vigour of his youth. He looked very much like an old warrior, living out his last bit of life in peace, yet wrapped in the aura of deadly skill and killing experience that let people know he was still a man to be feared.

While Arthgwr supposed his perceptions were fashioned by the effect of the mead and perhaps the fatigue of the journey and the heat of the hut, there was still no way of understanding how the man could possibly know about the priest. Arthgwr was becoming anxious.

"There is nothing to fear from knowledge, young Arthgwr. I am older and have travelled widely and therefore I have learned much. It gives me the illusion of being wise." He laughed long and hard at this pronouncement, as did Rhiannon.

Arthgwr did not miss that the man had called him "young" and again he was angered. What kind of trickery was this? He could feel rage mounting within him welling like some great wave from the sea. He did not enjoy being played for a fool!

"All right! You've had your bit of fun! How did you know about the priest?" Arthgwr's voice was a low rumble. Rhiannon looked up and immediately stopped laughing.

"Arthgwr," she said soothingly, "you are tired, and darkness is gathering. Why don't I take your two men here and go out in search of firewood? It will give you time to think and understand and to have a much needed talk. Arthgwr, if I may be so bold, you might wish to listen more closely to what is said to you. Believe me, you are among friends in this place, more so than I think you realise." Rhiannon signalled to the two men and the three of them walked out the door. Arthgwr was left standing in stunned silence.

Chapter 16

"My name is.... well, I haven't used it in so long and no one calls me by it anymore, but my name is "Laikolen". Does that name mean anything to you?"

Arthgwr shook his head no, and gestured for the old man to continue. The man who was called Lailoken looked very old to Arthgwr at this moment. Perhaps it was the firelight, or maybe his mind was playing tricks, but the man in front of him now looked like a wrinkled swath of leather.

"Aaaah, no matter, no matter. As I say, no one calls me that anymore. That was my birth name. I have become known by another name these days, just as you have, Owain Ddantgwyn."

Arthgwr was again stunned, that this enigmatic stranger knew him by his real name. The man called Lailoken, walked around the room and stoked the fire; he appeared lost in his own world. Arthgwr had seen old warriors before and had watched as they drank and talked and relived past glory. Lailoken was not one of those old men. He was otherworldly. There was no other way of putting it. The old man simply did not seem to be from this world. Even as he busied himself fussing with the logs in the hearth of this old stone house, Arthgwr could do little but stare in astonishment. Not that Lailoken took any notice. He just poked at the fire.

Arthgwr tried to speak, but the old man made a sign that he should hold his questions for the moment and off he walked into another room of his house. It was sometime before he came back, all the while

Arthgwr remained obediently silent, watching as the man appeared to change from ancient, to simply old, to middle aged and back again.

"You see I was born, as far as I can remember, in a place called Caer Fryddin far north of here. In my adventures as a young man, I travelled far. In those days, I used the name "Emrys" and many people I came to know, made a sort of riddle using my place of birth. So, I was called "Myrddin." You see the clever joke? No? It doesn't matter. When I travelled south and lived for a time amongst those more influenced by Roman customs and speech, I became known as "Merlinus." This they shortened to "Merlin." I detest that name!" The man spat into the fire for dramatic effect.

"What do I call you?" asked Arthgwr, much confused.

The old man stopped his narrative and looked up at Arthgwr. The old man suddenly looked much younger, and the change seemed to occur as Arthgwr watched. Arthgwr could not stop his mouth opening in astonishment. The old man, who now looked younger, slapped his knee and laughed. The laughter peeled through the stone house like thunder on a humid summer's night.

"You may call me Myrddin, as it is properly a Cymry name, yes?" said the man with tears of laughter in his eyes.

Arthgwr could do no more than to nod his head in agreement.

"Arthgwr. I like that name. It is an old name, yes? The language I mean...rather like the Old Tongue, not the gibberish we speak now, eh? Yes, I think the young ones would call you *Athrwys*, in the new tongue, or would it be *Art gwr*, from the old tongue, yes? It certainly suits you! I would say it describes you! I have heard much about you, Owain Ddantgwyn. You arrived at Caerwyn at the behest of your father, Yrthyr Pendragon, to marry the lady Gwenhwyfar of the Segontiaci. Aaaah, I remember little Gwenhwyfar, such an adorable little child was she. You defeated and spared the life of Gronw. He desired your wife you know, yes, don't look so surprised, I know all about that one. Leads everyone to believe he has some special connection to our Order, oh yes I know, such a fraud!" Myrddin spat contemptuously into the fire.

If Arthgwr had been astonished before he was now shocked to his very core!

"You...you are a Wise One? A *Druid*?" he managed to stammer.

"Yes, I am! Why, did you think us all dead? Did you? Well, we are certainly not extinct and that is a fear you can put to rest my lad! There are many more of us than you might suppose. Of course, if you had thought we were all dead then I am more than you might suppose!" The Druid laughed heartily at his own joke before continuing.

"There are not as many of us as there used to be and I can forgive you for thinking we were all dead. Those cursed Romans! They certainly tried to kill us all, mark my words they did indeed! We outlasted them though, have we not my boy? Our traditions have not entirely disappeared and there is always hope, yes...there is always hope and wherein lies hope, one finds life!"

The old man plunked a pitcher of mead on a table between where the two men sat facing each other. Arthgwr was tingling in anticipation of learning from a Druid. He could plainly see that the Wise One, called "Myrddin," was settling in, making himself comfortable no doubt to begin some grand tale. Arthgwr availed himself of a tankard of mead, which he nearly emptied in one gulp.

The old man looked morose now as he thoughtfully sipped at his mead, gesturing to Arthgwr to refill his own tankard yet again. The Old One put his cup down and looked deep into Arthgwr's eyes while his voice, deep, resonant, and as smooth as the honey from which his drink was made, entranced Arthgwr.

"I will tell you the story of why Rome hated our Order. I will tell you the story of our people and how we answered Roman treachery so long ago." Myrddin paused to take a long draught from his leather tankard.

He then began weaving a tale, his rich voice cascading over Arthgwr, transporting him through the mists of an age past, to a time long before he had been born...

...The warrior chief shook his head, his long hair swirling around him from the sudden movement.

"This is where our people will live!" he declared. His council murmured agreement as they looked down upon the fertile valley near the river Po. They had gathered every man, woman and child of their tribe. There were thousands of them, carrying their meagre possessions, pushing carts, herding their livestock. The tribe had travelled a great distance, swarming over the Apennine Mountains pouring into this land called Etruria.

Brennus, their leader, was a strong man, charismatic, forceful, and unyielding and he had done well to get them this far. No one called him by his birth name; they only addressed him as *"Brennus"* a name inspired by one of their gods. Only a brave and fierce warrior possessing intelligence and charisma would be so called; the name stuck.

"Brennus, there is a city near by, there may be resistance!" cried one of the chieftains. The Senones were a large tribe made from many families and many clans. They had decided on this migration because they were too many for the fields to feed them all back home beyond the ancient mountains. Brennus had been chosen to speak for all the chieftains and he had as in the past proved to be capable, brave, and intelligent.

"We come in peace, seeking land for our people. There is plenty of land here and we do not seek war with anyone. How can there be resistance?" He asked rhetorically, as he smoothed his beard and took a gulp of wheaten beer from his decorative drinking horn.

"We shall gather a few chieftains and we will ride down into the city and state our case. These Etruscans seem reasonable, we shall have no trouble here!"

The chieftains returned to their families to settle in for the night. Tomorrow with their leader, Brennus at their head they would make their wishes known to the people of the city.

Brennus and a score of chieftains, warriors, and their women set up camp within sight of the city, Clusium. Once settled, envoys were sent to meet with the city's leaders and invite them into their camp to parley. The tents were brightly decorated, hides were thrown on the ground for the comfort, and warmth of their expected guests while meat was boiled in large cauldrons in anticipation of the meeting. A few casks of beer were opened; Senones hospitality was nothing, if not generous. It was a point of pride and honour amongst the tribes.

The envoys soon returned bringing with them a small contingent of Etruscan noblemen and warriors. Pleasantries were exchanged, food shared and a trade of Etruscan wine, ruby red and fragrant and Senones wheaten beer, frothy and potent, was enjoyed. The Etruscans were slightly smaller and stockier in stature and appearance compared to the Senones tribesmen. They were darker of skin and their hair was black and their eyes deep brown. To a man, the Etruscans were clean shaved with hair cropped close to the skull and they wore the traditional Mediterranean toga and long draping capes of good quality cloth wrapped around them leaving one arm bare. The colour was subdued and sombre. Only golden bracelets worn on the arm, added any charm to their appearance. Their sandals were made of leather and laced up the calf. Each man carried a small dagger on a belt and a few of the men, obviously with some experience in warfare, carried short Roman-style stabbing swords in scabbards on their leather belts.

By contrast, the Senones were long limbed, lean and muscular, their skin much lighter in hue. The tribesmen were wild haired, most men sported beards or long flowing moustache. They wore *braccae*, which sheathed their legs in woollen cloth, wrapped round with leather strips that tied below the knee. Their tunics were short sleeved and brightly coloured. Men of importance wore woollen capes fashioned from large squares of splendidly coloured cloth arranged in checked patterns that identified their tribe. At the shoulder, these marvellous capes were tied off with ornately decorated brooches or clasps. Their shoes were simple leather affairs laced to the foot and ankle. The women wore bright dresses that tied at the shoulders leaving the arms bare, though some women of status wore the brightly garish, woollen capes just like their men. Women and men alike wore a belt and a knife and both sexes adorned themselves with as much ornamentation and jewellery as their status permitted.

The Senones warriors carried spears, three to a man, and a shield that was two metres in height. Wealthy warriors of status, boasted swords carried on the belt at the right side. They were fearsome weapons of iron and were long, strong, and sharp. The great length of the swords made them excellent for slicing, chopping, and cutting men down.

An Etruscan nobleman watched, as Brennus and his advisors sat around a low table. He had to admit the brooches and jewellery of these people were exquisite. On closer inspection, he noticed that the woollen cloaks were also of very good quality. They seemed to know their crafts well, he thought to himself. He noticed in disgust, however, that both men and women ate together, and chewed their meat from the bone while shovelling small loaves of bread into their mouths with both hands. The Etruscan was offered some wheaten beer; courtesy and diplomacy demanded he accept. He did not care for the foul tasting beer and it sickened him, watching the barbarians gulp down great draughts of the vile stuff from large common bowls that were passed amongst them from one man to another. Even women were allowed to take a turn and gulp huge draughts of the vile stuff directly from the communal bowl.

It was with shock and disbelief that he saw these animals gulp down good Etruscan wine without first diluting it with spring water as was customary in all civilised countries. The nobleman averted his eyes in contempt at seeing the thick unadulterated ruby red wine spilling down into the barbarian's beards, only to be unconsciously wiped away with the back of a hand. He remained polite and did not protest; wise considering the giant, hairy, well-armed men, standing behind the seated barbarian leader and his council.

"We want land for our people. We want to live in peace and wish no conflict. We are a determined people though, and we will not be put from our course." Brennus's manner was short and to the point. His request was as law allowed, after the proper proprieties had been observed in civilised negotiations. Brennus foreseeing neither problem nor conflict with his legal request therefore thought it best to come straight to the point. Brennus was a direct man. The Etruscans however were offended and startled by the Senones abrupt manner and what they considered an outlandish demand. Their leader, however, managed to cover the indignation they all felt as a group. After all, they were out in the open, outnumbered and they had underestimated how well armed were these savages. He paused and asked the Senones leader why he thought he had the right to ask for any part of Etruscan land.

Brennus stopped eating. Slowly he looked around him at the gathered Etruscan dignitaries. He stood up from his seat of piled animal hides and reaching his full impressive height, he spoke in a tone low and rumbling like thunder.

"All things belong to the brave who carry justice on the point of their sword!"

The Etruscan nobles felt the icy grip of fear clutch at their intestines as they listened to the leader of the hairy barbarian savages.

"Well, thank you for your views. Certainly, such a request cannot be decided upon here and now. We will need a proper council meeting to give the situation the serious consideration it deserves, of that you can be sure. We will reconvene in a few days. Meanwhile feel free to enjoy the lands you already occupy." The Etruscan hoped that nothing he said had been lost in translation and that his meaning was clear, that they needed more time. Yet, he hoped for the sake of his people that his meaning was not too clear as to reveal what he really had in his mind. He smiled to cover his anxiety and presented Brennus with a large urn of wine as a parting gift while he and his entourage prepared to return to the city.

"Hold!" cried the large barbarian chieftain. The Etruscan turned back to face Brennus, his fear taking hold of him anew. Surely now, he thought, he and his men were to be brutally killed. As he looked with fear-filled eyes into the blazing blue of Brennus's eyes, he saw the chieftain was grinning and holding one of the great communal drinking bowls full of frothing wheaten beer.

"Drink with me in honour of your gifts!" It was more than an invitation and the Etruscan knew that to refuse would indeed seal the fate of his entourage. He accepted the large drinking bowl in both his trembling hands; the fumes from the disgusting brew watering his eyes. The barbarians all laughed as he gulped and spluttered down what he could of the vile drink. Smiling weakly, he proffered the communal drinking bowl to Brennus. The Etruscan watched with abject horror as the longhaired barbarian drained the huge bowl of its corrupt liquid to the chants and encouragement of his people. Dropping the bowl at his side, the leader of these "people" let out a disgusting loud and smelly belch. The Etruscan nearly vomited. He hurriedly left with the cheering and laughter of the vile invaders still ringing in his ears.

The leaders of Clusium were outraged at the "request" made by the Senones. Fear, however, outweighed their outrage. The banter of the council did little to hide the true emotion.

"We have seen only a small group of their warriors," said one of the men who had met the barbarians and was now briefing the city council. "They were all heavily armed and ferocious!"

"Indeed," said another nobleman, "one cannot tell womenfolk from warrior, both are hairy, big, ferocious and festooned with ornamentation!"

"One wonders how there can be so many of them with such fierce-looking women!"

The quip managed to alleviate some of the tension in the room as council members laughed nervously. The respite did not last long and the mood soon turned sour as the members continued to discuss the appearance of the barbarians and described in detail their mannerisms and customs.

"If we mobilise our army against them we run the risk of defeat. We have no way of knowing their true numbers, their strength nor where the main horde is located."

"Not only that," another nobleman pointed out," but if we employ the army, the damn Romans will hear of it and they will surely consider that an act of rebellion...."

"Don't be ridiculous! Surely we are permitted to defend ourselves against such an obvious threat to our security as these barbarian invaders present?" The council erupted into shouting, banging, and chaos. Above the din, a young council member jumped onto a table and tried desperately to be heard.

"Listen to me!" he cried, "Quiet! Listen to me!" The shouting began to abate as men tried to hear the words of the young man. Soon all eyes were on the young man standing on the table.

"It has only been a short time since the end of the war. We have signed treaties with Rome and we have made concessions to her. Whether we like it or not, my friends, for all intent and purpose we have been all but conquered by the Roman She Wolf." Yelling and shouting rose to deafening levels with these last words as prideful men refused to acknowledge what common sense told them.

"It is true what I say, though it is a terrible thing to realise! It is true that it would be foolish to mount an attack on this barbarian scum! We don't know enough about their strength and their strategy to make an intelligent plan. So, my idea is that we call upon Rome! They consider us conquered! We represent their northern interests; well let them protect their interests!"

A fistfight erupted amid a cacophony of shouts and howls of anger. The chaotic scene continued for nearly an hour before calm born mainly from exhaustion descended on the gathering of men. Gradually, with the calm came sense and good judgement and with that came agreement. Soon there were shouts of jubilation as the council members pounded their fists and banged their approval on the wooden tables.

Late that night, letters were drafted informing the Roman Senate of what had happened and requested their counsel. In the meantime, during the following days an answer from Rome was anxiously awaited. The Etruscan council held regular meetings with Brennus and his chieftains, plying them with gifts of wine and foods. These barbarians seemed to enjoy the thick regional wine. The Etruscans were still disgusted and horrified in seeing great quantities of their precious wine sloppily drunk, undiluted with water. The heady, undiluted wine combined with the heat of the land, caused the Senones to become quickly drunk. Deadly quarrels were common, as Senones warriors were quick to anger when they were drunk. Another worry occurred to the council of Clusium, what would happen if drunken barbarian warriors simply attacked them? Fortunately, Rome answered the Etruscan request.

Rome sent three members of the influential Fabian family and a contingent of legionnaires as envoys to negotiate a deal with Brennus on behalf of the Etruscans. The three young Roman noblemen were rude, insolent, and arrogant. They did not intend to negotiate with northern barbarian invaders. They assembled a small force of their own legionnaires along with a cohort of Etruscan patriots. Spies had been sent out to watch and observe the barbarians and to report any troop movements or gatherings to the Fabians.

These spies were astonished at what they saw, reporting to the Fabians, that there were no such reinforcements or gatherings bigger than the camp itself. Other than, a few small groups coming and going the camp's population seemed to remain constant. The men hunted wild game during the day and early evening hours. They spent the nights drinking, cavorting with their women, and fighting amongst themselves. Their revelry and ribald behaviour carried on well into the night, abating only a few hours before dawn. It was noted that only a handful of sentries were posted and they patrolled a perimeter lit by few watch fires. The Fabians decided to attack the barbarian Senones just before dawn when they knew the hairy tribesmen would have exhausted themselves in their debauchery and drunkenness.

A small group of Roman foot soldiers crept silently in the predawn light, toward the Senones encampment. In unison, they attacked the barbarian sentries. The killings were silent, except for one. A Senones warrior managed to shriek a warning before his throat was slashed. Weary warriors still half drunk with Etruscan wine and Senones beer, rolled from their slumber only to fight desperately for their lives in the dawn's early light. For a moment, it seemed that the barbarians would gain the upper hand, for they fought ferociously despite their supposed drunkenness. It was then the Fabian brothers led a cavalry charge and thundered into the Senones encampment, trampling everything under the hooves of their mounts. Riders hacked and slashed at every living thing in their path. The cavalry wheeled and swept through the camp repeatedly. Tents toppled and caught fire, screams filled the night as the Fabian riders ran down women and children.

When dawn finally broke, the destruction of the Senones camp was complete. The Etruscans were well pleased. All, that is, but for one of their captains who appeared uneasy.

"Can you not see the might of Rome has won a great victory here in the morning light?" Marcus Fabian spoke with contempt to the Etruscan captain as he wheeled his horse around.

"You will have no more trouble from these barbarian pigs, I promise you! Did you not see how they ran away when my brother Quintas Fabian killed one of their chieftains? They are nothing but wild, untamed animals! They are not civilised men!" The Roman spat into the ground near the captain and then rode off. The Etruscan did not say anything. The arrogant young Roman would not have listened in any case. Instead, the Etruscan captain simply looked up to the foothills of the mountains in the direction the barbarians had run. His stomach was suddenly upset.

The attack itself and the killing of a Senones chieftain was cause enough for anger. The insolence of the Fabians and the slaughter of women and children had outraged the tribesmen. The surviving Senones, Brennus among them, had quit their camp and retreated to the safety of their main horde camped well up in the foothills. The Roman spies had not ventured far enough and had been lulled into thinking the encampment they saw was all that there was of the Senones tribesmen.

Now the council of the Senones gathered around their leader. Brennus had believed the Romans were a neutral party in the issue of the Etruscan lands. The request made of the Etruscans by Brennus was according to the international laws. The Romans had now broken those agreements and treaties. What was worse was their insufferable arrogance! Yet, Brennus held his anger and outrage in check. Barely managing to convince his council his course of action was correct, Brennus decided to send his own envoy to Rome. He demanded that the Fabian family be handed over to him so that they may be held accountable for their treachery according to international law and the ways of the Senones. Brennus used the time preparing his tribesmen while he waited patiently for an answer to his envoy.

He had not long to wait, his envoy returned to him empty handed and the message they carried only served to outrage the tribesmen further. Rome had rewarded the Fabian family by appointing them to the highest rank possible. Rome not only condoned the Fabian arrogance and outrage but also had rewarded their breach of international law, adding further insult to Senones pride!

The last of his patience and good will evaporated. Brennus was filled with a cold fury! He amassed the thousands in his tribe and roused them to war! Senones pride would be avenged!

"We will march against the arrogant Romans and teach them about Senones pride! We will not interfere with any other towns or villages in the lands we cross, for our vengeance will be saved for Rome alone! All will witness the wrath of Brennus and his Senones! We will forever burn fear into the heart of every living Roman!"

Three hundred and eighty-six years before the Christian priests say their saviour was born, Brennus and his Senones crossed the River Allia, ten to twelve miles north of the city of Rome. A force of three cohorts of Roman soldiers had marched to meet the invaders. But at the sight of the horde of wild haired Senones warriors, the Romans turned tail and ran. Neither a sword nor a spear was raised against Brennus and his tribesmen. The river drowned many of the fleeing Roman soldiers, whilst some were fortunate enough to make it to the nearby city of Veii. Only a handful of terrified soldiers made their way to the safety of Rome. In their haste to take refuge in the citadel on Capitoline Hill, they had left the gates to the city open.

The great city was eerily silent. The garrison charged with the protection of Rome was under the command of Tribune Marcus Manlius Capitolinus. His men were frantically preparing for the onslaught they knew was imminent. The warriors of the Senones gathered inside the open city gates. Their war chariots thundered back and forth while the tribal warriors on foot banged their spears and swords on their shields. The great vertical horns called *carnyx* were trumpeted. The wall of sound was insanely terrifying and it went on and on as the tribesmen whipped themselves into a frightening frenzy of rage.

Then Brennus attacked, unleashing his hordes of crazed tribesmen. The war chariots cut through the city garrison with frightening speed. Each two-horsed chariot carried a driver and a spear-totting warrior who could jump off, stab slash, impale his enemy, and then swing his body back up and into the chariot with lightening speed. Waves of Senones warriors ran through the naked and defenceless city, killing, cutting, and slashing every living thing, they laid eyes upon. The screams of their victims pierced the air, cutting through the deafening noise of horses, chariots, trumpets and metallic crashing of swords and spears. The Senones leader had taken Rome and true to his word, the wrath of Brennus was truly terrible to behold!

For seven months, he allowed his warriors to rape and kill as they pleased. Broken and slashed bodies piled up in the city streets. Blood ran freely in the gutters as flies and vermin gorged themselves on the carcasses of the enemies of Brennus, leader of the Senones.

Seeking to save the capitol, the only building not yet defiled by the Senones, a badly wounded Marcus Manlius and a city official, Quintas Sulpicius, beseeched Brennus to call off his men. The city, cried the two Romans, would pay any tribute he cared to name if he would just stop the carnage.

"We want ten times his weight in gold," laughed one of Brennus's men as he pointed at his leader. Brennus smiled and glared at the Tribune.

"Yes, that is our price! Ten times my weight in gold!" Laughter filled the hall, spears banged on shields and a mighty frightening din rose up from the assembled warriors. Some over enthusiastic Senones grabbed, punched, and pummelled the Roman negotiators.

Marcus and Quintas barely escaped with their lives, bruised and slashed, but with their heads still intact. One of their attendants was not so fortunate. Quintas saw the man's head roll down the steps, just as a tribesman gathered it up and proudly stuck it on his spear for display.

A desperate meeting was held in the inner city. The rag tag band of senators and tribunes were all that was left of what had been the fledgling republican government. The debate centred on who these barbarians were and how they were going to pay them off.

"Who are these bastards? It has been months of killing and slaughter! The streets are slick with Roman blood and I know of no woman among our citizenry who has not been ravaged by these scum!"

"Where did they come from, why haven't we heard of them before this?" The wounded tribune cried.

"They are the ones the Fabians went after on behalf of the Etruscans," replied an old centurion.

An older man, a statesman, wise and respected was hunched in the corner. He shivered and shuddered as though an incredible weight was crushing the life from him. He wept silently. The day before last, he had witnessed his grand daughter being brutally raped and killed. The home he knew as a boy had been burned to the ground. His only son, the father of his beautiful granddaughter, had been cut down trying to save the house. The barbarian who killed him cut his head off and tied it to his horse as he rode off laughing.

"They are called *keltoi* by the Greeks." The old man said through parched lips as he lifted his weary head to address the gathering.

A respectful hush fell n the gathering. One young man compassionately put his arm around the old statesman.

"Grandfather, what does that mean," he gently asked, "who are these people?"

"They are *keltoi*, that's what the Greeks say they call themselves. I think it means *hidden*."

"Hidden? They are far from hidden, we saw..."

"...did you see the markings on some of them..."

"...even their women..."

"...if you can call them women; they were no different from the men..."

"... don't let the jewellery fool you...I saw enough bare breasts to recognise them as women..." There was some laughter at this remark.

"Grandfather what do you mean..."

"I only know the stories of the Greek travellers. They call all peoples from over the mountains "keltoi" because they hide their ways from strangers and write nothing down of their customs. They are known as the "Hidden Ones" or the "Unseen Ones," though some of the Greek scholars think the name means "fighter" or "warrior.""

"But how do you know this..."

".... are there more of them...."

"...where do they come from..."

The old man was brought to the centre of the group and given some watered wine. A robe was wrapped around his frail body and some bread was pressed into his shaking hands.

"I heard a story long ago, about a Greek teacher of history.... *Hecataeus*.... yes, I think that was his name. He wrote about meeting a strange people far to the Southwest in the Greek port of *Massalia*. This was many, many years ago, ages ago..." He paused and took some bread dipped in wine.

"They say they are many tribes and they are spread throughout many lands. It is said that they fight amongst themselves.... it is said they drink too much and are not to be trusted as allies.... some say they even fight naked at times and that they.... they.... take.... human.... human heads..." It was no use trying to get more information from the poor man now. He slumped in his robe, shoulders shuddering with his quiet sobs of his torment.

"Why haven't they burnt the capitol buildings?"

"Why do they want such a ransom..."

"...should we pay such a thing..."

"We have no choice but to pay!"

"The pride of Rome will not allow..."

"There is little left of Rome never mind her pride! If we don't pay soon they will burn the capitol buildings and Rome will never rise again.... we will never rise again!"

"They haven't tried to burn the buildings yet, the capitol still stands...."

"...for now it stands but eventually they will realise that is where our political power lies...."

"....they'll have to burn it then!"

"I don't understand why they don't move to do it now!"

"Whose side are you on...."

A brief scuffle broke out as the desperate men sought some way of making sense of the worsening situation that ensnared them.

"Enough...enough... if they haven't realised it yet perhaps we can buy some time with the gold. Once they have the gold they will leave and we will still have the capitol...."

".... and with time we will become strong again and hunt these *kelts*.... these vermin down...."

"Where will we get such a ransom?"

There was more debate and discussion; it carried on until the early hours of the morning. Finally, the inevitable was realised and the decision to pay Brennus his ransom was made. It took several more days for the Romans to gather so much gold. They looted temples, the treasury, even the coffers of the oldest and wealthiest families. Finally, they had what they believed was the demanded amount.

It fell to Quintus Sulpicius to take the ransom to the barbarian, Brennus. A brave young tribune of proud bearing volunteered to accompany him. A few stalwart legionnaires also joined in the dangerous assignment. The gold was loaded and the sad contingent wended its way through the horror of the streets to the city centre.

The occupied hall was filled with longhaired barbarian warriors. Brennus their leader lounged insolently in what was once a fine handcrafted chair of great value. Guards stood behind him, their eyes moved over the Roman contingent and registered only contempt. Quintas Sulpicius and his men continued, the huge ransom of heavy gold hauled in a wagon pulled by donkeys. Brennus and his men erupted in laughter at the sight of the sad procession. The Chief of the Senones ordered that a space be cleared and scales set up at once to measure the booty.

Roughly shoving the Romans away from their cart, Brennus's men began piling gold into ten piles, each one equal to the other, and approximately the weight of their leader according to the scales they had devised for the purpose. Seeing the sloppy manner in which their gold was being measured, the young tribune angrily protested. He demanded that Brennus use proper legal Roman scales to weigh the gold. His outrage and anger caught the Senones off guard and for a moment, silence fell on all the warriors in the hall.

Suddenly and violently, Brennus roared, his face contorted in rage as he again bellowed in the Roman's own tongue.

"*Vae victus!*" The phrase meant "*woe to the vanquished*" and with that, he threw his own iron sword onto the weights requiring even more gold to be added. Grabbing the closest legionnaire to him, Brennus pummelled him with his fist and threw the unconscious man to the ground. One of his chieftains, a relative of the slain chief killed by Quintas Fabian in the Etruscan raid, drew his sword and cut the head off the protesting tribune. Holding the head by the bloody edges of its severed neck, he raised the gory trophy high for his comrades to see and screamed.

"*Vae victus, Vae victus!*"

Brennus and the Senones eventually withdrew from the city and they did not burn the capitol. It was a defeat devastating to the Roman psyche and they never forgot their encounter with the *keltoi*, the *kelts*, the *Celts*, the barbarians from the North. Centuries afterward, Roman mothers would warn their children if they did not behave the Celts would come in the night and spirit them away!

Chapter 17

"You look astonished, young Arthgwr," Myrddin said, breaking the spell that had so mesmerised Arthgwr.

"I know it is hard to believe," he paused before taking another long draught of his mead, "but our ancient ancestors on the continent, could have ruled their own empire in place of the Romans!"

Arthgwr was stunned. He was amazed by what he had heard certainly, but there was much more than that. The storytelling of Myrddin was so exquisite, so thoroughly captivating and engaging that Arthgwr felt he had *lived* the story and not simply heard it!

He was dizzy and slightly weakened from the experience and he took a long pull from his own tankard of mead to regain his senses. He could not shake the feeling that he had *experienced* first hand the story Myrddin had told him of centuries past.

Perhaps it was the mead, he thought or simply that he was tired, but Arthgwr still could not rid himself of feeling he had been right there with Brennus of the Senones.

The old Druid continued, not noticing Arthgwr's distress at the experience.

"Yes, our ancestors were part of many independent tribes and we shared similarities in language, culture and religion. We were known throughout the ancient world for our bravery and ferocity in battle! We fought with Alexander the Great, ransacked Illyria, settled the Carpathian Mountains and defeated and killed the Macedonian king, Ptolemy Ceraunos. We Celts founded the kingdom of Tylis and fought as mercenaries with Ptolemy I of Egypt. Our ancient relatives even supported Hannibal's invasion of Italy! Hannibal's feat of taking elephants across those mountains would never have succeeded without the expertise of our guides, tribesmen, and warriors! We minted coins, farmed, built forts and roads, excelled in metallurgy and made broaches and fine jewellery! Our noblemen and women were fastidious about their appearance and spent a great deal of time brushing their long hair, applying lime wash to it and adorning their bodies with ornaments and tattoos of intricate design! Our people washed their bodies with soap while Romans were still scraping the day's filth from their bodies with a *stipula*!"

Myrddin was now frothing at the mouth and shaking with the passion of reciting the past glories of his Celtic heritage. Suddenly, he stopped his ranting and fixed Arthgwr with a stare of piercing intensity.

"Listen to me and hear me well, Arthgwr! You need to understand the history of our race. Knowing your past will better prepare you for what is to come. It is important for our people's future that you learn from my stories! You will work this thing for our people, not for any personal gain!"

The old man turned abruptly and refilled his tankard with mead, releasing Arthgwr from his gaze.

Arthgwr had been trapped and captivated by the power of Myrddin's eyes. Their intensity had sapped the strength from his body. He felt, now that he was released from their hold, much like a drowning man breaking the surface of the sea and gulping at the precious air. The full weight and meaning of Myrddin's words had not yet formed in Arthgwr's mind. He was still reeling from the physical shock the hearing of them had caused. It had been taxing enough to live through the tales of Myrddin, but to experience the old Druid's frustrations, the anger that blazed from his eyes, that was something else! Arthgwr's head was swimming; he quickly drank down some more mead. The tangy liquor calmed him and settled his mind. Myrddin did not notice Arthgwr's reaction to his little speech; he seemed lost in another time. The Wise One took another draught of his mead and then launched into another tale, painting word pictures that entered the depths of Arthgwr's very being.

"Our biggest fault was our own sense of independence and individuality," Myrddin said, his rich and melodic voice carrying Arthgwr away again.

"It was difficult for the many tribes of Celts to come together for a common purpose. We did not have a centralised government although we clung to a common myth of a king of all the Celts. This "King of the Celts" would lead us, so we believed, to victory over our enemies. The reality was much different as tribe fought tribe over the smallest of infractions and for the most trivial of reasons. Each tribe elected their own king who ruled their tribe for the period of one year. With so many kings and chieftains changing yearly, it was impossible for our ancestors to come together as a cohesive nation. More than simply a bad political system, this tradition of freedom and independence kept our Celtic race from unifying and becoming a centralised power base creating a powerful society sharing common goals and ideals."

Myrddin took another gulp of mead but his eyes did not release Arthgwr and he could do nothing but sit and stare at the old man.

The Wise One continued with his tale....

Rome consolidated and increased her power conquering much of the known world, picking up the pieces of Alexander's decayed empire. Roman law was strict and punishment was swift and ruthless; it was the glue that held the fledgling empire together. There was no doubt Rome ruled with an iron hand. Yet, a Celtic tribe, the Tirgurini had fought and defeated a Roman army. Not only had the army experienced a humiliating defeat but also the Consul, Lucius Cassius, had been killed. What's more, this act of open rebellion had occurred and had been allowed to stand, unanswered for decades!

An ambitious man of some importance, from a good family, took it upon himself to bring these Celtic tribes to heel. He was in the land the Romans called *Gaul*, the lands below the River Rhine. To these new Romans, Gauls and Celts were the same, the Roman word *Geltae*, can be seen as similar to the Greek, *Keltoi*. This man of ambition named Gaius Julius Caesar was determined to increase his reputation as a brilliant general, Guardian of Rome and indispensable leader. Through his army of spies and informants, Caesar had received word that the tribe of the *Helvetii* had gathered with the *Boii,* the *Tirgurini,* and others intending to embark on a migration into the land of the *Avernians.*

Caesar's plan was to convince Rome that a major military commitment was necessary to safeguard her against the hordes of barbarians that included the dreaded Tirgurini who had years before committed such an affront to Roman honour.

Of course, Caesar had to cajole the Roman consul Pompey to lend him the money he required fielding an army. He managed to do this by offering his daughter Julia in marriage to Pompey, a much older man. The bargain struck, he convinced the Senate that he, Gaius Julius Caesar, was the best man to lead a great army in a campaign to tame the wild Celtic tribes. This appealed to the ancient fears Rome still harboured toward the Celts. The Roman province, Gallia Narbonensis, would need protecting. That sentiment convinced the Senate and Caesar had his army and his mandate.

Caesar thought to deny the Helvetii and their kin the permission to migrate. This, he thought, would provoke a battle with the three hundred and sixty thousand men, women and children intent on migrating. Such a battle would be very popular in Rome.

Roman spies and agents were everywhere, making alliances and agreements with the many Celtic tribes and bringing the information back to Caesar.

Armed with the knowledge of what was in the mind of his adversaries, confident of his leadership and the discipline of his legions, Caesar believed he would easily conquer the disorganised tribes. Their constant bickering, their pride and lack of centralised command would, Caesar thought, be the tribes' downfall. He was correct. *"Dived et impera"* became Caesar's mantra.

Caesar put down a Celtic/Gallic revolt by crushing the Celtic tribe of the *Belgae,* but this action only served to inspire a bigger rebellion. The son of Celtillo of the Arverni tribe dreamed of being the mythical "King of the Celts."

His name was Vercingetorix, a name that meant, "great king of a hundred battles." Vercingetorix led a rebellion, a successful campaign against the mighty Caesar. The young Arverian chieftain was a good fighter and he was much respected by his tribe. His personality also garnered him the respect from other tribes that allowed him to manage the great feat of uniting a few more of the tribes into one fighting force under his command. Vercingetorix was very close to living his dream of being the "King of the Celts"!

At the city of Gergovia, Vercingetorix handed the Roman general his first taste of defeat. This was a monumental achievement and it was a devastating blow to Caesar's huge ego, more so since he believed his victor to be an illiterate barbarian from the North!

The chieftains, however, were angered by Vercingetorix's tactic of burning crops and killing livestock in the villages they came across. This strategy of scorched earth was designed to deny Caesar and his legions food and supplies. Far from home Caesar depended on the local villages to resupply his army. The chieftains could not see the tactical advantage this strategy provided and they were blind to the devastating effect this policy was wreaking on the Romans. The tribal leaders demanded Vercingetorix end the tactic, for they could no longer stomach the hungry cries of their own tribesmen. The chiefs rebelled and fought faction against faction until finally Vercingetorix, against his own better judgement, agreed to their demands to gather the army and hold the city of Alesia.

This tragic change of strategy played right into Caesars hands. He was a brilliant tactician in his own right and the consummate master of the siege. Now free to resupply his forces without hindrance, Caesar quickly recovered his strength and began the siege of Alesia. He ordered his men to undertake a tremendous task to build not one, but two, concentric walls around the entire city.

Vercingetorix saw this and knew his only hope was with the men he had sent to outlying tribes. If they could manage to persuade the chiefs to gather their men and attack Caesar while he was preoccupied with his siege, the city of Alesia could be saved. Vercingetorix's men did not impress the other chiefs. They were hospitable and invited the men to council, but the chiefs just ate, drank, and argued amongst themselves. These other chiefs drank and boasted of their prowess as fighting men while Vercingetorix, his men and the city of Alesia were left to face the might of the Roman siege machines and the incredible walls Caesar's men were building.

It was inevitable that the siege soon starved the inhabitants of Alesia. There was nothing the great Arverian king could do but surrender to his own people as our Celtic custom dictated. The men handed their leader over to the Roman general. Vercingetorix rode his great white horse alone into the camp of Gaius Julius Caesar. He was dressed in the manner of a Celtic chief, the great gold torc around his neck showing his rank, tattoos on his arms and shoulders, his hair, long and flowing, and thick drooping moustache, and a great woollen cape flowing behind him.

Dismounting his fabulous white steed with dramatic flourish, Vercingetorix drew his long iron sword and placed it on the ground before him. He knelt in the dirt at Caesar's feet.

"I am the leader of my people", the proud King of the Celts said.

"I am responsible for them. You have conquered my people but I ask that you spare the lives of those in the city that have suffered so greatly. Allow them to surrender to you, to pay tribute to you, but let them live. I am your enemy and I give myself to you that you may do with me as you wish."

Caesar agreed to Vercingetorix's requests. The gesture, which was all his acquiescence amounted to, was ineffective. Seventy-five thousand men, women, and children starved inside the hundreds of acres that was once the mighty city of Alesia. Caesar took Vercingetorix back to Rome with him as a prize to the delight of the Roman citizenry. Vercingetorix was kept a captive for six years before he was dragged from his cell, paraded into the city, and ritually strangled in a huge public spectacle for the glory of the great Caesar.

Myrddin abruptly stopped his tale and turned to look at Arthgwr.

"You can see, Arthgwr, how our fierce independence, though admirable, has also been our greatest weakness. Do you know how we got the name of "Britons"?" Arthgwr could only shake his head no.

"A Greek named Pytheaus used the name, "*Prettanike*" which the Romans later translated to "*Pretani*," to describe our people living in the mysterious mist shrouded shores of our islands. They thought we lived in a horrible place at the end of the earth. The word comes from our own language and means "*people who paint themselves.*" Our warrior's ritual of painting their bodies with blue woad, made an impression, as did our tattoos. Roman writers, Caesar among them, converted the name Pretani to *Britannia!*"

Myrddin was angry again and he went about the hut in search of more mead. He stopped to stretch his back and then occupied himself with poking the hearth until a lick of flame leapt and engulfed a new log. Myrddin eased his back again, his mood somewhat under control. Arthgwr watched the old man but his own mind was in turmoil. Myrddin's story telling continued to make him believe he was really living the experience and not simply sitting in a hut by the fire, listening to stories at the feet of a grandfather. Not only that, but as Arthgwr watched Myrddin rant and rave about the hut, the old man seemed to grow younger. It might be the mead, the exhaustion, or even the excitement of the stories he was hearing, Arthgwr did not know, but he was certain the "old man" was looking younger than he had earlier! He looked down to see Myrddin had refilled his tankard of mead and had pushed a bowl of the broth in front of him. The warmth of the newly stoked fire and the generous tankards of mead helped calm his mind and Myrddin too seemed to settle.

After another long draught of mead, the Wise One began again to cast his spellbinding tale...

In the year fifty-five before the birth of the new religion's son of their god, Julius Gaius Caesar amassed legionnaires and supplies together with some *Gauls* and attempted an invasion of the misty islands. Caesar questioned the traders amongst the Celtic tribesmen about the island and its inhabitants. Those he questioned were either unwilling or unable to provide him with the knowledge he sought. Word spread amongst the Celtic slaves along the coastal villages of Gaul of Caesar's intention to invade the islands. Envoys from southern Briton tribes soon began appearing at Caesar's camp. He welcomed them with hospitality and plied them with Roman wine and fineries. Caesar cunningly negotiated with the chieftains extracting promises of allegiance and support. It was his trademark strategy of divide and conquer.

Having decided to send his own envoy to secure a safe landing, Caesar chose Commios, a chieftain from the Atrebatian tribe, and someone who he held in high regard.... for a barbarian. The choice was an easy one. Commios bragged that he was chief of the Atrebatians on both the continent and the islands. His people, he claimed, lived in both places and they were loyal to him. Caesar counted on this and hoped the island tribe would be further encouraged to allow him a safe landing. It was the promise of gold that had turned Commios to Caesar's ambitious plan. Gold that would help Commios remain in power on both sides of the sea.

However months later when Caesar's eighty transports and dozen warships came within sight of the chalky white cliffs of Britannia, he was dismayed to see hostile tribes of native Britons arrayed upon the cliffs above.

"Commios has failed," Caesar, thought to himself, "either that or he is working his own agenda." Commios had indeed warned the Briton tribe of the Cantii. He had told them of the Roman generals design on their lands. In doing so, Commios consolidated the alliance of other southern tribes and became a powerful chieftain. The planned landfall for the Roman invaders was now impossible.

Caesar had no choice but to sail his small fleet up the coast seven miles. And there, more savage Britons met him. The troop carriers were hard for the Roman soldiers to manoeuvre. The Britons rained a hail of arrows and spears down on the Roman invaders as they tried to beach their cumbersome ships. Caesar's VII and X Legions disembarked along the rocky beachhead. The legionnaires struggled in chest high waters. They were terrified by what they saw above the beach.

The Britons appeared naked and their skin was blue. Their hair was coated in lime wash causing their thick manes to stand stiff and straight adding to their height. Intricate designs and tattoos could be seen on their blue-tinted and naked bodies. The din was fierce.

Warriors screamed and shrieked their rage, banged spears, and swords on shields while their priests sounded their peculiar trumpets called carnyx. The wild tribesmen flung spears and slashed with their long iron swords at the Romans. Tribal archers dared death and stood boldly on the gravel beach and shot arrow after arrow into the legionnaires at close range. Caesar's men were able to set up several *catapultae*, wooden machines that harnessed the power of tightly wound ropes. The catapultae could send missiles ripping into their targets with tremendous force and were accurate to two hundred and fifty yards. The Britons had never seen such machines. They were forced to give way to protect themselves.

A Roman standard bearer had the pluck to jump from his ship and advance into the battle.

"Come legionnaires," he screamed, "the honour of your legion is at stake! Come and fight for Roman honour!" Many men followed his brave example and for the moment, they suppressed their fear of the terrifying Britons. A savage close quarter battle was fought. Briton and Roman alike were forced to step over the dead and dying to fight each other. The waves ran red with blood. More Romans poured from their boats forcing the outnumbered Britons further back. Caesar had his landfall.

The beachhead had come at a steep price. The Romans were without their cavalry and most of their supplies and food had been lost in the churning waves. Caesar could not move onward. Briton tribesmen and charioteers careened up the beach keeping Caesar's forces contained. The sight of the Britons and the chariots terrified his men.

The chariot had not been seen on the continent for a hundred years and no Roman soldier present had ever faced one in battle. Before terror gripped any tighter, a mighty storm erupted, putting the Roman ships in grave danger. The miscalculation of the tides during that time of year was a deadly mistake. More ships were lost.

The Romans managed to survive and the storm had kept the Britons distracted looking after their own. Caesar had snuck envoys out amongst the local tribes. The negotiations had paid off and a truce in hostilities had been arranged. The lull in fighting allowed the Romans precious time in which to refurbish and repair their ships. It had been noticed by the Britons that the Romans were vulnerable.

Tribal warriors surprised the VII Legion while they foraged for food. The Britons charged from the tree line driving the Romans into confusion as Briton chariots drove back and forth. Tribal warriors jumped down from the chariots platform to fight on foot and then swept back up as the expert charioteers wheeled around. Caesar himself noticed the expertise of the riders and charioteers. He saw the ingenuity of the tribesmen's chariots that allowed their warriors the mobility of cavalry and the power of infantry. The Romans had not seen this tactic before, as they were more accustomed to proper cavalry. The small but hearty ponies of the Britons might not carry a man to battle, but in harness, they were perfect for the open-ended chariot of the Britons.

Warriors from other tribes of Briton soon came to the gravelly shore. They stood arrayed against the Romans. The Britons banged their shields with their spears and swords, sounded their carnyx, and beat their drums. The din was incredible and terrifying to behold. The charioteers attacked while tribesmen rushed at the invaders. They hurled spears and shot arrows at the Roman soldiers. Roman discipline held. At Caesar's order, the legionnaires formed a wall of shields and they held firm against wave after wave of screaming Britons.

The Britons, disheartened by the unflappable discipline of the Roman legionnaires and frustrated in their attempt to break through their ranks, finally gave way. An envoy of Britons negotiated for peace with Caesar. Commios and his thirty horse soldiers appeared and were returned to the Roman general. Caesar was told that the Cantii had held his former ally and all his men captive the entire time. Accompanying Commios was a man called Mandubratios of the Trinovantes tribe.

Caesar was bottled up on the hard shore faced with a hostile enemy. The Roman cavalry were lost in the storm or had been forced back to the continent. His troops were running out of food and supplies and he had no equipment for a winter campaign. The ambitious Caesar ordered his men to cannibalise the damaged ships to repair the more salvageable survivors of his fleet. Caesar honoured the peace envoy and took Commios and Mandubratios aboard his ship as assurance of good faith. The Romans hurriedly set sail on a favourable wind and left Britannia.

Myrddin stopped his narration. He stood and stretched his back. Arthgwr sat motionless unable to move, he was still under the spell of the master storyteller. The fire roared at Myrddin's prodding, filling the room with warmth and light. Arthgwr regained his senses and accepted the tankard of mead thrust into his hand by Myrddin. He tried to focus on the Old One as he roamed about the room poking the fire some more, fiddled with a new jug of mead, the stuff seemed in endless supply and yet Arthgwr did not feel intoxicated. Finally, Myrddin came to rest in his chair. His blue eyes twinkled under bushy white eyebrows, but as Arthgwr focused on the old man's face, the eyebrows appeared less white. The deep and melodic voice of Myrddin began again, words cascaded from his lips, their cadence lulling Arthgwr into a kind of trance. He was soon transported back in time as though he saw for himself the happening of things that had passed long ago...

Caesar planned a second invasion of the Misty Isles. He intended to set sail from a point on the continent that provided the narrowest stretch of sea between him and the island. The staging point was the coast of the Morini tribe. This time Caesar took hostages to prevent any repeat of what he suspected was the treachery of his former ally Commios. The hostages were Celtic chieftains, among them a popular and powerful man, a chieftain of the Aedui.

Dumnorix was his name, the meaning of which was "King of the World." Dumnorix loudly protested being forced to accompany Caesar to the islands. Mockingly he informed Caesar that he would be unable to travel with him as he suffered from seasickness. Caesar was not amused and refused to excuse him. The leader of the Aedui was a proud man and he openly bristled at being ordered about by a foreigner in his own land. There was little doubt that the continentals Celts, those who Caesar called Gauls, were of the same stock and of the same tribes as the islanders. Caesar had been told that Diviciacus of the Suessiones had been a king, who had influence over large tracts of lands on both sides of the water. Caesar's own envoy and former ally Commios, had bragged he had reign over both island and continental factions of his own tribe.

The continental Celts, *Gauls*, seemed to have a peculiar reverence for the misty islands. The rumour circulating amongst Caesar's legionnaires was that the Aedui, Morini, and the others, revered the islands as sacred. It was said that the Gauls believed the islands of the Britons to be the sacred home of priests from a holy religious sect, a very powerful religious sect and that to attack the islands was an act of great sacrilege.

Myrddin stopped his telling again and smiled at Arthgwr.

"Oh yes," he said, "we were once very powerful and were held in high esteem even by our cousins on the continent. Our power was considerable in those days! In our society, no king was permitted to speak before a Druid spoke. We held huge gatherings which occurred each year when an "Arch-Druid" was chosen as a leader. These gatherings took place in Celtic Gaul on a holy mound a day's ride from the seat of power of the Parisi tribe. It amazed the Romans that priests from every corner of the Celtic world seemed to be in contact with each other, so co-coordinated were these massive gatherings. Oh yes, that confounded them and caused them to wonder in fear!" Myrddin chuckled to himself before continuing.

"Caesar believed it was our priest's religious influence that inspired our people to revolt against Rome. On that point he was right!"

Myrddin swallowed some more mead to calm him and then smiled again at Arthgwr.

"I'm not tasking you too much am I, my boy?"

Arthgwr was unable to reply. He could hear Myrddin, but his mind was still transfixed by the Wise One's story. Arthgwr could only manage a weak smile. Myrddin continued with his history...

Many of the hostages believed that Caesar was not keeping them merely as assurance against rebellion in Gaul, but that he intended on killing the chieftains. This was something he could not do in plain sight of the tribes for fear of insurrection. It was not lost on the tribesmen that in taking the most vocal of the chieftains with him into the waters between Celtic Gaul and the Islands that the General would benefit greatly if some mishap occurred at sea.

Dumnorix had been preaching and advocating Celtic unity for some time. The tribal bickering angered him, as had the infighting that had allowed the Romans to plunder tribal lands and divide the populace. The day before departure, Dumnorix and his cavalry rode from Caesar's camp. He arrogantly shouted, "Dumnorix and Aedui take hostages never do we give them!"

The chieftains and priests were making their own protestations. It was clear to Caesar that the chieftains and their followers were inspired to rebellion by Dumnorix's example. This threat to his invasion plans greatly concerned the Roman General.

To show the tribes his mettle and his ruthlessness, Caesar sent a troop of cavalry after the Aedui leader. The Roman troop rode hard and without rest and finally caught up with the Aedui and his escort before nightfall. Though they were surprised and overwhelmed by the Roman show of force, the Aedui fought fiercely. A centurion struck Dumnorix with a spear throwing the Aedui from his horse. Pouncing, the Roman managed to get the better of the fallen king. Catching his breath, Dumnorix fought back like a wild animal. The centurion managed to plunge his short Roman sword into the Audi's chest.

"I am a free man of a free nation!" Dumnorix managed to scream with his last dying breath.

The invasion was to start as planned. Many of the legionnaires were uneasy about Caesar's plan to bring Gauls with them to the Islands. They were especially worried now, after the killing of Dumnorix. They did not trust the Celtic Gauls and felt they would side with the island Celts at the first opportunity. The troops overheard the tribesmen speak reverently about the islands and their religious significance. What they heard made them afraid.

"I wonder if I'll lose my head during the crossing or when we land," quipped one soldier.

"Never mind Marcus, it will be of no great loss to you in any case." Laughter eased the men's growing tensions.

"So what are these bastards like, then?" asked one recruit.

"I do not know, I suppose they're the same as these buggers here..."

"I've heard that the priests of their religion are powerful magicians and they have warriors who paint themselves blue and fight naked with their worn wild like a horse's mane...."

"Don't you worry! Anyone fighting naked in this cold won't need to paint themselves, they'll turn blue with the cold!"

"But it's summer...."

"It maybe summertime for these smelly bastards, Lucius, but at home in my village this would feel like winter. Aaah, I do miss the warmth of the hot sun at midday, a glass of wine, perhaps a nap in the garden...." One of the men threw a helmet full of cold seawater and everyone laughed at the soldier's spluttering and cursing as his fantasy of home was rudely interrupted.

"Do they take heads, Captain?"

"Only if you let them, boy, only if you let them..." He managed to muster enough saliva to spit unenthusiastically on the deck of the transport ship.

The men continued boarding the war ships and loading supplies. Once underway, the legionnaires felt better, but a storm struck from out of nowhere and they were immediately kept busy, trying to stay afloat. They scrambled to their duties, slipping and sliding in cold seawater and warm vomit. More than a few men were lost over the side. Finally, they made landfall on the chalky coast of Britannia.

This time Caesar had an unopposed landing. He ordered the men to carefully beach the ships. The troops were put to work immediately making repairs caused by the sudden gale. Other soldiers spread out to secure their position. Leaving a tribune in charge of five thousand men to protect their main camp, Caesar took his army on a forced night march.

The Romans met with the tribe of the Cantii on the banks of the great Stour River. The legionnaires crossed the river and engaged the tribesmen. A running battle of cavalry and chariots ensued since the Cantii would not stand and fight in the Roman manner of formed ranks. Instead, they sent small groups to attack the Roman flanks, then they broke off their attack and retreated into the great forests. This tactic inflicted great losses on the Romans because the Cantii warriors would ambush any troop of legionnaires foolish enough to follow them into their ancestral forests.

Caesar however was a great orator, a persuasive and charismatic personality and he succeeded in marshalling the courage of his men. His troops mercilessly attacked the enemy pressing on even into the forest. The Cantii took many casualties and began pulling further back until they finally retreated into their hill-fort. These forts were fashioned from wood strengthened with ditches and steep earthen banks built on top o hills. The Cantii held the biggest hill-fort in southern Briton.

Caesar, ever the consummate tactician, had no problem in taking the fort. The fighting was fierce and in the confusion and din of the battle, the chieftains and main fighting force of the Cantii managed to escape into the woods. The Romans had gone two days without sleep or food and with the weather turning nasty, Caesar opted not to pursue the Cantii, but regroup his forces instead.

The Cantii warriors marched seventy-five miles from the sea, north to the River Tamesis and into the lands of the great chieftain Caswallon of the Cassivelauni tribe. The southern tribes had voted to elect Caswallon as supreme commander. He was a very clever and successful war leader and considered to be king over the tribes of the Cantii, the Cassivelauni, the Trinovantes and Artebates. The other tribes welcomed the Cantii. Caswallon began his war against Caesar by attacking foraging parties and slowing the Roman's inland expeditions.

This manner of fighting that Caswallon employed was not the usual way the tribes fought their enemies. Normally, rival factions would send wave after wave of fierce warriors screaming down upon their enemy. Overwhelmed by the maddening onslaught the weaker tribe would sue for peace. Sometimes a champion would be selected from each side and the two champions would fight each other to determine which side won. Caswallon instinctively knew that traditional tribal warfare would not work against Roman discipline. So, he rallied his warriors at the tree line in sight of the Roman legionnaires and there they began to bang their shields with their swords and spears.

The priests blew their carnyx and with the Celtic women, they screamed curses down upon the Romans. The noise was terrible and it had the desired effect. The Romans were unnerved and frightened. Caesar was taxed trying to keep his army together. He ordered a phalanx of men to attack the Celts in the tree line. As the Romans marched toward them, the Celts melted into the trees. When the Romans followed, they were slaughtered by slings, spears, and arrows and cut down by slashing swords of iron.

Caswallon refused to engage the Romans directly. He was a hunter and Caswallon had seen his own hunting hounds run down a great stag. The majestic animal exhausted itself trying in vain to kick and gore the hounds until it blundered spent and frightened into the range of his arrows. Caswallon now employed a strategy against the Romans, of nipping at his enemy's heels while staying away from its horns and hooves. He bloodied them terribly, interrupting their supply lines, devastating their foraging parties, killing all who foolishly entered the dark woods. He kept charioteers swirling around the Roman encampment but keeping out of range of Roman arrows. The continuous din of sword on shield and the blasting of carnyx grated on the Roman's nerve.

Night passed uneasily for the Roman soldiers in their camp. They had managed to build embankments and fortifications though many times they had to throw down their shovels and fight off another attack. The morning broke and they were attacked again by the Cassivelaunni accompanied by the same ear splitting noise of the night before. The hit and run strategy of the Britons harried and confused the Romans, but as the day wore on the Britons impatience got the better of them. One group of tribesmen, their blood lust up, bravely charged head long into Caesar's forces fiercely hacking and slashing with their long iron swords.

This was the type of fighting to which the Romans were accustomed. They fought a fearsome battle. The disciplined fighting of the Roman soldiers under the leadership of Caesar pushed the attacking Britons back, killing hundreds in the process. Caswallon had no choice but to retreat. Caesar had gained his first advance.

Caswallon was on the run and Caesar's troops gave chase, pursuing Caswallon to the Briton's tribal lands on the banks of the great River Tamesis. The Cassivelaunni tribesmen were prepared to prevent any crossing of the river. They had driven huge, iron-tipped spikes into the riverbed approaching the banks. Under the discipline of Caesar, the legionnaires worked their way around the deadly spikes, though it cost them dearly in blood, as arrows rained down upon them. They continued to press Caesar's invasion into the boundary lands between the Cassivelaunni and the Trinovantes.

The Britons knew Mandubraccios of the Trinovantes, by the name of Afarwy. He was furious with Caswallon for killing his father, Imanuentos, Chief of the Trinovantes. Knowing this and understanding the treacherous nature of Afarwy, Caesar successfully tempted him by promising him the chiefdom of his father. All that was required was for Afarwy not to throw his support in alliance of tribes that supported Caswallon.

This Afarwy agreed to. Caesar was now deep inside Trinovantian lands, Afarwy at his side. Caesar accepted tributes of grain ensuring his flanks were now protected against attack. Rested and fed Caesar's men marched to the hill fort of Caswallon. With newfound fortitude, they braved the natural barriers of swamps and forests and attacked the stronghold of the Cassivelaunni.

Caswallon escaped through the back of the hill fort. Caswallon had his own strategy in play. His allies, Cingetorix, Carnilius, Taximagulus and Segonox of the Cantii, were set to attack Caesar's base camp. These brave Celtic leaders would draw Caesar back to his base and allow Caswallon precious time to regroup and lead his coalition of Cantii, Cassivelaunni, Trinovantes and the Artebates.

The attack failed. Fortunately for Caesar, and though he was drawn back to the base camp, he stayed only long enough to refresh and resupply before heading back to Caswallon's hill fort. This was a major blow to Caswallon. Now unhindered by the leadership of Caswallon and free from his hit and run tactics, Caesar's men raided outlying farms and devastated Caswallon's lands causing defections amongst the Celtic alliance. To weaken the Roman advance, Caswallon resorted to burning crops and killing livestock, a burnt earth policy that backfired on him as it did on Vercingetorix on the mainland. The treachery of Afarwy prevented Caswallon from negotiating for supplies. The mighty tribal leader was faced with rebellion from his own tribesmen.

Caesar wasted no time in negotiating a treaty with the now weakened Caswallon. The Great Chief was forced to sue for peace by his own tribal council. Caesar was in a hurry now to return to Gaul where another rebellion was brewing. He demanded hostages. These hapless souls would be sold as slaves to defray the cost of the expedition. This was the first of thousands upon thousands of slaves that would come out of Briton in the next four hundred years!

A tribute was to be paid to Caesar yearly and a truce between the Cassivelaunni leader and the Trinovantes tribe was to be honoured.

Caesar hastily departed the shores of Briton. Many tribal leaders believed, despite the complicity of the traitor Afarwy, that Caswallon had defeated the Roman general. Caswallon, they said, had fought a battle of such intensity that Caesar was forced to protect himself and he engaged the Britons with his own sword drawn. During the battle, Caesar saved himself, but in doing so, he lost his sword on the battlefield. Caswallon, the Britons said, took possession of Caesar's sword. Caswallon celebrated this victory with his tribesmen displaying the sword of Caesar for all to see.

As to hostages, the only hostages surrendered were Afarwy and his army for their lives would not be spared if they stayed on the island.

No tribute was ever paid to Rome. Caesar failed to establish a Roman colony on the islands of the Britons. He could not truthfully claim to have added Britannia as a subjugated province in the Roman Empire.

Caswallon regained his kingship of the southern tribes by bringing to heel the treacherous Trinovantes. Britannia remained a rich and independent Celtic nation for another one hundred years!

Myrddin was on his feet again and pacing around the hut in his anger.

"Yes, Caswallon kept Caesar's sword and sent the Roman bastard packing! That's not how you hear the story told these days, is it? No, those lying Romans would have us all believe they are invincible!"

"Rome did conquer our island and they brought law and order with them," Arthgwr said pointedly. His head still reeling with the tales he had heard. His senses still so raw from experiencing those tales as though he had lived them, that he was checking his own body for war wounds.

"The might of Rome! The civilisation of Rome, Ha!" spat Myrddin. "Did you know that it was hunting dogs and human slaves, that the Romans took as booty from these islands? The Romans did not conquer us so much, as we were unable to fight them! It broke my heart to see the tribal chiefs turned against each other, squabbling and fighting like a pack of curs snarling at each other over the scrapings from their master's table! And for what? Riches, lands, power, or so they thought! It was their country and their souls that they sold to the Roman shopkeepers! Let me tell you about the invasion one hundred years after Caesar..."

Chapter 18

"The Roman aristocrat, Tiberius Claudius Drusu Nero Germanicus, became Emperor Claudius the year that the great chieftain of the Britons, Cunobelinos died," began Myrddin, his voice again transporting Arthgwr to another time.

Emperor Claudius soon realised he needed a military victory to establish himself securely and gain Rome's confidence. With this thought in mind, he raised an army of twenty-five thousand troops plus auxiliaries and cavalry that totalled a force of fifty thousand men. Platius, the officer in charge of the Emperor's new army, was told that when victory over the Britons was in sight, he should hold his position and send word to Emperor Claudius. The ruler of Roman would cross the channel and be present at the fall of Briton.

The troops were amassed for the quick voyage across the channel to the Misty Islands. Many of the men were fearful and disgruntled. They had been anxious about making the trip from Rome to the distant shores of the mysterious islands some still thought of as the end of the world. As the troops readied themselves for the perilous crossing, their passion for the adventure waned. Roman discipline ruled the day, however, and the invasion force set forth.

The landing was unopposed. Platius thought, the Britons certainly must have known the invasion was underway, how could they not? There was much trading of goods between the Celts and the Mediterranean world and gossip and news must have easily travelled to the inhabitants of Briton. Platius was not to be disappointed. When he had established a base camp he sent out patrols to get the lay of the land and to scrounge up whatever in the way of supplies they could find. The patrols were immediately attacked, men were lost and the attackers simply vanished back into the great forests.

The Romans called the new chief of the Britons, Caratacos, though his people knew him as Caradoc, son of the Great Cunobelius and an ancestor of the renowned Caswallon. Like his ancestors, Caradoc did not engage the Roman legions in open conflict. He employed the same guerrilla tactics his ancestor had used to harry the Roman patrols every time they left their base. Caradoc and his brother Togodumnos with their men and chariots inflicted heavy losses on the Romans. Even still, Platius to his credit, managed to secure positions at the cities of Rutupiae, Dubris and Lemanae.

The Britons did not believe the Romans capable of crossing the River Medway and so were careless in setting up their camp on the river's bank. Few guards were posted and no one looked after the horses.

Instead much beer and mead was drunk and the men sang and danced until they fell into a stupor. Platius upon seeing this devised a cunning plan. He called upon the *Batavia*, Roman troops who specialised in swimming while clad in armour. Once they swam the river, the Batavia stealthily crept into the Briton's camp. There were not enough men in their force to engage and kill the Britons, but they succeeded in maiming the horses used by the charioteers. The Batavia crept away under cover of night, their movements drowned out by the snoring of the drunken Britons.

The bloody battle began at daybreak. The Britons, deprived of their best weapon, the horse drawn chariots, soon lost ground to the disciplined Roman legionnaires. The Britons were massacred. Caradoc and some of his men escaped the slaughter and headed to the hill fort of Camulodunum. Smelling a victory at hand, Platius sent word to the Emperor Claudius. He then undertook the siege of the city and waited patiently for his liege.

The Emperor arrived with his Praetorian Guard, the VII Legion and several monstrous beasts never before seen in Briton. Having never seen elephants, the Britons were thrown into confusion and fear. The war elephants were an effective tool and proved deadly. The Romans quickly took the fort. Camulodunum became the capitol of the new

Roman province. Submissions for peace came from many of the tribes including Prasutagos, King of the Iceni. He and his wife Boudicca ruled the lands in the East.

Meanwhile, Titus Vespasianus, who was to be the future Roman Emperor, Vespasian, marched with his brother, Sabinus, westward engaging in thirty battles and capturing, for the Glory of Rome, twenty Briton hill forts along the way. Overlooking the River Frome, they came across the stronghold of the Durotiges, the hill fort called Mai Dun.

This was a huge, well-built hill fort, the strongest yet to be seen by Vespasianus and his brother. The Romans attacked the Britons found outside the safety of Mai Dun and killed everyone, peasants, men, women and children. Preparing to lay siege to the fort, Vespasianus decided to send an envoy to encourage the Durotiges to submit. He carelessly allowed a junior Tribune to pick the men for the task. Rather than carefully selecting a man suited for the dangerous task, the petty young Tribune picked the Centurion, Lucius, an officer he did not like.

By this time, the Durotiges had gathered their people into their hill fort and were well prepared to withstand a siege. The tribe had confidence in the strength of their fort and their fierce independent nature would never allow them to surrender.

Centurion Lucius, acting as newly appointed envoy on behalf of Vespasianus was inexperienced in the delicate art of negotiation. His role thus far in the invasion had simply been to guard supply wagons, set perimeter patrols and other menial logistical tasks.

Upon entering the hill fort under the banner of the Roman Eagle, he and his men looked around at the Durotiges. The tribesmen were tall by Roman standards, wild haired and well armed. To a man, they looked battle hardened and humourless. The talks were not going well due to the language barrier. A chieftain, in observance of the universal Celtic law of hospitality, offered a skin of mead to one of the Romans. The legionnaire took a drink and not finding the taste to his liking, spat the golden honey-liquor onto the ground.

The chieftain was infuriated and soundly punched the legionnaire in the face, breaking his nose. Lucius was yelling for his men to stand still, desperately trying to avoid an incident that could cause their deaths. The Durotiges simply stood round in a circle, hands on their swords, eagerly waiting the outcome of what to them was a time honoured custom, the challenge of single combat.

Of all the customs of the Celtic tradition, the law of hospitality was the most honoured. To refuse proffered hospitality in such a manner was a grave insult.

"If you kill us now," cried Lucius, "you and your tribe will be annihilated to the last man, woman and child! Do you want that on your conscience?" He was certain that he and his men were about to be butchered and eaten by these barbarians.

"Bugger off you filthy oily bastard..."

"...we won't submit to sheep shaggers like you...."

"Listen," pleaded Lucius, "listen to reason you barbaric idiots! You all stand to be killed! The might of Rome will not be put off by a dirt barricade!" Lucius franticly waved his arms around indicating the earthen walls of the hill fort.

Chaos continued to spread as chieftains and tribesmen yelled at the Roman envoys, neither understanding the other's language. The Romans were afraid they would die a less than honourable death by not fulfilling their duty. They were pledged to gain terms of surrender or to report back to Vespasianus and describe the fortifications they had seen from the inside.

The legionnaire, who had his nose broken for spitting out the mead, pushed his Durotigian assailant to the ground. Drawing his dagger and ignoring the shouted orders of Lucius, he went to lunge at the fallen Briton. The chieftain kicked upwards at the Roman and hit him hard in the groin. Spinning quickly away, the Durotigian got to his feet and drew his long iron sword in one smooth motion. The Roman still did not hear Lucius yelling at him to stop or maybe his blood was up and he refused to hear. He was filled with rage and he meant to kill this vermin in front of him. He lunged again with his dagger. The chieftain deftly sidestepped and swung his long sword in a graceful sideways arc that neatly severed the Roman's head from his body in traditional Celtic fashion.

The Durotiges cheered at the sight of the shower of blood as the severed head rolled on the ground and the body slumped unceremoniously. The tribesmen set upon the other Romans, but no more Romans were hurt or killed. One of the Durotiges chieftains allowed the Romans to leave the hill fort. Graciously he allowed them to take with them the body of their fallen comrade. The head, however, would remain as a prize to the Durotigian warrior who had taken it fairly in single combat. Tradition was to be observed.

The Tribune who received Lucius's report of the debacle at Mai Dun told Vespasianus how his envoy of peace was beaten and beheaded in brutal fashion. He reported that Lucius had thought the Durotiges intended to slaughter and eat he and his men, but the valiant sacrifice of one legionnaire spared the men such an ignoble demise. Vespasianus was outraged! He ordered ballistae and catapultae into place and began raining huge arrows, boulders, and stones down into Mai Dun.

It was a horrific barrage. Fires were set under the palisades and rather than going through the main gates, the Romans over ran the walls of the hill fort. In their frenzy, the legionnaires slashed and hewed every living thing in their path. Men, women and children were cut to pieces. Long after the fort fell, legionnaires continued to kill, rape and torture the hapless Durotiges. Finally, the horror abated and the order was given to march onward.

In their wake, the Romans left the few survivors to bury their dead and mutilated tribesmen. Heads and bits of bodies and limbs were seen lying in the mud. Corpses of bound women, their throats cut and faces pummelled, had been violated even after death.

The Maiden's Castle was no more!

Myrddin stopped his narrative for a moment to wipe his eyes with a piece of cloth. He heaved a heavy sigh and poked the fire moving toward another jug of mead all the while not even glancing in Arthgwr's direction. Arthgwr could not move he had become transfixed by the experience of living the tale he was hearing. Slowly, Myrddin returned and sat down to again spin his magic...

Caradoc was now in the mountains of the West across the River Severn. The tribes of the Ordovices, Deceangli, Demetae, Cornovii and the Silures supported him. The former consul of Rome, Publius Ostorius

Scapula, had been appointed as the new governor of the Roman province of Britannia. The mysterious isles were now officially Roman property and under Roman rule.

Refreshed and resupplied with the aid of the other tribes, Caradoc began a campaign of guerrilla tactics against the new governor Scapula and his Roman Legions. Caradoc's brave defiance of the invaders inspired other tribes in the South. They too engaged in their own uprising. The new governor was angered at the insolence of these savages whom he had thought of as "tamed." Scapula ordered all the tribes to be immediately disarmed.

Prasutagos of the powerful Iceni tribe was outraged at the insult. The Iceni had given their allegiance to Rome and they considered it a grave insult to their honour to be thus ordered to disarm. The Dobunni and the Silures tribesmen kept their weapons. And following Caradoc's example, they engaged in hit and run tactics on Roman garrisons with some moderate successes.

The largest tribe in Briton were the Brigantes in the Northwest. The tribe's lands took in most of the northern country and bordered on the lands of the wild Picts in the far northland. The Brigantes also began to fight Rome.

Legionnaires were taking loses and their strength was stretched nearly to the limit. A cunning bit of diplomacy resulted in a truce between Scapula and Cartimandua, the female warrior and Queen of the Brigantes. Her people knew her, as Aregwedd Voeydawg.

The leadership of Caradoc was impressive. By avoiding full-scale battle with the Romans, he had managed a series of victories, inflicting much damage and heavy losses on Scapula and his legions. The other tribes admired his military prowess and his bravery. Caradoc was hailed as High King of all the tribes. The Romans were now pressing into the western peninsula well into the tribal lands of the Ordovices near the fort of Clwyd. It was obvious to all that a battle between Caradoc and Scapula was inevitable.

Deep in the forest, a gathering of chiefs, advisors and priests took place. The robed Druid priest looked older than the land itself. Holding his staff high over his head, he called for quiet.

"Our sacred Order meets in secret now. Once we shaped men's destiny, plotted the stars, brought laws to replace chaos and soothed the spirit of our people. We guarded the traditions and the customs of the tribes and taught apprentices to do the same. We were powerful and even kings would not dare speak before us. Tradition still demands it! We grow weaker and I bring tidings to our gathering here this night. A rebellion has begun in the Sacred Isle, Ynys Mon. Our time is come." A murmur grew within the gathering at the news. Here and there, a glint of fear could be seen in the eyes of those in the circle.

"I am the earth. I am the sea. I have walked in many worlds and will do so again. Life is a great cycle, a never-ending wheel of birth, death and rebirth. The news told here tonight will bind us to a common cause. Victory will be ours again. We will live again. And we will die again to be reborn. I will again be the earth. I will again be the sea. The wheel of life will continue to turn, of that, we can be sure. Death is not an end of things only a transition. If what we begin here tonight is not completed in this life, then it will be completed in the next, you should have no doubt of that! I give you now the new High King. I bless him in the name of the Mother Goddess, for it is with her that our destiny will be decided and the shame of our slavery abated!"

All eyes looked to their king, the man they knew would lead them to victory over the enemy of their people. The mighty Caradoc walked into the circle, firelight glinted off the golden torc around his neck. His great woollen cloak, checked and patterned with tribal colours gave him an ominous, fearful appearance. Caradoc gazed around at the warriors who had fought beside him in past battles and he nodded his head in the manner of an approving father.

A cheer went up amongst the gathering of chiefs, warriors and their womenfolk. Raising his arms for silence the King prepared to speak.

"It is time my fellow warriors, it is time to decide the fate of our lands. Do we wish to continue living in an age of freedom or do we submit to a future of slavery? That is what we must decide upon in the hours to come! Do not forget that your ancestors, fearless warriors all, chased away the Roman dog, Julius Caesar from our shores! Do not forget those brave warriors who delivered our lands from tyranny, taxation and slavery! Do not forget those fierce fighters who rid our lands of the Roman Eagle and saved our wives and daughters from shame! Remember well, that all of you are part of this land and this land lives deep inside your own hearts! If we must die, then we die fighting for our freedom. We will be free! We are free! We will always be free!"

A silence followed the words of Caradoc. A spear began banging on a shield, then another and another and another. The din swelled like a storm's wave rising in the night air mingling with the wood fires of the gathered tribes and carried on the wind.

The morning bore witness to a terrible battle. The Britons, encouraged by the brave words of Caradoc, words of independence and freedom, fought so ferociously, the Romans began to falter. The blood of Roman and Briton alike mingled with the dirt and made a soggy mud. By day's end thousands of bodies were strewn over the countryside and flies and vermin swarmed and feasted on the gore.

The Britons were brave and ferocious fighters. But their passions got the better of their judgement and many tribesmen flung themselves uselessly at Roman infantry and were hacked to pieces. Waves of painted tribal warriors crashed into the tight disciplined lines of Roman legionnaires. A Silurian warrior held up a severed head of a Roman officer and shouted his battle cry. The warriors around the Silurian were overcome with emotion, blood drunk they charged headlong at the Roman formations.

Despite the fear they felt, the strict discipline of the Roman soldiers held. Their years of professional training and battle experience throughout the Roman Empire, took hold and prevented them from fleeing. The attacking Britons were butchered. The Roman machine advanced. Scapula had gained the upper hand. The Britons fought fearlessly, but in the end, the battle was lost.

Caradoc escaped and managed to take refuge in the land of the Brigantes. There he hoped to be resupplied with men and fresh horses by Queen Aregwedd Voeydawg. Caradoc's skill as a leader and his luck as a man failed him. Queen Aregwedd Voeydawg of the Brigantes had made a deal with the Romans. She ordered her council to seize the unsuspecting Caradoc. The great chief, who was the islands best hope for freedom, was handed over bound and gagged, to the gloating Romans. Humbled and in chains, Caradoc was sent to Rome to be executed at the pleasure of the Roman Emperor.

Myrddin stopped his tale and stretched. Walking around the hut, he poured himself some broth and slurped it down.

"The history is," he continued, "Caradoc and his whole family were taken as prisoners to Rome. Scapula was so worn out by the battles and his responsibilities that he died soon after Caradoc and his family were captured. Scapula never received his triumph and his enemy, although captured, was allowed to walk free with his family in the very heart of Rome. So taken with the barbarian's appearance were the Roman citizens that many of them began to wear Celtic style cloaks. An edict had to be issued from the emperor forbidding the wearing of barbarian clothing by all Roman citizens!"

The Wise One stopped his story and simply sat staring at Arthgwr as though looking for some reaction from him. Arthgwr was in shock and could only sit in abject wonder. He shook his head to try to regain his wits as he heard the old man speak to him.

"Now, do not misunderstand me. I am not the antichrist as some would have you believe!" The amused expression on his face gave way to laughter and he continued speaking to Arthgwr.

"No, there is much in their religion that has been influenced by our own philosophy, though I must say they do have some very strange notions of their own. As I travel throughout the land, I see our own philosophy, our own traditions and the essence of our people inlaid in the fabric of the land just below the surface. Our people are now pushed to the West, while the Sacsonaidd hold to their allotted lands on the Eastern shores. It is inevitable that a battle will be fought between us. Such a battle could be a death knell for our existence as the freedom loving people of the old ways! Yet, *ysbryd tragwyddol y keltaid....* the spirit of the Celts is eternal!"

Myrddin in his passion had shouted out the words, startling the transfixed Arthgwr.

Suddenly, Myrddin was close to Arthgwr, his nose was only an inch from Arthgwr's face. He had travelled the distance so quickly, it was as though he appeared magically next to Arthgwr. Myrddin's blazing eyes burned into Arthgwr as he came to the point of his message.

"If we fight these Sacsonaidd and their king who keeps taking our land, swallowing our country bit by bit, pushing our people into the western sea, then perhaps the old imagination would be ignited. This would serve as the rallying point of the survival of our traditions and of our essence. If we can unify the tribes to put up a resistance to the Sacsonaidd, then stories of our heroes and our valiant actions would bind our Celtic traditions and values to our people's souls. We are as we always were a freedom-loving people. Rome conquered our lands, but Rome never owned our hearts. Roman tradition became the commerce of the day, but our own Celtic ways were the currency of our souls. The wheel of life, the cycle of birth, death and rebirth, will not stop because of war. The fact of connectivity to all peoples, to all living things, and to the Mother Goddess Earth, will not be diminished by the fallibility of man. The spirit of our Celtic heritage will be victorious, even if our army is defeated. To accomplish this fantastic feat requires a catalyst! It requires a person not tainted by greed or glory, but dedicated to Celtic unity! This person must be popular with the people. Indeed, this person must have the love and adoration of the people, as well as the trust and confidence of the warriors and the tribes. That is not an easy balance to strike."

Myrddin sat back down in his seat and drank some more of the broth. He looked at Arthgwr intensely as he broke apart a piece of hard bread and mopped up more of the broth. Arthgwr gulped the mead in his tankard to calm his racing heart.

"Presently, we as Britons have a king called Emrys Wledig. At least, that is his name in Cymraeg. I would not suggest you use that to his face, for although he is a Briton, he is very much Roman by nature and prefers to be called by his Roman name, Ambrosius Aurelianus. What's more, he is Christian, but he is a brave man and a capable king. He defeated Gwrtheyrn and fought the Sacsonaidd to a stalemate, bequeathing them the lands they presently hold as their own in the Southeast. The situation is now grave. Ambrosius Aurelianus is a seventy-four year old man and he cannot wield the same power as he did in his youth. The chiefs of the tribes know this and true to their nature are vying for his kingship like carrion circling a kill not their own. The Sacsonaidd are pressing the advantage and attacking our border towns and villages in an attempt to push our people further west. Many of our people from the South have left our islands and fled to Amorica on the continent. If this continues, the tribes will fight amongst themselves and the Sacsonaidd will conquer us without resistance. This will be a deathblow to our ways, which are already eroded by the new Christian religion. I have not much love for Roman Britons, but I cannot stand idly by and allow this travesty to continue."

Arthgwr raised his eyebrow at this arrogant statement. He wondered just what this old man, Wise One though he may be, could possibly do to save what he had been describing as the Old Ways.

"If there was a war leader, a capable man of sound reputation and selfless determination and tenacity, who could unify the tribes, and yet be humble enough to fight and give the victory to Ambrosius Aurelianus, there might just be a chance. If I could deliver such a man with an army and ally him to Ambrosius, it would go a long way in uniting the tribes and securing victory."

Like a blinding flash of light Arthgwr suddenly realised what the Wise One was saying.

He wanted Arthgwr to rally his men, join with Ambrosius and fight the Sacsonaidd in the South and then hand over the victory to the king. Failing to win the battle would still be a victory, for it would give the people a hero to sing about and to stir their imaginations in such a way as to never let them forget their Celtic identity. He was to fight a losing battle, unto certain death, and if he were to win, which would be nigh impossible, then he was to hand over the hard won glory to another man.

The enormous responsibility of the task, the impossibility of the thing being asked of him hit Arthgwr hard. How could this wise old man possibly think that he, Arthgwr, once only a man named Owain Ddantgwyn, could accomplish such a thing?

Chapter 19

Owain Ddantgwyn remained sitting in his chair. He was stripped of his title, "Arthgwr" by the enormity of the task being asked of him. He was humbled. He was a man, just a man, sitting in a chair, a tankard of mead in one hand and an open-mouthed look of shock and incredulity on his face. The door of the hut opened and Rhiannon stormed in with the two servants in tow.

She and Myrddin exchanged looks, nodding her head in acknowledgement, she told the servants to put the firewood they had gathered on the hearth. Rhiannon poured cups of broth and gave them to the two serving men with slabs of hard bread and tankards of the ever-flowing mead. She made them comfortable in one of the other rooms of the stone hut and made sure they had firewood to last them into the cold of the night. With all of that done, she turned her attention to Arthgwr and Myrddin. Sitting down at a wooden table, she was handed a steaming cup of broth from Myrddin. Again, the two of them exchanged looks.

Arthgwr managed to regain his senses and seeing Rhiannon seated at the table, he decided to find out just how much she knew of all of this.

"You've been here since you left Caerwyn I suppose? Just what have you been telling this old man? He seems to think that he can use me as he sees fit! It seems I am to do his bidding without question! Did you not tell him of my responsibilities in Caerwyn? What of my wife and children? The villagers themselves have come to rely on me. Am I to turn my back on them, shirk my duty to them on the say so of someone who says he is a Druid? Now, with a new following of hundreds of souls at the camp down below, I am to turn my back on them as well?" Arthgwr was furious and had worked himself into a frenzy shouting the last few words, spittle spraying and his face contorted with rage.

Rhiannon bolted to her feet.

"Don't raise your voice to me, Arthgwr! I owe you nothing! I am my own woman and I owe no allegiance to you! I go where and when I wish and I ask no one's permission! I told you to listen to what Myrddin had to say! And did you? No, you are too full of yourself to consider words even when they come from a Wise One! You are a fool! You don't recognise what is at stake or what is being offered here to you this night!" She turned her head and spat contemptuously on the earthen floor of the hut.

Arthgwr leaped up, spilling the mead from his cup. Beside himself with uncharacteristic fury at Rhiannon's insults, his fists balled in rage and the veins on his neck popped out like corded rope.

"You impudent ungrateful wench........."

"Hold your tongue!"

The voice boomed so loudly inside his head that Arthgwr became dizzy and fell heavily back down into his chair. He thought his lungs were crushed and he gasped desperately for air. The voice was unlike anything human.

The sound came from within rather than a sound heard externally. The voice was something he felt, not heard. It was like he had been struck in the chest by a lance and had the wind knocked out of him, only much worse than that. It was simply indescribable! Suddenly, Arthgwr thought he was going to vomit and he could not find the strength in his legs to propel him toward the door. Quickly, he grabbed the now empty cup that had moments before been full of golden mead, and he vomited into it. Sheepishly looking around, he saw the terrible visage of Myrddin towering above him, eyes glowering red with malevolent rage.

Arthgwr for the first time in his life experienced sheer terror.

Myrddin's eyes dulled and returned to their natural blue colour as he stepped back away from Arthgwr. Arthgwr gasped a lungful of needed air. Myrddin became the Old Man again and as Arthgwr looked upon him, he seemed to be almost feeble. Yet, for Arthgwr there could be no mistaking the incredible feeling of awesome power that had just overwhelmed him. Even as he watched eyes wide with fear, Myrddin was trying hard to apologise to him.

"Yes, well...I...er...I am very sorry for losing my temper, young Arthgwr. Yes, I do apologise but you were being quite impudent and very impolite to dear Rhiannon. I should think that an apology to her might be warranted." Myrddin looked at Arthgwr and though he appeared more like a grandfatherly figure, there was no mistaking the sense of danger that still hung in the air.

"Excuse me, Rhiannon, I was impolite and I apologise. I suppose it's the strain of the last few weeks, I certainly have never acted like that before and I hope I never do again. I am sorry." Arthgwr was genuine and sincere. He was confused, tired and overwhelmed by all he had heard.

Rhiannon accepted his apology graciously, she nodded her head regally and walking toward Arthgwr, she stopped and bowed to him in courtly fashion as an unmistakable sign of respect. She returned to her seat, as did Arthgwr.

Myrddin smiled and began his pacing.

"You know, young Arthgwr, we Celts used to honour our women," Myrddin was preparing to launch another tale from ancient times.

"Yes, a woman could own property, have her say in decisions at a council and even lead men into battle. I know our Rhiannon here, has ridden into battle on more than one occasion. I will tell you of a woman who very nearly brought the might of the Roman invasion of our lands to its knees. Mind you pay attention, Arthgwr, for these tales contain the essence of our people."

Myrddin sat down and began to weave his magic.

The large cities in the south of the land became more docile under Roman administration, bribes, luxuries, and of course the power of Roman legions. A garrison at Camulodunum to the South had designs on the lands of the Iceni tribe. The Iceni's were a powerful and well propertied tribe. They were the only tribe to mint their own coins with their tribal name stamped on coins, for all to see. Warriors and important members of the tribe, wore heavy torcs made from gold, silver and electrum. Many tribesmen wore heavy gold rings. When the Iceni king, Prasutagos, died a terrible death in what some said was a hunting accident, the Romans prepared to make their move.

Boudicca Pennseviges, the wife of Prasutagos and the Iceni Queen, did not believe the story that her proud and noble and warrior husband could die in a simple hunting accident. She was not alone in suspecting a Roman hand was involved. It was all too convenient. For a time, the tall widow with the hip-length red hair, remained in shock. She gathered her two daughters to her and called for her husband's most trusted advisors.

"The only thing you can do for the sake of our tribe," she was told, "is to take the reign of power yourself! The Roman dogs will surely come sniffing around now our great king is dead. They will take our lands, our food and our metal and sell us as slaves. You who are the wife of the Great Prasutagos, our own Queen, you have the legal claim to lead the Iceni tribe!"

The old man who spoke was wise and loyal to Boudicca's dead husband. His outpouring of support, tinged as it was with grief and fear, overwhelmed Boudicca. She could not afford to act rashly, not with so much at stake.

"I thank you all for your counsel," she said in her low gravely voice," I will consider your words well and carefully."

It was the next day that the Roman garrison attacked. They poured through the villages killing everyone in their way. When Roman soldiers found Boudicca and realised who she was, they mocked her terribly. It was not possible for them to entertain the notion that a woman could be leader of a people. The Iceni tribal advisors insisted that proper respect be shown to their rightful Queen. They demanded that the Romans continue to honour all treaties and agreements of alliance and loyalty and security that had been sworn to by Prasutagos.

Abruptly, Myrddin stood up to stretch his back and again roam around the hut puttering at things. Rhiannon watched him with a look of concern on her face, but trepidation for the welfare of the Druid was lost on Arthgwr. He was sitting in his chair as though bound with chains and his expression showed he was not conscious of what was going on around him, but only to tale that the Druid spun. Myrddin stopped his poking with the hearth fire, took a long draught of his mead and took up the telling of his tale without missing a beat.

Catus Decianus, a man of some importance and stature, was in charge of the Romans and he would hear none of the entreaties made by the Iceni nobles. The land and wealth of the Iceni tribe were to him, spoils of war and therefore rightfully his to do with as he saw fit. His ambition determined that he should leave these islands a wealthy man, perhaps buy for himself a senate seat back home. That would take considerable money and the gold from this tribe would be a very good start. He ordered the council of the Iceni to be killed on the spot. Boudicca was horrified and shocked at the callous outrage. Her daughters Comorra and Tasca clung to her for protection.

"Only barbarians and cowards would have a woman leader!" spat the Imperial agent of Rome. "In Rome only men rule!"

With that, he grabbed Boudicca, pulling her daughters roughly from her and threw her to the ground. He ordered some legionnaires to strip the Iceni Queen naked, ripping away her fine cloak and her woollen dress. Catus then ordered his tribune Quintus, to take the scourge he handed to him, and whip the prostrate Boudicca. Quintus did as he was ordered and whipped the Iceni Queen until the flesh on her back hung in shreds. Catus grunted his approval, signalled to his tribune to carry on and with a haughty nod of his head, Catus walked away.

Boudicca lay on the ground unconscious and bloody. Her back was torn and ripped from the scourge. Quintus turned his attention to the two screaming, shrieking young girls. He ordered his guards to bring Boudicca's daughters to him. The youngsters were each gripped tightly by two strong battle tested legionnaires. The young girls struggled vainly for their freedom, but the legionnaires were far too powerful. Two more legionnaires approached each holding something in their hands. They were rods of hard wood. Another legionnaire went over to Boudicca and threw cold well water on her reviving her. The Roman grabbed the queen by her thick red hair and pulled her upright, so she could see. Her young daughters were then savagely beaten with the rods their screams of pain mixed with those of their mother's horrible shrieking. Mercy was not forthcoming.

Quintus grabbed Comorra and with the help of two of his men he ripped the clothes from her body. He then raped the child, right there in the dirt, amidst the blood and tears of the near dead youngster. He lifted himself up from the child and without remorse, turned his attention to Tasca. He grabbed her by her hair and threw her to his legionnaires.

"Go on men, taste the fruit of victory! Teach these barbarians the role of a woman! Do not kill them, for Rome is nothing if not merciful!" Tasca was beaten and raped repeatedly along with her sister Comorra and in front of their helpless mother, Boudicca, the Queen of the Iceni. The kingdom of the tribe and its holdings were ransacked and the tribal leaders, those who survived were stripped of all power and possessions. Hundreds of Iceni tribesmen and women and children were sold into slavery for profit.

Myrddin stopped his tale. Rhiannon's face was streaked with her tears. She went over to Myrddin and knelt before him. The old man put his hand on her shoulder in a fatherly way and shook his head. He stood up. Rhiannon followed him around the hut until she put a woollen cloak over the old man's shoulders.

"At the time the Iceni were being ravaged," the old man said, "our very own sanctuary in Ynys Mon, the Sacred Isle of our sect, where we taught all of our acolytes, was being attacked. Rome had decreed that our priesthood was to be hunted down and killed. Druids were murdered during the attack of our centre of learning. Brave warriors manned the walls and hurled their spears and arrows at the Legions. Women hurled insults and rocks, carnyx blared a frightful noise, and the scene was chaotic and terrifying. It was no use; the Roman Legions trampled us, killing anyone they could catch. All died that terrible day, all that is, but the very few who could escape. No more would the best and brightest of the Celtic tribes of our isle come to the mysterious Ynys Mon, seeking initiation to our order."

Again, Myrddin drank a draught of mead and continued with his history.

The iron fist of Rome was felt all over the south of Briton. The Roman veterans of Camulodunum, a great city in the South, threw the Britons off their lands and seized their homes. A temple was built there to the glory of the Roman Emperor Claudius. This outraged the southern Britons and they swore they would see the temple of Claudius destroyed; it had become a symbol of Roman oppression. The tribal leaders and chieftains, once proud and powerful warriors in their own land, saw their people sold into slavery and put to the yoke. They themselves suffered brutality, cruelty, and humiliation at the hands of the Romans. Britons came together in the market places in their homes and especially in the woods and at their secret gatherings, where they talked of the suffering and of the starvation and the shame of slavery. The life of a commoner was little more than enduring pain, violence, abuse, and torture. Anger and resentment grew in a climate desolate of all hope. The seeds were being sown for another full-scale rebellion. All that was needed for this tinderbox to ignite was a spark.

It was some time before Boudicca Pennseviges recovered from her wounds. Her daughters had also miraculously survived their horrible ordeal more thanks to the few druid that hid in their midst than the "mercies" of Rome.

Boudicca was still the Queen of the Iceni, though she looked with sorrow on her ravaged lands and broken people. Gathering some chieftains, she began talking about rebellion. She was met with resistance at first for the men were afraid, not only for their own fates, but for the retributions the Romans would surely exact on their families, their wives and young children. They did not have any weapons in any case.

"Men with nothing to lose, men who have lost all hope, who have lost their dignity are the most dangerous of all creatures. We will gain an alliance with the other tribes and we will fight these Roman bastards!" Boudicca quietly said.

The spark had ignited.

True to her words, Boudicca made a pact with the chieftain of the Trinovantians. Together the Iceni and the Trinovantians attacked the city of Camulodunum. Her orders were to give no quarter to the Romans; all were to be put to the sword!

An army of tribal warriors armed with spears, shields and swords and a few chariots that had been scrounged from scattered caches throughout the countryside marched on the city of Camulodunum. The city's garrison was made of contented Roman soldiers near retirement and smug in the victories they had won over the barbarous Britons. They were not prepared for the ferocious wrath of the tribal Queen of the Iceni.

Boudicca inspired her warriors and they fought with a savageness of desperate people. She rode through the city in her chariot, her thick red hair trailing behind, and her two daughters Comorra and Tasca at her side. The Queen commanded the Iceni and the Trinovantians warriors and led them to an unprecedented victory.

Roman blood flowed freely in the streets, as frenzied tribal warriors wreaked their revenge hacking and slashing with their long iron swords. Boudicca personally hacked dozens of Roman legionnaires to pieces in sadistic delight. The city did not stand a chance and soon fell to Boudicca and her forces.

Stopping her chariot in the middle of the captured and broken city, she gathered her strength and rallied her tribesmen. A group of Iceni warriors approached, she saw they drove before them a badly beaten prisoner. With a cold contemptuous smile she whispered in her gravely, voice.

"What is it you have before you, another Roman pig?"

"Oh, I think we have more than a just a pig. This Roman may interest you a great deal." The Iceni warriors dragged the beaten Roman to the feet of their Queen. One warrior grabbed the Roman's battered face and lifted it up so Boudicca could better see.

Comorra and Tasca gasped as they looked upon the face of the Roman. Boudicca smiled coldly, as she looked into the barely recognisable face of Quintus, the tribune who had beaten her and raped and beat her children in front of her eyes. The Queen of the Iceni motioned to her warriors to each take an arm and pull to stretch the tribune's naked chest and torso taut.

The sharp blade of her knife entered low just below the Roman's navel. Boudicca slowly drew the sharp blade of her knife upwards.

Blood gushed and spurted over her, the men, and the ground. The Iceni warriors had to hold fast with all of their strength as Quintus screamed, shrieked, and did everything he could to squirm free from their hold and the slow disembowelling he suffered. The Iceni Queen leaned forward and spoke lowly into the dying tribune's ear.

"This is not the first time Briton's have been lead to war by a woman!"

She continued to cut upwards ever so slowly. Quintus's intestines and organs spilled onto the ground and he gurgled in agony, but he was not yet dead. Boudicca took a long sword from a tribesman and expertly hacked off the tribune's head. She spat on it and ordered the head to be stuck on a spike and paraded around the city so all of her people could see how terrible was the queen's vengeance!

Standing tall in her royal chariot, Boudicca Pennseviges, the Queen of the Iceni, addressed the Celtic warriors.

"Our freedom is at hand! I speak to you now not as a woman from a noble line but as one of your own avenging the freedom stolen from me, avenging the flesh that was torn from my back," here she stopped and stripped herself to the waist, lifting her hair so that all could see the hideous scarring of the Roman scourge. A cry went up amongst the warriors and shields were hit with swords and spears, the din built to a crescendo. The noise abated as the Queen began to speak again.

"I avenge the brutalisation and stolen virginity of my daughters," the banging began again in earnest and it was some time before Boudicca could continue and be heard.

"Honour is on the side of righteous vengeance. Honour claimed for self and for tribe. I have reclaimed that honour here with this victory today! You have witnessed a Roman legion die harshly as they tried to fight us and you know that other legions are now hiding in their camps. Consider all the strength of the Romans and all the brutality you have suffered and you will know that in this battle you must be victorious or die!"

Boudicca's rebellion grew. She and her force of Iceni and Trinobatians routed the Roman garrisons at Verulamium and Londinium. The Queen's vengeance for the atrocities against her and her people burned cold in her breast. Boudicca Pennseviges killed maimed and tortured every Roman soldier she and her tribesmen came across. The new

Roman governor, Suetonius, ordered a Roman army of ten thousand soldiers to find and kill or capture the rebel queen. After many months, the Roman army, which was double the size of the rebel force, finally managed to catch up with the Iceni Queen and her tribesmen and allies the Trinobatians. It was not long after that the battle ensued and the rebel forces weakened and succumbed to the onslaught of the disciplined Roman army.

Boudicca had fought bravely overcoming great odds and she had many victories against the Roman legions. She and her fierce warriors had nearly managed to overthrow the yoke of Roman oppression and give freedom back to their fellow Britons. Boudicca Queen of the Iceni found herself surrounded and trapped by a Roman army and she had no way of escape open to her. The proud queen and her two daughters bravely drank poison, rather than be captured by the Roman army. With the rebellion in the South now crushed, Caradoc in the North betrayed and defeated, Britannia was firmly a Roman province.

Rome had at last won.

Myrddin had at last finished his tale. He remained quiet with a sad look on his old face for quite some time. The others respected his silence. Arthgwr was incapable of speaking, he was still coming to grips with the experience of Myrddin's tale. Finally the Wise One sighed, wiped away tears with his sleeve, and sighed again.

"That's it then," said Myrddin becoming a bit more energetic and youthful in his appearance, "now why don't we all sit back down with some mead and discuss this situation?"

They got themselves comfortable after stretching and scratching. Rhiannon had stoked the fire so that they were warm and comfortable as the night closed more tightly around the hut.

They sat talking for hours. Myrddin was doing most of the talking and Rhiannon too, Arthgwr mostly listened. He was mesmerised by their audaciousness and shocked at the plan they proposed. Arthgwr was at a disadvantage as he was still trying to regain his composure.

The suffocating power, Arthgwr had felt when Myrddin had raised his voice and glowered, still haunted him. He had, for the first time in his life, experienced real terror. The feeling of power that filled the room when Myrddin had become angered was not to be denied. Arthgwr could feel a residual power now; it was wreathed around the old man standing in front of him. He was exhausted from experiencing the living stories, the Druid had made real with his awesome talent.

Their shadows were cast on the wattle walls of the hut by the firelight and mixed there with the intricate designs and decorative patterns that were painted on the white washed walls. Watching Myrddin as he talked, Arthgwr could not help feeling an otherworldly sense of being lost in another time. The old man was young again, or at least, younger looking. As Myrddin turned, Arthgwr saw him as an old warrior, a tribal chieftain, regal and dangerous if provoked. When Myrddin turned full to face Arthgwr, his appearance was that of a humble caregiver, offering praise and support, very much like someone's grandfather, the kind seen in many a village wandering about stopping to talk of older times with anyone who would listen.

Suddenly, and just for the briefest of moments, Arthgwr saw Myrddin as a tall stropping young man, lean of muscle with long black hair, short black beard and blazing blue eyes under furrowed brows. As their eyes locked, Arthgwr felt as though a tree branch had suddenly crashed into him as he rode fast through a forest, all air was sucked from his lungs.

"Are you all right Arthgwr?" asked Rhiannon.

"My boy, my boy what has come over you? Are you unwell?" Myrddin was again the kind old grandfather worried about his young grandson who had just fallen and cut his knee. It was all Arthgwr could do to nod his head so weak was he from his vision of Myrddin.

Chapter 20

The morning light gently warmed Arthgwr's face and he stirred beneath the heavy wolf pelts. He quickly sat up and found that he was in the room where the servants had been sleeping. He could see their bedding neatly rolled and ready to travel. How he had come to be in this room, he could not remember. He didn't think he had walked in and surely Rhiannon could not have carried him. Myrddin, as Arthgwr remembered him from last night seemed so frail and grandfatherly that Arthgwr doubted he could have moved him, despite the aura of strength and power that swirled around the Druid. Perhaps, the servants had carried him.

The memory of the "conversation" last night came thundering painfully back to him. Arthgwr recalled he had given the Druid his word he would do what he could to work his plan. He remembered how moved he had been by Myrddin's historic tales of ancient Celts. He was overcome with a deep sense of obligation to the memory of his ancestors and to the people he lead here and now. While he still basked in the sense that he was undertaking something important, something much bigger than himself, Arthgwr felt a sudden chill of dread. He dressed quickly.

In the next room, the hearth fire was lit, hard bread, crumbly cheese and broth with boiled rabbit meat, were waiting for him beside a pitcher of mead. Arthgwr sat down to eat and was wondering where everyone was when the door crashed open and in strode Rhiannon and the two servants.

"The horses are all ready to travel. They have been fed, watered and loaded up, so when you are ready, let us be off!" Rhiannon stood there in the middle of the room, her dark hair flowing freely as she shook her head and laughed at the tardy Arthgwr.

He interrupted breaking his fast in mid-mouthful and was about to ask where it was they were going, when Rhiannon pre-empted him with her answer.

"We, that is, you and I and your two servants are heading back this morning to the camp. It will take about three days to get there. Then we will organise them for the trip back to Caerwyn where we will resupply and hand pick those men who will accompany you to meet Ambrosius Aurelianus. We will attend a gathering of tribal chieftains before our audience with Ambrosius. You will need your wits about you. You see, Arthgwr, you have to convince them that you are the one to lead the army into war under Ambrosius's authority. That will not be an easy task, I can assure you! Most of them are Christian and they will need to be assured that the cause is just or at the very least profitable. There are those who follow the Old Ways and they are a hard lot. They will need to see some proof that you are worthy of leadership, if you don't measure up, they will hack you to pieces! Of course, there are those who simply want to fight and any reason is good enough for them!" Rhiannon smiled.

Arthgwr had remained seated, his hand around a cup of broth that was halfway to his mouth. He was overwhelmed and barely managed to ask where was Myrddin.

"Oh, not to worry! Myrddin has gone to smooth the way for you!" She laughed uproariously at that which did little to cheer Arthgwr's sinking mood.

"Well, he did leave you a present," she added suddenly very serious, "and a powerful one it is too! However, you must complete a task to earn it. Are you ready for your task, Arthgwr?" There was no humour in her cold blue eyes as she said this to Arthgwr.

Gathering his wits, Arthgwr abruptly stood up and with his regained sense of self, he asked politely what the task was and what was involved.

"It is simple," said Rhiannon, "you need a symbol of power to convince the followers of the Old Ways and inspire those of the new religion. That symbol is a mystical sword named *Caladfwlch*. The name means "Hard Lightning," and it was forged, some say, by Gofannon, the god of smiths. It was thought, in our dark past, that the one who can lay claim to that sword would be the true leader of the Cymry. A day's journey from here is a mountain lake. The sword was put into the icy waters of that lake eons ago. All you have to do is jump in and claim it for yourself."

"Why did Myrddin not tell me this himself? Why does he leave when such an important task as you have described is required of me? What if I have questions for him? This task will delay us at least two days which means we will be four to five days from the camp."

"I think," said Rhiannon evenly, "that Myrddin is making a point."

"Oh, and what point would that be?"

Rhiannon paused looked around the room and then finally held her gaze on Arthgwr's eyes.

"I imagine he wanted you to trust."

Arthgwr was taken by surprise.

"What do you mean trust? I am a warrior. I have men under my command and women and children to defend! Trust? I have only the luxury of trusting my men and the steel of my sword and the truth revealed to me by my own senses! Trust, indeed!"

"Have you not heard what has been said to you here this past night? Did you learn nothing from Myrddin? Use your senses, use your intellect Arthgwr, and clear the dung from your ears! There is truth in what Myrddin has said! He has thought it all through and the plan is sound. Don't you see the wisdom and prophecy of Myrddin? Did you not feel his intellect, his power? Did he not allow you to experience the depth and richness of our past when he spent the night telling you our history? If you did not, then there really is little hope after all!" Rhiannon was exasperated by Arthgwr's reluctance to see what to her was so obvious.

For his part, Arthgwr was chastened by Rhiannon's passion and he sat back down. A lot had transpired in the hours of that long night. Much of what had gone on he did not understand. Myrddin had told him not to be afraid of the knowledge and that wisdom was learned by experience and passed onto others in the telling.

Arthgwr remembered that in telling the stories of old it seemed that Myrddin was relating personal experience as though he had lived through the sacking of Rome by Brennus, the attempted conquering of Britannia by Julius Caesar and the rebellions fought and lost by Caradoc and Boudicca.

Arthgwr remembered the vividness of the old one's story telling ability and realised that Myrddin must have spent most of his entire life learning the stories and the details of them, living them in his mind until they were part of his own memories. What an extraordinary man!

With all that knowledge stored in his mind, the ability to pass the experience to others as though he were sharing his own memories, the passion and energy to act on this knowledge for the best interests of his people; surely here was a man who had earned the right to be trusted. Myrddin did all of this on pain of death, for indeed, many of his kind had been wiped out during the years of Roman domination and now they were ostracised by the followers of the new religion. Who was Arthgwr to question such an intellect and in such a disrespectful manner? Suddenly he realised the reason for Myrddin's anger and Rhiannon's frustration. He had been a fool!

"Will I see Myrddin again?" he sheepishly asked Rhiannon.

"Yes, Arthgwr you will for we are to meet with him before he takes you to Ambrosius. First there is the task."

"Of course, we must go at once." Arthgwr's stilted formality amused Rhiannon.

She remembered him before he was "Arthgwr," when he was simply Owain, protector of Caerwyn. He was more carefree then, easy to laugh even if he was still a bit standoffish. Rhiannon missed the lively banter that had passed between her and Owain over the years.

One thing remained the same whether his name was Owain or Arthgwr and that was that quiet way of his when he got angry. There were times when she had just wanted him to blurt out his anger, to let it flow over those who had displeased him. Keeping such powerful emotions locked tightly inside was not a good thing for the body, she thought; better to let them out to air. Rhiannon smiled as she recalled how he had indeed lost his temper with her in front of Myrddin a short time ago. She smiled thinking to herself perhaps there is merit in controlling one's emotions in the presence of Druid!

"Arthgwr," she said demurely, "you needn't be so formal, though I must say it was refreshing to see your anger pour out from you instead of that tight-lipped quiet manner of yours."

She laughed and in looking up, she saw that Arthgwr was laughing as well. The little group rode off to the high mountain lake where Arthgwr's "present" from the Wise One lay as a mystery before them.

The servants saw to the horses while Rhiannon took the sticks and wood they gathered and put them in stacks forming a tight circle. Arthgwr stepped to the shore of the lake and admired the beauty of the place. Ringed with mountains and so protected from view and wind, the small lake shone and glimmered in the afternoon sun. The water, Arthgwr noted, was ice cold and very deep. He began to have his doubts.

Rhiannon was busy shouting orders to the servants and trying to set alight the stacks of wood. Arthgwr returned to help her. It took quite some time, but they managed to light the stacks of wood creating a ring of fledgling fire. Wolf pelts and woollen cloaks and blankets were thrown onto the ground in the centre of the fiery circle. Rhiannon looked pleased with the results. Arthgwr looked somewhat pensive but Rhiannon ignored him.

"Now listen to me," she was saying.

"The sword is not so far down as you may think. The waters only look infinitely deep. Mind, you be cautious! Remember you are not searching for a naked blade so rid your mind of that image. You are looking for a long bit of rough hewn stone. It will weigh a lot so conserve your strength. The lake has had the day's sun on it, but we do not have much light left so we must be quick before the light fails. Are you all right?"

Arthgwr signalled that he was fine though he stood shivering in leggings, breeches and a tunic to cover his body, no cloak or outer tunic to warm him. He tied his hair back to keep it from his eyes and began breathing in and out in exaggerated fashion to prepare for the long underwater swim. Rhiannon led him to the lake's edge a few short steps away. Opening her arms, she sang a prayer to the mother goddess Dôn, beseeching her to take Arthgwr into her safekeeping.

*"O Great Mother, smile down on this man your servant so that he may
bask in the warmth of your love;
O Great Mother, breathe your breath into him for he must travel in the
deep unable to fill his lungs with sweet air;
O Great Mother, let down your hair that he may take hold and find his
way back to us and into your arms;
These things I ask Great Mother as your obedient servant here in this
world and on into the next."*

Rhiannon lowered her arms and looked at Arthgwr who simply nodded to her and jumped into the cold dark waters of the mountain lake.

The shock of the cold hit him hard, it took most of his strength to keep from screaming out, and loosing the precious air stored in is lungs. Instantly, he lost feeling in his legs, toes, arms, and fingers. Yet girthed with dogged determination, he swam down and down. Murky shapes passed by him, things unknown bumped into him, but still he pressed on.

Finally, he reached the bottom, his eyes strained to see in the dim light. Most of what he saw was the shadows and shapes of submerged plants and timber. He desperately felt around with numbed fingers and hands hoping the bottom of the lake would reveal to him the stone with the sword locked within. Frantically he searched racing against time, the last bit of air about to run out in his strained lungs. It was no use. He kicked to the surface.

Arthgwr's head broke the surface of the water and he gasped mightily for much needed air. Thrashing about he realised he had precious little time or strength left to him. The frigid temperature of the mountain lake was taking its toll. He dove again.

Down and down he went as fast as he could swim. Again, he searched frantically along the lake bottom. Once he thought he had something, but it slipped from his numb grasp. He tried repeatedly. It was no use. He was out of air and was forced to kick to the surface.

Rhiannon was becoming frightened. Arthgwr looked white, his lips were tinged blue and he was obviously freezing. She called to him to get out of the water, but stopped in mid scream. It was too important a task. A tear fell from her eye onto her frozen cheek. Arthgwr dove a third time.

Swimming down as hard as he could, he twisted and turned until he hit the bottom with his hands spread as wide. He felt the sandy lake bottom for the oblong stone and it's prize. His right hand banged into something. He could not feel the details, but he could feel the mass and the weight of the object. Quickly he brought his body around and in line with the object. Using both of his hands, he felt desperately along the length of the object. He had it!

All he had to do now was to surface with the stone. He tried grabbing it first with one hand then the other, but it was no use. He could not hang on to the thing long enough to swim to the surface with it. Arthgwr could only try one more time before his lungs gave out. He finally managed to stand the object upright and hugged it with both his arms. He kicked furiously with both legs using his last bit of strength. He had to keep kicking or he would sink back down to the bottom of the lake. He would not have the strength to try again and therefore he would drown. Arthgwr did not entertain the idea of dropping his prize; he would not fail in his quest. It was an eternity before his head broke through the surface of the lake.

Arthgwr managed a quick gulp of precious air before the weight of the stone oblong pulled him down again. The fact that he could not use his arms to help himself added to the dilemma.

Rhiannon nearly screamed at seeing Arthgwr's head dip below the surface. One of the servants standing near the water's edge jumped in after Arthgwr. At seeing this, the other servant who had been in the middle of the circle of burning wood stoking the fires, dropped his torch and ran to the lake to help Arthgwr and his friend. When his heated body hit the frigid waters, he died. The shock of the extreme cold of the water on the heated flesh of the fire-tending servant caused his heart to immediately stop.

The surviving servant swam hard toward the spot where Arthgwr had gone under. He dove down, grabbed hold of Arthgwr's tunic, and pulled. Together the spluttering shivering duo made their exhausted way to the shore. Rhiannon and the servant struggled to get Arthgwr and themselves into the centre of the circle of fire. Immediately, they wrapped Arthgwr in wolf pelts and woollen cloaks. Arthgwr had not let go of the oblong stone with its secret prize held within. His frozen hands would not release their grip. Rhiannon had to pry his fingers of the encasement and had a very hard time in doing so.

The servant was frantically rubbing the extremities of Arthgwr trying to warm the blood and keep it flowing when he suddenly cried out. Arthgwr had stopped breathing!

Quickly Rhiannon pushed on his chest trying to stimulate his lungs into taking in air. Nothing happened. She rolled him onto his stomach and tried rubbing his upper back but that did not work either. Rolling him onto his back, she pressed her lips to his and blew breath into his mouth. It was an old Druid trick that sometimes worked. She paused and repeated what she had done. Spluttering wildly Arthgwr spewed lake water from his mouth and nose and gasped for precious air.

His colour was white, his lips tinged with blue and he was shivering uncontrollably. The surviving servant, Bevan, wrapped Arthgwr in the wolf pelts and then began stoking the fires that his friend had been tending before he had died. Rhiannon caught her breath and then began rubbing Arthgwr's hands and feet in an attempt to warm his blood. When Bevan asked if Arthgwr would live, Rhiannon smiled and nodded, wiping away the tears that were falling down her face.

As the last light died and the night engulfed them, Rhiannon and Bevan were kept busy tending the fires that kept Arthgwr from freezing. They had gathered much firewood and continued to do so in shifts. They were forced to go further and further a field to look for usable sticks. It was crucial for Arthgwr's survival that the fires stay lit. He was still shivering, but the hot broth helped and Rhiannon had also hung a pelt over one of the fires, singeing it in the process, but the fire-warmed pelt helped keep Arthgwr warm.

Rhiannon and Bevan built a cairn of stones to cover the body of Bevan's friend who had died jumping into the frigid waters of the lake. It was a solemn task more so because they were both so fatigued. Rhiannon allowed Bevan to sleep first, the emotional drain on him had affected him badly. After two hours or so, Rhiannon slept while Bevan stood watch.

Dawn was slow in coming. It took an eternity for the warming sliver of morning sunshine to claw away at the night. The three travellers were awake and bone tired. They warmed some broth on the last of the fires. They had exhausted the supply of firewood.

The cold and bedraggled trio travelled silently for hours. They stopped and made camp at the first spot where they found dry wood. Rhiannon heated watered mead for them to drink. The warm liquor chased the cold and damp from their bones.

Arthgwr looked down and saw the stone oblong he had brought up from the depths of the frozen lake. Here lay the object that had cost one life and had nearly cost him his own. It boggled his mind that this object was supposed to guarantee unity amongst the followers of the Old Ways. He wondered what the sword that was secreted away inside the stone looked like. Arthgwr stood up, he was intent on having a look. After all he had gone through to retrieve the object he felt it was his right to view it. Rhiannon agreed.

Arthgwr felt around the edges of the stone encasement. He could not see any obvious way of opening it or breaking the stone away without damaging the mystical sword held within. He noticed it was the shape and size of the moulds used long ago in making bronze swords. Arthgwr had heard a smith talking about the ancient ways used by his ancestors. It occurred to Arthgwr that this was such a mould and he wondered of what possible use could a bronze sword be to him.

Bronze was soft, pliable, and inferior to the iron weapons that people had been using for a thousand years. Arthgwr stopped what he was doing and stood up.

"We will not open the thing here in this cold place. We will carry it with us to the camp and there in front of witnesses, we shall claim our prize. If the tale of Myrddin is to have merit, then all should be privy to it."

Rhiannon smiled and began packing the horses. Bevan helped her.

The journey to the camp was uneventful. The three riders were lost in their own thoughts and they travelled in silence. It did not escape the notice of Rhiannon and Bevan that there was a change in Arthgwr.

He was quiet and thoughtful most of the time. When engaged in conversation, he was polite and calm. Yet, there was an arrogance about him, which was not there before. It was not the pompous blustery arrogance of a warrior bragging to all about his kills in combat.

Perhaps arrogance was not the right word at all.

Supremely confident, might have been a better description, but whatever it was, something had changed in Arthgwr.

They were a day's ride from the camp when Arthgwr slowed the pace and whispered into Rhiannon's ear that they were being followed. Rhiannon nodded imperceptibly.

Much later that afternoon when they were but a half-day's ride from their camp, Bevan rode up to Arthgwr and told him he had seen a rider off to their flank. It was obvious now, they were being watched.

Another hour or two passed and as the light began to fail, Arthgwr stopped. Up ahead, a lone rider blocked the trail. The noise coming from either side of them told Arthgwr they were outflanked. Alone Arthgwr slowly rode toward the mysterious rider, his arms outstretched showing he carried no sword.

"Arthgwr! It is you!"

It was Cai. He sat on his horse a long spear in his hand ready to give the word to attack and step into battle. He raised his left hand, obviously a signal to his men. Grim looking warriors emerged from their concealment.

"Well, you are a sight! We weren't sure at first that it was you and well it's best to be prepared for the worst in these times!" Cai had dismounted and walked to Arthgwr.

As Arthgwr dismounted, he asked Cai if he was expecting trouble.

"Well, there is always trouble isn't there? But a few days ago, we have had reports that two large groups of men were two day's ride from us. And they are converging on us from the east and the west. We can't flee because we would be over run by one group or another. The mountains are at our back, we can't effectively climb them but at least our rear is protected. So we are in a bad situation."

Arthgwr had nothing constructive to say so he simply followed Cai as they rode toward camp. After an hour or two's ride, they came across what appeared as a large bulge in the ground. As they rode closer, Arthgwr could see that the "bulge" was earthworks that had been erected around the camp for protection. It was clear Cai was going to stand and fight.

No firelight flickered and there was no trumpeting or merrymaking at Arthgwr's return. He and Rhiannon slipped into the compound as quietly as the night fell.

In the morning light, the compound did not look as formidable as it had during the night. There was a slight incline in the land and the earthworks would provide a rudimentary defence, but it was a desperate measure.

Riders had come in by midmorning to report that the two armies were not far off, one from the East and one from the West. They would be at the camp in a day depending on their negotiation of the mountain's passes. The rest of the day was spent in gathering firewood, water and preparing food. If Arthgwr and his people were to die here, they would at least die with full stomachs.

By early evening, Cai, Edern and Gwyn along with the rest of the council had gathered under the largest tent of their encampment where they waited for Arthgwr.

The sun was dying slowly in the heavens and the stars twinkled their return grateful for the leadership of the ghostly moon. The men sat in their traditional circle, a white cloth was thrown on the ground and cushions, and hides were arrayed about the circle for the comfort of the warriors. Ale was served with some hard bread and boiled meat. Arthgwr sat down and gulped ale. The ale, he thought, was refreshing after the tangy sweetness of the mead he had been drinking.

The men shifted and fidgeted nervously as Rhiannon appeared. Some warriors saluted her as she strode majestically over to Arthgwr. Gathering up her yellow and black patterned cloak, she sat down beside him and took a gulp of his ale. They engaged in a long conversation, Arthgwr was concerned about the women and children being so unprotected out in the open. Fighting a battle with these civilians so vulnerable meant tragedy. These poor souls were here at the camp because of Arthgwr's actions and promises. This fact was causing him great distress and his anguish was chipping away at his newly found confidence.

Rhiannon was sympathetic, but not very helpful. She reminded Arthgwr that Myrddin was in the South preparing the way at the court of Ambrosius. She told Arthgwr, it was Myrddin, who had arranged for him to gain the sword, Caladfwlch. And then she suggested Arthgwr use the sword for the good of all! Arthgwr thought about her words and dwelled on them for a long time before addressing the council formally. They were waiting to hear his wisdom.

"You all know the situation," said Arthgwr standing to deliver his words to the gathered council, "it is dire to say the least. Nevertheless, this is my plan. I will send two messengers with escorts to each of the oncoming armies with a request to meet us in the field just over this rise and away from our camp. I will make them a proposal of peace. If they accept we will, after a few days respite, march to the court of the High King. Each tribe will be represented and I will be the representative of all the tribes. There we will seek the council of the High King and if need be we will do his bidding. Should there be a chief or a warrior who does not agree with my proposal they may withdraw or if they wish they may challenge me to single combat. That is my decision!" Arthgwr sat down and looked at the faces of the brave men in his council.

The men were shocked. It was Cai, whose voice rose above the din of the other's complaints. He wanted to know just how Arthgwr would persuade not one but two armies who were now riding to attack them, to join them in an arduous trip to visit the High King to whom their loyalty was at best casually given. Many agreed with Cai.

They screamed their displeasure and their concern that by sending envoys they would be seen as weak and that would serve only to embolden their enemy. They wanted assurance from Arthgwr that he had some confidence in his power to unite the tribes in the way he had described. It had never been done! It was madness! It was hubris to think Arthgwr could succeed in such an undertaking! The council members resolve in their leader was wavering.

Arthgwr stood up and clapped his hands twice. The men of his council grudgingly fell silent and they looked around trying to fathom what Arthgwr was up to. Bevan appeared at the tent's entrance with an oblong stone in his hands. It was heavy judging from the look of exertion carved on his face. Arthgwr beckoned to him and Bevan carried the oblong stone to the middle of the circle and placed it on the ground before Arthgwr. Bevan stood to one side.

Rhiannon stood up. She walked regally around the circle and studied the face of each man present. The warriors were now completely silent and almost cowed, only Edern dared hold the gaze of Rhiannon. Arthgwr gestured to Bevan who stepped forward, head held high.

In a rich baritone voice, he began to tell the company the tale of the lake and how Arthgwr risked his life to retrieve what Myrddin had claimed was a mystical sword. He regaled them with the determination of Arthgwr and the resourcefulness of Rhiannon, whom he called "the Lady of the Lake."

Rhiannon bowed her head slightly at this new moniker and an enigmatic smile briefly crossed her lips.

The men were mesmerised by the tale. They had not heard of Myrddin before and were now in awe that a Wise One had chosen their very own Arthgwr, their leader, for a dangerous task. There could be no doubting the servant Bevan's tale. Both Rhiannon and Arthgwr vouched for it. The torchlight flickered in the tent. An eerie light settled upon the gathering, whether from the wood burning in the braziers or from some unseen force, no one could be sure. All eyes were now on the oblong stone.

Slowly, Arthgwr approached the stone oblong. He had not determined how to open the stone encasement and he did not know, for certain, if it contained the sword. All he had to go on were the words of the ancient priest, Myrddin and Rhiannon, the Lady of the Lake. Rhiannon, he had known for years, but she was now as much a mystery to him as Myrddin. Arthgwr walked around the stone. He knelt down and examined the encasement without touching it. The atmosphere inside the tent was taut and tense as a notched bow quivering to release death. Arthgwr said nothing and he not touch the stone. He simply walked around it again. Finally, he bent his knee and with both his hands, moved the stone. Arthgwr felt along the edges of the encasement. He straightened. Someone called out to hit the damn thing with an axe. Arthgwr shook his head. Another voice called for a boulder to smash the stone into pieces, but again Arthgwr shook his head. With a small rock in his hand, Arthgwr approached the stone oblong and gently tapped the edge. He then placed his hands on either end and pressed his weight down. The stone cracked length ways to the audible gasp of those hardened warriors watching. Arthgwr pressed down again gently and the stone split!

There inside the grey stone lay a magnificent sword; its blade shimmered a yellowish hue. It was a plain design with a double edge, longer than most swords and it had a two handed hilt. Arthgwr reached in with his right hand and withdrew the sword. He brandished it with a warrior's flourish and the blade sang through the air. The balance was perfect, the weight heavy, but not cumbersome. He felt a strength and vitality running through the sword and into his arm. Arthgwr twirled and spun the long sword cutting overlaying ellipses in the air as he tested the feel of the weapon. It was made of iron and not bronze. Arthgwr could immediately tell the edges were the sharpest he had ever seen.

"Caladfwlch, Caladfwlch, a strong name! A strong sword!" Arthgwr was clearly impressed with the weapon; his eyes shone and would not leave Caladfwlch.

Everyone in the room was transfixed. No one dared breathe. Arthgwr held Caladfwlch high and with his feet set apart, a fierce look of pride took over his face. The sword glinted and twinkled in the firelight like a thing alive. It threw a strange light as it reflected the orange-yellow of the tent's torch light on the faces of those present.

"Here before you is the sword, Caladfwlch which I retrieved from the frozen lake upon the counsel of "the Lady of the Lake"," Arthgwr used Bevan's new title for Rhiannon. The call went up for Arthgwr to test the blade's strength. Rhiannon nodded to him.

"It is a mystical sword, Arthgwr," she said. "Its' blade will cut through anything and as long as you wield it with a pure heart it will always serve you well!"

Arthgwr stood circling the blade around him, the singing of the blade rising above the murmurings of his council. He walked out of the tent followed by his curious council. Looking for something suitable to test his new blade upon he spied an outcrop of rock. The formation stuck out from a large boulder and the shape and size of the rock was closely that of a man's neck. It was rock! Surely no blade swung against solid rock could possibly remain intact. The steel would surely shatter.

The warriors became silent as they watched Arthgwr walk towards the outcrop. There were those men who would stop the demonstration, for certainly it was a bad omen to waste such an exquisite blade on the nape of rock and not in the glory of real battle. But others wanted to see the mystical qualities of a sword from the Otherworld, and they quieted any who thought of stopping the test.

Swinging Caladfwlch in front of him, Arthgwr brought the bright blade down in a masterfully strong stroke. Caladfwlch struck with a ringing clang so loud and piercing, that men covered their ears. Sparks flew into the air like yellow and red rain. The ringing faded and silence engulfed the scene. All eyes were on the rock that had served as the test. A gasp. A cry of excitement split the silence.

There in the dirt and snow lay the cleaved piece of rock while in Arthgwr's hand shone the unmarred beauty that was the sword from the stone, thrown to the bottom of an icy lake; Caladfwlch!

Arthgwr held the mystical blade above his head for all to see. A strange and eerie yellow light reflected from the sword, casting its luminous glow onto the faces of his companions.

"The task of retrieving Caladfwlch nearly cost me my life, as it cost the life of our dear servant. I realise now, that was not the task! Retrieving the sword Caladfwlch was not the task, but a test. It was a test of trust or if you will a test of faith. I ask you now," cried Arthgwr," to trust in me! To know in your souls that my cause is just and that my heart is set upon my path. I undertake this quest for the good of all and for all things right and proper! With your help and your trust in me, I will unite the tribes!"

Arthgwr's men were still dumb with awe in what they had witnessed. They were overwhelmed with emotion and passion. The incredible feat of the Sword from the Stone and Arthgwr's rousing words dispelled differences and inspired the gathering of warriors. They stood drawing their own swords almost in unison and shouted the refrain.

"All things right and proper!"

Spontaneously, each warrior walked to Arthgwr, knelt before him, head bowed, and swore an oath of fidelity.

Chapter 21

Arthgwr had been overwhelmed by the demonstration of love and devotion paid to him by his foster brother and the warriors on his council. Arthgwr walked away from the council meeting and finding a quiet place, he wearily sat down on a rock. Tears began to flow down his face. Looking to the night sky, he saw the constellation of the Bear, the reminder of the meaning of his newfound name, writ large for all mankind to see in the northern night sky. He suddenly felt very small and insignificant. The chill of the mountain air caused him to shiver, but he was not so sure if it wasn't more than just cold air making him shake.

The women and children and the men from the other tribes and nearby villages that had joined him were a huge responsibility. Such a burdensome responsibility and it weighed heavily on his soul. He thought he was a good man. He thought he had been a worthy warrior, one on whom a man could count in the heat of battle. Arthgwr believed he had been a good leader and that he had done well as leader of Caerwyn. He had upheld all the traditional values of his wife's ancestors. He had not alienated the followers of the new religion, which was a feat in itself. His decision to keep the Sacsonaidd alive had allowed the treachery of Gronw to be uncovered and Caerwyn was saved from attack.

Arthgwr bore no animosity to the Sacsonaidd he had held captive. He had thought of the barbarian, Ceolwulf, many times during this journey. He did admire the big man. The warrior within Arthgwr wondered how he would have fared in combat against the barbarian. The man within him hoped they would not meet in battle, but wistfully dreamed of a world where men such as he and the barbarian, Ceolwulf, could exist in peace.

No, Arthgwr harboured no great hatred of those people. He knew they had come to his country at his own people's bequest, or at least on behalf of the leader Gwrtheyrn. Arthgwr had no trouble allowing the barbarians lands to settle in the South-eastern shores. It was peace he was after.

Now, with all of these new obligations thrust upon him by Myrddin and Rhiannon, Arthgwr felt his resolve and confidence waning. He began to have doubts.

As a practical and self-reliant man, Arthgwr did not call upon the Christian god to relieve him of this terrible weight. He did not wish to be blessed or guided by any god, Pagan or Christian. He would not seek help from gods.

No! Arthgwr rebelled against that thought! They were his people! He would find what strength he had deep within himself to do what was right for his own! It was Arthgwr's responsibility and he would rise to the challenge as he always had.

He did give in to thinking about Gwenhwyfar, his wife. He wished mightily that she were here with him. Perhaps she would summon the goddess Dôn to hear his anguish. Perhaps the Mother Goddess could assuage his indecision or even infuse his being with the strength and courage he required to shoulder this burden. For that matter, the Christian god might be able to do the same for him. Arthgwr felt he could use some comforting at least in the face of the decisions he would have to make. For a moment, he thought of how similar the two faiths were to the people in these uncertain times. Arthgwr shook his head. He was a practical man. His courage, strength, and ability would determine the course. All that he desired at this moment was peace and prosperity for all his people. If only they could be united together as a nation, Pagan and Christian alike. It would be up to him.

Again, he thought of the barbarian, Ceolwulf. His admiration for the big man and his passivity about the Sacsonaidd settlements on the South-eastern shores of his people's land, did nothing to quell his passion for his country. Arthgwr would not stand by and let them, the Frisians, the Jutes, the Angeles or any others take by force, his countrymen's sovereignty or usurp their traditions.

Arthgwr stood up abruptly. This was no time for him to be weak minded. He needed to be resolute for his men had placed their trust in him and were ready to lay down their lives for him and his vision of unity. How dare he, Arthgwr, leader of these noble warriors, sit here under the stars of his country, his nation and doubt the faith his loyal warriors had in his ability to lead and unite them! He returned to his tent, renewed and confident.

Two capable warriors and their escorts were selected by the council and sent off with Arthgwr's proposal for the chieftains of the two advancing armies. There was nothing to do now but wait. Arthgwr briefed his men and the warriors. Preparations were made to further fortify the camp whilst Arthgwr and his council prepared the field to receive envoys from the two armies. Husbands kept their wives and children busy so that they would not dwell on the prospect of what might happen should Arthgwr's plan fail. Prayers were being said to both Christian and Pagan gods. The atmosphere of the camp was tense.

It was midmorning, when Arthgwr's men saw in the distance the dot of riders on the trail leading to the camp. They were coming.

Arthgwr had placed Cai in charge of organising the camp, making it ready should they need to stand and fight. By high sun, riders returned to the camp with the news that the two chieftains would talk with Arthgwr. They were on the way with their entourages. Time was short. A suitable place was found to host the meeting. Tents were erected and refreshments gathered and piled on tables. Hides and pelts were arranged in the traditional circle, but Arthgwr's place was strategically positioned so that he could escape through the wall of the tent and on to a waiting horse should things not work according to plan. The riders had arrived. The men of the camp cared for the visitors' mounts. The women and children designated to serve and help, offered the riders ale and hard bread. The envoys were lead into the tent and shown to the hides and pelts arranged for their comfort. They were a sullen lot and no smiles or banter arose from any of them. These warriors were serious men indeed. Gwyn accompanied Arthgwr to the parley.

After waiting for the warriors to refresh and avail themselves of the comforts provided Arthgwr stood and began to speak.

"We are at a crucial time in our history my fellow Cymry. Though we have survived the Roman invasion, not unscathed but intact for the most part, the threat to our way of life is clearly upon us," Arthgwr paused to remember the lessons Myrddin had taught him during the long night spent at the hut.

"These strangers have been brought to our shores to fight battles that we ourselves would not or could not fight. This is not the way of the Cymry, but the way of the Romans and it was the leader, Gwrtheyrn, who made that decision. The Romans are gone. We have rid ourselves for the most part of the Picts from the northern lands and the men from Iwerddon. Now we must contend with the Sacsonaidd and their tribes. They claim not to have been treated fairly by Gwrtheyrn and his council. The new king, Emrys Wledig," Arthgwr used the Cymraeg name for Ambrosius in an attempt to draw the tribes together in a common language, "hating what has become of our land, defeated Gwrtheyrn and his army in battle and then fought and defeated King Pascen of Buelt. These are our own compatriots and yet they fight our King. They fight our King even as he has fought the Sacsonaidd, King Hengest, and his sons. Our good king, Emrys Wledig, has given Cymru, our country, a victory over the new Sacsonaidd king, Aelle, and his sons. Our king has, as a gesture of good will and fairness, allowed the Sacsonaidd to live in the lands of the Southeast shores. They grow restless and they are threatening to push the Cymry into the western sea! This they may well do if they perceive the Cymry as being disorganised, petty thugs, and stealers of cattle! If we continue to fight amongst ourselves, the Sacsonaidd will consume us. Our way of life will be no more and even the songs of our heroes will die out ignobly." Arthgwr paused for a breath.

"What is all this talk of "Cymry"? I do not know this tribe! I am Venedotian and I will do as I see fit for my tribe!" A hush fell on the gathering as the warrior stated his case. Soon others stood and were proclaiming their tribal rights as well.

"I am of the Cornovii and do not recognise any tribe of "Cymry"!" With that, the warrior jumped to his feet with his men following his lead.

"I am here because of an alliance with Manw, he said, standing up and staring at Arthgwr defiantly.

"He is dead and so now I will take what action I deem necessary and you little man," he pointed his sword at Arthgwr, "are the one who threatens me and mine! You and your Roman King Aurelianus! Yes, don't fool us by using his Cymraeg name, the old bastard is Roman through and through!"

"So, you agree with me then!" Arthgwr yelled, a smile on his face.

"You agree that is better when Cymry are united, for you yourself entered into an alliance with Manw and he with the Venedotia! What you are saying differs little from what I am saying! We are all Cymry every man, woman and child among us! We are all Cymry, our land is Cymru, and I for one shall not stand idly by and allow others to take what is ours! We could, if we unite, show a force of such strength and resoluteness of purpose, that no nation would ever dare try to push us into the sea!"

The Cornovian was puzzled and could not quickly think of a retort, a sin in any Celtic society, and certainly a sign of feebleness now, amongst these warriors. He sat down. Even the Vendotian was confused, but quicker in intellect and possessing a sharper tongue than the Cornovian, he jumped up and attacked the obvious.

"What of Ambrosius, he is Roman. Why should we follow him?" The question brought some of the men back to their feet stomping and wildly whistling. Arthgwr waited for the demonstration to subside before speaking again.

"I am told that most of Cymru and even that part of the South called Britannia, knows Emrys Wledig, as King Ambrosius Aurelianus is called. Most know that his father was executed and his brother was murdered by Romans, yes, his own people, as you so delicately pointed out," Arthgwr nodded to the Vendotian.

"Ambrosius Aurelianus grew up in Amorica at the court of his cousin, King Budic I. He saw what Gwrtheyrn was doing to our land and he hated it! Ambrosius Aurelianus gathered an army and landed at Totnes in Dumnonia where he fought hard against Gwrtheyrn and the Sacsonaidd. He fought the Sacsonaidd King Hengest at Maesbeli and Caer Conan and besieged Hengest's sons Octha and Osla at Caer Ebrauc. Be forewarned, an invasion is coming! It matters not that there are Sacsonaidd here on our shores and that they have settled here. They want more! They threaten to drive us into the western sea! We are doing nothing about this! We are as a little people, a weak people, fighting amongst ourselves like dogs for the scraps at our master's table! Yet, if we united as one nation, all would know our strength! No tyrant will dare interfere with our destiny if we but united! Ambrosius Aurelianus wants this, I want this, and that is why I am willing to ally my army with this "Roman" king. That is why I want you to join me!"

The men were murmuring and talking amongst themselves. Arthgwr's words had made an impression on them. But the Cornovian was not to be appeased. He jumped to his feet sword in his hand and began to walk menacingly toward Arthgwr.

Gwyn saw the man moving and he looked to Arthgwr. Arthgwr saw what was happening and he glanced at Gwyn. The two of them had anticipated something like this occurring. They were surprised it was only the one Cornovian, who seemed intent on pressing his point by force.

Of course, the danger was that others might be enticed to join the determined tribesman. It presented a delicate situation. Arthgwr had to address the challenge from the Cornovian without antagonising the others whose support he may already have won. Arthgwr stood to unravel all the negotiations, if he mishandled the situation unfolding before him.

Arthgwr was glad he had the foresight to assign Edern to command the archers who were expertly hidden about the meeting place just outside. The plan was to create confusion and diversion so that he and Gwyn could escape, whilst at the same time, serve to warn the camp to pull out without haste and at full gallop. It was their only hope should their present plan fail. Had he been present, Edern would simply have cut the Cornovian down where he stood. The bloodletting would have ignited the entire company and Arthgwr would not have survived nor would the rest of the camp receive warning.

Arthgwr stood up and stopped the Cornovian in his tracks, with his words.

"If you intend on challenging me Cornovian, allow me to claim my sword. Or do you wish to simply cut me down without an honest defence?" The question created some derisive snickering that did little to diffuse the Cornovian's temper. He had no choice now, but to prepare himself for combat with Arthgwr.

The warriors were keenly interested in the outcome. They had been presented with a bold, shocking plan, which they instinctively mistrusted due to their rigid individualism. More to the point, they had not figured out the advantage to themselves and their tribe should they accept Arthgwr's plan. Having Arthgwr killed in single combat with a tribesman would absolve them from making any decision about Arthgwr's grand vision. They could carry on and gather what spoils they could from the gathered army of Arthgwr.

All eyes were on the two men preparing for the time-honoured ritual of single combat to the death. Arthgwr motioned to Gwyn who, with the help of a servant brought out the stone oblong and placed it where all could see. The dull grey stone edifice looked worn and ancient. The men's curiosity was piqued; they could not imagine what was in the curiously long solid piece of grey stone. Not a sound was made as Arthgwr took a small stone and tapped gently on the sides of the oblong. The stone encasement easily opened. Men strained to peer into the stone for a glimpse of what secret was held within. Arthgwr reached in and pulled out the shining sword, Caladfwlch.

A collective gasp rose from the warriors gathered to witness the drawing of the legendary sword from its stone encasement. Some warriors were deeply shocked by the sight of the great sword of the ancient legend and they feel to their knees in reverence. There was pandemonium as every warrior present witnessed Arthgwr standing tall, feet apart, eyes blazing and in his gloved fist the great shining sword Caladfwlch throwing its eerie yellow hue over the company.

To the shock and surprise of many, the Cornovian was not to be put off from his challenge. Though certainly less arrogant then he had been, he was still unconvinced as to Arthgwr's authority in the matter at hand. He said as much.

"You bastard! Do you think I, a Cornovian, and next in line to be king of my people, will be seduced by trickery? Stand and fight!"

Arthgwr bowed his head in curt assent and stepped to meet the challenge. Caladfwlch glinted ominously in the firelight.

The Cornovian swung bravely and missed. He cut down hard with his sword, but Arthgwr was nimble and not to be caught so easily. Again, the Cornovian whirled, this time his blade caught Arthgwr's tunic, slicing through it without touching his flesh.

Emboldened, the Cornovian thrust and then swung his sword in an overhead arc, narrowly missing Arthgwr's head. The missed downward swing cut another slice into Arthgwr's tunic. Arthgwr carefully circled. The Cornovian feinted and then spun, slicing his sword sideways to cut across Arthgwr's midsection. Arthgwr slammed Caladfwlch down to parry the blow. As the Cornovian blade struck Caladfwlch, it shattered into pieces with a resounding ring. The tribesman stood dumbfounded in shock and awe. The sound of the clashing blades still rang in the ears of the onlookers. Arthgwr did not strike the killing blow. He simply stood and looked at the Cornovian. The man looked defeated. The gathering was transfixed in silence.

Arthgwr turned to the warriors.

"Killing each other over disagreements helps only our enemies! We need to come together as one!" He had turned to face the gathering of warriors, his back now square to the Cornovian tribesman.

Arthgwr heard the unmistakable sound of a knife being drawn from its leather sheath. Turning to face his enemy, Arthgwr saw with mild surprise, that the tribesman was lunging at him, knife in hand.

Caladfwlch was in full swing. Arthgwr's spinning around caused the momentum. It was such economy of movement, no one thought that Arthgwr had moved, or even that he had seen the thrust of the attacking knife. Caladfwlch was already on the opposite side of the attacking Cornovian.

Nothing stopped. It looked as though the Cornovian knife would bury itself into Arthgwr. It had happened so fast. It was so effortless, no one had noticed.

Caladfwlch had sliced straight through the Cornovian's neck. The warrior was still moving forward when his head fell from his body and rolled toward one of the seated warriors. His body crumpled as it continued towards its' target. Blood splayed over the ground and the warrior's that were close by.

All were silent. They stared at Arthgwr. He stood before them, feet apart, arms at his side. Caladfwlch was gripped in his right hand, dark crimson blood flowing down the ancient sword's blood groove soaking the ground at Arthgwr's feet.

"Who will stand and pledge their allegiance to me as I stand before you with Caladfwlch, the Sword from the Stone, the fabled sword from the bottom of the ancient lake and blessed by Rhiannon, the Lady of the Lake. Who will stand with me against anarchy and purposelessness? Who will stand with me and unite the tribes of the Cymry and war against any who will take our lands?"

It started slowly. One man banged a sword on his shield. Then another did the same. And soon all of the warriors gathered were banging their shields with their swords, the noise was deafening inside the tent. The chant began softly, barely heard over the clanging of sword on shield. But soon the crescendo of voices rose in unison!

"Arthgwr! Arthgwr! Arthgwr!"

Chapter 22

The irony of his situation did not escape Ceolwulf. Alone, stumbling through brush and trees trying to find his way through the thick forest, he was where he had been when the tribesmen from Caerwyn had found him. At that time, he had a plan, a grand plan of creating an alliance and securing a place for himself beside the king or at the very least raising his stature among his own people. Ceolwulf thought grimly about his own blind ambition. Had he changed that much in so short a time? Time? He had forgotten just how long the men of Caerwyn had held him. The blow on the head had certainly skewed his perception of things and events. Still, he remembered with a warrior's pride that he had given a good account of himself with the fight that led to his "freedom." Yes, indeed that was a good one! And the battle in the forest was worthy of remembrance. Ceolwulf paused and reflected that it was a sad thing that the old soldier and his companion had been killed. They had been good men. Even in his state, he could see that. It was a good thing that they died in battle and in service to their leader, the lean man, the one they called Owain.

Ceolwulf looked around. All he could see was trees, brush, and the remnants of a snowfall. It was chilly and damp and close to sundown, he reckoned but he dare not light a fire. No, he was still too close to where the ambush had taken place even though he had been walking for an entire day.

Ceolwulf rummaged through the cloth bag he carried. He had gone through the belongings of the men he had killed in the ambush and retrieved much needed food, extra clothing and a few knives, even a sword. The tired warrior decided he could spare a bite of the hard bread and a mouthful of the stale ale he had found. That should keep him going a bit Ceolwulf thought to himself. His head hurt some, but that was because he was used to being fed regularly and able to sleep whenever he wished. It was not due to any injury received in the fighting. Ceolwulf was satisfied that he was mending very well and a little jaunt out of doors would serve him well. He chuckled to himself. Ceolwulf was fully aware that the leader of Caerwyn had let him go in the forest because it was improbable that he would be able to find his way out alive. Still he was happy to be free again.

He pushed on, trying to put more distance between him and the scene of the ambush. Ceolwulf hoped none of the warriors were following him and grinned. That would be doubtful given the number of them he had killed. Still he pushed on just the same. Moving south and east would, he thought, bring him to his people. Ceolwulf thought about his new home and wondered what did he really have to go back to? His wife Yetta had made it clear she was not the least bit interested in him and his own son, Aethelwulf did not show any great desire to acknowledge him. That left only his mistress Berit. Strange though it may seem he missed Berit. She was the only person in his life who had shown him any real affection. He had felt accomplished in her presence and it had assuaged his bruised ego. Ceolwulf was no lovelorn fool. He knew that Berit would get over him. She probably already had a new lover he thought grimly. Heretoga was a man he had trusted, but he wondered now if that trust had been well placed. It was Heretoga who had pushed the plan of the alliance with those men from Caerwyn. Ceolwulf wondered if his trusted comrade might have had ulterior motives. He did not know. Ceolwulf thought it was strange that the meeting had to be taken alone in the forest and by him alone. He thought it was also suspicious that the meeting went so badly since it was Heretoga who had made the negotiations. Ceolwulf wished he had not been so blinded by ambition. He should have thought through Heretoga's plan more deeply.

No, little good could come from his return. He would have to fight down the indignity of a failed plan and kill Heretoga. Besides, his absence had been long enough for things to change in his village. His return may not even be welcomed. Ceolwulf realised how much his ego and pride had fuelled his ambition and had blinded him to the consequences of his actions.

A feeling of overwhelming loneliness swept over him. Ceolwulf felt the full weight of his predicament and was chastened by his circumstance. The only thing he could do, would be not to return. It was a hard decision, but he felt the only decision left to him. The warrior stumbled under the weight of his thoughts. He shook his head, his long grey hair swirling around him as he did so. He exhaled heavily and with a clearing breath and a grim newly found resolve he trudged onward.

Ceolwulf stopped and throwing his head back, he laughed heartily. "Now that was an expensive lesson in humility!" he said aloud, but only the snow covered trees heard his confession. Judging that he had put enough distance behind him, Ceolwulf made camp. It was not much. He threw some scrounged brush under the outcrop of a rock. The light was failing and so was Ceolwulf's strength. He still did not want to risk a fire lest he be found and so he bundled up as best he could, using the extra clothing he had scavenged. Exhaustion allowed him some much-needed sleep. As he closed his eyes and surrendered to his slumber, he dreamt. His dreams however were troubled ones.

In his dream, Ceolwulf saw himself as an old warrior. The old warrior stumbled to his feet, he leaned on his mighty battle-axe now chipped, dulled and battle-worn. Looking around him he could see his men lay dead, their bodies lying on cold hard ground wreathed in a shroud of snow.

He had wanted to wage this campaign by hurling headlong through the thick forest. The warrior had never been defeated in battle but this was something different. The forest was sinister, foreboding and it was unknown to him. Why harbour such feelings? A forest after all is just a place of many trees. The warrior was convinced his cause was right and just, he had staked his honour and reputation on this campaign and he would see it through or die!

To a man, his captains advised against the quest. His bloodlust was up and he would brook no dissent. Many of the finest men had left him on the edge of the great forest and had turned back in disgust. They had thought him mad. They tried to warn him of the perils of the dense forest, they recounted tales of others who tried and failed to make their way through, but he would not listen.

Blinded by his bloodlust the privations, the cold, and hunger were as nothing to him. One by one, the men that had followed him dropped from fatigue, hunger, and the arrows shot from unseen enemies in the trees. The old warrior did not take notice. He pressed on.

It began to snow making seeing their way even harder. They were all close to freezing to death when just up ahead they spied something. It was a small clearing with a small hut, that promised at least some shelter from the cold. The ragtag band of warriors plodded towards the hope of warmth as fast as they could. Despite the sad state of disrepair, there was a pleasant smell to the rickety hut. That meant someone had been here recently. Immediately the old warrior posted guards. The next order of business had been to gain some warmth. He and two of his men started a large fire in the middle of the hut where a crude opening in the thatched ceiling served as a chimney.

The old warrior became comfortable as his bones warmed by the fire. The weak broth they had found in a pot hanging near the fire revived his constitution. In better spirits, he began regaling his men with exploits of past victories and honouring fallen comrades with sad tales of lost causes and great courage. At their leaders behest, the men drank the rest of the mead they carried with them and were caught up in the atmosphere created by the warming fire and tasty broth. A realisation struck the old warrior too late to be of any use. He had neglected to care for the horses. Those that had not run off were too weakened to be of any use. His men were afraid at his display of forgetfulness and irresponsibility. If he was not mad surely he was possessed, they murmured amongst themselves.

An attack took them by surprise and before they could shake their slumber, three-quarters of their force were dead. The great warrior was grief stricken. He knew this tragedy had come about due to his poor leadership. The responsibility for the deaths of the men he commanded, was his alone. Gone now was his ability to rouse his warriors to do his bidding. Gone now was his unflagging courage, his indomitable spirit and iron will. Head hung low, his great shoulders heaving in silent sobs, the big man was but a shadow of his former glory.

The last of his captains, nearly insane with fear, kicked the old warrior, his former leader, sending him sprawling in the snow.

"You bastard," he screamed, spittle spraying from his lips, "you conceited arrogant bastard! You have killed us with your vainglory, you have cut us down with your ego, and now you lay sobbing like a scorned camp girl! We are dead and dying and still all you can think of is yourself! You worry how the heralds will hound your name in the songs and poems they will sing about you, while it is we, who will join our brethren in Woden's Wild Hunt before light!"

A hound howled in the distance and the men became still as statues. Another howled, this time closer and from another direction. The enemy surrounded the warrior and his men. His captain, aware the old man was incapable of leadership, shouted orders to the few remaining able men left in their war band. Desperate orders, but perhaps they might save them all from a bad death.

Suddenly, brought back to life by his injured pride, the old warrior pulled himself to his feet. Gripping his trusted battle-axe with both his gloved hands, he swung the weapon in a wide arc of death and cleaved the captain in two. The men were stunned with fear and disbelief. The warrior stood and with head back, howled not as one of Woden's hounds of hell, but as only a tortured soul of a man could.

All around was death. The smell clawed at the nostrils' and worked its way into the bowels. It became colder and the snow fell heavily. The old warrior looked through his tear filled eyes at the scene he had created. The enemy closed in. The last thought he remembered was that he had lost the battle.

The horrible dream shocked Ceolwulf from his restless slumber. It was still dark. The sliver of a cold dawn was only now slicing through the cold air. He shook his head trying to rid himself of the terrible images his nightmare had left with him. What the dream signified, he did not know, but it left him feeling horribly unsettled. He was cold and stiff and it was no use trying to sleep any longer. In truth, he did not wish to sleep, even if he could, for he did not wish to be visited by such a nightmare as he had just experienced. He wondered if he would ever sleep. Ceolwulf stood up cautiously and stretched. Gathering his things and returning the earth he had lay upon to its original state, he shuddered. It would be some time yet before his nightmare released him from its dreadful clutches. He quickly moved on.

As luck would have it, he found a stream, its waters running free, clear, and cold. The gathering heat of the new day had been able to melt the snow lying around. Ceolwulf followed the banks of the stream after washing his face and drinking his fill in the refreshing waters. He carried some of the stream's water in an old ale skin he had scrounged from the ambush. He was happy to have survived the night and the nightmare. Ceolwulf was also happy that he had been able to spear two nicely sized trout. He carried the fish in a sack saving them for later despite his hunger pangs of the moment. He still did not wish to build a fire for risk of being seen and followed.

The morning of the next day began just as the day before. Ceolwulf had not slept well, waking up every time his nightmare threatened to take hold of his mind. He had not lit a fire and so had been forced to eat his meal of fish without cooking them first. His body did not take well to sleeping without benefit of a warm meal and a fire to ease his cold and weary bones. He moved stiffly this morning as a result. Ceolwulf moved about rubbing his extremities trying to get his blood flowing. He knew he would need to light a fire by this nightfall or risk growing too weak to move.

The day kept its promise and remained warm and Ceolwulf made good progress in his travels. Judging that he had put enough distance between himself and any who might have been following from the scene of the ambush, Ceolwulf finally lit a fire that evening. It was a small campfire, but sufficient to heat water in a small metal bowl. This he drank to warm his insides and he rubbed his hands together deliciously over the small flame. While enjoying the luxury of heat the fire afforded, Ceolwulf managed to dry out some of his clothes. Before extinguishing his flame, he warmed some of the pelts he had taken with him by hanging them over the fire. The hides were smoky, but they did warm his body. Wrapped in his warmed pelts and dry clothes he was able to enjoy a comfortable night even without a constant fire by his side. The nightmare did not return to haunt him.

It was many days later that he discovered the hut. It was a small hovel, but it indicated that there were other human beings in the area. That fact alone stunned Ceolwulf for he had not seen any sign of people since the ambush so many days ago. The discovery of the hut meant he was out of the forest depths. He had survived the forest!

Ceolwulf did not see anyone about and decided to cautiously slip down to the hut for a better look. It was a chance, but he thought he might be able to scavenge some food and supplies.

It took him hours in his weakened condition, but Ceolwulf managed to make his way down and into the lonely hut. Looking about he saw some items he could use, an old woollen cloak, a leather belt, a small carcass of what looked to be roasted rabbit meat and a small cask of ale. Hearing voices, he craftily made his way back into the woods. The voices he heard shouting behind him were in a language he could not understand.

Ceolwulf was too weak to travel very far from the hut. He had been on the go all day and nightfall was descending quickly. He was forced to stop and make a camp. Ceolwulf was shivering and he had no choice but to light a fire for warmth. Though the air had been warmed by the day's sun and the temperature was not as harsh as it had been at night, Ceolwulf found he could not stop shaking and he was cold and achy all the time. He picked up the meat he had stolen and tried to identify what sort of animal it was. Shrugging indifferently, he skewered it with a stick and put it on the fire to cook. He pulled out the woollen cloak and examined it. The cloak was of good quality and heavy. The hood would help keep him warm tonight, he thought to himself. The leather belt was of poor quality, but it helped cinch his clothing around his waist. Ceolwulf remembered when he first arrived on the island and had used his talent in leatherwork and metal work to earn a living. He was sure he could remember enough from his former trade to be able to produce belts, straps, harnesses and the like. It was a thought that flooded his mind with the fantasy of living a life other than that of a warrior. The thought was as frightening as his nightmare had been.

Turning his attention back to his cooking, Ceolwulf tasted the meat and judged it edible. He washed a mouthful of the mystery meat down with the ale he had taken from the hut. After eating, he settled in for the night, which promised to be warmer than his previous nights out in the cold. The fire was out, but he had used it to heat up the cloak and wrapped it around himself with the hood covering his head and face. Ceolwulf was warm and comfortable for the first time since his journey had started and he soon drifted off to sleep.

Late into the night, he awoke with a severe stomach ache. He writhed in pain until he vomited up everything he had eaten. Still in pain, he gulped down some ale, but that just made him vomit again. He squirmed and writhed in agony for the rest of the night, retching and vomiting long past the point where he had anything left to spew up. Exhausted, he finally fell into a sleep, just before the warming fingers of the sun clawed away the darkness of the night.

The full bloom of the warming sun on his face stirred him into opening his eyes. Everything was blurry and it took a bit of time for his vision to clear, but Ceolwulf could see the camp he had made before the fall of the night. The sun warmed the spewed contents of his stomach and the stench of it threatened to set him retching again. He quickly gathered his things and moved on, noticing in alarm that he felt much weaker than he had the previous day.

There were no more huts to be seen. Ceolwulf was out of the forest, as best he could tell, and following a stream in a south-easterly direction. He washed his mouth out with the fresh cold waters of the stream and then set to warming some water so that he might clean himself. The stink of his vomit was clogging his nostrils. Ceolwulf stomach had settled with a gulp of the stale ale and he was surprised that he felt hungry. He knew his stomach was empty, he was just startled to realise he had an appetite again. He had spent some more time fishing the stream and was rewarded for his endeavour. Ceolwulf took the fish and cooked it over the small fire he stoked. After spending the night in relative comfort, Ceolwulf pushed onward.

Over the next few days, he was able to catch a rabbit and made a sort of stew. He screwed up his courage and ate some trying not to imagine it to be anything like the meat that had made him sick. He felt better with something warm and filling in him, but he was aware that his body was still declining. He was weaker and getting weaker with the passing of each day. He yearned for some company. He had begun talking to himself aloud and knew that was not a good sign.

"Of course it would be worse if I answered myself!" he yelled aloud to the trees. Fits of laughter shook him and Ceolwulf had to sit down to rest. Once recuperated, he pressed onwards.

At dusk, he found himself on the edge of what appeared to be a small village, an outpost of some kind, he supposed. The scene surprised Ceolwulf. Part of him wanted to run screaming down into the settlement, just so he could be with people, prudence made him wait until dark before he could sneak down in to the encampment and steal what he needed.

Ceolwulf made his way out of the settlement with the booty he had stolen. He paused for a while some miles away from the scene of his crime to inspect the haul of goods he had taken. The treasure for the evening's work consisted of a knife, a flask of ale, some cheese, some hard bread, and a leather bag. He piled everything into the leather bag, swung the bag around his shoulders, and resumed his journey putting distance between him and the settlement.

It was later in the morning when he finally stopped, he was too exhausted to continue. He scrounged around as best he could, looking for suitable firewood. The day promised to be warm and indeed the cold morning's mist was lifting. Ceolwulf wanted to warm his bones and heat some food. A good rest with a small fire warm food and the warming sun would make him a new man he thought. He was moving about the thickets and brush looking for a suitable place that would provide him comfort and privacy from any prying eyes when he heard a voice. Ceolwulf froze in his tracks. He wrapped his cloak around him using the hood to cover his face hoping he could blend in to the brush.

"Wodens day!"

Ceolwulf ducked down, as he heard the whizz of an arrow. His face was in the dirt when he heard the unmistakable sound of the arrowhead burying itself in the tree trunk at the exact position his head had just occupied.

"No!"

Lying as flat as he could on the ground Ceolwulf remained motionless, his heart pounding in his chest. His mind was racing trying to figure out how he could escape from this danger. Ceolwulf could hear a man.... no....two men creeping through the bush towards him.

"Hail! Who are you...come...come we know you are there... you cannot escape...come out!"

Ceolwulf was shocked to hear his own language! Who was speaking to him in his native tongue? Was it one of his people, or was it a waelas speaking as one of his kinsmen? Ceolwulf did not know. There was only one way to find out. There was nothing that he could do. He was too tired and weak to make a fight of it and he would not survive against hidden archers in any case. Ceolwulf decided to do what the voice suggested and come out. Slowly, he stood up expecting to be shot through at any moment. That did not happen. Ceolwulf stood tall and looked around him. There were two men, one tall, robust and big boned, his hair long and grey, as was his rough beard. He was a bullish man, just past his prime. He was standing holding a staff; a sword dangled from his belt and a saexe was tucked in the front. Ceolwulf thought the man looked as though he could be any of a dozen men he knew from his own village.

The other man was slightly shorter, much thinner with sharp features. His hair was black as night and his eyes were pale blue. The man wore hair on his lip, but no beard and his hair was long and partly braided. The large long bow in his hands was unmistakable...he was a *waelas*!

"Friend, I say to you.... I thought you were Woden himself, hunched over with that hood over your face! Yes, indeed I thought for a moment I was being called to the Wild Hunt by Woden himself! Bryn lower your bow...."

"Where are you from?" The waelas's voice was harsh and the tone was menacing even though Ceolwulf could not understand the Cymraeg. His blue eyes had a steely hardness to them that matched his voice.

"Now Bryn.... everything will be alright, just lower your bow. You don't want to skewer the man before we even introduce ourselves do you?"

Ceolwulf's head began to hurt. He looked from one man to the other trying to orientate himself. Why was one of his countrymen travelling with a waelas?

"Oh, I know what you are thinking!" said the tall man, "you see you have been stealing from huts that belong to our village. Well, it's more a shire. My name is...Ecgtheow. This is Bryn. He is a Briton. Our shire is part Briton and part old country. I will tell you more of our history later. For now, you will need to come with Bryn and me, back to the shire. There is the question of compensation for the items you have er... liberated!" Ceolwulf looked blankly at the two men and then simply followed, as Ecgtheow led the way. Ceolwulf was acutely aware of Bryn following behind him at a good distance and he knew instinctively his great bow was notched.

It was a long day's march to Ecgtheow's shire. The shire turned out to be a large collection of huts surrounded by a wooden fence. All the huts looked to be in good repair and the little settlement appeared prosperous. There was a bustling market going on when the men arrived and Ceolwulf noticed there were many waelas about, or so it seemed. It was hard to distinguish his countrymen from the Britons. Ecgtheow marched Ceolwulf into the middle of the market whereupon he explained loudly to everyone within earshot that this was the man responsible for the missing items from the huts on their boundary. Ceolwulf could make out most of what was being said despite Ecgtheow's accent. Some Briton words he had heard while he was held captive in Caerwyn, but he could not yet understand the Briton language.

Struggling to make sense of what he was hearing and with some help from Ecgtheow, he learned that a discussion was ongoing about how he would be able to repay the village. When he further questioned Ecgtheow, he was told that was the way of the shire. Their laws were based loosely on the ancient Briton laws that dictated a man was responsible for his own actions and must make recompense for his deeds.

Ecgtheow was asking him if he had any special skills with which he could put to good use and thereby work off what he had stolen. Ecgtheow also mentioned Ceolwulf's present need for food and shelter indicating that would cost him also.

Ceolwulf was stunned. He thought he was about to be locked up in another cage. The idea of being confined and left to wonder his fate for days and weeks on end, was enough to make him lose his mind. He had felt his heart pounding and the blood racing through his veins at the thought. Instinctively, he knew his face was flushed and he could feel his hand tremor. Ceolwulf was alarmed for he had never before reacted to impending danger in such a weak-kneed manner. He did not take into account his weakened condition caused by his previous captivity, the single combat, the battle, and the incredible journey through the Great Forest. Nevertheless, he had been ready to fight, as best he could. And he was ready to die like a warrior. Then it dawned on him what Ecgtheow had said.

Pulling himself together, Ceolwulf managed to tell the people of the shire that he was a worker of leather and metal. This seemed to please everyone judging by the smiles and murmurs. Ecgtheow was certainly pleased with himself and before Ceolwulf could adjust to the idea he was not going to be caged, tortured or executed, he was introduced to an old couple. The old man and his wife led Ceolwulf away, the grizzled old warrior now more like a child who had been caught misbehaving.

He was shown the couple's hut, a modest, but tidy dwelling with a large workshop in the back. The old man indicated that the workshop was where Ceolwulf could eat and sleep. He saw the inviting pelts on the floor and fell on them, dead asleep. The old couple were shocked and wished the gaunt and smelly stranger had washed himself before going to sleep.

Ceolwulf slept soundly for nearly two days and he ate his fill of cheese, bread, hot soup, and stew. Of course, he drank a lot of the local potent ale, which the villagers sometimes served warm. Then he would sleep again. The old couple managed to persuade Ceolwulf to clean himself up. Using heated water infused with dried herbs Ceolwulf scrubbed the filth from his body and was thankful to put on clean clothes provided him by Ecgtheow, at a cost to be added to what he already owed the shire, of course.

Just when the couple was beginning to wonder it they were going to get any labour from the stranger, Ceolwulf presented them with two leather belts and a metal tankard. He had been working on them when he was alone and found that once his hands and fingers were warmed by the ale and good food, they were as nimble as ever before. Once he showed the shire he was competent at his trade of metal work and had the additional talent of being able to work with leather, Ceolwulf was kept very busy! There were items to repair, tankards, bowls, and other vessels not to mention knives, swords, axes, and farming tools. Ceolwulf was kept very busy and soon his debts were paid off in full.

Chapter 23

"Eala, you are doing well for yourself," Ecgtheow said to Ceolwulf over a midday meal of ale, cheese, and stew. "Yes, I'd say you have found your place." Ecgtheow was watching Ceolwulf's reaction keenly.

"Yes.... yes I suppose I have," replied Ceolwulf absentmindedly. "My hosts seem to be doing well from my labours as well!" Ceolwulf nodded in the direction of the old couple busily organising the afternoon's work for him to complete. They had added to his sleeping quarters in the days past and Ceolwulf was very comfortable. There was always plenty of food, ale, and clean clothing available to him. The old woman made sure Ceolwulf bathed at least a few times during the week. The two of them treated Ceolwulf as though he was their son and Ceolwulf as said as much to Ecgtheow.

"What you say is true... Old Redwald and his wife Aneira, yes... that's right she is Briton, they lost their son two summers ago. They used to make all our metal goods. You wouldn't know it now, but they were very talented in their younger days. Age was their enemy and their son had to make their living. When he was lost, the future for poor old Redwald and Aneira was lost as well. They were too old and their work was shoddy. No one in the shire said anything though! None had the heart to complain. Well, you seem to be an answer to their prayers!"

Ceolwulf could not help but feel satisfaction that his efforts were responsible for reviving the livelihood of the old couple. He was unaware that he was smiling.

'Friend, I say to you.... is that not a better thing than being a fighter for other men or even a thane who is driven by blind ambition?" Ecgtheow closely watched Ceolwulf's face.

Instantly, the smile on Ceolwulf's face disappeared, a look of surprise flashed, but was quickly covered by a scowl.

"What is it you are saying to me, old man? Why did you say such things about me? I am just a poor ordinary man who lost his way. I have no ambitions save to be happy." Ceolwulf struggled to put the smile back on his face.

Ecgtheow adjusted himself for comfort never taking his eyes from Ceolwulf. The sun was getting warm and it was quite pleasant sitting outside near the forge, the heat of which added to their comfort. Ecgtheow beckoned Redwald over and requested more ale. He told the pained-looking Redwald that he would himself pay for the ale and food, but that he and Ceolwulf needed to discuss important shire business. Redwald brightened at the prospect of being paid for his hospitality, though he was disappointed that shire business was infringing upon his own.

Turning his attention back to Ceolwulf, he indicated that the two should be more comfortable as this would be a long chat. Ceolwulf's keen senses picked up the movement of someone adjusting their position just out of his direct line of vision. He was aware that the angle and distance would benefit an archer. Ecgtheow ignored the look on Ceolwulf's face.

"You have spent many happy weeks amongst us now. I think you have found a place for yourself which means it is time for us to discuss some things of importance."

"Such as?" Ceolwulf asked, his eyes shining with keen focus.

"Such as why a warrior, a thane, I reckon, would wish to live such a life among us common folk. Oh, don't look surprised, Ceolwulf! Even now your eyes give you away! That steely look that speaks of a warrior assessing the battle ground, you have it now as we speak!"

"Is that why you have your man Bryn ready to shoot me through?" Ceolwulf looked hard at Ecgtheow.

"You see! That look! That is a warrior's look of cold contempt for death. That is the look of a thane, used to being in danger's way and fighting through just the same! No, that is not Bryn. It is his young son,

Gwyndaf. Bryn is some distance behind me over my right shoulder. Not to worry Ceolwulf," Ecgtheow quickly said noting that Ceolwulf had tensed like a wild animal ready to spring at its prey. "They are there only for my protection. I am old and no warrior."

Ceolwulf looked at the man in front of him and stated what he knew ever since the two had met.

"You were a warrior once and a leader of men."

"Yes.... I was, but I am no longer. I am here from my duty to the shire, Ceolwulf. I am charged with keeping the peace and keeping us safe, to the best of my ability. Surely, I would be a fool if knowing what I know, I came to talk plainly with such a warrior as yourself without some sort of ...er...alternative plan should you take offence at my questions?"

The look in Ceolwulf's eye confirmed to Ecgtheow he would indeed have been a fool and might yet end up dead. He swallowed hard, but did not shirk from his duty to find out just what the intentions were of this thane, sitting in front of him.

Ceolwulf took a deep gulp of ale. He needed time to think. What was it he wanted from this place? Indeed, what was it he wanted from his life? The trek out of the forest was quite an accomplishment and Ceolwulf had not failed to appreciate that in his own modest way. There was no disguising the battle scars on his body. Nor could he conceal his haughty demeanour, Ecgtheow had made that apparent. Ceolwulf realised that there was no escaping his past. Now he had to decide just what his future would be and that brought him back to the question. What was it he wanted from his life?

"Why don't you tell me what you know?" Ceolwulf said enigmatically to Ecgtheow.

"I know that it is no ordinary man who can walk out of the Great Forest alive. It is rare that anyone survives that place. Don't look surprised. The huts you raided were but a day or two from the Great Forest. It is the only way you could have come and not a man has come to us from the depths of those trees. You are the first. I know by how you carry yourself, your scars, the way you move, that you are a warrior. I say, "are" because you move so naturally and so smoothly that you have not had time to lose your warrior senses. I know by how you look at others that you are a man used to being obeyed. You were a leader of men, a thane in the old country and then again here in these Isles. There is more to you, however. I think you are tired of following a destiny chosen for you. I say that, because you chose to follow me here to the shire that day Bryn and I found you. I know you were weak and tired, but there was a certain fatigue about you that...well that...suggests you have come to a crossroads in your life." Ecgtheow looked sheepish as he spoke these last words.

Ceolwulf was shocked at how astute the older man was in his observations. He must have been a great warrior in his time, he thought. What Ecgtheow had said, Ceolwulf knew to be true and yet he was still hesitant to reveal his past to the old man. It was a past he wished to forget. Ceolwulf did not want to dredge up the fact he had been played for a fool by his trusted man Heretoga. He did not wish to bring up the details of his marriage to Yetta. He was embarrassed that a warrior, such as himself, could have been in such a loveless relationship as the one he had endured. The warriors that Ceolwulf knew would have beaten a wife for acting the way Yetta had acted towards him.

Indeed, they would have beaten her and taken what they wanted and left her for dead. Ceolwulf despite his brutality in battle could not bring himself to act in such a manner towards a woman. He could not explain why. Ceolwulf reminded himself that his marriage with Yetta had not been so bad in the beginning. He remembered how he had rescued her in the mead hall, the treacherous trip to Briton after the talk with her brother and how joyous they had been when their son was born.

All the fighting, the killing and the battles were things that made a man, a man. Acting from duty and for honour's sake, that was what made a man a good man. To be a great man, that required a man to build something, to make something of his life, so that his people would remember his name after he travelled to the Hallowed Halls in Woden's domain. A man, a real man, needed to build something that was good and for which those he left behind would be grateful. Ceolwulf had wanted to leave such a legacy for his son, Aethelwulf.

He realised with sudden clarity that was what the leader of Caerwyn had been trying to do. By keeping his village safe and prosperous, he was building something, a safe haven for his heirs and the families of the villagers. Surely this was a good and noble endeavour? This man in front of him now, Ecgtheow, the shire reeve of this settlement, was doing the same thing, protecting a haven for future generations. Ceolwulf had seen himself in that role, but in truth, his actions were more about expanding his borders and making a name for himself to impress an indifferent wife. It was not quite the same and Ceolwulf understood that now.

Looking at Ecgtheow, he understood he had a second chance. Now, Ceolwulf had a unique opportunity to attach his name to something good and worthwhile. Ceolwulf knew he had proven himself in battle, that he had led men to glory in war and that he had always tried to act honourably throughout his life. There was nothing left to prove to anyone. And now he was being presented the chance to choose to be free from the bonds of his own blind ambition. The opportunity being presented him, was to live the rest of his life trying to build something good, doing what others would see as good deeds, and not engage in vain, misguided, search for glory.

"I will not dispute you, but I maintain that my past is mine and I do not wish to share it with anyone. As to my being here, well that was simple happenstance, if not the will of Woden himself. I am alone in the world and in this shire. What I wish from whatever is left of my life is to be happy and to create something good. So I place my future in your hands willingly. I bring to the shire my skills as a worker of leather and metal and yes, I can wield an axe if it comes to that."

"Yes...I don't doubt you! Pity we didn't meet twenty years earlier!" Ecgtheow laughed at his remark and slapped Ceolwulf on the leg. Not being able to help himself Ceolwulf found he was caught up in the mirth of this old man.

"Yes, that would have been a match I would have paid to see!" Ecgtheow was nearly gagging, he was laughing so hard and Ceolwulf was now laughing loudly and freely himself.

"Friend I ask you..." began Ceolwulf, "what is the history of this place? How is it that waelas and our countrymen live side by side?"

Ecgtheow stopped laughing immediately, his friendly countenance replaced with a fierce scowl. It was clear he was angered.

"How is it friend...that after all these weeks you have spent in our shire that you cannot keep a civil tongue in your head? Do not refer to

Britons as waelas! For if one of them does not gut you like a fish then I will tend to the task myself!"

Ceolwulf was surprised at the emotion shown by the older man. He could see that old warrior within him was not entirely gone after all. He was saddened to have raised the old man's ire, though he could not understand the cause of his sudden and vehement anger.

"Dear friend...why is it that you become so angry I mean no offence!"

"The term waelas," said Ecgtheow through his anger, "is not appreciated here and you know well that apart from what the word means, it implies something more base and insulting. I caution you for the last time." Ecgtheow was beginning to clam down a bit and was regaining his composure. He beckoned over his shoulder and Bryn was soon at his side along with his son. Ecgtheow stood up and walked into the hut where Ceolwulf watched him talking to Redwald. The old man looked even more pained at what Ecgtheow was saying to him. Ecgtheow came back outside.

"Come the lot of you. We'll go to the dafarn for some food and good ale."

It was a long walk to the drinking establishment but it gave Ceolwulf time to collect his thoughts. He could feel the malevolence emanating from Bryn the whole time. Arriving at the dafarn, they seated themselves and ordered food and ale. The men drank their first ale in silence. Ecgtheow ordered two more jugs and then settled back and prepared to speak.

"I was born here...yes...I know that surprises you, but you see my father came here as a very young man. He was not the only one, for many young men from the old country made their way across the sea to these islands. They settled in relative peace and farmed the land. Oh, there were...er...disputes, but on the whole our countrymen were left to themselves. Here in the shire, we became friendly with the Britons. Goods were traded, customs observed and grudging respect developed into a sort of mutual alliance. Yes, we took wives as well and the Britons also took to wife some of our women from the old country. Most of us speak both languages fairly well. Bryn, as you may have suspected, is a relative of mine. He is my late wife's brother, which makes me the uncle by marriage to young Gwyndaf here." The boy smiled as Ecgtheow grabbed him by the hair and shook him affectionately.

Bryn had been watching Ceolwulf, but now he lowered his eyes, took a long drink and spoke in barely passable Sacsenaeg, as Ceolwulf strained to understand.

"Gwrtheyrn was not so responsible for inviting the Sacsonaidd here as the stories would have you believe. One thing is true and that is your people are hungry for our land." Ecgtheow put his hand on Bryn's shoulder to calm him.

"Some years ago now," Ecgtheow continued, "King Aelle from the South, fought the Britons in a great and bloody battle. The aftermath was so terrible that both sides desired a truce." Ecgtheow paused to take a long drink of ale.

"That truce seems to be in jeopardy. The Britons have been pushed west and now it seems there is to be a campaign to push them into the western sea. Our little shire has so far been saved from all the fighting. Indeed, we hardly realised the fighting had increased at all. There are signs now that indicate the end to the truce that has lasted so long. I can only hope that we will continue to be spared because our interests are so entwined it would be nigh impossible for most men here to choose sides. Doing so would certainly pit brother against brother."

Ceolwulf had listened intently to the tale Ecgtheow told and he regaled the old man with his own story of how he left his village and came to Briton. He kept his dignity and did not talk about Yetta or his son. He did mention his wish to form an allegiance with tribesmen on the borderlands and how such an allegiance would have put him in good stead with his king. Of course, Ceolwulf did not reveal the entire story of how he was duped by Heretoga and subsequently held captive in Caerwyn. The abridged story nevertheless amused both Ecgtheow and Bryn.

"You see that is why I would know of your intentions, now that you are among us," Ecgtheow leaned forward to look deeply at Ceolwulf. Bryn simply stared as did his son, Gwyndaf.

"It seems," began Ceolwulf carefully, "all my life I have been fighting against one tribe or another, and rarely have I found the cause to be in my own best interest. Nevertheless, I have fought with honour and for the sake of honour whatever the cause. I take the matter of honour very seriously," Ceolwulf paused and turned his steel gaze toward Bryn, "very seriously indeed."

Ceolwulf paused again, with measured movements poured himself a tankard of ale, and drank. He wiped his mouth and still holding Bryn with his eyes, he eased his back and continued.

"Upon reflection, it seems that my sense of honour has worked against me. I thought myself an intelligent man, but I have been a fool. I thought I honourably defended my people, but all I accomplished was to search for my own glory. I wished to earn myself a name that would impress those who heard it spoken. Instead, I am estranged from all who knew me and I am alone. I have led a hollow life and now I wish to live out whatever time may be mine in a honourable way. So I say to you Ecgtheow, shire reeve, I would live here in the shire. I bring my skills as a worker of leather and metal. I lay at your disposal my experience as a former thane and warrior, handy with a battle-axe, knife, and sword. I would swear to Woden to uphold the peace of the shire against all comers be they Saxon, Jute, Angles, Frisian or Briton."

Ceolwulf looked at each of them even young Gwyndaf. He waited for their reaction not knowing what it may be and feeling strangely detached about the outcome.

To Ceolwulf's surprise, Bryn reached over to take Ceolwulf's hand firmly in his own and with a look of friendship in his eyes simply said, "*Croeso*." Welcome.

Ecgtheow took some more time to explain to Ceolwulf that it was an older man named Alfred who had inherited the shire from the original founders. He was a sort of king and lived in the big wooden hall near the centre of the shire. Alfred as titular head of the shire had a modest retinue of guards but the actual day-to-day running of the shire and all its holdings was left to Ecgtheow. Alfred was often travelling around the shire either hunting or visiting with his people. He was a fair man and even tempered.

The people of the shire, Briton and Saxon alike loved him as their own. Alfred was getting on in years and it was noticed. Many thought that Ecgtheow would be named in his place, as poor Alfred did not have a son. Of course, Ecgtheow did not mention that to Ceolwulf. Bryn had told him when Ecgtheow went outside to relieve himself. Upon his return, Ecgtheow ordered more ale and food and the men spent a pleasant afternoon drinking and getting to know each other. Ceolwulf was again surprised to find he liked the previously surly Bryn. As the conversation loosened, Ceolwulf, by way of Ecgtheow's translation, could not help but appreciate Bryn's wit and sense of humour. By the third jug of ale, the two men were laughing and pounding each other on the back as though they had been life long friends.

The following days passed quickly for Ceolwulf. He was kept unduly busy with his work repairing leather items and making metal tankards, bowls and even working on an exquisite battle axe for one of the older men. The increase in business was due to the word of mouth endorsement from Ecgtheow. Even Bryn spoke favourably and increasingly of the Britons were requesting goods from Ceolwulf, Redwald, and Aneira. The old couple were very pleased and Ceolwulf was kept well fed, well clothed and with plenty of ale to drink. They even introduced him to Eurfron, a beautiful young Briton girl with golden hair that she wore in long tresses. Her red lips and rosy cheeks were breathtaking. She moved with a slight sway that Ceolwulf thought seductive. He flushed with embarrassment when, over a tankard of ale, Bryn told him that Eurfron's name meant "golden breasted." Bryn laughed hard at Ceolwulf's reaction.

Ecgtheow had left the shire and was gone for several days. He was travelling the countryside checking on small hamlets whose inhabitants were originally from the shire. Though living outside the shire the hamlets were still under its protection and the artisan and farmers of the hamlets enjoyed a strong and vital trade with the bigger settlement.

Ecgtheow called this, "making the rounds." Along with the bountiful trading arrangement it was his duty to collect a small tax from each of the hamlets in the name of Alfred. The tax was used to provide for some of the needs of the people. The shire had a hall where twice a year a sort of council was held and grievances were heard and settled in civilised manner. The taxes helped offset the cost as well as provide for the stockpiling of winter grain. No one under Alfred's sphere of influence starved in winter. Ecgtheow, of course, did not travel alone. He had a small contingent of armed men with him for protection.

Sometimes Bryn and some of his relatives accompanied Ecgtheow. At other times a motley collection of Briton and Saxon men rode with him. There was rarely any trouble. Once or twice in the last two years there had been attempts at robbing the band, but that proved fateful for the would-be robbers. Ecgtheow always chose experienced seasoned warriors, men with clear heads, agreeable dispositions, and deadly fighting skills.

A small feast was organised to celebrate Ecgtheow's return as it coincided with Alfred's return from a long hunting trip. There was much speculation in the shire, that Alfred's "hunting trip" was merely a rouse, and that he was really visiting his mistress in one of the outlying hamlets. No one spoke openly of the matter, so as not to offend Alfred's wife. The celebration was held in the main hall of the shire and most of the shire's residents attended. Guests brought food, ale, and musical instruments. Many of the Britons sang or told tales of their ancient heritage. Ceolwulf was beginning to understand a few words thanks to the tutoring of Bryn and the ever patient Eurfron.

One of the Sacsonaidds, an old warrior born on the continent and steeped in the old ways, stood up on a bench. He held in his hand an old ornate drinking horn filled with mead. Pausing for a long drink of mead, the old man began reciting a poem of valour. He told of a young battle-king from the frozen North Country who answered a call for aid from a distant king of a troubled land across a great fjord. This battle king wished very much to make a name for himself quickly to secure the loyalty of his own people. He was a valiant young man, confident, but not cocky. The battle king, with a company of fifteen of his own seasoned warriors all battle tested and true, travelled into the land to fight the monster that had been troubling the distant king. The young battle king first dealt with some political intrigue at the king's court, for new allegiances were hard forged. Wasting little time, the battle king and his men were soon on the monster's trail. A bloody battle ensued, but the warrior-king prevailed because of his battle skill and good character. It seemed the enemy, a ferocious she-beast from the depths, was defeated in a test of sheer will and determination that took place beneath the waves of the sea. The king was well pleased, heaping songs and praise upon the battle-king and his brave men. Alas, as the celebrations were under way the warrior king collapsed in a heap. Stripping away his skins and armour his closest friend revealed a terrible wound that had gone undetected. The battle king had won the day for the king, but in so doing, he had forfeited his own life. The heralds, however, saw to it that his exploits would be remembered forever, assuring the young battle-king a place in the mead hall of the brave.

By the end of the poem everyone was quiet and reflecting on the bravery, courage and honour of the young battle king in the tale. Then the banging began, sword to shield, tankard on table, and the ale and the mead flowed again. Singing and dancing broke out and there was much laughter.

Bryn and Ceolwulf were drinking and talking about Bryn's son Gwyndaf. Ceolwulf had need of a helper now that he was kept so busy with the demands of the shire's people. Gwyndaf had agreed to assist with stoking the furnace, chopping the wood, scraping the hides and other menial tasks. Ceolwulf had noticed how the boy watched him closely when he was working with the metal. Curious to see what the boy could do, Ceolwulf handed him a small repair job on a tankard. To his delight young Gwyndaf took to the project right away and did a marvellous job. Ceolwulf thought that Gwyndaf would make a good apprentice and decided to speak to Bryn about the idea. As Ceolwulf discovered such bargaining and negotiating were common at such gatherings. Bryn had agreed to allow his son to work as Ceolwulf's apprentice for room and board. Gwyndaf would see to the daily chores and learn what he could from Ceolwulf.

Earlier that morning, Gwyndaf had forged a quantity of small iron arrowheads about the size of the first joint on his little finger. Ceolwulf had been impressed and wondered how effective these little bits of iron might be. This innocent curiosity expressed by Ceolwulf caused a row with Bryn and his son. Both insisted they were the deadliest weapons in the land and when Ceolwulf smiled and ran his finger over the head of a battle-axe that lay nearby, well emotions ran high. Bryn and Gwyndaf were determined to demonstrate, not only their skill and accuracy with the great long bow, but the power of the mighty weapon as well.

Twenty-five paces away a leather sack was filled with dirt and placed on a pole about chest high. It was then covered with an armoured breastplate of the old country fashion. Ceolwulf was sceptical that a simple arrowhead of the kind that Gwyndaf had made, could have any effect on the leather bag protected as it was by the armour. It was not just any armoured breastplate either. Ceolwulf himself had made that armour, personally finishing it only the day before. A small wager was now riding on the outcome. The people of the shire had overheard the arguments and many had gathered around to watch, bet, and cheer.

Gwyndaf was to go first. He took a position about twenty-five paces from the breastplate-protected bag. The crowd was excited and bets were made although none of the Cymry would bet against Gwyndaf a fact that went unnoticed by Ceolwulf. Gwyndaf was ready

"Easy win, eh, Da?" he called out to his father. Bryn laughed and winked back at his son. He was proud of Gwyndaf.

"Now, don't you make it look too easy there, son for I am to go next!" Everyone laughed.

Drawing back on his bow, Gwyndaf held it steady, arrow nocked, its energy making the weapon quiver. For a moment more he held steady. Then the young man loosed the arrow. There was the swish of the fletch, as the shaft whizzed by at an amazing speed, too fast for the eyes of the crowd to see. A decidedly metal "thunk" was heard twenty-five paces away and it looked as though the "enemy" had sprouted feathers. A cheer went up and Ceolwulf was jostled and pounded on his back good naturedly as it became evident that the arrow had indeed pierced the armour breastplate. The yelling and cheering subsided as Bryn now took his place. Ceolwulf watched incredulously at Bryn who had positioned himself sixty paces from the armour clad leather bag.

"Never!" said Ceolwulf shaking his head. Money quickly changed hands but again none on the Cymry in the crowd would bet against Bryn.

"We shall see!' replied Bryn in a low voice, a big smile on his face.

Like his son before him Bryn pulled back on his bowstring so that it was in line with his ear. The bow quivered and the sinews in Bryn's arm bulged as testament to the strength of the man and the power harnessed in the weapon. Bryn loosed his arrow and it streaked in an upward arc. Sixty paces away the same metallic "thunk" was heard. Ceolwulf shook his head and handed over a small pouch of silver coins. He paused and then took back the pouch. Everyone froze; tension and anxiety filled the air in anticipation of the big Sacsonaidd reneging on his wager.

Ceolwulf looked around and then took out three small coins.

"This will compensate me for the ruined breast plate!" he said with a smile and handed the pouch back to Bryn.

Amid the laughing and guffawing someone yelled out about the prowess and strength of an axe wielding Sacsonaidd warrior. It was all good-natured fun, but Ceolwulf soon found himself with a battle-axe in hand, watching as three posts were set in the ground. Each of the posts was slightly thicker than a man's neck and the third post was "wearing" Ceolwulf's ruined breastplate. Money and ale were being freely passed around and everyone was laughing and joking. The crowd grew silent as Ceolwulf, realising he was not able to talk his way out of making such a display, resigned himself to his fate.

Gripping the battle-axe, he checked it for balance. Swinging it around in circles, first with just his wrist, and then changing from hand to hand, and overhead, in bigger and bigger circles, he satisfied himself as to the workmanship of the weapon. It was well made and finely balanced. To test the sharpness of the axe's blades, he pulled a hair from Bryn's head, much to the amusement of the onlookers, and allowed it to be cut on the battle-axes' blade.

Feet apart, battle-axe now secured in a harness behind his back, Ceolwulf was all concentration as he stood motionless. Then with blinding speed and precise manoeuvring, he released the axe. One swing and the top of the first pole toppled to the ground. Before it hit the earth, another swing dispatched the second post top and it fell, on its way to joining the first one. Even before that second post top hit the ground, the battle-axe's blade had swung a deadly arc and came down burying itself deep into the breastplate protecting the third post. The strike of Ceolwulf's axe cleaved the post and the breastplate in two. Both halves of the breastplate hit the ground slightly after the first and second post tops.

The crowd was silent.

"Well, I want my three coins back", cried Bryn, "for I didn't cause that much damage!" The crowd erupted with laughter and the two men backslapped each other as tankards of ale were pushed into their hands by celebrating villagers. Bryn and Ceolwulf took a few coins from the bag and then donated the rest to the supplier of the ale so all could drink freely and enjoy themselves.

Relaxing at a table with Bryn, his son and family, Ceolwulf was lounging comfortably with Eurfron in his arms, her back pressed against his chest as they all listened to Ecgtheow. Ceolwulf absently curled his finger in Eurfron's golden hair and bending forward he kissed her gently on the forehead, she snuggled in closer to him.

"Well, you see that there could be a problem," Ecgtheow was saying. Bryn looked thoughtful but said nothing. Ecgtheow continued, "This Cedric and his son Cynric are making quite a bit of noise. They have trampled more than a few villages and hamlets and engaged a number of Briton warriors winning most of the encounters." He looked forlornly at Bryn and his family. "I am sure this spells trouble for his her in the shire."

"There has always been fighting in the lowlands and in the Southeast. This is no concern of ours," said Bryn finally. "Old Emrys Wledig fought Hengest at the Battle of Maesbeli and Caer Conan. Not to mention, he besieged Octha and Osla at Caer Ebrauc. He is fair though, that old man, for he let the Sacsonaidd who surrendered to him, stay in peace at Bryneich."

"Yes, but this time it is beyond those lands and it is spreading. This Cedric wants to establish a new land. Already there are reports of him wanting to capture the territory and call it Wesseaxe! He is pushing the Britons across the River Wye! This is what I have been saying would happen for some time now, you know that! Now I fear our time is at hand!"

"What Bryn is saying is true, Ecgtheow. Hengest is dead and his son Aesc is not made from the same mettle as his father. This Cedric hasn't really done anything, apart form going on a few raids and making boasts! There will always be fighting in the South, it won't affect us here, my own experience shows that surely!" Ceolwulf said, holding Eurfron close to him as though what he spoke of might threaten her in some way and that he was her only protection. Eurfron looked up to him concern showing on her face. Ceolwulf squeezed her tightly and she settled back calmly.

"I've heard a story," said Bryn with a smile on his face, "King Gwynllyw of Gwynllwg has fallen in love with a princess."

"Oh, really, oh, please go on Bryn, let's hear a story of love and romance, please!" Eurfron cried enthusiastically.

"Yes... alright then...the princess is the daughter of King Brychan. She is the apple of his eye and of course she has been brought up in the Roman religion...Christian, she is, and tutored at the royal court of Garthmadrun. Gwynllyw is a rough Pagan, a follower of the Old Ways and of course, King Brychan refused Gwynllyw's request for his daughter's hand in marriage."

"How did that go over with the Pagan Gwynllyw?" asked Ceolwulf straining to understand Bryn's accent. Despite his warrior ways Ceolwulf was enjoying the romance of the tale.

"Oh, well, it did not sit well with him at all and he's not one to give up on something he desires, not our Gwynllyw! He takes three hundred men with him and damned if he doesn't steal the beautiful Princess Gwladys from her father!"

There were gasps and murmurings from those who listened to Bryn's tale. All seemed caught up in the yarn. All that is except Ecgtheow, who stubbornly refused to smile and instead sat with a scowl on his face.

"Well, then what happened?" squeaked Eurfron, backed by a general clamouring of those who were listening.

"An astonishing thing happened," continued Bryn, "a man, a sort of king, though no one knew him as such, well, he intervened. This king or whoever he was, had been leading his people from village to village in an attempt to gain allegiance of the tribes and villages in the region. In any case, he speaks with Gwynllyw and promises to take his case to King Brychan and negotiate a settlement between the two men before there is any blood spilled over the matter." Bryn stopped his story and grinned at the gathering before he continued.

"So he did! King Brychan promised not to chase Gwynllyw and he would agree to the marriage of his daughter Gwladys to him, so long as Gwynllyw agreed to raise the children of their union as Christian!"

"And that's how the battle was stopped?" asked Ceolwulf incredulously.

"Yes...exactly how it was stopped and stopped before one drop of blood was ever spilled!"

"But what was the name of this king or leader and where is he now?" asked Eurfron. Ceolwulf looked down oat his woman as though he were jealous of the attention she showed for this bold new leader. Eurfron giggled with amusement at Ceolwulf's mock jealousy.

"Aaaaah, well that's just the thing! We don't know his name or where he comes from!" Bryn's eyes sparkled as he was enjoying the telling of this romantic mystery.

"Is he a ghost or demon from the Otherworld?" asked Eurfron.

"Oh, no not that," laughed Bryn. "No, he is flesh and blood but he goes by a title, not a name. They call him, "Arthgwr," from the old tongue. It means he fights like a bear and that he is from the North. I suppose that is where he disappeared to back into the Northlands."

"Is it true?" asked Ceolwulf, a half smile on his lips. A cold shiver ran through his spine as though he sensed foreboding. Eurfron, sensing something was the matter, snuggled closer into her man. She looked up at him trying to fathom the problem. Ceolwulf just smiled and kissed her reassuringly.

"Oh, yes...it is true, I swear it and the news could only be a few weeks old."

"Well, pity we didn't have such a strong leader to face up to Cedric!" quipped Eurfron and then she giggled as Ceolwulf squeezed her tight pretending to be the jealous lover.

"Old Emrys Wledig could handle that little bugger Cedric, there is no threat there I tell you!" said Bryn forcefully.

"You don't see it," an exasperated Ecgtheow sputtered. "The tribes in the North have fallen amongst themselves and they pose no opposition against any who seek to usurp the land. There is nothing stopping Cedric, his son or anyone else for that matter from taking our lands! Einon Yrth has seen his kingdom of Gwynedd torn in two! The land is vulnerable to plunder and I fear we in the shire will fall under the sword of any usurper who will call himself king!"

"You are speaking of our very own kinsmen, Ecgtheow. What are the likes of you and Alfred to do? And what about me? Am I now to take up arms against my own kin or those whom I have come to love as kin?" Ceolwulf looked down on Eurfron and kissed her head again before looking up and catching Bryn's eye.

"That's just it!" cried Ecgtheow. "We are neither fish nor fowl here in the shire. No matter what king comes calling, we all of us will be considered suspicious because we live in harmony! Don't you see? I for one owe no allegiance to anything, but the shire. This is where I was born. This is where my family lives and where my good wife is buried. I honour my Saxon heritage, but I recognise no king or leader, save Alfred, and no country, but what I can see here in the shire. I will defend this place and the people I love, Briton and Saxon alike, to the death, for they are my family, my kin and my tribe!"

Bryn could see his brother-in-law was working himself into a fit. Calmly, he put a hand on his shoulder and offered him ale. Looking up into the eyes of his kin, Ecgtheow felt overwhelmed with emotion and dread. Slapping away the ale, he jumped up and stumbled out of the hall. Bryn, concerned now for his brother-in-law's well being, sent Gwyndaf after his uncle.

"Well," said Ceolwulf, "poor Ecgtheow seems to have quite a lot on his mind. Have you heard what Alfred has to say about all of this?"

Bryn shook his head.

"It is late, and there is work to be done tomorrow. We will sleep on this, ponder the problem and tomorrow with clear heads we will speak to Alfred and seek his opinion."

Standing up rather woozily, Ceolwulf leaned on Eurfron for support. Smiling, he spoke.

"I do not wish to stand against any who can put an arrow through a breast plate at sixty paces!" He clapped his hand on Bryn's shoulder and looked deep into his new friend's eyes as though he were seeking to read the man's mind.

"I do not wish to be split into kindling by a man I call friend!" The two men hugged and slapped each other's backs. Ceolwulf pulled away and, hugging Eurfron, the two of them wobbled out of the hall on their way back to Ceolwulf's lodgings. Bryn looked after them with a frown on his face. He turned to the rest of his family.

"I'm going to bed!"

The days passed by and nothing much more was said about the conversation the night of Alfred's return. Ecgtheow however was withdrawn and dour and he was often busy conversing with Alfred. Ceolwulf was kept busy as usual with the endless requests for leather and metal items and repairs to the shire's utensils and tools. It was hard for him to keep up with the workload even with Gwyndaf's help. He joined Bryn at the dafarn from time to time to listen to shire gossip and learn the news such as Bryn had knowledge of. Ceolwulf enjoyed drinking and talking with Bryn and he improved his knowledge of the Briton language.

Bryn was busy as well working his bit of land and getting crops ready to plant. The weather was warming nicely and the farming tools were sharp and ready to use. Bryn's family fussed over Ceolwulf and Eurfron, as did Redwald and Aneira. It seemed there was a conspiracy afoot to see the two of them hand fasted. Ceolwulf took it all in stride but not without some pride.

Ceolwulf was worried about how frail Aneira was looking these days. Gone was her usual spark and quick witticisms that were so often directed at keeping her husband in line. The last few weeks Ceolwulf had observed Aneira simply sitting in the sun half dozing seemingly unaware of what was going on around her. Her face was gaunt and her skin was slack and grey. Her husband Redwald doted on his Briton wife, the two of them had been hand fasted for most of their life, neither of them had known another as partner. It touched Ceolwulf's heart to see the two of them together fussing over each other or sometimes poking fun at each other's foibles in good natured fun.

Ceolwulf was working in the forge as usual when he heard a dreadful wail unlike anything he had heard before. He went running to the source of the sound armed with his battle-axe, Gwyndaf close on his heels. It was what Ceolwulf had been afraid of for a long time.

Aneira had died. She had been sitting quietly in the warm sun while her husband Redwald fetched some cheese for her to nibble. Redwald had called out to his beloved, but got no response. Not worried, he continued to slice a piece of cheese and hard bread for his wife. He called her again, but still he heard no response. He was about to continue in his task, when he was overcome with the most dreadful feeling. Moving as fast as his old body would allow, Redwald hurried to his love's side. He reached out his hand and gently shook her shoulder. Her head fell forward on her chest. She was gone.

Being the first to arrive at the scene, Ceolwulf helped old Redwald to a chair, but the poor old man could not sit. He was a heap, a ragged blubbering heap of sorrow and he fell to the ground. Ceolwulf sent Gwyndaf to fetch his mother and some of her friends to help. Already, villagers were gathering and a few of the women took over from Ceolwulf.

They lay Aneira down on her bed and loosened her clothing but it was plain for all to see that she was indeed gone. Concern now was for poor old Redwald. He was totally beside himself with grief. The women took him to another room and laid him down. The man just sobbed and sobbed softly calling out his dear wife's name over and over. Bryn and Ecgtheow ran in and Ecgtheow held a tankard of mead to the old man's lips. It was no use, he couldn't drink. One of the Briton women came in with a heady broth of herbs and tried to get Redwald to drink, but he would not accept it. Ecgtheow held Redwald's head and placing his fingers over the old man's nose, he gestured for the woman to pour the concoction into Redwald's mouth. That seemed to work.

Ceolwulf asked what it was that they had given the old man and was told it was an ancient recipe to aid in calming the spirit and soul. Redwald did indeed calm down and Ceolwulf watched as Redwald's body relaxed and went limp. The hut was now full of villagers eager to do what they could to help. Women began preparing poor old Aneira's body for burial.

One of the older women noted Aneira bore a smile on her lips and said it was a good omen that meant Aneira recognised that she had lived well and had died happy. No one yet was talking about poor old Redwald and what he would do with himself now his life's partner had gone on before him. There would be time enough to figure that out.

Another shout raided up this one was also very urgent. Ceolwulf was following the directions of the women tending to Aneira and watched as Ecgtheow went running to see what was the matter. He noticed Ecgtheow talking to one of the shire's men. Suddenly Ecgtheow turned a ghostly white and ran flat out to the Great Hall. Ceolwulf excused himself and ran after Ecgtheow.

"What is it?" He asked when he arrived to see Ecgtheow ashen and shaking.

"What is it man?"

Ecgtheow looked up.

"It's Alfred. He is dead."

Ceolwulf watched as the village gathered much as they did at Redwald and Aneira's hut. The crowd filled the Great Hall to overflowing. Aneira had already been laid to rest. It would be Alfred's turn now. Ceolwulf noticed the Briton singing songs to their gods and making offerings for their leader's spirit. He saw people from the Old Country, the country of his birth, praying to Woden and singing.

Woden is the chieftain of speech
mainstay of wisdom
and comfort to wise ones
for every noble warrior
hope and happiness.

Ceolwulf saw a small group of Britons who stood together away from the others. One of them was speaking and Ceolwulf could just hear a sort of cadence as though a prayer was being said. What struck him as unusual was the odd way the members of the group moved their hands in front of their bodies in a ritual pattern. The group was on their knees and at given times they touched their head, midsection, right shoulder and finally their left shoulder pausing to put their ring finger to their lips as if in a kiss. It was obviously a sign, but of what Ceolwulf could not guess, but he was sure he had seen that ritual before.

Alfred had been bathed and dressed in his finery and buried with his sword and shield. The villagers cried and cried, none more than Alfred's wife. Sad songs were sung throughout the shire, the people were reeling from the sudden deaths. Alfred was not long in the ground, when news came that Redwald, too, had passed away in the night.

The old couple had become adoptive parents of the old warrior Ceolwulf and he was sad at loosing them. Eurfron comforted her big warrior as best she could. Ceolwulf tried to shake off his melancholy mood; after all he had seen many men die gruesome deaths. Indeed, he had caused the demise of many men, too many to count. Yet, he felt for the first time in his life, a sense of loss at the passing of the old couple. He wondered if the loved ones of the many men he had dispatched to the otherworld had felt the same way. Three beloved ones had died within a day of each other. The shire was staggered by the loss. It was not the same as losing men in battle for losses were anticipated in war. Everywhere people were crying and praying to their gods.

Ecgtheow and Bryn had been looking for Ceolwulf. With the entire shire turned out for the funerals, Ecgtheow had been distracted. Now, it was to business and he had called a meeting of all the important men and women in the shire. They all met in the Great Hall. It surprised Ceolwulf, to be called on to attend.

The mood was, as expected, sombre and subdued. The first business was some outstanding debts and promises of labour owed from one of the villagers to another. That sorted Ecgtheow turned to look at Ceolwulf. Standing Ecgtheow addressed the council.

"This man Ceolwulf who has lived among us now for many months, a short time in the big scheme of things yes and yet he has become so valued a friend and respected artisans. He is now bereaved and alone in our shire. What shall we do and how shall we look upon him from this day forward? Redwald and Aneira had no living relatives in the shire. Their poor son having died they had no kin left to claim their property. Ceolwulf here was as close to a son as they had in the last moments of their long lives. They were fond of him I can tell you that and they were grateful for the work and the living Ceolwulf provided for them. Therefore if no one objects I say Ceolwulf shall inherit Redwald's hut and keep for his own use all property belonging to the hut. I say this provided Ceolwulf can supply us with the leather and metal goods we need...at a fair price mind you."

There was general agreement and pounding of the tables signifying that Ecgtheow's suggestion was accepted. Ceolwulf was dumbfounded. He realised immediately the wealth he had just inherited. Before he could get his wits about him Ecgtheow was up on the table addressing the council again. Ceolwulf strained to hear what was being said.

"Alfred, a good man and wise leader will be missed. The shire mourns his passing. It is a bad time to lose such a man. Therefore I have another suggestion for the council to consider. Consider it well for the times are turning and danger is about us remember this! So I say to you that I, Ecgtheow with Bryn at my side to advise me am willing to take over the duties of Alfred. My own former position as shire reeve will be given to Ceolwulf, for as I have already said, he is a good man and we have all seen what he can do with an axe!" A hush fell over the Great Hall.

Then chaos erupted. Shouts and cries, conflicting points of view, grew into a deafening noise. Pandemonium ensued as speeches were yelled out, tables were overturned and fistfights broke out between impassioned villagers. The bedlam carried on for a long time. Slowly arguments made sense, egos were assuaged and a decision was reached.

One of the Briton women stood up and spoke for the council saying they agreed to what Ecgtheow had suggested.

Ceolwulf was astounded by the events and the decisions of the council. He had this night been made a rich and powerful man in the shire!

Later, away from the council and alone with his woman, he spoke his mind. Eurfron was supportive and loving as always and yet she made Ceolwulf look at all sides of any question. Eurfron, like most Briton women was shrewdly intelligent and independent by nature. Ceolwulf remembered the teasing he had taken from Bryn about the meaning of Eurfron's name. Bryn had told Ceolwulf clearly to be careful, for the passions of the Briton women run deep. His friend told him, when Briton women are crossed there is nowhere a man can hide to escape their vengeance. The same is said of their love for their man. A Briton woman once smitten or successfully wooed by some young warrior, will love their man until death. Woe betide any who threaten their man, whether king or low born, they will bear the wrath of the Briton female!

Ceolwulf did not know at the time if Bryn was mocking him or if what he said was true. He chose the side of caution and decided to believe Bryn's warnings. From that day on he always treated Eurfron honestly and as an equal.

With the consent of the council who had heeded Ecgtheow's recommendations, Ceolwulf was able to do some good for himself and those around him. He had been feeling very good about the work he had been doing and he took a renewed pride in his craftsmanship. Ceolwulf had been happy to work for Redwald and Aneira and now he would be working for himself. He thought of the responsibilities of becoming the shire reeve and his newfound stature in the community. He thought about the respect and friendship he had received from fellow Saxons and Britons alike. For the first time in his life he realised what it was he really wanted. Filled with an overwhelming feeling of true happiness Ceolwulf swept Eurfron up in his arms. He tried explaining his feelings to Eurfron and finally got around to asking if she would have him as her man. The young woman loosened her ribbon allowing her golden locks to cascade around her smooth white shoulders. She moved seductively against his taut body and melted in his arms. Ceolwulf received his answer.

Chapter 24

Caerwyn had never looked so beautiful. Yet, it was not the same village as when Arthgwr had left. There were so many people! Palisades had been erected and they protected the perimeter of the entire village. The size of the village had doubled and there was a new buzz and bustle to the place. Arthgwr ordered Cai to set up camp just outside of Caerwyn, so as not to overwhelm the village with the horde his army had attracted along the journey. Arthgwr wanted to assess the resources of his home before committing them to housing a mob. The logistical planning and responsibilities attached to his leadership melted away before the vision of his beautiful wife.

Gwenhwyfar stood resplendent in a long flowing blue dress, her hair intricately woven, gold earrings, bracelets on her arms and ankles, and rings on her fingers. Arthgwr could not help falling in love with her again. Several young women attended his wife, but it was the men Arthgwr noticed immediately.

All around the courtyard, where Gwenhwyfar and her retinue stood, were serious looking men, all of whom were well armed. Just as the warrior in him coldly calculated the situation, Elidir rode up. The young man had grown. He was every inch the experienced warrior in his demeanour and he was taking his duty very seriously indeed. Arthgwr looked around and for the first time noticed the archers located in high perches throughout the courtyard. All of his men were under scrutiny and should any one of them make a false move, Arthgwr was sure they would die instantly.

Part of him was impressed and thankful that such protection was afforded his lovely wife. His ego, however, objected to the very idea that he and his men should be held at bay in such an insolent fashion. His visage was grim when he looked upon his dead friend's son.

"Elidir," he said in a low voice, "I am glad to see you are protecting my wife so well."

"Yes, my lord," the young man said simply, touching his forelock in salute. "I take no chances with my charge, no chances at all. I had to see for myself that it was indeed you, sire, and not some ruse to throw us of our guard." Already Arthgwr could sense that the archers were laying down their great long bows and moving from their firing positions.

"Yes, I see, very good Elidir. I am glad I selected you for the task. Your father would be proud of you, as I am."

There really was nothing else Arthgwr could say, he had chosen well, and Elidir had proven his mettle by taking absolutely no risks in executing his task of protecting Arthgwr's family. He motioned his men to dismount and did so himself, handing the reins of his horse to a young boy close by, eager to be of service to the now famous "Arthgwr."

"I do hope you have protected my son and daughter Gwyneth as well."

Arthgwr looked sharply at Elidir watching for any sign of emotion when he mentioned his daughter by name.

"Yes, sire, I have indeed protected your daughter well. She is accompanied by two guards where ever she goes."

Arthgwr looked carefully at Elidir and said, "Really? And who might these guards be?"

"One of them is...well...er...me..."

"And the other one?" asked Arthgwr.

"That would be me, father." It was Cynglas his son who spoke. Arthgwr had not seen him and would not have recognised him if he had, the boy had grown in his father's absence. The young boy removed the armoured helmet he had been wearing and shook out his hair. Cynglas his son was now standing tall and proud, sword at his waist and bow in his hand. From behind Cynglas came his daughter Gwyneth.

Gwenhwyfar was laughing as she ran with her two children into the arms of her husband. Arthgwr was standing, mouth open in surprise at how grown up his daughter appeared. Laughter filled the air. Gwenhwyfar, Cynglas and his sister, Gwyneth ran up to him and embraced him lovingly, laughing all the while. Arthgwr looked from one to the other and back again, a bewildered look still on his face. It was a happy scene and even Elidir's warriors were smiling and laughing.

Elidir watched from his mount, happy in his heart to witness such a loving moment. He wondered about his future father-in-law. He had known him all his life and he remembered well, the stories his own father Dyfyr had told of the man, Owain, who had become this "Arthgwr." To Elidir, he seemed to be a complicated man. Now, with this new meaning of his name, which seemed to have changed the man himself in many ways, Elidir was uncertain if he knew Arthgwr at all. It was then he noticed that Arthgwr the warrior, whose very name now implied bear like ferocity, the fierce northern warrior, this man of arms, was weeping. There could be no mistake. From Elidir's vantage point he could clearly see tears in Arthgwr's eyes as he hugged his daughter and his wife. Arthgwr hugged his son, much to the chagrin of the young boy. The boy was almost a man and wanted so desperately to be treated and respected as a warrior. Elidir watched as Arthgwr hugged his boy tight to his chest, tears flowing down his cheek. Elidir thought to himself what manner of man is this Arthgwr? Could he really be the fearsome warrior his new name suggested and of whom everyone spoke with reverence, even awe? Could he be the man whose bravery and ferocity had earned the respect, the undying loyalty of his own father?

As he pondered those questions, Elidir watched, as Arthgwr, his family and retinue were swept inside their hall. The singing and noisemaking was getting louder and more rambunctious as more villagers pressed in to see the returning Arthgwr. Elidir stuck close to the family especially to Gwyneth. He did manage to send word to Anwas Adeiniog informing him of what was going on in Caerwyn. Anwas had been a whirlwind of activity reorganising the structures and layout of the village. He took into account the increased population, predicted even more growth and compensated for increased needs of water, grain and grazing. His men and the conscripts of Britons that found their way to the edges of Caerwyn had built and reinforced huts, walls and fortifications all around the village. Elidir knew that Anwas would have no trouble working out what to do with the small army Arthgwr had left on the outskirts of their village.

Inside the hall that Anwas had redesigned, Arthgwr and Gwenhwyfar hugged and kissed. The children managed to escape the latest round of hugs and kisses. Cynglas was now equipped with the tools of the warrior and hovering around making sure his sister was looked after properly. Gwyneth was being coy and allowing her brother and Elidir to see to her needs. It was a strategic move intended to keep Elidir close by her side. The little girl inside her still felt close to her father. She looked at her father adoringly. Rhiannon had moved closer to Arthgwr and Gwenhwyfar. The Lady was very glad to see her safe. Arthgwr was fussed over and attended to by Rhiannon, Gwenhwyfar and Gwyneth.

Food and drink were brought and everyone began to feast. The singing and dancing continued and the din grew so loud Arthgwr could not hear what his wife was saying to him. It didn't matter though for the mere sight of her was enough to fill him with joy. They hugged, touched, and caressed each other as much as modesty would allow. Now and then Gwenhwyfar and Rhiannon would put their heads together, talk, and laugh raucously, leaving Arthgwr to wonder what was being said.

Arthgwr pulled Elidir aside and asked him to make provisions for his men. Elidir assured his liege that Anwas had already seen to the task. He told Arthgwr that Edern ap Nudd and his brother, along with a few men, had insisted on seeing to Arthgwr's safety. Arthgwr grinned and nodded his head. He was very glad Edern had not been present earlier when he had been confronted with Elidir's men. Edern took Arthgwr's safety very seriously. Arthgwr was sure Elidir had done the right thing and he was glad the young man was so attentive in his duty to safeguard Arthgwr's wife and children. He looked at Elidir and wondered what sort of son-in-law he would make. Then he remembered the young man's father and suddenly Arthgwr missed his old friend. Apart from his foster brother Cai, Dyfyr had been his most trusted confidant.

Of course, he told his good wife Gwenhwyfar what he was thinking and often he sought out her advice. There were times when a woman's point of view was important. But warriors related best to others who had faced death and that's when he confided in Dyfyr. Frankly, Gwenhwyfar's perspective was sometimes a mystery to Arthgwr, she was at times too mystical for his pragmatic mindset. The feeling of loss overwhelmed him again and Arthgwr realised how much he missed his talks with Dyfyr. The old man's candid and earthy advice was always appreciated, no matter how hard it was to hear. A good friend, such as Dyfyr, was a very rare commodity and Arthgwr recognised this fact.

More food had arrived and women were seeing to it everyone got something to eat. The hall was crowded with people singing, jostling each other for food or drink or to dance. Music flowed through the crowd, a harp, ram horn flute played a bawdy song, and everyone applauded the musicians. Arthgwr caught sight of Edern and his brother Gwyn and motioned for them to join him. He could see that Edern had already deployed his men and Arthgwr could feel a new blanket of security descend over him and his family. He made note to send Elidir to learn from Edern and his brother. He was sure Elidir would make an excellent addition to his inner circle of warriors. Elidir took a moment from his duties and walked over to Arthgwr. Gwyneth watched her father from a distance as Elidir leaned down to speak into Arthgwr's ear. She could not detect any sign or emotion from the look on her father's face. She was worried.

"So husband, you have had adventures." Gwenhwyfar nuzzled closer to Arthgwr and pulled the wolf skin pelt closer around them as they lay in each other's arms on their bed. Arthgwr was basking in the afterglow of his wife's love and enjoying the sweet scents of their room.

"Yes.... I suppose I have at that," he said with a smile. Arthgwr had told his wife about the ordeal of the sword Caladfwlch.

"It is not the adventures that trouble me, cariad, so much as the task itself. I feel as though my own will has been ripped from me and replaced with the will of others. Myrddin is a powerful Wise One and I cannot refuse him. He expects me to gather my men, all the tribes, Christian and Pagan alike to do his bidding. I am to garner the respect of all these warriors and bind them to a common cause. How can I accomplish such a thing? Myrddin provided the task of getting the sword Caladfwlch, which brought many of the men together. It won't be enough to bring all the Christian warriors to my side and that task he has left up to me! I feel I am being torn apart between the old ways and the new! I know what he is playing at! He is using my ambition of uniting the Cymry as one nation, to manipulate me into working some intangible glory. He wants me to provide an army loyal to me, though I am to fight for Ambrosius Aurelianus. Yes, he is Roman! And Myrddin admonished me not to use his Cymraeg name; he wants him identified as the Roman he is! Once I have won the battle, I am to turn the glory of it over to this Roman! All this I am to do so that the bards will forever sing of our valour, that our deeds should not be forgotten."

Gwenhwyfar looked at her husband with compassion. There was so much in this world that seemed beyond the ken of men. She had confidence that her husband would make sense of the matter and act appropriately.

"This Myrddin...did I tell you he is a Wise One? Oh, yes, and he knew all about us, that's certain. He even knew about Father Bedwini. Something else...don't laugh but when I look upon him, his countenance seems to change from old to young, to older and back again. His real power is in his story telling. It is as good as being present at the adventures he describes. But there is a dark side to him, cariad, a strong power lurks underneath the surface of that being."

"Husband, surely you know the Ancient Ways run deep in my family, there can be no surprise to you there! With that knowledge you must surely know in your heart that much abounds on this earth that is not so readily knowable to the minds of men."

"You sound exactly like him! And that Rhiannon! You are all so.... so...mystical!" Arthgwr was angry and he spat the words out. As soon as they left his mouth, he saw the pain they caused flicker across his wife's beautiful face.

"Cariad, forgive me, I did not mean to upset you. I just don't see the world as you do. Dealing with Myrddin and Rhiannon has taxed me greatly.... I don't know what to believe anymore! How am I to bridge the gap between Pagan and Christian when in my heart I believe in neither? The only thing I know for certain is that I don't know anything at all!"

Gwenhwyfar looked compassionately at her husband and stroked his long hair. She could see the stress in his face and it worried her, never had she seen him so drawn, so serious and concerned.

"You are wise Arthgwr, and wisdom, my husband, is knowing what you know; is not all there is to know. Trust your feelings, Arthgwr. They have served you well in the past. Because you are a man of courage and honour and goodness, whatever you decide to do will have those qualities even if the outcome is not a perfect one. You may not understand the

Old Ways or even the ways of the Christians, but are they so different? Are both beliefs not motivated by honouring the goodness in men even if their methods differ and even if the ideals should be different from the reality? Both Christians and the Pagans choose to act for the higher good and believers of both religions agree to accept the authority of something that is greater than themselves. Men thirst for strong leadership and they will seek it in the Old Ways and in Christianity too. They will even seek it in a good leader of men, someone like you, my love. You will find a way to convince both that your decisions and actions are right and just, Arthgwr, for you will not believe in a lie. Believing a lie is to deny a truth and that is something you are incapable of doing. You will be that strong and good leader of men if you will just follow your heart. Remember, the ancient Celtic virtues that were taught to us by the Druids, honour, loyalty, hospitality, justice, courage and honesty. You possess all of those virtues, my husband. So trust in yourself, my love, faith in yourself will serve your cause well."

Gwenhwyfar looked at her husband and noticed not for the first time since he had been back, how hard looking he had become. She saw he was more angular and his skin was stretched tight across his frame. Arthgwr had no fat on his body; he was all sinew and muscle. Not that he had ever been pudgy, but there had been a slight softness to his features. Chiefly around the eyes she thought. That was gone now. The many hard weeks away from the comforts of home and living out in the open, leading his men into battles and engaging in single combat all had taken a harsh toll on his body.

Of course, Gwenhwyfar knew the experience of getting the sword in the stone from the icy lake had nearly depleted his strength, if not physically then certainly emotionally and spiritually. It was his eyes that caused Gwenhwyfar the most concern. Her husband seemed to have lost that twinkle of innocence that had so warmed her heart.

In its place was a decidedly cold and calculating appearance that made anyone he looked at feel uncomfortable, as though they had been assessed and had been found wanting in some way or another. She new he was weary and in need of rest. She also knew that he would be gone from her in a few more days. Gwenhwyfar was certain war would break out by that time.

Rhiannon had told her as much during the festivities. According to her, Arthgwr and his army would need to march within three days time. They had far to go, though Rhiannon had been vague as to the where, Gwenhwyfar instinctively knew that it would be to wherever Myrddin was and that along the way a major battle would be fought. She stroked her man gently and noticed he was finally asleep. Wrapping her body around his, she pulled the wolf pelt over them and settled quietly, enjoying the warmth of her husband's body, lulled by the rhythm of his breathing.

Her mind would not allow sleep and Gwenhwyfar woke. She wondered if she would be strong enough to weather Arthgwr's absence. This next time her husband was to be away, she knew would be much longer in duration. Gwenhwyfar shivered and drew the wolf pelt tighter. She had found it very lonely without her man these past months. More than that, she had the peculiar feeling of being a stranger in her own birthplace. Gwenhwyfar could barely bring herself to ponder the thought, but it was dawning on her that the Old Ways and her place within that ancient religious culture, may be drawing to an end. She had not yet had time to speak to Rhiannon about her feelings. She had seen how the priest Father Bedwini was becoming very popular within the village. Only a week ago, displaced villagers from the lands her husband was seeking to bring under his banner, began arriving. Many of the newcomers were Christians. There were more Christians now, than followers of the Old Ways. Gwenhwyfar's feeling of loneliness was not all due to her missing her husband. She remembered the words she had just spoken to Arthgwr, they sounded hollow and insincere to her. Gwenhwyfar lay back and closed her eyes again, the sound of her husband's breathing carrying her back into slumber. It would be a disturbed sleep, she worried of what the future might bring.

Arthgwr was enjoying the walk. He and Anwas Adeiniog were inspecting the village and Anwas showing him all the innovations and changes he had made in the months that Arthgwr had been away. Edern's men were shadowing Arthgwr attending to his safety whilst to be discrete and stay out of his way. What Anwas had accomplished was impressive. There were now proper earth works protecting the village, new stone foundations for bigger buildings and some granaries were being erected. Even the dafarn had added a room, much to Geraint's delight. More room meant more revenue.

The village of Caerwyn was bustling with activity. Village farmers were close to being ready for the start of the year's planting. Metalworkers were kept busy pounding white hot metal into the farming implements that would soon be used to provide the villagers with food. Arthgwr stopped briefly to talk with a villager about his hounds. It had been a long time since Arthgwr had been hunting. He had loved following the ancient trails with his brace of huge hunting dogs on the scent of a boar or a deer. Those hounds had died years ago and Arthgwr had never replaced them nor had he hunted again. He patted the big dog, for a moment his face relaxed, and the old visage of his former self returned, as he spoke with the hound master. Anwas noticed the change.

Arthgwr seemed interested in a large white hound with red tipped ears. The sheer size of the beast was intimidating. The dog's muzzle reached above Arthgwr's waist. The hound had a wide chest and the width of its head meant strong jaws. As Arthgwr patted the dog, it nuzzled him with its massive head and the long curved tail wagged a steady beat. Anwas looked at the breeder who seemed to understand immediately. He brought out another hound, an older male and stood the two together for Arthgwr to see. They made an impressive brace and Arthgwr delighted in the sight of the handsome hounds. The dogs nuzzled him and jostled each other in competition for his attentions. Bending down, Arthgwr allowed the dogs to lick his face as he banged on their chest and roughly petted their flanks.

The breeder cleared his throat and after catching Anwas's eye, spoke casually.

"Sire, I would be well pleased, since these buggers have taken to you, if you would keep them for yourself."

Arthgwr quickly looked up to see if he had heard the hound master correctly.

"I cannot, I am to leave within a day or two. I could not find the time to train these beauties and that would be a shame." He sounded regretful.

The breeder looked up at Anwas and then at Arthgwr.

"Yes, sire, but they would look after you. They're quite clever, if I do say so myself, and once they take you in their affections, well no man alive will ever get close enough to do you harm, not with my pretties by your side!"

He motioned for Arthgwr to hold the hounds tightly by their collars. The hound master walked over to a couple of men who were mending a fence a short distance away. The breeder enticed them to try to strike Arthgwr, who stood dumbfounded, holding tightly to the brace of huge hounds. Anwas, understanding what the breeder was up to, made sure that Edern's men were aware of what was going on. He did not want any unnecessary bloodshed.

The men sauntered over to Arthgwr, though they nervously looked at Edern's men who were alert and watching the events like hawks watching their prey. One of the men had an old leather tunic wrapped around is arm as suggested by the hound master. At a signal from the breeder, the man lunged at Arthgwr with his leather wrapped hand. Without warning, both hounds dove for the man, mouths wide open; lips curled back, white teeth, the length of small knives, flashed in the daylight. The strength of the hounds nearly pulled Arthgwr off his feet. The beasts, barely held back by Arthgwr, barked and strained to get at the man who had now jumped back nearly into the arms of his friend. The poor worker was white with fear. The breeder was laughing heartily, happy to see his pretties showing off for the leader of Caerwyn.

Edern's men were clearly unnerved not knowing what to do, whether to watch the men or watch the two huge dogs fiercely barking at the end of the leather tether that Arthgwr could barely hold.

Fortunately, the villager had not been foolish enough to allow the dogs to bite into the rolled up leather tunic on his arm; it would have afforded him no protection from the hound's iron jaws.

Arthgwr was clearly impressed, but he would not take the brace of hounds. Instead, he finally accepted the older male hound. The breeder was well pleased as he had plans for the younger dog. He also knew that this act of kindness would not go without reward and he looked forward to a time when he might claim his due. Anwas and the hound master exchanged another look and it was understood commerce had taken place. Arthgwr was pleased.

"He is a fine looking animal is he not, Anwas?" Anwas nodded his approval, but was careful to stay out of reach of the beast's ominous jaws. Edern's men were cautious. On the one hand, they were glad

Arthgwr had more protection, but they were worried the beast may turn on their leader.

"I think I will name him "Cafall"!" cried Arthgwr, acting now more like a happy child than a leader of warriors. Anwas was glad to see Arthgwr laughing and enjoying himself. Arthgwr shook hands with the breeder and thanked him profusely for his fine gift, receiving assurances from the man that the huge dog would be perfectly safe around Arthgwr's family. He cautioned that only Arthgwr should feed the hound and by his own hand and that he always do so away from other people. Arthgwr listened to the hound master and thanked the man again. The breeder would not accept payment and insisted Arthgwr take his new dog unencumbered. Anwas and the breeder exchanged looks, both knew a favour was owed.

Chapter 25

Gwenhwyfar had told Arthgwr that their daughter would be found near the kitchens. She was learning to prepare mixtures from dried herbs collected last autumn. The kitchens were a communal enterprise for there were times such as feasts or when the men came back from patrol, when the women worked together for the good of all.

Once the wheat had been harvested from the fields and ground into flour, the village's women gathered to make bread. Though most made their own breads and kept the loaves at their own homes, the surplus was used to supplement the entire village. Trade would be brisk, when others ran out of their own supplies, and of course, there were always the celebrations and gatherings requiring bread. The surplus wheat was kept dry and stored in timber-lined storage bins cut into the dirt floor.

One of the older women was in charge of stoking the fires, general repair of the ovens and the storage of flour and herbs. She was a widow and was the only woman who held a permanent position in the kitchens. It allowed her a modest living. Gwyneth was in the kitchen talking to the old woman and helping her chop fragrant smelling herbs on a large wooden table. She moved about her work, not noticing her father was watching her from the doorway. As Gwyneth began powdering some birch for use as purification in childbirth, she glanced up and caught sight of her father.

Immediately, her bright blue eyes lit up and her smile shone its brilliance. She came running to her father, her long curly tresses of light brown hair flowing in her wake. Gwyneth suddenly caught sight of the huge hound at her father's side, but instead of being afraid, she squealed with joy and before Arthgwr could do anything, she flung her arms around the beast.

Time froze. Everyone stopped dead in their tracks, no heart beat, no lungs breathed air, and even the dust and particles of herbs caught in the sunlight, dared not fall to earth.

The huge beast began licking Gwyneth, succumbing to her pets and cooing. There was movement again and the men dared fill their lungs with air.

"Oh da," she managed to say as the huge beast leaned into her nearly knocking her down with its huge body. "He is beautiful...just beautiful. What is his name and where did you get him?"

It was difficult for Arthgwr to find his voice at first. "His name is Cafall," was all he could manage to say to his precious daughter.

In truth, he had not anticipated his daughter's reaction to the hound or he would not have introduced the dog unannounced. He had thought of a more subdued and controlled introduction between his daughter and his new dog. Now that it was all done, and thankfully without incident, he was amazed at how easily the animal had taken to his daughter.

Nevertheless, Arthgwr was relieved that his own inaction had not spelled tragedy. Looking sheepishly over his shoulder, he could tell that his guards had also been taken by surprise, though they did have their swords halfway out of their scabbards and were less than three paces from where his daughter knelt, petting the huge dog. They returned an equally sheepish look to their leader and backed off a pace or two. The big dog's head turned in their direction and an almost imperceptible low rumble was heard. It was a warning that a new bodyguard was on duty.

The old woman Gwyneth had been assisting, was standing mouth agape, in a state of shock. Gwyneth had to go over to her and give her a kindly shake of the arm to break the spell. Startled from her distress, the old woman became a whirlwind of action and words trying to impress Arthgwr with her knowledge of plants and herbs. Still, she never took her eyes from the huge hound. Cafall was content to sniff the air and lick his chops.

Finally, Arthgwr was able to get a word in and arrangements were made for a feast that evening. Gwyneth and her mother would be responsible for organising what to serve and who would be invited. Of course, Elidir would be present, Arthgwr could well see in his daughter's eye that she loved the young man. For a moment, Arthgwr had the feeling that something of importance was to transpire. It was an unsettling feeling and he dismissed it immediately, not understanding from where the thought had come. He tugged at the leather strap with which he held his huge dog and then together with Anwas and the guards left the women to their herbs.

"Arthgwr!" There was no mistaking the voice. It was Father Bedwini. Arthgwr saw him just as the priest called out. He had been talking to a woman who looked embarrassed to be seen by Arthgwr. The priest bent down and kissed her briefly before smacking her on the rump as she left hurriedly. Anwas could not help but snicker and even Arthgwr could not suppress a chuckle. The priest made his way over to them. He still limped from the wound he had suffered in the ambush in the Great Forest. Apart from his injury, the priest looked in fine fettle and the smile on his face implied he was glad to see Arthgwr.

"Well, you've taken your time in coming to see me!" The priest was winded after his short exertion and he paused to catch his breath. It was only then that he noticed the huge beast that was intently watching his every move.

"Great Lord!...but that is a huge dog!"

Cafall for his part strained at the leather strap trying to sniff at the priest. Father Bedwini approached cautiously. Walking around the hound with his hands outstretched, palms up, he quietly knelt down whilst averting his eyes from the beast's intense gaze. Arthgwr and Anwas clearly expected the dog to rip the priest apart. Arthgwr's arms strained at the leather strap and he was about to give the order to his befuddled guards to strike down the dog should it attack the priest. But Cafall, having managed to pull Arthgwr so that he could get closer, only licked the priest's face gently and nuzzled him as though to command that petting was now in order.

It was Arthgwr's turn to swear now. The priest looked up, giggled, and then admonished him for the mild language.

The men made their way to the dafarn where Geraint and his wife greeted them. The new addition was completed and Arthgwr and his retinue were shown to a relatively private area. Weapons were checked at the door according to the new law made after Math had killed Guto. Edern's men set up a perimeter just outside the room within the line of sight and hearing. They felt a bit easier knowing that Cafall was close to their leader. They had been impressed with the demonstration orchestrated by the hound master and thought the dog was capable of watching out for Arthgwr's safety.

Ale and food were ordered, Anwas took care of that with a stern look at the dafarn owner. Soon the men were enjoying boiled beef and barely ale, while listening to Arthgwr tell the priest of his exploits.

Father Bedwini, although he laughed and marvelled at the appropriate places in Arthgwr's story, nevertheless wore a scowl on his face. Arthgwr could not help but notice and was slightly offended by the look on the priest's face.

"What is the matter?" asked Arthgwr.

"Well, you seem to have won the hearts of the Pagans with all your fighting and retrieving ancient swords with magical powers! I don't see what you have done as being of value for Christendom or for those of your people who are good Christians! Are you going to have the whole country revert to Paganism and silly superstition and put in peril the souls of good Britons everywhere?"

There was a pause, more like the calm before a storm as Anwas and the men outside who had heard the priest, entered the room and carefully watched their leader. Even Cafall seemed to be waiting, looking up to his new master for direction.

The jaw muscles in Arthgwr's face twitched, his hand clenched and unclenched. There was no mistaking that he was visibly angered by the priest's impertinence. Still, he said nothing.

A battle played out inside Arthgwr's mind. He was a leader of men and though it was a role he had not wished for, he was nevertheless determined to do the best that he could to live up to expectations. Arthgwr knew as a leader he had to consider all sides of a problem. He also knew that a good leader needed to put his people before his own desires. That is, assuming he were a good leader, and not some despot tyrant working a battle for his own aggrandisement, political power, and wealth.

Arthgwr thought of Myrddin's words and understood that he needed to do more to have the Christians on his side as well as the Pagans. Even Myrddin recognised this fact and he was certainly not a Christian.

Arthgwr was unsure what he believed in other than his prowess in battle and the power of a good sword in his hand. He had never really given such things much thought one way or another. He was a pragmatist and saw that things happened in nature in accordance to the laws of nature. It was enough for him. Now was not a good time for him to weigh such philosophical questions; there was too much at stake. Pragmatically, though Arthgwr knew he needed all of his people to work this thing for the good of all Cymry. Myrddin was right about that.

He sighed. If there was some animosity or difference of opinions because of religious beliefs, then Arthgwr needed to address that. Whether he understood the differences or not was not important.

"Father Bedwini, what would you have me do?" he asked the priest. "How shall I do right by the Christians?"

Even the priest looked shocked at Arthgwr's reply. The good father had expected a huge row over this issue. He was ill prepared for Arthgwr's supplication and he was now speechless. Stammering, he mentioned the chapel again, pointing out that Arthgwr had never formalised any plans to begin building since last they spoke on the matter.

The anxious look on Anwas's face told Arthgwr that he too was a Christian. For some reason this came as quite a surprise to him. Arthgwr wondered just how many of his men were followers of the new religion. Certainly, the many tribesmen he had won to his side were followers of the Old Ways. Their reverence for the sword Caladfwlch attested to that. If there were as many Christians as there were followers of the Old Ways, then he had best do something to placate them and win them to his cause. Arthgwr was sure Myrddin would agree. If building a chapel for this priest and the villagers would do the trick, he had best build it, he reasoned. He remembered what the priest had said about the chapel being a memorial to his good friend Dyfyr.

For a moment Arthgwr was lost in his memory and longing for his old friend. Cafall stirred and broke his reverie. Arthgwr had come to a decision. He told the priest to go ahead with planning his chapel. Father

Bedwini was elated, but his look quickly changed to one of concern, and again Arthgwr had to ask him what the matter was.

"Yes, its very fine...but you see Arthgwr, while that would be good for all of Caerwyn, it doesn't do much for those who are not from the village. A symbol would be needed so that Christian brethren may rally round it and feel bound by your cause. The Pagans have your sword, it's only fair that Christians have something as well."

"And what do you suggest Father?" asked Arthgwr in a tight voice, his patience about run its course.

"A symbol, Arthgwr, something you may carry into battle that would inspire good Christian warriors...a crest depicting the symbol of our Lord...a red cross carried on your shield."

"A cross on my shield?" asked Arthgwr incredulously.

"Indeed! It would be a great symbol for all Christendom!" beamed the priest.

"No."

The priest looked crest fallen, but then all present could see his ire beginning to rise.

"But I will wear a cloth with the symbol of the Cross sewn to my right shoulder. Would that serve your purpose priest?"

Father Bedwini began to weep and to Arthgwr's embarrassment, the father knelt and kissed Arthgwr's hands in thanks. Even Anwas looked emotional and when Arthgwr told him he could start work on the building of the chapel immediately, he was sure that Anwas would cry like the priest. Arthgwr pulled himself together and suggested they conclude their business, so the men drank a toast to seal their agreement. Arthgwr made his way back home.

Gwenhwyfar did not seem to mind the hound Cafall, much to the surprise of Arthgwr. What amazed him was the fact the hound genuinely seemed to be fond of Gwenhwyfar. He watched as his wife ruffled the huge dog's ears and then laughed like a small girl when the beast washed her face with his huge tongue. Sitting in his chair drinking ale, Arthgwr could almost forget the stress of the last several weeks. Pleasantly distracted, he did not think about the coming problems and dangers that as yet lay unseen in his future.

After enjoying his ale and playing with his hound, Arthgwr got up and stretched. The issues of the day came flooding back into his mind, no longer was he able to keep them at bay. They were nagging thoughts that made him feel uneasy. The conversation with the priest had bothered him and he was at a loss to understand why he had agreed to wear a Christian cross on his shoulder. Surely it was a case of simple political expediency, he wasn't sure now. He was uneasy that so many of is own men were Christian and could not figure out why that bothered him so much. Watching his wife and realising he should tell her about his decision was something he did not look forward to doing. Arthgwr was sure that his decision about wearing the Christian symbol and the increase of all things Christian in the last few days would be upsetting to Gwenhwyfar. It certainly felt to him that the Old Ways were under assault from this new religion and he wondered how that would change the land.

"I spent some time today with our priest the good Father Bedwini," he said by way of introducing the subject he wanted to discuss with Gwenhwyfar.

"Why is that upsetting to you?" She asked uncannily, it seemed to Arthgwr.

"Has he made you promise him something that weighs on your mind?" As always his wife had succeeded in unsettling him. Arthgwr could do nothing but stare at his beautiful wife and wonder how she could always be so in tune with what was going through his mind.

"As a matter of fact he has," said Arthgwr and he told Gwenhwyfar about the chapel.

"I don't see why it's necessary at all," she said, "we have had Christians in our village for many years and there has been no need of such a thing. Christians and Pagans alike, have lived side by side without ever getting in each other's way. I am uncomfortable with the idea of having a building dedicated to their religion in the midst of what many of us think is sacred ground given to my family by the Goddess." She turned and looked fully at her husband.

"And you, Arthgwr, had no right to agree to such a thing without first consulting me."

Arthgwr was stunned.

"You forget yourself, Gwenhwyfar! I am leader of the people and I am charged with the responsibility of bringing them together Christian and Pagan alike, to work this thing for the good of all Cymry! Your own

Druid, Myrddin, has asked me to do this thing and now you question the way I decide to carry out this task?" Arthgwr was angry.

Gwenhwyfar did not show any emotion, she simply looked at her husband. "What else do you have to tell me?"

Arthgwr sat down heavily. It was exasperating talking to his wife when she seemed to always know ahead of time what was happening. There was nothing he could do but to tell her about the emblem of the Christians that was to be sewn on the shoulder of his tunic. Gwenhwyfar said nothing more; she simply petted the head of the big hound.

"You may well win the peace for the good of all Cymry," she said without taking her attention from the dog, "but I fear it will nevertheless be the end of our people. We were never fully conquered by the Romans and always managed to live according to the ways of our ancestors. In the face of invasion by Sacsonaidds and the onslaught of this new religion, I fear our old ways will disappear completely. If that is to be the case then of what use are your victories?"

"What are you saying? I am working this thing, fighting these battles, so that I may save our people! Even if we are unsuccessful in battle, the fight itself will serve as inspiration to our people and draw them together in spite of the Sacsonaidd."

Arthgwr had never before seen his wife so dejected and he was concerned. He moved to her and wrapped her in his arms.

"Did you not give me a speech about how the Old Ways and the ways of the new religion were not so different? Why now are you so worried about these things?"

Gwenhwyfar pulled back from her husband and looked up into his blue eyes.

"Our daughter wishes to marry Elidir...."

"That is great news indeed," cried Arthgwr, "though it is hardly news...did you in all your otherworldly wisdom, not predict this very thing happening? Did you not convince me it was a good thing when I thought she was too young to marry? So why now the long face?" He was trying to be jovial and he pulled his wife back into his arms, hugging her and kissing her head.

"They wish to marry in the chapel. Elidir is a Christian like his father and our daughter wants to convert. The priest knew of this before he talked to you. Having you build a Christian chapel, wear a

Christian votive on your arm and seeing your own daughter convert to the Christian faith, will be the end of our Caerwyn. The priest knows this and he has won the battle for Caerwyn, something Gronw with all his scheming and treachery could not do."

She felt her husband's body stiffen and looked up into his face. For a moment, she was afraid. The look on Arthgwr's face was like nothing she had seen before and instinctively she knew that the man she had known as her husband was surely dead.

Her loving husband had become this other man, this *Arthgwr Penteleu,* the Man Bear of the North, the War Leader.

The feast was well under way. Villagers were thronged together throughout the village, drinking and singing songs of valour. At the hut of Arthgwr and Gwenhwyfar, tables overflowed with foods prepared by the village women. Musicians played their instruments and everyone was dancing.

Math and Enid received a huge welcome as they walked through the crowd. Gwenhwyfar smiled warmly, she was always glad to see Enid. The change in the woman was dramatic. Enid had blossomed into a beautiful, thoughtful, and courageous woman during her time with Math. Her new man, Math, had earned himself new accolades, having been instrumental in staving off the attack by Gronw and the Essylwg. He looked more sombre and older since his friend Llew had been killed.

Suddenly, there was a commotion and Gwenhwyfar heard raucous laughing in the midst of the confusion. It was Rhys and his wife Katryn along with their children. Katryn was pregnant and the commotion was created when, as Rhys teased her about her size, she swatted him on the ear, causing him to fall over a table. It was all good-natured fun and Rhys was soon fetching food for his wife, hugging, and kissing her, despite her mock attempt at anger. Math and Rhys saw each other and embraced before downing a huge amount of cider.

Gwenhwyfar sat at a large table flanked by her son, her daughter and Elidir. Edern had men assigned to her and there were one or two maidens also attending Gwenhwyfar's needs. Rhiannon came by and sat beside her as Gwyneth moved to allow the two older women to talk in private. Gwyneth sensed her mother was upset with her.

Gwyneth knew her mother felt strongly about the Old Ways and she also knew it was expected of her to follow in the traditions of her mother's ancient family. All her life, Gwyneth had been schooled in the traditions. She was a strong willed young girl and she loved Elidir. When her love told her of his beliefs, Gwyneth could not help but become curious about the new religion. The resolute look on Elidir's face when he spoke of his religion had so endeared him to her that she was captivated and bound to him even more.

Instinctively, she knew Gwenhwyfar wanted this marriage as much as she did, so why was her mother so troubled? Surely, her mother could see that there really was not that much difference between the Old Ways and the new religion. Well, she thought to herself, not enough of a difference to cause a fight and her mother had to see how much she loved Elidir. Now that her father had agreed to Father Bedwini's suggestion about wearing the Christian Cross on his battle gear her mother could not possibly object to her conversion now, could she? The building of the chapel was also a sign from the Christian God that all was right. How could her mother fail to see that?

Arthgwr had been absent from the feast. So had Cai and some of his men. Many of the villagers had seen Arthgwr accompanied by his warriors, riding out of the village, Arthgwr's huge hound trotting along happily behind the horses. The village people assumed their leader was going hunting. They anticipated a supper of venison upon Arthgwr's return. Word now spread that the hunters were back in Caerwyn. Arthgwr made it known that he had something important to say to the people and had commanded a huge bonfire to be built in the middle of the village. He sent for his family and the rest of his men.

The firelight cast eerie shadows on the gathering. Musicians continued playing and the sound of the drums beating a lively rhythm cold be heard all over Caerwyn. A small platform had been erected close to the fire and Arthgwr could now be seen pacing up and down on it. He paused to call down a greeting to his family who were ushered to a spot secured for them. It took some time for word to travel through the village, but eventually it was obvious all the people in Caerwyn were present. It was a large crowd. A murmur of anticipation slowly rose above the sounds of the beating drums. Cai banged his sword on his shield and his men followed his lead, creating such a din that it drowned out the villager's and their drums.

"*Lechyd da....* good health..." Arthgwr called out, "I have something for you!" He motioned to his men who brought forward not one, but two, deer they had killed and already butchered. A cheer went up as the men placed the venison on spits over the fire. The drums began beating again. It was sometime before Arthgwr could be heard.

"You all know that I will soon be going off to war again. Though this pains me, for I would much sooner remain here at home, but I have a duty, which I cannot shirk. It has long been my belief that Cymry should unite as one and stop the bloodletting between the tribes. A common enemy from across the Eastern Sea now threatens us, reminding us of the Roman occupation of our lands. No tribe can stand against the Sacsonaidd hordes by themselves. Our only chance of survival is to unite and fight as one people. Perhaps when the Sacsonaidds see our united resolve, a peace can be negotiated, if not, there will certainly be war." Arthgwr paused and looked at the gathering of his villagers. Some were surprised to see the symbol of the new religion, a bright red cross, sewn onto the shoulder of his tunic.

"My duty then is to unite the tribes to save our people. I therefore proudly carry into battle the ancient and legendary sword, Caladfwlch!" Arthgwr raised the sword above his head for all to see. A loud cheer rose up from the men. Again, the beating of swords on shields mingled with beating drums caused a chaotic racket. Arthgwr motioned for behind him and a large banner unfurled.

At the sight of it, lit by the light of the fire, the crowd went silent. They were looking upon a symbol from Roman times.

It was *Y Ddraig Goch*...the red dragon...and symbol of the *Pendragon*, a title derived from the word *penteleu,* and given to a wartime leader. Arthgwr, leader of Caerwyn, was now standing before the people from Caerwyn, and those from the many villages throughout the region, as the Fierce Bear-Man and feared war time Leader of Leaders.... *Arthgwr Pendragon!*

Before the beating of the swords and drums could drown him out, Arthgwr pulled the priest to his side.

"Father Bedwini will give a blessing, but before he does let it be known that the good father has volunteered to follow us into battle and minister to the spiritual needs of our Christian warriors. The Ancient customs of the tribes and members of the new religion will ride together under the banner of the Pendragon with me as their leader carrying the symbol of the Cross on my right shoulder for all to see!"

There was no stopping the crowd now, as drums and swords beat wildly, and cheers rose up from the excited villagers. Amidst the tumult, Father Bedwini stood beside Arthgwr looking frail and strangely subdued. At the bidding from Arthgwr, the priest raised his arms and began the blessing.

The feast had ended and Gwyneth and her mother were alone in Gwenhwyfar's room.

"Why do we have to wait," cried Gwyneth, "it's not fair!" Gwenhwyfar put her arms around her daughter.

"Life is rarely fair, cariad. Life carries on with no regard for the wants and wishes of mere mortals. It is the way of things and a wise woman will soon accept it as so. We must strive to make our actions worthwhile and add our own meaning to our lives. Surely, there can be no better meaning, than to experience the wonderful mystery of life, of living here and now, to the fullest degree possible?"

"Is it not God's will, that Elidir and I should marry?" Gwyneth was distraught at realising her father would be gone for a long time and that her marriage would be postponed until his return.

In her youthful exuberance, she had thought Elidir and she would marry by week's end. It did no good to explain to her that the chapel was not even a foundation yet and the priest was accompanying her father on a long and dangerous journey. The poor child was confused.

Sleep did not come easy to Gwenhwyfar nor did morning bring wisdom. Gwenhwyfar was trying vainly to understand the last evening's events and their significance. Her husband had abruptly ridden off, after being told of their daughter's intentions, and the complicity of the priest. She had worried he would do something rash and she feared for the priest's life and if truth were told she worried for the very safety of Elidir as well.

The sudden appearance of Arthgwr and his men was both a shock and a relief to her. Gwenhwyfar had been awed, along with the rest of Caerwyn, at the unfurling of the *Y Ddraig Goch*. Later, when she was close to her husband, she noticed with surprise, the fresh tattoos on his arms. They were of ancient design, three blue interlacing swirls tattooed on his forearms. Still freshly scabbed, they were beautiful symbols from ancient times. Drawn in one continuous stroke, the design represented the movement of time, the triple spirals also served to represent the ancient idea of birth, death, and rebirth, and the elements of earth, water and sky.

Rhiannon had paid her a visit midmorning and Gwenhwyfar was glad for her company. Together they had ridden out of the village under escort of course to visit and pray at a *nemeton*, a sacred grove dear to the hearts of followers of the Old Ways. The two women instructed their escorting warriors to wait thirteen steps away from the sacred grove of oak trees. Rhiannon and Gwenhwyfar then prepared themselves with prayers and drew small blue designs on their foreheads and arms in blue dye. They entered the sacred grove and spent a few hours talking and trying to make sense of the world.

Gwenhwyfar broke a piece of bread and Rhiannon added a small portion of meat together with a bit of barley ale and offered it all as sacrifice to the Goddess. Both women prayed for the safe keeping of the men and a positive outcome for the war ahead.

"If I were younger," Rhiannon mused wistfully, "I would wear my husband's armour again into battle."

"Bare breasted?" teased Gwenhwyfar trying to lighten her friend's mood.

"Is there any other way to go to war?" a sly smile appeared on Rhiannon's face as she answered. Leaning over she hugged Gwenhwyfar, grateful for the comfort of such a dear friend. "The Sacsonaidd have landed up north and we are to leave tomorrow and intercept them."

Gwenhwyfar nodded, she had expected as much.

"We should leave now, but I want you and Arthgwr to spend another night together. I want you both to reconcile. He will be no good as a leader, if he is pining for the love of his wife while on campaign!"

Gwenhwyfar looked sadly at her friend.

"I cannot see the outcome of this thing." She said quietly. Rhiannon took her by the hands.

"Nor can I," she said, "and neither can Myrddin. We can only do what we can and hope for the best."

"I fear this will be the end of our traditions and our heritage."

Rhiannon put her arms around Gwenhwyfar and gave her a hug. She smoothed Gwenhwyfar's hair and kissed the Lady on the cheek.

"I am not so sure, cariad. Our ways withstood the Romans and so it may be the same here. Your husband is a good man and he may very well stop the Sacsonaidd in their tracks. I feel that there will be a peace, though how long it will last or how the thing will be worked, I cannot say. I do not think our traditions will entirely disappear."

Gwenhwyfar sighed and nodded weakly. She returned the kiss and held the hands of her friend.

"He has changed so, Rhiannon. I barely recognised him and you should have seen his face when I told him of our daughter's decision to convert." Gwenhwyfar's own face showed the strain that decision had caused her.

"Yes, he has changed. The ordeal of the sword took nearly all of his strength. It cannot be understated that the battles and the single combat he has endured have taken a terrible toll. I fear there will be greater trials ahead of him. Yes, he has changed and perhaps he is changing still. He will need to be as strong as steel to even attempt the task that lies before him. He is a good man, Gwenhwyfar, not a perfect man, but a man with a good heart, a strong sense of righteousness and endowed with a courage only told in our ancient stories. Myrddin and I will do all in our power to assist him and keep him safe."

Gwenhwyfar squeezed Rhiannon's arms in acknowledgement and gratitude. A tear glistened on her cheek as she thought of what lay before her husband and wondered what was to happen to her, her family, and their way of life in the face of the unknown future ahead. Gwenhwyfar sniffed and with her hand wiped the tears from her face.

"What happened to the priest," asked Rhiannon in an attempt to cheer her friend. "Did you see his face? It was bruised and his clothes were torn. Either your husband had at him, or some other husband caught him rutting with his wife." Rhiannon laughed bawdily.

"He was a sight wasn't he?" Gwenhwyfar said, wiping the last of her tears away. "I tell you I feared for his life when my husband left, I felt certain he would do the priest violence. If Edern were to learn how angry Arthgwr was with the Father, he would surely have killed him on the spot." Gwenhwyfar noticed a slight flush come across Rhiannon's face when she mentioned Edern's name. The flush deepened, giving her cheeks a warming glow.

"You don't think that priest is dallying with married women do you," Gwenhwyfar asked her friend, giggling slightly at the unseemly prospect.

"Have you seen him around the village? He is always lurking about the kitchens. I am sure he is trying his best to find himself some company, married or otherwise!" Rhiannon smiled mischievously and then broke out laughing.

Gwenhwyfar laughed along with her friend. The thought that Rhiannon was experiencing feelings of romance after so long a time alone, warmed her heart. She wondered how Rhiannon and Edern would get along together.

The two women said their final prayers and washed themselves with the clear mountain water they had brought with them. Bundling up they gracefully walked out of the sacred grove under the respectful eyes of their escorts.

Father Bedwini had feared for his life. When Arthgwr appeared before him, the look on the leader's face, caused a ripple of cold fear to shiver down the priest's spine. The priest was relieved to see Edern was not among the men accompanying Arthgwr.

Without a word, Arthgwr backhanded the priest, knocking him to the ground. Before Father Bedwini could say a word, the wind was driven from his lungs by a vicious kick in the stomach. The sound of a knife being drawn from its sheath caused the priest to gasp in terror. Suddenly, there were other voices and through the pain, the priest could make out two more men straining hard to hold onto an enraged Arthgwr. Father Bedwini was roughly pulled to his feet. He realised there were two men struggling to restrain Arthgwr. The priest expected to be martyred.

Several longhaired, tattooed warriors, all of whom were well armed, roughly dragged the priest to his feet and tied him over the rump of a horse. The warrior band rode away with their captive at breakneck speed. It seemed like hours before they finally came to a lurching halt. Father Bedwini was unceremoniously thrown to the hard ground and left there while the warriors tended to the sweat lathered horses. Fires were lit and the priest could smell the ale that the men were drinking. A dread passed over him again, and he mumbled another prayer.

Arthgwr soon stood over him this time he seemed more in control of himself. He did not strike the frightened priest.

"You devious sanctimonious bastard!" spat Arthgwr. "You have done nothing but turn our village upside down with your divisive doctrines!"

The priest swallowed hard but managed to answer arrogantly.

"You are a fool! If you cannot see that your silly superstitious religion has run its course, then you are surely doomed! Your days are numbered and your only chance now is to commit your everlasting soul to the service of the One True God!"

A sharp kick to the back stopped the priest's ranting. Looking up he saw a wild haired, tattooed warrior standing over him with a knife in his hand.

No further words were spoken. The warriors left the priest bound and sitting on the rough earth. Drums began beating an ancient rhythm and soon a haunting melody was played on a ram's flute accompanied by a carved wooden flute. The fires had been lit in a circle and the strange shadows caused by their light drifted eerily against the rising wood smoke.

A group of warriors brought two carcasses into the circle. The priest gasped again with fear until he recognised the bodies as those of deer. He watched as tattooed warriors bled and butchered the deer. The blood was saved in large basins, the entrails were thrown onto the ground; the livers of the forest animals were passed around to each man who ceremoniously took a bite from the animal's organ. A wide basin of ale was passed around in ancient tradition. Each man took a gulp and passed the basin to the next warrior. This happened frequently and the wild looking warriors drank deeply.

Father Bedwini could see Arthgwr sitting motionlessly on a pile of skins. Beside him sat a warrior with a bowl of blue dye and a small sharp knife in his hand. Another man had been drawing patterns on Arthgwr's arms with a small piece of burnt wood. The first man began pecking along the drawn lines with the small knife, dipping it frequently into the bowl of blue dye. It was a painstaking task and lasted for hours.

Every time the priest turned his head away or closed his eyes, a sharp kick reminded him to pay attention to the ritual he was so obviously intended to witness.

After a time, Arthgwr stood up shakily and raised his arms to show his tattoos to the gathering of warriors. They yelled and chanted his name and then unfurled a huge piece of cloth. Straining to see through the dark of night and the smoke of the fires, the priest managed to catch sight of a flash of red that was the *Y Ddraig Goch* of the Pendragon. The warrior's chanting was deafening.

Arthgwr came over to the priest and leaned down to him.

"I don't trust you, priest. Since I don't trust you, I am going to keep you close, at hand. I am bound by my promises to you, so I shall wear your cross on my shoulder, and I shall build the chapel. You won't see it completed, because you will be with me in battle. If you run from the fighting I will have my dog hunt you down and eat your liver!" The priest shut his eyes as Cafall, aware of his master's anger strained at the leash that kept him from reaching the priest.

The hounds' hot fetid breath washed over Father Bedwini spraying him with spittle. The dog's benevolence of the afternoon was replaced with a ferocious desire to protect his master. After a moment, the priest was unceremoniously bundled off and tied across a horse as the warrior band rode off toward the village gathering.

It was well after sunrise when Gwenhwyfar woke Arthgwr. Gwenhwyfar had let him sleep late. Rhiannon had pointed out Arthgwr would need to be clear headed and well rested to begin this journey. Gwenhwyfar knew this was this last she would see of her man until the battles were won. She bent down and washed his face with some warm scented water she had carried in a basin. Arthgwr opened his eyes and grinned at her sheepishly. For a moment, Gwenhwyfar thought she may break into tears, at seeing the innocent grin melt away the etched worry lines from her husband's face. He reached up for her and as he did so she saw more clearly the tattoos on his arms.

They were beautiful despite the newness and the scabs. They would heal in a week into very handsome tribal markings. She was proud of her warrior.

"I need to wake myself and prepare for this journey," he said as he stood up. He was naked and Gwenhwyfar could see the chiselled physique and the many scars of battle carved into his flesh. She began washing him with the warm water. He smiled appreciatively. The couple soon returned to their marriage bed, wrapped in each other's arms.

He had spoken to Elidir during the night. The boy was as stubborn as his father had been. In his innocence, he could not understand Arthgwr's point of view regarding his Christianity. Elidir had pointed out that his father Dyfyr had been a Christian as were a number of Arthgwr's trusted men. Arthgwr knew he was right and could only express his anger and frustration by telling the boy that those other men were not the ones marrying his daughter. Elidir was. There were the responsibilities Gwyneth had to her mother's ancient family traditions. Elidir simply stated that in times such as these when war was about to break out and the future was anything but certain such responsibilities really did not matter to two young people in love.

Arthgwr was left armed with only bland admonishments about how he as the young girl's father had come to learn of her and her young man's intentions. Elidir was chastened and sobered by that and he muttered about how the matter could have been handled more honourably. He refused to concede that Father Bedwini had been anything but steadfastly straight forward in the matter. This angered Arthgwr.

In his wrath, Arthgwr had grabbed young Elidir by the throat and threatened him with a horrible death should any harm come to his family. Elidir looked calmly into Arthgwr's eyes and without a trace of the fear, stated simply that there was nothing that Arthgwr could do to him that would match his torment should anything happen to those he loved so well.

Arthgwr was stunned into silence. In front of him, was the son of his dead best friend, the love of his daughter's heart. The boy was struggling to control his fear and yet he managed to speak truth in the face of the powerful, Arthgwr Pendragon.

Arthgwr pulled Elidir to him and hugged him. As he did so, his eyes caught movement and looking up he saw his own son Cynglas watching him. He beckoned the boy to him and hugged him as hard. There they stood three men hugging each other. The younger men, boys really, were uncomfortable and respectfully untangled themselves as they looked at each other with embarrassment. They were still held fast in Arthgwr's strong arms. Elidir noticed tears in his leader's eyes and wondered, not for the first time, just what kind of man it was who was about to lead warriors into battle.

Arthgwr addressed the villagers again and gave his last orders. Gwenhwyfar thought how magnificent he looked in his polished leather armour and new tunic. The Christian cross looked huge on his shoulder, and though he had been wearing it for only three days, it was still clean and bright. The sword Caladfwlch hung loosely by his side as the war banner of the Pendragon fluttered overhead. The villagers were all cheering and drums began beating out ancient beats.

"I ride with the Christian Cross on my shoulder. You have seen me wearing it now for three days. I have won the prize, the ancient sword Caladfwlch, which I risked my life to rescue from the icy lake and the stone that encased it. I am Cymry! And I wear the markings of the tribes on my arms with pride. The times we live in are perilous and we have seen much change in the last while. I am *Arthgwr Pendragon*, "The Bear-Man, Leader of all Leaders" and I have a vision of a united country living in peace! Will you help me work this thing? Will you ride with me into battle against the Sacsonaidd and help make our country safe?"

The roar of the crowd was deafening. They were banging shield, swords, and farm implements, blowing horns anything that could make a noise. Arthgwr stood with his arms raised high for all to see the tribal markings. He beckoned and was joined by Father Bedwini who began to give a blessing to the soldiers and offered a prayer to the villagers for safety, ending with the words, "*in nomne et patris et filii et spiritus sanctii amen....*"

The farewell to his family was heavy on his heart, but Arthgwr knew he had no choice in the matter. His daughter was crying. She was upset he was going, upset she couldn't marry sooner, but she would get over her disappointments, he thought. His son was stoic, which warmed his father's heart. Arthgwr did not kiss him this time, he was now a warrior. Ironically, the priest had garnered a new respect amongst the villagers for his decision to ride with the warriors. Arthgwr had left in place the same men as before including Anwas and Elidir.

Arthgwr hugged his daughter who stood wrapped in her mother's arms, watched over by Elidir and her brother Cynglas. The men began to ride out and Arthgwr turned one last time to gaze upon his family. Then with a shout he galloped off, his huge hound Cafall running along side his horse.

Chapter 26

Rhiannon rode at the head of the column beside Arthgwr. Cai was somewhere up ahead with a few men, scouting the way. It was a sizeable army Arthgwr was leading and he rode with grim determination. Rhiannon had not said anything in some time, for she was respecting Arthgwr's own silence. She knew he had a lot on his mind. Rhiannon was keenly aware the upcoming battle was important and would be a hard fight.

She had told Arthgwr it would be necessary to ride north, to the area near the old Roman legion city of Deva. Scotti tribesmen from the North, along with the Sacsonaidd from across the sea, were rampaging through the countryside. It was a serious situation and one that demanded immediate action. This was the reason she gave for the diversion. What perplexed Arthgwr was how Rhiannon received her information. He had questioned her on the matter, but Rhiannon only alluded to messengers and foreknowledge she had garnered from conversations with Myrddin. The Lady of the Lake deftly avoided answering any question directly.

"What I don't understand," Arthgwr began saying, "is why we need to make this fight at all, when Myrddin is waiting in the South to give me audience with Ambrosius Aurelianus."

Rhiannon paused before answering.

"Up to now, Arthgwr, you have fought other tribes of Cymry. You have won them over to your side and though you have certainly been victorious, the battles were not that difficult." That caused Arthgwr to snap around and look hard at her. Rhiannon continued nonplussed by his gathering anger.

"Myrddin, that is Ambrosius Aurelianus, wishes to see how you fare against the real enemy. To be sure, this marauding is getting out of hand and someone must put a stop to it. From there, we will travel south and meet up with Myrddin."

There was no mistaking the look in Arthgwr's eye or the low tone in his voice, he was angry.

"I notice," he said in that menacing low tone of his, "you say Myrddin's name when it would seem more appropriate for you to use the name of Ambrosius Aurelianus. Surely you don't mean to suggest that Myrddin knows Ambrosius's mind and decides for himself what is best."

It was Rhiannon's turn to become angry. Her flashing blue eyes showed clearly, she was angered by the Arthgwr's remarks.

"I don't pretend to know the workings of these men's minds, but I do caution you Arthgwr, not to underestimate Myrddin." Arthgwr thought Rhiannon was flustered by his question. They rode on in silence.

Rhiannon looked around and noticed Father Bedwini riding some distance back from them. His head was hung low and he looked dejected, his hood pulled over his head, bobbed up and down in time with his old black horse's gait.

"Your priest does not look too happy," Rhiannon finally said, trying to relieve the boredom of the travel. She looked up at Arthgwr as he turned to see what she had meant by her comment.

"Did you two have a disagreement or something?"

Arthgwr looked back at the priest without emotion. "No... not really. I just don't find the man to be trustworthy."

"Oh, did you catch him in a lie?" Rhiannon's interest was piqued now.

"It was more an omission than a lie. I am surprised you don't know all about it, as you seem to know everything else."

Rhiannon looked casually at Arthgwr and realised he was still vexed.

"What is troubling you Arthgwr? Is it your family?"

"Of course, it is my family! Don't play me for a fool Rhiannon! I know you and your Druid are using me to work something for his own agenda. I know it my vision of a united Cymry with which he manipulates my mind. What he manipulates Ambrosius Aurelianus with, is something I can only guess! I will wager it to be something to do with power and fortune!" Arthgwr's face was creased with furry and worry and frustration. She knew he was under much strain, still, Rhiannon found it hard to empathise with him. Her pride would not allow her to respond, despite her own anger and the nearly overwhelming urge to take this man down a notch. She rode on in silence.

It was noon the following day, their fourth day travelling when Arthgwr and his army came across the small village. Screams and yells greeted the warriors as they came into view. Villagers could be seen scrambling to gather loved ones and hide behind their pitiful earthen works, the only protection they had from the army of Arthgwr Pendragon.

Arthgwr raised his gloved hand, his army stopped. A delegation was formed, Gwyn ap Nudd and a few men along with the Father Bedwini were selected. The delegation would ride down, under the banner of the Leader of the Pendragon, and parley with the occupants of the village. Edern ap Nudd split the rest of their company in two, dividing them on either side of the hamlet. The cavalry was under Arthgwr's command and it was to remain in the tree line. Arthgwr wanted only to re-provision the warriors and to continue on to their destination before the night fell.

The precautions were unnecessary. The town proved to be friendly, once contacted by the envoys sent by Arthgwr and their safety assured. Father Bedwini was in his element. It turned out the entire town was Christian complete with a chapel and their own priest. Arrangements were fast made allowing the horses to be watered and fed in shifts. The warriors themselves were able to fill their leather skins with water and grab a small bit of bread as well. The village was well stocked, a testament to the hard work of its people.

Father Bedwini told the villagers they were in the presence of the illustrious Arthgwr. They immediately began clamouring for an audience. Arthgwr was hard pressed to ignore their wishes given the hospitality and generosity they had shown his men. He rode his big white horse into town accompanied by his hound Cafall. Edern of course saw to Arthgwr's personal safety and archers were posted and deployed ensuring Arthgwr's safety.

The village priest was called Dafydd. He was rotund and baby-faced but possessed a jovial manner. For all his girth Father Dafydd was energetic and moved surprisingly quickly. Upon seeing Arthgwr and the cross he still wore on his shoulder, the priest fell to his knees to give thanks to God that a Christian army had come to rid the countryside of the heathen foreigners and the filthy Scotti. Not even the sight of Arthgwr's tattoos dissuaded him from this belief. The Christian soldiers in the army mingled happily with the villagers and told tales of their exploits boosting the image of their leader as a pious Christian leader come to save the country from godless savages. Soon songs of joy broke out and even those soldiers who followed the Old Ways began singing. Their long hair and braids whirled around their heads as they danced. No one seemed to mind their blue tattoos of intricate designs and animal motifs. Some mead was passed around before Arthgwr was forced to pull Father Bedwini aside and insist they take their leave and move the army out.

The priest stood up on a table and with the help of Father Dafydd managed to bring the crowd to silence with the promise of a quick prayer and blessing. As the prayer ended, one of the villagers came forward and touched the cross on Arthgwr's shoulder. He quickly made the sign of the cross on himself and moved off with tears in his eyes. That started a trend. All the villagers quietly and reverently queued up to touch the cross on the right shoulder of the leader of the new Christian army.

Arthgwr could do nothing but stand and allow the villagers their moment. He worried about those of his men who followed the Old Ways. He needed them on his side just as much as he needed the Christians. He could ill-afford to alienate them now. He wondered how many of the villagers still worshipped the Goddess.

Standing up, he drew Caladfwlch from its scabbard and held the famous sword overhead in front of the banner of the Pendragon, the Y Ddraig Goch. Looking around he could see those he knew to be followers of the Old Ways were comforted by the sight of the legendary sword and sight of the Red Dragon, proudly flapping in the slight breeze.

To his amazement, he saw the Christians were kneeling and looking in awe upon his raised sword! Arthgwr held the sword, Caladfwlch by the blade, showing the famous gilded hilt shining brightly in the sun. He was unaware it appeared to the Christians, that he was holding on high, a golden cross!

Father Bedwini seemed in a much better frame of mind as the army resumed its journey. Rhiannon and Arthgwr were riding in silence again, each concerned with their own thoughts. It began to rain.

Cold, fat raindrops fell steadily from the dark sky, soaking their woollen cloaks making them heavy and cumbersome. The army rode on sombrely. As visibility began to worsen in the rain, Arthgwr decided it would be fruitless to carry on. He gave orders for the army to bivouac near a stand of trees. It took some time for the warriors to gather, set up makeshift shelters, light cooking fires, and establish a perimeter. Scouts were replaced and the fresh men, after gulping down some hot broth, struck out in the pouring rain to ensure the safety of the resting army. It was getting late. The weather had not cleared, as Arthgwr had anticipated. He decided to stay overnight at the camp, hoping the weather would be better by morning. Arthgwr chuckled to himself as he spied Father Bedwini fumbling about in the downpour, his mood the worse because of the weather.

It rained and rained. The warriors and camp followers spent a miserable night without sleep. In the morning, they were wet, cold, and hungry. The wood was sodden. There was no time to re-light the fires that had burnt out during the night. Arthgwr ordered the cavalry to tend to their horses, while everyone else broke camp. He instructed them all to be ready to move out within the hour. Any military leader worth his salt knew not to let warriors mope about when they were wet, cold and hungry. Arthgwr could do little about the camp girls and followers, but as long as his warriors were following orders, they would not have time to heed the complaints of the civilians.

Arthgwr's army was on the move just after dawn. They had not gone more than a few miles, when outriders came to report to Arthgwr, that the scouts had run into some townspeople wandering around. Arthgwr was visibly angered that there was no more information in the scant report. He decided to push on and not wait for the scouts; they could catch up with the main body on the move.

Arthgwr could not help but notice that Rhiannon had grown quiet and pensive at hearing the news. He wondered what she would have to say about the situation, but since they were not speaking to each other, he did not ask her. Rhiannon did not offer any opinion and rode in silence keeping her thoughts to herself. After another two hours of riding, Arthgwr was informed that scouts had been spotted in the tree line riding towards his army.

With the appearance of the first scout, Arthgwr knew something was wrong. The man looked ashen, his eyes were wide yet unfocused and he looked around him as though he had lost something. Rhiannon drew up beside Arthgwr. Upon seeing the scout, she motioned immediately to the warriors nearest to her, to get the man down from his mount. She dismounted and quickly went to the aid of the warrior scout. Arthgwr leapt from his horse and walked briskly over to where Rhiannon was now ministering to the scout. It took some time and patience, but Arthgwr learned from the man, something terrible had happened up ahead of the army. From the bits and pieces of information he and Rhiannon coaxed from the man, they learned a massacre had taken place in a camp not far away. The camp had been the temporary shelter to those poor souls fleeing the old Roman legion city of Deva. Whatever they were trying to flee had caught up with them.

Rhiannon poured mead for the warrior who sipped at it, though much of the golden liquor ran down his chin. Arthgwr had had enough. Whatever was out there, whatever had happened to cause such a shock to one of his strong warriors, would not be enough to make Arthgwr wait idly by for a similar fate to befall his army. Arthgwr the Fierce Bear Man of the North would bring the fight to his enemies!

He put the entire army on alert. The warriors were told to be ready to march. The horses were saddled, the cavalry was ready and the foot warriors all had their gear packed into the wagons. The civilians were frightened, but were kept busy seeing to the wagons and the oxen. A small band of outriders under Arthgwr's command, prepared to move out. Arthgwr wanted to see for himself what had happened.

They rode for a few hours stopping every now and then to make sure they were not followed or being spied upon. The directions Arthgwr received from his scout indicated they should hug the tree line for another few miles and then follow a small path through the trees and brush. It was not a thick forest. Certainly it was nowhere near the magnificence of the Great Forest of Caerwyn. Everything smelled fresh from the night rain and it was still cool. The sun was struggling valiantly to warm the earth. A light fog rose from the ground, eerily shrouding the underbrush at their feet. The sounds of the forest were muted, which added to the otherworldly feel of the place. An odd odour wafting its way through the air caused Arthgwr to wrinkle his nose. He sniffed. The odour was faint but grew stronger with the change in the gentle midmorning breeze. Arthgwr wrinkled his nose again.

"You might well turn your nose up," whispered Father Bedwini quietly, "it's the smell of burned flesh." He spurred his horse ahead as Rhiannon rode up to Arthgwr's side.

"The priest is right," she said quietly, the eeriness of the setting caused them all to lower their voices, "something terrible has happened here!" The horses snorted and stamped their feet nervously punctuating the words Rhiannon had spoken.

Pressing forward, the small band soon saw wisps of smoke intermingling with the ground mist. The warriors warily made their way through the trees, circling around to avoid a direct approach toward the unseen encampment. As they came upon the camp, Arthgwr heard Rhiannon gasp sharply.

Peering through the fog and smoke, Arthgwr managed to glimpse what had shocked Rhiannon. The priest was kneeling over what Arthgwr could only imagine was once a human being. Father Bedwini was rocking back and forth mumbling his religious incantations, tears streaming down his face and his breath coming in racked sobs. Rhiannon was frozen to the spot where she was standing. She looked around, but her mind did not comprehend the images. It took a moment for her to realise the body the priest was praying over was that of a badly butchered young child. A few of the warriors were hunched over vomiting on the burnt ground.

There were bodies everywhere, men, women and, as Rhiannon had already seen, children. The camp itself was simple, there were no defences, just a fence line made of some bushes and a few primitive huts fashioned from hides thrown over young saplings. There were scattered fire pits here and there with cooking utensils and pots, but no food to be seen anywhere. A few dead dogs and a pig was the only evidence of livestock. The people must have been destitute. Arthgwr wondered why people of such little worldly worth, should be so brutally butchered. It was sickening what had been done to them. Arthgwr watched, as Rhiannon helped the priest to his feet. The father took a few steps and then dropped to his knees again and began praying through sobs that racked his body. Rhiannon looked helplessly at Arthgwr.

A seething anger, built on revulsion and moral outrage, took hold of Arthgwr. Curtly, he ordered his warriors to assist Rhiannon with the priest. He ordered the army to move up and join him. While his men helped with the priest, Rhiannon walked up to Arthgwr.

"Do you still believe you are being played for a fool? Are you still convinced Myrddin is manipulating you simply to do his own bidding?" Her voice was trembling and her face was ashen like the face of the scout's earlier. She searched Arthgwr's impassive face, seeking some form of acknowledgement from him. Arthgwr simply stood and stared at the chopped and burned bodies that were strewn all around them. He could see the limbs of young children and women hideously sticking up amongst the blackened wood of the burned out camp. Rhiannon saw tears welling in Arthgwr's eyes. She realized the ghastly scene had made an impact on him.

It was dusk. Arthgwr's army had marched hard the rest of the day and the scouts had done a good job tracking the butchers of the massacred peasants. Arthgwr listened as Edern and his brother Gwyn outlined the details of the enemy's encampment.

"They have a few guards posted, but no fence, earthworks or anything else that would hinder our cavalry. Most of their men are lying about, eating or sleeping, though there are several men drinking and playing some sort of game. There are more of them, than there are of us. But I saw no horses. I don't think it is a main force."

"They outnumber us, but you don't think they are the main force, why do you think that?" Arthgwr was already preparing a battle plan. He needed to know where the rest of the enemy's force was hiding.

"They are too lightly armed from what we can see," answered Gwyn. "They've no cavalry and only a few oxen for a small number of wagons. I think they are just a large roving band. No doubt they were sent to run the peasants down and I suppose, they are to scavenge and pillage anything they come across. That suggests no strong leadership, no sense of purpose other than to loot and kill."

"They are bold and confident," added one of Edern's men, "they depend upon their numbers and the fact the countryside has already been raped by the larger force that is closer to the town."

"We can't go around them and attack the town, that would leave this bunch at our rear," Arthgwr grimaced.

"We will have to attack them. Get the cavalry ready and divide them into two groups, you lead one and I will lead the other. In the mean time, divide the archers into two groups as well. If the archers can get close to the camp will they be able to pick their targets?"

"A bit of a chance there," said Ifans one of the best archers with the army. Edern looked at his brother and then said to Arthgwr, "There might be enough firelight to see something. The silly bastards do have a few big fires going and there's a fine moon tonight." He grinned devilishly.

"It won't be enough," Arthgwr said finally. "There won't be enough light. Instead, we will use the cover of the night to set our positions and attack at first light in the morning. This is how we will do this thing."

Arthgwr outlined his plan. At his signal, archers were to fire into the camp. The two groups of archers were to be set at angles from each other, so that when the arrows were loosed, they would crisscross creating a field of death. Those of the enemy that survived the initial attack would panic and run. The lay of the land afforded them only one sure way out. The two groups of cavalry would ride down from opposite sides of the battlefield. They would easily override horseless warriors and would continue riding, angled in the formation of a spear. At the point the two groups of cavalry converged, they would wheel their horses and form one line. Then at a slower pace the unified cavalry would ride back into the escaping prey. The rest of Arthgwr's warriors were on foot behind the cavalry. They would advance with swords and spears, cutting down the fleeing enemy. The cavalry and foot warriors would stop their advance at a signal from Arthgwr. This would allow the archers, still in two groups and angled to prevent their arrows from striking their own men, to loose their arrows in another deadly volley. The cavalry would then ride through at a gallop with the foot warriors right behind them cutting down the enemy like farmers cutting their summer wheat.

The plan was a bold one that required timing and precision. A lot rested on the stamina of the men. The warriors would need to work throughout the night getting their bearings and maintaining their positions in the dark.

It was a hard night. Arthgwr's men worked tirelessly and were ready at first light. Rhiannon insisted on riding with the cavalry. She had worn the sword she had brought, unbeknownst to Arthgwr, and she would not be dissuaded from her plan. The sight of Rhiannon, dressed for battle, bearing the sword that many supposed belonged to her dead husband inspired the warriors. Edern felt a strong stir of emotion as Arthgwr assigned Rhiannon to his command. He was deeply moved by her courage and loyalty.

Rhiannon had secreted the sword in her baggage along with a small leather bag. Just before first light, she took the leather bag, walked to the closest tree, and knelt down. It was not an oak. It was nothing grander than a sparse twig of a tree, but she deemed it would suit her purpose given the circumstance. Spreading a small piece of clean cloth upon the ground Rhiannon placed her bag down and opened it.

Inside was powdered woad, a type of plant similar to a cabbage. As she mixed it with some water the concoction turned a beautiful colour of blue. Taking a bronze mirror from her baggage, she applied the woad to her skin with a small brush, creating artistic swirls and designs on her cheeks, arms and throat. A few warriors tentatively approached the Lady of the Lake. They had been watching her from the shadows. Without turning to acknowledge their presence, Rhiannon lifted the cup of prepared woad, offered it to the Goddess and then passed it to the closest warrior, along with the pouch containing more of the powdered plant. The grateful warrior bowed deeply and applied woad on his face and arms, drawing an intricate design before passing it to the next man. The mist of the morning swirled around them, shrouding the band of warriors in its embrace. Those Christian warriors, who witnessed the ancient ritual, crossed themselves and murmured to each other. They were uncomfortable and frightened by the Pagan rituals. And yet, they were awed by the glimpse into the ancient past they had witnessed.

The battle plan was executed perfectly and the battle itself did not last long. The whispered swish of arrows flying through the early morning mist was followed seconds later by the agonising screams of impaled men. Pandemonium broke out in the camp, as men lay gurgling and thrashing on the cold ground. Screams and shouts rang out and another volley of death streaked out of the mist skewering the sleepy enemy. The men began to run wildly away from the direction of the arrows. Blindly they ran, through the morning mist slipping on the dew-laden ground scrambling in vain to escape death. Thunder added to the cacophony, only it was not thunder, but the thundering thrashing of horses' hooves. Bodies were thrown about randomly and trampled under the weight of the heavy beasts, as Arthgwr's warriors leaned from their saddles and hacked at the running men.

A war goddess was seen, painted blue and wielding a huge sword with which she cut down man after man. She was flanked by demons that were also painted with frightening blue designs. They too, cut down fleeing men, each swing of their swords, and each stab of their spears, caused a blossoming of crimson red blood.

The sound of the thunder faded for a moment, but the frightened men kept running. Suddenly, the thunder started up again, only this time it was louder and closer.

The cavalry had wheeled about and was now charging directly at the enemy. Steel rang on steel and the sound mixed with the screams of butchered men as the cavalry cut through the enemy's ranks. In the blink of an eye, the fighting was over.

An eerie silence ensued for a few seconds, before the swishing noise was heard from both sides. Arrows rained down on the survivors, piercing their flesh adding to their fear and panic. Another strange noise, a loud metallic clanging was heard. It was the clanging of swords on shields. The horses had pulled back, the arrows had stopped streaking through the early morning sky and now Arthgwr's warriors were on foot, marching deliberately toward the enemy their swords hacking and slashing at anything in their way. There was no mercy shown to any of the enemy that was still alive.

The sun rose on a grisly scene of death and devastation. The field was strewn with mangled bodies and hacked off limbs and severed heads. The hooves of the horses and the feet of the warriors made mud, a red mud, as they churned the earth and the blood of the enemy. There were no wounded enemy warriors. They were all dead, every one of them. Those who had survived the initial attacks were brutally stabbed to death. They lay hacked and broken in the red mud, screaming in fear, pain and desperation for mercy. No mercy, no quarter had been shown them. The enemy was dead. The only sound coming from them now was the buzzing of flies.

The day was grey and dismal; the sun was too ashamed to shine its light on the ghoulish sight.

Arthgwr's men were exhausted. There were a score of injured men crying out and groaning in pain. The camp women tended to the grievous wounds of their butchered warriors. He gathered his warriors up to him and walked amongst them assessing their strength. He offered words of praise and encouragement. He offered comfort to those of his men who found it difficult taking part in such bloodletting. Arthgwr reminded his warriors, they had not killed innocents. He told them they had killed and defeated an evil force, a force bent on destroying their race. Many of the men found solace in his words, some gathered round him touching his sleeve, bloodstained and ragged, the Christian Cross still visible. They held a prayer service lead by Father Bedwini who was assisted by one of the officers. Rhiannon and the men who had ridden with her, watched impassively and then turned away.

Slowly the army shook off the morning's deadly business. Grimly the warriors marched toward Deva. At midday, they stopped and made camp in a suitable spot near a fresh brook and a grove of small trees a mile from the town. Riders had already been sent out to bring in the rest of the camp. After a day of much needed rest, Arthgwr marched his warriors into the once Roman held town of Deva. News spread of the army's arrival and the people came out to see the great war leader from the North, the Pendragon, Arthgwr.

The main army made camp outside the city walls. Arthgwr took a small band of warriors with him into the city proper. They rode past the walls that surrounded the city and stopped near the amphitheatre. The Roman walls and buildings were decaying. The city government, such that it was, showed Arthgwr their gratitude. The city leaders provided food and drink for the army. The information they were able to supply was less helpful.

It was true that Sacsonaidd warriors had raided the town, but they had not taken possession of it. Instead, they scoured the outlying areas and harried settlements. Most of the Sacsonaidd army had headed south some days ago, leaving only the smaller force to carry out raids of terror. The townspeople had suffered much at the hands of the invaders. The town had been picked clean. There was not a family still living inside the walls that had not lost a loved one to injury or death at the hands of the invaders. Many had fled the town in search of safe haven. It was Arthgwr's sad duty to tell the townspeople about the massacre of their people.

Arthgwr returned to his own camp outside the walled city. He called Cai, his trusted foster brother, Edern ap Nudd and his brother Gwyn, Rhiannon and the rest of his advisors to his tent for a meeting. It surprised him to see Rhiannon still wearing the ancient blue designs on her body, though she clearly had washed the blood and grime away. The painted men who accompanied her also caused Arthgwr to take note and glancing up he thought he saw a smile of pride on Edern's face as he caught sight of Rhiannon. Whatever Edern's thoughts were, Arthgwr was glad to see he had not forgotten his duty. Two of Edern's men had immediately flanked Arthgwr and a few archers had taken up positions just opposite Rhiannon and her men. Rhiannon noticed this and she smiled to her self.

Arthgwr started the meeting by simply stating that the army was soon to be moving south. Rhiannon nodded to herself, but the gesture was not wasted on Arthgwr.

"Clearly it is to the South where our duty lies. We have rid this area of invaders. Their main force has retreated south. We have pledged ourselves to the service of Ambrosius Aurelianus and it is to him we must travel now." Here he glanced meaningfully at Rhiannon and she held his gaze unblinkingly.

"The battle we have won was bloody," heads bowed as Arthgwr continued. "Remember that we fight for those who cannot defend themselves against oppression and tyranny. We fight for the right to be one nation united! Let us not allow our heads to swell too much with pride! For we now know that there can be no doubt that we are fighting for our very survival! Let us also not forget that we do not slaughter innocents. We do not rape, murder, pillage, and torture! We kill those who would do these things to our people! To all things right and proper!"

Arthgwr stood and watched as the men shouted the slogan and chanted his name.

"All things right and proper! Arthgwr! Arthgwr!"

He felt hollow inside, devoid of real feeling or passion. The killings had affected him.

Chapter 27

Arthgwr and his army had been travelling south for two days. Rhiannon had not spoken a word to Arthgwr in all that time, though she often rode beside him. Her men, with their wild hair and blue tattoos, were accepted and appreciated by Arthgwr. And even Edern was impressed and intrigued by them, though he kept a close eye on them. To Edern, anything that did not conform or stood out as different was viewed as a possible threat to his leader.

The silence between Rhiannon and himself was beginning to wear on Arthgwr. He missed their conversations and wondered what had caused the rift between them.

Arthgwr turned, as Rhiannon rode up beside him, slowing her horse to keep pace with him. A few moments passed before Arthgwr could contain his resentment no longer.

"What is it that bothers you so?" he asked Rhiannon.

"Have I done something to cause you to treat me as a pariah? Was it the killing? You know I am here working this thing on your behest and your relationship with the Druid, Myrddin!"

Rhiannon pulled her mount up short.

"You men!" she spat. "You are all the same! Everything revolves around you! Nothing under the celestial lights of the Goddess happens, that doesn't pertain to or affect you personally! Are you incapable of thinking without your ego clouding your thoughts?"

She wheeled her horse around prepared to ride further back in the column away from Arthgwr. He was too quick for her and snatched the reins of her mount so that her horse could only turn back towards him.

"What is it then? What is bothering you? Tell me now and allow me the opportunity to think without my ego clouding my thoughts this time."

Rhiannon looked at the man she knew and tears welled in her eyes. She saw him wave off Edern's men as they closed the distance to his side. Obediently, they backed off, but kept in sight of their leader. Rhiannon's tears began to fall. Arthgwr moved in closer to her and stretched out his hand stroking her hair. She knew him to be a kind man and she respected him as a honourable warrior and strong leader of men.

In truth, Arthgwr's actions did not cause her mood. Rhiannon looked up into his face and managed a weak smile as part apology for her earlier tirade. Arthgwr accepted the gesture wordlessly and indicated they ride together for a few hours more before making an early camp to rest the horses. The killings had affected Rhiannon too.

Arthgwr rode around the camp to speak to his men and offer encouragement. The mood had been sombre since the battle and the long hours on horseback during the last two gruelling days, had not improved their mood. Warriors were sharpening their swords, mending the leather strapping on shields and scabbards and engaging in the general activities of Men of War. Arthgwr noticed that many of the men had gathered around the priest Father Bedwini. The Christian holy man was offering up prayers and salvation for their troubled souls.

"The battle has taken a toll on the men," Rhiannon spoke softly to Arthgwr as he came up beside him.

"Yes...it was a gruesome thing we did. I wonder have we become the very monsters we fear?"

"You ask that question after only one battle?" Rhiannon's mood was turning again. Arthgwr wondered how much she knew of Myrddin's plan and how much she was holding back from him. Whatever she knew he doubted she would reveal the details to him. The thought angered him.

"I would remind you that I have been in many battles, nearly eleven by all accounts and I have fought nearly as much in single combat to the death. I am no fledgling boy!" Arthgwr's anger was palpable.

"I know you have killed, Arthgwr, but have you done so with such reckless abandon and what is more important, have you the stomach to do so again?"

Arthgwr was silent for a moment. He walked over to where his guards were holding Cafall, his huge hound. Taking the beast from the warrior, he stroked the hound's massive head and allowed it to walk freely beside him as he returned to Rhiannon.

"You saw what they did to those peasants. What would cause a man to behave so? I have killed, as you well know. I have killed many men, perhaps nine hundred in the battles I have fought with my army and in single combat. I find no glory in killing. It is a messy business, but it sometimes is necessary to secure the peace. Indeed, that is the only reason I can see for waging war. But butchering children, ravaging women and burning and mutilating their bodies unto their death, this I cannot understand."

Arthgwr stroked the hound's head. He remained contemplative for a few more moments.

"The answer to your question," he said quietly, "is yes. I do have the stomach to mercilessly kill barbarians when they would do such unspeakable things to our people. Only I would wish to know why a man would behave in such a way!"

Rhiannon looked at him not without compassion.

"The most frightening thing about men we consider as monsters because of their gruesome deeds is not the atrocities they commit, or their reasons for committing them. The most fearful thing about such men is that they turn out to be nothing more than ordinary men. Just men. And it is a fact that any man has the potential to be a monster, that is what you fear."

"That barbarian we held captive," Arthgwr's voice was full of unspoken emotion, "what did you mean when you spoke those things about him?"

"What I meant was what I saw in him," she answered quickly. "He was a man who sought honour in circumstances that allowed little room for such noble thoughts. He tried his best, but lost his way and then regretted that fact."

Arthgwr was intrigued and it was obvious to Rhiannon that these questions had been burning in him for some time.

"Do you think he survived the Forest?"

"Yes, I do think he survived and found his way out." Rhiannon brushed her hair from her face, her blue painted designs visible in the firelight.

"Do you think he ever regained his honour?" Arthgwr's eyes burned intently and she could see the vulnerability behind the fortress of strength in the man.

It was Rhiannon's turn to be reflective and she paused a great while before she answered him.

"Yes, Arthgwr I think he regained his honour, but not in the way you might think. He has found himself. And I believe he has found a way to build something good that he can leave behind so that people will remember him and speak his name with kindness. That is immortality. That is true honour."

"But how is it you know such things? Gwenhwyfar is the same way. She intuitively knows things and yet when I ask how it is she knows she changes the subject."

Rhiannon smiled at the pensive look that crossed the great war leader's face. This is Arthgwr Pendragon, she thought to herself, the Great Bear Man from the North, the war leader of a thousand warriors. And yet he looked like a troubled youth trying vainly to make sense of the world around him.

"Arthgwr," she said kindly, "we need to ride hard tomorrow and so we must rest as best we can tonight. You will want to have all your wits about you when you meet Ambrosius Aurelianus." And before Arthgwr could answer, she was gone.

Arthgwr's army marched onward. They trudged morosely along the path, heads cast down spirits low. Suddenly, in the middle of the path there appeared before them a very old man. Upon seeing him, Rhiannon immediately heeled her horse into a gallop leaving Arthgwr to wonder how a man, especially an old man could have slipped past the advance guard. It only dawned on Arthgwr who the mysterious old man was, when he saw Rhiannon dismount and run to him.

"Good afternoon, Arthgwr, how are you?" cried Myrddin, throwing back the hood of his robe revealing his long flowing white hair. His blue eyes sparkled and twinkled in the afternoon sunlight and Arthgwr could not help feeling that the old Druid was privy to some celestial joke.

"Good afternoon, very well thanks and you?" answered Arthgwr rather flatly, which caused Myrddin's eyes to sparkle even more. Arthgwr watched the old man as Gwyn, Edern and his men brought their horses to a stop and gathered protectively around their leader. Somehow Arthgwr did not feel any more protected and for a moment he had the fleeting thought that he and his men were right where Myrddin wanted them to be.

"I know what you are thinking!" cried Myrddin his voice crackling with humour. Arthgwr was stunned, wondering if the druid would be offended by the thoughts he was holding in his mind.

"Yes...I know.... you are thinking, why am I on this road when the way to Dinas Emrys lies a half day's journey over the west?" Myrddin laughed and crackled with the energy of a man twenty years younger that what he appeared. "It is because we are going to Caer Melyn!"

"And what pray tell awaits us there that is so important?" demanded Gwyn.

"Ambrosius Aurelianus is there with his retinue and he is awaiting the Great Arthgwr. Caer Melyn is one of his fortresses he visits from time to time." Myrddin was nearly giggling as he spoke which of course infuriated Gwyn and his brother.

Arthgwr looked up sharply and caught the eye of Rhiannon who simply nodded to him. She knew this was the plan all along, he thought to himself. What other surprises lay in store for him he wondered.

Cachu.... thought Arthgwr. Well there was no sense in delaying and though he abhorred the idea of doing just as Myrddin wanted him to do, there was nothing to suggest he had a choice in the matter.

Arthgwr motioned his men to stand down. He motioned to Myrddin indicating he would share his mount with him. But the wily Druid simply laughed and clapped his hands. A dozen tribesmen on horseback appeared like magic. They drew up alongside Myrddin and one of them handed the old man the reins to a mount. The men were all tattooed. Their long hair was pulled tightly back from their faces. It seemed all of the men were blond haired. On closer inspection it could be seen that they had dyed their hair with lime wash making their hair stiff and giving it a whitish-blonde appearance.

They carried with them spear, swords and oval shields. Edern was fuming, it was his sworn duty to protect Arthgwr and yet he had not foreseen the arrival of these fierce looking tribesmen. He was about to remedy that situation as his sword hand began moving toward his weapon. A hand clamped firmly on his shoulder and through his embarrassment, Edern saw it was the hand of Arthgwr himself.

"We will ride for a time, but we will rest early this night for we will have a hard ride tomorrow," said the Druid.

"Yes...I have heard as much," said Arthgwr and he looked at Rhiannon. Arthgwr wheeled his horse around beside Myrddin. The two men led Arthgwr's stunned personal guards and the rest of the army along the road that lead to Caer Melyn.

They rode only a few more hours covering just a few miles. With so many stragglers the army could not move fast. But that did not seem to bother the Druid, Myrddin. He seemed well pleased with the chosen resting place. Arthgwr was less amused. Since the appearance of Myrddin, his mood had changed for the worse. Edern and his brother were on edge because of that fact. There was no mistaking the feeling of tension swirling around Arthgwr.

The tattooed tribesmen were welcomed amongst the army's Pagans and they followed Rhiannon, her own tattooed men-at-arms and Myrddin, wherever they went. While the camp was being set up for the evening, many of the non-Christians of Arthgwr's army were seen talking and drinking with Myrddin's men. The Christian warriors were becoming agitated. They felt uncomfortable with so many of the Followers of the Old Ways around them. Father Bedwini seemed nonplussed, but he did offer a special mass for the men and the camp followers who were Christian. That seemed to ease the anxiety and bruised feelings.

"Is there something troubling you, Arthgwr? Do you wish to speak with me?"

Arthgwr was startled by the voice. He had been caring for his great hound with his mind on his problems and he had not heard Myrddin come to him. He quickly looked around for Edern. He could just see his man standing by a brazier a few yards away intently watching the two men.

"It is all right my son, I have convinced your man I mean you no harm and I am after all unarmed." Myrddin's mild tone and honeyed voice soothed. Cafall got up and walked over to the old Druid. He lay down exposing his belly and neck to the priest of the Old Ways.

"You have me at a disadvantage, Old One and I am not a man who likes to be in that situation. I especially don't like it given the fact I am leading an army into another battle, a battle that seems more and more to be of your making!" Arthgwr's tone was low and even, but it was clear that he was vexed.

"Shall we step into your tent and make ourselves comfortable?" asked Myrddin. The two men stepped through the opening of the leather tent Gwyn's men had set up. It was a large affair with two braziers and capable of housing at least a dozen men. Hides had been thrown on the ground and there was even some hot broth in a small cauldron sitting on a low wooden table. Bread and ale were laid out next to the cauldron with some leather cups. The men made for the table and tore chunks of bread dipping them into the broth. Edern stepped close wanting to ensure Arthgwr's safety but was halted by the soothing tones of Myrddin's voice as he asked that he and Arthgwr be allowed to talk in privacy.

"Well?" asked Myrddin as he and Arthgwr sat across from each other eating bread and broth and drinking ale. "What have you to say to me?"

In the light of the dim braziers inside the tent, Myrddin did not seem to be as old as he normally appeared to Arthgwr. He moved about spryly and sitting in a field camp did not seem to bother his old bones. Arthgwr was feeling decidedly less like a leader of an army and more like a wayward youth ready to be chastised by his grandfather.

"I see you managed to get your sword," Myrddin pointed to Caladfwlch and smiled.

"Yes...and it was no easy task I must say..."

"No. Arthgwr, in truth, it was not and I congratulate you." The Druid's voice was even and his face sombre, Arthgwr felt that the Old One was sincere.

Arthgwr looked into the Druid's eyes. Arthgwr the Druid's ice blue eyes were looking deep into his soul. So stunning was the effect that for a moment Arthgwr was at a loss for words.

"Don't look so surprised my son! I understand the dangers you have faced, the battles and the single combat you have endured thus far. Believe me when I tell you I understand all too well."

"But what is it all in aid of, why am I doing all of this, what do you gain from scripting such a thing?" The anguish that appeared on Arthgwr's face was evidence of how much he had been affected by the commitment he had made to Myrddin.

"I know it is hard for you to understand, Arthgwr. I know that you sense there is something more going on here than what we have already discussed. But it is as I told you in my hut. You are needed to unite the tribes and lead an army into a great battle that will secure a peace. The glory of the victory, however, is to be given to Ambrosius Aurelianus, the leader of Briton and the king to all the Romano-Britons in the South."

"It is a lot to ask of one man," Arthgwr said quietly.

For a moment, Myrddin was at a loss for words. He stammered and muttered before he stopped and simply looked at Arthgwr. Then he began laughing uproariously.

Arthgwr looked incredulous at the Druid's reaction to the serious situation he had outlined to the Wise One. Myrddin was on the verge of choking he was laughing so hard. Arthgwr went to his side to offer assistance, which caused the old man to laugh even more. He declined the hand offered him and when Arthgwr placed his hands on the Druid's arm, Myrddin took hold of Arthgwr's arm to move him away. The strength of the grip nearly caused Arthgwr to cry out in pain. He was shocked.

Immediately, he sat down on a bundle of hides, a look of total disbelief frozen on his face. Myrddin stopped laughing and looked long at the younger man. He stood up and poured ale, giving the cup to Arthgwr.

"You are right, Arthgwr, it is an enormous thing I ask of you. I have done my best to explain things to you by giving you the history of our people." Myrddin moved around a bit as though he were stretching tight muscles. He looked fitter to Arthgwr, than the old man who had appeared in the middle of the road early this afternoon. With another ale in hand, Myrddin found some hides and made himself comfortable.

Turning his ice blue eyes to Arthgwr, he allowed his intense gaze to soften before he began to speak.

"I suppose there is more you should know. What I am about to say to you is dangerous. Men have already been killed for speaking of this subject. So I tell you these things with caution and suggest you speak to no one of what we will talk of here tonight."

Arthgwr looked blankly at the Druid and then nodded his head slightly to indicate he understood. Myrddin stretched and began his tale.

"Back through the mists of time, back hundreds of generations, before our people populated these isles, there was a tribe of our ancestors who were very good with horses. Now, our people have always been good with horses, your own cavalry is proof of that point. But these wild tribesmen were as one with their mounts. They lived in a land in the middle of the continent, on the slopes of the Caucus Mountains. The ancient Greeks were the first to talk of these wild horsemen ancestors of ours. They described them as white skinned, tall and lean with brilliant blue eyes and thick long black hair, just like their horses manes. But to the Greeks, the most impressive thing about these tribesmen was their horsemanship.

"They began telling stories of how man and horse seemed to move together as one being. Many wild stories were told around campfires, about beings that were part man and part horse. The Greeks came to know one of these horsemen as a great teacher possessing infinite wisdom. They called him *Chiron* and he was widely revered throughout the width and breadth of the land. He taught many people in the ways of wisdom and healing. One student stood above the others and his name was Aesculapius. It was he, who began building institutions that would teach the people the wisdom of Chiron by drawing the words the great teacher had spoken. Chiron was worshipped then, as the Christians worship their Jesus now.

"And there have been other men, other legends, telling of heroes who were born of virgins seeded by the gods. There was the crucifixion of Antigonus, who was proclaimed the King of the Jews. Prometheus and Hercules both were forced to wear a mock crown of thorns. Prometheus was crucified and Hercules was born of a virgin. Attis was born of a virgin, hanged on a tree, later escaped into a cave and died, but later rose, and was called Father God. Mithra was also born on the winter solstice, his father was the Sun God and some say he had no mother, only Petra Genetrix, a female Rock, seeded by heavenly lightning. Shepherds and Magi witnessed this event; they brought gifts to the cave where the babe was born. Mithra raised the dead, healed the sick, made the blind see, cured cripples, and cast out demons. As Peter, son of the Petra, he carried the Keys to the Kingdom. Upon his death, he ascended to heaven at the spring equinox after celebrating a last supper with twelve disciples representing the signs of the zodiac. The meal included buns marked with a cross. Mithra was buried in a rock tomb, but was withdrawn and lived again. His followers were men only, his priests were celibate and he decreed the virtuous would be saved, but the sinners would be cast into hell."

Myrddin took a long gulp of his ale. He became agitated when he noticed the look of puzzlement on Arthgwr's face,.

"Don't you see, Arthgwr? Events that were already celebrated by Old Religions were born again in a new movement that was familiar and popular with the people. The celebration of the birth of the Sun God, which occurred on the Winter Solstice, became the celebration of the Son of God, also celebrated during the winter solstice, now called Christ Mass.

"The spring equinox, always celebrated as the re-birth of life, became the resurrection of the Son of God. Just as the sun was born and died only to renew itself in the spring, so did the Jesus in the new stories. Many of the Old Gods of the tribes were given new life as Saints in the stories and teachings of the new religion. The new religion spread to Rome and after a time it was strong enough to challenge Mithra and the other ancient gods for supremacy. In an effort to unite Rome and solidify his power, the Emperor Constantine decreed the new religion, Christianity, the official religion of the Empire. Constantine converted to the new religion, although he waited till scant minutes before his death to do so. And he did not go out of his way to destroy Pagan beliefs. Nevertheless, he usurped lands and temples to be used by this new religion. He also moved the political power of Rome to a new city, a Greek city called Byzantium, which he renamed Constantinople in honour of himself.

"The new church grew in power in both Rome and Constantinople. It was not long that their differences and petty jealousies brought about a schism. The bishops of Rome saw their powers rise, for now they had riches, men-at-arms, and political influence. The Emperor Julian wanted to stop the power of the bishops and re-instated Pagan beliefs as the official religion of the Empire. He was unsuccessful and was replaced. The new emperor turned the Empire back to the Christian religion."

Arthgwr looked like a drowning man. He could not understand the intrigue and had never before heard of these other religions. To Arthgwr, Christianity was the new religion and he was still trying to cope with it and the likes of Father Bedwini. This story of Myrddin's served only to confuse and befuddle him.

"But Myrddin what does all of this have to do with me? Why does this have any bearing on what you will have me do?" Arthgwr's pain was visible on his face. It was the anguish he had been feeling these past months finally coming to the surface of his conscience.

Cafall heard the strain in his master's voice and although the great hound had been lying next to Myrddin, he raised himself up and walked over to Arthgwr. With a nudge of his massive muzzle the beast licked the face of his master with his tongue and settled close to him.

Myrddin looked at the young man before him and though his heart was sympathetic, his voice was harsh when he told Arthgwr to be patient and listen closely. He saw the rebuke register with Arthgwr and felt a pang of guilt.

"Don't you see?" Myrddin said as he continued with his narrative, "their religion is being shaped! Constantine had been working the thing for his own power and the unity of the Roman Empire. The bishops Irenaus, Augustine, Germanicus, they were all just as power hungry! But Hilary of Poirier and Pelagius, two prominent bishops of Celtic blood, had written down their thoughts of the trinity and free will, both of which have been tenets of our ancestor's philosophy since time began. The thought was born that there may be room for an accommodation between the old and the new. The Grand Council has agreed to entertain the idea that we could assimilate into the new religion as long as there is some common ground."

Arthgwr's head began to ache with the intricate plotting and the amount of information Myrddin was imparting to him. He was overwhelmed and out of his depth. He drank some ale and then stood up abruptly, startling his hound.

"I still do not see where all of this is leading!" he shouted.

"What do I care about one religion over another? To me it is the same as men going to the dafarn, one may prefer cider, one may prefer ale and yet another may prefer mead, but they all will drink!"

Edern could hold himself back no longer. Hearing Arthgwr's shout, he and two men rushed into the tent. Cafall leapt to his feet and stood his ground between Arthgwr and the men, a low menacing growl filled their ears like rolling thunder. Arthgwr stood stock-still and slowly raised his hands to calm his man Edern. Myrddin stayed motionless where he was sitting, both his hands in plain sight.

Arthgwr calmed Edern down and ensured him all was well, the assurance came in the form of a direct order to stand down. But peeking out of the tent Arthgwr saw the reason for Edern's zeal. There were several white-haired and tattooed tribesmen forty feet from the tent, lounging by one of the braziers. The occasional glint from the weapons caught Arthgwr's eye and instinctively Arthgwr knew Edern's brother Gwyn would be hidden somewhere with a few archers at the ready. The night was dark, though and no sign of this was evident to him.

Arthgwr assuaged Edern and the men withdrew from the tent leaving Arthgwr and his great hound alone once more with the old Druid. The Wise One continued with his lesson.

"Rome nearly destroyed us all. Even now, there are Britons who are more Roman that Briton. Ambrosius is such a man. But at least he has in his heart a love for the land, for the people, and a grudging respect for their traditions. He is a Christian, but a Pelagian. Our Order has sent envoys throughout the continent and they have determined that there was more than one story of Christianity and the Celtic Church here in our islands embraces some of that diversity. After all, our own Wisdom has influenced their thinking from ages ago. Therefore, it is possible we can compromise, even assimilate to some degree. Failure to do so will supplant the Imperial Order of Rome with the Holy Roman Empire. The bishops of Rome will not tolerate any diversity regarding their faith. It was Germanicus, who had Pelagius killed and his work denounced as heresy. As provincial barbarians in the eyes of the Holy Roman Empire, we will be similarly destroyed, utterly and for all time. The tyrannical bishops of Rome will destroy even the memory of our people, their traditions and their heritage. It will be as though we never walked the face of the earth! Before the Grand Council will allow further involvement, I have to show that we can unite, as a people.

"Gwrtheyrn's tactic of inviting the Sacsonaidd to our shores has proved disastrous. But it may be the catalyst we need to unite the tribes under one banner and have followers of both the old and the new religions come together as one. I have to prove such a unity is possible before the Grand Council will approve. And that is why I need you Arthgwr."

Arthgwr was struggling to understand the intricacies of what Myrddin was trying to explain to him. He sensed the importance of the issues at hand but could not quite grasp their implications. He looked at Myrddin and then after a pause he asked the question.

"Is the Grand Council unanimous in entertaining the idea of an alliance with the Christians?"

"No, they are not and in fact, only about half of the Council is ready to endorse such a plan, whether or not my demonstration is successful. Many Druids have left the Grand Council and have taken to the countryside. But, if I am successful there is a slim chance that the Council, or whatever may be left of them, will decide to ally themselves with the remaining Pelagians. The Council's wisdom and teachings will quietly influence what the Celtic Church is disseminating. The Christians already have sent an envoy they have named Patrick from Cymru to Ireweddon. Our only chance of survival is to make this alliance, hide our Wisdom within Christian teachings and so prevent the Roman Bishops from gaining too much power. Otherwise they will erase all memory of us from the minds of the people and it will be as I said before, like we never walked the earth as free men!"

Myrddin took a long draught of ale, slurped the last bit, and belched loudly. It was not a seemly end to such a serious discussion.

"Can we succeed?" asked Arthgwr in an almost plaintive voice.

"Probably not," replied Myrddin, "but by trying, we may at least be remembered. Tales of our courage will abound and inspire future generations. Our teachings may be able to survive in some form and at least the influence of our thoughts might be felt. Only by doing nothing at all, will total failure be realised! You see Arthgwr this is not just a battle that if lost we can still recover from and mount another attack. This is a fight for our very survival as a race! If we lose we might as well never have existed!"

Myrddin looked up and the intensity of his gaze bore into Arthgwr, the strength of him nearly overwhelming the war leader.

"Surely it is a task worthy of the effort?" the Druid said in a low voice.

"You did not mention any of this when you first recruited me to your cause." Arthgwr said in an even tone. He was beginning to feel as if he had been duped, played like a game piece in the strategy of this Druid.

"Arthgwr what I told you was true. We need a man of integrity and talent to lead a united force in the field against the Sacsonaidd. I would wish Ambrosius were up to the task, he certainly wants more than anything to defeat these invaders and set the Islands free. But he is old and proud and he cannot do this thing of his own accord. There is no one else we can trust. Already tribal chieftains are circling like crows to carrion. It has been your valiant effort and success, Arthgwr that has stopped these chieftains. The ones in the North at least are united and under your banner of the Penteleu...the Pendragon. With you lies our hope for success, not in the victory of the battle perhaps but in the future where our essence, the memory of our existence may live forever. Without you as I have already said, we will be as if we never existed! The Roman Bishops will see to that and they will run roughshod over our land."

Arthgwr still looked confused.

"What of the Sacsonaidd? Do they not figure into this plan of yours? You don't seem to hold much confidence for our winning the peace against them, so why then would the Pagan Sacsonaidd allow Roman Bishops to hold power in the victory the Sacsonaidd would win with their own blood?"

"You underestimate the power of the Bishops, my son. As we speak, many Sacsonaidd on the main land have already converted to the Roman religion. It will not be long before they are converted totally to Roman doctrine. If we do not fight the Sacsonaidd, our race will be weakened. The onslaught from the Roman Bishops, the newly converted Sacsonaidd and our own Christian peoples will unite with such a force they will completely do away with our Wisdom, our traditions and our way of life. By fighting them you will demonstrate to the Council that Cymry can unite. This will spur the Council to supporting the Celtic Orthodox Church and our ways will be saved, though hidden as they may be, within the Christian doctrines. But whether we win the battle or not, our essence, our wisdom, our memory, at least will survive!"

Arthgwr's head hurt straining to understand the subtleties of the Druid's arguments. He glanced at the old Wise One and was shocked to see that he again looked much younger and healthier then he had first appeared. Arthgwr shook his head to clear his vision and looked once more at Myrddin. He saw an old man smiling kindly at him as though he were a child receiving his grandfather's blessing. Arthgwr nodded to Myrddin and with Cafall at his side, he left the tent.

The morning mist slowly melted away under the heat of the dawn's rising sun. The air was fresh and the day promised to be warm and pleasant. Arthgwr had decided to remain camped one extra day in order to rest the army and the horses and to make much needed repairs to the war equipment.

He needed more time to digest what the Wise One had told him the night before; his head still throbbed with the subtle arguments and intricate plotting of Myrddin's labyrinthine mind. He had informed Cai of his decision upon leaving the Druid's presence. Cai was all for resting the men and horses. Edern on the other hand, was wary and suspicious as was his nature. Rhiannon personally vouched for Myrddin's tribesmen, which eased Edern's concerns. She herself had not washed off her blue woad designs, in fact, more of her men were seen with permanent tattoos, and they were mingling with the men who had accompanied Myrddin.

Father Bedwini was upset with all of this and he had held an early morning mass to bolster the spirits of the Christian followers in the army. This did seem to settle most of the Christian warriors, giving them peace of mind and a calmer demeanour, which certainly helped the general atmosphere of the camp.

Arthgwr needed to clear his head. He had decided to go hunting in a nearby forest. It was not a huge forest by any means merely some dense woods in comparison at least to the Great forest of Caerwyn. It was Arthgwr's thinking that the diversion of a good hunt might ease his mind. A hunt might better prepare him for the arduous task he had agreed to undertake at the behest of the mysterious Myrddin.

Edern was entirely unhappy at the prospect and had argued vehemently with Arthgwr to the point of insubordination. The woods, he claimed, were unknown and with the exception of a cursory patrol, they had not been explored by any of Arthgwr's warriors or Edern's men. But Arthgwr had been adamant and with uncharacteristic stubbornness, he had ordered Edern to either accompany him on the hunt or stand down. Edern had no choice. He and two of his men had opted to ride with Arthgwr and his hound, Cafall on the hunt. Edern was furious and anxious.

By midday, the men were miles from the main army much to the added concern of Edern. Arthgwr was riding ahead searching for sign of Cafall. The huge hound with the red tipped ears had run off on the trail of a wild boar they had flushed from the underbrush. Arthgwr was not sure, but he thought he had managed to wound the animal with a hastily shot arrow. Therein lay the concern for there was nothing more dangerous in all of Cymru than a wounded boar. Arthgwr feared for his hound. He had ridden hard following as best he could the trail of his big dog. In so doing, Arthgwr had out ridden Edern and his escort and he now found himself on the edge of a great meadow.

Dismounting from his horse, Arthgwr cautiously skirted the edge of the tree line, keeping himself out of sight from anything or anyone that may be lurking within the grasses of the meadow. As he moved stealthily along, Arthgwr noticed movement on the far side near some bushes. Closing the distance, Arthgwr saw his hound. The warrior/hunter of his nature prevented him from calling out his dog's name. Instead, he continued to move cautiously, undetected by the big dog. Arthgwr noticed Cafall seemed to be staring into the bushes, as though guarding something. Stopping for a better look, Arthgwr was pleased to see that it was his boar. He began to move more swiftly to the scene of his kill. Suddenly, he stopped dead in his tracks. The boar, his boar, sported not only his arrow as he had expected, but a second arrow that sprouted from behind the head of the great beast. Cafall was growling at something and it wasn't the already dead wild boar. There was some one nearby.

"Are you in the habit of stealing another man's kill?" demanded Arthgwr, his bow up and ready to shoot.

"It is not stealing, if the other man poaches on your land!" came the haughty reply.

"Move to where I can see you!" commanded Arthgwr.

"Bugger off! You drop that bow and call off your hound and then we will see what I will or will not do!" The voice was young, but it held a confidence and a bravado that impressed Arthgwr.

"I am Arthgwr, known to some as *Arthgwr Pendragon* and my army is but a short distance away. That boar is my kill and I have been tracking him for some time. You can see my arrow in him."

"Yes...and a piss poor shot it was too. I don't expect that the mighty *Arthgwr Pendragon*, whoever the bloody hell he might be, would loose such a poor shot as that. If he did he should be embarrassed to own up to it! I am Gwyndaf and you are in my shire!"

"Well Gwyndaf, I don't know what a "shire" is, but if you mean your lands hereabouts then I do apologise. My army, as I said, is just a mile or so away and we are passing by with no intent to harm. May I see who it is I am speaking to?"

"Lower your bow," came the almost amused voice of what sounded certainly to be a younger man, "and call off your hound and I will show myself."

"That I will do, Gwyndaf-Who-Has-Never-Missed-A-Shot!" declared Arthgwr, now amused by this give and take. He called Cafall to his side.

From the cover of the bushes and trees strode a tall angular looking youth, with long black hair and blue eyes.

"*Shw mae*," said Arthgwr politely.

"*Shw mae*," replied the young Gwyndaf.

"So my young hunter, what is a "shire?" asked Arthgwr innocently.

"That is what we call our lands, it is a local dialect."

"I have never heard that word before. From whence does it come?"

Gwyndaf looked Arthgwr up and down and he noticed the big dog at his side. The dog seemed even larger up close and the youth was impressed.

"We have hounds here, but that is the finest I have seen! You should be proud!"

"Well, young Gwyndaf...thank you very much...I am proud of him, he has become my best companion since I got him from a breeder some weeks ago."

Cafall suddenly became alert. The big dog's red tipped ears stood erect on his massive head, which tilted back and forth, as his big nose twitched the air. A low growl rumbled from deep within the mighty beast. The big brute could sense the presence of someone else close by. Arthgwr's hand slipped unnoticed to his sword, just as another man came into view.

"What's all this then?" asked Bryn of his son. He knew much already having waited in the brush, his huge bow trained on Arthgwr's chest, ready to kill the man, should any harm come to his son.

"It's alright *da*, this is *Arthgwr Pendragon*, the Great Hunter, see, his arrow is in our boar."

"Yes...what your son says is true, though my name is Arthgwr, it is sort of a title given me by my followers." Arthgwr smiled.

"Followers?" asked Bryn amused by his son's sense of humour in the situation.

"Certainly, a man such as myself would have to have followers, you know, someone who can shoot straight lest I starve to death here amidst the bounty of your fine forest."

The father and son laughed at Arthgwr's self-deprecating humour. Tensions were eased and weapons lowered.

"You are from the North then?" asked Bryn eyeing the big hound whose eyes had never left Bryn since he had made his presence known.

"Yes...I am. I am travelling with my army a bit south from here..."

"Oh, it's an army you have then?" Bryn looked into Arthgwr's eyes trying to determine if there was a danger lurking beneath the banter.

Arthgwr immediately sensed the change of mood and understood Bryn's concern. He sat down in the grass, his arm carelessly draped over the hound's huge neck. Bryn and Gwyndaf sat as well, Bryn pulled out a leather drinking skin and offered a drink to Arthgwr who accepted graciously. Taking a deep drink Arthgwr was mildly surprised to discover the drink was mead.

"You know I have heard a tale some weeks ago now about a royal love that threatened war in the North. Have you heard such a story?" Bryn took a gulp of mead and passed the skin to his son.

"There are many reasons for war in the North, I am sorry to say. I have done my best to unite the Cymry and I have had some success if I may say so..."

Bryn and Gwyndaf laughed at what they thought was brash braggadocio.

"The story you are thinking of if I am correct and I must say I am surprised you have even heard of it," Arthgwr had noticed their confusion and he was amused by their ignorance of who he was, "concerns the marriage of Gwynllyw of Gwynllwg to Princess Gwladys, daughter of the King Brychan."

Arthgwr's eyes sparkled as he saw the surprise register with his two "hosts."

The boy and his father sat there on the meadow grass mouths open and a comical look of shock on their faces. Just then, Cafall stirred as Edern came into view, sword in hand, ready to cut down any threat to his leader. Arthgwr raised his hand to assure Edern he was in fact no danger. Standing, he thanked the still astounded huntsman and his son for the drink. Bryn came to his senses.

"Here," he said with a look to his son, "don't forget your kill."

"Master Hunter Bryn, thank you and perhaps you may persuade your village, your "shire", to come and join Arthgwr and his army in fighting the Sacsonaidd."

Arthgwr misunderstood the expression of the two men as overwhelming awe in the presence of a great battle leader.

He was amused.

Chapter 28

Arthgwr did not want to rush into a journey south to Caer Melyn. Instead, he wanted to take a company of men back into the forest he had been hunting and where he had met the two men who spoke of their "shire."

Edern had been angry and frustrated that he had not kept ahead of Arthgwr on the hunt. He felt he had been incompetent and his frustration with himself was palpable. Arthgwr tried to jolly him up, but when that failed, Arthgwr, the wise leader, simply and clearly apologised to his warrior for making his job that much harder by wandering away. Arthgwr pledged to never wander off without adequate protection. This eventually assuaged the ruffled ego of his man Edern.

Still Arthgwr had wanted to reconnoitre the area in detail and see for himself what sort of encampment lay in the deep woods.

What struck Arthgwr as odd was Myrddin's insistence that the army push on to Caer Melyn. He did not seem at all interested in finding the shire. The two men had argued the merits of exploring the hunter's forest. In the end, Myrddin had convinced Arthgwr of the importance of getting to Caer Melyn to seek audience with Ambrosius Aurelianus. The missed opportunity of exploring the forest still nagged at Arthgwr more than he thought it. And he was still baffled over the entangled discussions of the previous night with the Druid.

The yellow earth found in the pits in the nearby hills surrounding Caer Melyn, gave the place its name. The pale yellow compound made it look like the gods had spilled honey on the ground. Myrddin explained to Arthgwr that the yellow earth was called *"sylffur"* in Cymraeg, but the Romans called it "*sulpur.*" He said the ancient Greeks had used it to keep insects from their crops and that some even used the yellow powder like stuff in the dyeing of cloth. Arthgwr wrinkled his nose and Myrddin laughed aloud. The sylffur, when burned, smelled like rotting hen's eggs.

Nightfall was but a short time away, when the army came upon the first outriders from the fort. Arthgwr's men were questioned by the fort's advance guards. The guards were striking in their appearance.

They all wore the same uniform, strong leather breastplates with wide leather fringes over a Roman style toga that hung to their knees. It was the uniform of the Roman cavalry complete with high crested helmet, cheek protectors and large red horsehair plumes. Their forearms were protected with armbands of leather and metal and they wore protectors on their shins tied off with leather above their thick-soled sandals. The men were armed with short Roman swords, javelins and rectangular shields.

Myrddin acted as intermediary and on his word Arthgwr, Cai, Gwyn and five warriors of their choosing were allowed to accompany the riders into the fort of Caer Melyn. Arthgwr had thought it wise to put Edern in charge of the army as it would boost his confidence and Arthgwr knew Edern would be vigilant. He also did not wish to have Edern's zeal for is leader's protection to be misinterpreted. Rhiannon was to stay with the main camp and assist Edern. Father Bedwini however was selected as one of the five men to accompany Arthgwr.

Upon entering the gates of Caer Melyn, Arthgwr, Myrddin and the men were shown to a building off from the main hall. They were informed they might rest and prepare themselves before their audience with Ambrosius Aurelianus.

Arthgwr was unimpressed with Caer Melyn. He thought it small and nothing more than earthen works and timber, certainly not the stronghold he had expected. There were no great stonewalls, no strong stone buildings and though the fort was well kept, Arthgwr thought it beneath the reputation of the man in charge, the proclaimed king of the Southern Britons.

"I'm not sure I like the looks of all this," Cai whispered into Arthgwr's ear. It had not escaped Arthgwr's attention that Ambrosius's men seemed less than enthusiastic by his arrival. He wondered if Myrddin's plan was sound.

"Did you understand what those bastards were saying?" asked Gwyn, referring to the guards who had escorted them into the fort. "They sounded like the priest," he jabbed his thumb in the direction of Father Bedwini.

"Yes," said Arthgwr looking at Father Bedwini, "they were speaking Latin, though with an accent I have not heard before."

The building they were in could have held twenty men comfortably. There was a long wooden table, fresh straw on the floor, chairs crudely carved but comfortably padded, and braziers burning supplying heat and light. On the other table were some hard bread, cheese, salted pork, an unidentified broth, decanters of drink, and several goblets.

Arthgwr poured the liquid into a goblet. It was a ruby red colour. Father Bedwini explained to the soldiers that the liquid was wine, a drink fermented from grapes. Priests in the bigger communities, to celebrate their rituals, used wine but they used it sparingly and no layperson was allowed to drink. Some of the men had not been to the big cities and therefore had never before tasted the Mediterranean drink.

Raising their goblets, the men drank a toast, a weak affirmation of their task and more a fervent prayer for a positive outcome.

Myrddin finished his wine and directed the men's attention to the bowls of water on small tables near the braziers. The water was scented and warm. Myrddin gently instructed the men that they should wash themselves and attend to their appearance. He said this would make a good impression on the king. Dutifully, though with much ribald behaviour and banter, the men took off their equipment, lay down their weapons and began to wash their bodies.

The sight of his men struck Arthgwr, all of them were battle hardened and scarred. What caught Arthgwr's attention was he had seen his men only as his army of loyal fighting men. Now in comparison with Ambrosius Aurelianus and his men, with their matching armour, weapons, plumes of red feathers, shaven faces, shorn hair, his own men appeared unkempt and a motley crew of barbarians.

Myrddin saw the look on Arthgwr's face and instantly understood. He walked over to Arthgwr and stood beside him without saying a word. Arthgwr was unaware how crestfallen he appeared. Lost in his melancholy, he had not noticed Myrddin's presence.

"They are not pretty," said Myrddin quietly.

The men were washing the dirt from their bodies. Their long hair, knotted and filthy from the battles they had waged on the long journey, swirled about them as they cleaned themselves. Tribal tattoos were visible and plenty and two of the men had skin still tinged faintly with blue woad. Another two warriors had full beards, but the rest had smaller beards and moustaches and the sides of their faces were clean-shaven.

Arthgwr looked at their weapons and armour stacked on the straw strewn floor. The weapons were all in good repair, but none matched with any of the others. Instead, it was a hodgepodge of swords, knives, spikes, round leather shields, oval wooden shields, spears and short axes, each the preferred weapon of its' owner. The weapons had been collected from defeated enemies or found on ancient battlegrounds and passed down generation to generation. Some odd looking instruments were made to the specifications of the owner expressing his particular style of fighting and killing. The only weapon common among them was the long bow made from the wood of the yew tree.

The clothing the men wore was an assortment of woollen breeches, cloaks, shirts of multi-colours and the occasional leather jerkin and breeches. Cloak clasps were simple affairs made of thick iron, nothing ornate. Even the men's rings were thick and though inscribed with sentiments or inspirations, they were not gold or jewelled.

Myrddin moved over to a basin of water. He took out from under his cloak a cloth bag and laid it on the table. Opening it, he removed three curiously looking squares of an amber coloured substance, two brass devices that had long spines on one edge, a small very sharp looking knife and several long strands of thin leather rope.

Aware that Arthgwr and his men were watching him, Myrddin stripped to the waist and picking up a square of the amber substance, rubbed his hands together with it in the basin of warm water. White foam appeared and Myrddin rubbed this vigorously together on his face, neck, arms and chest paying special attention to his underarms. Washing the white foam off with the water, he took hold of the small knife and scrapped it over his cheeks taking away the many days growth of hair. He scraped his face with the knife again before cleaning it in the bowl of water. He repeated this until his cheeks were clean of hair. And then he picked up the brass device, dragging the brass spines through the mane of his long grey hair. Combing all the knots from his hair, Myrddin then used the scented water to wash his locks, drying them with a piece of cloth that had obviously been provided for the purpose. Lastly, he tied off his hair with a bit of leather rope. Saying nothing, he took a thick piece of rough leather and sharpened the small knife. He gestured to Cai to duplicate the ritual on himself.

The men laughed while Cai enthusiastically duplicated Myrddin's actions. The rest of Arthgwr's men followed suit. The cleansing ritual had been a part of their culture for many hundreds of years, even before the coming of the Romans, though it had not been practiced so thoroughly in recent time.

Arthgwr smiled as he took his turn along with his foster brother Cai. Even Father Bedwini laughed as he washed his shorn hair and scraped the hair from his face with the sharp knife.

Arthgwr paused to inspect his men and he was proud again. They had put on their breeches, shirts, and woollen cloaks. Their hair was now clean, uniformly tied back with thin leather rope, their cheeks hairless and their small tribal beards and moustaches were trimmed, combed, and worn with a sense of prideful identity. They stood in line, smiles on their battered faces and their fearsome weapons at their side. Their clothes and weapons did not match, they were not uniform, but there was no mistaking they were serious hardened warriors, fiercely individual and yet sharing a common cause and a singular vision of freedom.

Myrddin moved to Arthgwr's side and put a consoling hand on the leader's shoulder.

"They are still not pretty," he said softly.

"No," said Arthgwr, "they are not. But they can fight!"

The men laughed and sat at the long table drinking wine and eating bread and salted pork with cheese.

There was a pounding at the door, not impolite by protocol standards, but authoritarian just the same. All laughing stopped and the men looked to their weapons. Myrddin calmed them and bade them to sit at the table. He went alone to the large wooden door and opened it.

By firelight, it was plain to see the Roman-style clad soldiers of Ambrosius Aurelianus, four of them at the door with a glimpse of a larger band of armed men at the edge of the firelight's ethereal reach. They were polite enough, asking in accented Latin, if everything was all right with the men inside and was there anything they required.

Myrddin indicated they were comfortable enough and thanked the generosity of King Ambrosius. The man, a captain in the guard by the looks of him, nodded his head in acknowledgement. In a respectful tone, he instructed Myrddin that Arthgwr and his men were to be escorted to the main hall. First, however they were to be searched to be sure they were free of any weapons. The captain was respectful in his demeanour, but it was clear he was resolved to carry out his orders whatever the consequences.

Myrddin turned from the door. Instantly Arthgwr knew he would not like what Myrddin was to say to him next.

Cai was outraged when he learned what was being ordered. He bellowed and stomped up and down, waving his long iron sword in the air. Gwyn too was angered, kicking over a table holding one of the basins of water, toppling it to the floor with a crash, shards of pottery raining down everywhere.

Father Bedwini remained calm, while the other men looked to Arthgwr. Two of them, Steffan ap Dafydd and his cousin Tryffin simply smirked. They were followers of the Old Religion and they had expected some form of treachery once they heard the Latin-speaking guards and saw their decorative outfits.

Myrddin quickly began to explain, while the captain remained respectful, but with mounting impatience by the doorway. His orders were clear and what's more they were from his king.

Arthgwr raised his hand, a signal for his men to stop what they were doing and allow him time to think. Myrddin continued to explain that this was all reasonable, pointing out to Arthgwr, it was exactly what Edern would insist upon should any delegation wish audience with Arthgwr in Arthgwr's own camp. Gwyn nodded in agreement at that thought and he looked at Cai. While Arthgwr seemed somewhat convinced by Myrddin's argument, he was not ready to submit to a body search. That insulted his sense of himself and the mission he had sworn to undertake on the say so of Myrddin the Druid.

Myrddin instructed the men to stack their weapons on the table slowly and carefully and in full view of the captain and his men. Speaking with authority Myrddin reminded the captain of his own special relationship with Ambrosius. The captain smoothly acknowledged Myrddin and his status with his king but he did not budge from his sense of duty to carry out King Ambrosius Aurelianus orders to the letter.

Taking a deep breath Myrddin straightened to his full height. It seemed that the braziers in the room burned with greater intensity in sudden fury.

"I am your lord's special counsel!"

His voice filled the head of all present. It was more, much more, than the mere sounds of his thundering words; the Druid's voice had become a presence within their bodies.

"I am Myrddin, whom you call Merlinus. I have walked these islands since time began! These are my people! You are of my people! The mighty Romans themselves did not destroy me! I will not now subject to indignity! You insult me by doubting my word. My word is my bond, a sacred trust, and a sacred vow taken before you were but a gleam in your father's eye and before your own mother had ever dreamt of lying under him! I vouch for these men who stand before you! I vouch for these brave warriors who stand with me ready to do service for your lord and who have at great sacrifice to themselves and their own tribes, come to your king's aid! And yet you have the unmitigated audacity to question my word? I suggest to you, youngster, that you think long and hard before you choose your next act for it may be the last act of your life and the demise of your world as you know it!"

It was if all the air in the great room had been suddenly sucked out. Braziers flickered wildly, shooting fire high only to fall, splutter, and smoke before flaring again. Not a man dared to breathe. Indeed, drawing a breath was impossible and the men were frozen, rooted where they stood, transfixed as if they were nailed to the very floor. Arthgwr looked at Myrddin and saw the strong, black haired man he had seen back at the hut on the shore of the icy cold mountain lake the day before he claimed the sword Caladfwlch. The braziers suddenly flared again as though they were going to burn the entire building to the ground in seconds. The shadows cast by the fiery bursts swirled and mingled with the black smoke of the braziers creating eerie shadows that enveloped the entire scene.

The captain turned white with fear and stammered out his apology allowing Arthgwr and his men to file out of the hall without being searched. The beads of sweat on the captain and his own men were matched by the awe and sweat of Arthgwr's own company. The men were too eager to leave through the door and escape the terrible wrath of Myrddin. Father Bedwini had a look of sheer terror on his face, his lips were moving in silent prayer, but his shaking body cast doubt on his religious resolve in the face of what he had witnessed. There was the smell of urine in the air. Arthgwr's own men cowered and averted their eyes, meekly following Myrddin's instructions. Steffan and Tryffin were trembling in fear, realising for the first time they were in the presence of a true Wise One.

Arthgwr stood alone with Myrddin and he looked at the Druid, who now appeared to him like a favoured grandfather, grey of hair and kindly.

"What does this mean Myrddin? Has Ambrosius decided against your plan after all?"

"Arthgwr," Myrddin said softly, almost gently as though he were talking to a frightened child.

"Ambrosius is not aware of my plan. It will be up to you to convince him of it."

Myrddin pushed by Arthgwr and followed the others being escorted courteously now, by the cowed guards to the main hall for the audience with the King.

The main hall was very much like the building that had housed Arthgwr and his men only it was considerably larger. The walls and structure were of timber and earth; no stones had been used in the construction of Caer Melyn. There was a long massive table of hewn wood that was positioned length ways dividing the hall and chairs were situated on either side. Another table not as big, yet still of substance, ran horizontally across the top end of the former table forming the unmistakable symbol of Christianity, the cross.

A great fireplace warmed the head table and threw heat and light into the room. Braziers were set in the corners and stanchions were inset in the walls their firelight amply and pleasantly assisted in filling the great hall with warmth. Straw was strewn on the earthen floor and tapestries hung on the walls between stanchions. The great room was comfortable and inviting. Hounds roamed freely seeking any food that might escape from the table or thrown to them by guests of the king. There were soldiers sitting at the main table and several milling around in groups talking. The men were armed with short swords and knives but no armour, javelins or shields were present. All were dressed in the Romanesque style favoured by Ambrosius. Serving girls moved amongst the warriors offering warm bread, wine and salted meats. A silence fell on the conversations as Arthgwr and his men were led into the hall.

Myrddin had entered into the hall first. His hooded woollen cloak was modest, but of good quality. His long grey hair was still pulled back from his face and tied off with a leather strand. Myrddin stood straight and dignified as he ushered in Arthgwr's men. They looked splendid, their long hair tied off, revealing the strong character of their faces. Their clothing, while not uniform, was in good repair. There was no mistaking, but that they were tested warriors, independent but sharing a strong bond as only those who had fought and bled together for a just cause could understand. These were hard serious men and it showed.

Father Bedwini entered and muttered a prayer ending with the hand gestures forming the cross in the air. Ambrosius's men took note, bowed their heads respectfully and crossed themselves in the same fashion.

Cai was last to enter and he stood proudly for a moment before announcing in a deep booming voice the arrival of Arthgwr. The language was Cymraeg and few of Ambrosius's men had understood what Cai had said.

Arthgwr strode through the doorway, his cloak dramatically thrown over his left shoulder leaving his right sword arm free but without a sword at his side. His tunic was worn and faded, but it still showed the cross that had been sewn into the shoulder of the garment. Standing by his men, deerskin clad feet slightly apart; Arthgwr looked every bit like a man accustomed to leading other men. His blue eyes were hard, his face impassive and strong as he gazed around the room.

Ambrosius's captain escorted Arthgwr to a place at the huge table. Arthgwr's men followed and arranged themselves on either side of their leader. Cai waited for his foster brother to be seated and then sat on Arthgwr's left side while Myrddin sat on Arthgwr's right. Father Bedwini, much to his chagrin, sat next to the Druid.

Food was brought along with more wine. One of Ambrosius's men leaned across the table and in accented Latin began speaking to Father Bedwini.

"*salve, quod nomen tibi est?*....Hello, what is your name?"

"*mihi nomen est padre Bedwini*....my name is Father Bedwini," replied the priest saluting with his goblet of wine. The soldier leaned in closer so that only the Father could hear what it was he was saying.

"Who are these men and why are they here? I know they are to have an audience with the King but surely they have no status. My God they're nothing more than country peasants!" The soldier wrinkled his nose to show his disgust for Arthgwr and his men.

Father Bedwini glanced furtively to his right to see if the Druid had heard what the soldier had just said about Arthgwr and his company of warriors. He knew instinctively the danger involved should any of the men hear such insults. He breathed a more easily when he saw Myrddin engaged in an animated conversation with Arthgwr. There was no sign that the Druid or any of the others had any inclination as to the attitude of Ambrosius's soldiers, save for the unpleasant stand off before being brought to the hall. The Father took a great gulp of wine and wiped his mouth with a piece of cloth set next to his goblet.

Myrddin looked placidly at Arthgwr infuriating the man even more.

"How could you do this to me? Have I not been a willing enough servant to our people? You made me believe that this plan of yours was made with the cooperation of Ambrosius!" The leader of the men from Caerwyn was angry.

Arthgwr saw anger in the face of Myrddin and for a moment he feared the power of the old Wise One. Instead of exploding in rage, Myrddin took a long draught of wine, wiped his lips and with a kindly, almost condescending tone, began to speak to him.

"Arthgwr," said Myrddin, "I know these past few months have not been without hardship for you and I am well aware of the trust you have placed with me. I know that for a warrior such as you, trust does not come easy. Realise Arthgwr that I too am at risk here. I am gambling my life that I may save something of our people's traditions, heritage, and way of life before it is washed away forever. I too, am forced into a trust I do not find easy. I need to trust in you Arthgwr. We all do. Think, Arthgwr, as a man of war, would you be so likely to take the measure of a man from another man's say so? Would you listen to that man's story of battle, Arthgwr? Especially if he was not a man of war himself?"

Arthgwr knew Myrddin was right, but it still did nothing to assuage the anger he felt and the feeling he had been played the fool.

Looking around the hall again, he took notice of Ambrosius's men. He thought he detected a derisive look from the man beside Father Bedwini. It did nothing to help his mood.

"*dic nihi, unde venis*...tell me where do you come from?" asked the soldier seated opposite to Cai.

"Never mind, how could you understand me? You speak that noise from the Northwest. Your language sounds like you have something caught in your throat." He laughed, turned, and slapped his comrade on the back sharing his jocularity at the expense of Cai.

"Only civilised men speak Latin!" Many of Ambrosius's men were snickering at the soldier's insults to Arthgwr.

Before Arthgwr or his men could respond, for there was no mistaking the insults despite the difference in language, Myrddin stood up knocking over his chair with the force of his movement.

"Tell me, where do you get the audacity to insult guests of your master? As your Lord's confidant and advisor I find your behaviour rude and impertinent! These men have important business with the King and you will answer for your impudence!"

"Sit down old man!" sneered the soldier; "I mean no harm, just having a little fun with the peasants!" He gruffly passed a jug of wine to the Druid as an off-handed gesture of good will.

Arthgwr's mind was in turmoil. He was furious at Myrddin for not fully preparing him for the task he had agreed to undertake on the druid's behest. After all the battles over the last few months, the privations, the danger, the death and atrocities that had so affected him and all his company of hardened warriors and most importantly the separation from his beloved wife and children Arthgwr now doubted himself and the wisdom of the druid. The secrets the Druid had confided to him the other night still lingered and haunted him causing him to feel he had been duped and used for the druid own agenda.

Arthgwr felt that as a man, he could endure the hardships of waging war, but being away from his wife Gwenhwyfar and his children Cynglas and Gwyneth was proving to be more than he could bear. He felt one of his limbs' had been ripped from his body, such was the anguish he felt at being apart from his children.

Young Cynglas, his son was growing up. Arthgwr had barely known how to respond to his young son on his last visit. And his daughter Gwyneth was preparing to marry! It was all happening too fast and he was not even present. He was waging war on the say so of an old man who claimed to be a Druid! Now he was to have an audience with a powerful king, the self-appointed king of all the Southern Britons, a man he had never met, who had adopted Roman customs and judging by his men, had nothing but contempt for those of the North!

Myrddin expected him to convince this old warrior that he, Arthgwr, virtually unknown in these parts, should be the one to lead the king's army into an important battle against an enemy force of overwhelming force bent on taking the islands for their own. What's more, the king wanted to lead the army himself, but Myrddin wanted Arthgwr to persuade this king to allow Arthgwr to lead. The outcome was a losing proposition. The battle would no doubt be lost. Yet Myrddin insisted that the fighting of this lost battle would save the Cymry from obscurity.

Indeed, the Druid's argument now seemed to Arthgwr like a ploy for power not unlike that which Myrddin himself had accused the Roman Bishops of trying to perpetrate. Ambrosius's soldier, ignorant as he was, might very well be right in his assessment of Arthgwr as nothing more than a country peasant! What hubris, he thought to himself, that he, Arthgwr, an unknown warrior from the hinterlands of the Northwest wild country, could unite these tribes and change the course of destiny, a destiny written by mighty Rome and the onslaught of Sacsonaidd hordes!

He felt decidedly foolish and small. The feeling did not sit well with him and that thought combined with the anguish of being separated from those he loved created in him despair that fuelled a cold burning fury.

He was now being mocked by a Southern Romanised pretender to a warrior, clean-shaven, shorn of hair and in a ridiculous horse-haired helmet!

In a quiet low tone, Arthgwr spoke to the soldier in Latin.

"It is not which language a man speaks that determines if he is civilised or not. His actions tell others if he is a civilised man worthy of knowing. I am your king's guest and I am here because I have led men into at least eleven battles and have personally fought many single combats to the death. With my men, those you see with me now, I have been victorious. You are a soldier serving your king, very commendable. By what right do you question your king's judgement? Pray, tell us what you have done that is worthy of your king's attention?"

The soldier was dumbfounded. It was not clear which was the greater shock; that Arthgwr spoke Latin or the substance of what he had said. Before the soldier could gather his wits Arthgwr stood up and with him, all of his men, even the Father Bedwini.

"Tell your master," Arthgwr spit out the word so that it would sting. He continued in the same low voice, "we will be waiting at our camp. Ambrosius can call on us at his leisure. Tell him he may bring with him what men he might, armed or unarmed, it makes no matter, for we have seen the worth of those he keeps close to him!"

Arthgwr and his men were walking toward the door. Myrddin though, was left standing, still looking at Ambrosius's man. The other soldiers did not quite know what to do but it was plain by the look on some of their faces that anger was creeping into their thoughts.

There was a loud crack of an oak staff on the wood floor. All eyes turned to the front of the hall as heralds led Ambrosius Aurelianus to his seat at the head of the big table. Every man in the hall stopped and turned to face the King.

Myrddin spoke first.

"My lord, I have the honour of introducing to you, Arthgwr Pendragon, the Fierce Bear-Man from the North. Unfortunately, before we can discuss urgent business that will directly affect my Lord's plans, there is a matter of protocol requiring a judgement."

Ambrosius Aurelianus gazed at Myrddin and then took in the scene in front of him. His white hair was short, falling just below his ears and he was clean-shaven in the Roman Christian fashion. He was not resplendent in his manner of dress, but attired in good quality clothing of the Roman fashion. His biggest extravagance was a red cloak fastened with a gold broach in the shape of an eagle. Upon his wrists, he wore simple leather guards, nothing ornate or jewelled.

Arthgwr turned with the other men and gazed at the king. He was impressed that at least the king of the Southern Britons was no peacock. The king was past his prime, well past, but he still maintained the hardness and discipline of a military commander and it showed in his every movement. As Arthgwr looked into the king's brown eyes, he heard him speak in a smooth baritone voice.

*"quaeso, vente ad mensam...*please come to the table, sit and be comfortable then tell me of this difficulty with protocol."

Arthgwr looked at his men and with his eyes directed them to go to the table. Ambrosius's soldiers backed away allowing Arthgwr's men to pass unhindered. Arthgwr stood where he was feet slightly apart, his face stern and his eyes bright and blazing. He held his place for a heartbeat more then strode to the table with dramatic flair. He cast a glance at Myrddin.

Taking his cue from Arthgwr, Myrddin addressed Ambrosius.

"Forgive me my Lord, I have not been free with information and have asked that you take this meeting without telling you much about the reason except that it was important to you. My Lord favours me with his confidence, but I will allow this man," he gestured to Arthgwr, "a man of war and winner of great battles to explain in his own terms, warrior to warrior. First my Lord, I have to say that this guest, this important guest here on my request and my oath of good will to you, has been rudely insulted by one of your men." Myrddin paused and looked at the offending soldier.

"Indeed," said Ambrosius, "and how were you insulted Arthur, is it," he asked using the Roman accented word for Arthgwr, "or should I call you "Artorios?""

Arthgwr stood and spoke in Latin to the Roman-Briton King.

"Whatever name you give me will suffice. The offence given here is that my men and I were judged uncivilised. Because of our appearance it was thought we did not understand Latin. It was assumed, since we are not finely dressed or uniformly turned out, that we are somehow less then men of war. Though we have been vouched for by your own trusted counsel, our weapons have been taken from us and we were to be subjected to a search of our bodies."

401

Ambrosius looked at Arthgwr for a moment. He saw the chiselled body of a hard man, the long hair, the short beard and tattoos of a Pagan and the cross on his tunic indicating a Christian. He looked then at the other men and saw the same long hair, beards and tattoos. The king noted the rough look of the men, the lack of what he considered sophistication. Yet, he sensed an air of fierce dedication and saw in the men's eyes that they were all accustomed to hardship and battle. None of this was lost on the king.

"I doubt you would be foolish enough to allow a group of armed warriors into your presence with only the assurances that their intent was peaceful, even on the say so of your own most trusted advisor. Surely your own men would act to protect you and in so doing is it not reasonable to think they may be over zealous in their fealty to you?" The king paused and again took the measure of Arthgwr.

Arthgwr knew he was now caught on a battle of wits that would determine the outcome of this meeting. He smiled and opened his arms and responded.

"If such had happened as you were visiting my hall, would you not bring your displeasure to my attention?"

Ambrosius smiled, enjoying the clever exchange.

"I would indeed," he said, "so we are both of us, leaders who have in their employ, men who are over zealous in their fealty to us. What shall we do?"

"Let us put our men at their ease and talk between ourselves in private. You have a priest, I see, as do I. The interest of the Church and the souls of the people will be watched over, I have no doubt. Surely Myrddin here, will keep us both honest in any dialogue we enter into, after all he has advised us both."

It was a bold and daring move. Myrddin looked at Arthgwr in puzzlement. Arthgwr was smiling but his attention was focused squarely on Ambrosius.

The Romano-Briton king smiled quickly to mask his surprise at the audacity of this man. The king stood up and opened his arms in a gesture of friendliness.

"Agreed! I will send you this man," Ambrosius pointed at the soldier who had insulted Arthgwr, "on the morrow with a place and time where we can meet and talk." He did not wait for a response, but turned with the abrupt air of a ruler of men and strode through the doorway, his entourage following him.

The smile was no longer on his face.

Arthgwr and his company wheeled about and walked out of the building into the night. Upon reaching his camp, Arthgwr sent word that all of his councillors and military leaders were to attend to him immediately. It would take some time to gather them. Arthgwr found himself alone in his tent for a moment.

Chapter 29

Arthgwr was furious. Not only did he feel used and deceived by Myrddin, but also the insults from Ambrosius Aurelianus's men had rankled him. According to Myrddin, Arthgwr should fight a battle, risk his men, his own life, only to serve up victory to this Roman king! In effect, Arthgwr was doing the old man a huge favour, one that no other Briton in all of the kingdoms would even contemplate! Yet there he sat taking abuse from some fancifully dressed young upstart who had in all probability not spilled blood in battle either for his king, country or in his own honour!

His men were gathering and the tent was filling rapidly. They were quiet. There was no mistaking the mood of their leader. Even the dog Cafall was quiet and lay under a trestle table.

Arthgwr barked orders in a very low tone. None had to be repeated, no one dared to question him out right, but there were concerns. It was going to be a very long night. The men had their instructions and they hurriedly left Arthgwr's tent for there was no time at all to waste.

It looked like Beltane with all the bonfires that had been lit throughout the camp. There was urgency in the air and tensions were running high. The peace was kept, there were no fights or outbursts. Edern's men saw to that.

The camp followers; families, women, a few old men and boys too young to fight, were busy. There was work to be done. And work needed to be carried out into the night, so there was no time at all for hurt feelings or bickering. The camp women were working as fast as their nimble fingers could sew. Groups had formed based on tribal connections. Where it was impossible to establish membership in a tribe, villagers were adopted into the closest tribe they had connections with. The captains and advisors of Arthgwr's inner circle had spread the word that this was Arthgwr's order.

Christians and Pagans alike did the best they could and everyone worked hard, even the children. The fighting men were busy practicing and drilling with spear, sword and bows. It was very difficult and dangerous with only firelight to guide them. A few men were injured, but none seriously. The most dangerous routines, of course, were the formations of cavalry.

Arthgwr pulled up his cloak and went to see how his plan was forming up. He was not filled with any great amount of confidence. He did not let that show in his bearing, as he strode amongst the people, his people.

As dawn approached, Myrddin appeared outside the tent of Arthgwr. He looked tired, like the old man he had so often appeared to be, the kindly grandfather. The two men stood, each refusing to look at the other. It was obvious to Myrddin that Arthgwr was angry.

"The king will be here at noon," he said without looking at Arthgwr. "The man who insulted you will be here at midmorning. The king is expecting to see some sort of demonstration of your prowess. It will be up to you what that may be. He was intrigued when I told him you would lead the battle but allow him the credit."

"You told him that?" Arthgwr's voice was almost a growl.

"Yes, I did," said Myrddin defiantly and looking at Arthgwr for the first time.

"I thought I could use what little influence I may have with the king to smooth the way for you." Myrddin was now standing erect and he looked much younger.

Arthgwr turned to face the druid. His face was lined and did not hide the strain and lack of sleep he had endured since this venture had begun. His voice was low and gravely and as menacing as a winter storm.

"You listen to me, Myrddin or should I say Merlin," Arthgwr used the bastardised Latin pronunciation of Myrddin's name as a knife.

"Wise One, Druid or whatever you may call yourself, I am not intimidated by your charlatan trickery. How you do the things you do may be beyond my ken, but I will tell you this, it is trickery nonetheless! I do not live in a world of trickery. I live in the world of reality. Reality is the sharp edge of my sword! I have faced down the naked blades of over a dozen men in single combat for you! I have, with my army, fought eleven battles, again facing the reality of the sword's keen edge knowing at any minute I might be cleaved! I did that for you! I even convinced my own men that your cause was our cause! Yet, you stay far from the battle, spin your intrigues and your stories, and conjure up your tricks to bend the minds of lesser men. You just keep in mind that I am the warrior here and my sword cuts what I wish it to cut!"

Myrddin stood stock-still and held Arthgwr's glowering gaze for a long time before he spoke.

"You mind, my young tempestuous warrior, that a sword can cut both ways and neither you, nor your army, is anything at all without hope!"

Then he was gone. A swirl of his cloak in the early morning mist and Myrddin disappeared. Arthgwr was alone and shaking with rage and frustration.

Daylight broke and Arthgwr was running out of time. He called for Cai, his foster brother, and demanded to know what progress had been made. Cai was noticeably put off by the common way in which Arthgwr addressed him. Arthgwr sensed the change in his foster brother and heard his terse reply that all was well. He allowed himself the luxury of touching his foster brother on the shoulder by way of expressing his apology and his respect. Cai touched his forefinger to his forelock as salute and acknowledgement. They rode silently together to the field to see to the preparations.

To the untrained eye, it may have looked like chaos. But to Arthgwr and Cai, they saw no chaos only a very astute strategy at play. Both men were pleased. The two warriors were filled with pride to see the fighting men were wearing their ancient tribal colours.

The field was ablaze with colour, which lent itself to the initial impression of chaos. There were men dressed in cloaks of yellow and black squares, blue and gray checks, red and green plaids. There were even Christian warriors wearing plain grey cloaks with black crosses signifying their religious preference. They were all of them, Arthgwr's men and they were drilling like the fighters they were with bow and sword and spear and horse. It was impressive.

"You never really explained why you wanted the men to wear traditional colours, Arthgwr. Would it not have been easier and even more impressive to the king if they were all dressed the same?" asked Cai.

"I ask you brother, did you not see those men of Ambrosius? Pompous idiots the lot! All of them were kissing up to the royal arse! I doubt any of them have seen battle in a year! Now Brother, would it not be more impressive to see men from different tribes, different religions, all of them warriors, battle-tested, who would as easily turn on each other as any enemy and yet they choose to fight under the command of one man and for a single binding cause?"

Cai was shocked at his foster brother's characterization of King Aurelianus. After all, the king had fought many battles, routing the tyrant, Gwrtheyrn and fighting the Sacsonaidds to a peace that had lasted more than a decade. The look on his face gave away his thoughts and Arthgwr laughed.

"You think I am too harsh on the old king. No, I give him his due and no one can take away his deeds or his honour. His men on the other hand are soft and yes, I do not much care for the Roman clothing that is the king's chosen fashion. I fight for all Cymry, my land is Cymru, what is known as Briton, and now because of these Roman-loving Southerners, it is nothing more than a dead Roman province on the outer borders of the world! I give the king his due, all right. But I was born here, I have lived here, loved here, and bled here, and here I shall die! The same can be said of all my men! That is our heritage, it is in our blood and it is in our soul! It is what makes us who we are, how we think and how we choose to act. That makes the difference between us and them!"

Cai looked at his brother and remained silent.

The sun was high in the sky. The men were tired and sweating. Arthgwr called a rest in the drilling. He had seen enough and was confident of the military prowess of his warriors. He forbade any drinking of ale, mead, or cider and ordered the women to serve only water. Myrddin had returned to witness the demonstration and to do what he could to ensure the outcome of this dangerously delicate plan.

A rider came up to Arthgwr and told him that the soldier of the night before had arrived as promised by the king.

Edern had set the place of the demonstration. It was a small meadow sufficient for the task. He had set Arthgwr's tent just above the meadow on slightly higher ground. Any who approached would have to come up a slight rise and thus be disadvantaged. On the other hand Arthgwr, if caught in a trap, could easily ride swiftly down the slope into the meadow, covered by the troops already in place for the demonstration. That left the main army just out of sight, but close enough to give protection and engage any enemy.

Arthgwr noticed all of this as he dismounted and walked into the tent to wash his face and clear his head. He smiled. It was tempting to allow Edern to deal with the king's insolent guard of the night before, but that would be too quick and bloody and not politically astute.

The king's man was shown into Arthgwr's tent, he stood at attention. Arthgwr was forced to be impressed, the man looked grave but not frightened. He wore the costume of the king's men, the Roman fashion with the horsehair crest in his helmet, the toga over tight fitting breeches and thick leather sandals with iron studs in the sole and of course his face was clean shaven and his hair was shorn to the skin. He was of average height and carried a bit of weight but was not excessively muscled. Arthgwr noticed his hands, while worn, were not calloused.

Cafall growled menacingly, but was quieted by Arthgwr's hand. Looking up Arthgwr caught sight of Edern standing close the king's man and he knew instinctively his trusted man had been told of the events the night before at the king's audience. Arthgwr beckoned Edern. It would not be safe to have him standing so close to the man who had insulted Arthgwr. There was a pause of a heartbeat before Edern could tear his glare away from the man and obey his leader.

Arthgwr motioned Edern to come closer so that Arthgwr might speak directly into his ear. The conversation was short and Edern did not look too happy, but neither did he look too angered.

Arthgwr offered the king's man food, drink, and bade him to make himself comfortable. He then asked his name.

"Lucius is my name and I am here on my king's pleasure." He spoke in the accented Latin of Ambrosius's men and there was no hiding the contempt he held for the present company.

Arthgwr looked at Edern and nodded. Edern took a step forward and began to speak, Myrddin who had still not said a word to Arthgwr since dawn, nevertheless obeyed Arthgwr's wish that he translate Edern's words into Latin.

"It is our custom, you fancifully dressed gelding, that if you insult one of us, let alone our leader Arthgwr, you fight in single combat to the death! As we are here at your king's pleasure, we will forgo our customs this once and allow a contest to be held without weapons. A friendly contest you understand, you puny hairless bastard, nothing of consequence riding on the outcome. My liege, Arthgwr, has decided that as guests in your country, there are bound to be cultural differences. That was all there was last night, a cultural misunderstanding, and nothing more and no injury to honour on either side, as your own king pointed out. So, we shall simply have a friendly competition and to make things even more friendly, you boy-lover, the winner will be saluted here and later, there will be food and drink for all that have gathered, you piece of dung."

There were snickers and giggles from those of Arthgwr's men standing behind Lucius. Of course, the king's man had no idea what had been said to him as Myrddin's interpretation had censored the insults Edern had thrown at him.

After the angry words he had traded with Arthgwr, Myrddin had spent the rest of the morning at Caer Melyn. There he had spoken to a representative of the king and had persuaded him that a contingent of men should accompany the offending officer, Lucius and that one of those men should be a captain in the king's army. Myrddin then sent word to Rhiannon to forewarn Arthgwr. It would be best that Arthgwr's men, especially Edern, were not surprised by the sight of an armed contingent representing the king, arriving so soon before Aurelianus himself.

Lucius was the only one surprised to see the arrival of a full contingent of armed men lead by a representative of his king and accompanied by his own captain. All the king's men were treated as honoured guests. Arthgwr was very stern on that point and especially so with Edern. He had let Edern in on his plan and the psychology behind it so that Edern's temper would be kept in check. To be on the safe side Gwyn and Cai were also present to ensure things went smoothly.

The men formed up into a square, making a clearing for the fight. Food and drink were passed around and the men friendly to Lucius were in one corner having the rules of the contest explained to them. In the other corner, was Steffan ap Dafydd, one of the men who had accompanied Arthgwr to the King's audience.

Steffan was not as tall as Lucius and he was not as heavy. None of this seemed to bother Steffan, whose body was wiry and sinewy, covered in blue tattoos, his hair long and braided had been tied back with leather. Steffan was smiling and joking with his brother Tryffin.

The rules were simple. No weapons were allowed. The men had to be stripped down to their breeches and searched for hidden weapons. The contest was not to the death. And quarter had to be given, even if it were not requested.

Lucius looked over at his opponent and smiled. He was sure he could defeat the smaller man with the strange blue markings on his chest, arms and back, his long dishevelled hair and small beard that covered his chin, repulsed Lucius and he thought of the man as little more than an animal. The men in Lucius's corner were laughing and boasting of Lucius skills. They gathered some drink for him and slapped him on the back in good humour. In the opposite corner, Steffan simply spoke to his brother and a few friends, they were all smiles but not excessively boisterous. The brothers exuded confidence. One of Lucius's men who had been watching Steffan, had stopped smiling. The contest was about to begin.

The men moved to the centre of the square clearing and circled each other in crouching positions. There were a few feints and slaps thrown by each man as they tried to gauge the other's mettle. Lucius feinted to his right as though to grab Steffan's left leg. Instead, his left fist crashed into the right side of Steffan's face and he fell to the ground to the raucous cheers of the king's men and Lucius's friends. Immediately, Lucius began kicking at Steffan's head, but Steffan had regained his senses and was able to cover his head and then scramble to his feet.

Lucius struck with a right fist to Steffan's face and then his left fist crashed into Steffan's ribs. Steffan doubled up in pain and Lucius came straight in to finish him off with a kick. Again, a roar of approval went up from the men of Ambrosius Aurelianus. Steffan stood straight up; his hands blocked the kick while his head smashed into Lucius nose, splaying blood everywhere. A right fist by Steffan hammered into the side of Lucius's face. Steffan grabbed Lucius behind the neck interlacing his fingers while bringing his knee crashing up into Lucius's face. After three devastating knees to the head, Lucius crumpled to the earth. Steffan delivered two devastating kicks to Lucius's midsection before Tryffin, his brother, pulled him off the unconscious Lucius.

The King's men were silent. Arthgwr's men whooped and hollered but were soon civil when they caught sight of the look of Arthgwr and Edern. No egregious celebrating or boasting was to be tolerated. However, none of Arthgwr's men could help but notice the satisfied look on Edern's face.

Friends helped Lucius up, gave him drink, tended to his broken nose, and cut face. Steffan ap Dafydd walked over and held his hand out. Lucius slowly and begrudgingly took the offered hand and shook it. Steffan hoisted the man to his feet and hugged him like a brother. Now there were more cheers and yells from all the men. Arthgwr allowed that celebration to continue unabated. He looked at the captain of the army and the King's representative, the captain nodded in respect. The representative simply looked at Arthgwr. The captain, Arthgwr decided was at least a fighting man. He stood and walked over to the captain, ignoring the rank of the king's representative and offered a drink to the fellow warrior.

Arthgwr was right, the captain stood, saluted Arthgwr with his cup and turning to Steffan ap Dafydd, he saluted the victor. He then took a gulp of ale, walked down to Lucius, and offered him the goblet of ale. Arthgwr was surprised. Not only was the captain a fighting man, he seemed intelligent and fair and most probably he was a very good captain.

Trumpets sounded and horses could be heard approaching, Arthgwr had already been informed that it was the king coming to see the demonstration at the agreed upon time. Edern had the men line up in formation. Cai ordered some camp women to clean up the tent and make sure there were food and drink, cushions and chairs for the honoured guest.

Outside the tent, Gwyn had unfurled the banner of the Pendragon and an honour guard, a number of representatives of each of the tribes stood splendidly at attention.

Arthgwr, Myrddin, Cai, a few aides, and Father Bedwini greeted Ambrosius Aurelianus, his priest, and retinue. Edern and his brother Gwyn were busy readying the men for the demonstration.

All due ceremony and proprieties were observed. The formal nature of this meeting, the incident of the previous night, made the atmosphere tense. It was the king's captain who, after approaching the king with due ceremony, explained the contest between Lucius and Steffan ap Dafydd. The king seemed surprised to see Lucius. He had thought his fate was to have been certain death at the hands of the man he had insulted. Instead, the king saw Arthgwr's man, Steffan ap Dafydd sharing a goblet of ale with his man, Lucius. The king could not help noticing his man's face was badly broken.

He looked again at Arthgwr and nodded. Food and drink were immediately brought to him. As the king was served, he raised his goblet to Arthgwr, who bowed his head in respect and returned the salute with his own goblet of ale.

Myrddin looked happy, Father Bedwini looked puzzled and the king's young priest, Dubricius, looked frightened.

In the meadow below, straw figures had been set up to represent the enemy. Bits of cloth and some old weapons were attached to the figures to give the less imaginative mind an idea of what was happening. Arthgwr's men could be seen two hundred and fifty yards away and they were methodically marching towards the "enemy."

Suddenly, the straw figures all sprouted what looked to be twigs. Instantly, the onlookers realised the "twigs" were arrows. From an angle to the right of the field, just by the tree line, came the charge of Arthgwr's cavalry. They ran right through the straw figures chopping off bits with their long swords. As the riders passed out of the way, another wave of arrows rained down on the straw men, this time from a much closer distance. The cavalry came to a hard stop; wheeled suddenly and attacked, this time from the opposite angle. Again, as the horsemen reached the other side of the field, a rain of arrows flew nearly horizontally at the straw men. The cavalry did not charge again. Instead, a wild group of men came running full tilt from behind the archers, cutting down anything standing with their long iron swords. The archers in the meantime, slung their bows over their shoulders and with their own swords drawn, methodically waded through the "enemy," finishing off any straw men left standing.

The entire operation was over in the blink of an eye. There was no mistaking the timing, the precision and the ferocity of the attack.

The King of the Romano-Britons of the South, Ambrosius Aurelianus looked at the field of hacked straw and saw nothing standing. He then looked upon the men. They were all grouped, horsemen, archers and foot soldiers, each proudly displaying their individual tribal colours. the warriors stood, long hair unfettered and blowing in the slight midday breeze, their blue tattoos and most of all the burning pride that shone in each man's face. The king could not help noticing that there were many Christian soldiers present, he could tell from the black cross sewn onto their grey woollen tunics.

The King looked about, his gaze falling on Arthgwr and Myrddin.

"Gentlemen," he said in Latin, "shall we walk a bit?" Arthgwr stood up as did Myrddin, the king rose regally and turned to admire Cafall.

"What a fine hound you have Arthur," he said using the mispronunciation of the title. The three men walked, the dog followed its master.

Aurelianus was not excessive in his praise for the prowess of Arthgwr's warriors and his strategic execution of the demonstration. He was simple and brief in his remarks, moving quickly to the obvious politics at the core of what Myrddin had already alluded to in his talks with the king.

"Merlinus," said the king using the Latin name for Myrddin, "tells me the Saxons, Jutes and Angles together with some Frisians are gathering to invade our lands. It has been many years since they have tried to be so foolish. I would have thought the slaughter suffered on both sides to be deterrent enough for such recklessness. I understand small raids have already taken place far to the North. You, Arthur, have seen this and engaged in battle with some of these raiders I understand."

The king looked at Arthgwr taking his measure but Arthgwr gave nothing away and evenly looked back at the king not deigning to comment on the obvious facts. Arthgwr was aware of the intelligence of the king and the shrewdness with which he formed his thoughts.

"Merlinus," continued the king, "while not coming right out with it, wants me to understand, that I am too old to lead men into victorious battle against such odds and with so much at stake. No, do not protest Merlinus, I know your thoughts."

Myrddin simply bowed his head and pulled his cloak and hood more tightly around him. It would be hard to tell him from the two Christian priests who also walked with their cowls covering their heads.

"The problem, if I understand the situation and am not yet as senile as our Merlinus would have me so defined, is that our forces here in the South are not adequate to repel an invasion, at least those forces loyal to my banner. No other king," here Aurelianus looked pointedly at Arthgwr, "has the political power to mount a successful challenge against me. If I am to understand the situation, it would not be in the best interest of Briton for there to be such a challenge as that would certainly be seen as a fatal weakness to these Saxons and they would descend upon us like biblical locusts." At these last words the two Christian priests looked up from their cowls.

The men walked on silently. The day was pleasant, the fragrance of the meadow flowers scented the air. Occasionally, Cafall lifted his great head and sniffed, no doubt he could sense the guards that followed these important men, maintaining their safety, at a respectful distance.

"Of course, you Arthur with your army already here, could mount an attack on my meagre forces and claim the kingship for yourself here and now."

Arthgwr stopped in his tracks. The others also stood still. Father Bedwini and Dubricius nearly collided with each other. The king continued.

"However, my forces that lie in and around Caer Melyn would rush in against your flanks, whilst word would be sent that Aurelianus was under attack. Though I suppose, not all my noblemen would come running to my rescue, I fancy enough of them would mount a force that could still be impressive. I am enough of a fighting man to realise there would be no guarantee of who would emerge victorious if such a challenge by you were executed. Again, as a fighting man, I could guarantee there would be many good men lost and too much blood spilled. Then the country would be easily overrun by the Saxons."

Arthgwr opened his mouth to speak but the king cut him off.

"No, Arthur do not protest, I have seen ambition before...."
Now, Arthgwr spoke over the words of the king.

"I do not protest. The idea you suggest is intriguing. Many of my own countrymen have already expressed the very same idea to me. If I were to come at you, Aurelianus, it would not be trumpeted by our friend here," Arthgwr pointed at Myrddin, "there would be no arranged demonstrations of my strategies or any indications of the fighting skills of my army. I would take into account your strengths, weaknesses, and those of your allies, real and pretended, and you would learn of our strategies and fighting prowess the hard way. I have done this many times in the last year and a half and I can guarantee, as a fighting man, that I would be victorious."

There was no shock or tremor of anger nor smell of fear about Aurelianus. Neither in his voice nor his demeanour, did the king exude anything, but regal confidence. His mood was tinged with mild interest, associated with playing *Scaci,* a Roman board game of strategy, similar to the Cymry *Gwyddbwyll* and the Saxon *Skaktafl.*

"You are telling me, there would be no contest and that you are to be the king?" Aurelianus was smiling as he asked Arthgwr.

"You think I have not heard such a boast before or that I should be intimidated by how your men cut down straw. Let me remind you my young Arthur, I have been trained in the Roman fashion, as have all my men. The Romans are the most successful fighting force the world has ever seen. Briton is a Roman province and has been for four hundred years! These islands have been Christian for nearly two hundred years! I myself am a Roman citizen and a devout Christian. I ask again Arthur, who dresses like a Pagan, who thinks himself an ancient tribal war leader, do you think I am to be intimidated by painted men with long hair who cut down straw?"

Myrddin was getting nervous, though it did not show. He had to keep silent and he could not argue on behalf of either man. This was not just a battle of will, a test of dominance. What happened here between these two men would affect the fate of the land.

Myrddin was now at the point where he was powerless to influence the outcome any further than he already had done. He glanced at the two priests and noted they were too stunned by the tone and tenure of the conversation and especially by the brashness of Arthgwr.

"Impressed by long haired men cutting down straw? No, of course not. Why, who would attempt to impress the great High King with such a meagre show? True, to a trained eye, the precision and strategy of the demonstration would signal the potentiality of good planning. But impressed? No! Though, I do note you were not born on this island. You were born in Amorica. And though you may have some Cymry blood in your veins, everything about you reeks of Rome. You speak of "the country", but you know nothing outside of the crumbling ruins of your own Southern *civitas*. You are forgetting, my Roman King, the fact that many of your precious civitas were built on ancient tribal forts! You and your men have no respect for us from the North and consider us barbarians. You pride yourself as Roman citizens, when the Roman civilisation you cling to is nothing more than a feature of your own slavery! Rome is no more! Not the way it once was, lording over the world with an iron fist and looting tribute under the guise of providing for the peace! This is not "the country" as you so quaintly state. This is *my* country! We are all Cymry and this is Cymru our land! This is my country! My men were all born here, they speak the language of their mothers and they breathe the air of their ancestors and work their land as freemen! I give you your due, King Aurelianus. You have fought well in the past. You have earned a reputation as a honourable man, a good warrior, and a reputable leader. You cannot defend my country against what is surely coming! Your failure will cause the extinction of our race. And, as you so correctly pointed out, I cannot, even with my army and the alliances I have forged between the many tribes, defend our land any the better. The only hope for our country is for us to join forces under the terms that Myrddin has laid out and to which I have agreed. Roman and Briton, Christian and Pagan united as one against the onslaught that is to come! The question now is, do you really love this land or is it the power of being a king who fancies himself a Roman, perhaps even a Caesar, that keeps you here?"

There was no mistaking the storm clouds gathering in the king's eyes. He was furious! Before he could speak, Arthgwr left him with one more thought.

"No, don't answer me now. Take Myrddin back to Caer Melyn and listen to his argument. If you agree, as I have, to his conditions and his plan, then send word and I will meet you in your hall with a formal retinue of officers and we will do this thing as honourable men. We will hammer out an agreement we both can live with and one that will not dishonour either us or our men."

The king looked directly at Arthgwr with steely blue eyes, his fury barely under control.

"If I do not agree with this man's plan?" He jerked his thumb towards Myrddin.

"Then," stated Arthgwr evenly, "you will surely determine if your fate can be fulfilled by mere artful words and trickery. I will do what I deem best in order to defend the country that I so love!" Arthgwr turned on his heels and walked back toward the tent and his men.

Only Cafall followed him.

Chapter 30

Arthgwr was tired. It had been a long day, made more so by the fact he had not slept the night before. He had posted guards to make sure of no alternative strategies on the king's part. All was quiet allowing Arthgwr and his men to catch up on some much needed rest.

No word had reached Arthgwr, indicating the king's decision. Myrddin had not been heard from since they had last talked. Arthgwr had rested, even dozed for a while in the early evening, but sleep, real sleep eluded him. That Myrddin had not appeared, worried him. He did not regret speaking his truth to the king of Southern Briton, but wondered if he might have gone too far. Perhaps artful words, even trickery, were better strategies, if they secured the goal at hand. Arthgwr had no patience for such things and truly believed in honesty, forthrightness and the reality of his sharp iron blade.

It was close to midnight when Rhiannon appeared at Arthgwr's tent. Her presence was announced first by Cafall and then by the guard. Arthgwr smiled for the first time in days, at seeing Rhiannon. She was wrapped in a dark blue, almost black woollen cloak, her long shiny black hair hung around her shoulders and bosom, melting into the darkness of her cloak. The contrast of her dark hair and cloak with her marble white skin, made her seem ethereal in the moonlight. She accepted a tankard of ale from Arthgwr. Rhiannon knew he had expected her to appear.

"You have won the day," she said simply, as she lounged on some cushions, her beauty brightening the soldier's sparse tent. Cafall walked over to receive his petting. Arthgwr simply sipped his ale and smiled at her giving no hint of his feelings about her news.

"When I say the day is yours, I mean of course, that the king has agreed to the terms and you will be so informed officially in the morning. Myrddin did his part well," here she smiled and radiance filled the tent.

"Of course, you still have the task of convincing the noblemen, but that should not prove to be too difficult a task," here Rhiannon smiled slyly. "That is to say, with the exception of one, whom you have already met and made of him, a new enemy."

Arthgwr feigned surprise, though it was no great act, for if Aurelianus was in favour of Myrddin's ideas and plans, then Arthgwr could have no clue as to who this new enemy might be.

"Please, leave me in suspense no longer and reveal this new enemy's name to me," smiled Arthgwr, playfully formal. He felt a twinge in his gut, which usually told him there was danger ahead. All warriors had such intuition and he was no exception, but tonight the feeling did little to help him. Arthgwr was very much aware of the beauty of Rhiannon more so now than ever before. He could not help wonder if that was the gut feeling he was experiencing.

What greater danger could there be than a beautiful woman to an already married man, so long and far from his home? He took another sip of ale and tried hard to remember if there was anyone specifically whom he had insulted and who held significant rank with the king. He could not.

"You do remember the person who acted as the king's representative during your friendly contest?" A flicker of recognition registered on Arthgwr's face as Rhiannon continued.

"His name is Llew ap Cynfarch, though here he is called Lot, and he is of noble birth. Rumour has it he is a descendent of Caradoc, whom the Romans called Caractus, the chief of the Catuvellauni tribe. Not a man to have as an enemy."

"Yet," said Arthgwr smoothly, "he backs the king, who for all intents and appearances is a Roman king, and yet he does not vie for the throne himself. Some may conclude that such a man lacks either ambition or the power necessary, to be successful in his challenge," Arthgwr smiled and gulped down more ale.

"I have been told the very same has been said of you, Arthgwr."
Rhiannon was not smiling when she said this. Cafall looked up to her
for she had stopped scratching the beast's ear.

"Lot is considered a king in his own right, at least in his lands.
Though, I daresay he covets the crown of Aurelianus."

"The man I remember as acting as representative for the King
during our little contest was a pompous ass. Now the captain they sent
with him, well now there was a man. He was a warrior and from what
I saw probably a good leader of men. Him, I remember the other was
not really note worthy."

"Ah, yes the captain. His name is Pellinore and he is distrustful of
Lot. If you showed Pellinore favour over Lot, that might explain the
problem he has with you now." Rhiannon was smiling again.

"He is originally from Orkney in the North and most probably
was acquainted with your father. That might be a start for a calm
conversation. Presently, he lives here in the South, in his ancient lands of
the Catuvellauni. Lot's tribal lands border the lands that used to be the
tribal kingdoms of the Trinovantes, the Dobunni, and the Artebates. I
suppose if he wearies of our king, of our cause or of you, then he will
return to the North. It would be good to have him on your side."

"Well," smiled Arthgwr, "I am sure the good king will help sort this
out since he has agreed to the terms of Myrddin's plan."

"Actually, no," smiled Rhiannon, "King Aurelianus has already
left. He needs to consolidate his power in the capital and rally troops
in preparation for a Sacsonaidd attack. This will be the second line of
defence should you be defeated. You are to be informed officially by
Myrddin and the priest Dubricius sometime tomorrow. In the meantime,
Caer Melyn is yours. You have the power of Aurelianus's name and may
call the noblemen to the fort at your leisure. The king wishes you to lead
his men under his banner, though you can fly your own if you wish.
He insists his men stay dressed according to his fashion, including their
hair. He was quite adamant on that point. You have won. You are the
Dux Bellorum of King Aurelianus provided of course you persuade the
nobles you are capable." Rhiannon laughed when she said this. Arthgwr
was stunned and still trying to get over the shock of the news.

Rhiannon laughed at his dour expression and despite himself
Arthgwr smiled. It was pleasant having her here, happy, beautiful and

intelligent to talk with, though part of him knew there was a web that was being spun and he was most probably the fly caught in it.

"Relax, my dear Arthgwr. Myrddin, Pellinore, and the others will send word for the noblemen to gather here at Caer Melyn in a fortnight. That will lend us plenty of time to put our special touch on the place, make our plans and," her she smiled again, "perhaps invite your wife to come for a time."

"Are you serious? Bring Gwenhwyfar here? As if she would leave Caerwyn!" Arthgwr was shocked at the idea and yet the thought of seeing his wife filled him with warmth. Rhiannon noted the modest flush that slightly coloured his face. For a moment she felt alone. It had been a lifetime since she had felt that kind of warmth for another. Her husband's memory was more legend now and it was difficult to separate the man from the myth. Seeing Arthgwr flush at the mere suggestion of him seeing his beloved, caused a flood of memories to sweep over Rhiannon, memories she had not thought of for years... pleasant memories. She turned her head away from Arthgwr and pretended to pay her attention to his huge hound.

"I would not be surprised if Gwenhwyfar would wish to spend sometime with you outside of the village. Caer Melyn is not that bad. By the time she would arrive we could have it looking quite decent indeed!" Rhiannon's smile had returned.

"I will go to Caerwyn myself with the invitation and escort her back here to you."

Arthgwr opened his mouth to speak, but Rhiannon raised her hand.

"No Arthgwr, do not worry. I will speak with Myrddin regarding the preparations and to Edern regarding the security. You concentrate on resting yourself. You look terrible and you cannot be effective if you are not at your peak physically, mentally and spiritually." A swirl of her cloak and she was gone.

Arthgwr stood in the middle of his tent looking at his hound. It was as though he had dreamed Rhiannon's visit. He took a sip of ale and turned to look out the tent's door. He could only glimpse a suggestion of Rhiannon as her cloak and black hair masked her in the night. Arthgwr saw that she was with someone, one of his men. The fire burst with a pop and a piece of wood burped into flame.

In the sudden firelight, Arthgwr saw it was Edern, who so tenderly administered to Rhiannon. Was that a lover's demure smile he saw on her face?

Turning, he looked down at Cafall. For a moment, Arthgwr felt as though his hound was more aware of the world.

It was midmorning when Myrddin and the priests, Bedwini and Dubricius, came to officially inform Arthgwr of the King's decision. Edern's men kept the Druid and the priests waiting while Edern saw to it that Arthgwr was fully prepared and rested. The Druid found Arthgwr to be in excellent spirits and more alert than he felt himself at this moment. He did not understand the knowing smile Arthgwr seemed to have on his face every time he looked at Edern.

Arthgwr took his time in preparing himself. The decision had already been made and as Rhiannon stated, he had won the day; there was no need to hurry; all that needed to be done could be done as he, Arthgwr wished.

Myrddin was wearing white robes with gold thread sewn into intricate designs at the cuffs of his sleeves. Arthgwr could not tell if the thread was actual gold or simply gold-coloured thread, but it was a stunning effect. A golden torc hung around the Druid's neck. Arthgwr was very certain the torc was made from real gold. Myrddin's white robes were tied with a wide leather belt, hanging down from the belt was a small sack, and a curved dagger sheathed in a golden scabbard.

There was a large gathering outside the tent. Edern's men along with Cai had kept the gathering orderly and calm. It was obvious that word had been spread regarding the king's decision and the warriors, the camp followers and the leaders of King Aurelianus's army wanted to see the actual handing over of power. It was equally obvious that Myrddin shared the centre of attention. Dressed as he was in the sacred robes of his order, there could be no mistaking the fact Myrddin was indeed a Druid.

The priests Bedwini and Dubricius looked dull and uninteresting in comparison. Their plain woollen robes and simple rope belts did nothing to enhance their dour expressions. The Christians seemed uncomfortable at least until Dubricius began speaking, in Latin, of course. He gave a short prayer and he and Father Bedwini intoned the words together ending with the phrase, "...*in nomine Patris et filii et spiritus sancti...*"This soothed the many attending Christians. They knelt and moved their hands in front of themselves in the sign of the cross.

There was no denying that this was Myrddin's spectacle. And he was going to make the best of it. Standing tall and addressing the gathering in Cymraeg and Latin, he called them to order in that deep bellowing voice of his that sounded as though it came from inside one's own head.

"I speak on behalf of Ambrosius Aurelianus, King of the Southern Britons and with his full knowledge and authority. What I say here today, are the wishes of King Aurelianus, witnessed by the leaders of his army, and the Church, represented by Father Dubricius and Father Bedwini. As of today, Arthgwr Pendragon has been given the right to lead the king's men under the king's banner and Caer Melyn is now his." Myrddin paused dramatically for effect. His audience was enthralled and they strained to   hear correctly the words of Myrddin.

"This is a temporary assignment and Arthgwr serves at the pleasure of King Aurelianus. Arthgwr may carry his own banner but his authority comes directly from the king and under the auspices of the Royal banner. The cause for this is a simple one. We, as a race, are going to be invaded by Saxons, Frisians, Jutes, and Angles. Ships have already landed in the North and battles have been fought. Arthgwr has to date fought many battles against this foe. Our only chance of survival is to unite as one people, seek out the invaders, and fight them before they over run us! These are the wishes of the king! Arthgwr will call at his pleasure, all the king's noblemen to Caer Melyn. We wait on the pleasure of Arthgwr to command us!"

The speech was melodramatic and Myrddin added to the mood with swirls of his brilliant robes as he waved his arms about. It did not go unnoticed that the Pagans were moved by the Druid's speech. They began dancing and chanting Arthgwr's name when Myrddin had stopped talking. Their long hair, blue dyed skin and intricate tattoos were cause for the Christian's discomfort while the pounding of the Pagan drums added to the chaotic scene.

It was now time for Arthgwr to step forward and take the responsibility that had been handed to him by Myrddin and the two Fathers under the authority of King Ambrosius Aurelianus.

All eyes were on him as he strode from his tent wearing his best battle gear and carrying the sword Caladfwlch loose in his right fist. Arthgwr walked straight up to Myrddin and the two priests. Then he did an extraordinary thing. He knelt at the feet of Father Dubricius and waited for his blessing. Dubricius was caught unawares and for a moment stood stupidly staring at the back of the kneeling warrior's head. His senses finally returned to him allowing the bestowal of the blessing. This was well received amongst the many Christians.

Arthgwr rose and raised his sword arm and all the Pagans saw the tribal tattoos on his sinewy forearms as sunlight glinted on the blade of the famous Caladfwlch. The Christians of Aurelianus's army saw all of this as well and were left baffled by this man who seemed to walk between two worlds, the very old and the new. One of the Pagan warriors yelled and began banging his sword against his shield. It was repeated by another and another, the din rising, a sound that bound warriors to the common cause.

"I have come here to Caer Melyn, to King Ambrosius Aurelianus out of love. It's true, I have known war all my life, but it is love that bends me to her will now. Love for my people, love for my country, love for our traditions and hope, for a future where our children can live in peace. It is from such love, that I pledge my life to defending our island. It is from humility that I ask for your support in defence of our country. Whether Roman, Briton, Christian, or Pagan we need to stand as one. No matter if you are a Silurian, Ordovician, or Votadinian, this land is ours and we must put aside our squabbles and protect our people from the coming onslaught! Let us unite for the benefit of our people and for our land!"

Arthgwr thrust the sword Caladfwlch into the air for effect. The men, women, and warriors that had been listening intently were moved by his words. The support of the priests, the introduction by Myrddin, whom they knew as Merlinus, and the sight of the famous sword Caladfwlch, created a spectacle that swept them up with emotion.

Hearing the crowd roar its approval Arthgwr knew that he had won their hearts. He also knew that convincing the noblemen would not be so easy as this. Arthgwr walked over to Myrddin.

"We will need to talk very soon..."

Myrddin did not allow him to complete the sentence. Instead, he waved in an offhanded manner and curtly dismissed the two priests. Grabbing Arthgwr by the arm, he led him back inside the tent.

"Arthgwr, listen to me, this is only the beginning! It will not be so easy to convince the noblemen especially now that you have made an enemy of Lot! You will need all your wits about you, my boy, to convince them once Lot has had his say! Not to worry, Arthgwr. For now the most important thing you can do is to rest. I think Rhiannon's idea of bringing Gwenhwyfar here is an excellent one. Arthgwr, you have time, now that Aurelianus has given you Caer Melyn, his banner, and his authority, there is nothing for you to do at this point. Just rest, I will handle getting your wife here. Your man Edern will handle looking to her safety. Arthgwr, allow some of my men to act as her personal teulu if you will. It is her right as an ancestor of the Mother Goddess Dôn!"

Arthgwr was still stunned by the idea of seeing his wife after being apart for so long. That she would agree to leave Caerwyn and travel to Caer Melyn seemed an impossible dream to him. Filled with hope that he would see his Gwenhwyfar soon, Arthgwr numbly nodded his assent. Myrddin was about to leap into action, but paused and turned toward the still troubled Arthgwr.

"Oh don't you worry, she will agree to come here without hesitation. You have nothing to fear on that point!" Off he went, organising work parties, even as he rode back up to Caer Melyn.

A small contingent of servants and a few of Aurelianus's men, assisted Arthgwr and his council in moving their meagre belongings into the fort. Men and women scurried about in frenetic activity for the rest of the day. The actual move would take place at daybreak. It was handled well by Cai, Gwyn, and Edern. Rhiannon and Myrddin were preparing for the trip to Caerwyn, which would also begin in the morning. Myrddin's men were placed under the command of Rhiannon, while Edern had a small band of his own chosen men and the added responsibility of being accountable for the safe arrival of Gwenhwyfar.

Arthgwr, for the first time in over a year, found himself with little to do. Myrddin, Dubricius, and Father Bedwini had instructed selected warriors and representatives of Aurelianus, on what to say to the noblemen. There was a protocol about inviting them to Caer Melyn that needed to be followed. It was important the nobles hear for themselves, this matter of urgent business.

The men were under the command of Cai, who had ordered them into the field to contact the noblemen loyal to Aurelianus. The assumption was that the nobles would be gathering in Caer Melyn within three days. This left Arthgwr with the luxury to sleep, eat, drink, and rest his weary bones. Just the sleep alone was like a tonic to his body and mind. He felt refreshed and stronger than ever.

The perimeter walls of Caer Melyn were being overhauled by a group of men under the command of Gwyn. The brothers had wanted higher walls for better protection. The extra height and width would increase the security and integrity of the fort. The men and women of Arthgwr's army followers, merged with the folk living around the fort, and together they worked to clean and repair fences, dwellings, clear the pathways between out buildings, and put a new face to Ambrosius Aurelianus's Caer Melyn.

Walking through the Great Hall, Arthgwr was startled by the sudden appearance of Myrddin. The old one's eyes twinkled and he was a bundle of energy, causing Arthgwr to wonder about the age of the Druid. The hall had been thoroughly cleaned and even the wooden walls had been freshly white washed giving the inside a roomier appearance.

"What do you think," asked Myrddin, "is there something else that may be done here that would put your own particular stamp on the proceedings with the nobles?"

Arthgwr looked about and noted the long table and the head table that formed the suggestion of the cross. The configuration implied whoever was seated at the head of the table, as someone of supreme importance. It was what he had thought when he had first been ushered in so many days ago.

"I think we are going to be dealing with the pride of many ambitious men, all of whom will be vying for prominence in the physical absence of the king. That will be a distraction and will make it difficult for me to have my words heard, much less my argument agreed upon." Arthgwr walked around the hall with a look of seriousness on his face.

"Any ideas pop into mind as how to deal with such a problem?" asked Myrddin. Arthgwr had the distinct impression Myrddin was mocking him and not for the first time, did he feel his ire rise. He resisted the bait and instead put his mind and energy into conjuring a solution for the predicament. Arthgwr walked on without answering.

"The one thing I have been talking to the people about, is the importance for us to unite as one in the face of this danger. I truly believe that. I know you have an ulterior motive and will work your own agenda. But for anything to work, we will need an alliance between tribal leaders. They have already entered into allegiance with Aurelianus. The king has given me his banner and his authority. I need to find a way to keep and exercise it. The nobles do not know me. Though I have made allies of the men here in Caer Melyn, it will not be enough to carry the day, once the nobles meet. I need to flaunt the confidence Aurelianus has in me and yet not tip the balance so much as to cause an open challenge to my position." Arthgwr continued walking around the hall oblivious to the merriment in Myrddin's eyes.

"When they march into this hall they will be seated and I will be at the head of the table in a position of power. This will be a challenge to the most ambitious of them and an invitation to challenge the legitimacy of my position. Once that happens, it will be impossible for me to convince them, my position is the right one. I need to circumvent any suggestion of challenge without seeming to do so." Arthgwr turned and looked at Myrddin as though he were about to say something. He did not and simply kept walking his brow furrowed with the pretence of paying apt attention.

"Most of these nobles will be Romanised; they will see every nuance as a potential invitation to snatch political power. What of their original blood? What of their own tribal heritages? Just by appearing in this hall, they acknowledge my power and position granted me by their king. Need I rub their noses in it? It is their allegiance I need here not their subservience! They will need to command their own troops. It is co-operation, not coercion, I seek at this point. What if...?" Arthgwr was suddenly quiet but his face betrayed the fact his mind was racing and had hit on an idea, perhaps even a solution.

"What if we harkened back to our past, as we have done many times within our own army? What if we resurrect one of our ancient customs?" Myrddin was smiling, as Arthgwr continued heatedly with his outrageous idea.

"Let us rid our selves of the tables! Instead, let us have a large circle, just as our tribal ancestors did in ancient times. We will all sit around a large wooden, circular table, that way no one will be so obviously in power. It will not by itself, raise the issue of challenge, though it will be cause for some confusion. While the nobles are trying to understand the significance of the table as they are seated around it, I will be in position to speak and make my words heard! The idea of alliance will be planted in their minds because I am not seated in an obvious position of power over them. That alone will make my position more palatable, since they will not need to rescind their allegiance to Aurelianus nor swear fealty to me. The nobles need only agree to the king's cause, which is my cause!"

Myrddin smiled. Arthgwr looked at the old Druid and immediately had the impression that this most outrageous idea was not entirely original with him. The thought momentarily dampened his enthusiasm. The twinkle in Myrddin's eye was infectious and Arthgwr began laughing, despite himself. The two of them walked around the hall and finding a small doorway and corridor that lead to the kitchens, they searched out a meal together.

While some craftsmen were tasked with building a large round table from two long tables, Arthgwr strolled around Caer Melyn with his hound Cafall. Edern had assigned a few men to watch over his leader and they were never too far behind him. Cafall nosed his way along, sniffing and snorting. The air was ripe with roasting meats, cheeses, and baked bread. Arthgwr was not hungry, he had eaten amply with Myrddin only an hour ago. Work was progressing well on the third day and Caer Melyn was ready to receive the important guests. Arthgwr wondered where his wife was and what she was doing at this moment.

In less than two weeks, she would be again by his side. He longed to hear news of his children. It had already been decided that his son, Cynglas, would stay in the role of warrior apprentice to Elidir. Arthgwr's daughter, of course, was obliged to stay on at Caerwyn to protect the unbroken maternal ancestral line. Proper supervision was in place. Arthgwr and Gwenhwyfar had not forgotten that their daughter was betrothed to Elidir. For a moment Arthgwr allowed himself to become melancholy. He missed seeing his children, their bright faces, their boundless energy and their innocence. Arthgwr pledged he would compete his task to the best of his ability and in a timely fashion so he may be reunited with his family.

Father Bedwini nearly ran into Arthgwr he was so caught up in his thoughts. It had taken one of Arthgwr's men and a low growl from Cafall before the priest looked up and avoided further embarrassment.

"Excuse me...I was not paying attention..." mumbled Father Bedwini. He eyed Arthgwr suspiciously, but also kept an eye on the hound Cafall.

"Don't mention it; where are you going, may I ask, in such haste? Nothing is wrong is there?" Arthgwr was being most polite; he had not spoken directly to the priest for sometime.

"No, Arthgwr nothing is wrong. All is going according to your wishes. Caer Melyn will look very different indeed by nightfall. The people have been working hard." The priest relaxed and became more himself.

"And yourself, Arthgwr, how goes it with you? I must say you look very refreshed and vibrant, the rest has done you well I think."

"Thank you very much, Father. I do feel well rested." Arthgwr even smiled at the priest.

"Is it true that the Lady Gwenhwyfar will be coming to stay here at Caer Melyn?" The question was asked innocently enough, but it irritated Arthgwr to have the priest mention the name of his wife. He paused and took a breath before answering. He did not wish to lose his peace this day over the irritation of a priest.

"Why yes, it is true," Arthgwr said openly, "and I can say with honesty, I miss her a great deal. My children are also foremost on my mind today. It has been a long time since last I saw them."

"True, Arthgwr, true, and there is the wedding to think about after your campaign ends." The priest did not intend to let Arthgwr shy away from his promise of a chapel. Ground had been broken, it was true, but it could just as easily be filled in again. Even worse, it could become a grave for a certain priest rather than a chapel for the faithful. Father Bedwini shivered.

"Yes, Father, it is true and I was just thinking of that myself," the tone of Arthgwr's words was enough for the priest to detect the melancholy hidden within the man.

"Arthgwr, life waits not one moment for man. Time marches on. Children grow into men and women and beget their own offspring. Warrior's, if they are not killed in battle, see their bodies lose to the enemy of time and realise the loss of that battle is inevitable. You cannot stop this process Arthgwr. Your children are growing and in so doing, they are becoming their own masters. They are now living their own lives. Is that not how you would have it? You begat them, brought them into the world, taught and cherished them and ultimately you need to let them go out into the world."

Arthgwr stopped walking and looked at the priest directly. He did not like the priest talking to him about his children. What could this priest possibly have to say about family life? He was sure the Father Bedwini had bedded women, but he was just as sure he had no family and therefore no knowledge of what family life entailed. Yet, he could see the earnestness in the man's eyes and realised he was speaking from the heart. Moreover, Arthgwr realised that what the priest said was true.

"Sometimes, Father, you surprise me. You are not as dim witted as you appear." For a moment, there was silence and then the priest burst into laughter. Arthgwr enjoyed the moment laughing with the priest even his men were chuckling. He bade the priest well and continued on his rounds.

Chapter 31

The Great Hall was filled to capacity. As had been expected, the configuration of the new table confused the nobles. Some thought it a design of the devil and were not easily assuaged, when it was pointed out to them, that the ancient tribes often sat in a circular fashion. The nobles were content that Arthgwr was not sitting at the head of a table in a position of power. His position did not outwardly threaten any noble present. It could not be said they were content. The new configuration meant they could not challenge for the coveted spot at the table's head. The circular table, the Round Table as they called it, served to address all the nobles and Arthgwr as equal in that regard.

It had taken some coaxing from Myrddin, but finally everyone was seated. There were fifteen nobles present along with five representatives of nobles unable to attend personally, for one reason or another. It was a good showing and Myrddin was well pleased. Food and drink were being served and helpers and attendants were present in the hall, some standing directly behind their lieges.

Myrddin had called the group to order and had made introductions with a brief explanation of what was expected of them by their King Ambrosius Aurelianus. The two priests, Father Dubricius and Father Bedwini recited a solemn Christian prayer for the benefit of the Christian majority already seated and attentive. The torches burned brightly in their sconces. It had been decided to hold the gathering at nightfall, it would be that much cooler in the crowded hall. The nobles and their attendants were calm, now the initial shock of the Round Table was over. The guests were plied with food and drink. The happy gathering

431

was now ready to listen intently to the new *dux Bellorum,* as some had referred to Arthgwr.

"My Lords," began Arthgwr solemnly, "in coming here to Caer Melyn this eve, you have complied with your king's wishes, and I respect and honour you for that. The king remains the king, and I his humble servant, am charged with leading our men as an allied force into the field against the Sacsonaidd horde." Myrddin and Father Bedwini were taking turns translating Arthgwr's words from Cymraeg to Latin.

"Your own eyes," Arthgwr indicated to the table, "show you I have no desire to challenge the established authority of King Aurelianus, nor any one of his trusted nobles gathered so grandly around this table here tonight. I hope it is understood by all, that I seek to illicit from this revered company, no challenge to the authority vested in me by the king."

"Are we to understand," asked Lot, a contemptuous sneer on his face, "that you will surrender your position once the battle is won?"

Arthgwr had anticipated this question. He had also predicted who would ask it. On this point, Arthgwr knew he needed to be clear.

"It is what King Aurelianus wishes and what we agreed. Yes, I will surrender my post once the battle has been waged. Further, the king himself has stated my position is only temporary and that I serve at his pleasure. I am here, my lord Lot, for a single purpose; unite the tribes, the people and fight the Sacsonaidds as one! This we must do together if we hope to have any degree of success!"

Lot would not be put off and rose to make his point.

"And then you will relinquish all claim to the throne?'

Arthgwr stood to answer and all eyes turned to him. Those of Caerwyn, those who knew Arthgwr, instantly recognised he was angered by the prodding given him by King Lot of Orkney. They were anxious and the tension could be felt rippling throughout the great hall.

"You may be at your ease, Llew ap Cynfarch," said Arthgwr using Lot's Cymraeg name, "for challenging me will not get you any closer to your prize. Ambrosius Aurelianus is the one you need to challenge, but I suggest you do so with sword in hand. I might add it will not be an easy task for you to undertake. If I am any judge of character, there are many here who are loyal to the Ambrosius Aurelianus."

This response brought much banging on the table and murmurings of approval. It was clear that King Aurelianus was beloved and still held sway over the majority. Tension in the hall mounted. There were many curses shouted out and the rattling of swords in their scabbards added to the chaos. Captain Pellinore jumped up and with sword in hand, declared for Aurelianus and Arthgwr. The brash captain now stood in open challenge to Lot. Others followed and it looked as though the hall was to be the first battleground and that Arthgwr had already lost his mission of unity.

Jumping to his feet and unsheathing Caladfwlch, Arthgwr yelled for silence. With help from his men, he was able to restore quiet to the great hall. Arthgwr held the ancient blade high. The firelight glinted off the iron blade of the famous sword, casting an eerie yellow glow over the gathered nobles. It caught the eye of the men in the hall and shamed them into silence.

"It is the right of King Lot of Orkney to ask his questions!" Arthgwr yelled. "If taking the throne is his desire then he has the right to say so. If he is not challenging the king, then what better way to demonstrate his fealty to him than to throw in with us? He need not prostrate himself in submission to my authority. All that is required of him is that he acknowledges the wise decision of his king by following the king's wish. And it is the king's wish, that he help me work this thing for the good of all Britons! The same can be said for every noble in the hall!"

The murmuring of voices was loud, but it was obvious that the words Arthgwr spoke had hit their mark. Pellinore looked surprised, though it was Lot who appeared the most baffled. He had nowhere to turn, anything short of supporting Arthgwr would be seen by the others as treason. How could he go against the king's wishes and not be seen as vying for the throne for his own gain? Arthgwr was wagering Lot was not yet prepared to do that.

Myrddin looked over at Arthgwr, his eyes betrayed his apprehension. The Druid knew all too well that if King Lot of Orkney pressed his case and gained support from the others, it would mean the end of unity. Lot did not have to go against the king to cause this entire undoing. He only needed to create doubt in the nobles. It was possible Lot could persuade the nobles to his side simply by deflecting comments about his own ambition and pointing out, that Arthgwr held all power. If his argument was clever enough, he could convince the other nobles that Arthgwr had usurped the king's power already. This would be catastrophic for Myrddin's cause and he was powerless to stop it. Arthgwr's wager took them to the brink. If Lot were prepared to vie for the throne, then now would be the time to execute his plan. That would spell the end of Arthgwr and Myrddin's plans.

Fortunately for the plans of Myrddin and Arthgwr, King Lot of Orkney was master of a divided house. With his origins in the North, he was not as powerful as those present, who were born in the South. Lot maintained a home, fort, and garrisons in both the North and the South, not unless he could consolidate his wealth and men could he openly consider the throne of southern Briton. While Arthgwr was also born in the North, he had the decided advantage of having a large army already with him.

"Well, as I am not required to supplicate myself to Arthgwr's authority per se," Lot was smiling, but he was far from being amused. "I can only honour my pledge of fealty to King Aurelianus and do as he wishes me to do!"

Arthgwr had won. His gamble had paid off and he had his first victory. Tomorrow the hard work of getting this rabble of men to fight as a cohesive army under one command would begin. Arthgwr and his men had their work cut out for them. Arthgwr's mind was not on the task ahead. He was consumed with the event that would unfold two weeks hence, when his beloved would arrive.

The dying light of the late afternoon sun caused her thick yellow hair to look like molten gold cascading over the bodice of her pure white woollen dress. She did not walk so much as she appeared to float just above the courtyard of Caer Melyn. If he did not know better, Arthgwr would have thought her an apparition, a wraith from the Otherworld. She was no phantom. She was Gwenhwyfar, his wife. The news of her arrival had reached him as he was training the troops in the field. He had ridden his horse hard for the three-hour journey to be at her side. She stood more beautiful than he remembered, more ethereal and graceful than he had recalled.

He leapt from his mount and ran across the yard, crashing into her with unbounded passion. All activity in the fort stopped as men and women watched the embrace with a mixture of embarrassment, empathy, and envy. A cheer rose up, as Arthgwr waved to the impromptu gathering. And with Gwenhwyfar taking his arm, he walked as regally as he could manage toward his house.

Gwenhwyfar looked at her husband and noted that at least he looked rested. She was surprised to see how angular his features had become and saw there was no fat whatsoever on his taut muscular body. The smile on his face was a welcome sight. It assured her that he was still who he was when she had first met him so long ago. She was happy that he had not forgotten his children. Indeed, the first hours of their meeting were occupied with her explaining in detail all that Cynglas and Gwyneth had been doing in his absence. He seemed to Gwenhwyfar, to be well pleased with the progress of his children, though perhaps a bit melancholy that he had missed such a large part of their growing up. Gwenhwyfar had told him all the news of Caerwyn. After that, the two of them spent their time reacquainting themselves with each other's bodies.

"When Rhiannon suggested that we had time and that I should send for you, I thought it impossible. I did not think you would ever leave your ancestral home of Caerwyn." Arthgwr was murmuring into his wife's ear, as they lay sprawled on the big bed in the chamber set aside for the king's guests. It was dark now and the torches provided the only light.

"Well, cariad," sighed Gwenhwyfar, "apart from my desire to see you, the decision was not a hard one to make. Times are changing even in Caerwyn. I fear the new religion has all but taken over our land. Fewer and fewer of our people follow the old ways now and I find my position and power waning. It was happening all the time, although somehow in Caerwyn, we had managed to slow time. In the last year, with all that has been going on, it seems time has found us out. Soon, our daughter will marry Elidir in the chapel built by our villagers. It will be a Christian wedding and my own daughter will convert to the new faith. It will be the end of my ancestral line."

The wetness of her tears glistened on her cheek and Gwenhwyfar laid her head against the chest of her husband. He gently caressed her head and uttered all the cooing sounds that a man makes to a frightened horse, a woman murmurs to an injured child, and a lover to his sorrowful beloved. Arthgwr tried to say words that might cheer his wife, but none would leave his lips. He held her tightly. It was all he could do.

Cafall issued a low growl a sure sign that someone was nearby. There came a loud knock on the bedchamber door but before it could be answered, the door burst open. In strode Myrddin, all merriment and mirth, with two jugs of ale, and a tray of food precariously balanced in his seemingly unsteady hands.

"I thought I would find you two here! You know it is well past supper and rumours of a ribald nature are spreading like wild fire around Caer Melyn. Here, Arthgwr, help me with these things before I drop the lot. Now, let me get a good look at the daughter of Bevan, the ancestral heir of Caerwyn, whose grand mother I had the pleasure of knowing so long ago!" He made his way unhesitatingly to Gwenhwyfar and pulled her into his arms. Arthgwr stood forgotten as the two, Myrddin and Gwenhwyfar, hugged and laughed like long lost siblings. The energy that filled the room and circled around the two of them was palpable. After a long pause, Arthgwr reminded his wife and the Druid, of his presence.

"Come, Arthgwr, come, do not stand on ceremony on my account," said Myrddin humorously magnanimous, waving Arthgwr closer with his arms, laughing all the while.

"Now correct me if I am wrong, but you were just thinking how different the world is these days and how you cannot find your place within the new order."

Gwenhwyfar smiled despite her tear stained cheeks.

"Was I as melodramatic as all that?" she asked demurely and she stood holding Myrddin's hands in her own as she looked deeply into his enigmatic blue eyes.

"Not at all my dear, not at all," cried the Druid before he added, "well, just a bit over the top perhaps. Nothing that would embarrass the ancient Greeks though, not at all!" Myrddin accepted a tankard of ale from Arthgwr. Arthgwr managed to balance the tray of foodstuffs elegantly, as he turned, so his wife could accept a drink and some food. Finally, he placed the tray down and allowed himself a tankard of ale, which he drank down in the blink of an eye.

"You must admit the times are changing, Myrddin. Gwenhwyfar has pointed out, our own daughter will be married as a Christian. You told me yourself that our mission is in part to redress the balance that once held in our sway. Now the new religion is taking over completely." Arthgwr belched uncharacteristically and looked for pardon from his company.

"Now Arthgwr, Gwenhwyfar, there is no use lamenting the inevitable. It is a waste of your energy and talent to do so! Don't you see? The whole idea of our plan is that we will do what we can in the face of the inevitable. We cannot control all things. We have no power to change what is about to happen. Arthgwr, have you not listened to my stories? You know what we are facing. Surely the two of you must realise that the more things change the more they stay the same. Look at me! I am a Druid. Many of our people have thought us all dead for decades. Yet, here I am advising a king and if I may boast, influencing him to do exactly as I want!" Myrddin giggled like a young girl, it was incongruous to his wrinkled face, grey hair, and beard and not at all becoming.

"And you Arthgwr, Owain Ddantgwyn, look at you! A son of a chieftain pushed off to a small village where you rose to power on your own merit. Now you command an army that is the biggest in all Briton! You have a king's power and are poised to thwart a great enemy. With you are all the tribes of the island! Some would say it is a great climb you have enjoyed, but you and I both know it is nothing of the sort. It is exactly what you should be doing, at exactly the precise time for you to do it! Nothing has changed.

"Daughter, you leave your ancestral home, your lineage and for that you lament. Yet, here you are in Caer Melyn, the wife of Arthgwr and some would have you as his queen! Queen of all Briton! Is not the island a gift from the Goddess to us all? Nothing has changed! Oh, I know what you will say. The New Religion is replacing our old one. The people now worship one God and have forsaken all the gods and goddesses of their heritage.

"Have they now indeed? I see they worship a statue of a mother and child and hear the pious give thanks to many different saints. Is that any different from worshipping the Mother Goddess or giving thanks to the God of the Storm, the God of the Forest, the God of Light? I think not! Nothing has changed! Listen my children; the oncoming war with the Sacsonaidd will only serve to seal our place in the hearts of our people. Stories will be told of the great battle. Heroes will be forged in the telling. Our people live through their stories, their legends, and myths. It is the very essence of who we are as a people. No matter what happens, the stories will be born and they will live on. In living on, they will maintain what is essential in us as who we are; we will never die! Do you not see? If we win, we win; but if we lose, we still win, which means we have already won and cannot lose! Nothing has changed!" Myrddin sat down with a satisfied look on his face.

Gwenhwyfar looked thoughtful, she was trying to take in all of what Myrddin was telling them. She had long known that destiny had plans for her and her husband. She never could see clearly, the meaning or scope of the plan and had only glimpsed bits when Arthgwr had told her of Myrddin. Now, she saw and was held in awe, at the breadth of Myrddin's intellect and power. She realised her intuition about how much her friend, Rhiannon, had known about all of this, was correct. Gwenhwyfar her friend had known for a long time; a peace descended upon her, a deep contentment surrounded and embraced her and she could not help, but smile broadly to herself.

Myrddin instantly knew that Gwenhwyfar had finally understood. He was glad he had suggested to Rhiannon, that Arthgwr's his wife should visit Caer Melyn. Myrddin knew that Arthgwr would never completely understand the plan. He knew that would not matter, as long as Gwenhwyfar saw the wisdom in it's undertaking. Myrddin looked upon Arthgwr, he saw nothing but confusion in his eyes. They were on the eve of carrying through with the most ambitious plot since Caesar had attempted to conquer Briton and still Arthgwr did not wholly understand. It was not that Myrddin thought Arthgwr dim-witted, not at all. He was an excellent leader of men, the best bar none. Only Arthgwr Pendragon, the Bear Man of the North, and Iron War Leader, once known as Owain Ddantgwyn, could presume to attempt the task ahead. It took a certain kind of bravery, a certain kind of dedication and loyalty, to do someone's bidding even though you did not completely understand the details.

Arthgwr may not understand the nuances of the plan, but he most certainly had an appreciation of the consequences. His closely held ideal of unity was key to the success of Myrddin's plan, even if the battle was lost. The people would remember they had been inspired to unite as one in the face of overwhelming odds.

That elixir would intoxicate a generation and last an eternity, despite the winds of change sweeping the land. It was what Myrddin counted upon; without such a past, there could be no future, even in essence, for their race.

"Come now let us go down to the hall and be seen by the people. I am sure there is food, drink, music, and dance there to entertain us! We would not wish to disappoint Rhiannon and Edern and the men."

The Great Hall was full and lively. The Round Table, as it had become known, was full with trays of food and drink. Seated around the table were Arthgwr's best men, Myrddin's warriors and officers of the king's army. There was much animated talking and good-natured fun amongst the men. This was a good sign that they were coming together as a single fighting force. A number of hounds wandered about scavenging for hand outs; they scattered when Cafall appeared making his rounds.

A cheer went up, when Arthgwr and his wife Gwenhwyfar entered the hall with Myrddin. Edern entered the hall from the opposite door and with him was Rhiannon. Both of them beamed enormous smiles at seeing Arthgwr happy with his wife. Soon, Arthgwr was seated and plied with drink, while Edern sat at his side, more relaxed than Arthgwr had ever remembered seeing him. Rhiannon closeted herself away with Myrddin and Gwenhwyfar. The three of them talked and ate amid much laughter. Edern leaned forward to speak with Arthgwr.

"Arthgwr, I wanted to tell you how well your son Cynglas is doing. He, Elidir, and Anwas Adeinoig, have Caerwyn well in hand. Cynglas has built fences, palisades and trenches, for defence and there are many patrols. I dare say Arthgwr, Cynglas and Elidir have made Caerwyn safe. Anwas has done a marvellous job on logistics. There are housed inside its protective walls, a host of people and many of them can fight. As I say, your son has done a marvellous job and so has your future son-in-law."

Arthgwr looked up sharply at that last remark. Seeing nothing but pride in Edern's face, he decided to take the comment at face value. It was a compliment from an expert warrior assessing a defensive structure of importance. Arthgwr was sensitive about the impending wedding of his daughter, Gwyneth, to his late friend's son, Elidir. Any father would be anxious for his daughter's happiness. Arthgwr was slowly warming to the inevitable. He had nothing but respect for Elidir. He knew if he had to choose someone for his daughter to marry, he could do no better than Elidir. Arthgwr smiled to himself. Gwyneth had chosen her own husband and with no help from him. Perhaps that was why it was taking time for him to warm to the idea of her marriage. It warmed his heart to hear that his son was doing well and living up to his responsibilities. Arthgwr missed his children and regretted he could not have watched them grow into their roles as the future of Caerwyn. Destiny it seemed had other plans and he had other duties.

There came a mumbling of voices and Arthgwr looked up to see King Lot of Orkney and his retinue enter the hall. So far, in the last two weeks of intensive training, there had been no trouble with either Lot or his men. Not since Lot had voiced his allegiance to the king and thrown in with Arthgwr's plan. Lot and his men were working hard and fitted well in the company of the fighting men to whom they were assigned. Arthgwr, however, remained wary of Lot. He knew that if Lot managed to turn just one other noble to his side, then he would have enough power to challenge the position vested in him by King Aurelianus. Lot would have to be creative in his argument and frame Arthgwr as someone who was only interested in stealing the throne from the king of the southern Britons. That would be a hard charge to make, now Arthgwr's speech had won the nobles to his position. The fact remained, Aurelianus had thrown his support to him, Arthgwr Pendragon of Caerwyn. Arthgwr figured Lot to be a shrewd man, capable of just such an act, despite his apparent allegiance to Aurelianus.

Lot seated himself across from Arthgwr, while his men took up seats on either side of their leader. Though Lot's men were closer in appearance to Arthgwr's men, than to the men in Aurelianus's army, they were all Christian. Lot did not have much liking for Myrddin because of this. The difference in religious beliefs rankled him and Lot's mood was most definitely black, whenever he spied the Druid. Seeing Myrddin laughing and talking with Rhiannon and Gwenhwyfar, evoked Lot's distaste for all things he considered as un-Christian.

"Merlinus," Lot called out in Latin, "could you not make yourself useful and conjure up some wine?" This caused his men to snicker in amusement.

Myrddin smiled enigmatically.

"Ah, my Lord Lot, alas I cannot. But I daresay, I have no need of conjuring up a drunkard, for one appears already in the hall."

Lot's humour left him immediately and jumped to his feet.

"You forget yourself Merlinus," snarled Lot," I am your better and as such you will treat me with respect!"

"My better? I think not! As for respect, well, that must be earned, it cannot be commanded not even by a king. You forget yourself, my dear Lot. I am Myrddin, the Advisor and Special Counsel to King Ambrosius Aurelianus, in whose hall you are now demanding wine. I notice your are not so free with your tongue when the king is present!" Myrddin had stood up and pulled himself to his full height. In the torch light, Myrddin's visage became intimidating to behold.

"Is that so? Why then are you cloistered away with Pagan women folk and not sitting with real men, Christian men?"

The hall went quiet. All present knew the two women Myrddin was speaking with were Rhiannon, protégé of Myrddin and Hero of Caerwyn, and Gwenhwyfar, the wife of Arthgwr Pendragon, the Ancestral Heir to Caerwyn, and descendant of the Mother Goddess.

It was too late.

Edern had already jumped the table and held a naked blade at Lot's throat before his men could make any protective move. Arthgwr had no way in which to prevent Edern from slitting Lot's throat. Myrddin's honeyed voice somehow stopped tragedy from occurring.

The Druid's voice was not loud, at least not to those who were present, but to Edern, the voice of Myrddin stopped him in his tracks. Only a tiny trickle of blood appeared on Lot's throat where Edern's blade had been poised for the kill. Myrddin continued speaking, entreating Edern to sheath his blade and return to his seat. Myrddin's pleading in honeyed voice, magically filled Edern's head to the exclusion of all other sound, and its cadence persuaded the warrior to drop his hand and with it the deadly knife.

Arthgwr silently signalled Gwyn to retrieve his brother. Gwyn slowly and quietly moved to Edern's side and gently, ever so gently, lowered his brother's knife arm. Calmly, Gwyn led his brother back to his seat.

Arthgwr stood up.

"Well, I am sure we all agree that was exciting! Now, Lord Lot, allow me to introduce you to my wife and Ancestral Heir to Caerwyn, the Lady Gwenhwyfar. By her side sits, the Hero of Caerwyn, Myrddin's protégé and my Special Counsel, the Lady Rhiannon. I am sure Lord Lot meant no offence, and in that event, no offence has been taken. Of course, if I am mistaken, I am sure we can continue our discussion."

Arthgwr was glaring at Lot. There was no misunderstanding his fury or the veiled threat behind his words.

"As I was saying, if I am mistaken, I am sure we can continue the conversation outside or tomorrow perhaps, on the field?"

Lot was white, whether with anger or fear, was undetermined. He managed to gather his wits and with a curt nod of his head in the general direction of Arthgwr, he answered.

"No offence intended nor taken." He turned to nod his head to Gwenhwyfar and Rhiannon. He then swirled his cloak around himself and arrogantly stomped out of the hall.

Everyone began talking at once and many were casting glances at Edern who remained seated, his eyes glazed like he had been drinking ale all day. Myrddin went to him and kept talking in a low voice to the warrior. Rhiannon also hurriedly attended to him, whispering into Edern's ear and caressing his face, a fact quickly noted by Arthgwr. Gwenhwyfar returned to her husband's side. She did not look shaken or upset, like many in the hall.

"You shall have to keep a sharp eye on that one," whispered Gwenhwyfar.

Chapter 32

The training in the last five weeks had gone very well. Cai and Gwyn were especially pleased. Edern was more reserved. He had not been able to let go of what Lot had said in the hall. Edern believed Lot should be killed immediately for what he considered to be an insult, not only to Arthgwr, to the men of Caerwyn, and to Myrddin, but to the Lady Gwenhwyfar, and of course, the Lady Rhiannon. Edern could not understand what had stayed his hand that night. Clearly, he had the man at his mercy, but something prevented him from cutting Lot's throat and it was not his sense of morality. He could barely remember the night; it was all vague and foggy. That he did not kill Lot was certain, but the why of it was something he could not figure out. Rhiannon and Myrddin had talked to him at length after the incident explaining the politics of the situation and why he should not kill Lot.

Arthgwr issued strict orders that Lot and his men should not be touched. None of these things explained why he had not killed Lot, when he had his knife pressed to Lot's throat, poised to despatch him on the spot. Myrddin tried explaining to him about the night, but the wily Druid never quite answered Edern's question directly. Nor did Rhiannon, though it was abundantly clear to Edern that they both knew something they were not sharing with him.

It was late afternoon. The dying orb of the day cast a golden light, tinged with streaks of faded red that wended its way through the trees. Purple shadows moved throughout Caer Melyn and the smell of cooking teased the villagers.

Arthgwr was in conference with the nobles and his own advisors. Myrddin had some news regarding the Sacsonaidd advance.

The news from Myrddin meant the army under Arthgwr's leadership would need to mobilise at once. The nobles were passing orders to their advisors and captains that their men should be ready to move out at Arthgwr's command. Caer Melyn was bustling with activity as warriors hurried to gather their war gear.

"The information that comes to me suggests that King Aelle of the South Sacsonaidds has begun to push westward. We need to stop him before he gains a strong hold or we are surely doomed." Myrddin was unusually dour and serious and his demeanour lent weight to his words. All those warriors present felt the serious nature of the Druid's information. The Christian priests were busy with blessings, benedictions, and readying their flock for battle.

"To be effective, we will need to move quickly and secure some point of high ground so that we can control Aelle's movements," said Arthgwr thoughtfully. "Is there such a place lying before Aelle? Can we reach it and secure it before he does?" he asked of the gathered nobles.

"Yes, there is a place near Aquae Sulis to the south of here. It is an old hill fort the Romans called it, Mons Badonicus, it should serve us well," surprisingly the information came from Lot. The others agreed immediately.

"*Mynydd Baddon*," cried Myrddin using the Cymraeg name for the hill, "of course! It is perfect and so close to the ancient hot springs of our ancestors! How appropriate!"

"Can we get there in time? Is it defendable?" asked Arthgwr his mind working furiously to fashion some sort of plan quickly.

"Yes," said Pellinore, "if Merlinus is correct and Aelle has just begun his westward push we could easily travel to Mons Badonicus within three days and secure it. The site is an old hill fort and it still has some rings of protective earthen works and commands a view of the surrounding lands. We could hold it easily!"

"Then we have no time to spare! We move immediately! Tell the men to prepare, we move out before dawn. Tonight will be their last supper with loved ones. They should make the best of it!"

The supper Gwenhwyfar had laid out for Arthgwr was left untouched on the table. Upon entering their home in the heart of Caer Melyn, Arthgwr stood stunned that his wife had already prepared food for his imminent march to war. The expression on her husband's face, when he realised she already was informed of the coming battle, caused Gwenhwyfar to smile. She deftly avoided his questioning and instead directed him to the table laden with foodstuffs. Arthgwr nevertheless blurted out his plans and the fact that he and his men were leaving for battle before the sun rose in the morning.

Suddenly, the thought of eating did not seem so important and the two of them entwined in each other's arms. They had made love every night since Gwenhwyfar's arrival, but tonight was special. Gwenhwyfar sensed the battle of Mynydd Baddon would be pivotal and that her husband's fate might include what the Christian's would call martyrdom. She knew the many battles her husband had waged to this point, could easily have turned against him. Arthgwr had faced death several times, not only in the chaos that was battle, but also in the personal act of single combat to the death.

Gwenhwyfar knew this and she accepted the fact. She recalled the severe wound he received from the strangely marked spear of Gronw's. She recognised the markings as the work of one trained as a Druid. She had wondered how Gronw had known to make markings that guaranteed death to the enemy of the one who drew them. Her husband had indeed died that day. Owain Ddantgwyn was no more. In his place was Arthgwr Pendragon, the Dux Bellorum of King Ambrosius Aurelianus. This too, she accepted, though not gladly, if truth were told.

"Promise me," Gwenhwyfar murmured into her husband's chest, "promise me that when this battle is over you will come to me here and take me back to Caerwyn for our daughter's wedding. Do this for me and I will be happy to live the rest of my days with you here in Caer Melyn, if that is your wish."

Arthgwr was set to make some witty retort to make his wife smile, to lighten the mood. At once, he saw that this was not the time for levity. He gently caressed his wife's golden tresses and kissed her forehead. Pulling her head to his chest, he hugged her with passion.

"I do promise," he said solemnly.

The army, preparing to march, noisily met the threat of morning. What light there was came from the bonfires lit by the people of Caer Melyn and the torches carried by the foot soldiers. Commander's barked orders, while the families of the warriors wailed their sorrow at seeing their men go off to battle. The banging of spears, swords and shields, the whinnying of horses and shouts of the men created a cacophony of sound that would surely frighten the sun and prevent it from showing itself.

The sun, fearing nothing that men could muster, did show itself. When the villagers and people of Caer Melyn beheld the brightness of its magnificence, the warriors were already well on their way to battle.

The hill fort of Mons Badonicus was not much more than a modest hill, with concentric earthen work rings at the summit. It did command a view of the immediate countryside and Arthgwr could see immediately that it was certainly a military advantage. The tree line had been cut back to give a good view of any attackers. Arthgwr planned to hide a contingent of cavalry in the trees. Most of his archers occupied the walls. A number of them were also hidden in the trees opposite the cavalry. Scouts had provided information that indicated the Sacsonaidd route.

Arthgwr left his scouts in a string along the route, with orders to abandon their position at the first sight of the invaders. This knowledge of the progress of the enemy, would give Arthgwr a chance to time his counter attack. Cai had the warriors cut and gather hay and wrap it into great balls mixed with pitch and some of the *sylffwr* they had brought with them from Caer Melyn. It was an idea of Myrddin's who said that the pitch and sulphur would burn hotly. He had demonstrated with a small batch, the effect of which was instant fire. The men dubbed the concoction *"Merlin's Fire."* Myrddin had hidden these balls within the first ring of earthen works where they could easily be sent down the hill. The slope of the land would be a great asset when the time came.

Myrddin, Rhiannon and Gwenhwyfar had remained at Caer Melyn with Father Dubricius. The priest, Father Bedwini, accompanied the army and was with Arthgwr's warriors at Mons Badonicus. He was kept busy attending to the salvation of the Christian warriors. The Pagan warriors were busy sharpening their weapons and grounding woad into the blue paint they applied to their bodies. They laughed and danced and banged their drums and were further heartened when they saw Arthgwr walking toward them with the sword, Caladfwlch.

It was not long before sunset when Arthgwr heard news that Aelle's men were getting closer. Myrddin had heard first and had relayed the information to Arthgwr and Edern. Immediately Arthgwr called a council, attended by all the captains. Lot and Edern sat apart, neither looking at the other.

This was no time for personal grievances and the two men were both professional enough to realise the importance of that. Pellinore also kept a civil tongue and listened carefully along with Cai, Edern and the others, as Arthgwr laid out the battle plan.

By midday the following day, the scouts had bunched up in the field below the first rings of the hill fort. It was estimated the first troops of Aelle would soon appear.

A steady drone of drumbeats could be heard, though there was still no sign of the invaders. Aelle and his army marched, they had no horses, no cavalry; they simply marched forward. They killed and burned everything in their path.

All was quiet in the hill fort of Mons Badonicus. The warriors waited. Tension filled the air. The faint sound of the approaching Sacsonaidd's drums played heavy on the men's nerves. Arthgwr's warriors, Christians and Pagans alike, were well trained, experienced and they remained calm.

The scouts that had bunched up in the meadow below the fort, also kept their wits. The brave scouts were steely in their resolve and convincing in their ruse. They moved about, as though they were tending to the late summer's last cutting of hay. They sang as they feigned work and appeared oblivious to the line of warriors that had appeared a thousand yards away.

The drumming stopped.

More invaders could now be seen and yet the scouts of Arthgwr remained unflustered as they busied themselves in the field.

The invaders took the bait and began running at the unprotected peasants that lay ahead of them. The scouts cried out in alarm and began running from their fast approaching attackers. As the Sacsonaidd warriors of King Aelle converged on the meadow below the hill fort,

Arthgwr's well-trained scouts managed to escape into the safety of the first ring of earthen works. They immediately began randomly firing arrows at the pursuing warriors. It was just enough resistance to whet the appetite of the attacking Sacsonaidd. They did not press their attack, but instead, let loose their own volley of arrows and spears at their prey. While the first invaders were thus engaged, the rest of the force kept marching forward and soon the meadow was full of Aelle's Sacsonaidd warriors.

The sun had begun to hide itself from the warfare of men. In the failing light, bonfires took up the task the sun had abandoned. The field below the fort now looked like the blackness of the sky dotted with the brilliance of countless stars.

"Arthgwr," called Edern, "have you seen this?" He waved his hand to take in the sight below them.

Arthgwr looked out over the earthen works at the top of the hill fort and saw the vast number of fires.

"It seems we are outnumbered ten to one at least. Hardly what I would call an even battle! Perhaps we should send word to Aelle and tell him he needs more men!" Arthgwr smiled and slapped Edern on his back. His loyal warrior laughed heartily and took a gulp of ale to regain his voice.

"Is there enough light?" Arthgwr asked looking at the dying sun, its rays too weak to allow more than a meagre glow.

"If we hurry we can manage and in any case, the fires down there will help us," replied Edern. "Shall I give the signal?"

Arthgwr nodded his head. Edern lit an arrow afire and waved it in his outstretched hand. He waved it twice from side to side.

Suddenly, below them and behind the second ring of protective earthen works, firelight appeared. Cai and his men lit the great balls of hay and pitch and sent them down the slope into the enemy below.

The showering sparks streaked from the rolling balls of fire, as the slope of the hill caused the balls to gather speed. The firelight lit the darkening sky and sent fear and shock through the Sacsonaidd warriors below. The first of the balls of fire found their mark crashing through the Sacsonaidd lines and penetrating into their encampment. The giant fireballs ignited a tent, sending flames spurting into the air. One Sacsonaidd, caught in the firestorm, was himself ignited. He screamed in terrible agony as he tried flailing and thrashing about in a vain attempt to extinguish the flames. "Merlin's Fire" had another property, it was not so easy to extinguish. Many others soon joined the burning enemy as the fireballs crashed their way through the Sacsonaidd encampment. The entire meadow crackled and roared in flames casting an unnatural flickering light on the horror. The smell of burnt flesh and hay mixed with a tinge of rotten eggs that was the sylffwr, waft on the late summer's night breeze.

Piercing screams of men burning alive filled the ears of Arthgwr and his warriors. They remained unmoved by the sound. Arthgwr gave another signal and the swish of fletched arrows added to the chaos of sounds. The archers could see by the light made from the horror that was Merlin's Fire. Deadly arrows rained down on the burning Sacsonaidd. Volley after volley of flesh piercing arrows tore through the enemy.

King Aelle did what he could to rally his troops. A few of his stalwart warriors managed to shoot arrows back at the men behind the earthen works. Aelle corralled a small number of his captains and ordered them to extinguish the flames. There was not much water, only what each warrior carried for drinking. It was useless against Myrddin's concoction.

The battleground below the ringed fort was blazing. The firelight was a decided benefit for Arthgwr. He took full advantage.

Thunder was heard above the chaos. Through the darkening night and the burning hay and thick acrid black smoke of the pitch and sylffwr, shadowy figures could be seen forming a line just in front of the trees. The line was moving toward the fray in unison along with the sound of the thunder.

The crazed, confused Sacsonaidd realised too late, that a cavalry charge was underway. The hacking and slashing of the mounted riders cut the enemy invaders down as the cavalry methodically and unhurriedly stomped through the battlefield. Once they reached the far side of the battleground, the archers loosed yet another series of barrages. Screams of impaled men, moans and groans of slashed and hewn warriors, added to the hideous sound of burning men. The night darkened, even as hungry flames consumed the hay and bodies.

The cavalry wheeled about chancing one last charge before the encroaching darkness made it too dangerous. They rode through the thick of the Sacsonaidd, slashing and hacking with their long swords and stabbing and jabbing with their spears. As the fires caused by the rolling balls of hay treated with Myrddin's concoction were spluttering out and the darkness of the night grew, the horsemen were forced to ride more slowly. While they were devastatingly effective in hewing men down before them, they incurred casualties of their own. Four of their number were pulled from their mounts and gruesomely hacked to death by the Sacsonaidds.

It was time to stop. There was no more light available from the fires by which Arthgwr's men could see. The battle was forced to an end until the first light of the morning.

"Do you think we have won the day?" asked Edern of his leader. It was still dark, though the sky was growing grey in anticipation of the sun's arrival. The smoke from the pitch, sylffwr and the burning hay still billowed about the meadow. It was impossible to see clearly and the stench caused eyes to water and men to hold their noses against the brutal assault to their senses.

"I am not sure. We won't know until daylight breaks and we can ride through them a few more times. Have you the second cavalry ready below? We do not want any of these bastards to escape!" Edern nodded and went about his duties.

Arthgwr looked out over the field at the still dying enemy and refused to give in to his compassion. He would not allow sentiment to interfere with the fate of this enemy. These Sacsonaidd were bent on the destruction of his race. The stench of burnt flesh was carried on the morning breeze and invaded his senses. Still, he turned his soul against the horror that was slowly becoming visible to him, as the sun was reluctantly birthed into his world.

It soon became clear that fully one-third of Aelle's invaders had been killed in the assault. That still left the Sacsonaidd force with more than enough men to win a victory over Arthgwr and his army. The rising sun revealed the extent of the destruction wreaked by Arthgwr's archers and cavalry. Aelle was not to be underestimated and even now he sought to mount a counteroffensive against the hill fort. A band of Sacsonaidd warriors managed to breach the first ring and were now working to gain the second ring. A series of volleys of deadly arrows, fired from the fort, ended their ambitions.

In the meantime, another group of Sacsonaidds took advantage of the diversion, their brothers had paid for with their lives. Soon, these brave warriors reached the fort itself and engaged in hand-to-hand combat with a group of archers. They were repelled, but not before the lives of six archers were taken.

The day wore on and there were more concentrated attacks on Mons Badonicus. The fort was now under siege and the men within were threatened with starvation. Aelle's men could not find the archers or the cavalry that had so plagued them in the night. It was as if they had never existed and the horror that had struck at them in the dark, a nightmare.

Arthgwr's men had simply rode and marched further into the forest. There they had been ordered to stay until the sun began to go down.

Aelle's men pressed their advantage of superior numbers, but they could not break through the walls of the fort, despite having successfully breached the concentric rings. Arthgwr's men fought on, impervious to fatigue, the lack of food, water and sleep. All the members of his army fought shoulder-to-shoulder, Christian beside Pagan, Roman beside Briton. He saw the horsehair plumes of the helmets worn by the Roman-Briton soldiers of Aurelianus's men, as the cavalry made another charge. He saw the clean-shaven Romanesque foot soldiers throwing their Roman javelins, and slashing with their short Roman swords. Arthgwr proudly watched his men both Christian and Pagan slashing away with their long iron swords, their long hair swirling about them. They fought ferociously!

The sun was becoming low in the sky. Arthgwr gathered his men behind the walls of the hill fort. A signal had been put forth to the archers and the cavalry in the forest.

Soon it would begin. Arthgwr and his men mounted the horses they had kept inside the fort, whilst archers prepared themselves along the wall, protected by sword and spear of their compatriots. The fighting was intense.

It was late in the afternoon, when the first volley of arrows was fired at Aelle's flank from the tree line. Another volley of arrows was loosed nearly simultaneously from the fort. So it went, the deadly arrows criss-crossed the battlefield, raining death onto the enemy. The horsemen began at full gallop. The Sacsonaidd bunched closer together trying to escape the onslaught of arrows. They did so in vain.

Arthgwr's mounted warriors flew down the hill, madly negotiating the rings of earthen works. In short time, they were on the slope of the meadow unhindered by the rings. Slashing and hacking as they came, they were soon joined from the flank by the others in full cavalry charge.

Edern wasted no time and lead his contingent of foot soldiers at a full run toward the Sacsonaidd. Made malleable by the arrows of the hidden archers, the invading Sacsonaidd enemy was now caught between the anvil that was the cavalry, and the hammer of oncoming warriors. The fighting and butchering went on and on until early evening. The cavalry could no longer ride through and charge for they could not see, there were no fires burning brightly this evening. The men dismounted and joined the fray, slashing and hacking as they went. Surprise was their advantage for they were already deep inside the enemy's ranks. This added to the confusion of the Sacsonaidd. The hidden archers also abandoned their bows and drew their swords, adding to the slashing and cutting of the battle. A second wave of men from the fort, these were the fort archers, who had laid down their bows, came screaming at the Sacsonaidd.

Arthgwr, of course, was in the middle of the chaos. He had been knocked from his mount, his sword Caladfwlch had cleaved the offender in two. Aelle's men broke rank and were running for their lives. The second cavalry that Arthgwr had hidden below the Sacsonaidd position in the meadow, prevented the Sacsonaidd from escaping. The lack of light did not hinder their task; the enemy was running toward them. The horsemen simply slashed at anything that moved in front of them, horseflesh pummelled the rest into the earth. Still the fighting was far from over.

Surrounded by the enemy, Arthgwr fought wildly, slashing and hacking with Caladfwlch. The mighty sword from ancient times hacked off the limbs of any who got close to the man who wielded it! Arthgwr slashed a Sacsonaidd who was determined to separate his head from his body with a huge double bladed battle-axe. He parried another blow, struck again with Caladfwlch, and opened his enemy from shoulder to hip.

At that moment, an intense burning feeling surprised Arthgwr. A sword ripped into the flesh of his side. Though the wound brought him to his knees, Arthgwr managed to block a killing blow and countered with his own deadly strike. Another Sacsonaidd warrior went to his reward at Woden's table.

The red orb of the morning sun peaked shyly over the horizon. Morning mist obscured the vision of men, preventing them from seeing the full gore of the battle. As the sun grew bolder in the early morning sky, the mist could no longer protect the young sun from what the men had done, it gave in and retreated. Glistening with morning dew, the hacked and hewn bodies of thousands of warriors littered the meadow, obscene testimony to the cruelty and futility of human kind.

It was impossible to tell from the carnage that lay strewn about in the blood and gore soaked meadow, which side had won. The priest wandered aimlessly amidst the grotesque scene of the battlefield, tears streaming from his face, his lips mumbling ineffective holy words.

Others came and slowly picked their way through the slaughter. They were from the hill fort of Mons Badonicus. The fort had held fast and the only survivors left alive were Arthgwr's men, the Sacsonaidds had been butchered in the meadow below. Aelle's body had already been recovered.

Arthgwr and his unlikely army had won the day.

This was cold comfort to those wandering through the bloody battleground. They were searching for their leader, the man who had won victory against the invaders, despite insurmountable odds. They were searching for Arthgwr Pendragon.

The morning air warmed under the sun's attention. The sweet smell of hay and meadow flowers and the pines and oaks of the nearby forest were completely undetectable, so great was the horrible stench of decaying men. Soon the sound of the flies became so loud, their buzzing drowned out all other noise. There was still no sign of the Bear-Man of the North.

Chapter 33

Arthgwr groaned and opened his eyes. All he could see was green. He closed his eyes and then tried again. He groaned and a hand was placed tightly over his mouth. He lost consciousness.

It was daytime and the sun shone brightly. The brilliance gave him a headache and he groaned aloud. Water was given and it trickled down his throat spilling over his mouth and down his chin.

"You were a right sight, my lord," the voice was young and speaking Latin. Arthgwr turned, to better see the source. A young man wearing Roman armour without a helmet, was busy filling skins with water from the nearby brook. The boy's hair was shorn close and his face was clean-shaven except for the stubble that had grown in the last few days. He was obviously one of Aurelianus's men. Arthgwr could not place a name to the lad. Arthgwr propped himself up to get a better look and saw that, though younger than himself, Aurelianus's warrior was no boy.

"What is your name, soldier?" Arthgwr asked in a voice that was unfamiliar to him. Immediately, he realised his throat was bone dry and the desire for water almost overcame him. The younger soldier predicted this and again held a full skin of water to Arthgwr's lips.

"I am Jason, my lord. My friend over there is Petrus." He pointed back to the brook where another young man was collecting firewood. He too was dressed in Roman armour complete with the red horsehair plumed helmet worn by Aurelianus's men. The soldier, he noticed still carried a Roman sword.

"You have a very nasty gash in your side and you were unconscious when I found you. It was in the very thick of the battle and you had killed many of the enemy, my lord. There must have been ten or more cleaved Sacsonaidd piled around you. More were coming and you had passed out from your sword wound. I fought as best I could. So did Petrus, but it was hopeless. We couldn't let them kill you or worse, capture you. If that happened, they would surely have rallied and the day would be lost. So, Petrus and I bundled you up and fought our way clear of the battle and into the forest. Oh, not to worry sire, the day was ours! We stopped to tend your wound. I have been a leather worker in my life and know how to make a good stitch. We washed you clean and I stitched you up as best I could. It is my suspicion that you have a broken rib or two, my lord, so I bound you tightly and put the breastplate on you to keep the wound secure."

Arthgwr looked down and saw he was wearing a Roman style armoured breastplate. He took a breath and felt the sharp stabbing pain of his ribs. The young man was right; his ribs were broken. The binding was tight and he laboured for breath.

"Now, don't you worry, my lord. Petrus and I will take care of you. You must keep the binding tight sire, it holds your ribs together and helps keep your wound stitched. Just don't work yourself up so that you need to breathe hard and you will be fine." The soldier offered Arthgwr more water and a piece of hard bread, which he gratefully accepted.

"The bad news, sire is that we are lost in this great forest. I am embarrassed to have to tell you this, but we cannot find our way out. Petrus and I, we ran deep into the woods after we stitched you up. The Sacsonaidd were following us and close on our heels. We managed to lose them sire, but in so doing we ourselves became lost. We have some small amount of food and the brook here has given us water. Petrus is looking for firewood so that we can cook the rabbit he caught earlier. After that, we have some hard bread and a bit of cheese, enough for two days or so.

"I need to get to Caer Melyn. I made a promise I must keep," Arthgwr wheezed the words and realised just how weak he had become. Jason came over to him and eased him down on a bough of pine branches. He poured water into Arthgwr's mouth and wiped his face when he coughed and spit up bloody spittle.

"Yes, sire, of course. The brook here flows southward, so Petrus and I thought we should follow it upstream. By going north, we should eventually find our way closer to Caer Melyn, perhaps we might even run into some of our own men on patrol. We just don't know how far we are from the fort."

Arthgwr nodded to signal his support of Jason and Petrus's plan. He was in no condition to argue and he did not have a better strategy in any case. Petrus came back with an armload of firewood. He was a big strapping young man, clearly used to hard work.

In short time, Petrus had fashioned a lean-to from branches, complete with soft pine bed. Jason placed Arthgwr in the shelter and turned to help Petrus build another structure from the boughs he had collected nearby. After that, Jason started a small fire and began skinning the rabbit. Soon, the sweet smell of roasting meat filled their nostrils. Arthgwr was not hungry and could not eat the meat. The smell of the roasting flesh reminded him too much of the horror he had committed on the battlefield and his appetite left him. He fell into a dreamless sleep.

Walking was slow and painful for Arthgwr. Jason and Petrus took turns assisting him. They rested frequently and when they did, Jason foraged about for things they could eat. Petrus was the hunter and Jason was very good at finding edible herbs and vegetables. Later that evening, Jason cooked a fine wild leek soup, which Arthgwr managed to keep down. It was important he maintain his strength.

Continuing up stream, the three men believed they were getting closer to their destination. After three more days of travelling, they began to despair.

They broke camp early on the fifth morning. Shaking the morning dew from their cloaks, they set out without breakfast. It was getting colder at night and the mornings were damp and uncomfortable, summer was dying. Only when the sun reached its glory at noon, did its magnificence warm their bones. Pushing on upstream, never wavering from their agreed plan, the three men finally stopped at the edge of a meadow.

Petrus heard a sound and saw movement in the tree line. He stopped and cocked his head to better hear. There was no further disturbance. The men agreed it might have been a boar or perhaps a deer.

Just as Petrus was preparing to hunt for their supper, all three men heard another noise, this one much closer. They froze in their tracks, each man grabbing at his weapon. This was no deer or boar. The sound they heard was man-made. Before they could react, they heard a voice.

"Right! You three just stay right where you are and drop your weapons now, like good lads."

The voice was speaking Cymraeg. This surprised Arthgwr and delighted him at the same time. He laughed at the baffled expressions of his friends Petrus and Jason and answered in Cymraeg.

"Good afternoon, how are you?" called out Arthgwr.

"Not bad, what about you?" came the humorous reply. The trees bustled for a moment and then Arthgwr saw the unmistakeable point of an arrow aimed at him. Looking around he saw there was an arrow pointing at Petrus and Jason as well. They were surrounded. The two soldiers could not completely understand Cymraeg, they could pick out a few words and were comforted it was not Sacsenaeg being spoken.

Two men and a woman came into sight from the trees. They were obviously Cymry and amused by the banter they had exchanged with Arthgwr.

"What is your name and how is it you happen here?" One of the men asked as he slung his great yew bow over his shoulder. Arthgwr noted that the other man did not follow suit. His bow was still nocked, though the arrow pointed to the ground. He was just far enough away that he could easily release his arrow and arm himself before Arthgwr, Petrus or Jason could reach him. It was then Arthgwr noticed the woman was holding a spear.

"This," declared Jason proudly, "is none other than Arthgwr Pendragon, who has just won a great battle against King Aelle of the South Sacsonaidd! We are making our way to Caer Melyn."

"Now is that a fact? We have just come from Caer Melyn. Yes, we spent some time there, talking with the folk. It seems your Arthgwr did indeed win a great battle and killed the bastard Aelle. Along with him, your Arthgwr is said to have killed nearly a thousand Sacsonaidd! They say the Pendragon was killed. His body has not yet been found and some folk say he has been spirited away to the mystic Isle of Avallon. Perhaps, he will come again if the Cymry have need of a hero. Of course, the priests say he was martyred in a glorious battle for the Church and has found his reward in Heaven. Anyway, he is said to be dead."

"Well, not to disappoint, I am not dead." Arthgwr said from behind a sardonic smile.

"Though I am wounded and we three are hungry for some good food. You said you were recently at Caer Melyn. How far away and in what direction is that?" Arthgwr sat down and took some water.

The woman was looking him up and down. Her golden hair was tied back with a brightly coloured cloth. The cloak she wore did little to hide her ample bosom. She walked around and finally stopped in front of Arthgwr.

"Did you stop a war from happening without spilling any blood?" she asked boldly.

"I did indeed stop a war between King Brychan and King Gwynllyw the cause of which was the daughter of Brychan. She had fallen in love with the Pagan Gwynllyw, which upset her Christian father. He was especially vexed when Gwynllyw stole his daughter. I suggested he agree to the match, provided that Gwynllyw pledge that he raises his children as Christians. That did the trick and war was prevented."

"You are Arthgwr! Well, my lord, you are not far from Caer Melyn, a day, perhaps two, if you follow the sun directly from here. We will help, but first you must meet my husband. He is hunting with some others. We are a small band and have been put from our homes during the fighting. We are gathering our selves up and moving back now the slaughter has stopped. Please, my lord, here drink this, it is good ale," the young woman offered a skin of frothy ale.

"My husband will be back before dusk and we will make camp and start for your Caer Melyn in the morn."

Arthgwr was overwhelmed by the hospitality of this little group and by the fact he was so close to his beloved.

Two days! He would keep his promise to her! Two days! He tried to stand but could not. Arthgwr had kept himself going with the promise he had made to his wife, Gwenhwyfar. It was that thought alone, that drove him onward, despite the pain from his wounds.

Now that Arthgwr was able to realise his goal and keep his promise, he was overcome with fatigue and pain. Petrus and Jason assisted him. The woman looked at the wound and approved of the binding. She mixed some herbs in a mug of water and bade Arthgwr to drink the concoction down. It would help him she had said simply. Arthgwr was grateful.

"Your man is indeed fortunate to have such a fine woman for a wife," he said weakly. "Pray tell, what his name?"

"Oh, thank you very much indeed, my lord, though it is I who am the fortunate one. My husband will be here very soon," the young woman blushed.

"His name is Ceolwulf."

Ysbryd tragwyddol y keltiad